W9-BQM-725

TO END IN
FIRE

BAEN BOOKS by DAVID WEBER

HONOR HARRINGTON
On Basilisk Station • *The Honor of the Queen* • *The Short Victorious War* • *Field of Dishonor* • *Flag in Exile* • *Honor Among Enemies* • *In Enemy Hands* • *Echoes of Honor* • *Ashes of Victory* • *War of Honor* • *Crown of Slaves* (with Eric Flint) • *The Shadow of Saganami* • *At All Costs* • *Storm from the Shadows* • *Torch of Freedom* (with Eric Flint) • *Mission of Honor* • *A Rising Thunder* • *Shadow of Freedom* • *Cauldron of Ghosts* (with Eric Flint) • *Shadow of Victory* • *Uncompromising Honor*

EDITED BY DAVID WEBER
More than Honor • *Worlds of Honor* • *Changer of Worlds* • *The Service of the Sword* • *In Fire Forged* • *Beginnings*

MANTICORE ASCENDANT
A Call to Duty (with Timothy Zahn) • *A Call to Arms* (with Timothy Zahn & Tom Pope) • *A Call to Vengeance* (with Timothy Zahn & Tom Pope) • *A Call to Insurrection* (with Timothy Zahn & Tom Pope) *forthcoming

THE STAR KINGDOM
A Beautiful Friendship • *Fire Season* (with Jane Lindskold) • *Treecat Wars* (with Jane Lindskold)

House of Steel: The Honorverse Companion (with BuNine)

BAEN BOOKS by ERIC FLINT

THE RING OF FIRE SERIES
1632 • *1633* (with David Weber) • *1634: The Baltic War* (with David Weber) • *1634: The Galileo Affair* (with Andrew Dennis) • *1634: The Bavarian Crisis* (with Virginia DeMarce) • *1635: The Ram Rebellion* (with Virginia DeMarce et al.) • *1635: The Cannon Law* (with Andrew Dennis) • *1635: The Dreeson Incident* (with Virginia DeMarce) • *1635: The Eastern Front* • *1636: The Papal Stakes* (with Charles E. Gannon) • *1636: The Saxon Uprising* • *1636: The Kremlin Games* (with Gorg Huff & Paula Goodlett) • *1636: The Devil's Opera* (with David Carrico) • *1636: Commander Cantrell in the West Indies* (with Charles E. Gannon) • *1636: The Viennese Waltz* (with Gorg Huff & Paula Goodlett) • *1636: The Cardinal Virtues* (with Walter Hunt) • *1635: A Parcel of Rogues* (with Andrew Dennis) • *1636: The Ottoman Onslaught* • *1636: Mission to the Mughals* (with Griffin Barber) • *1636: The Vatican Sanction* (with Charles E. Gannon) • *1637: The Volga Rules* (with Gorg Huff & Paula Goodlett) • *1637: The Polish Maelstrom* • *1636: The China Venture* (with Iver P. Cooper) • *1636: The Atlantic Encounter* (with Walter H. Hunt) • *1637: No Peace Beyond the Line* (with Charles E. Gannon) • *1637: The Peacock Throne* (with Griffin Barber) • *1637: The Coast of Chaos* (forthcoming)

EDITED BY ERIC FLINT:
Grantville Gazette I–IX • *Ring of Fire I–IV*

For a complete listing of Baen titles by David Weber and Eric Flint, and to purchase any of these titles in e-book form, please go to www.baen.com.

TO END IN FIRE

DAVID WEBER
& ERIC FLINT

BAEN

To End in Fire

This is a work of fiction. All the characters and events portrayed in this book are fictional, and any resemblance to real people or incidents is purely coincidental.

Copyright © 2021 by Words of Weber, Inc. & Eric Flint

All rights reserved, including the right to reproduce this book or portions thereof in any form.

A Baen Books Original

Baen Publishing Enterprises
P.O. Box 1403
Riverdale, NY 10471
www.baen.com

ISBN: 978-1-9821-2564-6

Cover art by David Mattingly

First printing, October 2021

Distributed by Simon & Schuster
1230 Avenue of the Americas
New York, NY 10020

Pages by Joy Freeman (www.pagesbyjoy.com)
Printed in the United States of America
10 9 8 7 6 5 4 3 2 1

For my son, Michael Rice-Weber, USMC.
Your mom and I could not be prouder of you.
—DW

To Rick, Karen and Kevin.
—EF

February 1923 Post Diaspora

"You know, I believe that's the first time I ever heard the words 'Ballroom' and 'watchdogs' used together."

—Anton Zilwicki

City of Mendel
Mesa System

CATHERINE MONTAIGNE WAS APPALLED.

Her personal shuttle had been designed as the luxury tender of a luxury yacht owned by one the galaxy's more...idiosyncratic billionaires. The term "no expense spared" was most often used to indicate only that something was very expensive. In the *Harriet Tubman*'s case, however, it was literally true, and her shuttle was an almost equally expensive vessel. Indeed, ton-for-ton, it was actually *more* expensive. It was much larger than most "shuttles"—a bit larger than a naval pinnace, actually—and boasted quite a lot of features lesser vessels did not. Unlike a standard shuttle's rows of seats, its passengers sat in luxury armchairs scattered around a tastefully decorated "salon" with smart wall bulkheads. At the moment, those bulkheads were configured to display a panorama of snowy mountains and a magnificent waterfall. The viewscreen at the forward end of the compartment and the "portholes" spaced along that panorama displayed a much uglier view, however.

For all that she'd led a rather adventurous life, Montaigne had seldom seen destruction on this scale. Well, she *had* toured the ruins of Yawata Crossing after the Yawata Strike had virtually destroyed the entire city. That had been worse, but it had also been...different. The tsunami which destroyed that city might have been spawned by de-orbiting wreckage as the result of an attack, but the tsunami itself had been a force of nature.

What had happened to the city of Mendel had not. And Mendel was far larger than Yawata Crossing had ever been.

That size actually gave the destruction passing beneath her luxury shuttle even more impact, in a way, because so much of the city was untouched. It provided a stark visual contrast

3

between what Mendel had been and what its devastated sections had become. Of course, she reminded herself, the true devastation was concentrated on the seccy side of town, so *that* part of it probably hadn't mattered very much to the city authorities. Or to the previous city authorities, at least. But there'd been more than enough additional damage to go around.

The broken stub of a residential tower directly in front of the shuttle looked as if it had been hammered by a small asteroid. The once massive ceramacrete structure was a rim of rubble around a deep, ugly crater, and a vast swath of the city had been blanketed in a deep layer of the finely divided dust, like lung-tearing snow, vomited skyward from its destruction. Much larger and more dangerous debris had showered outward from the kinetic weapon strike which had wreaked that destruction, as well. More than enough "minor" craters marked where that wreckage had found the earth once again, and trees and recreational structures in the parks and green belts had been flattened like reaped grain by the blast front.

Gutted industrial areas were interspersed with the green belts. It had been the seccy side of town, after all, which made it the logical home for the industry first-class citizens objected to finding in their own backyards. Most of *that* damage, she knew, had been inflicted by direct combat, which probably explained why most of the ravaged structures were still recognizable. As structures, at least.

For a moment, her mind fluttered away from the chaos and the human agony and suffering that must have accompanied it. What would be the term for an expert on methods of destruction? Demolitionist? No, that would be the person who did the destroying.

She shook her head slightly, as if to shed those useless questions.

She knew the city bore other, lesser—but no less obscene— wounds left by the "small" nuclear detonations and fuel-air bombs attributed to Ballroom terrorist attacks. Those were beyond her view, even from the shuttle's two thousand-meter altitude, but whatever else they might be, they hadn't been *Ballroom* attacks. If anyone in the galaxy was in a position to know that, she was. That was another problem she'd need to address, but not yet. Not now.

At her command, the shuttle and its sting ship escorts were

passing over the city slowly, but from their meager altitude, the terrain below them was still passing fairly quickly.

She waved a hand at the shattered tower which had drawn her eye.

"Is that...?"

"Yes, that's Hancock." Saburo X, sitting next to her, nodded. "Bachue the Nose ran that district, and we're sure she's the one who gave the order to drop most of an entire floor onto the Misties below. Killed somewhere around two thousand of the bastards."

"Misties" was the nickname for the troops of the Mesan Internal Security directorate, whose official acronym was MISD. They were the most hated and feared of Mesa's enforcement agencies.

Had been feared, rather. They weren't any longer. But they were still hated.

"And that," Saburo pointed toward another huge tower, "is Neue Rostock, Jurgen Dusek's district. I'm told—" He paused as the shuttle passed over the ceramacrete structure and it disappeared from view through the viewports, then shrugged and continued. "I'm told—"

"Sandra," Cathy said, "full vision, please."

One might have expected such a palatial saloon to be carpeted. It was not, however, for reasons which became apparent as the deck, bulkheads, and overhead all vanished. Only the passengers' comfortable seats remained visible... floating unsupported two thousand meters above the cityscape.

Two thousand meters of crystal clear, completely empty, thin air above the cityscape.

Saburo tensed a bit in his seat. Behind her, Jeremy X uttered a quickly stifled little hiss.

Cathy's stepdaughter Berry had a more pronounced reaction. "Mom!"

Cathy glanced at her. The young woman's thin face was paler than usual. Her eyes were wide, and her hands were locked with clawlike power on her seat's armrests.

"For Pete's sake," Cathy said. "It's just the smart walls! Well, and the smart *deck*, I guess. But still—"

"Mom!"

"Oh, pfui." Cathy gave Neue Rostock Tower a quick glance. It was now—appeared to be, rather—passing directly below her. "Sandra, restore the sissy floor."

The space below their feet and under their seats instantly seemed to be a deck again, although the deck was now a magic carpet suspended in mid-air. The view all around them remained unimpeded.

Saburo whistled softly. "Perhaps a bit of warning next time, Countess."

"I gave up the title, remember?"

"As you said yourself, *pfui*. People who make perfectly serviceable shuttles disappear are obviously aristocracy. Sensible commoners like us—" he pointed toward himself with a thumb and Berry with a forefinger "—would do nothing of the sort."

"Berry is hardly a commoner," a voice spoke up from the luxurious landing shuttle's flight deck. It belonged to Cathy's assistant, Sandra Kaminisky. "She's a monarch. And, Catherine, I really don't think it's proper to call your stepdaughter queen a 'sissy.'"

"Who asked you?" Cathy demanded.

"You did. When we left Congo you told me to maintain proper protocols."

Sandra more-or-less ran the *Harriet Tubman*, as well as serving as a combination social secretary and aide-de-camp. And, in truth, Cathy *had* told Sandra to keep her from straying too far into her normal habits. This was, after all, officially a royal visit. Queen Berry had brought much of Torch's government with her, prominent among them, Prime Minister Web Du Havel and the Secretary of War, Jeremy X.

Now that the deck had been restored—more precisely, now that the optical illusion that the deck had vanished had been abnegated—Berry was able to relax a little. She turned her head and looked at her prime minister, whose expression was serene. Undeniably, it was *serene*.

"You knew she'd do that," Berry said accusingly, and Du Havel shrugged.

"I had no idea what she'd do. But I've known her for decades. Any time Cathy is in close proximity to technology which she doesn't understand but knows how to use, you've got to be on your guard."

Cathy had ignored the interplay while Neue Rostock Tower reappeared to her left as the shuttle banked. Now that she had a better look at it, she could see just how badly damaged it was.

Repair and construction remotes swarmed about it, but even now, the next best thing to three T-months after the fighting, they were still mostly at the "hauling away debris" stage. Actual repair, assuming that would ever happen, lay in some distant future. At least it was still standing, though, unlike Hancock. Its upper stories were basically a heap of rubble, but it was obvious that it had never been hit by the monster that had destroyed Bachue's tower. Instead, it had been systematically hammered by far more—but far smaller—KEWs. Among other things. Scores of jagged breaches had been blasted through the incredibly tough outer shell of its lacerated ceramacrete flanks by other weapons, as well.

There were more of those holes than she could possibly have counted. A *lot* more. Neue Rostock hadn't been destroyed...only blasted into ruin.

"Ruthless bastards," she muttered.

"Being fair about it," Saburo said, "they did try to limit the collateral damage as much as they could once they launched their assault on Neue Rostock. That's why they refused to release even the tactical KEWs to General Drescher for so long. Which was just as well for Dusek and our friends. Drescher was a nasty enough handful even when her superiors insisted she had to send her assault force in on the ground, and when they finally relented enough to let her use the tactical KEWS..." He shook his head. "Just as happy she wasn't in charge from the beginning. She might've hit Hancock with something a lot smaller than the big bastard they actually used...and then the collateral damage wouldn't have stopped them from doing the same thing to Neue Rostock."

Cathy had already known that much, from the report Thandi Palane had sent to Torch right after the fighting was ended by the arrival of Admiral Gold Peak's fleet in the Mesa System.

The Mesan authorities had begun trying to crush the rebelling seccies by using the Office of Public Safety's regular troops, the so-called "Safeties." Those barely even qualified as policemen; they were essentially just official thugs. The Safeties had very rapidly gotten chewed to pieces once the crime bosses who ran the seccy districts realized they were in a fight for their lives. At which point the authorities sent in the MISD's troops. They were, if anything, even more brutal than the Safeties, but they were also better trained and armed.

Unfortunately for those authorities, the Misties had gotten hammered even more badly than the Safeties, at which point they had sent in the army—the Mesan Planetary Peaceforce. The MPP had still heavier combat equipment than the MISD's forces, and they'd been trained as a real military force. By Mesa's admittedly loose standards, they even followed the established laws of war. Prior to the recent emergency, they'd never been deployed to break heads—and necks—among the slaves and seccies of Mesa, so the slaves and seccies hadn't felt the same hatred for them that they felt for the OPS and MISD.

That wasn't saying much, of course. The distinction between sheer hatred and bitter hostility could get awfully thin.

Cathy sighed. Creating a functioning society with a generally accepted government out of the human cauldron Mesa's former rulers had created wasn't going to be easy, to put it mildly. She had no idea where to even start.

Fortunately for her and Mesa, she didn't have to figure it out. That was in the hands of other people. People who, despite outward appearances, she suspected would do a much better job of it than she could have.

Two of those people were now sitting with her, looking down on the wreckage. Seated just behind her was Jeremy X. Today, he was the government of Torch's Minister of War. But in his former life, he'd been the head of the Audubon Ballroom—which, depending on how you looked at it, was either the fighting organization of Mesa's genetic slaves or the galaxy's most savage terrorist organization.

Or perhaps both.

An even more dubious candidate for peacemaking was the man seated to her right. Saburo X had been in charge of organizing and coordinating the activities of the Ballroom on Mesa itself. The sharp point of the spear, you might say.

But perhaps that was the key to it, she thought. Jeremy X and Saburo X hadn't simply hated Manpower Incorporated and Mesa's government the way all the ex-slaves and seccies did. Unlike most of those folk—and more than any of them—they'd spilled blood themselves. A *lot* of it. They didn't really need revenge, any longer, because they'd already gotten plenty.

So—maybe—they'd do the best job of making peace.

What was the old saying? *Magnanimous in victory*, if she

remembered right. It might prove true that people who used "X" for a surname could manage that better than anyone else.

On the other hand, if she remembered the saying right, the other half of it was *Gracious in defeat*.

Could the people who'd once ruled a planet like Mesa manage that? She had her doubts.

"We'll be landing soon," Sandra said. "You might want to get properly dressed for the occasion. That especially applies to you, Catherine. Even if you did renounce your title, you still shouldn't disembark in the company of a reigning monarch wearing a sports jumper. What they used to call 'sweatpants,' except that I can't remember the last time I observed you sweating."

Catherine frowned. "Who the hell needs an assistant to be that sarcastic?"

"You do," Berry said. "I remember you spending quite a while interviewing candidates until you found one with the best—or worst, maybe—reputation." She thought for a moment, then added: "Sandra's really good at it too. I approve of her. Especially right now."

✦ ✦ ✦

Saburo spent the rest of their flight to Mendel's spaceport giving Catherine a detailed explanation of the various ruins.

"Most of the damage in the seccy districts was caused by the Hancock KEW and the debris it threw up. Well, there was plenty of battle damage, too, but you can't really see that from this far up. A lot of the damage to the industrial sections around Neue Rostock is from that. Dusek's people fought a delaying action against the Misties to cover the evacuation of as many people as possible into the tower."

"How many nuclear strikes were there?" she asked, then, seeing the frown gathering on her companion's brow, hastened to add: "Blasts, rather. I guess I'm not supposed to call them 'strikes,' since that suggests they were sent down from orbit."

The frown faded, and after a moment, a little smile took its place.

"I can't say I care that much, myself," he said. "But, yes, the Manties—The Grand Alliance, I mean—will get touchy on the subject.

"There weren't any nukes in Mendel itself in the final wave, after Gold Peak got here," he continued. "But there were three in the 'terrorist campaign' her arrival interrupted. That one—" he pointed at a spot in the distance "—is the only one you can see from here. The other two were smaller. One of them took out an entertainment complex on the outskirts of the city, and the other one—go figure—was detonated above a lake in one of the richest citizen districts. Other than the fish, all it killed were some boaters and people having picnics. As a military target, it made no sense at all. Not even from the standpoint of running up the body count just for the hell of it."

"And the big one?" As far away as they were, all Cathy could see was what looked like rubble.

"That used to be a district that had a concentration of research labs and high-priced think tanks. Sort of the crème de la crème of their brainiacs." Saburo shrugged. "It wasn't really that big a blast, by nuke values. Five kilotons, they figure. If the labs and such had all been in a single big, sensible ceramacrete structure, the bomb—missile, whatever it was—wouldn't have done nearly as much damage. But, no! They had to use up prime real estate right in to middle of Mendel—well, the middle of the suburbs, anyway—to show how prestigious *their* work was. All low airy buildings—not a one of 'em more than nine or ten stories—with lots of walkways and gardens. So they fried."

It was impossible to miss the coldness in Saburo's voice. However much the man might have it under control, he hated the people who had enslaved him and his folk just as much as any of them. You'd not find any sympathy in his heart for the thousands of slavers—that's how he'd think of them, even if they hadn't directly participated in slavery—who'd died in the aftermath of the Grand Alliance's seizure of the Mesa System.

Maybe the children. A tiny little bit.

Building a society out of that was . . . not going to be easy.

"We're coming in for the landing," Sandra announced. "Everyone please check your seatbelts. That means you, too, Catherine."

Mendel Spaceport
Planet Mesa
Mesa System

CATHY WASN'T SURPRISED TO SEE THE PEOPLE ASSEMBLED TO greet them as they disembarked from the shuttle. The small group standing at the foot of the ramp were the ones she'd expected to be there. Jurgen Dusek was the all-but-officially-recognized leader of Mesa's seccies, and four of the other people were also heads of seccy districts—understanding that "leader of a seccy district" overlapped with "crime boss." Thandi Palane was the commander of Torch's military, and the person who'd led the military side of the seccy rebellion. Which, while...convoluted, actually made sense, since the only star nation which had actually been in a formal state of war with the Mesa System, prior to Tenth Fleet's arrival, had been the Kingdom of Torch.

She was sorry, but not surprised, that Anton Zilwicki wasn't there. He'd sent her a message after *Harriet Tubman* entered the system that he'd be away when her shuttle landed—somewhere unspecified on unspecified business, and for an unspecified amount of time. There were drawbacks to being in love with the man who was one of the galaxy's most accomplished spooks, even if the spook in question insisted in public that he was just a retired naval officer...and never mind that one of the Star Empire's most popular news shows had once exposed his rather flamboyant history. (Which had gotten quite a bit more flamboyant since, but most of that—thankfully—was still unknown to the public.)

She wasn't surprised by the other people who weren't there, either. There were no senior officers from Admiral Gold Peak's forces, and only a small security detachment of Marines. Victor Cachat was there, true, but the role he'd played in the rebellion,

11

coupled with his by now well-known relationship with Palane, made his presence more of a personal one than as a representative of Haven's government.

No one was calling it that—not openly, anyway—but this visit to Mesa by Torch's queen and government officials amounted to a show of force. Not a show of military force. That was hardly necessary, with the Tenth Fleet orbiting the planet along with three quarters of a million ground troops. No, this was a *political* show of force. Nothing could more pointedly underline the impending transformation of Mesa's society than a visit from the rulers of the planet that had been seized by Mesa's own former slaves.

Being honest about it, although this was certainly nothing anyone would say openly, either, the visit was also in the way of a showing of teeth to the Grand Alliance. Not an outright baring of teeth; just a slight lifting of the lip to show the tips of the canines.

It was certainly not a visit that suggested or implied any military conflict. But, politically, it was a reminder to the people who'd occupied and now controlled Mesa that whether they liked it or not, they had no choice but to give the now-freed slaves and liberated seccies a dominant position on the planet—and do it soon. Fine, fine, as soon as possible. That still left the "as possible" issue open to debate.

What Cathy *hadn't* expected was the crowd that had poured onto the ceramacrete apron. It was...

Immense.

She had no idea how many people were spilled all over the spaceport's grounds, but the number had to run into six figures. Half a million? Even more? It was quite obvious that the spaceport's security force was no longer making any attempt to control the crowd, if it ever had.

Judging partly from their appearance, but mostly from their apparel, the crowd was entirely made up of slaves and seccies. She'd be surprised if there were even a dozen full citizens present.

She made a remark to that effect once she reached the bottom of the ramp, and the response was immediate.

"I'd be surprised if there was even one of the bastards," Dusek said.

Cachat's contribution was a sniff.

"But plenty of them will be watching on the newscasts," Thandi said, grinning quite cheerily. "The datanet available to the full citizens has always actually been a lot more independent and fractious than you might have expected. The news channels available—legally, at least—to seccies and slaves were something else entirely, of course. Those were both centralized and rigidly controlled. And, at the moment, *we* control them, since the Alliance didn't grab them right off. We can't control what the full citizens' nets are showing, but I'd be surprised if they weren't playing it pretty much straight up. They've got pretty discerning subscribers who won't be happy if they find out they've been lied to. As for the seccy channels, they were instructed to cover your arrival. Exclusively and until we tell them they can resume regular broadcasting. Which won't be for a while yet."

"Unless the Military Administration seizes the restricted channel network—which I would've done right off," Victor said. He sniffed again. "That was slack on their part. On the other hand, they didn't have the advantage of being trained by Oscar Saint-Just."

Everybody looked at him. Except for Thandi and Dusek, their expressions ranged from startled to (on Cathy's part) somewhat aghast.

"Yeah, that's what I would've done, too," Dusek agreed.

Jeremy had recovered almost instantly. His mental reflexes were as quick as his physical ones.

"How long will it be before they do elbow us out?" he asked, and Victor shrugged.

"They've had almost three months to do it already, and they haven't," he pointed out. "So it's possible they never will. Of course, this—" he waved a hand to indicate the massive, gathering crowd "—may change their mind. If it does, and if they're smart, they'll do it after we finish broadcasting the rally."

"What rally?" Berry asked.

Dusek pointed to a bustle of activity in the distance. A number of people seemed to be erecting some sort of structure.

"That rally," he said. "They should have the speakers' platform ready shortly." He smiled. "So you'd better start working on your speeches."

It was Berry's turn to look aghast. But Cathy just nodded. Giving impromptu speeches was something she'd done more times than she could remember. She was quite good at it. Actually, she was *very* good at it.

"And if the Manties are *really* smart," Victor continued, "they'll dicker with us instead of being heavy-handed. All we really need is unimpeded access to a few outlets, only one of which needs to be a news channel. They can leave most of the others in the hands of the citizens."

He smiled as well. It was a very thin smile.

"Excuse me. Every Mesan is a citizen now. I should've said 'the former full citizens.'"

Cathy had gotten to know Victor fairly well by now. She was amused but not surprised to see the way the man—who was, after all, an official in Haven's government—slid so easily and naturally into the role of a revolutionary activist.

You always had to remember that about Victor Cachat. While the man's loyalty to Haven was absolute, it was not tribal. It was based on his deeply rooted political convictions. He'd already, as a very young man, turned against Haven's government when he decided it had betrayed Haven. No one doubted that he could and would do it again, if he felt it necessary. Perhaps oddly, that was part of the reason everyone who knew the man trusted him as much as they did—from Haven's president, Eloise Pritchart, on down.

"We'd better get to it, then," Cathy said. "From the looks of that crowd, it's going to take us a while to get to the platform."

"*Speech?*" Berry whined.

HMS *Artemis*
Mesa Planetary Orbit
Mesa System

MICHELLE HENKE, KNOWN ON FORMAL OCCASIONS AS COUNTESS Gold Peak, stopped watching the newscast and looked back at the officers gathered around the briefing room table aboard her flagship.

"They're not snarling...yet," she said. "But they will be, before long, if we don't handle this right."

Oliver Diamato, one of Lester Tourville's task force commanders, frowned.

"Snarl with *what*, Admiral? They can't possibly think they've got the firepower to go toe-to-toe with us!"

"Doesn't matter one damned bit," Tourville said curtly, still watching the display with a baleful expression.

The treecat perched on the back of his chair made a soft, scolding sound, and the Havenite admiral—Henke's second in command for Tenth Fleet—turned his head to look at it. It cocked its head at him, gazing at him steadily until he smiled ever so slightly and reached up and back to rub its ears for a moment. Lurks in Branches regarded him for another moment, then gave a human-style nod, and Tourville turned back to Diamato.

"It doesn't matter," he said in a less...fraught tone. "They know perfectly well that the Grand Alliance has no desire to maintain a permanent military occupation of Mesa. We've managed it for three months, now, and I'm honestly a little surprised we've kept a lid on things as well as we have. But the pressure is building, Oliver. Sooner or later, we'll have to cede authority to a civilian government. They know that, too. And this—" he nodded toward the display "—is their none too subtle way of

15

reminding us that that government will have to be acceptable to that crowd. Which numbers—"

He raised an eyebrow at Henke, and she raised her voice slightly.

"Do we have a count yet, Dominica?" she asked.

"It's still growing, Milady," Commander Dominica Adenauer, Henke's ops officer, replied over the briefing room com. "Currently, it's somewhere between eight hundred and twenty and eight hundred sixty thousand people. But before it's over, there should be close to a million. Give or take thirty thousand.

"It's impossible to make crowd-counting an exact science," Adenauer's voice took on a slightly aggrieved tinge, "because human beings keep moving around. Especially civilians."

"We should have seized the system's news services," Diamato said, and Tourville shrugged.

"We did seize everything that had any possible military application."

"And I wasn't about to try to seize anything else, Oliver," Henke said. Diamato looked at her, and it was her turn to shrug. "Their datanet is as diversified as any datanet in the galaxy, and there were way too many news and entertainment services, at least for their full citizens. We couldn't have seized control of all of them, and shutting them down would have required us to shut down their ISPs, and *that* would have shut down their entire planetary communications net. The only news services with a plug we could have pulled *without* shutting down the entire web were the restricted 'seccy channels.'" She shook her head. "That kind of blackout would have been catastrophic for any hope of maintaining something like public order down there. Even if that weren't true, shutting down the communications—or even 'just' seizing control of the news services—could only have fanned the flames for the people who already think we're responsible for the 'nuclear strikes.'"

"Well, with all due respect, Admiral, we should at least get control of those restricted channels now," Diamato said. "After the rally's over, anyway," he added a bit grudgingly. "It'd be too heavy-handed to do it right now."

"Actually, it'd be too heavy-handed to do it at all," Michelle said. "One of the main reasons General Hibson's been able to keep that lid on is the fact that the MMA's kept its hands off the news and information services." General Susan Hibson's Mesan Military Administration had been—functionally, at least—the

Mesa System's government for the last three months. "There's a reason we've been careful about not tampering with the full citizens' services, and making it very clear that we haven't. And the same reasoning applies to brute forcing some kind of control of the seccy news channels. Probably applies even more strongly, actually."

"Absolutely," Tourville agreed. "Remember what it was like when Ransom controlled all of our news channels back home, Oliver. Anybody with two neurons to rub together knew they were lying to us. Well, those seccies and ex-slaves down there in Mendel knew exactly the same thing, especially the ones who managed to pirate the full citizens' feeds. This is the first time anyone except the people whose boot was on their necks had any input into the news they're receiving over 'their' services. We need to leave them in control of those feeds—clearly and visibly in control—or they won't trust us. In fact, if we don't leave them in control, there wouldn't be any reason they *should* trust us. And right now, we *need* that trust, since there's none at all coming from the rest of the population."

"What's your estimate, Cynthia?" Henke asked, looking at Captain Cynthia Lecter, her chief of staff. "I think we can figure that 99.9 percent of the former full citizens think we're responsible for the nukes. But what about the seccies and ex-slaves?"

Captain Lecter shook her head.

"I think you're too pessimistic about the assumptions of the former full citizens, Milady," she said. "We need to come up with a shorter term for that, by the way. One or two syllables instead of six. Anyway, I figure as many as ten to fifteen percent of them are at least skeptical that we're the guilty party. They've had time to do some thinking now, and too many things about the slaughter don't make any sense with us as the culprits."

"*That* high?" Tourville's expression was dubious.

"Yes, Sir. But I'm simply speaking of people who have doubts that *we* did it. Call them agnostics, if you will. That doesn't mean they believe our theory that the Alignment did it. In fact, a number of those agnostics are furious with us for making the accusation, since they considered *themselves* the Alignment."

"And the seccies and ex-slaves?" Henke asked.

"That's not easy to determine, Milady," Lecter replied. "Obviously, a much higher percentage of ex-slaves and seccies are willing to believe us. But it's hard to probe beneath the surface, because most of the ones who do think we did it are keeping their mouths shut. They're in an impossible situation, if you think about it. We *did* liberate them, after all. And even if they think we were responsible for the nuclear attacks, they don't think *they* were the target. All the blasts were clearly aimed at one or another full citizen target. It's just that a lot of seccies and ex-slaves got caught in the destruction because they were too close."

"It's a common pattern," Rear Admiral Michael Oversteegen put in. "Go back through history, and you'll find that whenever some outside military force liberates a conquered people, th' ones bein' liberated almost always suffer a lot of collateral damage. You almost never hear about it afterward, though. Like Captain Lecter says, what's someone who's lost a husband or a mother or a child supposed t' say? 'I hate you bastards because you killed some of my family when you freed us.'" He shrugged. "So would you rather we *hadn't*?"

War was a mucky business. Henke had known that since she was very young—and if she'd ever needed further proof of it, she had it now.

"All right, people. Cynthia, after that's over—" she pointed to the rally being shown on the display "—schedule a meeting for me with Dusek and some of the other seccy leaders. And we'll need General Hibson in attendance, too. We need to...formalize our understanding of how news on events like this will be handled."

"Understanding?" Tourville smiled crookedly. "Sounds more to me like we're talking about continued capitulation, Milady."

"I prefer to think of it as an enlightened *mutual understanding*, Lester." Henke's smile was even more crooked than his. "Speaking of which, I think it would probably be a good idea to have you present, too."

Tourville nodded his agreement.

"I wish at least some ex-slave leaders had emerged by now," he said then. "We really need input at the top from what you might call the very bottom. Even Dusek really speaks more for the seccies than the slaves at this point. Oh," he waved one hand, "I'm not saying they don't trust him, but the truth is, from their perspective, he was closer to a full citizen than a slave, given his position in Neue Rostock. We need some leaders who are genuine ex-slaves if we want them fully onboard."

A loud roar from the display drew Henke's eyes back to it. Catherine Montaigne had left the platform, and a new speaker had come forward.

"Ex-slave *leaders*?" she asked, with something that might, by a sufficiently charitable soul, have been described as a laugh. "Oh, I think you might reasonably say there were some of those around with *him* on the planet!"

She sat back and watched as Jeremy X began to speak.

Varuna Tower
City of Mendel
Planet Mesa
Mesa System

BRIANNA PEARSON STARED AT TWO OF THE PEOPLE SEATED IN her penthouse living room.

"Are you *serious*?"

Her inflection made it clear that she wasn't really asking a question. She rose from her own chair and went over to one of the huge windows that overlooked the city. From this elevation, she could see most of Mendel as it stretched to the north of the city's center.

What was left of Hancock Tower lay in that direction—so did Neue Rostock—but she could see neither of them. In the case of Neue Rostock, which lay to the northwest, too many tall buildings obscured her view. But she would have been able to see the very top stories of Hancock...once. Now, though, after the KEW called down by that damned idiot Bentley Howell, she would have had to be a lot closer—or a lot higher—to see its ruins.

Something else she couldn't see at the moment but had seen all too clearly before the arrival of the Grand Alliance's fleet was the damage caused by the debris thrown up by Hancock's destruction. Among Howell's many other idiocies, it had apparently not occurred to him that a KEW strike of that magnitude would fling tons of material into the sky, and that what went up would come down again, unless it achieved orbital velocity. The ceramacrete exteriors of the towers facing the blast site had survived reasonably intact—and served as something of a protective dyke for the buildings beyond them—but there'd been a lot of secondary damage even to them. The damage done to anything

20

in the open, between those towers and Hancock, had been far worse. The number of ground vehicles destroyed outright by the falling debris had numbered in the scores. The number which had been "merely" damaged reached into the hundreds, and no one had a final count, even now, of exactly how many private air cars had simply been swatted out of the air by the blast front. They *did* know that seven of the city's mass transit air buses had gone down, though. Worse, half a dozen above-ground high-speed personnel tubes had been thoroughly wrecked, as well.

And they knew the human casualties had been just as bad as the physical damage.

She considered her visitors' distorted reflection in the window's crystoplast. She'd just been introduced to the man sitting on the right side of the divan. He was a large, heavyset fellow named Ingemar Bukelis, who worked for the Mesan Office of Investigation's Domestic Intelligence Branch. Brianna already knew the woman on the left, Skylar Beckert, but only slightly. Beckert was the director of MISD's Domestic Intelligence Analysis and, as such, had been several rungs down from Brianna's own position in the hierarchy of Mesa's government.

Former government, she reminded herself. The political situation was chaotic. There were three separate power centers on the planet, now. The first, and by far the most powerful, was the MMA, what amounted to a military dictatorship exercised by Susan Hibson in Admiral Gold Peak's name. Being fair about it, Hibson was trying to rule with as light a hand as possible under the circumstances, and the occupiers had left as much as possible of the pre-invasion civilian infrastructure up and running. The Mesan *military* was also still in uniform and, technically, under the same officers, but *its* leash was short. Very, very short.

The second source of power was the new Citizens Union set up by the leaders of the seccy insurrection. Jurgen Dusek, the boss of Neue Rostock, had been chosen as its Chairman. Chosen by whom? So far as Brianna knew, by a two-person electorate: himself and Thandi Palane, the military leader of the insurrection. But none of the other bosses seemed to be objecting. Not publicly, at any rate.

The relationship between the MMA and the Citizens Union was a cooperative one but, under the surface, a competing one, as well. The Military Administration held ultimate authority and wasn't shy about showing it—wisely, in Pearson's opinion, given the powder keg the planet represented. But Gold Peak and Hibson clearly wanted to minimize any appearance of heavy-handed military dictatorships. And it looked to Pearson as if they also understood that they simply could not exclude the seccies and slaves—*ex*-slaves—from the levers of power. Not if they wanted to maintain any sort of long-term stability, at least. And it appeared the Citizens Union recognized that any transition to "self-rule" had to be handled very carefully if things like bloodbaths were to be avoided. So for at least the moment, the CU was the MMA's junior partner, although everyone realized that would have to change—and sooner, rather than later—if the Grand Alliance was ever going to be able to step back from its role as military occupier.

At least, that was how it looked to Pearson from what was admittedly quite a distance—a literal distance as well as a figurative one. She hadn't left her penthouse, except for quick errands, since the day after the Grand Alliance's fleet entered the Mesa System.

Which led her to consider the third of the power centers—the one that was by far the largest, in terms of people, and by far the weakest, in terms of power. That was the bureaucrats and administrators of the previously existing Mesan government, a surprising amount of which was still operating. Gold Peak and Hibson had been careful about preserving the organs of government and the regulatory agencies. Executive authority *over* those agencies was quite another matter, but most people who'd had government jobs had kept working, once the initial uncertainty created by the conquest had eased.

Not all, though—and Pearson herself was a case in point. She was Vice President of Operations (Mesa) for Technodyne Industries, and by virtue of that position had also been a member of Mesa's General Board. People like her, from the highest echelons of Mesa's government, were for the most part staying out of sight, although many of them hadn't exactly tried to hide. They'd just gotten out of the way, like Pearson, who'd placed herself under what amounted to voluntary house arrest. Anyone running things now could easily discover her address. If they wanted her, all they had to do was send someone to summon her . . . or arrest her, if that was what they preferred.

Others had truly gone into hiding, though. Pearson had

been attending an emergency meeting in the General Board's conference room when word arrived that a *big* hyper footprint had just been detected. That footprint had belonged to Admiral Gold Peak's Tenth Fleet and its dozens of superdreadnoughts and battlecruisers.

The Mesan Navy couldn't possibly fight off that kind of firepower, and four of the Board members had raced out of the conference room within five minutes. No one had seen Regan Snyder, Fran Selig, François McGillicuddy, or Bentley Howell since, so far as Pearson knew. They'd "taken a powder," to use an ancient and obscure cliché.

That was hardly surprising. Regan Snyder had been Mesa's Director of Commerce—and, more to the point, Manpower Incorporated's representative on the General Board. Fran Selig had been the Commissioner of Mesa's Office of Public Safety, while Bentley Howell had been her counterpart for the Mesan Internal Security Directorate. And François McGillicuddy, as Mesa's Director of Security, had been both Selig and Howell's boss.

In short, they were the most prominent figures on Mesa of the galaxy's most hated and reviled system government, and the three most visible officials in charge of suppressing the slaves and seccies. It appeared the MMA had more pressing concerns than catching them, just at the moment, but they had to be sweating the moment that changed, because if Admiral Gold Peak—or, still worse, Dusek and Palane—wanted to settle grudges, those four would be first in line for the guillotine.

They might still be, when they finally *were* caught. And so might Pearson herself, for that matter. She'd never had the public notoriety of many Board members, and behind the scenes she'd tried her best to keep the repression within bounds. But Mesa's slaves and seccies had had centuries to build up a reservoir of hatred for their masters. She didn't suppose they'd be prone to making fine distinctions at this point.

The one thing Pearson had feared the most, though, hadn't happened. Neither Mendel nor—so far as she knew—anywhere else on the planet had endured the raging slaughter that the freed slaves on the planet now called Torch had inflicted on its full citizens. *Manpower's* headquarters building had been stormed even before Hibson's troops had been able to reach the surface, and the casualties there has been . . . ugly. But that had actually been a surprisingly isolated event. No doubt there'd been some additional lynchings, here and there, but nothing on the scale of the madness on Torch.

Part of the reason for that was simple: the Tenth Fleet had close to a million ground troops, and Susan Hibson was prepared to land as many of them as she needed. Her Military Administration had very quickly established martial law, disarmed the Misties... and made it very clear what would happen to any freelance vigilantes. Too late to save the Manpower HQ, perhaps— and Pearson had to wonder if that had truly been an oversight on Hibson's part—but still very quickly indeed, And at least two other factors had mitigated against a mass pogrom, as well. The first was that Mesa's economy was complex and multifaceted. It was not the rather crude high-tech plantation-style economy that Torch had had. Slaves were scattered all over, mostly working alone or in very small groups. It would have taken them time to organize a lynch mob—time which hadn't been given to the slaves' victims on Torch.

Or to Manpower. Which was probably because no "organizing" had been required in Manpower's case. *That* mob had been more a matter of... spontaneous—and instantaneous—combustion. Or like dropping a lump of metallic sodium into a beaker of water, perhaps.

Before any *other* mobs could have assembled, Tenth Fleet's ground forces were already beginning to land... and the third factor had come into play. Ironically, the very same huge ceramacrete structures that had made the seccy rebellion so difficult to crush now worked in favor of the full citizens. By the end of that first day, most of them had retreated into their towers and armed themselves. It had always been legal for full citizens to own light weapons, and among them were the surviving members of the MISD and the OPS forces, most of whom had headed home with their military-grade weapons before Hibson's confiscations. If any slaves had tried to assault any of those enormous buildings, they would have suffered terrible casualties. Indeed, the Manpower mob's casualties against the corporation's far smaller force of security guards had been atrocious enough to discourage anything not fueled by a sheer, incandescent, bone-deep hatred. A need to destroy that didn't truly *care* if it died in the destruction, as well.

Pearson had seen video of *that* mob. She never—ever—wanted to see something like it again.

Now she turned back to face Bukelis and Beckert.

"You *are* serious, aren't you? You really think the Grand Alliance is telling the truth about these—these—" She waved her hand. "I still choke on saying it, because it's so ridiculous. About this so-called 'Mesan Alignment' of theirs, which they claim is the ultimate source of all the galaxy's wickedness?"

She shook her head vigorously. The motion was not so much one of denial as that of a dog, shaking off rainwater. Then she pointed at the fourth person in the room, a short and wiry fellow with an undefinable academic aura.

"For God's sake!" She jabbed her finger again. "There—right there!—is your Mesan Alignment. The most thinly disguised 'secret cabal' in history. Chicherin is even one of its officers, even if he does pretend not to be. Which is pointless, now. I figure it took the Grand Alliance less than twenty-four hours to turn up the names and ranks of every member of the Alignment in good standing. Am I right, Jackson?"

The vice president of Research and Development for the Mesan Genetic Consultancy made a slight motion with his shoulders. Jackson Chicherin's gestures all tended to be minimalist. This one was his version of a shrug.

"Probably," he said. "Our 'security' was basically designed just to keep the Office of Investigation from having to take official notice of us. As long as we kept our heads down—just a little—we got ignored by the security establishment. And for the record, I am *not* an 'official' in the Alignment."

He cleared his throat.

"We don't actually have officials, as such. I am merely Mendel's Deputy Lodge Leader for the Alignment."

Pearson rolled her eyes.

"Why am I not surprised?" she demanded of no one in particular, then resumed her seat. "All right. Try to convince me."

"Let me do the trying, Brianna," Chicherin said before either Beckert or Bukelis could speak up. He nodded toward the two people sitting on the divan. "What they'll tell you—I know, because they've spent several hours telling me already—are the following things. All of which, by the way, I believe to be true, as well.

"There are three critical issues involved." He raised a hand

and started counting off his fingers. "First, neither the Audubon Ballroom nor any other slave or seccy organization had the skills and resources carry out the wave of terrorist attacks prior to the Grand Alliance's invasion.

"Second," he counted off another finger, "the reason Ingemar is here is because he was Harriet Caldwell's assistant. Caldwell was probably the best analyst for the office of investigation's Domestic Intelligence Branch."

"Harriet was a real whiz at it," Bukelis put in. "*No-Sparrow-Shall-Fall Caldwell*, we called her. It was only partly a joke."

"I'd heard of her all the way over in Domestic Intelligence Analysis," Beckert added.

Pearson was a bit impressed. Despite the similarity in their names, DIB and DIA were not close at all. The Domestic Intelligence Branch was part of Mesa's Office of Investigation, which was charged by law to deal only with full citizens, whose legal and civil rights were scrupulously observed. Domestic Intelligence Analysis, on the other hand, was part of the MISD, which was legally *forbidden* to deal with full citizens. The two agencies were supposed to "liaise" with each other, but that was mostly a fiction. If an analyst for DIB had a reputation good enough to be familiar to DIA agents and officials, she had to be really good.

"You said, '*was* a whiz at it,'" she said. "Am I to take it she is no longer of this world?"

Bukelis shook his head.

"Harriet and her boss, Tony Lindstrom, were ambushed in MISD's own parking structure. Their armored limousine was shredded by a ten-millimeter tribarrel. The weapon was recovered and turned out to be of Manticoran manufacture."

His shrug was not minimalist at all.

"The official report put it down as another Ballroom terrorist incident. But that's pure bullshit. Not even Dusek had more than a handful of genuine military-grade weapons, and they were all ours. Acquired from sources right here on Mesa by . . . creative bookkeeping, shall we say? We didn't encounter a single Manty weapon, even during the worst of the fighting in Neue Rostock. And how would the Ballroom have known they were exiting the building in the first place? It was an impromptu expedition, not a planned one." He grimaced. "There's no way Harriet and Tony were killed by the Ballroom. No way at all."

"Of course not," Skyler Beckert said. She looked at Pearson. "I can't tell you how many times I tried to convince my boss, Bentley Howell, that there was no way the Ballroom could have been responsible for the preinvasion terrorist incidents. And the invasion itself pretty much demolished the alternate theory I'd developed."

"Which was?"

"That the Manties were carrying out what amounted to an undercover commando operation on Mesa, which they were disguising as some sort of terrorist plot. Mind you, there's some evidence for that at the beginning. I was never able to figure out exactly what happened, but I'm certain Zilwicki and Cachat were somehow involved with the Green Pines Incident, which was the first use of nuclear devices."

"How did the invasion demolish your theory?" Pearson asked.

"A commando operation of that nature only makes sense as part of a long-term plan to destabilize Mesa. Why would the Manties bother, if they were going to conquer the system outright a year later?"

"Maybe they didn't know that at the time. It's quite possible, you know, that Gold Peak's invasion was a last-minute decision," Pearson pointed out, and Beckert shrugged.

"Could be," she conceded, "but what's still obvious—now, in hindsight—is that the Manties could have taken Mesa any time they chose. I find it hard to believe that they'd have taken the risk of using nukes in a commando operation—a totally *unnecessary* commando operation they would have known was going to piss off a lot of Solly public opinion and that could be traced back to them—under those circumstances. That's the sort of tactic and exposure you resort to only for 'must-succeed, can't-do-any-other-way' objectives. Which kicking the crap out of us clearly wasn't on, oh, so many levels."

It *did* seem implausible, Pearson thought, and looked back to Chicherin.

"You said 'three reasons,' Jackson. What's the third?"

He raised his hands and then spread them while turning in his chair. The gesture indicated the huge expanse of windows overlooking the city.

"It's right out there. Unless you've got the brains of a goose, you can't believe for one moment that the Grand Alliance was responsible for the nuclear strikes that followed immediately on their conquest. None of it makes any sense, for the very reasons Skyler just summed up for any 'commando operation.' They had no motive—indeed, they had every reason to keep casualties to a *minimum*. The Manties have no track record of doing that sort of wholesale murder. In fact, even their worst critics had to admit—before this, at least—that their record was the exact reverse of that! And while the Havenites were notoriously brutal under the old regime, not even they ever carried out this kind of indiscriminate slaughter. And even if they'd been crazy enough to do it here, the method makes no sense. Why use nukes, when they could've used KEWs? And, finally, the targets make no more sense than any of the rest of it. One of the bombs exploded on an uninhabited *island*, for God's sake."

He lowered his hands.

"And then, there's this. Whatever government emerges here in Mesa, we full citizens have to be part of it. No one can govern Mesa without us. We're still thirty percent of the population, and we have a much higher percentage of the educated and skilled work force."

Pearson had already figured that out, but—

"Where are you going with this?" she asked.

"You and I—" he flipped a finger back and forth to indicate the two of them "—are probably the best candidates from the old General Board to be included as full citizen representatives in the new government, whenever it starts getting formed. Neither of us had a reputation for being harsh, and in your case, there'll be plenty of people willing to testify you did your best to restrain Selig, Howell, McGillicuddy, and—" his tone darkened "—that snake Snyder. We don't even have to lie. You *did*."

"I'm not sure how much weight that's likely to swing with anybody," she replied. "But what does any of this have to do with what you came here to talk to me about?"

"Isn't it obvious? At the risk of seeming like a cynical, calculating, cold-blooded maneuverer, Brianna, *it's entirely to our advantage* to support the Grand Alliance's claims concerning the nuclear bombardment after the conquest. As it happens, I think it *is* true somebody else is responsible for the killings. Whether it's the Manties' version of the 'Mesan Alignment' is another issue. That's obviously nonsense. We had nothing to do with it. But *somebody* did it. Somebody else—not us, not the Grand Alliance. Somebody *else*. That's enough to start making peace, Brianna."

She stared at him for a while, then, abruptly, snorted.

"What did you get your degree in?" she asked.

"I have lots of degrees. Most of them in biology and genetics, of course. But I also picked up a master's certificate in history along the way. I did my thesis on an Ante Diaspora statesman. Man by the name of Machiavelli."

HMS *Artemis*
Mesa Planetary Orbit
Mesa System

.I.

"WELCOME ABOARD, YOUR MAJESTY." MICHELLE HENKE, LESTER Tourville, Susan Hibson, and Cynthia Lecter had risen to greet the monarch of Torch. Now Henke gestured toward one of the chairs around the large table. "Please, have a seat."

Next to her, Lecter coughed gently. Henke glanced at her, then back at the Queen of Torch, whose expression seemed a bit stiff, and realized she'd committed a breach of protocol.

"Excuse me," she said. "I believe the correct form of address is 'Your Mousety.'"

"Yes, thank you." Queen Berry had quite a friendly smile. "I prefer it to, ah, the usual."

A small troupe of people had followed the queen into the flag briefing room: Catherine Montaigne, Thandi Palane, Victor Cachat, and Web Du Havel, along with two men Michelle had never met before. She recognized one of them from holos she'd seen—the infamous, although now somewhat respectable Jeremy X. The other man was a complete stranger to her. All she'd been told was his name, Saburo X, and the fact that he was a close associate of Jeremy's. Presumably the reason for his presence at the meeting would be explained in due time.

Michelle smiled back at Queen Berry, waited until she'd been seated, and then sat once again, herself.

"You've met my cousin Elizabeth, I believe?" she said.

"The Queen—no, I guess she's the Empress now?"

"Only cousin Elizabeth I have."

30

"Yes, several times." Queen Berry nodded. "But that was back when I was just plain 'Berry,' before..." She waved her hand. "Before all the stuff that happened."

"And before anyone was referring to you as 'Your Mousety.'"

"Oh, long before," Berry said, and Henke chuckled.

"Lord in Heaven, I would love to be a fly on the wall when you first get introduced in Landing that way. She's quite a formidable woman, my cousin, but some things are too challenging for even her to overcome. One of them's 'proper protocol.' She and Duchess Harrington have tried to...revamp it for years now, with an unfortunately uniform lack of success. But you—you're a 'foreign potentate'! So all of those propriety-obsessed protocolists are just going to have to suck it up. 'Your Mousety.' Ha! They'll drop dead in droves!"

Web Du Havel shook his head.

"We tried to talk her out of it," he said.

"We *did* talk her out of it," Jeremy corrected the prime minister. Henke was struck by his voice. It was quite a bit higher pitched than she would have expected from someone with his fearsome reputation. She'd seen the imagery of the man, but never heard a recording of his voice.

Of course, that was hardly surprising. Unlike Montaigne, who was a noted orator, Jeremy X had been noted for killing people, not giving speeches.

"We did talk her out of it," the former head of the Audubon Ballroom repeated. He gave Torch's monarch a glare that seemed utterly insincere. "Much good it did us, too! Kept calling herself 'Mousety' until everyone gave in. The girl is as implacable as an iceberg. If I were you, I wouldn't let her anywhere *near* Landing. Protocol's all very well, but sooner or later, she'd have your poor, brutalized bureaucrats calling the Star Empire the *Asteroid Empire*."

Victor Cachat cleared his throat.

"If we could dispense with terrorist jocularity, I believe we have business to deal with," he said.

"Says Comrade Mayhem and Havoc," Jeremy transferred his glare to the Havenite, although it didn't seem to gain any more in the way of sincerity.

Cachat ignored that. He'd nodded respectfully to Tourville upon his arrival, but his attention was on Henke herself.

"I assume you have some remonstrances to raise with us, Admiral Gold Peak. Probably a long list of them. So we should get started."

"I'm curious about the pronoun you just used, Officer Cachat. I wouldn't think 'us' was appropriate. Given that, unlike these other folks, you are an officer of the Grand Alliance."

"Good point. I shall correct that immediately."

That statement struck Henke as being even less sincere than Jeremy's earlier glare, and she smiled very slightly.

"I wouldn't call the issues I wish to raise 'remonstrances,'" she said after a moment. "They're more in the way of . . . concerns."

She shifted her gaze back to Berry and her expression turned much more serious.

"I've read ONI's reports about the uprising on Torch," she said somberly. "'Verdant Vista,' as it was called then. That was a bloody business."

"It was horrible," Berry said, and there was no trace of a smile on her face now. "We tried to stop it—*did* stop it, as fast as we could."

"Yes, I know. My question is, could you do the same thing here?"

"There's no chance of that happening here, Admiral," Palane said. "First, if it *had* been going to happen, it already would have. Even General Hibson—" she nodded respectfully to the diminutive, dark-haired Marine "—and the rest of her ground troops would have had a hell of a time stopping a Verdant Vista scale mass uprising. But leaving everything else aside, the military conditions don't exist. It would be even harder for us to break into the citizen quarters than it was for them to break into Neue Rostock. Unless you'd be willing to let us borrow . . . oh, I don't know. Somewhere around five thousand tactical KEWs?"

Michelle shook her head with another smile.

"Tempting," she said. "Unfortunately, we've got enough grief as it is."

"Well, darn," Palane said, with an answering smile.

Henke placed her hands on the table and sat up straighter.

"I'm not worried about any sort of pogroms right now, or in the near future. What concerns me is that the Grand Alliance has no desire at all to maintain a long occupation of Mesa. We've seen how well that usually works out, and we have no intention of replacing the Sollies' Frontier Security with our own version of the same thing. That means we have to create a workable planetary government so we can pull the MMA back off-planet—or at least shift it into a secondary position, clearly acting in support of a legitimate, locally constituted government and not as an outside dictatorship—ASAP, and, given Mesa's history, that's going to be difficult. If whatever government we leave behind us doesn't work out, sooner or later there's going to be a lot of bloodshed. The animosities between Mesa's full citizens—*former* full citizens—and everyone else are...intense."

"'Intense' is putting it mildly," Jeremy said. He didn't say it with a snarl, though. In fact, his tone seemed almost insouciant. And so did his next words.

"But I really wouldn't worry too much about it Admiral. You—we, I should say—have several things favoring us."

"Which are?" Henke asked, and Jeremy nodded toward Web Du Havel.

"We've discussed it at some length, and I think it would be best for me to let the judicious scholar here explain it." An impish grin flashed across his face. "I'm likely to put everything too...ah..."

"Too *not* judiciously," Du Havel finished. He sat up straight himself, although he kept his hands in his lap. "The way we see it, Admiral, we have three factors working on our side. 'Our side' meaning that of the entire population of the planet, in this case."

"I'm listening."

"First, the former slaves are completely disorganized politically. The only significant group that exists in that respect is the Audubon Ballroom, and the Ballroom's strength on Mesa was... how shall I put this—?"

"No need to be diplomatic about it, Web," the man named Saburo X said.

His voice was a striking contrast to Jeremy's: a baritone so deep it was almost an outright basso. Now he looked at Henke and shrugged.

"We never had much strength here, Admiral," he said. "And even less once the scorpions launched their repression after Green Pines. The great majority of people they butchered and imprisoned were perfectly innocent, but willy-nilly they did sweep up some of our people in the process. Only two of the ones captured survived, and the scorpions didn't bother capturing very many people in the first place."

Scorpion was the term used by the Ballroom—and many slaves, for that matter—to refer to anyone working for Manpower or any institution associated with genetic slavery. The casual way Saburo tossed it off was a good indication of just how... *broadly* the epithet was applied. Members of the Ballroom didn't have a lot of use for the notion that anyone suspected of being a slaver in any way, shape, or form had to be considered innocent until proven guilty. Their attitude—certainly their operating philosophy—was more along the lines of *kill them all and let God sort them out.*

Yet what struck Henke most about Saburo's use of the term— for that matter, everything he'd said—was that, like Jeremy, there didn't seem to be any rage underneath it. He seemed quite dispassionate, in fact.

"The point Web is beating around the bush about," he continued, nodding toward Du Havel, "is that those of us in the Ballroom—yes, I'm still a member, even if Jeremy's resigned—are in no position to compete with Dusek and the other bosses for the political allegiance of even the former slaves, much less the seccies."

"That's absolutely true," Du Havel said in a more serious tone. "And while it's equally true that there are a lot of uncharitable things that could be said about Mesa's criminal bosses, the one thing they are *not*—not one of them—is prone to recklessness. They are pragmatists from the top of whatever hair they have down to the soles of their feet. So long as they're the effective leaders of the ex-slaves as well as the seccies, they'll see to it that the peace is kept. Given the new dispensation, their personal situations—and fortunes—look very promising, and widespread violence is bad for business. The last thing they'll tolerate is anyone upsetting apple carts just because they're furious and seeking vengeance."

That was... an interesting way of looking at the situation. Henke could recall very few times she'd ever heard anyone point to the *virtues* of criminals, when it came to government. The one enormous exception to that was Erewhon, of course. The onetime member of the Manticoran Alliance—and current charter member of Oravil Barregos's Mayan Autonomous Regional Sector—had been founded, long ago, by an association of criminal cartels. Its present system of government was no longer composed of outright criminals, but it retained much of the cartels' original DNA, and it worked quite well.

"I may be a bit skeptical about that," she said out loud, "but I can see your point. What are the other positive factors?"

"The second," Du Havel said, "is that it is the perception of Mesa's entire population—that includes the former full citizens—that the planet's authorities got their asses handed to them by the seccies in the rebellion."

"Interesting." Henke sat back. "I happen to agree with you—and them—but aren't you concerned that someone's going to try to . . . reshape the narrative? After all, someone is eventually going to point out that General Palane's forces were on the verge of total defeat when Tenth Fleet entered the system."

"Of course they were," Cachat said. "I know; I was there myself, and I'd overseen the setting of our final suicide detonations. Neue Rostock *was* on the verge of being overrun by the Peaceforce. But Neue Rostock is only one of over a dozen seccy residential towers in Mendel alone. There are plenty more in every city on Mesa. And while the MPP would have taken Neue Rostock, we'd already gutted them—just like Bachue the Nose and her people in Hancock had already gutted the Misties. They'd have won a tactical victory, but only at the cost of placing themselves in a terrible strategic position."

"I understand that." Henke nodded. "That's exactly my own and General Hibson's analysis of the situation. My question is what's going to keep someone from trying to deny it down the road, once the immediacy of the situation is past? God knows everyone in this briefing room has seen plenty of 'narrative shaping' that doesn't have a single damned thing in common with reality!"

"Oh, you're right about that, Admiral!" Palane said. "But this particular 'narrative' is going to be just a bit harder than most to reshape." She shook her head. "Don't think everyone on this planet doesn't know the truth. Ask General Drescher. She's no dummy."

Henke had spoken to Drescher already. Multiple times, in fact. Not about this subject, granted, but she'd been impressed by the Mesan general's judgment and good sense. Now she raised an eyebrow at Hibson.

"Gillian—I mean, General Drescher—and I have talked about this, Milady," the MMA's commander said. "She's said exactly the same thing more than once."

"But it's not just the military who understands what happened—understands it deep down inside, where the nightmares live," Palane continued. "Every one of those *former* free citizens of yours who's sitting home right now with a pulser in her lap, ready to defend *her* tower if the seccies and slaves come for her family, knows it just as well as Drescher. That's *why* she's sitting there with that pulser. Because she knows there's no organized military force between her and the seccies and ex-slaves except the Grand Alliance. And she knows—or she's *afraid* she knows—exactly what would happen if the Grand Alliance pulled the MMA back offworld and left tomorrow. That kind of 'knowing' goes to the bone, Admiral." Palane's expression was one of grim satisfaction. "They aren't going to forget it, no matter *who* tries to 'reshape the narrative,' for a long, *long* time."

"I'll grant your assessment, for now, at least," Henke said. "But I'm still not sure exactly how the former full citizens' understanding that they got their butts kicked is going to help you prevent pogroms from the people who did the kicking."

She looked back and forth between Berry and Du Havel, and Du Havel spread his hands.

"After a victory, especially one as overwhelming as *this* one, people are generally more willing to let bygones be bygones," he said. "To a degree, at least. Not always, of course, but it's our assessment that that's the situation here. That's not just the result of the fighting, either. Regardless of who they think is responsible—you, or the Alignment, or unknown persons—what's obvious to everyone is that the former full citizens suffered most of the casualties in the wave of nuclear detonations, and the casualties themselves ran into the millions. Most people's appetite for vengeance only goes so far, Admiral.

"On top of that, there are simply too many full citizens for that sort of pogrom. They're a third of the population, and there are the next best thing to twelve billion people in the Mesa System. Even the most vengeful ex-slaves would get pretty tired before they'd slaughtered four billion of their vile oppressors, Milady.

"Besides, relations between slaveowners and slaves are always more complicated than either the slavers themselves or—" he glanced at Jeremy "—abolitionists like to think they are. Even on Torch, there are plenty of accounts of slaves helping to rescue full citizens after the butchery—even during it, when it was at its height. More, actually, than there are of slaves finishing anyone off."

Saburo grunted in agreement.

"Quite a bit more," he said, and a very thin smile crossed his face. "I'd call it deplorable slackness except the truth is that by now even my bloodthirstiness has been assuaged."

"All right." Henke looked back at Du Havel. "I'll accept that assessment, too, at least provisionally. Anything else?"

"Well..." Du Havel glanced at Saburo. "Well..."

"God save us from diplomats," Jeremy said. "What Web's hemming-and-hawing about, Admiral, is that the best way to make sure there's no unfortunate trouble is to create a new police force. General Hibson's ground forces have done a good job, better than I would have thought they could, this far. But they're still obviously foreign *troops*, not cops, and they can't have the sort of...neighborhood presence a *community* force needs. That means we need to replace them with a new one, one whose legitimacy is at least acceptable to all parties, as soon as we can.

"OPS and MISD have to go, entirely and completely. All of us know that. But all of us also understand—or I hope to *God* all of us understand—that you can't simply junk the existing police forces unless you're ready to stand up something else to fill the power vacuum. That's what we need here, and you've already said that the Grand Alliance has no desire to provide one on any long-term basis. So, what does that leave?" He shrugged. "It leaves a new police force. One positioned to monitor the situation and nip anything in the bud."

He paused, watching Henke's expression, and she nodded gravely, hoping he wouldn't realize just how indecently pleased she was by what she was fairly certain he was headed toward.

And that *Susan Hibson* wouldn't have to suggest it, after all.

"Well," he continued, "who better to put in charge of such a force than someone who's proven his own aptitude for trouble-making and won't have anything to prove to the sixty percent of this planet's population that used to be enslaved? Seeing as how I doubt if any thousand ex-slaves on Mesa put together could match Saburo's body count when it comes to scorpions. I think I could myself, but it would be nip and tuck.

"Not—" he smiled just as thinly as Saburo had done "—that anyone was keeping score, you understand. We're not *barbarians*."

Henke raised a hand to hide her smile, but inside she felt only exultation. True, she hadn't considered *Saburo* to head the

new police force. She'd been afraid it was something else that
was going to end up on Palane's plate. But now that she'd met
the man, heard Jeremy's analysis of his suitability, she had to
admit that it sounded good to her, as well.

"Well," she began, lowering her hand, "that all sounds—"

A soft chime from the briefing room hatch interrupted her,
and she frowned. But none of her officers would have interrupted
a meeting like this unless it was important, and she pressed the
com key.

"Enter," she said.

The hatch opened, and Lieutenant Archer, her red-haired flag
lieutenant, stuck his head through it.

"Yes, Gwen?"

"Pardon me, Milady. Captain Zilwicki is here and wishes to
speak to you as soon as possible."

"He's *here*?"

"Standing right behind him, Milady," Anton's unmistakable
rumbling basso replied.

"Sweetie!" Catherine Montaigne exclaimed.

"Daddy!" was Queen Berry's contribution.

.II.

HENKE REFLECTED UPON HER EARLIER COMMENTS VIS-À-VIS PRO-
tocol as the Queen of Torch and the leader of the Manticoran
Liberal Party converged upon the newest arrival for their own
highly informal greeting. On Queen Berry's part, it mainly consisted of a hug any uninformed observer might have mistaken for
a determined attempt to strangle him. On Catherine Montaigne's
part, it consisted of the sort of long, lingering kiss which normally saw beer mugs thumping on tabletops while the raucous
crowd whistled shrilly.

The admiral waited patiently, then cleared her throat and
pointed at one of the still unoccupied chairs.

"Have a seat, Captain," she invited with a small smile, and
Zilwicki settled into the indicated place with only the slightest
trace of color in his cheeks. Well, she thought, he'd had years of
practice with Montaigne's...idiosyncrasies. No doubt he'd learned
to take them in stride. However...

"Do we need anyone to leave, Captain Zilwicki?" she asked, glancing around the compartment. "I'm not sure anyone here besides Admiral Tourville, General Hibson, Captain Lecter, and me has the proverbial 'need to know.'"

"Actually, Admiral, some of what I have to report—even more, the proposals that come with it—will require the input of everyone here, to one degree or another."

"One of Anton's positive qualities, Admiral," Cachat said. "He's not obsessed with security for its own sake. Still, I wonder if Her Mousety needs to be present."

"Since when did you go all formal on me, Victor?" Berry demanded with a look of disapproval, and Zilwicki shrugged.

"There's no point in excluding her. She'd just wheedle it out of someone we *didn't* exclude, eventually. Better she gets it straight from the horse's mouth."

"I never understood that particular cliché," Henke said. "Unlike Cousin Elizabeth, I never really liked horses very much. And I certainly never met one with anything interesting to say."

"And I'm not sure *you* ever met one at all, Anton," Cathy said, regarding him skeptically.

"Hey!" Zilwicki protested. "We have horses on Gryphon—and not just in zoos, either." He nodded toward Cachat. "He's even ridden one."

Henke and Lecter both looked at Cachat.

"When and where?" the admiral asked.

"And *why*?" Lecter demanded.

"Sorry." Cachat's normally expressionless face looked slightly smug. "Need to know."

"He did it on a dare, by the accounts I heard," Zilwicki said. "I don't believe them, though. Victor's not a gambler except for really, *really* big stakes."

"I've heard that about him," Henke agreed with a nod. "On the other hand, why don't you go ahead and tell us what you've discovered?"

"Of course, Milady." Anton leaned forward a bit. "For the past several weeks, I've been analyzing the curlicues and oddities from the wave of explosions. Most of my time's been spent at my computers, because I had two very capable agents—Damien Harahap and Indiana Graham—to do whatever field work was needed. For the past stretch, though, I've been out in the field myself, and the upshot of it all is that I think I've found several... ah, let's call them nexuses, all of which put together start giving a picture of what happened."

"Really?" Henke tipped back in her chair, her expression intent. "I don't suppose your analysis was able to determine the origin point for the detonation signal?"

"Not from the timing of the explosions themselves, if that's what you mean, Milady, and we're not going to, either, I'm afraid. Lieutenant Weaver and Captain Lecter were correct that the planetside explosions were deliberately randomized. I'm less certain of Lieutenant Weaver's suggestion that it was to conceal their point of origin—I'll get to that in a moment—but they were definitely intentionally randomized. I was, however, able to determine the origin point for the explosions elsewhere in the system."

"Let me guess," Henke said. "It came from one of the planetary orbital habitats that was destroyed itself?"

"Exactly. And again, Lieutenant Weaver's analysis was correct about that, although he hadn't determined the actual habitat from which it came, since all of the ones in planetary orbit went up at virtually the same moment. No one really tried to disguise the actual source, though, so it was simply a matter of plotting the explosions and backplotting at the speed of light. And the answer was that it came from the biggest of them all—Station Delta." Zilwicki shrugged. "What I can't be positive of is whether the planetary detonation commands were also sent from Delta. I think it's very probable that they were, however. That a signal sent from somewhere on the surface of Mesa activated a timed detonation sequence from Delta, which triggered everything else. That's why I say that no matter how we analyze the timing of the planetary explosions, it's not going to tell us where the order to blow everything the hell up actually originated."

"Sounds reasonable." Lester Tourville nodded. "Except for the fact that if they'd done that, they wouldn't have had to bother with 'randomizing' anything down on the planet, either. They could have just detonated everything simultaneously, since they were going to blow up the transmission point, anyway." He grimaced. "Would've been a lot simpler, wouldn't it?"

"I don't think the...stretched out envelope for the planetary explosions was intended to conceal the location of their HQ, Admiral," Zilwicki said. "I'm pretty sure it was actually intended

to play into the notion of a Grand Alliance Eridani Edict violation. Missiles and KEWs don't arrive simultaneously on target
unless some ops officers invest the time and effort to make sure
they do, so if they wanted to make it look like an irrational,
impulsive, driven by hatred, 'just kill the bastards' order, staggering the explosions..."

He raised an empty, cupped hand, and Tourville nodded.

"Good point," he acknowledged. "That *would* appeal to these
bastards' twisty thinking, wouldn't it?"

"That's one way to put it," Zilwicki agreed. "Of course,
another way to put it would be to call it wringing every possible
advantage out of something they figured they had no choice but
to do anyway."

Tourville grunted sourly, and Zilwicki shrugged.

"Anyway, no matter how much I massaged the detonation
times on the planetary surface, I couldn't turn up any pattern
that would lead me to their secret headquarters. However, while
analyzing *when* things were blown up wasn't very helpful, analyzing
what things were blown up proved...rather more informative."

He tapped the controls on his briefing room chair's armrest
to bring them online, inserted a chip into a data port, then
entered a string of commands, and a holographic globe of Mesa
appeared above the table. The surface was transparent, so that
all places on the planet could be seen from any vantage point.
The continents were delineated by glowing traces.

"Should I call for a drumroll?" Henke asked with a quirky
smile.

"It would be nice." Zilwicki smiled back. "But...no. In retrospect, it was obvious enough we all should have seen it."

He tapped another key, and the globe was suddenly stippled
with incandescent pinpoints in an explosively expanding net.
They leapfrogged crazily across Mesa's surface, connected by thin
strands of light to indicate sequence, and Henke's smile disappeared. She'd seen that same data displayed far too many times,
and every time she had, she'd thought about the millions of lives
that had vanished into those blinding pinpoints.

The net stopped expanding. It burned steadily, and Zilwicki
waved a hand at the globe.

"A lot of those explosions were in places that don't seem to
make any sense at all," he told them all, rather unnecessarily.

"But what occurred to me was that the reason they don't seem to make any sense is because we don't know what they were blowing up. What I mean is that they obviously *would* make sense if we knew what had been there before the explosions. These people may be vicious, and they may be callous, and they're sure as hell ruthless, but not even they would be erasing things they didn't figure needed to be erased."

"Makes sense." Henke nodded.

"There are two basic approaches to hiding sensitive installations," Zilwicki continued.

"One is to put them in a place where there's so much other traffic, so many other people and so much other infrastructure, that all of *your* activities disappear into the background noise. The problem there is that so many possible things can go wrong, so many random bystanders who may notice something you don't want noticed. Not only that, any modern urban area is so heavily monitored that there are scads of stored data a suspicious analyst can sort through looking for patterns that shouldn't be there, and the longer you keep your HQ in one place, the more likely you are to generate a pattern he can spot.

"The second approach is to stick your installation somewhere where there *is* no other traffic or infrastructure, no inconvenient monitors or bystanders to notice anything they shouldn't, and camouflage the hell out of it to keep anyone from even realizing it exists. The problem *there* is that if anyone does notice your comings and goings, it's a lot more likely to cause them to wonder what the hell is going on."

He looked around the compartment to be sure everyone was with him, then shrugged.

"We're all pretty much in agreement that these people have been around a long, long time and that they're very good at hiding. It's also evident that they're really into . . . concentric levels of security. That they've built what Duchess Harrington calls an 'onion' around their most critical facilities. All of which suggested to me that they probably had what you might call an *operational* HQ and a *strategic* HQ. The former would be the communication and coordination nexus and might be moved periodically; the latter would be the long-term, secure site where they kept their really senior—their *generational*, let's say—leadership. There'd have to be a lot of traffic in and out of the operational HQ, and it would have to have a lot of communication links, but they'd do their damnedest to limit traffic in an out of their secret, strategic HQ to the barest possible minimum, and *it* would probably have only a single link of its own. It would communicate—directly—only with the operational HQ, which would relay anything that needed relaying.

"Bearing that in mind, it seemed likely their operational HQ had been in one of the urban or habitat sites that got nuked. It was possible I was wrong and that they'd done the same thing with their strategic HQ, or even collocated them. But if they *hadn't*—if they'd separated them the way their *modus operandi* suggested they probably had—then the strategic HQ might well have been one of those 'nothing to see here' sites we've been unable to explain. So, I started looking at the most obviously 'unimportant' explosions, instead. And, *this*—" he touched a key "—is what I found."

A single pinprick, in the middle of the McClintock Sea, flashed suddenly red.

"The *island*?" Tourville said, and Cachat barked a laugh.

"You're right—it's obvious!" he said.

"It was obvious that it *could* have been what I was looking for," Zilwicki corrected. "There were quite a few other targets where the official records insisted there was nothing to be blown up in the first place, but this one stuck out for several reasons, once I really started looking at it. One of the major points in its favor was that the nature preserve around it covers almost a million square kilometers, and it's in the *middle* of the McClintock, not one of the coastal preserves. It's completely closed to development. *Nobody*'s allowed to live there. So—"

"So if they had any traffic in and out there wouldn't be any of those bystanders or traffic monitors to see it," Henke said, her expression thoughtful.

"Exactly," Zilwicki agreed. "And none of the other 'empty spots' had that kind of complete geographic isolation from human habitation. That could have appealed to them for any number of installations they really wanted to hide, but it was so perfect for their needs that I couldn't shake the conclusion that they wouldn't have 'wasted it' on anything less important than their central headquarters."

"That may be a *bit* of a leap, Captain Zilwicki," Lecter said, but her tone was thoughtful, not dismissive.

"Agreed. So I sent Damien and Indy to look it over on the ground. Judging from the size of the hole it left behind, the nuke that took out the island had to be buried pretty damned deep. Our best estimate is that it was about two hundred meters below ground level. That's an awful deep hole to dig if all you're going to do is put a bomb at the bottom of the shaft, so my belief is that whatever they'd built there went *down* two hundred meters and they just parked the bomb in the subbasement. That indicates that its target was probably pretty damned big, especially given the challenges of going that deep on an island, with all the seepage issues that implies."

He entered another command, and the transparent globe disappeared, replaced by an overhead view of a large, semitropical island. A deep, almost perfectly circular and obscenely beautiful blue "lagoon" dominated its center, and its once luxuriant tropical tree cover lay like the petulantly scattered jackstraws of some enormous child. The parts of it that hadn't been incinerated by the fireball, at least.

"As you can see, the crater's already almost entirely full of water," Zilwicki continued. "And it hasn't been possible to form any detailed picture of whatever they needed to blow up. But not even a nuclear explosion really obliterates *everything*, and there are the ruins of a handful of . . . satellite structures." He tapped a key and an icon in the holograph highlighted the outlines of what might have been relatively small foundations in a ring, spaced equidistantly around the central crater. There were a couple of gaps in that ring, where the destruction had been worst. "And Damien and Indy also found the ruins of an extensive—and very well camouflaged—detached boathouse. They used a separate—and smaller—bomb on it, so there are a few more traces of it left, and unless we miss our guess, it was about the farthest thing imaginable from 'utilitarian.' We're talking about first-class luxury here, and that further supports the notion that this was an important site and that the people assigned to it were stationed there for the kind of extended period that would justify amenities like that. In short, the sort of site where a generational conspiracy might park its core leadership.

"And they also found *this*." He reached into a pocket, produced a scrap of what looked like silvery fabric, and handed it across to Henke.

"And 'this' is exactly what?" she asked quizzically, turning it in her hands as she examined it. "Heavy, isn't it?" she added, looking up at him.

"It is. And what it is, Milady, is a *very* advanced piece of smart fabric. When it's attached to a power source, it's completely transparent to light and every other form of radiation...from one side. The *other* side, however, becomes what's effectively a highly flexible, easily configured flat screen. An HD screen, one might say. I never saw anything quite like it before, so I don't have any idea how expensive it might be, but the mere fact that they have it—and that no one else does, to the best of my knowledge—and chose to use it *here*—" he jutted his chin at the holo of the island "—certainly seemed to underscore how important they thought the place was."

Henke considered that for a moment, then nodded, and Zilwicki sat back once more.

"Once I got Damien and Indy's report, I started searching for imagery of the island," he said. "At which point I discovered another interesting thing. The most recent overhead imagery in the official Park Service archives is well over two hundred T-years old. Apparently, no Park Service ranger has overflown the island in the last two centuries. Not only that, but there's no more recent imagery in *any* official archive anywhere on the planet. Or none we've been able to access yet, at any rate. And that is *not* something that could've happened by accident.

"So I extended my search beyond the official records. At the moment," he smiled thinly, "the system constitution's prohibitions against warrantless searches of full citizens' electronic data are...in abeyance, let's say. That was one hell of a lot of data to crunch, and it turned out that there was a fair amount of imagery of the island in private hands. A 'fair amount' given that it's in the middle of an enormous nature preserve which just happens to not be crossed by any commercial air routes, at any rate. Which is to say, not a vast treasure trove, but one hell of a lot more than I really expected. Most of what I found is pretty bland and useless for our purposes, but my algorithms finally turned up something very interesting from a privately owned shuttle that overflew the area about five years back."

The desecrated view of the crater disappeared, and Henke and Tourville leaned forward as one as it was replaced by a low-angle view of a gorgeous gem of greenery afloat upon a sea of deep blue water. And almost at the center of that gem—exactly where the lagoon now lay, in fact—was a luxury air car.

Rather, there was *half* a luxury air car. Its rear half was hidden inside an obviously solid canopy of treetops.

"*That* is an air car passing through an opening in the middle of a hologram," Zilwicki rumbled. "You can't tell there's a gap in it because the opening's too small and the angle is so oblique. It seems pretty clear they opened a hole just big enough for the limo...and closed it again as soon as it was clear. But the hologram as a whole is maintained in every single stray bit of imagery I've been able to find. I'm pretty sure those satellite structures Damien and Indy found were footings for the masts supporting a canopy of *that*—" he gestured at the scrap of fabric still in Henke's hands "—that covered the entire center of the island and the holo projectors that produced the image it displayed. And that—" his gaze swept the people seated around the table "—is a *lot* of work to hide a structure on an island in the middle of nowhere that no one was going to be visiting anyway. The sort of work I might expect out of, oh, say a paranoid, megalomaniac, secret conspiracy that's managed to hide itself for centuries."

There was silence for a moment. Then Henke shrugged and dropped the fabric on the tabletop.

"It's all circumstantial and conjectural, but it sounds to me like you're probably right, Captain. If you are, is it likely to lead anywhere else?"

"That's...possible, although not anything *I'd* call likely." Zilwicki picked the fabric back up. "We're busy analyzing the hell out of this stuff, hoping we can track it back to a particular nanotech outfit, for example. Frankly, I don't see much chance at all of that panning out. On the other hand, I'm still running a search of all the existing air traffic records. I don't expect to find anything in the island's immediate proximity, but we're looking for any air cars that just pop into existence on the theory that they had to come from somewhere, and it might just have been this black hole in the middle of the planetary airspace. If they did, finding out where they were *headed* might be sort of helpful.

"And, speaking of traffic records, that brings me to my next point."

He paused, and Henke shook her head at him.

"Do you have any idea how much I hate unnecessary pauses for emphasis on the part of smug briefing officers?" she inquired with a smile.

"I do believe Captain Lecter might have mentioned something about that to me, now that I think about it, Milady."

"Then I suggest you get to it."

"Of course." Zilwicki bobbed his head to her, then continued in a more serious tone.

"As our capture of that single air car's image demonstrates, even the most cunning super-genius villains aren't gods. They can't control *everything* that happens on a planet inhabited by billions of people. They can't keep *track* of everything, either. And it occurred to me that the entire 'blow everything to hell' plan and its timing were too elaborate to have been improvised at the last moment. They must've been in place for quite a while. And one thing about longstanding plans is that the assumptions upon which they rest are subject to change, especially in a system as chaotic as an entire star nation filled with naturally chaotic human beings. That means someone needs to check periodically, to review their underlying assumptions and be sure all of their preconditions stay in place. Which, in this case, they hadn't."

He tapped his armrest controls, and a different hologram appeared above the table.

"This is Station Delta, before it was destroyed," he said. "I'm positive that one reason it was used as the nexus for relaying at least the off-planet demolition signals was because this is the habitat where the Mesa System Traffic Control Service hung its vac helmet. Like our Astrographic Service back home, the TCS keeps track of all extra-atmospheric traffic in the entire star system. Originally, TCS was located *here*—"

He highlighted a position near the center of the huge, sprawling orbital habitat. Like most such—the Beowulf System habitats were an exception to the rule—it had long since departed from whatever neat and tidy design it had originally possessed. In the vacuum of space, streamlining and gravity were equally irrelevant, so whenever a new addition was needed, it was simply constructed wherever it was convenient. By the time of its destruction, Station Delta had become a jumble of erratically sized structures and subsections haphazardly attached to one another by the sort of spindly booms a spider would have shunned.

"But a year ago," he continued, after they'd had a moment to look, "the decision was made to expand and upgrade the TCS's capabilities. While the work was going on, TCS's traffic control facilities were moved to..."

He adjusted the highlight.

"Here."

"Way out from the center—and on the other side of that big...whatever it is," Henke said.

"Exactly. And 'whatever it is' is basically just a warehouse boom." Zilwicki's smile was almost broad enough to be called a grin. "In fact, a warehouse boom big enough it—"

"Shielded the new TCS facilities from the explosion," Henke concluded with a nod. From her long naval experience, she understood something many civilians didn't. Even a powerful detonation in space—even a nuclear blast—generated no shock-wave to anything not physically connected to it. There was no air, no water, no fluid of any kind to serve as a blast-conducting medium. There definitely were radiation effects, including the radiant heat energy of the explosion, but it wasn't at all uncommon for portions of a structure—especially ones which had been shielded in some way—to survive an external blast, which was effectively what it had been for the TCS facilities, given how far from the primary blast site they were located and how...flimsy the intervening structure had been.

Which hadn't been the case with the murdered Beowulf habitats. They *had* been built, and updated, to a coherent plan, and the explosions which had killed them had been located near their hubs. There might not have been any atmosphere outside those habitats, but there'd been plenty *inside* them to transmit blast and generate disastrous overpressures. The only reason Hamish Alexander-Harrington and Jacques Benton-Ramirez y Chou were still alive was that even Beta had been fringed by industrial booms, and they'd been stuck on one of them, far enough from the primary blast zone to survive.

Barely.

Tourville grunted, a sound that resonated with his own understanding...and satisfaction.

"There were survivors," he said.

"Better'n that," Zilwicki replied. "There were surviving TCS operators *and* all their records."

"That's what you meant about no one checking the prerequi-sites." Victor Cachat was not given to effusive displays of emo-tion, but his satisfaction was just as evident as Tourville's. "You think that's why they used Delta as the relay point. Or blew it up, anyway. By destroying it, they also erased their own tracks—some of them, at least. Just like—" He broke off. "Let me guess. The blast was centered right about where the TCS facility was originally located."

"Within a hundred meters of it, as near as we can reconstruct."

Cachat nodded, but Berry was looking puzzled.

"I'm not clear why you're all so pleased about that," she said. She sounded a bit plaintive, and Zilwicki looked at his adopted daughter.

"The reason *I'm* so pleased about it, Berry, is that I've been convinced for quite a while that the Alignment has been—had been—evacuating their people off-planet. And doing it in a way designed to cover their tracks. Wrapping one onion ring around another, you could say. The main ring they used—" his face turned hard "—was as ruthless as it gets. They launched a series of so-called 'terrorist attacks' to disguise the fact that many of the people supposedly killed were actually taken off-planet. And then they concluded the whole business with a monstrous wave of nuclear detonations. Not just so they could blame them on Admiral Gold Peak—they didn't have time to put together some-thing this elaborate *after* Tenth Fleet got here, so it had to have been orchestrated well in advance. They used it to help tar the Grand Alliance with responsibility for an Eridani violation when the opportunity presented itself, but its *true* purpose was always to wipe out their physical footprint here...including anyone they hadn't been able to get off-world in time."

"Always the nice thing about nuclear explosions, or fuel-air bombs—or sinking a cruise ship in kilometers of water." Cachat's tone was mild, his hands lightly folded on the table. "They don't leave any awkward and untidy remains."

"Oh." Berry made a face. "That's *gross*."

"These are very gross people we're dealing with," Cachat replied. "Slick and subtle in their methods and means, but in the end they're just a pack of vicious mass murderers."

He turned toward Zilwicki.

"Do you want me to interrogate the Traffic Control people?"

Berry's face tightened. She'd once witnessed Cachat's inter-rogation methods. They'd been...extreme. Thandi Palane only laughed, though.

"For Pete's sake, we're talking about civil servants who've probably never wielded anything deadlier than a tablet. I really doubt it'll be necessary to use the Black Victor *spill-your-guts-or-you-die-in-five-seconds-and-counting-now-four-seconds* inter-rogation technique."

Zilwicki chuckled as well.

"Not hardly," he said. "They were rescued by a Manticoran destroyer, and they've been in our custody ever since. They're babbling like a brook."

"What records do they have?" Cynthia Lecter asked. "Anything beyond ship movements and flight plans?"

"Oh, yes, indeed." Zilwicki worked at the controls again, and the hologram of the now-destroyed Station Delta vanished, replaced by what seemed to be a corridor aboard the station. Or possibly aboard a vessel, although it seemed too spacious for that.

"One of the things TCS was assigned to monitor," Zilwicki explained, "were the movements of all people transferring to or between ships at places like Delta. The records would be kept on the TCS servers for one T-year, and then transferred to an archive down on the planetary surface. An archive which just *happened* to be located at Ground Zero of one of the other nuclear explo-sions blamed on Tenth Fleet.

"The next transfer was due a bit less than three months from now, however, so there were still six T-months worth of records aboard the station at the time of its destruction. That period is plenty long enough to cover most—maybe all—of the so-called 'terrorist incidents.'"

The image of three people appeared in the display: a man and two women, coming around a corner and moving toward the camera. Their faces were quite visible. A few seconds later, they'd passed out of the camera's field of view.

"And speaking of the Devil, we've just seen the ghosts of two such victims. Not sure about the third." Zilwicki backed up the recording to bring the three figures into view again, then froze it. "We haven't been able—yet—to identify the tall woman with the reddish hair. But the shorter woman is Lisa Charteris. She was the head of a mysterious scientific project about which we still haven't learned anything. More to the point, she and her husband Jules were supposed to have died in the 'terrorist' blast that killed more than nine thousand people in Saracen Tower. Her husband *was* killed, in fact. We found recorded imagery of him entering the auditorium where she was supposed to be one of the speakers at a scientific conference on the servers of one of the full citizen news channels that had a team in place to cover it. The blast happened about two minutes after his arrival, so we know he went up with it. Lisa Charteris was presumed to be one of the unidentifiable bodies in the wreckage. But—"

He nodded toward the holographic image.

"Here she is, aboard Station Delta, about to board a luxury liner headed out-system. Two days before the blast that supposedly killed her.

"But here's what's *really* interesting."

He expanded the image of the man and looked around the table.

"Milady, Admiral Tourville, Your Mousety, Ladies and Gentlemen... meet Zachariah McBryde."

Cachat twitched upright in his chair, and Zilwicki nodded to him, then looked back at the others.

"This is the fellow whose brother Jack, with our help, smuggled the scientist Herlander Simões off Mesa. And then, when his own defection was stymied, blew up what we're now certain was one of the Alignment's central security facilities. To put it another way, someone we know—know for sure and certain—was a high-ranking member of the Alignment. The *real* alignment, not those poor souls on Mesa—poor saps, rather—who think *they* are the Alignment."

Zilwicki leaned back in his own chair, gripping the armrests.

"Zachariah McBryde supposedly died in another terrorist incident. His remains were never found—terrible, what a fuel-air bomb will do—but a couple of items of his jewelry survived the blast and were given to his grieving family, all of whom were members in good standing of the Alignment. And *one* of whom—"

In a rare dramatic gesture, he paused, raised his fist to his mouth, and coughed portentously.

"One of who," he continued, "his youngest sister Arianne, just so happens to have been both a highly qualified adviser to the system CEO under the old regime as well as an influential figure in the *other* Alignment. That is to say, the very outfit I've become convinced is the key to...well, not *everything*. But certainly one hell of a lot."

.III.

"I THINK YOU'D BETTER ELABORATE ON THAT, CAPTAIN ZILWICKI," Henke said. "My intelligence people's view of this so-called 'Alignment'—and my own—is that it's basically an innocent bystander. It got used as a front for the real Alignment without its knowledge. Over the last several months, we've interviewed literally hundreds of its known members in front of treecats. And because we have, we know they're telling us the truth when they tell us that none of them had any clue that was happening. Aside from that, I have to say that, as far as I'm concerned, it's been just one hell of a shrill nuisance. It's among the loudest voices criticizing us."

"I'm aware of that, Milady, and I agree. But that doesn't mean that this"—his fingers mimed quotation marks—"'Benign Alignment' isn't tightly associated with the Alignment we already knew about, whether its members realize that or not."

"How many of them are there, Anton?" Cachat asked. "Do we know?"

"We have pretty reliable numbers on that," Hibson put in. "The Domestic Intelligence Branch of the Office of Investigation had very thorough records on the Benign Alignment's membership, and my people have everything DIB ever had. Trust me, we made looking for the Alignment our number one priority."

"DIB had records on them? Why?" Cathy asked.

"Because while they were tolerated by the Mesan government, they were never fully trusted," Hibson replied, "so they were under constant surveillance. And the Alignment itself made no strenuous efforts to keep their identity secret, anyway."

"So how many of them are there?" Du Havel asked.

"Just north of eight hundred thousand," Zilwicki replied.

"*That* many?" Du Havel's eyebrows rose. "I had the impression they were just a fringe group."

"Out of a system population of over twelve and a half billion, eight hundred thousand is only point-zero-zero-six percent, Web," Zilwicki pointed out. "So, numerically, it *was* a fringe group. But it's still what you might call a...largish absolute number, and the Benign Alignment's members punch above their weight—in the area of science and technology, at least, if not politics. Their membership has a very high percentage of biologists, both theoretical as well as technical, and an especially high percentage of Mesa's geneticists."

"And how many of the bastards worked for Manpower?" Saburo demanded with a scowl.

"None, so far as we've been able to determine."

"*None?*" Saburo's eyebrows rose even higher than Du Havel's had.

"None," Hibson confirmed before Zilwicki could reply. "Not one single known member of this Benign Alignment of Captain Zilwicki's was ever an official employee of Manpower, and every one of them we've interviewed has...strongly asserted the same in front of our furry lie detectors."

"I'm pretty sure that was why DIB—or the General Board, anyway—didn't trust them," Zilwicki said. "But to understand why I think that, you have to understand the *nature* of the Benign Alignment. They fully share Leonard Detweiler's advocacy of genetic engineering and uplift, but they've always been harshly critical of Manpower and its methods. It's fair to say, in fact, that they hated Manpower themselves—with a passion. Which is why, given Manpower's position on the General Board, the system government didn't trust them any farther than it could spit. The Benign Alignment viewed Manpower as the single greatest obstacle to getting the galaxy's population to accept Detweiler's vision because of how thoroughly it had blackened the very idea with the perversions of genetic slavery."

"That's very interesting," Henke said, "and I mean that sincerely. But I'd like to get back to where we started. Why and how do you see this 'Benign Alignment' as being the key to—what did you call it?—'one whole hell of a lot,' as I remember?"

"I think they're key to several of the things we need," Zilwicki replied. "First, and most critically, I take it from what you've already said that we're pretty much in agreement that the members of the Benign Alignment still here on Mesa have no connection with the other Alignment. That is to say—"

Henke's lips quirked.

"Let's call them the 'Malign Alignment,'" she suggested. "And, yes, you may assume I agree that there's no connection between them and the murderous bastards we're looking for."

"Actually, there *is* a connection," Zilwicki disagreed. "It's one the Benign Alignment's members don't know about, but it's still there. In fact, it's one of the things I'm counting on."

"Okay, now you've lost me," Henke said.

"I think we're all satisfied at this point that the Malign Alignment has been using the *Benign* Alignment as a front," Zilwicki replied. "But it goes farther than that. Judging by the involvement of both McBryde brothers—both of whom were listed as known members of the Benign Alignment—it's also been their primary recruiting pool. Makes sense, when you think about it, since they'd start right out being in favor of 'genetic uplift.' That probably makes it an easier step to become a 'designing genetic supermen' fanatic.

"Assuming I'm right about that, it also means that a lot—I don't know what *percentage*, but a lot—of the Malign Alignment's members were like the McBrydes: members of the Benign Alignment, as well, like wolves hidden among the sheep. It wasn't simply a cover for them, either, because it also let them take advantage of the Benign Alignment's social and professional networking, which undoubtedly increased their own reach.

"But there's a flipside to that, as well. I've analyzed the casualty lists from the various 'terrorist' incidents, and the Benign Alignment's losses are *significantly* higher, proportionally, than those of the population as a whole. Again, that's only reasonable if the Malign Alignment was evacuating key personnel, many of whom would have been concealed as members of the Benign Alignment. But there's *another* reason for that, too. One which suggests an interesting possibility to me."

He sat back, eyebrows raised, looking around the compartment expectantly. There was silence for a long moment, and then Jeremy X whistled softly.

"You are a cunning man, Anton," he said. "I am once again reminded of all the reasons I am so glad that you're on our side."

"Okay, so I'm the dummy in the room again," Berry said, looking back and forth between her minister of war and her father. "Where, exactly, are you going with this, Dad?"

"He's suggesting that this 'Benign Alignment' is the one segment of Mesa's full citizenry that *can* be trusted," Jeremy told her, never looking away from Zilwicki. "He's going to propose that we bring them into the fold. Offer them a political alliance, if you will. Tacitly, if not openly."

"You are?" Berry's eyebrows rose.

"Just a minute," Henke said, before her father could reply. "I understand the logic of our being able to trust them. What I don't see, is why *they'd* trust *us*. I'm trying not to let my personal... irritation get in the way of my judgment, but their denunciations of us have been particularly shrill. And that's because of how furious they are with us for suggesting that something called the Mesan Alignment is a cesspool of evil. I would anticipate a certain degree of—skepticism, let's call it—on their part if we suddenly approach them with an offer of political alliance."

"That's where my analysis of their casualty rate comes in, Milady," Zilwicki said. "Because they were joined at the hip, whether they knew it or not, the Benign Alignment suffered one hell of a lot more 'collateral damage' in those 'terrorist" attacks and nuclear explosions—proportionately speaking—than the rest of the system population. The fact is, they got *hammered* by the Malign Alignment. Anyone like Jules Charteris, whose wife was about to be disappeared without him, had to be 'tidied up.' Probably quite a few parents—or children—fell into that same category. The 'collateral damage' from the coverup *had* to hit the people closest to the evacuees hardest, and the Benign Alignment was too close to the Malign Alignment to not take heavy losses. Even when they weren't threads that needed to be snipped *themselves*, they were far more likely than the general population to be in close proximity to someone who *did* need snipping. You can't use fuel-air bombs or nukes in someone's neighborhood without killing a hell of a lot of his neighbors...and relatives. Not only that, I will guarantee you that for a lot of the Benign Alignment's members, people they loved—people they never guessed were part of the Malign Alignment—were taken from them not by death, but by their superiors.

"I can't begin to imagine how many of them will be furious with the Malign Alignment's *leadership* for what's been done to them, and how many of them will be furious with the people they loved for being *part* of the Malign Alignment—for helping to *empower* what the Malign Alignment did to them. But either way, it's going to generate one hell of a lot of anger.

"If they become aware of it, that is."

"And assuming they *believe* us about that," Henke murmured, but she was nodding as she spoke.

"I think there's . . . a pretty fair chance of that, Milady," Lecter said with a thoughtful expression. "They're really pissed with us for suggesting *they* had anything to do with the terrorist attacks or the nukes, but what they've attacked is our use of the label 'Alignment' for the people who were behind the bombs. Not many of them have joined the chorus that claims we did it ourselves."

"She's right," Zilwicki said. "Almost none of them have, in fact. And by and large, these are highly intelligent people. They may not want to look at the evidence, but once they admit it *is* evidence, I don't think very many of them will be able to deny it."

Henke nodded again, more firmly.

"It's certainly the first hopeful thing about the Alignment—Malign or Benign—anyone's floated to me lately, anyway."

"Wellll . . ." Zilwicki drew the word out uncharacteristically and gave Jeremy a look that seemed somehow wary. "There is one other point I'd like to address."

Henke looked at him as warily as he'd looked at Jeremy, then sat back and invited him to continue with a hand wave that was almost resigned. Zilwicki turned his chair to face Jeremy directly.

"There's another reason I think an alliance between us and the Benign Alignment would be workable, Jeremy. The fact is, that both we and they have something positive to gain."

Cathy's expression got a little pinched.

"Anton, I don't know that this is the right time—"

"There'll never be a '*right*' time, Cathy." Zilwicki glanced at her, and he looked more like a dwarf king than ever as he almost growled the words. "That's in the nature of the beast. But I think this is as right a time as we'll ever get."

Their eyes held for a heartbeat or two. Then she sat back, and he returned his gaze to Jeremy.

"The fact is that the Benign Alignment is right, in a lot of ways, and has been all along. Beowulf's restrictions on genetic engineering need to be . . . reappraised. Although, to be fair, *Beowulf*'s attitude toward those restrictions has already evolved one hell of a lot over the last several centuries. And, also to be fair, the Code was always more concerned with preventing the weaponization of genetic engineering than with restricting genetic improvement per se. Part of the problem is that it was so difficult to separate those aspects, especially in the wake of Old Earth's Final War. Most people today don't realize, for example, that the 'Scrags' actually represent what was probably the *least* extreme of the 'super soldier' modifications. Some of the other mods were so far from the human norm that they could be produced only by cloning, and those... variants ought to scare the crap out of just about anyone. One reason we still have the Scrags and not the others, is that most of the others were too genetically differenced from humanity in general to maintain a viable population.

"Still, there's no question that Beowulf, like the rest of the galaxy, overreacted to the Final War. It was inevitable, really. But Leonard Detweiler was right when he called the Beowulf medical establishment on it. As nearly as I can tell he was an autocratic, stiff-necked, arrogant pain-in-the-ass who was only too well aware of his own brilliance. That probably had a little something to do with how... poorly received his pungent criticisms were. But he was also right, and there are plenty of examples of what you might call improvements on the base model to demonstrate that. Some of them were deliberate and planned, and some of them were nature taking a hand. I might point to Duchess Harrington as an example of the former. The Meyerdahl mods predated the Final War, so they were 'grandfathered in,' anyway, but the Beowulf Code has never objected to genetic modification to suit planetary environments. Not until the modification would get extreme enough to edge into weaponization territory, anyway. And Thandi here is a perfect example of the natural selection model, although even that's an 'artificial' result in the sense that no human beings would ever been subjected to the conditions on the Mfecane worlds if they hadn't learned to travel between stars."

"But if the Beowulf Code allowed something like the Meyerdahl mods to stand, what was Detweiler's problem with it?" Tourville asked. Zilwicki looked at him, and the Havenite shrugged. "I'm not trying to play devil's advocate here, Captain Zilwicki, but this isn't really one of my areas of expertise. Prior to our visit to Mesa I was the prototypical uninformed layman on the ins and outs of 'genetic uplift.' Since then, though, I've come to the conclusion that Beowulf's objection had to be more to his proposed methods than to the technology itself."

"That's fair enough, Admiral." Zilwicki nodded. "Part of what

Beowulf objected to about Detweiler's proposals was the radical nature of some of the improvements he advocated, and part of it was, in fact, the methodology he proposed using. For example, some of the earlier efforts to raise intelligence levels had...unfortunate consequences on things like mental stability. Victor and I saw an example of exactly that sort of 'unfortunate consequence,' secondhand, at least, in the case of Herlander Simões's daughter." His expression turned hard and cold for a moment. "I don't know how serious Detweiler was and how much of it was a way to deliberately goad a medical establishment which had already rejected his arguments, but he actually proposed doing...trial runs on clones who could be terminated if it turned out their genetic modification was a blind alley. Which is *exactly* what the Malign Alignment did in Francesca Simões's case. He was really, truly pissed with the 'Luddite thinking' of the Beowulf medical mainstream by that time, so I think it's entirely possible *he* was venting in hopes that pure outrage would carry off some of his critics. As Francesca demonstrated, though, at least someone took him seriously.

"But another part of what Beowulf objected to was the potential social consequences of a deliberate policy of genetic uplift. Of a search for a *Homo superior* whose attributes would be defined by its designers and directed towards a programmed goal."

"Social consequences?" Tourville repeated.

"The human race has an unfortunate tendency—one which appears to be pretty thoroughly hardwired into us—to fear 'the other,'" Zilwicki replied. "We've tried, off and on, for millennia to eradicate that tendency, but without very much success. Where we *have* made progress—and a hell of a lot of it, actually—is in expanding the definition of what you might call 'us' so that fewer and fewer people fall into the category of '*not* us.' One of the things Beowulf feared was the emergence of a new 'not us' that would be feared and hated. A reemergence of what used to be called 'racism.' That sort of concern made a lot of sense at the time, in many ways, given the prejudice against 'genies' which had come out of the Final War. And that same sort of prejudice is alive and well today—and stronger than ever, for many people—where genetic slaves are concerned. Which, by the way, is why the *Benign* Alignment hates Manpower with every fiber of its being.

"But they were also concerned that targeted improvement—improvement for the sake of improvement, not simply to fit specific environments—would become deeply politicized. Who defined what was an 'improvement'? Who had the authority to control and direct programs like that? Did *anyone* have that authority? And what happened when someone decided to follow in Plato's footsteps, organize a government on the basis of his *Republic*, but with its citizens genetically engineered to suit their roles within it?"

"Plato?" Tourville repeated. "Never heard of him. Where was his republic and what happened to it?"

"It never actually existed," Zilwicki replied. "It's the name of a very old book in which a philosopher named Plato described the ideal republic."

"Never heard of him," Tourville repeated.

"I can shoot you a translation of his book after we're done here," Zilwicki said. "The point is that the Beowulfers were worried about a continuation or reemergence of the pre-Final War competing genetic programs which had come so close to wiping out Old Earth. And they were afraid that the creation of a genetically stratified society—one based on actual, documentable genetic differences—would definitely re-create the sort of prejudice and bigotry associated with old-fashioned 'racism.' And you have to admit, Admiral, that what we've so far learned about the *Malign* Alignment and its stratification into alpha, beta, and gamma lines—and there might be still more 'lines' below the gammas—suggests that that's exactly the outcome it's looking for. So the Malign Alignment is a poster child for why the Beowulf Code *shouldn't* be reappraised.

"But the Mesan Alignment that was established here on Mesa during Detweiler's lifetime, the one we're now calling the Benign Alignment, rejected his radicalism—assuming he was ever serious about it in the first place. It was dedicated to supporting a *gradualist* improvement of the human race—one which deliberately conserved strengths, weeded out weaknesses, but without any defined final objective. What you might call the maximization of each individual's natural potential as a part of moving the entire race forward. I can't be sure yet, but I suspect we'll discover that the *Malign* Alignment began as a splinter faction of the original Alignment that was impatient with the concept of gradualism. But that original Alignment definitely was a benign organization, and I'm pretty sure it was only because of the... intensity of feeling where genetic modification was concerned during Detweiler's lifetime that it was organized in secret."

"But why stay that way?" Tourville asked. Zilwicki looked at him, and the Havenite grimaced. "As far as I can tell, the prejudice against your 'gradualist improvement' has been fading for a long time now. If anybody wanted to propose something as radical as your 'super soldiers,' or if they wanted to begin combining human and nonhuman genetic material, I'm sure a lot of people would object. And we may very well discover that that's exactly what your Malign Alignment has been up to. But from what you're saying, that's not what *these* people have been doing, at all."

"It isn't. But I think the answer to your question is twofold, Admiral. First, its existence has been a fairly *open* 'secret,' at least here on Mesa. That is, it wasn't costing its members anything in terms of pursuing its goals or their own lives to remain 'secret.' But, second—and more importantly, I suspect—there's the fact that it *is* here on Mesa...which is also the home of Manpower and genetic slavery." Zilwicki shook his head, his expression grim. "Obviously, they've been afraid that any Mesan organization advocating for an expansion of genetic engineering would be tarred with the Manpower brush. Which is another reason that they hate Manpower so passionately."

"Where you going with all this, Captain?" Henke asked.

"I think it's time we—the Grand Alliance—brought the Benign Alignment into the open, Milady. I think we need to make it clear that what the *Benign* Alignment's been doing is not—for that matter, never has been—a violation of the Beowulf Code. And then I think we need to offer it the opportunity to...repair some of Manpower's more egregious transgressions."

There was a sudden silence, in which most of the people in that compartment very obviously didn't look at the two former genetic slaves at the table.

Jeremy glanced around the compartment, then shook his head.

"How about people don't take it upon themselves to presume to know what the wretched and downtrodden products of Manpower think? I assure you, we're quite capable of speaking for ourselves."

He turned to Zilwicki.

"Just how much good do you think they could really do us?" he asked.

"I don't know, exactly." Zilwicki had been resting his wrists on the table edge. Now he spread his hands wide, without raising them. "But as you'd expect from people with their viewpoint, they're heavily concentrated in the biological sciences. And medicine. And however much they may have despised Manpower, they've been right here. Able to study Manpower's work up close. None of them ever worked for Manpower, so far as I've been able to determine, but that doesn't mean they haven't had access to its researchers and technicians."

"Interesting," Jeremy said. He leaned back in his chair, slowly, and folded his hands across his slim midriff. He sat that way for several seconds, then looked at Henke.

"Anton and Cathy know—at least roughly—Admiral Gold Peak, but what do you think my life expectancy is?" he asked.

"I really couldn't say," Henke replied. "Did you escape slavery early enough for prolong to be effective in your case?"

"No," he said.

"Well, I know Manpower's never wasted any effort on extending the lifespans of its slaves," Henke said, meeting his gaze levelly. "So I would assume that your life expectancy is short, at least by the standards of someone who *has* received prolong."

"You might say that." Jeremy smiled, but there was no warmth in that smile. "Of course, for you prolong recipients, all 'natural human lifespans' seem extremely short. But for those like me—" he gestured with his thumb at Saburo "him, too—the matter gets parsed a lot more closely. By the time prolong was developed, the average lifespan for humans had edged past a T-century. A bit more for women; a bit less for men, as always. But it was still a century, maybe a hundred and ten or twenty T-years."

He was silent for a moment, then inhaled deeply.

"After I escaped—eventually, not right off—I consulted the best doctors I could find. All of them came up with the same rough estimate of my own expected lifespan. All but two thought I'd make it past the age of sixty." His smile widened and showed some real warmth. "Assuming I didn't get myself killed in the course of my activities, that was. But only one thought I'd make it to seventy."

He swiveled his gaze to Saburo.

"What about you, Comrade? I don't think we've ever discussed it."

"Not much point to discussing it," Saburo replied with a grimace. "But mine is better than yours. Not by much. No one I consulted thought I had a chance to reach eighty."

By now, most of the expressions around the table were pinched.

"I knew it was short, but I hadn't realized it was that bad," Tourville said, and Saburo shrugged.

"My reflexes and hand eye coordination are way outside normal human parameters." He nodded toward Jeremy. "*His* come close to being supernatural. But we paid a price for it."

Jeremy made a growling noise in his throat.

"What's most annoying is that Manpower could have engineered us—rather easily, in fact—to have normal lifespans. Which prolong would have extended tremendously...if anyone had been wasting it on slaves. But they didn't bother."

"Sugar plantations," Cathy almost snarled.

"Exactly." Jeremy nodded, then looked around at the others. "Ancient Ante-Diaspora plantation owners in the Caribbean found it was more profitable to work a slave to death in a few years and buy another than it was to keep her or him alive. Manpower has the same point of view. Almost all genetic slaves have unusually short lifespans, because the kind of people who buy us can always get another if—when—we break." He bared his teeth briefly. "But that's also true for former slaves and most seccies, because the damage—Manpower's engineers call it the 'parameters'—was done before birth. Except that Manpower's engineers call that process 'decanting.'"

"I already knew a lot of that," Henke said, then snorted. "You may have heard that I have a friend whose family is fairly prominent among the abolitionists, both in Manticore and on Beowulf. But I don't think I've ever discussed the damage as such with her. How much of it can be repaired? After the fact, so to speak."

"Quite a bit, probably." Jeremy unclasped his hands and sat upright. "Maybe not as much for current generations, but certainly for their kids. Assuming the geneticists and medical technicians are good enough. And if enough money is available. It's not cheap."

"It's not cheap by the standards of an individual," Zilwicki said, "even if they're billionaires. But 'cheap' is measured on a very different scale if you're matching it to the wealth of an advanced star nation. Which—" he cleared his throat "—Mesa still is. Yes, there's been some damage done by the nukes. But much less than you might think. Modern industrial societies are extraordinarily resilient. They bounce back in no time."

He tapped his forehead, near the temple. "It's the brainpower, what does it."

"So who do we approach first?" Jeremy asked. "In this very Benign Alignment of which you speak?"

✧   ✧   ✧

"You didn't seem taken off guard when I raised the subject of genetic engineering," Zilwicki said to Cachat as they followed the other participants out of the briefing room.

Cachat twitched his lips in a facial version of a shrug.

"I wasn't expecting you to raise it, but it's not as if I hadn't thought about it before. Don't forget, I'm the one who shares a bed with Thandi and engages in other activities there than just sleeping on any number of occasions. Until I learned what to expect, the experience could be . . . startling, let's call it. And I know exactly how well Jeremy X can shoot a pistol. I owe my life to his marksmanship."

He shrugged again, this time with his shoulders.

"Why shouldn't those abilities—and many others—be shared by all humans? As long as it can be done safely and with the full cooperation and consent of the individuals involved, I certainly have no objection. Of course, the simple passage of time hasn't eliminated all of the other considerations that worried the people who wrote the Beowulf Code in the first place. You were right when you said some of those considerations are 'hardwired' into us, and I've had entirely too much personal experience with the sort of nightmares corrupt ideologues can create. Letting someone like Oscar Saint-Just direct a program of 'targeted uplift' would be . . ." He paused, as if searching for the exact words he wanted, then snorted.

"It would be a really bad fucking idea," he said.

"So you think it would have to be kept out of the state's control?" Zilwicki asked, and Cachat shook his head.

"I don't know if it could be trusted to proceed *without* state control, at least where those full cooperation and consent aspects are concerned," he said. "Bottom line, one reason I've never been incensed by the Beowulf Code's . . . myopia is that it truly does take something *like* the Code, with its broad acceptance and legal recognition, to prevent something like this from being abused into genetic slavery or that 'genetically stratified' society the Malign Alignment seems to be aimed toward. Maybe 'state control' is the wrong way to phrase it, but somebody—and maybe your Benign Alignment is the place to start—has to articulate what's acceptable and what isn't, codify it, and then hold all of the would-be Saint-Justs out there as accountable to it as they've been to the Beowulf Code. Somebody with genuine enforcement power. Of course, anything like that would have to be set up carefully. With the proper sort of watchdogs."

"Like you?" Zilwicki asked with a thin smile.

"I was thinking of former Ballroom members, actually."

"Hah. You know, I believe that's the first time I ever heard the words 'Ballroom' and 'watchdogs' used together." Zilwicki took Cachat by the arm and began walking down the passage. "But it's not such a strange idea, now that I think about it. We developed our original watchdogs—genetically engineered them, even if the methods were crude—out of wolves, didn't we?"

Victor eyed him sideways.

"I think you're trying to distract me," he said. "Speaking of watchdogs—or should I call them hunting dogs? I've noticed the absence of your two minions for some time now."

"Damien and Indy?"

"Yes. Them."

"Oh, them!" Zilwicki grinned. "I don't see where you have a need to know."

"You bastard."

"That's a harsh thing to say to a long-time partner of yours."

"You bastard," Cachat repeated.

"Oh, fine. I'll tell you." Anton glanced over his shoulder. "But not here. Anyone might be listening."

"Who cares?"

"Neither one of us, I suppose. But principles are there for their own sake, I always say."

They continued down the passage, with Zilwicki's hand still grasping Cachat's arm. Steering him, if not propelling him. The Havenite agent made no attempt to resist, however. His paramour wasn't the only person he knew whose strength fell outside normal human parameters. He'd have as much success resisting a tidal bore.

Balcescu Station
Debrecen Planetary Orbit
Balcescu System

"I DON'T MEAN TO INSULT OUR HOSTS OR ANYTHING," INDIANA Graham said, "but this dump makes *Seraphim* look good."

Damien Harahap looked around. In its better days—which he doubted had ever been all that good—the area of Balcescu Station through which he and his companion were passing at the moment had been a vending area. A string of small shops on either side of the corridor had catered to the needs of the station's crew and visitors.

Those glory days, such as they had been, were long gone. As time passed and Balcescu Station's business had become more and more enmeshed in the slave trade, it had suffered from the same condition slavery always brought with it. Wherever it spread, everything not bound up with slavery itself began withering on the vine. The wages of free people stagnated or declined, and while the wealth of the relative few who benefited from slavery increased, that wealth wasn't typically spent in the places where slaves did their work or the slave trade was concentrated.

The only exception to that rule of which Harahap was aware was the planet on which genetic slavery had originated. Mesa itself had remained a wealthy and advanced star nation, despite being the headquarters of Manpower and despite the fact that the majority of its population were slaves or descendants of slaves. And while he didn't know why that was true, he agreed with Anton Zilwicki and Victor Cachat, both of whom were convinced the reason it had was at the heart of what they called the Manpower Mystery.

"Manpower makes no sense," Cachat had once told him.

65

"Economically, it—and slavery—should have died a natural death long ago. Which is why Anton and I are both sure it isn't really a business to begin with. It's a disguise—a way to hide malice and malevolence beneath mere greed and corruption."

As badly as slavery might undermine a healthy economy however, its sudden disappearance left a vacuum. Whatever business had allowed the small shops to survive had declined since Torch's navy had seized the station. The navy's personnel substituted to a degree for the now vanished practitioners of the slave trade, but only to a degree. Mostly because there simply weren't as many of them, but also because they weren't transients. They'd buy food and drink regularly, so restaurants and taverns survived, although even they had fewer customers, because there were fewer mouths to feed. But the market for other goods, the sort travelers tended to pick up in transit—never great to begin with—had all but collapsed.

"I wouldn't call them our 'hosts,' exactly." Harahap's tone was even drier than usual. "Given that Torch seized the place by force, its people are more in the nature of an occupying force than a bunch of guests."

"And *scary* occupiers, to boot," Indy agreed, and Harahap snorted.

"Scary" was one way to put it, he supposed. The civilian inhabitants of Balcescu Station had come perilously close to being massacred by the Torch Marines who'd witnessed the destruction of the pinnace they'd sent to seize the *Luigi Pirandello*. Harahap couldn't find it in his heart to blame the Torches for their reaction. In fact, the thing that truly surprised him was that there *hadn't* been a massacre. Not even a handful of freelance murders. Given how many of Torch military's personnel were ex- (and, in some cases, not so very ex-) members of the Audubon Ballroom, the temptation must have been high. The fact that they hadn't yielded to it spoke well for their discipline.

According to reports, they *had* come close, however. Which was all very regrettable, of course . . . but was likely to increase the locals' eagerness to cooperate.

They've got to be worrying that something might trigger us into having them summarily executed after all, he thought. Not that he ever would. But neither would he refuse to capitalize upon the fact that they didn't know that.

They made their way through the rundown shopping area to the entrance to the section of the station in which the Torches had established their headquarters. The two guards waved them through without bothering to check their credentials, which they'd already seen. Harahap thought Torch's military—its ground forces, at any rate—were quite good. Not surprising, perhaps, in troops who'd been trained by Thandi Palane. But they weren't what you'd call a spit-and-polish outfit.

That was fine with Harahap. He vastly preferred competence to perfection of drill. He nodded approvingly to the guards, and the treecat on his shoulder bleeked in amusement. No treecat would ever need something as silly as "credentials" to know if someone was who he said he was, and Fire Watch had even less use for pointless formalities than his two-leg.

They continued down the passage to the office of the station's new commandant, and Harahap pressed the door buzzer. Lieutenant Colonel Kabweza was perched on a chair behind a desk covered with old-fashioned handwritten notes. Like a bird. Kabweza was so short that when she raised her chair to a comfortable work height, her feet would have dangled a few centimeters off the deck if not for the footstool under her desk.

Now she looked up and waved them inside. Her expression was not happy. Neither was it particularly surprised, however.

"No luck," she said with a scowl. "We've scoured the records every which way from Sunday. They've been scrubbed completely clean." She nodded toward the chairs in front of her desk. "Have a seat."

Harahap detected no enthusiasm in her invitation, which didn't astonish him. From her point of view, investigators sent out from Mesa were more of a nuisance than anything else. But she'd been polite and cooperative, and she obviously didn't like telling them her efforts had been fruitless.

"Completely scrubbed?" Indy said as he took his seat. "That seems odd. I wouldn't expect a station like this to maintain tight security."

"Normally, I'd agree with you," Kabweza said. "Especially when you add in the warning not to mess with their computer files we gave them as we approached the station. Understanding that the distinction between 'warning' and 'bloodcurdling threats of ghastly horrors' couldn't be discerned without special optical equipment."

She smiled, although the expression was fleeting.

"But there it is. By the time we were able to check the records ourselves, there wasn't anything left."

"I assume you didn't carry out the bloodcurdling threats of ghastly horrors," Harahap said, and the colonel shrugged.

"What would have been the point? What's done is done—and, besides, we don't think the station crew were the ones who did it. My technicians tell me they're pretty sure it was a prearranged scrub. Probably programmed to happen automatically under certain conditions." She smiled again, more broadly. "Conditions like, oh, imminent occupation by hostile forces."

Harahap wasn't surprised. The Alignment was anything but sloppy, when it came to security. They wouldn't have overlooked programming the computers of a transit station they were using for a special evacuation to scrub themselves if it even looked like someone else might get a look at them.

He didn't waste anyone's time with phrases like *are you sure?* and *have your technicians doublechecked?*

This trip was looking more and more like wasted effort. Well, he'd been on wild goose chases before. He'd be on more in the future. And he'd always known the expedition to Balcescu was something of a long shot, anyway. Zachariah McBryde had last been seen leaving Mesa aboard a luxury liner. The liner had made its first stop at a planet named Descombes, and they'd found a recording that showed McBryde disembarking from the ship.

Then . . . he'd vanished. Further investigation determined that there were three alternate ways he could have left Descombes, and Harahap had picked the one he thought was the most likely choice for a clandestine evacuation—a nondescript general cargo ship that had offered limited—and cramped—passenger accommodations.

That had led him and Indy to Balcescu. Which now looked to be a dead end.

"The one thing I'd still like to do," he said, "is to question the former station CO. Somogyi, I think his name was. I assume you still have him in custody?"

"Zoltan Somogyi," Kabweza agreed with a nod. "And, no, we don't. We just released him a few hours ago. There didn't seem to be much point in keeping him." She tapped the touchscreen built into her desk. "Zoltan Somogyi's address," she said.

"Somogyi, Zoltan," a computer voice replied. "Section Alpha Two, Suite One-One-Three."

Kabweza tapped another command, and the terminal transmitted the same address to Harahap's uni-link. The station schematic he'd loaded to it on arrival blinked alight, highlighting the route to Alpha 2, Suite 113.

"Thank you," he said, standing once more. "It's probably a long shot, but longshots sometimes pay off. Come on, Indy. Let's go pay a visit to Mr. Somogyi."

❖   ❖   ❖

"I know you're the fearless, brilliant interstellar secret agent," Indy remarked to no one in particular as they hiked through less than pristine passages towards their destination. "But to an amateur such as myself, this seems like a waste of time. If the Marines couldn't sweat anything out of him when he was still scared to death, what are the odds we can?"

"It probably *is* a waste of time," Harahap agreed. "But, like I told the Colonel, you never know. And we don't have anything else to do right now, so why not take a chance? Besides—"

He reached up to caress the ears of the treecat on his shoulder.

"I'm willing to bet Somogyi's never met a treecat, but he may have heard about their reputation by now. Maybe he hasn't, too, in which case we might just...enlighten him. Someone who can stand up to familiar interrogation techniques can be rattled by something *un*familiar. And if he happens to buy into the notion that Fire Watch here can actually read *minds*, and not just emotions..."

He shrugged, and Indy snorted.

"Did I ever mention that you're a very devious fellow?" he asked, and Fire Watch bleeked a laugh of agreement.

❖   ❖   ❖

"Hurry," Zoltan Somogyi hissed, leaning over Sophie Bordás's shoulder. Bordás was—had been, at any rate—Balcescu Station's sensor officer. At the moment, she sat at a work console in one corner of his three-room suite, keying in commands.

She also restrained herself—barely—from snarling, *If you think this is so easy, why don't you do it yourself?* Instead, she said, "We made these security protocols hard for anyone to access for a reason, remember?"

"Sorry." Somogyi straightened and wiped his face with one hand. "I just—"

The entrance buzzer sounded. Bordás broke off what she was doing and both of them stared at the closed door.

"Just ignore it," she whispered.

Somogyi hesitated, obviously drawn to the idea. But after a moment, he shook his head.

"Better not. I told that bitch Kabweza I was going home. If she's sent somebody to check on me, I damned well better be here."

He moved to the door and activated the bulkhead viewscreen that showed the corridor beyond it. Two men stood there, neither of whom he recognized. One of them was an obviously young, wiry fellow. The other—probably the older of the two, Somogyi thought, although prolong made such judgments chancy—was probably the most *ordinary* looking individual Somogyi had ever seen. As he watched, the ordinary looking one pressed the buzzer again.

"Come on, Zoltan," he said into the mic above the buzzer button. "We know you're in there. We just want to ask you a few questions."

Somogyi looked back at Bordás. She stared at him for a couple of seconds, then shrugged.

"I've been covering my tracks as I went," she said. "They probably won't figure anything out even if they look. But give me a second to get away from the console."

She crossed swiftly to a nearby couch and slid into it. Then, after a brief hesitation, she sprawled across it, as if she were a very regular visitor to Somogyi's apartment. A lover, maybe.

Fat chance of that ever happening. Somogyi was tolerable, but that was about the best she could say for him.

"Go ahead," she said. "Let 'em in."

Somogyi unlocked the door and opened it.

"What do you wa—"

He broke off, staring down at the animal seated upright on the deck next to the older man. It was vaguely catlike, allowing for the fact that it had six limbs and was quite a bit larger than any Old Terran cat he'd ever seen. It was also staring at him, quite placidly, to his relief. The thing was dangerous looking.

That was his first thought. Then he noticed the harness it wore...and what looked like a very small *pulser* holstered under its left forelimb.

He gawked at it, and the man standing next to it smiled at him.

"Never seen a treecat? I thought you probably hadn't. Which is why Fire Watch got off my shoulder and out of your door-cam's field of view." He smiled again, a pleasant expression which somehow failed to set Somogyi at ease. "We didn't want you to be nervous or anything, Zoltan. I *can* call you 'Zoltan,' can't I?"

"Uh..." Somogyi replied.

"Good!" The older man patted him on the shoulder. "This probably won't take more than a few minutes of your time, Zoltan," he said breezily as he pushed past Somogyi into the apartment. One eyebrow rose as he saw the woman sitting on the couch.

"Good afternoon, Ms....?"

"Bordás," she supplied.

"Ah! The sensor officer." The interloper beamed. "The very person I wanted to talk to next."

Somogyi stared at him, then back down at his monster, trying to remember... Treecats. What had he heard about *treecats*? He'd certainly never heard that they packed pulsers! But—

They can read minds. The damned things can read minds!

Panic roared through him, and he slammed his shoulder into the younger fellow, who was still standing in the doorway. The impact knocked him aside, and Somogyi raced toward the lift shafts. He'd gotten at least three whole meters down the passageway when something slammed into his shoulders from behind. He twisted under the solid, sinuous weight of the impact, then—

"*Bleek!*"

A hand—a four-fingered hand, with long, multi-jointed fingers—reached around from behind, into his field of view. Those fingers wiggled there, as if to be sure they had his attention... and then an obviously razor-sharp claw popped out of each fingertip. One of them just brushed his cheek, ever so lightly, and he froze.

He didn't move. He didn't speak. He barely even breathed, and a single thought went through his mind.

I am so screwed.

✧   ✧   ✧

"Those are copies of the station's surveillance records," Colonel Kabweza murmured. It had taken her security techs an hour or so to break Bordás's codes, and she frowned down at the imagery flowing across her display. "Now, why would Somogyi have made them?" she asked herself thoughtfully.

"Petty extortion and blackmail," a voice said, and she looked

over her shoulder. Damien Harahap had entered the compartment;
now he crossed it, Fire Watch flowing along beside him, to stand
at her shoulder. "He and his partner in crime—well, more like
partner in peccadillos, really—made them because they'd realized how regularly and thoroughly the station's security protocols
scrubbed the originals."

He handed a chip to her.

"Run this," he said. "Let's see if anything turns up."

Kabweza looked at him dubiously for a moment. She wasn't
a big fan of running someone else's executables on her own
terminal. But she plugged it in, tapped YES at the run prompt,
and sat back with her arms crossed.

"That's why they made the backup records," Harahap continued,
his eyes on the display. "As for the elaborate security precautions,
that was because both of them—especially Somogyi—were wary
of the people he thought really controlled Balcescu Station. He
wasn't trying to blackmail *them*, just spacers and slavers passing
through who engaged in petty offenses of one kind or another.
But he also figured anyone scrubbing data so furiously would
be...less than happy to discover that someone was circumvent-
ing their security measures."

"And just who were 'the people' he thought really controlled
the station?" she asked, and Harahap smiled at her.

"That, Colonel, is a very interesting question, isn't it?"

A tone chimed, and he and Kabweza looked back at the
display. The image of a man, sitting at a small table in one of
the station's passageways, filled the left half of the display. Two
women sat at it with him. The one to his right was obviously
talking, and he was listening to her. A far larger version of the
man's face filled most of the other side of the screen.

A line of alphanumeric characters blinked below the face:
Zachariah McBryde. Probability 98.8%.

"It's McBryde, all right," Harahap said. "I've studied enough
of his imagery by now to be sure of it, even without the recognition software. I recognize the woman talking to him, too. Don't
know the other one, but that's his boss, Lisa Charteris. But—"

He frowned, and used a finger to indicate another man, standing a few meters away, watching McBryde and his companion at
the table. His posture seemed stiff; his bearing, alert.

"But *this* is the guy I really want to find out more about,"

Harahap continued. Fire Watch bleeked questioningly, and he looked down. The 'cat's fingers flickered, and Harahap chuckled. "I want to find out more because if he isn't a watchdog, I've wasted my life," he told the treecat. "I've seen a lot of them, and he's nowhere near as good at it as most of them have been. Not if part of his job is to be unobtrusive, anyway."

"Why would McBryde need a watchdog?" Kabweza wondered. "He's in no danger by this point." She glanced at the time mark. "This recording was made twenty-six hours before we seized Balcescu Station. By the time we got here, he could have left on either the *Prince Sundjata* or the *Luigi Pirandello*. And once we did get here, no bodyguard could have helped them, anyway."

"I said 'watchdog,' not 'bodyguard,'" Harahap replied, his eyes back on the display. "He's not a protective detail. The reason he's watching McBryde and the others is to make sure they don't get captured . . . or try to run away on their own. And I'm willing to bet we just found out what happened to the *Luigi Pirandello* and the pinnace that seized it." He nodded at the display. "That man—or someone else like him—was aboard the *Luigi Pirandello*. Once he knew capture was inevitable, he blew up the ship and took your Marines with him."

Kabweza frowned, rubbing her chin with the tip of an index finger.

"But was McBryde aboard when he did it?" she asked.

"I don't know. Let's see if we can find out."

He reached past her to her console and raised an eyebrow at her. She grimaced, but she also sat back and nodded permission, then watched him enter another command.

✧   ✧   ✧

It took a while, and the recognition rating wasn't quite as firm—but 87.4% was more than good enough for Damien Harahap. Especially when the only reason the rating was a bit low was that the images had been captured from the rear, showing only a partial profile, as people boarded ship for departure. The rating for Charteris was a bit better—91.1%—although she was in a different boarding queue.

"Okay," Harahap said. "Zachariah McBryde got out of the system aboard the *Prince Sundjata*. And Lisa Charteris had the bad luck to be aboard the *Luigi Pirandello*. So now her real status matches the official one. Dead as a doornail."

"That's a bit cold, don't you think?" Kabweza asked, and he shrugged.

"There's nothing any of us can do to change what happened to her at this point," he said, still gazing at McBryde's image. "And she worked for an organization that killed God only knows how many innocent bystanders covering her disappearance. I've carried out operations with a lot of 'collateral damage' in my time, but not like this. So it's a little hard to work up a lot of sympathy for her. I feel a lot sorrier for the other passengers and your Marines, Colonel."

"Point," she agreed with a nod. "Definitely a point."

✧   ✧   ✧

Harahap and Indy stood gazing through the crystoplast wall of the departure lounge while they waited for their courier boat to mate with the boarding tube. There wasn't much to see. The planet below them, Debrecen, was as drab and nondescript as the station that orbited it, and Fire Watch had opted to nap in one of the lounge's—many—unoccupied seats instead of watching nothing at all happen.

But Harahap wasn't actually looking at the planet, either. He was gazing at the starfields beyond it.

"Wonder where McBryde is now?" Indy said.

"I don't know," Damien replied. "And it's a big galaxy. But someday, I intend to find out."

March 1923 Post Diaspora

"A petty detail. We're both *Marines*.
Once a Marine, always a Marine.
We're bound to get along famously."

—Major Bryce Tarkovsky, Solarian Marines

Courier Boat *Charles Davenport*
Galton System

THE STREAK DRIVE COURIER BOAT DECELERATED STEADILY TOWARDS the heart of the Galton System.

The system primary was a K5v, with six planets and two asteroid belts. Its innermost three planets were of no particular interest to anyone, but Galton-IV, known as Tschermak to its inhabitants, was an Earthlike world. Its surface gravity was about twenty percent greater than Old Terra's, which produced an atmosphere a bit thicker than humanity's birthplace, and it was only about six light-minutes from the primary, which gave it a year only half a T-year long. Its size and slow rotational speed, on the other hand, produced a "day" that was over sixty-seven hours long. That was...inconveniently lengthy, so the Tschermakians divided it into two somewhat more manageable thirty-three-hour "day-halves" divided by a seventy-seven-minute Compensate.

The combination of that long day and heavy gravity explained why many of the system's inhabitants preferred to live elsewhere, although Tschermak did have some spectacular scenery, and the surf and sailing to be found among the Leonard Ocean's Sanger Islands had to be experienced to be believed.

Of course, ninety-nine percent of all Tschermakians were barred from ever setting foot on those islands...except in menial and closely supervised positions.

The inner asteroid belt, between Galton-IV and Galton-V, was well within the system's 15.4 LM hyper limit, but not particularly rich in resources. The *outer* belt, however, was quite another matter. Once upon a time, Galton had boasted nine planets, but that had been before its current outermost planet, Galton-VI, had arrived. Between them, Galton-V and the "nomad" gas giant—a superjovian

77

so massive it fell just short of brown star status—had wreaked havoc on what *had* been the system's outermost planets. The astrographic models for what had happened were...confused, but all of them agreed that the nomad's arrival had knocked the previous outermost planet out of its orbit. Exactly what had happened then was less clear, but evidence suggested a collision—or at least a very, very near miss—between the displaced planet and the next planet in. After that, all bets were off. Everyone agreed it must have been lively as hell, at least on the time scale of a star system, but it had all happened long enough ago that the murdered planets' broken bones had long since settled into a stable, extraordinarily wide, and even more extraordinarily valuable asteroid belt.

Benjamin Detweiler sat in the small but palatial craft's main lounge, watching the viewscreen as Galton's brighter and steadily growing pinprick of brilliance emerged from the starfield. It wasn't his first visit here, by a long chalk, although only a handful of people in the system knew who he truly was. And, as always, the *Charles Davenport*'s approach could have served any dictionary as an example of "extreme caution," because Galton was not a welcoming star system.

The courier boat had emerged well outside the hyper-limit, on a least-time vector for Tschermak. At that range, not even a superdreadnought could have posed a threat to the system, but the diminutive courier's crew had been only too well aware of the multiply redundant sensor platforms watching their approach. And of the ranks of multidrive missile pods poised to obliterate them if those sensor platforms saw anything they didn't like.

By the standards of the Grand Alliance, the sensor net was big and clunky, because the Alignment's FTL communications technology still lagged well behind its adversaries'...and because weapons refits took first place just now and there were only so many things even a system like Galton could upgrade at the same time. As a result, Galton's current FTL net required a far larger transmitter and a much higher power budget, both of which drove up the size of the platform in which it was mounted, and its bandwidth was far narrower. But it worked, which was what really mattered. And the Alignment's stealth technology was at least as good as the Grand Alliance's, which made the passive sensor platforms themselves—and the whisker lasers which connected them to their control platforms—almost impossible to detect.

The control platforms, on the other hand, were almost impossible to *hide* once they brought their FTL transmitters online; the Alignment's inability to generate *directional* grav pulses was another aspect in which its capabilities lagged the Grand Alliance's. That was why each cluster of sensor platforms was linked to a total of three widely separated control platforms. Only one of them at a time would transmit data to Tschermak and the enormous habitats in orbit around it. The other two provided redundancy, standing ready to replace the first if an enemy managed to localize and destroy it.

Galton's multidrive missiles were also big and a bit crude by the Grand Alliance's standards. The Alignment remained unable to match the capabilities of even the Republic of Haven Navy's current-generation MDMs, far less those of the Royal Manticoran Navy's FTL-commanded Mark 23. On the other hand, the Alignment had been able to engineer its graserhead down to something that could be stuffed into a really, really big MDM. Those graserheads couldn't match the multi-targeting capacity of a conventional laserhead, but each hit they did achieve would be devastating.

And all of that concentrated lethality stood ready to blow *Charles Davenport* out of space if it strayed a single kilometer from its designated vector.

Detweiler wasn't particularly worried about that, though. It was the job of *Davenport*'s crew to sweat the details of their approach, and the courier's recognition code had been transmitted and acknowledged the better part of two hours ago.

No, what worried Detweiler was the reason he'd come and the message he had to deliver. That, and the fact that he was about to find himself admitting—and apologizing for—a rare and potentially painful error. An error whose cost could be high, indeed. He wasn't looking forward to delivering either of those, but neither would he flinch from the task. Avoiding things like that had never really been an option for him or his clone brothers, and that was even truer now. With their parents' deaths, leadership of the entire Alignment had devolved onto Benjamin Detweiler's shoulders, and he would not shirk his responsibilities...or fail the memories of Albrecht or Evelina Detweiler.

GSNSS *Francis Crick*
Tschermak Orbit
Galton System

DETWEILER AMUSED HIMSELF, AS HE FOLLOWED HAUPTMANN Chou through the labyrinthine interior of Galton's largest orbital habitat, by imagining the breadcrumbs he would have had to leave behind to find his way out again. Of course, in reality, he wouldn't have needed to do any such thing, even if he hadn't had an officer showing him the way. That was what location monitors and uni-link apps were for. Still, it was a challenging mental exercise.

And one that helped divert him just a bit longer from the true reason for his visit.

He *thought* he'd written every twist, turn, lift shaft, and interior airlock to memory. Like all of the Detweiler clones, he had a near photographic memory. But he wouldn't have wanted to stake his life on it, because *Crick* was huge. True, it was on the small side by the standards of habitats for systems like Sol or Beowulf. For that matter, it was far from the biggest platform in Tschermak orbit. Several other habitats were considerably larger, and the orbital industrial platforms dwarfed the station. But at somewhere north of 48,000,000 tons, it was certainly the largest *mobile* structure ever built.

On the other hand, *Francis Crick* hadn't been built primarily as an industrial node or to provide space for population expansion, like those other habitats had been. Oh, there were close to two billion people in the Galton System, counting both its orbital habitats and the genetic slaves who lived on Tschermak, at the bottom of the planetary gravity well, and it was true that almost a million of those people did live aboard *Crick*. But the true reason the station was so immense was because it was really a fortress, not what people usually meant by the term "habitat," at all.

There were many ways to defend a vessel or an installation. Armor, obviously, as well as defensive weapons, like counter-missiles, point defense lasers, ECM, gravity sidewalls, fitting even something *Crick*'s size with impellers to generate a wedge . . . The list was a long one. But one of the surest ways to strengthen something was, and probably always would be, the most straight-forward method: make it massive. There was an old saying that *quantity has a quality all its own*. That wasn't *quite* as true of fortresses as it was of other things, given the destructiveness of modern weaponry, but it was still true enough to be going on with.

And the other way to defend a vessel or an installation was to provide it with the most potent possible *offensive* weapons, as well. To pack it with the sort of horrific firepower that would destroy any adversary before he got into his own range of it.

Orbital *habitats* seldom mounted weapons at all. Since the best way to insure one would be shot at was to have the ability to shoot at someone else, habitat designers normally incorporated only *defensive* systems of the sort unlikely to turn their handi-work into magnets for incoming fire. Galton wasn't like other star systems, however, and *Crick*'s designers had incorporated both approaches into not just *Crick*, but many of the other platforms. Although few of those designers had known that every human being, every orbital weapons platform, every shipyard here in Galton was its own defense for something else entirely.

Every time he visited the system, Detweiler thought of the peculiar logic that had led to Galton's creation. No, not to its *creation*, but to its . . . repurposing. It was simultaneously the crudest—and yet, perhaps, the most cunning—of the Alignment's strategies. Build one of the most powerfully fortified star systems in the human-occupied galaxy, make it the Alignment's primary industrial and command node outside the Mesa System itself, central to all of its goals and purpose . . .

And all with the *final* purpose—if need be—to be sacrificed.

Hopefully, it would never come to that. But in the end, Galton had become a disguise—an illusion. His brother Collin called it a cloak for destiny, but Collin, despite his pragmatic mindset as the Alignment's spy chief, was given to occasional bouts of what their undutiful youngest brother Gervais called "artsy-fartsy" language.

And it wasn't as if that had always been Galton's purpose. But if the day came that the Alignment ever found its back to the wall, Galton would take the fall to conceal the existence of the Alignment's *true* final redoubt.

When Galton was first selected as the Alignment's ultimate off-Mesa operational base, no one had even considered that sort of a requirement. The Detweiler Plan had always called for the secret colonization and massive industrialization of the Alignment's own star system, for a multitude of reasons. One huge consideration had been the unavoidable need for the sort of base that could build and crew the level of firepower the plan would eventually require. And another had been as a bolthole, an escape hatch down which the Alignment could disappear in the eventuality that it was forced to flee the Mesa System.

Galton's discovery had been a happy and unexpected bit of serendipity. Star density was sparse in the system's region, and the majority of those stars were typical, useless red dwarfs. Long-range observation had suggested that the K5v listed as ACR-1773-16 might possess both significant asteroids and a planet in the liquid-water zone. The odds had been at best marginal, however, and there'd been very little pressure to expand into the region two hundred and sixty years ago. Indeed, there was little reason to do so even today...although that owed a little something to the Alignment's intervention.

But despite the lack of pressure those two and a half T-centuries ago, the Qaisrani Consortium, a barely profitable exploration group based on Larkana in the Istvan System, had decided to give it a look anyway, since one of its vessels would be passing within a half dozen light-years on its way to survey a much more promising star. The *Anoosheh Kashani*'s skipper had never expected to stumble across a system with both a habitable planet and the orbital cornucopia of ACR-1773-16's asteroid belts. The outermost belt, especially, would have made it exceptionally valuable to any industrial base, even without the world that ultimately became Tschermak. Indeed, the entire star system would have proved the sort of treasure trove that might come along once in the corporate lifetime of a hardscrabble consortium like Qaisrani... except that it had never learned of it.

Qaisrani was one of dozens—scores, really—of small, independent freight and exploration concerns which served as local carriers and agents of the Jessyk Combine, the Mesa System's largest single shipping company. Jessyk's reputation was no better than that of most Mesan transstellars, but neither was it any worse, and its clandestine connections to Manpower were a well-hidden secret. But its web of contacts had proved invaluable to the Alignment on more than one occasion, and Galton was a sterling case in point. Indeed, it and the system known as Darius were the crown jewels of Jessyk's gifts.

Anoosheh Kashani's captain, one of the Qaisrani Consortium's skippers who'd done business directly with Jessyk in the past, had been selling survey data to Jessyk on the side for years. Most of it had been fairly penny-ante, given the fact that Qaisrani scarcely stood at the pinnacle of the exploration industry. But she'd strongly suspected that for *this* sort of system, Jessyk would be able—and willing—to pay her much more than the finder's commission payable under her contract with Qaisrani. The fact that Qaisrani legally owned any survey data *Anoosheh Kashani* turned up had been a minor problem for that plan, but she'd convinced the rest of her nine-person crew (whose shares of the finders' commission would have been even smaller than her own) to conceal the data until they'd had a chance to... discuss it with the Jessyk agent in Istvan.

Fortunately for the Alignment, the agent in question had seen interesting possibilities, despite the system's remote location. He'd agreed to pay Captain Zardari and her crew ten times what Qaisrani would have paid them... and he'd *still* been able to take it out of petty cash. In return, they'd submitted an official survey report showing no habitable planets and substantially understating the number—and, especially, the *richness*—of ACR-1773-16's asteroid belts. There were plenty of other, more conveniently located systems with resource bases at least as rich as the one *Anoosheh Kashani* had reported, so the agent had expected the falsified report to head off any interest in the system until Jessyk decided what it wanted to do with it.

It was unfortunate for him that his report to the home office had come to a senior manager who'd happened to be a member in good standing of the Alignment... and who had decided that Jessyk didn't need to know about it, either. Instead, he'd handed it to the Alignment's leadership, who'd known exactly what they wanted to do with it and taken steps to be sure they could.

Anoosheh Kashani had, tragically, failed to return from her next survey mission. And, equally tragically, the Jessyk agent in Istvan had suffered a fatal air car accident about the time the ship should have returned, thus eliminating anyone who might have disputed the survey report Zardari had filed.

It had been the perfect sleight of hand, Detweiler thought now. One of the potential problems for any "secret colony" was that stars with habitable planets might attract hopeful survey crews or even entire colony expeditions who weren't aware those stars already belonged to someone else, and who would then have to be "disappeared" lest the secret be lost. But ACR-1773-16 had already been surveyed—the official survey record on was on file to prove it... and confirmed there was zero reason for anyone else ever to visit it.

And so Galton had come into existence.

While it was true Galton was a long way from Mesa—just over nine hundred light-years, in fact—that was actually a huge point in its favor. Especially since it could be reached in less than thirty-eight days by a warship or courier boat, and in little over a hundred even by a freighter, thanks to the Mesa-Visigoth and Warner-Mannerheim hyper bridges. A direct voyage through hyper would have required a ten-month voyage for the same freighter, however, which put it far, far outside Mesa's astrographic neighborhood.

Galton's initial population had been rather larger than that of most newly colonized star systems, because it had been possible to import a starting workforce composed of Manpower Incorporated's finest products. And it was remarkable how rapidly additional population could be produced on-site, using the cloning technology Manpower—and the Alignment—had refined to a pinnacle of efficiency. The initial startup cost had been a little steep, but it had also been well within the Alignment's capabilities, and the need to ship in workers had lasted only a couple of decades. Once a modest industrial base had been established, Galton had become a self-sustaining, self-replicating entity that no longer required much in the way of outside funding or imported population or parts.

Of course, at the time, no one in the Alignment had expected to turn up a previously unknown wormhole in the Felix System, twelve light-years from Mannerheim, less than thirty years later. The wormhole in question connected Felix to the Darius System, approximately three hundred fifty light-years from Galton. It, too, lay at the other end of the Warner-Mannerheim bridge, but thanks to the Felix-Darius Bridge, it was over two hundred light-years—and three months, for a freighter—"closer" to Mesa.

It had been something of an embarrassment of riches, but the possibilities for maximum concealment had been too good to pass up. There'd been some thought of moving the Galton project to Darius, instead, but from the beginning, the Detweiler Plan had thought in terms of concentric security. And so the Alignment had launched a *second* secret colony system, with its own industrial infrastructure and its own shipyards, but without any known connection to Galton.

Galton had become precisely what it had initially been intended to be: the Mesan Alignment's personal industrial complex and private shipyard and the primary point of contact through which the leadership in the Mesa System communicated with its out-system infrastructure.

For all of its many virtues, however, Galton was poorly placed for rapid communication with the rest of the human-occupied galaxy. From the viewpoint of concealment, that was a good thing. From the viewpoint of coordinating networks of agents and multiple field operations, it was...less desirable. That was the reason—so far as Galton knew—why the Alignment's uppermost echelons had chosen to remain in place, hidden away on Mesa, rather than simply relocate to Galton.

The Alignment had, however, used Galton as the site for its military command structure, the location of its vital industrial structure, the home of its cutting-edge research and development, and the repository for its most sensitive records. Almost all of the entire Alignment's actual organizational structure—the staff and hierarchy which formed its true skeleton, its most critical physical assets—had been moved entirely to Galton.

That was what Galton believed, at any rate...and it was largely true.

It simply wasn't the *only* truth.

There was an entire hidden network of Alignment bases tucked away around the galaxy. Most operated clandestinely, in inhabited star systems whose citizens never suspected the Alignment's presence, although others were in uninhabited systems chosen as strategically located support bases for the Alignment's black ops. And all of them truly were administered through Galton. Its inconvenient location meant there was always provision for direct communication of orders and directives from Mesa in time-sensitive situations, but those were rare and always attended with a certain degree of risk. The critical strategic decisions were always made on Mesa, but most operational planning to *implement* those decisions originated in Galton, and any message traffic that *wasn't* time-critical went from Mesa, via a single secure channel, to Galton, which saw that it was distributed to its recipients.

Because of its location and function, Galton also housed the Alignment's equivalent of its general staff college and the offices—and staffs—of its army's chief of staff and her naval counterpart. The Office of Strategic Planning, responsible for overseeing the entire Detweiler Plan's operations on a day-by-day basis, was located in Galton, as well, although like the Navy and Army, it received its ultimate direction from Mesa.

In short, Galton was the very heart—and the soul—of the Alignment. It simply wasn't the Alignment's *brain*. Or, at least, not its entire brain. The temporal, parietal, and occipital lobes, yes, and the brain stem, as well. But not the *frontal* lobe, where the executive functions resided. That remained on Mesa, although it communicated with the rest of the Alignment's body through Galton.

But what only a tiny handful of people in Galton knew was that even though all of that was true, it was simultaneously a lie. Only they knew that a system named Darius existed. Only they knew that every single record, every single bit of research, every single plan created in Galton was transmitted to Darius, as well, where it was tucked away in the Alignment's *true* secret archives. Only they knew that other researchers, other military planners, pursued their own R&D programs and evolved their own operational plans *based* upon and integrated with the ones coming out of Galton, but separate from them. And only they knew about the secret communications channels which let Darius insert its own contributions into Galton's research programs and operational planning.

And only that tiny handful knew that Galton was the Alignment's queen, not its king.

Which was just as well, because that meant that only that tiny handful understood that the Alignment was prepared, if it must, to sacrifice its queen to avoid checkmate.

No one had really expected to need to do anything of the sort, but the Alignment hadn't survived this long by preparing only for problems it expected to arise.

Of course, sometimes it still got bitten on the ass by one of those unexpected problems, Detweiler reflected sourly. Some of those could hurt—badly, and that was particularly true for the unintended consequences of its own actions. Like the consequences of the war the Alignment had done all in its power to keep alive between Manticore and Haven. The weapons technology the combatants had developed was ultimately at the root of the Alignment's currently...precarious position. Both because its threat had forced the Alignment to act precipitously—and much more openly than was its wont—in an effort to neutralize Manticore, and because those actions had, indirectly, led to the formation of the Grand Alliance. And *that* had led not simply to the invasion and conquest of the Mesa System, but to the utter and ignominious defeat of the vaunted Solarian League in only a fraction of the time the Alignment's strategy had allowed for...and depended upon.

In point of fact, the Detweiler Plan had gone well and truly off the rails it had followed so smoothly for so many centuries. The situation wasn't irretrievable, but it was going to require a *lot* of rethinking...which was, ultimately, what brought him here today.

They needed time—a minimum of twenty or thirty T-years, and preferably at least twice that—to recoup their losses and go so deeply to ground that even those pestiferous Manticorans and Havenites would decide the Alignment no longer existed.

Twenty or thirty T-years that could prove very expensive.

Fortunately, Galton was a treasure.

"Here we are, Sir," Hauptmann Chou said, as they reached the command deck hatch.

Like that of the Andermani Empire, Galton's military system had derived from an ancient German model, rather than the Anglo-French system adopted by the Solarian League and the military forces of most star nations descended from it.

That, too, was part of the deception.

Darius's military used the more customary system. So did Mesa's. Galton's use of the German variant was simply another of the Alignment's many deceptive maneuvers. The ancient Russians had called such maneuvers *maskirovka*—disguise. That had always seemed fitting to Detweiler, since a large portion of his family's genetic line had a Russian origin. He'd wondered, occasionally, if that was why they were such masters of the art of *maskirovka*.

Galton's underlying structure had been deliberately crafted to be as different from Darius's as possible. Or perhaps it would have been more accurate to say that Darius, the younger child, had been deliberately designed to differ from *Galton*. And as part of that deliberate differentiation, Galton was a harsher, harder, and far more militant entity than Darius had ever been. It was also the reason that even though Galton's cloned workforce might not be *called* slaves they were still indentured servants—workers indentured for a lifetime and, at best, a step below Mesa's seccies. Galton never treated them with the brutality of Manpower, their physical standard of living was actually quite good, and the perversions routinely practiced upon "pleasure slaves" were strictly prohibited, but they remained noncitizens, with no voice in their governance, their employment, the place they lived...

Darius's cloned workforce had never been slaves, never been indentured. Like every Dariusan, their lives were more regimented than they might have been elsewhere, but that was because of the great cause in which they, just as much as any alpha- or beta-line member of the Alignment, were fully invested. And that, too, was part of the plan.

Ultimately, both Galton and Darius must emerge from the shadows, and there would be no way to hide the fact that both were systems secretly colonized from Mesa, both deeply committed to overturning the Beowulf Code's prohibitions on targeted genetic uplift. But if only a tiny handful of Galtonians knew about Darius, the number of Dariusans who knew of Galton's existence was almost equally small.

Not *quite* as small, but nearly, and there was a reason for that, as well, because Darius had been colonized by a faction within the Alignment which had learned of Galton and been horrified by it.

When the time came to step into the light, Galton would be the lair of the dark, ruthless warrior of the Detweiler Plan, while Darius would be the refuge of the compassionate, caring heart of a Mesan Alignment which would never have dreamed of imposing its views upon the galaxy by force. Indeed, the historical record Darius presented to the galaxy—a record which consisted of contemporaneous documents, the validity of which could be conclusively substantiated by internal dating—would prove that its founders had subscribed to the Detweiler Plan but been deeply disturbed by the level of militancy—and, especially, the Manpower-like denial of full rights to its cloned workers—implicit in the early plans for the Galton colony.

They'd realized they would never be able to accomplish their goals—peaceful, beneficent goals—operating in semi-secrecy on Mesa *or* in the militant, authoritarian environment Galton was intended to become. And so they'd taken a page from the same playbook but rejected that book's willingness to impose its views upon others by force. Their response had only been possible because of the serendipitous discovery of Darius. The faction in Galton which had become aware of the dark strands weaving their way into Leonard Detweiler's shining dream had managed to conceal that discovery from anyone else in Galton and sent the survey data home to Mesa. And the members of the Alignment revolted by what Galton was becoming had seized it eagerly.

The timing had worked well. Given the later date of Darius's discovery, it had been simple to create a proper paper trail from the very beginning, with no need to go back and doctor existing records. It had even been early enough to begin pushing Galton into a far greater militancy than the original plans for the colony had envisioned, enhancing the differences between Leonard Detweiler's estranged stepdaughters. And when the time came, the people of Darius would be horrified by the excesses Galton had committed, just as their own colony's founders had feared it might. But the fact that Galton had resorted to such criminal, malignant tactics would not sway the Dariusans' adherence to the purpose for which their own star system had been settled—the genetic uplift of all humanity.

Hopefully, that would still be the way things worked out.

But if it wasn't...

Two guards flanked the hatch leading into *Crick*'s command deck. "Command deck" took in rather more territory, in this instance, than the term usually suggested, since this section of the station contained not only *Crick*'s tactical command center but also, two decks above that, the primary central command nexus for the entire system. That nexus was backed up aboard two other orbital installations, but the one aboard *Crick* was the one that really mattered.

The one where the secrets no one else in Galton could be allowed to know were hidden safely away.

The sentries flanking the hatch were alert. They also weren't given to cutting corners, so it took Detweiler more than a minute to pass their security scrutiny.

He found that a little amusing. Every time he visited Galton he wondered if they'd insist on taking urine and blood samples on top of all the other techniques they used to make sure he was really who he claimed to be. So far they hadn't—which was fortunate, since he would have refused to give them any genetic material.

There was some information the Alignment didn't allow into anyone's database, even the one in *Crick*. And first and foremost among that information was the fact that the Detweiler genome still survived. Galtonians understood that operational security—the god in whose name their entire star system had been settled—meant the identities of its leadership on Mesa must be and remain an incredibly closely held secret. Benjamin had been here many times, but all anyone in Galton knew—well, *almost* anyone in Galton knew—was that he was a senior courier for the Mesa-based leadership.

His Iridium Level ID, which did contain biometric data that matched the security file assigned to the (false) name it bore, sufficed once again, however. Although, to their credit, the guards didn't seem all that impressed by the towering seniority an Iridium ID indicated. Detweiler didn't mind that one bit. Galton's culture had been deliberately shaped to be as militaristic as possible. One could hardly complain if people one had spent two centuries turning into Prussians insisted on behaving like Prussians.

The atmosphere lightened quite a bit once he entered the command deck. Most of the officers stationed there were part of the onion's penultimate core. Only two of them were part of the true center, what he thought of as Detweiler Territory. So most of them were unaware of Galton's possible final destiny. But they knew almost everything else concerning the Alignment's goals, strategies, and methods.

A very tall, uniformed woman wearing the insignia of an oberst came toward him, her hand outstretched.

"Welcome aboard, Benjamin," she said as they shook hands.

"Chuntao. Nice to see you again."

Oberst Xú Chuntao gestured toward a hatch on the other side of the compartment.

"Generalfeldmarshall Adebayo's waiting for you," she said. "So is Grossadmiral Montalván."

That pair were the two—the only two—permanently stationed in the Galton System who lived in Detweiler territory, and Adebayo must have deduced that he hadn't come on a routine visit.

Normally, she and Montalván maintained a certain distance from each other—not because of any actual friction between them, but because of the *public* friction between their services' competing needs—as a simple safety precaution. As a last resort, the Alamo Contingency was supposed to trigger automatically, but even the best automatic plans could fail, and it would be far better to have at least one of them in charge all the way to the end.

As he followed the oberst across the compartment, Detweiler reminded himself not to use the term "Detweiler Territory" in front of the two people he was about to meet. That was merely a label he and his brothers used in private. The Detweiler line was the final authority in the Alignment, true—and it had been, going all the way back to the beginning. But there were around a dozen other lines that were also very influential... including the Adebayo and Montalván lines.

From the outside, someone might have characterized the Alignment's power structure as dynastic rule. But it wasn't, at least... not quite.

That same outside observer could have been excused, had he been allowed to delve a little deeper, for deciding the Alignment's system was very like that used on Erewhon, and there were definite similarities. In some ways, Detweiler and his brothers had joked among themselves, it could be argued that the Detweilers (as a group, not individually) were the *capo di tutti capi* of the Alignment's central genetic lines, but their authority went deeper than that.

Both the Alignment and Erewhon's system were sternly, even harshly, meritocratic, but the Erewhonese system lacked the scientific precision that characterized the Alignment. They paid no attention to anyone's genetic background; they simply used the catch-as-catch-can methods of extreme pragmatists.

To the Erewhonese, a person was simply as she or he was. The Alignment understood that what lay beneath was a coherent evolutionary logic... which the Alignment had been created to guide.

Where the process would lead over time, no one—outside the Alignment—yet knew. But that was the entire point of the Detweiler Plan. Evolution was too important, too fundamental to the human condition, to be left to chance. Oh, there would always be chance mutations, unplanned genetic combinations, and the variety those introduced would be of inestimable value to the final process. But they would be variations on the central theme, and that theme would be firmly under the control of conductors who understood the score.

Conductors best suited by both evolution and training to provide the necessary guidance, to decide what chance mutation should be conserved, which lines it should be adapted to, and which mutations should be pruned. And that was why the Detweiler Line was not simply "first among equals." The other central lines might be advisors, strategists, analysts. They were, in many ways, the people who trained and educated each generation of Detweilers, who formed the true heart of the Alignment's collective memory. But they were the peers of the realm, not its princes. All of their lines held chairs around the Round Table which had been created by Leonard Detweiler's true heirs so long before, but only one of those lines bore Excalibur.

The Detweiler Plan's original intent had been quite similar in some ways, really, to that of Plato in *The Republic*: the evolution of a collective version of his philosopher-kings. But it had become evident as time passed and understanding deepened that something more . . . fundamental was required. That producing a collective version of any one ideal human race, even one of philosopher-kings, was a suboptimal outcome.

No, what was needed was another speciation of humanity—one that was planned and coordinated, this time, and resulted in the emergence of a cluster of closely related species. Specialization had great benefits, after all. Each species would have its own strengths and abilities, and its proper place in the structure of intelligent life.

With one species to rule them all, of course.

It was too bad he wouldn't live to see the final outcome. Not even the most optimistic projections foresaw a final triumph of the Detweiler Plan for several more centuries. And while Detweilers were long-lived, even by prolong standards, no one was *that* long-lived.

Yet.

✧   ✧   ✧

Oberst Xú ushered Detweiler to the hatch of Generalfeldmarshall Karoline Adebayo's working office and tapped the admittance button lightly. The door slid open almost instantly, and the oberst braced to attention, nodded to him, and withdrew as he stepped through the door.

"Welcome, Benjamin," Adebayo said, rising from an armchair and nodding for him to join her and Grossadmiral Montalván in the office's comfortably appointed conversational nook. "Come have a seat. Rest your weary bones."

Given Galton's militant nature, it was inevitable that its governor would be a military officer, and Adebayo made a very good one. She was a striking figure, not just because of her height but because of the combination of her very dark skin with an aquiline nose and light green eyes. The contrast with Gunther Montalván was so great it was almost comical. He was short and squat—muscle, not fat—with very pale eyes, hair, and skin.

Detweiler smiled and lowered himself into a facing chair.

"I'm not all that creaky, Karoline," he protested, as she sank back into her own chair, and she issued a little snort.

"If your bones aren't weary from muscular tension, I'm going to have some harsh words for my orbital commanders. Anyone who goes through the sort of gauntlet you had to pass through to get here should damn well be exhausted. In spirit, if not in body."

"So, what's up, Benjamin?" Montalván asked. "We weren't expecting to see you again this soon."

"Basically—" He drew a slow, deep breath. "Basically, I came to apologize. Well, that and to give you a *qui vive*."

Adebayo's and Montalván's postures stiffened. They glanced at one another, then back at Detweiler, eyebrows rising.

"Apologize for what?" Adebayo asked.

"Now that some time's passed, my brothers and I have come to realize that we screwed up with the Beowulf strike." He shifted in his chair, uncomfortably. "I'm afraid we let our tempers get the better of us. We were very close to our parents, you know. And we lost them when Albrecht blew the island because the damned Grand Alliance arrived early."

"Ah."

Adebayo settled back in her own chair with a nod of understanding.

For self-evident reasons, she and Montalván had known the organizational framework of Houdini from the beginning. And almost eighty percent of everyone Houdini had extracted had ended up in Galton, so the fact that Houdini had been activated was general knowledge here in the system.

What had not yet become generally known was Houdini's

end game. Beyond Adebayo and Montalván, no more than half a dozen people knew how many of the Alignment's own had died in the final stage of the operation, and of that half-dozen, only Adebayo and Montalván had known the Detweiler genome existed... or that Benjamin's parents had sacrificed themselves to make Houdini work.

"Exactly." Benjamin's nostrils flared. "We let our anger—and our pain, but anger was the real driver—dictate our plans, not logic. Not... rational thought."

"And you think we showed our hand a little too much," Adebayo said.

"More than a little, and that wasn't the only... miscalculation we made," Detweiler replied grimly. "We shouldn't have given the order at all, we shouldn't have supported it with tech the Solarian League didn't have, and we should have aborted it when the original attack failed, not pressed on. And—" his nostrils flared "—we should have seen where that kind of casualty total was going to lead."

She nodded and crooked her fingers in a silent invitation to continue.

"The support we provided *might* have been ascribed to the Sollies," Detweiler told them. "If that bitch Harrington hadn't taken Ganymede station and gotten her hands on every single SLN tech file and R and D program, that is." He shrugged. "We didn't anticipate that happening. Once it did, there was no way anyone could believe the Sollies were behind it—or not without one hell of a lot of outside help, anyway.

"And—" he looked at them squarely "—we should have been smart enough to instruct our agent in-system to abort if the Sollies had been driven off by the time he was in position to transmit the detonation command.

"It was the casualty totals that drove the Alliance to send Harrington to the Sol System in the first place. All of our intelligence indicates that she—and Elizabeth, Pritchart, and Mayhew—all knew who'd actually orchestrated it." He grimaced. "Truth to tell, we *wanted* to 'send a message.' That's why we sequenced the explosions the way we did. Which was angry—and incredibly stupid—of us. I think that's pretty evident from what happened to the League. The Grand Alliance knew the Sollies hadn't actually planted those bombs, but they didn't really care. They knew we were using the League as a catspaw, even if they didn't have a clue why we'd maneuvered them into conflict in the first place, and they decided to end it. That was...unfortunate enough, but one of the reasons they decided that was to free their hands to look for us. And the way we did it is likely to lend more credence than we'd like to their insistence to the rest of the galaxy that the entire war was the work of some long-standing, deeply hidden conspiracy."

Montalván shrugged.

"I wouldn't worry too much about it, Benjamin. After what's happened over the past T-year, there's so much confusion and rumormongering in what still passes for the Solarian League that the Beowulf Strike will sink out of sight fairly quickly, at least as far as the Solly public is concerned. Oh, they'll remember that the casualties were horrific, but it happened during a war, you know. And they're so busy trying to put the actual war behind them that any impact the death toll might have had on Solly thinking will fade soon enough. That won't happen in Beowulf, of course. Or in the Grand Alliance. But they already believed the worst of us."

"And I think you may be overlooking a benefit," Adebayo added.

"Benefit?"

Detweiler arched both eyebrows at her, and she smiled thinly.

"You don't live here in Galton, the way Gunther and I do. Sometimes, I think, even you don't fully appreciate the differences between here and Darius. Galton is a *warrior* society, Benjamin. When word hit that Beowulf's three largest orbital habitats had been destroyed, there were celebrations all over the system. Almost as big as the ones after Oyster Bay!"

She shook her head.

"Nobody in Galton knows how Oyster Bay was actually staged, but they *think* they do, and they see the Beowulf Strike the same way."

Detweiler nodded. The Oyster Bay strike on the Manticore System had, of necessity, been launched from Darius and not Galton because Galton didn't know about the spider drive. That had sprung from R&D conducted here in Galton, but it had been *developed* in Darius. As a result, the Galton Space Navy had no equivalent of the graser torpedo or of the *Sharks* which had deployed them for the strike. But Galton's industrial base had shipped off over a thousand of its graserhead MDMs well before Oyster Bay, and Adebayo's files—files which were replicated on the backup command stations, not stored solely on *Crick*—contained the operational plan for those MDMs to be deployed by "conventional"—but highly stealthy—freighters for the attack. And there were equally official files detailing the post-strike damage assessments . . . and how the specialized graser platforms which had plowed the road for the Beowulf Strike had been deployed from Galton, not Darius. The MDM conversions described in the Galton files (and built and shipped off) were far less capable than the platforms which had actually been used, but since those platforms had destroyed themselves in the moment they fired, no one would ever know that.

But if they ever had the chance to capture Adebayo's files, they *would* know neither strike had come from Darius.

"I understand that," he said. "It's just—"

"Don't worry about it," she told him even more firmly. "Yes, there could be a downside. I understand that. I'm just saying that there's a hell of an *upside*, as well, in terms of morale and purpose here in Galton. Gunther and I couldn't have stifled those celebrations even if we'd tried."

"Which we didn't," Montalván said. "Karoline is right about the way our people here reacted, and she's right about the long-term advantages, at least here in Galton. Are there going to be negative consequences down the road? Maybe. But we don't know that . . . and there's no point borrowing trouble before it comes on its own." He smiled crookedly at Detweiler. "Look, let's be blunt about this, Benjamin. The reason you came to apologize was because you think you probably brought the Alamo Contingency closer and that makes you feel guilty. Well, maybe you did, but maybe you didn't, either. And if it turns out you *did*, so what? Karoline and I knew—and accepted—that possibility when we took this assignment. I won't say I'm looking forward to it, but if it happens, it happens. I'm good with that."

"I'm good with it, too, Benjamin." Adebayo rose and headed toward a sidetable. "Apology accepted—and now that the formalities are over, what would you like to drink?"

Hadcliffe Residential Tower
City of Mendel
Planet Mesa
Mesa System

THE YOUNG WOMAN WHO ANSWERED THE DOOR WAS FAMILIAR to Anton Zilwicki. Not because he'd ever met her before, but because he'd been studying her from a distance lately.

She looked like her older brother Jack, he thought, allowing for being ten years younger and female...and for her hair color. Jack's hair had been red; hers was blond. But she had the same blue eyes and a more feminine version of the same chin, coupled with a slim and athletic figure. Pretty, in a low-keyed sort of way.

Allowing for the scowl on her face, anyway.

"Ms. McBryde?" he said. "My name is—"

"I know who you are, Zilwicki. What do you want?"

"I was wondering if you might give me a bit of your time. There's something I'd like to discuss with—"

"No."

She started to close the door, but Zilwicki stopped that with a palm placed on it.

"Fine!" she snapped, reaching for something on the inside of the doorframe. Zilwicki couldn't see it, but he was quite sure it was a control panel. Once she touched it, not even someone with his strength would be able to keep the door open. And if he tried to force his way through, the door would pin him in place, allowing her to summon the police.

He dropped his hand, and the door closed.

"I know what happened to your brothers, Ms. McBryde," he said through the shrinking gap. The door closed completely right after "brothers."

97

Three seconds later, it slid back open.

"Both of them," he added. "I know exactly what happened to Jack, and I have a general idea of what happened to Zach."

Her face was noticeably paler than it had been when she opened the door. The scowl was gone, too.

"How do you know?" she asked. It was almost a whisper.

"I was in touch with Jack when he died, and I've been able to trace where Zach went after he left Mesa—up to a point, at least."

"Zach's still alive?" That *was* said in a whisper.

"Probably," Zilwicki said. "I can't be positive, but he was at the last point I tracked him—which was days after he was supposed to have been killed in a so-called terrorist incident."

She put her hand on the doorframe, leaned her head against it, and closed her eyes.

"Why should I believe you're telling the truth? You—all of you—have been slandering us ever since you conquered Mesa. Besides, Planetary Security told us the Ballroom killed Jack. And that you and your friend Cachat were responsible for it!"

She opened her eyes, without removing her head from her hand, and gave him an accusing look.

"Victor and I were on Mesa when Jack died," Zilwicki confirmed. "However, if you'll think about it, the same people who said we were responsible for his death are undoubtedly the people who announced that we'd been blown up in a nuclear explosion of our own making. Which, obviously, we weren't. So I think it could be argued that what they told you might be just a tiny bit inaccurate."

Her accusing eyes narrowed slightly, and he shrugged.

"Apropos your other point, about people slandering the Alignment, I've come to believe that you're right about that. It's...a bit more complicated than that, though, because until recently, we didn't think we were. Slandering you, I mean. And we had our reasons to call the people who really caused all of this the 'Mesan Alignment.' For that matter, we still do."

He paused for a moment, returning her stare with a calm gaze.

"Ms. McBryde, I really do think you should talk to me." Moving a bit slowly, so as not to alarm her, he pulled a chip from his pocket. "This is the final record we've found of Zach's whereabouts. It's also a recording of my last meeting with Jack, which happened shortly before he died."

She stood up straight and seemed to brace herself. Her shoulders squared, her hands at her side.

"So he met with you? You're telling me he was a *traitor*?"

"The Alignment would certainly think so. Not your people, but what I think—now—is a different Alignment. One that used you exactly the same way it's used a lot of people over the years. Including the Star Empire, the Republic of Haven, *and* the entire Solarian League."

"You're a lunatic," she said flatly.

"No, I'm not." Zilwicki shook his head. "And Jack really did work for Alignment Security, not Planetary Security. That was just his 'day job.'"

"Of *course* he worked for Alignment Security! We all knew that. But if you'd paid any attention at all to what we've been telling you ever since you got here, you'd know that 'Alignment Security's' entire job was just to help us stay under the radar! Jack worked with Planetary Security because it gave him the tools and the access he needed for *that*, not for some horrible, sinister fabrication of your own sick imagination."

"No," Zilwicki said gently. "Oh, there was an Alignment Security that did just that, and Jack *was* a member of it. But that different Alignment I'm talking about used your Alignment's 'Security' just the way it used all the rest of you. As a cover and a mask. Ms. McBryde, Planetary Security knew all about your Alignment. So it made perfect sense for the *other* Alignment to plant its people in Planetary Security under the cover of working for a harmless, idealistic organization. Especially people like Jack, who were very, very good at their jobs. In fact, he was so good that none of you—none of the people who loved him, and who he loved, because, believe me, he *did* love you—ever suspected the truth any more than Planetary Security did."

She stared at him, her lips trembling, and he shook his head.

"He deceived you because that was his job. His responsibility. And to keep all of you safe, because he knew the stakes he was playing for. He didn't want that side of his life to splash onto you, endanger you. But he did work for that other Alignment... until he truly realized where it was headed. That's when he realized he couldn't do that anymore. Ms. McBryde, that's why *he* contacted *me*...and why he was the one who set off the explosion that destroyed the Androcles Tower."

Her face was now almost as pale as the proverbial sheet. Androcles Tower's destruction had been the first blast of the Green Pines "terrorist attack."

"W-why would he do that?"

"Because he was one of the bravest men I ever met," Zilwicki said quietly. "Because he'd been discovered by that other Alignment attempting to smuggle a dissident scientist off-planet, and there was no way he could escape. So instead of surrendering, which would have amounted to a death sentence anyway—those people are utterly ruthless—he chose to take a lot of them out with him. That also had the effect of covering the escape of the scientist—his friend. And my escape, as well, since I was helping him."

Arianne was silent for a while staring at him.

"But why Androcles?" She shook her head. "I never understood that. It didn't make any more sense than the explosion in Buenaventura Tower!"

"The explosion wasn't *in* Androcles Tower; it was *under* it, in something called the Gamma Center."

"Gamma Center," she repeated, her voice almost numb, and Zilwicki nodded.

"As nearly as we've been able to figure out, it was the central security installation for the Align—oh, for the moment, let's call them the 'Malign Alignment.'" He shook his head again. It was a minimal sort of headshake. "Personally, I consider your brother a hero, and I think the whole galaxy will agree with me once the truth comes out. 'Betraying' the Malign Alignment is like accusing someone of betraying Satan. Good for him."

Her shoulders sagged. But she also stepped away from the door, opening it wide.

"Come in. I'll listen to what you have to say."

❖   ❖   ❖

After the chip's recordings ended—she'd played them on her living room smartwall—Arianne's hands were clasped tightly in her lap.

"How do I know these recordings aren't faked? You have a reputation—I don't know if you deserve it, but you've got it—of being a wizard when it comes to manipulating electronic data."

"I do have a certain reputation," Zilwicki acknowledged. "And, sure, I could have created every single thing I've just shown you. But simply creating imagery can only take you so far."

"Explain," she said, and he pointed at the now-dark screen.

"First, I'd have to have already had extensive recordings of your brothers. Now, admittedly, I have access to most of the planetary database at this point, so, yes. I could have gotten my hands on those recordings—now. But even the best CGI is going to contain teeny tiny flaws that can be picked out of it by sufficiently careful analysis. Especially if it was created by combining imagery from different sources. I don't say it would be easy, but it would certainly be possible using tech right here on Mesa.

"More to the point, though, I've never met Zach, and I didn't meet Jack until shortly before that recording of him was made. You're their sister. You know their mannerisms. The way they talk, the words they'd choose, their expressions. Their body language. There's no way I could have built a 'Jack' that would deceive you if you looked at it as suspiciously as I know you just looked at this one. There'd be holes, false notes.

"As for Zach, that imagery was taken from an original Traffic Control Service database. It's still there, if you want to look at it. So are the TCS personnel who were in possession of that database when we rescued them. A database that has all of the original embedded security codes and date/time stamps, and you are entirely welcome to examine the source files yourself. Or to have anyone you care to nominate evaluate them for you."

"Really?" It was her turn to wave at the inactive screen. "Maybe that's all true, and maybe it isn't. And maybe I'll take you up on that offer to examine the source files. But whatever that says about Zach, it doesn't say anything about the original imagery of *Jack*."

"No, it doesn't. I'm afraid you'll just have to take my word for that one, because I recorded it after Jack initially approached us."

"Approached you where?"

"At a diner in a seccy district. I was a waiter there. I was there with—ah, my partner—"

"Why don't you just name him Victor Cachat, so we can skip the bullshit? You think I haven't seen the program that aired on that Manticoran so-called 'news discussion show'? And if you studied me as intensively as you're suggesting, then you know I was one of CEO Ward's senior scientific advisors to the old General Board. You think I didn't have a pretty damned high security clearance?"

"Yes, Victor. We were here to investigate Manpower when Jack spotted me on an intercepted bit of security footage and approached us."

She closed her eyes again. Then she shook her head. It was a sharp, abrupt gesture, as if she were trying to shake water out of her hair. Or mud.

"All right," she said. "I figure you wouldn't offer me the opportunity to look at the original data files if they wouldn't tell me what you're saying they would. And you're right about individual mannerisms, too. There's not enough of Zach for me to recognize any of his personal quirks, but that's Jack. I recognize him. I couldn't tell you exactly how, but I do. So I believe you didn't fake any of it. Still..."

She looked away. She sat gazing at the window that covered an entire wall of the apartment and looked out over the city, but Zilwicki didn't think she was actually looking at anything. Her eyes were tearing up.

She sat that way for several seconds. And then, abruptly, she reached up, wiped her face, and looked at Zilwicki.

"What about Zach? From what I gather you're saying, he's still loyal to—" She waved her hand in an angry gesture. "Whoever those fucking people are."

Zilwicki opened his mouth, but before he could reply—

"And don't call them 'the Alignment'!" Her tone was as angry as the gesture had been. "The Alignment—the real one—is what *I* belong to."

He spread his hands.

"Ms. McBryde—"

"Call me Arianne. For this, 'Ms. McBryde' is idiotic."

"Arianne. Look, I myself have come to the conclusion that we're dealing with two different 'Alignments' here. So have a number of other people."

"Who?"

"Victor Cachat, for one. Catherine Montaigne, for another. She's now the effective head of Manticore's Liberal Party. Then there's Torch's Queen Berry."

"Well, sure." Arianne sniffed. "Cachat's your partner, Montaigne's your girlfriend, and Queen Berry's your daughter. You're even better connected than I am."

Zilwicki put his hands back on his chair's armrests and smiled.

"It's not just Berry. Pretty much the entire government of Torch—the top echelons, anyway—have come to the same conclusion. Web Du Havel, General Palane, and Jeremy X all have."

That caused her eyes to widen again.

"*Jeremy X* thinks that?"

"The man is anything but stupid, Arianne. Yes, Jeremy thinks that."

She looked to the window again. This time her eyes seemed to be focused. Zilwicki thought she was looking in the direction of Hancock Tower. She couldn't have seen it, because taller buildings would have blocked her sight—and there wouldn't have been anything except rubble to look at, anyway.

"What about Jurgen Dusek? The other seccy bosses?"

"That, I don't know. But I'd be surprised if Dusek doesn't come around once I lay it out for him."

"Lay out what?"

"Well, to begin with, there's the fact that every single member of the... Benign Alignment we've talked to has indignantly denied membership in an organization which would do the things we know *our* Alignment has done. And the reason that's significant is that they've done it in front of treecats."

"Treecats. You're telling me that treecats really can read minds?" Arianne said skeptically.

"No. They *are* telepaths, but only between one another. What they *can* read are human emotions... including the triggers that indicate whether or not someone is lying." Zilwicki shrugged. "That's not exactly something we want to get into discussing with the rest of the galaxy just now, but, trust me, it carries a lot of weight with Manticorans and the Grand Alliance in general.

"But there are some other factors in play, as well. To begin with—"

It took Zilwicki several minutes to explain his reasoning. After he was finished, Arianne's expression had gone from angry skepticism into one that combined ruefulness and... something else. He thought she was appalled.

"So you're telling me one reason you trust *my* Alignment is that so many of us got killed by this *other* Alignment of yours?"

"That's one way to put it." Zilwicki nodded. "Of course, another aspect is that despite the overall casualties the Benign Alignment took, very few of your senior leadership cadre were among them. If your Alignment was the primary mover in everything the Malign Alignment's done, then logically it should have been your senior leadership that was being gotten off-planet, and it wasn't. On the other hand, if we're right in our suspicion that the Malign Alignment was using your organization as a front, hiding behind it, then that would explain why so many known scientists, technocrats of all sorts, political and civic figures *associated* with your organization but not in official leadership roles disappeared. And—" his expression turned grim "—the reason that so many of your friends and relatives really were killed, Arianne. Because the Malign Alignment couldn't leave that many loose ends. Couldn't afford to have that many smart, capable people trying to figure out what the hell happened. And because they were totally willing to kill as many Mesans—as many of *you*—as it took for them to disappear down the rabbit hole."

She looked at him, her eyes dark. Then stood and headed towards her kitchen.

"I'm going to make some coffee. Would you like some?"

"Please. Flat white."

She programmed the robochef. As he had many times before, Zilwicki found himself amused by the stubbornness with which human beings retained obsolete terminology. "Making coffee" now meant ordering a robot to do it; the "robot" was a complex console, dispensing all manner of food and drink; and the alcove in which this was done was still called a "kitchen," even though the number of people who actually cooked was small.

Foodie fanatics, Cachat called them, with his usual distaste for what he considered silliness—especially silliness that required a great deal of wealth. More recently settled planets inclined toward more basic facilities, at least until the planetary technology and wealth level caught up with the rest of the galaxy, and kitchens there tended to be fully functional places where actual *people* prepared food. On more developed worlds, renovating an apartment's "kitchen" to actually *be* a kitchen was expensive. Sometimes *very* expensive.

You'd never see a Havenite super spook stoop so high!

Arianne came back with the coffee herself. A lot of people would have let another robot do that task. Zilwicki wasn't positive, but he thought that personal gesture was a sign that she was shedding her previous hostility. Some of it, at least.

She handed him his cup, settled back into her chair, and raised her own cup to sip. Then she lowered it a few centimeters, gazing at him through its wispy tendril of steam.

"Why did you come here?" she asked. "And don't bother telling me it was because you wanted to console the grieving sister."

"Not much consolation, anyway," Zilwicki said. "One brother dead for sure, the other vanished into an unknown fate. And it *is* an 'unknown' fate, Arianne. There's some evidence that not all of the people who were shipped off planet were what you might call totally willing."

He took a sip of his coffee. It was just as good as he'd expected.

"I will say that I think you were owed the truth about Jack, and that I owed it to him to tell it to you. He's undoubtedly one of the reasons I'm still alive right now, and, ultimately, we owe virtually everything we've learned or suspect about the Malign Alignment to him...including the mere fact that it exists. But, no, you're right. That's not the main reason I came here. The truth is, I came in hope of recruiting you."

"*Recruiting* me? To what? Or should I ask to *whom*?"

"What, for now." He set down the cup. "Arianne, I think you believe me by now that there's another 'Alignment' out there that's been using you and *your* Alignment as...Well, not catspaws, since I don't think you've actually *done* anything for the bastards. You've been a veil for them, though. And I'd think you have to be angry as hell at the thought of how many of your friends, how many members of your Alignment, got slaughtered just to conceal the other Alignment's withdrawal. They didn't care how many of you they killed. Hell, they were willing to kill every one of their *own* that they couldn't get offworld in time! But that's the way they operate. They're masters of the art of concealment, and one of the techniques they use—often—is to cloak themselves, exactly the way they did by hiding in and behind your Alignment. And then they place another cloak, another mask, over that one. And then another. And another. Duchess Harrington calls what we're doing 'peeling an onion,' and the truth is that's a pretty good analogy. So the reason I'm here is that I'd like you to help me—help us—hunt them down. Help us peel that onion right down to the core."

"Who is 'us'? Never mind. We can get into that later." She sipped from her own cup. It was quite a long one, this time. When she set the cup down, her voice was very quiet, almost soft.

"'Angry' doesn't begin to describe how I feel, Captain Zilwicki. I'm not sure there's any word that does. 'Rage,' maybe—but it's too cold for that."

"Are you familiar with ancient mythology?"

"Yes, as it happens. I was fascinated by the subject for a couple of years."

"Do you recall the Erinyes?"

"The Greek Furies? Oh, yes. There were three of them ... I'm trying to remember ... hold on." She raised her uni-link. "Names of the Greek Furies," she said.

"*Alecto, Megaira, and Tisiphone,*" the uni-link replied. "*Alecto represents endless anger, Megaira jealous rage, and Tisiphone*—"

"Is vengeful destruction," she said. "Yes, I remember now."

She lowered the uni-link and looked at Zilwicki.

"That one, I think. What would I be jealous of? And I don't have any interest in an endless hunt. But vengeful destruction, now ..."

Zilwicki smiled as he picked up his coffee cup once more.

"Can I call you 'Tisi' for short?" he asked, and she laughed.

"Yes, you can."

Joint Intelligence Sharing and Distribution Command Center
Smith Tower
City of Old Chicago
Old Earth
Sol System

"THIS IS JUST...WRONG." DAUD IBN MAMOUN AL-FANUDAHI'S EYES were sour as he looked around the huge towers—the many huge towers—that surrounded them. "I feel naked up here. No, *out* here. We're supposed to be a clandestine outfit, remember?"

Lieutenant Colonel Natsuko Okiku looked up at her far taller companion and shook her head. They stood together at the railing of the observation deck that provided them with a spectacular view of the capital city of the Solarian League from the four hundred and fifty-second floor of Smith Tower. Unlike al-Fanudahi, Okiku wore a smile.

"Look at it this way, Daud. It could be worse. Brigadier Gaddis might have suggested we set up in George Benton when he planted his own headquarters there."

George Benton Tower had been the headquarters and personal kingdom of "the Mandarins," the top bureaucrats of the Solarian League. They were the people—the *unelected* people—who'd really ruled the League, in practice if not in theory.

Until just under two months ago, anyway.

Now the Mandarins were ensconced elsewhere—in a Manticoran prison, in fact—awaiting trial for an entire panoply of war crimes, including violation of the League's own Eridani Edict against mass-casualty attacks and the wholesale murder of civilians. One might have expected those trials to have already begun, but the Grand Alliance had decreed otherwise. They would be tried only after the League's new constitution had been

107

confirmed and its new government could participate directly in that investigation and trial. "We will do nothing in the dark," Empress Elizabeth had declared, speaking for the Grand Alliance, and al-Fanudahi had to admit that was very wise of them. Unlike all too many Solarians, he *knew* what the Mandarins had done, how they had systematically lied to their own star nation. Letting the new Solarian government find the proof of that in its own archives might well go a long way toward damping down Solarian revanchist sentiment.

Which didn't make him any happier about the subject of their current discussion.

"'Planted his heaquarters.'" he grunted. "That's a good term for it. As in 'he planted his boot on their necks.'"

Okiku's shrug emphasized her slight build. With her sandalwood complexion, almond-shaped eyes, midnight black hair, and diminutive size—just under a hundred and fifty-six centimeters and a bare forty-two kilograms—the colonel was the stereotypical image of a delicate Oriental girl. And she truly was young enough, for a prolong society—just past forty, which made her look like a pre-prolong teenager—to fit snugly into the frame. Of course, the Gendarmerie uniform and severely short, military-style haircut might have suggested to the acute observer that surface impressions could be misleading.

Which they were. Very, very misleading. The "delicate Oriental girl" in question was actually one of the Criminal Investigation Division's most capable, tenacious, and ruthless investigators. There was a reason she'd been Brigadier Simeon Gaddis's personal protégé. The CID's commander had considered—still did consider—her one of his top half dozen subordinates, and no one who'd ever worked with her would have disputed his judgment.

"You know exactly why the Brigadier did that, Daud," she chided, still smiling. "Intimidation is a fine art."

"And just who does he *need* to intimidate?" al-Fanudahi demanded. "The Mandarins are in prison, the Grand Alliance's fleet is still in orbit, and the 'Provisional Government' isn't about to turn into another exercise in empire building!"

"I'll grant all of that," Okiku said. "But the Provisional Assembly's just a little preoccupied with that whole Constitutional Convention thing just now. Besides, there's that old saying about the spirit being willing but the flesh being weak." She shook her head.

"I think most of the Provisional Assembly's members are reasonably honest, at least by Solarian politician standards, but the Mandarins have only been gone for two months—hell, *not quite* two months. They're making all this up as they go along, really, and none of them have a lot of experience in genuine representative government. Not on the Federal level, at least. That's not something we've seen a lot of here on Old Terra lately, if you'll recall."

She arched an eyebrow and held it there until al-Fanudahi nodded.

"We're luckier than hell that whatever may have been happening on the Federal level, at least the Assembly had the good sense to choose delegates who had a lot of political experience in their home star systems when they set up the Provisional Government and chose Yon Sung-Jin as Acting Prime Minister! That doesn't mean he or any of the other 'acting' ministers—*or* the Provisional Assembly—don't have a bazillion things they have to do on the run, including how to get some kind of handle on bureaucracies that've run without anything remotely like legislative oversight for literally centuries. And on top of that, they really are preoccupied with getting the Constitutional Convention organized. Which makes sense. The courier boats haven't even reached a *bunch* of the League's systems to tell them what happened here or that there's going to *be* a Constitutional Convention. It'll be months yet before the convention delegates can be selected and actually assemble here, but with that damned fleet in orbit looking over their shoulders, this wouldn't be a good time to let any grass grow under their feet.

"And, just to add to the mix, virtually all of the lower-level bureaucrats and apparatchiks in all those regulatory agencies they're trying to get a bridle on—and, I might add, your own, beloved Navy, as well as civilian administration—are still in place. They have to be, because nobody else knows how to run the bureaucracies in question, and if those bureaucracies just suddenly *stop*, the wheels really will come off. But a lot of them, especially the senior ones, were just as corrupt as the Mandarins, if on a lesser scale, so they have to be worried about their... futures in public service, let's say. And any of them who already had secret bank accounts—which couldn't possibly be more than, oh, ninety-seven percent of them, you think?—are worried about what happens when the new management really does take over and they get audited. So a bunch of them have to be thinking in terms of how much more they can..."

acquire before they disappear into the Verge somewhere. And, on top of all *that*, there are always going to be career politicians hunting for personal advantage, apparatchiks too stupid to realize the old empire-building days truly are a thing of the past, and any number of ambitious outsiders, outraged 'patriots,' conspiracy theorists, revolutionaries, anarchists, and assorted political nut jobs." She paused. "Did I leave anybody out?"

"Only any operatives still working for the Other Guys that we don't have a clue where to find, I suppose."

Al-Fanudahi's tone was even more sour than it had been.

"Well, then!" Okiku spread her arms in a gesture which encompassed the entire city around them. "I'd say there are quite a few people who need intimidating. And the Brigadier's right about its being a fine art—especially now.

"The last thing any of us can allow this to become, or to allow the Grand Alliance to be afraid it *may* become, is a military dictatorship." Her own tone was dead serious now. "The Grand Alliance won't stand for it, not for a heartbeat, and if they decide that's what the Brigadier and Admiral Kingsford are doing, they'll...make their displeasure known. Firmly.

"And if the citizens of the Sol System—or, worse, of the League in general—decide that whatever new constitution gets written was imposed upon them by some sort of junta, its legitimacy will be a lot harder to establish. Probably even for a lot of the people who have to admit the Grand Alliance was right about what an unmitigated shit storm the League's supposed government had turned into. That's the real reason the Brigadier and the Admiral refused places in Prime Minister Yon's cabinet." She smiled suddenly. "I don't know about Kingsford, but I *do* know the Brigadier's spent a lot of time recently studying Thomas Theisman and how *he* went about restoring the old *Havenite* constitution.

"But if they can't afford to look like a military dictatorship, they still have to be able to...to loom ominously in the background. The Brigadier likes to quote some pre-space politician. He says they need to walk softly but carry a big stick.

"Right this moment, no one in the Navy's going to even think about bucking Kingsford's authority, which turns what's left of the Navy and the Marines into *his* big stick. As for the Brigadier, every honest cop in the Gendarmerie—and, contrary to prevalent pre-conquest belief, that was probably a good seventy or even eighty percent of the total force, here in the Sol System, at least—has recognized him as the *most* honest cop in the Gendarmerie. He was the guy who was willing to take down *anybody* he could prove was dirty, even before the war, and they know it. That gives him a pretty big stick of his own. When General Mabley 'took early retirement,' he was the only real choice to replace her as the Gendarmerie's CO, even if his position is still officially 'acting' and he didn't get the promotion that would normally go with the job. And he's also the one who personally arrested the Mandarins."

"No, he didn't. *You* did," al-Fanudahi pointed out with the air of a man set upon picking nits. "You and Bryce."

"Oh for God's sake, Daud!" Okiku rolled her eyes, but she also chuckled. "Okay, I'll grant you that Bryce and I actually slapped on the manacles—" in fact, they'd been very sophisticated, quite comfortable restraints, but she liked *manacles* better "—but the Brigadier was the officer in charge of the arrest. He had Admiral Kingsford's total support, and he knew it, but the two of them only acted on Attorney General Rorendaal's—well, *assistant* attorney general, at the time—authority, with a warrant duly issued by a judge right here in Old Chicago. Sure, the judge had the Brigadier, me, and three other armed Gendarmes in her office when Rorendaal screened to, ah, *discuss* the warrant in question, but she signed it, and that means the Mandarins' arrest was completely legal."

"And the point of all of this?" al-Fanudahi asked, although his more resigned tone suggested he knew exactly where she was headed.

"The point is that both the Brigadier and the Admiral need to be...highly visible, but without going overboard about it. They need everyone to know they stand behind the Provisional Government—fully—and that they're in a position to step in, as quickly and as hard as necessary, if any of those various factions decide to screw the pooch. That's the best way to make sure none of them do. But at the same time, they need everyone to know that the *last* thing they are is a military dictatorship.

"That's the entire reason they got that warrant, to prove this isn't just some sort of coup. But it's also why the Brigadier has his office in George Benton. He's visible, he's right there if the Provisional Assembly wants to 'consult' with him, and everyone in the entire star system knows he's ready to arrest anyone he needs to arrest to maintain public order and keep this whole constitution-writing process moving forward to both the Grand Alliance's and domestic public opinion's satisfaction."

"But do *we* really have to be part of his 'stick'?" al-Fanudahi asked, almost plaintively.

He shoved his hands into his pockets, which were capacious, given the jacket he was wearing. It was a mild day...for the first week of March in Old Chicago. But that was by right-off-lake-Michigan standards of "mild." Al-Fanudahi was a history buff, which made him one of very few people in the universe who knew that the ancient nickname Windy City had actually been a reference to Chicago's notoriously verbose city council. Originally, it had been called the White City, because of its distinctive architecture and—for the time—extensive use of street lighting.

None of which changed the fact that, this time of year, Chicago was still all too often cold and windy, especially when you stood on an open deck a kilometer and a half in the air.

He looked around again, still a bit pickle faced.

"Damn it, Natsuko, I spent *years* being ignored by my pig-ignorant superiors and working as far out of sight as I could manage. I miss our old haunts in the Hillary Enkateshwara basement!"

"Oh, come on. It wasn't in the tower's *basement*. I'll grant you that the office was...pretty hard to find, though."

"It might as well have been in the basement. I *liked* being in the middle of a warehouse for stuff nobody wanted. Just our own little rogue operation. No official organizational charts. Out of sight, out of mind. Nice, quiet, no incompetent superiors sticking their noses into our business, nobody likely to come looking to assassinate us... I was a contented mouse in a world of apparatchik cats. Now—"

He jerked his head to indicate the tower upon whose balcony they stood.

"*Now* we've got an office. No, a bunch of offices; big ones, too—right smack in the official headquarters of the Joint Intelligence Sharing and Distribution Command Center. Which, I might add, is *another* thing the two of them have cooked up out of nowhere!"

"Damned straight and damned well time, and you know it," she shot back. "The JISDC, I mean. You just finished pointing out how your superiors ignored you every time you warned them the Manties and Havenites were about to hand us our heads, and *none* of this would've happened if they'd listened to you. So, yeah, I think creating a new command where people at your level—*our* level—share information and the people at the top *have* to read—or at least sign receipts for—our output is a *damned* good idea. At least the bastards know they'll get shot at sunrise, professionally speaking, if they ignore the info anyway and we were *right*."

"Yeah, but why include *us*—the Ghost Hunters—in something that public?" It wasn't the least bit "public," of course, except within the Solarian intelligence community, but she understood his perhaps somewhat petulant point. "You just pointed out that there are plenty of apparatchiks still out there, and most of 'em don't like us very much. Especially since we committed the unforgivable sin of being right when all of *them* were wrong. And then there are the Other Guys. I'll guarantee you some of those still-in-place apparatchiks have really been working for them for *years* . . . at least. While we were hiding out over in Enkateshwara they couldn't find us to do anything about us . . . even if they'd realized we were sharing notes in the first place. But now—" He glowered afresh. "They know about us *now* . . . and we've got everything but spotlights pointed at us!"

"Who cares? These days, in case you hadn't noticed, we're the ones with fangs and claws and the oh-so-formerly-feline bureaucrats and apparatchiks are the ones tiptoeing around *us*. Not to mention—"

"Time!" a voice called out from behind them.

It was exactly the sort of voice you'd expect from an overly large male Marine who wasn't one bit shy about resorting to intimidation when it seemed the handiest way to break an impasse. Or an arm or two.

Granted, Major Bryce Tarkovsky was a personal friend, very smart, and a really, really nice guy.

As a rule.

"And here we go," al-Fanudahi muttered.

✧   ✧   ✧

It was just as bad as al-Fanudahi had feared it would be. In fact, it was worse. Lots worse. Because it would appear they weren't destined for desks in JISDIC, after all. Oh, no! Not them!

Brigadier Gaddis presented his proposal in a calm, reasonable, and utterly inflexible tone of voice. When he was finished, every-one in the room—well, except Bryce Tarkovsky, of course—looked apprehensive. Al-Fanudahi truly did like Tarkovsky, a lot, although there were times he thought the major might as well have had "Born to Raise Hell" tattooed on his biceps. But this time, even Okiku's usually imperturbable self-confidence looked a bit wobbly.

So they were field agents, now. Gaddis had even suggested this was some sort of promotion—or at least a recognition of services rendered.

It was a truth al-Fanudahi was quite sure went back to pre-historic times. *No good deed shall go unpunished.*

He tried not to glower at Tarkovsky and Okiku. At least they'd both held plenty of field assignments before! Just one more notch on their guns for *them*. But he was an analyst, damn it. He was the one field agents *reported to*, not the fellow who went out there digging the data up in the first place! What did *he* know about—?

His inner indignation paused as he saw the expression on Irene Teague's face. In fact, he had to struggle not to laugh. Teague was twenty years younger than he, not even out of her thirties yet, and she was third-generation prolong, which made her look younger still. At the moment, in fact, she looked like a ten-year-old introvert who'd just been told she'd been tapped to perform in Shakespeare's *King Lear* ... cast in the thankless role of Cordelia. Also known as *exit, corpse.*

"*Me?*" she didn't—quite—squeak.

Unlike al-Fanudahi, who was a Battle Fleet officer, Teague was an officer in Frontier Fleet. Up until the recent unpleasantness with the Grand Alliance, Battle Fleet had seen very little in the way of combat, whereas Frontier Fleet had been almost constantly engaged on active operations of one sort or another, policing the Solarian League's borders ... and all too often helping Frontier Security break heads (and necks) on planets whose citizens got "uppity." But Teague had spent her entire career in Intelligence, all but two years of it right here on Old Terra. And the two years she'd spent *off* the motherworld had been at the Frontier Fleet nodal base on the planet Bergusia in the long-settled Kenniac System, barely eighty-two light-years from Sol. The planet had been named after the Celtic goddess of prosperity, which was quite a fair description of it.

"*Me?*" she repeated. Her brown eyes moved around the room. It was unclear whether they were searching for rhyme, reason, or an escape route. "Why me? I'm just an analyst."

"Which is exactly what we need on Mesa." Gaddis sat up

straight in his chair, which, given that he was almost two meters tall, made him loom over the conference table—and Teague—like a frowning deity. "Especially because you, like Captain al-Fanudahi, have been assigned to ONI's Operational Analysis for years. We'll need that expertise. Besides, he's Battle Fleet, you're Frontier Fleet. That may give us some balance in the Grand Alliance's eyes."

Al-Fanudahi snorted.

"As if they're likely to care, Sir," he said. "I figure by now the GA's assessment of any of the Solarian League Navy's intelligence branches—Battle or Frontier Fleet—is about as distinguishable as mud, mire, and morass."

Gaddis glowered at him, but Tarkovsky spoke up before the brigadier's glower could build to full Force 10 glare status.

"You might be surprised, Daud. The one thing their own intelligence people aren't is dimwitted. They know the Navy's top officers were about as alert to changes as well-fed dinosaurs. But they'll also realize that somewhere in the bowels of a huge military organization like the Solarian League Navy, there had to be at least some dissidents who were paying attention to the real universe. I mean, we couldn't *all* have been as stupid as Admiral Cheng!" Al-Fanudahi's eyes rolled at the mention of his thankfully ex-CO, and Tarkovsky shrugged. "Well, right now, they have every reason to want to hook up with people like that—like *us*—in hopes that we can be persuaded that the GA's theories about the Alignment are correct."

"We haven't come to any such conclusion," Teague said stoutly.

Tarkovsky and Gaddis swiveled matching hawklike gazes onto the fair-haired Frontier Fleet captain, but al-Fanudahi decided to come to the rescue. He'd had time enough to absorb another new reality. Whether or not he or Irene liked it, they *were* bring reassigned to Mesa.

"No, we haven't 'concluded' that," he agreed. "But by now that's only because *good* analysts demand strict standards of proof before they 'conclude' anything, and you know it. Oh, we never get *definitive* proof until the war's over and we get to go through the other side's archives, but we at least need a clear preponderance of the evidence before we offer up any propositions as facts. And even then, we qualify them. But having said that," he glanced around the table, "there isn't anyone in this room—including; no, even especially you, Irene—who isn't firmly convinced the Other Guys are out there and up to no good. We may still question whether or not the GA's theory of the Alignment is the one that best fits the bill, and it'll still take a *ton* of evidence to convince me it is, really. But *somebody's* out there; they're just as cunning and vicious as the Manties and Havenites think they are; and we have to find them. Because if they've been doing this for remotely as long as it seems they have, they aren't going to stop until someone *stops* them, and we can't do that when we don't even know who the hell they are."

He took a deep breath and let it out slowly.

"Besides," he told her, "having you on Mesa would be a comfort to me."

"Well..." She drew a deep breath of her own. "Well, okay. I guess. But Ghulam and the kids—"

"Oh, come off it! Your beloved husband's been crabbing for years that you never get to travel anywhere because of your blasted job. As for your kids—we're talking about George and Tahmina, right? They'll love it."

"*Mesa?* The evil slaver planet, with the rubble and ruin of nuclear strikes scattered around the entire globe? My kids—"

She paused, then grimaced.

"Well, yeah. They'll be hopping up and down with glee when I tell them. Especially George. What is it with eight-year-old boys' infatuation with pirates and gangsters?"

Gaddis settled back into his normal seated posture. He was still imposing—the man was really tall—but he no longer looked Jovian.

"All right, then. We're all agreed. We'll send a delegation to Mesa—an informal one, to start—that will try to get the GA to agree to let us participate in an investigation into what really happened after Gold Peak's fleet seized the system."

He, too, looked around at everyone seated at the table. "Two people from OpAn, one Battle Fleet and one Frontier Fleet; Natsuko, to represent the Gendarmerie's CID; and Bryce, for the Marines."

Weng Zhing-hwan cleared her throat. Like Okiku, she was a lieutenant colonel in the Gendarmerie, but the patch on her shoulder indicated that she belonged to Intelligence, rather than the Criminal Investigation Division.

"I have no objection at all to Bryce going, Sir. But I'm curious. Why someone from *Marine* Intelligence?"

"Think of me as a goodwill ambassador," Tarkovsky said.

The look Weng gave him was to "skepticism" what a glacier was to "icy."

"I'm serious!" he insisted. "The Manties and Havenites may have a dim opinion of the SLN, but that doesn't extend to the Solarian *Marines*. Oh, no, not at all. They know the kind of crap we've been ordered to do from time to time," his expression dimmed—briefly—"but they also know it wasn't our idea...and we did it damned well, anyway. Usually with as little brutality as possible. And that high opinion certainly hasn't been lowered by recent events on Mesa, where—" he buffed his nails on his tunic and blew on them "—the brilliantly planned and led seccy rebellion had for its military commander one Thandi Palane, formerly of the Solarian Marine Corps."

His smile became an outright grin.

"You could say we're old friends."

"You've never met the woman in your life, Bryce!" Weng accused, and he shrugged.

"A petty detail. We're both *Marines*. Once a Marine, always a Marine. We're bound to get along famously."

Captain Daud al-Fanudahi cherished a few minor reservations on that point, but he said nothing. What was there to say? For the first time in his career, he was about to become a field agent, investigating what was probably the most malignant force in the human-settled galaxy. And he was going to do it on what was probably the most notorious planet in the human-settled galaxy... and had been even before it was ravaged by war and indiscriminate bombardment. A mission that would depend at least in part on gaining the goodwill of a woman who'd just led what was already being recognized by military analysts as a masterpiece of defensive tactics. Brutally effective ones, to boot.

And for their goodwill ambassador, they were relying on a Marine officer who'd once kidnapped a fellow officer he suspected of wrongdoing. He'd then subjected the fellow to an interrogation that might not have come up to Torquemada standards but was still *way* outside any official channel...and still enough that the interrogated individual had dropped dead as a result. From an implanted nanotech suicide protocol, granted, not anything Bryce had done directly.

Still...

Suddenly, for the first time that day, Daud Ibn Mamoun al-Fanudahi found himself feeling rather cheerful.

CNO's Office
Admiralty Building
City of Old Chicago
Sol System

DR. CHARLES E. GANNON LEANED BACK IN HIS SEAT AND CROSSED his legs as the chair reconfigured to support his weight in perfect comfort. It was an exceptionally tasteful—and expensive—armchair. As you'd expect of a piece of furniture in the inner sanctum of the Solarian League Navy's commanding officer.

Once he was settled, Gannon gestured with his forefinger in the way he'd captured an audience's attention over decades of university instruction.

"I have a theory about this," he said.

"Of course you do." Admiral Winston Kingsford smiled. "Chuck, you have a theory about everything."

"I'm hurt! And the accusation's false, anyway. I think I'm fairly restrained in my conjectures. I've made it a point, for instance, never to develop any theories about my wife."

"That's not restraint." Kingsford sniffed. "That's just self-preservation. No husband in his right mind hypothesizes about his spouse. I don't develop any theories regarding Samantha, either. Not out loud, anyway."

"Okay, point. How is Sam, by the way? I haven't seen her since..." Gannon furrowed his brow. "Eight months? That 'gala affair'—" he shuddered "—at the new Art Institute?"

"I'm afraid she's a bit irked with me, at the moment. We were supposed to have been on vacation this month." Kingsford twirled his own forefinger in a manner which indicated...pretty much everything in the universe. "The situation got in the way."

"Surely she doesn't blame you for everything that's happened

118

lately? Minor things like foreign invasion and occupation will tend to upset personal plans, especially when you're the Chief of Naval operations. Pesky of them, I know, but there it is."

"No, of course she doesn't. But she was really looking forward to relaxing on Grand Anse Beach in Grenada. So was I, for that matter."

The admiral smiled crookedly—and briefly, then leaned forward, planting his forearms on the big desk in front of him.

"All right. Let's hear this new theory of yours about the Mesa Massacre."

"Is that what they're calling it now?"

"Don't you follow the news?"

"As little as possible. It's mostly twaddle."

"Well," Kingsford sighed and wiped his face with one hand, "yes, that's what they're calling it. Stupid turn of phrase. A 'massacre' is something that has an up-close and personal character. And it's usually targeted on a specific group of some sort. What happened on Mesa after Gold Peak seized the system was way too indiscriminate to deserve the term."

Gannon peered at him for a moment, all traces of humor gone from his face.

"Actually," he said, "that's the theory I was going to present to you. I've come to the conclusion that the slaughter on Mesa wasn't indiscriminate at all. Nor was it a massacre. It was cold-blooded, first-degree murder, and it did have clear and specific targets and goals."

"*Millions* of targets?"

Kingsford's tone was dubious, and Gannon's light brown eyes, normally a close match in color to his hair, seemed to darken. That was an optical illusion, of course, produced by his now-grim expression. Unlike the style currently favored by most male academics, Gannon was clean-shaven, so it was impossible to miss the tight set of his jaw.

"The targeting wasn't 'indiscriminate,' Winston. You can't even call it collateral damage. That mass murder was planned and deliberate."

"You're serious."

"As death." Gannon nodded grimly. "You know how closely I've been following the developments on Mesa. What you may not know is that I have my own pipeline into Manticoran intelligence."

He waved his hand in a dismissive gesture, "Don't ask; I won't tell you. I don't get everything, of course, but I've gotten enough to know the parameters of the killings, and there was absolutely no logical or coherent pattern to that so-called bombardment. It just looks insane."

"Insane?" Kingsford snorted. "I guess you could call nuking an uninhabited island that!"

"There were more absurdities than just one island." Gannon waved a hand. "I think we'd have to accept, for the sake of argument, that if the Mesan version of what happened is remotely accurate, then the Grand Alliance carried out this 'indiscriminate bombardment' as soon as it was in orbit and that it was probably in support of the 'terrorist campaign' which it had fomented preceding Gold Peak's arrival. Correct? I mean, I find that entire argument ludicrous, but that was the official line."

Kingsford looked skeptical. Obviously, he found the "official line" as unlikely as Gannon did, but he nodded.

"As I say," the professor continued, "I found that argument... suspect, let's say. But the more I looked at it, the more I came to the conclusion that, however ridiculous it looked at first glance, the 'terrorist campaign' and the 'indiscriminate bombardment' actually *were* linked, really were part of a coherent strategy.

"It just wasn't the *Grand Alliance's* strategy."

Kingsford's skeptical expression went into overdrive, and Gannon snorted.

"Let me lay out my thinking before you jump in," he said, and Kingsford settled back again with another nod. It wasn't *quite* the sort of nod one used to humor a lunatic, but that was only because of how long he'd known Gannon.

The professor quirked a brief grin at the CNO, but then he sobered.

"First," he said, holding up an index finger, "let's look at the 'terrorist' targets. Especially at four of them: two amusement parks, and two sports stadiums, all attacked with weapons of mass destruction in the same two-day window, weeks before Gold Peak arrived."

"Those sound like exactly the sort of targets terrorists would have been looking for," Kingsford pointed out.

"Not logical ones, if what they were looking for was just to rack up a body count, which appears to have been the terrorist's objective, at least according to the Mesan system authorities. Those four bombings happened during the middle of the day, on a Tuesday and a Thursday, respectively, Winston. A workday and a *school*day, the both of them. Which means the amusement parks were way below capacity, and the same was true of the sports stadiums. If they'd wanted to just rack up the bodies, they'd have struck at bigger urban centers, caught all those people at home, or at work...or in school. They'd at least have waited for the evening crowds. They didn't. Why?"

Kingsford frowned and ran the fingers of his right hand through his dark hair.

"My head's starting to hurt, Chuck. I don't see the big difference between killing a lot of people at work or at home versus killing them in amusement parks and sports centers."

"Ah, but there *is* a difference. A big one. Because it's easy to reconstruct who was at school, or at their workplace, when the blasts went off. There are plenty of records for that. Whereas *anybody* could have said they were going to an amusement park or sporting event." He leaned forward, his face intent. "*And how would you know if they did or didn't?* Nobody keeps a record of such things. There might be camera footage from the arrival gates, or security cams on the grounds, but if you're going to blow *them* up, too..."

"But why—? Oh."

"Yeah. *Oh.* Nuclear explosions and fuel-air bombs eliminate the evidence. Ursula Unknown tells her friends or family or coworkers she's taking the day off to go to an amusement park, or sports event, or whatever other place of entertainment. Her body is never found, of course, because it's been vaporized. But was she actually there?"

Gannon's middle finger came up.

"Another 'terrorist attack' took out a big park on the edge of the plateau Mendel sits on. It was the equivalent of a beach. You couldn't swim, but you could paraglide, grav ski, and sunbathe. Same thing. 'I think I'll go to Overlook Park today.' How do you know if they did or didn't? The bomb 'just happened' to be directly adjacent to the park admin offices...which means the repository for all the imagery from its security cams. And the explosion was so powerful it collapsed a vast stretch of the cliff. People were buried, as well as vaporized."

He lowered his hand.

"The same pattern crops up over and over again when you look at the attacks ascribed to terrorists. Concerts. Business and professional symposiums. Places where people would logically gather, but no one would be keeping official records of who was actually there as opposed to who simply *said* they'd be there. And every time, any security cameras covering the place stored their data on-site. Some of them sent it to a central site eventually, but even they'd have at least their last several days' imagery only on their on-site servers, and those were taken out in the blast, as well. An awful lot of that could have been sheer coincidence, especially given the power of the explosions, but *all* of them?"

He shook his head.

"At first, the fact that they were all public gatherings or public places inclined me to accept that they *could* have been terrorist attacks. Some of the information from that Manticoran pipeline I mentioned to you was telling me the exact opposite, you understand, but misinformation is an ancient and respected intelligence tool, and even the good guys have been known to use it to . . . shape their allies' positions. Still, it did strike me as odd that terrorists who could get their devices into position for attacks like that *couldn't* get them into position for real mega-casualty attacks.

"And then there was the Grand Alliance's 'indiscriminate bombardment.' A bombardment that took out uninhabited islands. Resort towns in the middle of the mountains, far away from any major population center or industrial center. Completely empty spots in the middle of a prairie. Orbital platforms—some habitats, with hundreds of thousands of citizens; some freight platforms with no more than a few dozen employees aboard. But a bombardment which somehow missed the major industrial platforms; the orbital smelters; the Mesan military's remaining infrastructure, planetside or orbital; urban and industrial centers on the planet. As I said, it made no sense. Militarily, the targets were pointless from any tactical or strategic perspective. From the perspective of a 'terror strike,' they made even less sense, given how easy it would have been to drive the casualty totals up into the hundreds of millions, if that was what they'd wanted.

"In fact, it made as little sense as the terrorists' targeting made before Gold Peak ever got there."

It was very quiet in Kingsford's office, and Gannon settled farther back into his comfortable chair.

"Since both sets of explosions seemed equally...irrational, I decided to look at them as if they were, in fact, part of a single set of events, but not events set into motion by the Grand Alliance or the Ballroom. And what I found was that with only two exceptions, the population centers taken out by the 'bombardment' were not only very small, by the standards of something like Mendel, but also rather like those stadiums and amusement parks. They were resort towns, which customarily had sizeable floating populations. Places Ursula Unknown's cousins could have told people they were going for a few days, or possibly a week or two. I couldn't come up with any reason for blowing up uninhabited islands or empty spots on the prairie...unless, of course, the islands *weren't* uninhabited and those particular bits of prairie *weren't* empty.

"I'd already realized that a disproportionate—*completely* disproportionate—percentage of the mass-casualty 'terrorist' sites were places where no records could be checked on who was or wasn't actually present. When I combined that with the relatively few mass-casualty sites of the 'bombardment,' I realized why that was. I'm convinced the pattern of the terrorist strikes was designed to conceal as many survivors as possible—and do so in the middle of such a monstrous butchery that it wouldn't occur to anyone that its real purpose was to keep some people *alive*. The *right* people—so they could disappear without a trace."

"Wait a minute." It was Kingsford's turn wave a hand. "Just how in hell did you get to that conclusion because of the sites the *bombardment* hit? The terrorist attacks, okay. I'll give you that one, at least as a workable hypothesis. But no one got snuck out of any of the bombardment sites, Chuck, and nobody got off-planet after the explosions, either. Not without being *totally* documented by the GA, anyway!"

"All true. But think about this—the one thing that more than any other casts doubt on the Grand Alliance's claim that the Alignment they talk about was responsible for the 'bombardment' is simple. If their 'Alignment' did it, it had to have killed thousands, maybe even millions, of its own people. What possible reason could it have had to do something like that? If I'm right about the reason it 'disappeared' so many people so tracelessly, it's because it had already used the 'terrorists' as a cover to extract key people from the planet and the system. I think it was still in the process of doing that. That it had concentrated additional evacuees in those resort towns the 'bombardment' destroyed. And that Gold Peak's arrival took it by surprise.

"So it executed its fallback plan."

"My God, Chuck." Kingsford stared at him. "Do you realize what you're *saying?*"

"Of course I do." Gannon's expression was grimmer than ever. "Winston, your own analysts are telling you that at least a dozen of the 'bombardment' sites where they've been able to look at the available evidence were obviously surface explosions. And they were nukes, not kinetic strikes. That's enough to rule out Tenth Fleet's responsibility, right there, as far as I'm concerned! But when I put all the rest of it together, I realized that this Alignment of the Grand Alliance's—whether it's actually what they think it is or not—had to be behind what happened. That it was pulling people off the planet. And that it had gathered the other people it needed—or who might have been breadcrumbs leading to those people—into discrete, concentrated locations. Locations from which they could be evacuated under cover of more 'terrorist' attacks, or—"

"Or eliminated, if it wasn't possible to get them out," Kingsford finished harshly, and Gannon nodded.

"My God," the CNO said again. He sat there for several seconds, frowning in thought. "Assuming somebody cold-blooded and vicious enough to entertain a strategy like that, your argument makes sense. It's disgusting, and terrifying, and while it may be *purposeful*, it really *is* insane, when you think about the mindset behind it. But—"

"But how could they get that many people off the planet without leaving records of suspicious passenger and departures?" Gannon smiled thinly, and quite savagely. "Well, guess what? One of the orbital targets that the 'bombardment' obliterated was—"

"Station Delta!" Kingsford slapped a large, powerful hand on his desk. "Mesa System Traffic Control's headquarters."

"Along with all the current records of ship travel." Gannon nodded. "Of the previous eight or nine T-months, at least. They would have backed up the records on-planet at the end of the current quarter...assuming the entire station hadn't been taken out by another 'terrorist bomb' first, of course. You see how well that fits my theory? *Everything* about those terrorist attacks and the supposed bombardment makes sense if you look at it from the angle I'm suggesting."

"Not the uninhabited island—and that was one of the biggest explosions, if I remember correctly."

"Yes, it was. But I'm willing to bet that island wasn't what it was said to be. I'm damned near certain there *was* an installation of some sort on it—and one that was so important that they used a huge blast to destroy all traces of it."

Kingsford tapped his desktop and the expensive-looking "wooden" surface turned translucent. He tapped again, on one of the touchscreens which had appeared, and entered a brief command. Then he stood.

"Come here," he invited as one wall of his office disappeared behind a three-dimensional hologram.

Gannon climbed out of his own chair and walked across to it. By the time he got there, it had stabilized, and he folded his arms as he gazed at a display of the human-settled portion of the galaxy—which sounded more majestic than it really was. Even two millennia after the beginning of the Diaspora, humans still hadn't penetrated all that far into the immensity called the Milky Way. The star systems humanity had settled—or even visited—were a ragged-fringed bubble no more than thirteen hundred light-years across in the Orion Arm...which was ten thousand light years in length and thirty-five hundred wide. And the Orion Arm itself was just a minor spiral arm, dwarfed by the Perseus and Scutum-Centaurus arms.

That small a section of the arm could be displayed on a large enough scale that the locations of humanity's major political divisions could be indicated with a combination of color coding and outlines. The Solarian League was far bigger than any of the others, of course. But Gannon was interested to see that Kingsford had programmed the display to delineate subdivisions of the League whose allegiance was getting what one might have called shaky.

Apparently, the degree of shakiness was represented on a scale from green to yellow, to various, steadily deeper shades of orange.

And then there were the handful of individual star systems—like Beowulf—which blazed a brilliant, bloody red. And the equally crimson stars of the recently declared Mayan Autonomous Regional Sector. What an appropriate color for an entity with the acronym MARS, he thought. Red like the proverbial "red planet." He wondered if Oravil Barregos had thought about that when he chose the name for the first Office of Frontier Security sector to ever declare its independence of the Solarian League. Had he deliberately named it for the ancient god of war?

There was no room in the office for the sort of holo tank one might find on the bridge of the ship, so it was impossible to walk around the holograph to view it from different angles. But another command from Kingsford, entered over his uni-link, started it rotating slowly.

"In one sentence, tell me what you see," he said.

"A very imposing Solarian League that's in the process of disintegrating," Gannon replied.

"Well, that was certainly succinct. Now elaborate."

"All right." Gannon unfolded one arm and pointed into the display. "Beowulf was only the first Core System to secede. There are going to be others—like Hypatia, not exactly a Core System, but still a charter member of the League. Beowulf's obviously going to be looking at some kind of political union with the Star Empire; they're already joined at the hip economically, commercially, and by blood, thanks to the Manticoran Junction, so that's inevitable. I expect quite a few additional ex-Solarian systems will seek membership in the Star Empire, too, assuming they're close enough to make it practical. A lot of the other single star systems, especially in the Shell and inner Verge, will simply announce their independence and strike out on their own. But there are others that are... more interesting. Like MARS."

His forefinger indicated the bloody icon of the Maya System and the web of equally red star systems radiating from it. There were almost a dozen of them.

"It looks to me like MARS will attract at least another half-dozen of the local star systems," he said. "Erewhon's decision to sign on with Barregos makes that even more likely, given the way it's going to up their industrial potential and give them the Erewhon Wormhole Junction." He shook his head slowly. "With that base to build on, an at least friendly relationship with the GA, and somebody like Barregos in charge, MARS is going to stand up, Winston. We're looking at another independent multi-system star nation. And one that'll be respectably large when the dust finally settles."

"Agreed." Kingsford nodded. "And just between you and me, I don't really blame Barregos or Rozsak. Mind you, it's a bit embarrassing to admit they played us so well, but I think they take their responsibilities to their citizens seriously. I even think that was a major part of *why* they played us. I don't see any way they come back to the League, but we're already getting feelers from them about maintaining economic and military ties."

"Better than I'd expected, really," Gannon said.

"Assuming it happens, anyway." Kingsford snorted. Then— "What else, O Sage?"

"Well, there's this section down here."

Gannon's finger swooped over five hundred light-years "down" from Maya to the Mannerheim System, the center of the ten-star "Renaissance Factor." The Factor's systems had never belonged to the League, and they formed a two hundred-light-year bubble of surprisingly affluent sovereign systems in the Fringe. All of them were independent polities, but the chaos and uncertainty of the League's war with the Grand Alliance had drawn them together in a defensive association that was busy transitioning into an actual star nation.

"You can kiss at least another dozen or so star systems goodbye to the Renaissance Factor within another two to five years," he continued. "Then—"

His finger started toward another portion of display, but Kingsford stopped him.

"Never mind," the admiral said. "You've proved my point for me."

He headed back to his desk, waving Gannon back to his armchair as he went.

"And what point did I prove this time?" the professor asked with a chuckle as he resumed his seat.

Kingsford didn't answer immediately. Instead, he leaned over his desk and planted his elbows again, then brought his hands up in a steeple, with the fingertips covering his mouth.

Gannon's jocular mood vanished instantly. He recognized that posture, and it wasn't that of an old friend. It was the way the Solarian League Navy's Chief of Naval operations paused before making a weighty decision.

A moment passed. Then Kingsford lowered his steepled hands enough to clear his mouth.

"I want you to resign your post at the University," he said.

Gannon's eyebrows rose. Not far. Maybe half a centimeter.

"And do what, instead?" he asked. "I'm not old enough to retire."

"Not hardly." The admiral smiled. "What I want you to do instead is become the Director of the Office of Naval Intelligence."

Gannon's eyebrows went up farther. Quite a bit farther.

"You want me to head up *ONI*? You've got to be kidding."

"No." Kingsford lowered his hands to rest on the deck, still in a steeple. "I'm not kidding. Chuck, I need an outsider to step in and shake that damn somnolescent bureaucracy by the scruff of the neck until it wakes up and finally gets its head out of its ass."

"Winston, somnolescent or not—and I certainly won't argue that it isn't—it's still a military bureaucracy. In case you hadn't noticed, this—" he flicked fingers across the jacket he was wearing "—isn't a uniform. That's because I'm what people call a 'civilian.'"

"You've been in the Navy."

"Yes, I have. Decades ago, when I signed up in order to get away from home as soon as I turned legal age. I was still a kid, Winston. I only served a decade or so, and entirely as a rating. A rating who got busted twice, clear back to spacer third." He smiled. "I've always taken a certain perverse pride in that. Busted twice—but they promoted me back to petty officer twice, too. I was damn good at my job, if I say so myself. Just... ah, young. Only thirty-four when I left the service."

"So you were still a baby when you deserted to the civvy side," Kingsford said. "You were still in the Navy. That's plenty good enough for me to beat down any opposition. And the fact you were a rating works in your favor, as far as I'm concerned. Especially because I know what you were busted for. It wasn't the usual AWOL or drunk and disorderly. You got busted—both times—because you lipped off to superior officers and told them they were numbskulls who didn't know what they were doing."

"They *were* numbskulls." Gannon shook his head. The gesture wasn't so much one of disagreement or negation as it was of simple disbelief. "You have got to be kidding," he repeated. "For Pete's sake, Winston—I'm not just a university professor, I teach *intellectual history*. That's about as relevant to naval intelligence as... as... Hell, I don't know. Music appreciation, maybe."

"Cut it out. You're a polymath, and you know it as well as I do. You teach so-called 'intellectual history' because it's a catchall term that lets you teach anything you want. Since you won the Banerjee Award, the University doesn't even argue with you anymore."

He un-steepled his hands and leaned back. His arms were now firmly planted on his chair's armrests, like a helmsman at his post.

"I need you, Chuck. I need somebody who can *think*. And— just as important—who won't hesitate to tell me *what* he thinks. The last time you gave a damn whether someone agreed with you or not was when you wrangled with your mother about doing chores. And, like you said, you left that off the day you turned eighteen."

Gannon looked at him, then drew a deep breath.

"That's not quite true," he said. "I give a damn what Andrea thinks—and I don't think she's going to like this one bit."

"Be a raise in pay."

"Big deal. The money from the Banerjee could carry both of us for a half-century. She makes twice what I do, anyway. It's not money, it's..." He sighed. "It's the aggravation. I can get cranky, you know, and some of it's bound to spill onto her a bit. Even in the ivory tower, I get peeved now and then. As head of ONI? Oh, dear Lord."

"I need an answer, Chuck. And I need it now. In case you hadn't noticed, all hell is breaking loose."

"Bit of an overstatement, Winston. It stopped 'breaking loose' the moment Harrington crossed the hyper wall. Now it's just coming apart."

"Yes or no?"

"Yes, damn you." Gannon glared at the admiral. "You knew I'd agree, didn't you?"

"Yep. I've known you a long time. Since the day you told an ensign he was full of shit and didn't know his ass from his elbow."

"And you were the one officer who *didn't* bust me." Gannon smiled reluctantly. "You even listened." He shook his head. "Okay, maybe this'll work out."

General Board Boardroom
Madison Grant Tower
City of Mendel
Planet Mesa
Mesa System

THE TABLE WAS OVAL-SHAPED, WITH SEATS FOR UP TO TWENTY-five and room behind them for chairs to seat whatever staff their occupants might bring to the meeting. It was also luxuriously furnished, as one would have anticipated for the meeting place of the General Board of the Mesa System.

At the moment, however, someone else occupied the General Board's meeting place, and Captain Cynthia Lecter felt a combination of deep satisfaction and trepidation as she looked around the almost fully populated table. The rest of the conference room was empty. The meeting she was about to convene was not the sort in which one wanted any participants who weren't absolutely necessary.

General Susan Hibson, present as the CO of the Mesan Military Administration, sat to Lecter's right. Hibson really ought to have chaired this meeting, in many ways, but Michelle Henke had chosen to send Tenth Fleet's chief of staff to discharge that role, instead. Tenth Fleet was the actual power in the Mesa System, and Lecter's position as Henke's chief of staff provided all the authority she needed for their purposes today—the main one of which was to begin the process of transitioning away from the MMA and back to civilian *Mesan* government. Hibson obviously had to be a part of that conversation, but there were definite arguments for putting someone else in charge of it.

The others around that table...

Only two were from what had once been the General Board:

Brianna Pearson, formerly Vice President of Operations (Mesa) for Technodyne Industries, and the Vice President of Research and Development for the Mesan Genetic Consultancy, a man named Jackson Chicherin.

Chicherin still held his position with MGC, which was a locally based firm. Lecter didn't know if Pearson still held hers with Technodyne. Pearson herself might not even know yet if she remained their employee. Transstellar corporations were notorious for cutting the throats (figuratively speaking...as a rule) of executives who foundered on reefs.

For the purposes of the moment, however, it didn't matter whether or not Pearson was still a Technodyne employee. She *had* been, which had made her a prominent member of the General Board. Which, in turn, meant she still held a certain degree of authority among Mesa's full citizens. And, perhaps more to the point, she was one of the tiny number of former Board members who would be—very grudgingly—accepted by Mesa's seccies and ex-slaves.

"Tiny number," as in *two*: her and Chicherin. Every other former member of the General Board would have been flatly rejected, and a fair number would've taken their lives in their hands if they'd dared to show up.

None of the other people sitting at the conference actually *approved* of either Pearson or Chicherin. But they all understood the necessity of including some prominent representatives of Mesa's former full citizens in the process of constructing a new government, and these were the only two all of them—*any* of them, really—could stomach. Chicherin had always been far in the background, and Pearson was known to have objected on several occasions to the brutal tactics of the previous government in dealing with seccies and ex-slaves.

The commander of the Mesan Planetary Peaceforce, General Gillian Drescher, was there, as well. It would have been impossible to have the meeting without her, since she commanded the only more or less intact armed force on the planet, other than the occupation troops supporting Hibson's MMA.

The seccies were the best-represented at the table, by far. Along with Jurgen Dusek, the recognized "Head Boss" of Mesa's seccy bosses, six other bosses were there as well: Andrea Nur, from Potosi District; Hyndryk Abbas, of the Jewel District; Anibal Eisenberg, from Kelly District; Jacelyn Amsterdam, from Watson; Theodora Moreau, from Crick City; and Cáo Li-Qiang, from Franklin. The cities of Watson, Crick City, and Franklin had the largest seccy populations on Mesa, after Mendel itself. The capital city was far larger than any other, of course, and the only one whose seccies had been organized by the Bosses into districts.

Seven seccies out of twenty-one people, total—out of nineteen, if one subtracted Lecter and Hibson from the equation. Seccies were only ten percent of the Mesan population, but at the moment they held more than thirty-six percent of the positions in what amounted to a provisional government. Very provisional, to be sure—but it was still the body out of which the planet's new government would emerge.

Former full citizens, on the other hand, held a little over twenty percent of the seats, despite constituting thirty percent of the population. And as for the majority of Mesa's inhabitants, the former slaves . . .

Well, that was a problem. Except for the Audubon Ballroom, Mesa's slaves had had no political or even social organizations at all, other than their religious ones—and most of the denominations tolerated by Mesa's authorities had embraced a form of pietism that emphasized personal, individual relationships with God, a sense of duty and order . . . but definitely *not* social activism. For the moment, at least, the ex-slaves' religious organizations were not well suited to playing a role in organizing a political movement. And those on the planet who'd been members of the Ballroom had been few in number. More importantly, because of their underground existence, they were unknown to all but a few of the ex-slave population, which gave them zero name recognition, and they had little political experience, in any event.

Given that material, how could representatives of Mesa's ex-slaves be catapulted overnight into important positions of the new government?

The answer was that they couldn't—not for now, at least. Ex-slaves—ex-slaves native to Mesa, at least—with the capacity to fill that role simply didn't exist yet. So, willy-nilly, the ex-slaves who constituted sixty percent of Mesa's population were "represented" at the table by people who had either made their names in the Ballroom off Mesa or held a high status among the ex-slaves for other reasons. Of those eight people, only two had ever lived on

Mesa—Lakshmi X and Saburo X—and neither of them had been born here. Like Saburo and Lakshmi, Jeremy X, Donald Toussaint, and Web Du Havel had been born into slavery, but off-planet. And three of the "representatives of ex-slaves" had never been slaves at all, and neither had any of their ancestors. Queen Berry of Torch, Thandi Palane from Ndebele, and Catherine Montaigne—who was here as a prominent figure in the antislavery League, not as a Manticoran politician—were also present and could be expected to speak for the ex-slaves, but they were scarcely Mesans.

To make things still more difficult, all of them, except for Thandi Palane, had arrived on Mesa only a short time before—Donald Toussaint and Lakshmi X had landed just the day before—and all but three would be leaving Mesa, some sooner than others.

Berry and Web Du Havel really ought to be leaving for the six-week return voyage to Congo as soon as possible, since they were the heart of the system's government. They wouldn't be, however. Not immediately, at least. Their insight and advice—especially Du Havel's—would be far too valuable on Mesa. And Berry Zilwicki, the Queen of Torch, the planet where the victims of genetic slavery had finally found a voice and a place of their own, was far too valuable as a sign of what slaves and ex-slaves could achieve. So, yes, they had to be leaving soon . . . and, no, they wouldn't be.

Catherine Montaigne, on the other hand, truly did need to leave soon, because the Mesa System wasn't the only one building a new government for itself. She was bound and determined to arrive on Terra before the formal start of the Constitutional Convention that would create a new government for the *Solarian League*. Assembling that Constitutional Convention was taking, literally, months, if only because of travel times, so she didn't actually have to race directly off to Old Chicago, but she was also determined to return to both Manticore and Beowulf on her way. Manticore, because as the leader of the Manticoran Liberal party she needed to consult with Prime Minister Grantville first. Whatever else, she would be seen as an official representative of Empress Elizabeth, so it would probably be a good idea to know the Grantville Government's latest views. And Beowulf, because she needed to consult with the Antislavery League's central committee, since the ASL was planning the largest convocation in its history.

Which would just happen to take place in Old Chicago.

Jeremy X and Thandi Palane would be staying on Mesa rather

longer even than Berry and Du Havel, although no one knew exactly how *much* longer just yet. They couldn't stay indefinitely, since they were the leaders of Torch's military. But given that Torch had just won its declared war with Mesa hands down—granted, it was the Grand Alliance that had actually done it—everyone agreed that it would be more important for them to help stabilize the situation on Mesa before returning. For the moment, Torch's military forces had nothing to do except train.

That left the last person sitting at the table, whose status was...complicated. Kevin Olonga was—had been, rather—a full citizen of Mesa, but he'd occupied no government position and had never been a prominent figure. Not for the population at large, at least. He was there because he was a member of the Mesan Alignment's central committee...and the only one who'd been willing to accept the offer to participate.

He'd gotten the invitation only because Admiral Gold Peak had insisted. "We *have* to have one of them at the table," she'd said. "That's the only way we'll be able to start untangling the mess of who is and who isn't part of the 'Alignment.'"

As Web Du Havel had put it many more times than once: "Nobody ever said slave rebellions didn't have lots of problems."

✧   ✧   ✧

The first hour went smoothly enough. But the tension mounted quickly when the issue of creating new police agencies for Mesa was brought up.

Actually, it mounted the *instant* that issue was brought up.

"*Are you out of your mind?*" Brianna Pearson demanded before Web Du Havel even finished with his proposal.

"You want to—" here she glared at Saburo—"put a *known terrorist* in charge of Mesa's police agencies? Absolutely not!"

"Excuse me, Ms. Pearson," Susan Hibson said, before Lecter could speak. "Are you under the impression you have a choice about this?"

The two women locked eyes. Hibson was much the smaller of them, but despite her current exalted rank, she carried herself with the hard-trained, muscular grace of a treecat. Her hair and complexion were darker than the fair-haired Mesan's...and her eyes were much, much harder.

Pearson started to reply, but General Drescher raised a hand before she could.

"Brianna, you're being foolish," she said. "General Hibson's right. You—we—*don't* have any choice in the matter."

Pearson's eyes swiveled to her in what might have been betrayal, but Drescher was looking at Lecter.

"We don't, do we, Captain?" It wasn't an actual question; it was a way to rub Pearson's nose in reality.

"No, you don't," Lecter said. "This is an issue Admiral Gold Peak discussed at length with the parties involved, and she's made a firm decision. The reasoning—"

"I think I understand the reasoning," Drescher interrupted. "What I really need to know, from *my* perspective, is if you intend to place Mesa's military under the Ballroom's command, too."

"No. You'll remain the MPP's commander—under General Hibson's orders—" Lecter twitched her head at Hibson "—just as you've been under the Military Administration. The MMA isn't going away tomorrow. Not until we *know* this new arrangement will be workable." She let her own eyes sweep the former full citizens at the table. "Bottom line, the Grand Alliance knows it's going to be here for a while, no matter what. And General Hibson's troops are the ultimate guarantee to all parties that no one will be allowed to victimize anyone else. But we need to move her as far into the background—in reality, not just appearances—as we can, and do it as quickly as we can without destabilizing the situation. And part of the way we're going to do that is to let everyone see your people and the new provisional government stepping into your responsibilities as *Mesans*. The only thing we might need less than the appearance that you're our puppets would be for us to think we could *make* you our puppets."

"Captain Lecter—and Admiral Gold Peak—are right about that, General." It was Jeremy, this time. "And an army is quite different from the police force we're talking about here. General Hibson will have to maintain oversight until everyone concerned is convinced this transition has worked, of course, but I'm sure she'll be keeping only a light hand on the reins. Provided, of course that the MPP remains strictly nonpartisan in political terms. For which purpose—"

He pointed, with a very thin smile, at another person sitting at the table.

"May I introduce you to Donald Toussaint? Until very recently, he was a colonel in Torch's military, but he's resigned his position in order to become a citizen of Mesa and serve as your People's Commissioner. If you're not familiar with the title, it—"

"I know what it means." Drescher studied Toussaint for a moment with a quirky half-smile. "Am I right in assuming that Commissioner Toussaint's previous surname had only one letter?" she asked, and Jeremy grinned.

"You're very astute—as, of course, one would expect of an army's top commanding officer."

"What about my personnel? Are you planning to dismiss them and replace them with... others, let's call them?"

"That would be extraordinarily stupid," Web Du Havel replied. "Demobilizing an army is a tricky proposition under any circumstances. Even if you do it only to return the troops to civilian life after *winning* a war, you've suddenly made lots of people unemployed where there may not be enough jobs to absorb them. If you do it in the middle of a period of political turmoil, or—especially—in a society that's just *lost* a war, you compound the problem by an order of magnitude. In that case, you have many thousands—perhaps millions—of angry and very possibly desperate people on your hands, all of whom are familiar with military-grade weapons. It's what we political scientists call Dereliction of Demobilization. After too many drinks at a faculty party, that slides into the Freikorps Fuck-Up."

The tension in Drescher's shoulders eased a bit.

"All right," she said. "What about new recruits?"

"Any citizen of Mesa is eligible to enlist in the MPP, assuming they are of age and meet the minimum physical and educational requirements," Du Havel replied. "*Regardless* of their previous status. We expect a number of former slaves and seccies to do so."

He didn't add *and we will damned well see to it that happens*, but Drescher was anything but dense.

"A lot of my current troops will find that hard to accept," she said, although her tone indicated that it was simply an observation, not a protest.

"Of course they will." Du Havel nodded. "Indeed, we expect a large number of the existing MPP's personnel to resign rather quickly. But that will be as a result of *their* choice, not something that was forced upon them by the new government. That makes a big difference."

"You're still talking about a lot of very unhappy people."

"We are," Susan Hibson agreed. Her tone was much warmer than the one she'd used with Pearson. "And it can't be helped. But your people who *don't* resign will just have to make sure they don't act on that unhappiness. Believe me, the last thing we want is for *my* people to have to do that. If they do..."

She shrugged, and Jeremy nodded.

"Yes, you will. And they're *already* very unhappy, General," he said. "As slaveowners usually are when slaves upset the order of things."

"Most of us weren't slaveowners!" Pearson protested, but Jeremy only shrugged.

"With a few exceptions, you all stood by and made no serious effort to abolish slavery—and reaped the side benefits, as full citizens of Mesa. That's not much of a difference, from my point of view. But I'm not trying to pick a fight here." He leaned forward with a small, dismissive gesture.

"Ms. Pearson," Du Havel said, "please accept our judgment on this matter. I've spent decades studying this problem—along with all the others involving the abolition of slavery. Not just genetic slavery, either. I've looked at the institution of slavery clear back past African slavery in the last three centuries Ante-Diaspora to the days of the ancient Roman Empire and even earlier. And I've devoted more than a little attention to how states and societies rebuild themselves—or don't—in the wake of crushing military defeats, as well. So believe me when I tell you that unless we keep stirring up animosity, most of the full citizens will try to make an accommodation with the new regime. Regardless of their political views, people have lives to get on with. All of the former full citizens are going to have to make adjustments. They won't be all that sympathetic to a soldier who quit of his own volition because he couldn't stand the idea of being in the same outfit as former slaves and seccies. For most former full citizens, the attitude will be along the lines of: *Get over it. Things are tough for everybody.*"

"Just drop it, Brianna," Drescher advised. "I think they're probably right. Besides, I've coped pretty well under General Hibson, I think. I'm pretty sure I'll be able to manage under the new dispensation, too." She eyed Donald Toussaint. "Depending."

"We'll get along famously, General," he said with a grin, and Pearson scowled.

"Fine. I'll drop that issue. But what about this nonsense of having him—" she jabbed her chin in Saburo's direction "—be the new head of all police agencies? Talk about creating a unified opposition!"

"You interrupted Web before he could finish," Saburo said. "He didn't say anything about my taking over *all* the police forces on Mesa. That was your assumption. It'd be impossible, for practical reasons, if nothing else. What Web was going to say was that we'd be dissolving the Office of Public Safety and replacing it with a new police agency specifically tasked with maintaining social order. That's what I'll be heading up."

"But—" She stared at him, then shifted her gaze to Du Havel. "But you just got through saying that disbanding an army was a bad idea."

"That applies to a *military* force." Du Havel shook his head. "First, the OPS was never truly a military force. At best, it was a *para*military force, with every single vice to which such forces are too often heir. But more importantly, neither it nor its major subdivision, the Mesan Internal Security Directorate, ever had any purpose for existence beyond grinding under the planet's slaves and seccies. How in the world do you think we could possibly *not* dissolve them? We don't want to demobilize the MPP precisely because we don't want to trigger off a rebellion among the ex-full citizens. What the hell do you think would happen if we kept OPS intact? There'd be an even bigger and more ferocious rebellion—on the part of the ex-slaves and seccies."

"You bet your sweet ass," Jacelyn Amsterdam hissed. "We've already put out the word that any Safety or Misty who comes into Watson goes out in a body bag. That's if there's enough left of them to bother bagging."

"Same for Creek City," Theodora Moreau said.

"*And* Franklin," Cáo Li-Qiang added, and Jason Dusek slapped the table with a meaty hand.

"And the same goes for every seccy district in Mendel. Forget it, Pearson. The OPS and MISD are in history's trash can. They're gone—and we're more than willing to upgrade that to '*dead* and gone,' if that's what they prefer."

"And here I always thought you were brighter than Regan Snyder, Brianna." Jackson Chicherin spoke up for the first time since the meeting had begun. "What the hell's gotten into you?

The dissolution of OPS was a given. I took that for granted from the outset. What I was worried about was the possibility of mass reprisals and 'war crime' trials against those so-called 'agents of the law' *after* they were dissolved."

"Oh, trust me, we'd *love* to try some of those bastards—and hang them," Susan Hibson said flatly. "And if were up to *me*, they'd be decorating a lot of light standards in downtown Mendel. Unfortunately, what they did was covered under what passed for laws where slaves and seccies were concerned." She showed her teeth. "So they get a pass...for *past* actions. You may have noticed what happened to the handful of them stupid enough to try anything after my people hit the streets, though."

"And one of the conditions of transitioning to the provisional government is a commitment to continue that policy," Lecter said with a firm nod. "So any would-be vigilantism will be strictly freelance...and punished by the *Mesan* police and courts."

"That's fair enough," Chicherin said. "Better than I expected, really."

Pearson glared at him, but he ignored her and looked at Saburo, instead.

"If I understand what you're saying correctly, you intend to leave the existing local police forces in place. And the same with the Office of Investigation."

"Yes—except that those police agencies will be part of a consolidated hierarchy, with my people looking over their shoulders. We'll be the central coordinator as far as policy and accountability are concerned, so they'll have to deal with that. As far as what they do—their function—is concerned, I'll make absolutely as few changes as possible. Stability is what we need here, after all. But that said, all of the existing forces will have to begin accepting applicants from outside the full citizenry. The *former* full citizenry, I should say. Not only will they have to accept ex-slave and seccy applicants, but I'll see to it that those applicants get prioritized."

Chicherin winced.

"I think...getting local police forces to accept..."

"I don't care about the street cops," Saburo said. "Not for now, anyway; that *will* change down the road, but we can ease into it. What I damned well *will* see now, though, is that the Office of Investigation gets leavened with ex-slaves and seccies. That's going to happen fast. *Very* fast. There's no way in hell I'm going to allow Mesa's planetary police to remain a preserve of former full citizens."

"Ah." Chicherin breathed a little sigh of relief and leaned back in his chair. "That's . . . okay."

Du Havel had watched Pearson throughout that exchange.

"You have to face reality, Ms. Pearson," he said now. "More than half of Mesa's people were slaves until a short while ago. The only thing that will settle them down and help avoid violence is the knowledge that the OPS has been dismantled and that the recognized top law enforcement agency on the planet now has a former Ballroom member in charge. That will go a long way to calm their fears."

"Not the fears of the full—*ex*-full—citizens!" Pearson snapped.

"Actually, I think you're wrong about that," Drescher said. "If the former full citizens also see that I'm still in command of the MPP and that OPS has been dissolved, what armed force could threaten them—even assuming General Hibson wasn't still here to step in? It's a hell of a lot better than seeing OPS under new management operating against *them*, don't you think? And don't forget that if they come under attack this time, they'll be the ones who enjoy all the advantages of defending themselves from within huge ceramacrete towers." She grimaced. "I can tell you from experience that that's one hell of a defensive position. So, who could really come after them? The Office of Investigation really is a police agency. It's not a military or paramilitary outfit."

Pearson looked around, then let out her breath and slumped a bit in her chair. After a few seconds, she nodded.

"Okay," she said. "I'll let it go."

"All right, then," Captain Lecter said. "Now that we've addressed that issue, I want to move on to reconstruction. Boss Dusek, why don't you kick off the discussion."

"Just a moment before you do, Jurgen," Saburo interrupted, raising one hand slightly. "I think I should make an announcement at this point."

"Yeah, sure," Dusek grunted. "What is it?"

"I'm dropping my surname of 'X.' As Donald—" he nodded toward Toussaint, sitting next to him "—has already done. It's been a Ballroom tradition—well, a very recent one—that the new surname chosen be that of some historical champion of slaves. Hence, in his case, Toussaint.

"But I've chosen to do otherwise." He smiled. There was no humor at all in the expression. "My name is henceforth and forever more, Saburo Lara."

❖   ❖   ❖

Jackson Chicherin made it a point to speak to Berry at the break. Like almost every other human being who'd encountered her, he found the young monarch of Torch to be a friendly and comforting sort of person.

They began with cordial, idle chitchat. Then Chicherin said: "I have to say I'm relieved that Saburo has decided to change his surname." He shrugged. "I do have to say I was a little surprised he chose that particular moment to make the announcement, but I think it'll be reassuring to quite a few of the ex-full citizens. It's a break with his Ballroom past...and 'Lara' sounds so much less harsh than 'X.'"

Berry's lips tightened.

"It is...and it isn't. And he didn't just happen to choose that particular moment to announce it. Lara is the name of the woman he loved. She died saving me from an assassination attempt launched by the Alignment. So, yes, you can take a little reassurance from Saburo's new last name. But I wouldn't take it too far, if I were you."

❖   ❖   ❖

Later in the break, Chicherin sidled up to Kevin Olonga.

"We have *got* to start calling ourselves something else," he said quietly.

"What?" Olonga frowned. "We've gone by the name of the Alignment for—"

"It's *over*, Kevin. And that name is an albatross around our neck."

"What's an albatross? Some kind of necklace?"

Forge One
Sanctuary Orbit
Refuge System

SONJA HEMPHILL PROPPED ONE SHOULDER AGAINST THE BULKHEAD and raised the coffee cup in both hands to inhale its rich, deep perfume. She'd never been much of a coffee drinker back on Manticore. She'd preferred tea, actually. But that had been before she met *Havenite* coffee. She didn't know what had happened to the coffee trees imported by Haven's original settlers, but whatever it was, it had imparted a deeper, richer, and more mellow taste to the coffee brewed from it, and she thought about the woman who had introduced her to it as she gazed out through the crystoplast of her office's deck-to-overhead viewport.

She'd expected to respect Admiral Shannon Foraker when they finally met. How could she not respect the woman who'd been her own counterpart for the Republic of Haven's navy? And who'd come up with so many pragmatic, sometimes crude, but almost always workable counters for the Manticoran weapons her less capable industrial base had been unable to duplicate?

What Hemphill hadn't expected was how much they were going to *like* one another. For all the differences between them, they were also very much alike, and each of them recognized in the other a kindred soul—a sister, under the skin.

The treecat sprawled comfortably on the deck beside her, sharing her view of the planet called Sanctuary, rolled over onto his back and stretched all six limbs in a prodigious yawn. Hunts Silently was her self-assigned bodyguard against the Mesan Alignment's assassination nanotech, not her bonded companion, but he'd also become the closest friend she'd ever had. Closer than she'd ever dreamed she *could* have, really. Yet he did have his occasionally . . . inelegant moments, she thought, glancing down at him with a smile. And there were times when it was even easier than usual to see why Stephanie Harrington had called his kind "tree*cats*" when she first encountered them all those centuries ago. In fact, he looked about as ridiculous as any Old Terran cat, just at the moment.

Hunts Silently gave one last, spine-arched stretch, then rolled up into a sitting position and his true-hands flicked signs at her.

<*There is nothing wrong in being comfortable,*> he told her. <*And two-foots are* much *sillier looking than the People.*>

She chuckled as his cupped true-hands swept emphatically apart in the sign for "much." Not that he didn't have a point. Sometimes, at least.

"The wisdom of treecats is not to be despised," she told him solemnly, and chuckled again, louder, when he nodded in undeniably complacent agreement.

She took one hand from her cup, reached down, and rubbed his tufted ears. He buzzed a purr and leaned his head against the side of her knee as she returned her gaze to the planet below them.

Sanctuary. Perhaps the most fitting name for a planet that she'd ever heard, and yet simultaneously how bitterly, bitterly ironic. It was nothing short of a miracle that the generation ship *Calvin's Hope* had managed somehow—no one would ever know how, because those records had vanished—to reach this cool K8 star, almost ten light-years from her original destination. And the planet her crew had found here, hidden from the rest of the galaxy by the heavy concentrations of dust that obscured the KCR-126-06 system, was a gorgeous emerald-and-sapphire gem. A bit on the chilly side, perhaps, especially for Hemphill's sensibilities. She'd grown up on the Star Kingdom's capital world, and Manticore was warmest of all the Star Kingdom's habitable planets, so even Sanctuary's high summer seemed cool to her. But eighty-three percent of its surface was water and it had very little axial tilt, which combined to produce extraordinarily mild seasonal variations. If it was cooler than Manticore, it was far warmer than Sphinx, and its climate could have been specifically designed as the antithesis of tempestuous Gryphon's.

Her mood turned more somber as she thought about what *Calvin's Hope*'s passengers must have felt, how they must have reacted when they found this beautiful, perfect jewel at the end of their impossible voyage. The joy with which they must have stripped their vessel, shuttled themselves and their children down to the surface, settled into the rich, mountain valley they'd christened Paradise Valley and built the settlement they called Home on the banks of the river they'd named Hope.

Only to discover that that beautiful, fertile valley was the mouth of Hell itself when the snowcapped mountain above Paradise Valley—the snowcapped *volcano* above Paradise Valley—erupted with a fury that dwarfed Old Terra's Krakatoa. Indeed, that eruption had approached that of Thera, the most devastating eruption and earthquake in the history of Old Terra's humanity. Dust and lava had annihilated Home, wiped out the colonists' imported technology, and driven the terrified survivors back to an almost hunter-gatherer level of existence. How they had clawed out a living, preserved any of the terrestrial food plants they'd brought with them, managed to not simply survive but fight their way back to a steam-age level of technology, in the thirteen centuries between that cataclysm and their discovery by the People's Republic of Haven was more than she could begin to imagine. But they had.

Somehow they had.

Of course, it helped that in most ways Sanctuary truly was the welcoming haven it appeared to be. As if in partial compensation for its high level of tectonic and volcanic activity, its mild climate and fertile soil offered effectively year-round growing seasons, and human physiology was immune to every disease native to its ecology. Its population had increased to almost two billion by the time they were discovered, and that number had climbed steadily—and sharply—in the forty T-years since. One thing the Legislaturalists of the People's Republic of Haven had done right—Hemphill couldn't think of a *second* thing, not right off hand—was to bring modern medicine, including prolong, to Sanctuary.

Well, they *had* educated the people of Sanctuary, as well. To a rather higher level than their own Dolists, in fact. But not out of the goodness of their heart.

One day, and not so very far in the future, this obscure star system about which most of the galaxy knew absolutely nothing would be wealthier and more heavily industrialized than ninety percent of the Solarian League's core worlds. It was the next best thing to inevitable for a planet whose system primary boasted no less than five massive asteroid belts...and which lay within fifteen light-hours of six *additional* asteroid belts. The Epsilon Belt, fifteen light-minutes beyond the Refuge hyper-limit, was especially resource rich, the broken bones of an entire shattered planet, torn apart when the A-class central component of the system captured Refuge and added it to its original pair of red dwarf companions.

The industrial possibilities of Refuge had not been lost upon the Legislaturalists, who'd turned Sanctuary into a top-secret shipbuilding complex code-named "Bolthole." That process had begun even before the outbreak of hostilities between the People's Republic and the Star Kingdom. In many ways, Hemphill supposed, Bolthole was the Havenite equivalent of Roger Winton's Project Gram. Which made it even more ironic that this was where Sonja Hemphill, who'd grown up in Project Gram, had ultimately found herself.

She gazed down at the planet, watching the terminator line creep steadily toward her as *Forge One* approached the dawn. Darkness lay heavily across the planetary surface directly below the geostationary industrial platform, but she saw the red glare of fiery clouds, lit from beneath as one of the volcanoes in the Avarshal Chain spilled lava into the Eastwind Sea. She wondered how much area this eruption would add to the islands. Not that anyone would be settling there anytime soon. The Avarshal Chain was the most active of Sanctuary's *several* volcanic chains. She wondered if—

A soft, musical chime interrupted her thoughts, and she turned from the viewport, crossed to her desk, and pressed the com button.

"Yes, Rafe?"

"Good morning, Milady." The voice belonged to Senior Chief Yeoman Rafael Biggs, who ran Hemphill's office with an iron hand. "Admiral Foraker is here."

"Oh, she is, is she?" Hemphill shook her head with another, broader smile.

"Yes, Milady. And Commander Gharsul is with her."

Hemphill's eyebrows rose slightly at that. One of the more endearing things about Shannon Foraker was her...obliviousness, probably wasn't the exact word, but it came close, to all of the protocol—what Hamish Alexander-Harrington was fond of referring to as "fuss and feathers"—which went with her towering seniority. Hemphill suspected that outside the bounds of the R&D and logistical management of her position, Foraker still thought of herself as the naval commander she'd been before Thomas Theisman overthrew the Committee of Public Safety. Nor did she understand how the fact that she genuinely didn't see why anyone might think she was in any way "special" produced such near idolatrous devotion from her staff.

And it was also why she so often forgot to go through "channels" when she needed to speak to Hemphill.

On the other hand, she didn't usually bring Gharsul with her unless she had something serious on her mind, and Hemphill's smile faded as she wondered what that "something serious" might be this time. They were scheduled for their regular joint morning brief in less than three hours—*Forge One* synchronized its clocks with the city of Mountain Fort, the Sanctuarian capital, almost directly below its equatorial orbit—so why hadn't Foraker waited? Admittedly, the Havenite was a night bird who apparently thrived on about a third of the sleep a normal human required, but this was early, even for her.

"Well," Hemphill said, "in that case, Senior Chief, please ask them to step into my lair."

"Of course, Milady."

Hemphill turned toward the hatch as it slid open and a slender admiral in the gray and green uniform of the Republic of Haven navy, as blond as Hemphill herself, stepped through it.

"Good morning, Admiral." In light of Gharsul's presence, Hemphill greeted her a bit more formally than had become their wont. She held her coffee in her left hand and extended her right. "I didn't expect to see you quite this bright and early."

"Oh, damn." Foraker grimaced as she shook the offered hand. "I forgot to tell you I was coming. Again."

"You *are* the commanding officer of Bolthole," Hemphill pointed out with a gentle smile. "As such, I think you can pretty much come and go on your own schedule. At least you haven't woken me up in the middle of the night to discuss our latest project."

"You mean I haven't woken you up in the middle of the night *yet*," Foraker said with a crooked smile. "You might want to ask Five about the last time I did it to him."

"I'm sure you had a very good reason," Hemphill said soothingly, and Foraker chuckled.

"Good morning, Gharsul," Hemphill continued, smiling at Gharsul.

"Admiral."

Like all Sanctuarians, the commander used a single name. Their culture used a combined patronymic and matronymic "surname," but only for legal purposes and on *extremely* formal occasions. He had the striking combination of dark skin, dark hair, and very light eyes characteristic of the natives of Sanctuary. They were green, in his case, rather than the more common azure or cornflower blue, and he was quite tall.

Like every Sanctuarian young enough to receive it, he'd been given third-generation prolong, but in his case, he was almost as young as he looked. There was a reason for that.

Neither the Legislaturalists nor the Committee of Public Safety had considered Sanctuarians citizens of the People's Republic. Refuge might be their star system, but the People's Republic had regarded it as an imperial possession and its inhabitants as subjects, not citizens. They'd been better off than quite a few of the planets the Solarian Office of Frontier Security "administered," but that hadn't been saying all that much. And because they weren't citizens, they'd been ineligible for service in the Peoples Navy . . . despite how many of them worked aboard the industrial platforms committed to *building* the Peoples Navy.

They still weren't citizens of the Republic, although Hemphill felt confident that would be changing in the not-so-distant future. But from the moment of Eloise Pritchart's first visit to Refuge, even before Thomas Theisman had finished off the last of the State Security warlords, Sanctuary had been an *ally* of the restored Republic of Haven. It was no longer an imperial possession, and as allies, its citizens *were* eligible for service in the Republic of Haven Navy. Indeed, it had been Pritchart and Theisman's policy to integrate as many Sanctuarians as possible into the RHN to make that new relationship crystal clear to all concerned.

Gharsul's relatively senior rank, barely seven T-years later, might have led some to conclude that he owed his rapid promotion to "affirmative action." They would have been wrong. Even if Theisman or Pritchart had been prepared to cut corners (which they weren't), Shannon Foraker would never have selected Gharsul as her senior intelligence analyst if he hadn't thoroughly demonstrated his fitness for the position.

"Can I interest either of you in a cup of coffee?" Hemphill continued, raising her own cup slightly.

"You certainly can," Foraker replied, then snorted. "In fact—"

"I've got this," Hemphill said dryly, and pressed the com key again.

"Yes, Milady?"

"Unless I miss my guess, Senior Chief," Hemphill said, never taking her amused gaze from Foraker, "the Admiral forgot breakfast again."

"Croissants, cheese plate, fresh fruit, and coffee already inbound, Milady," Senior Chief Biggs replied.

"Thank you." Hemphill released the button and pointed at the comfortable chairs at the small conference table in the corner of her office. "That looks like a good place to perch," she said.

"Am I really *that* predictable?" Foraker asked a bit plaintively as the three of them crossed to the table.

"Only in certain aspects of your life, Shannon," Hemphill reassured her, and Hunts Silently bleeked a laugh as he sprang lightly into one of the chairs. "And to be honest, I had a bit of a hint that you'd probably forgotten unimportant little things like food. You've got that 'Oooh, shiny!' look again."

Gharsul raised one hand to hide his smile, and even Foraker's lips twitched. But then she shook her head as she settled into a chair of her own.

"Takes one to know one," she said, and Hemphill raised one hand to acknowledge the hit.

They really were *much* too much alike, she thought.

The office door opened again, and Senior Chief Biggs walked in with a wheeled cart laden with food, plates, and flatware. He pushed it over to the conference table, parked it, and poured coffee into a cup. The cup bore *Forge One*'s platform number on one side and Foraker's name on the other, and Hemphill hid a smile as he extended it to the admiral. Biggs kept that cup in his desk drawer for occasions just like this one. He'd come to know Foraker as well as Hemphill had, and like her Havenite subordinates, he regarded her with the affectionate respect any sorceress deserved.

"Thank you, Rafe," Foraker said, and he bobbed his head.

"My pleasure, Admiral."

He offered the pot to Gharsul, but the Sanctuarian shook his head.

"*I've* already eaten, Senior Chief," he said with a slight smile.

Something suspiciously like a chuckle came from Foraker's direction, and Biggs glanced at Hemphill, eyebrows arched, but she shook her head.

"I'm good," she said. "Thank you."

"Of course, Milady."

He braced briefly to attention, then withdrew, and Foraker reached for a plate and one of the piping hot croissants.

"So," Hemphill said as the Havenite added smoked salmon, several slices of cheddar, and a small bunch of grapes to her plate, "to what do I owe the pleasure?"

"Just something I wanted to kick around with you before the morning brief," Foraker replied. "Take a look. See what you can make of this?"

She pulled a chip from her pocket and slotted it into her chair arm's data port, and the office's smartwall came alive. It displayed a star map, flanked by two quite different displays, and Hemphill pursed her lips as she regarded them.

The star map was straightforward enough, although she had no clue why four star systems had been highlighted. Congo and the Manticore Binary System glowed green, but the Sol and Yildun systems were a bright, bloody red.

She filed that away and turned to the next display. It showed a comparison of two different—very slightly different—versions of the same missile. Hemphill recognized the Solarian League Navy Cataphract, its answer (of sorts) to the Grand Alliance's multidrive missiles, but she wouldn't have noticed the differences if they hadn't been visually highlighted for her. Even with that assistance, it took her the better part of three minutes to identify the variations between the two, because they were almost identical.

Once she was confident she had the differences nailed down, her eyes moved to the third display. It was a complex chronological graph—that much was obvious—but the numbers meant nothing to her off the top of her head.

"All right, I see them," she said. "I can't say they mean all that much to me right at the moment. Some context?"

Foraker grimaced around a mouthful of croissant. She took a quick sip of coffee and used the cup to indicate Gharsul.

"There's a fascinating discrepancy here—one Gharsul spotted," she said.

"Really?" Hemphill sat back with her own coffee. "Explain it to me, Commander."

"Of course, Milady."

Sanctuarians were much more comfortable with the notion of hereditary aristocracy than most Havenites, and the formal address came more readily to him than it did to some of Foraker's other subordinates. Not that it mattered one way or the other to Hemphill. If she really needed to waste time worrying about inconsequentials, she could think of at least a dozen that were more pressing.

"First, there are the missiles," Gharsul continued, using a light wand to indicate the diagram. "The one on the left is an example of the Cataphracts provided to the People's Navy in Exile for the attack on Torch. The one on the right was captured from the SLN after Admiral Filareta's attack on the Manticore System. As you can see, they're almost—not quite, but almost—identical."

"I don't suppose that's too surprising," Hemphill said. "In fact, I'm not sure I'd call it a 'discrepancy' at all. It's fairly obvious they were still refining the design when Mesa decided to hit Torch. For that matter, they were still refining it right up to the end of the war! So it's not too odd Filareta had a later mark eight months after 'Operation Ferret.'"

"I'd tend to agree, if that were the case, Milady," Gharsul said. "But the discrepancy is that the *PNE's* Cataphract is actually a later mod than the one Filareta took to Manticore."

"Excuse me?" Hemphill sat upright, and Gharsul nodded.

"As I said, the difference is very slight, but we've compared both of these to the most recent Cataphract marks, and there's not much question where they fall in the development sequence. Of course, Filareta was in transit for over two months, so the window between the PNE's departure for Congo and his departure for Manticore is a little tighter than the actual attack dates indicate. But both sets of missiles had to come from somewhere, and it's their *origin* that really has us puzzled, Milady."

The wand highlighted one of the dates on the chronological display.

"These are the dates we've been able to reconstruct for both the PNE's move on Congo and Filareta's deployment from Tasmania for the attack on Manticore. And as we looked at them, we realized something odd.

"Technodyne's never had a manufacturing facility in Mesa, so the Cataphracts used in the Congo attack had to have been produced somewhere else and then mated up with the PNE. But according to the captured data Duchess Harrington brought back from Operation Nemesis, all Cataphract production for the League Navy was at Yildun or Technodyne's facilities in Sol. That didn't bother us especially until we realized that the PNE's missiles were actually the *later* version. There's no way they could have reached the PNE from Yildun or Sol before the Congo attack. The timing simply doesn't allow for it."

Hemphill sat upright, her eyes sweeping the dates, then moving back to the star chart, while the admiral in her estimated transit times.

"I see your point," she said then, slowly. "But if they didn't come from Sol and they didn't come from Yildun, where *did* they come from?"

"We don't have a clue," Foraker said. "That's what inspired *this* 'oooh, shiny' moment."

"It certainly looks like Technodyne must have a third production facility we've never known about," Hemphill mused.

"Technodyne or... somebody," Foraker said. Hemphill looked at her, and she grimaced. "The ships that carried out the Yawata Strike and the graser platforms that plowed the road for the Beowulf attack had to come from somewhere, Sonja. According to all the data Duchess Harrington captured at Ganymede, that 'somewhere' doesn't belong to Technodyne, and it's not located anywhere in Solarian territory. So the Alignment must have its own Bolthole tucked away in a back pocket. And the fact that the PNE had the upgraded Cataphract when it hit Congo may just give us a maximum volume in which that 'somewhere' has to fall."

"This has to get to Manticore and Nouveau Paris as quickly as possible," Hemphill said.

"I agree." Foraker nodded. "I just wanted to bounce the notion off you before I sent the courier boats. I'd like you to read through Gharsul's report, see if there's anything you think needs to be modified, before they depart."

"Of course." It was Hemphill's turn to nod. "And I think we probably need to get this to Admiral Gold Peak and Captain Zilwicki in Mesa at the same time."

L'Ouverture Station
Torch Planetary Orbit
Congo System

RUTH WINTON SAT BACK AND SCRUBBED HER FACE WITH BOTH hands, then stretched hugely. She'd been sitting at her console aboard *L'Ouverture Station*, the Congo System primary orbital station, for hours now, and her back was beginning to ache a little. Her butt ached a little more than that—although she allowed that the butt-ache was probably psychosomatic. The chair was designed for her backside, and was actually quite comfortable.

The real problem was that her whole life was a pain in the ass.

She lowered her hands and punched for the next screen of data.

"God forbid Princess Ruth Winton should have so much as one hair on her head put in harm's way," she muttered. "Evildoers abound everywhere, and the dynasty has to pile care upon vigilance lest I suffer the least misfortune from reckless—or not-so-reckless—adventures."

She gazed at the data before her. No one could physically read through the mountains of captured data she was currently analyzing, but neither could she depend on even her algorithms to recognize the significance of every correlation they turned up. They were very good at spotting correlations within the parameters she'd provided, but defining the parameters was a major part of the problem. It was, in fact, one of the reasons her tendency to "think outside the box" made her so good at her avocation. For her, the entire universe was one huge data set, and—usually—she took an almost sensual pleasure from running her mental fingers through all that marvelous data. And, she acknowledged, she loved figuring out secrets. Which probably said interesting things about her basic personality.

"Don't see what all the fuss is about, though," she muttered as she glared at the output before her. She rather doubted that a close analysis of hydroponics consumption in a *Mars*-class heavy cruiser's environmental plant was going to provide any mind-boggling revelations. "I'm—what, only fourth in line for the throne. Oh, wait—no! I'm not in the line of succession at all, because my biological daddy was a Masadan maniac. But does anyone listen when I point that out? No, of course they don't!"

She scowled at the thoroughly useless analysis before her. Despite her fascination with ferreting secrets out of huge piles of data, she'd gotten to the point where she almost—not quite, but almost—wished Admiral Rozsak had just obliterated the PNE fleet when it attacked Congo. If he'd just blown them out of space, the Torch Navy wouldn't have been able to salvage so many of their records.

Nothing here. Move on, she thought, and pulled up the next screen of no-doubt fascinating data.

"Bored, bored, bored. How many letters can be prefixed to that? Let's see... Cored. Doored—no, that's pushing it. Ford. Gored. Horde—hoard'll work, too. Lord."

A fresh analysis popped up before her, and she swallowed a groan. Logistic reports on ammunition were less boring than reports on environmental plants. She couldn't think of anything else they might be less boring than, however.

"Can I get away with 'moored'? No, that'd be cheating. Oared's okay, though. So's poured and roared. Sword... soared, too. Toward? No... don't think so. Ward—maybe word. I think that's—"

She broke off, frowning at a single line of the data.

"What the hell? Now, why was there that much discrepancy...?"

She tapped in an additional query, confirming the raw data, and her frown deepened. The PNE's possession of the Technodyne-designed Cataphract had cost Admiral Luis Rozsak's defending task force dearly, but she hadn't realized that the advanced missiles had been delivered to Citizen Commander Luff quite as late in the game as they had been. Or, rather, she'd known when the *Cataphracts* had been delivered. What she hadn't noted—and what the computers had just flagged for her—was how much earlier all of Luff's *other* ordnance had been delivered. In fact, that big a discrepancy suggested...

She leaned back, cudgeling her brain, her ennui vanished as she hunted down the memory she wanted. Where had she stored—?

Aha! She chuckled in triumph and entered the search string that brought up the astrogation data captured along with everything else in the PNE database. Luff's people had been meticulous about where they'd gone, but deplorably sloppy about recording *why* they'd gone some of the places they'd been while awaiting their orders for "Operation Ferret." One would almost think they hadn't been interested in helping someone like, oh, Ruth Winton, figure out what they'd been up to. Antisocial of them, perhaps, but then again, they *had* been unregenerate StateSec holdouts working for Mesa and Manpower and bent upon planetary genocide.

She snorted at the thought, but then her eyes narrowed as she found what she'd been looking for.

"I will be damned," she murmured to herself. "Why would they have gotten their Cataphracts there? I mean, there's nothing *there*. I think, anyway."

She opened another window, brought up *L'Ouverture's* astrographic charts, and entered the coordinates from the PNE database, then grinned as the chart blinked confirmation at her.

"Nope," she muttered in the far more cheerful tone of a Ruth with a puzzle to solve. "This makes no sense at *all*. Oh, goody!"

"Are you talking to yourself again, Ruth?" a voice asked from behind her. "Better be careful, or people will start thinking you're screwy."

"Not a problem." She never took her eyes from the display. "When you're Princess Ruth, and your family's as stinking rich as mine is, the term is 'eccentric.' Not 'screwy.' Besides, I'm the best conversationalist I can find."

She gazed at the star chart a moment longer, tapping the tip of her nose with an index finger to help herself think, then turned her head as the person who'd spoken came forward to stand beside her. Even sitting, Ruth's head was no lower than the young woman's shoulder. Cynthia X was so short that, combined with her squat torso, she put Ruth in mind of a mini-Anton Zilwicki, female edition. *Antonia* Zilwicki, maybe?

A lot of the former Ballroom members had changed their surnames by now, but Cynthia hadn't, and probably never would. Her experiences at Manpower's hands had been worse than those of most genetic slaves—which was a very low bar to begin with.

After her escape, she'd become one of the Ballroom's most proficient strikers, as they called themselves. (Manpower—the entire establishment of Mesa—had preferred terms like "murderers" and "terrorists.")

She'd never said it in so many words, but Ruth had grown to know her well enough by now to realize that Cynthia was almost sorry Manpower had finally been driven under. She wouldn't be able to kill any more of the scorpions. There were plenty who'd survived the recent unpleasantness, but Jeremy X had placed a ban on revenge killings.

It wasn't often that anyone applied labels like "spoilsport" to the galaxy's most deadly assassin.

But however lethal Cynthia might be, and however disappointed the young woman might be at having to turn in her hunting license, she was also very smart and had a natural aptitude for intelligence analysis. That was why she'd become something in the way of Ruth's understudy over the last few months.

"I want you to look at something." Ruth rose and gestured for Cynthia to take her chair. "Start with—" She leaned over and brought up the logistics analysis which had initially piqued her interest. "This here."

"What am I looking for?" Cynthia looked over her shoulder at Ruth, then chuckled at the look the princess gave her. "Okay, okay! I'll *find* it," she said, and started through the data. Then she frowned.

"I feel like I'm cheating. If you hadn't been looking at star charts, it would've taken me a lot longer to find. But—" her eyes narrowed—"'no sense at all' is putting it mildly. NZ-127-06? There's no habitable planet in that system. Nothing even close."

"No." Ruth shook her head. "Can't be. It's an M4V, both its planets are small and so close they're tide-locked to the primary, and according to the astro database, it produces even more solar flares than most red dwarfs. So why—"

"—did the PNE get its Cataphracts in *that* system?" Cynthia finished.

"Exactly." Ruth nodded. "I mean, part of the answer's obvious. They had to rendezvous with whoever delivered the missiles to them, and NZ-127-06 made a handy navigation beacon. One with no inhabited planets to notice who might be dropping off or picking up cargo. But what's really interesting to me is that—"

"—it's nowhere near Mesa, Sol, or Yildun," Cynthia said, and Ruth gave her another nod.

"Exactly," she repeated. "We'd all assumed they had to come from Sol or Yildun, although they could have been transshipped through Mesa. But way out there?" She shook her head. "There are a bunch of equally useless stars that would have been more conveniently placed for a shipment coming from any of those three star systems."

Cynthia swiveled the chair to face Ruth directly.

"Captain Zilwicki needs this information," she said.

"So do Manticore and Nouveau Paris," Ruth agreed. "But you're right that Anton and Victor need to be brought up to speed as quickly as possible. So I'm thinking maybe I should—"

"Forget it, Princess. If you want to get onto that courier boat, you'd have to shoot your way aboard—and I didn't sign up for that."

Ruth glared at her. Then, at the display. Then, at the universe. As much of it as she could see, anyway.

Which wasn't much, trapped aboard an orbital habitat.

April 1923 Post Diaspora

"I'm going to have to sit down after all.
Victor Cachat thinking is the stuff of nightmares."

—Yana Tretiakovna

City of Leonard
Darius Gamma
Darius System

"LUCKY YOU." GAIL WEISS LEANED OVER ZACHARIAH MCBRYDE'S shoulder and planted a kiss on his left ear. "Wish I got to work at home."

"That," Zach replied with a grin, never looking away from the display in front of him, "is because *you* are a lowly peon, toiling in the tactical fields, while *I* am a lofty superintendent of strategic imperatives."

Gail smacked the top of his head.

"That's just a fancy way of saying I know what I'm doing and you're whistling in the dark," she informed him.

"Well...That's putting it a little strongly. The 'whistling in the dark' part, I mean." He frowned as he studied one of the items on his display. "Right now, I think 'whistling past the graveyard' might be more appropriate."

"That bad, huh?" She straightened up, and for a moment the hand which had delivered the head slap gently caressed his shoulder. She was tempted to ask him what was causing him problems, but the temptation fled as soon as it arrived.

Partly that was because Gail had only a very general feel for Zach's occupation, which was quite unlike her own. She was a specialist, whose line of work was tightly focused. Zach was just the opposite: a generalist who spent his time organizing others to develop projects, the specific nature of which he himself often understood only partially. He seemed to be a combination of supervisor, counselor, gofer, and ombudsman.

Think of me as the Spanish Inquisition and you won't be far off, he often said. Given that he was obviously well-liked by those of his coworkers Gail had met, she took it as a joke. Mostly.

159

But the main reason she didn't inquire was because she'd realized, in the six T-months since they'd arrived on Darius Gamma, that the Alignment's surveillance of its citizens was not only extensive, but intrusive. She was quite sure they had no privacy even in their own apartment.

The personal aspects of that surveillance didn't particularly concern her. She was far from a prude, and, in any event, whatever AI program monitored them would be quite indifferent to their sex life. The real problem was that the Alignment took what it called "Security" very seriously, and its definition of the term was...expansive. The end result was a regime that, while not a police state in the usual sense, she was certain would be quick to intervene if it felt its citizens—who were also its employees—had wandered too far from their assignments and proper interactions with other citizens/employees.

So instead of asking him what he meant, she simply headed for the door.

"I may be home later than usual," she said over her shoulder. "There's a rumor going around that I'm being given a new assignment. You know how that usually goes."

"Yeah," Zach grunted, still not looking away from the display. "I sure do. Welcome to your new glorious undertaking. First, we have to figure out what it is. That may take a while, but as soon as we do..."

She smiled as she stepped out the door into the corridor beyond. The corridor was wide enough to allow for a slidewalk down its center, but Gail stayed close to the wall. Slidewalks were always tempting, but she preferred to maintain a brisk stride as a way to keep fit. Many, many things had changed since human beings left Old Earth, but one thing remained fixed and certain: exercise was good for you.

✧   ✧   ✧

Zach tried to concentrate on his work after Gail left, but he found himself too restless. He rose and went to the huge window—one entire wall of their apartment, really, programmable for anything from transparency to complete opacity—and looked out over the Darius System's capital city.

It was a beautiful city, although it looked very little like any other city he'd ever seen.

He'd once visited Old Chicago, the capital of the Solarian

League, which was universally considered one of the most majestic cities in human-settled space. He found no reason to dispute the opinion.

To begin with, it was enormous in every respect—down, as well as up. Chicago's labyrinthine subterranean regions were often called the Fifth Wonder of the League, and only partly in jest. Zach had spent the better part of two days in those depths. He'd been completely lost within ten minutes, and he'd remained so for the entire length of his stay. The supposedly state-of-the-art navigation app he'd been given for his uni-link had proved just as useless as he'd been warned it would. Fortunately, the man who'd warned him had also served as his personal guide, so the visit had gone smoothly enough, even if he had never known precisely where he was.

The city spread horizontally, as well as vertically. The boundaries of the vast urban stretches west and south of the city couldn't be seen, even from Chicago's tallest edifice, the Aspire. But Zach hadn't spent much time gazing at that landscape. He'd been far more impressed by the man-made archipelago that reached out over Lake Michigan. Kilometer after kilometer of structures: towers, residential and commercial; parks; marinas—everywhere. The enormous towers' foundations were fixed in the lake's bedrock, but square kilometers of the spaces between them were filled with more modest structures, many of them floating on the water, instead. Only a civilization with counter-grav architecture could have built and sustained such a place.

Still, that urban beauty had really been *beauties*—the things in the city, more than the city itself. Chicago was ancient, and like all such human-created places, it was also a mishmash. A gorgeous and superbly designed upscale residential tower might find itself sandwiched between two shorter, squatter towers that could most charitably be described as "functional." And the farther one got from the lake, the . . . lower-scale stretches of the city became as more and more people were shoehorned into increasingly "affordable" housing.

Not so, Leonard. Leonard was a unitary whole, planned and designed from the very beginning as a single work of art. Its layout was totally unlike the Solarian League's capital, because Old Chicago had risen from the grid pattern of pre-space, pre-counter-grav, Ante Diaspora history. Leonard was untrammeled by that ancient legacy. More than anything else, it made Zach think of a gigantic snowflake.

Mesa's capital city, Mendel, where Zach and his family had spent most of their lives, had begun with a similar design—albeit on a less ambitious scale. But the centuries had battered Mendel's original geometric precision. Battered it badly as slaves became the majority of Mesa's population, and then battered it still worse once a large number of manumitted slaves became second-class citizens. Throughout human history, anywhere and at any time that such rigid inequalities had arisen, they were inevitably accompanied by slums and tenements. They might be cleaner and less dilapidated slums and tenements on a planet like Mesa than they would be in the Verge or Fringe. But they'd still be slums and tenements. Any comparison with what they *might* have been only underscored that reality.

But Leonard was . . . perfect. And the longer Zach spent here, the more oppressive he found that perfection. No, worse than oppressive. Leonard—the whole of Darius, had begun to frighten him.

Badly.

The fact that the entire system population was comprised of proud and open Alignment members—nearly four billion of them—should have been exhilarating. And, in some ways, it had been. There'd been no need any longer to maintain the secrecy he and his brother Jack had lived with for so many years, hiding their true affiliation even from their own family. Every one of the McBrydes had thought of themselves as loyal members of the Alignment. But what only Zach and Jack had understood was that the "Alignment" their parents and sisters belonged to was a shell, a façade hiding the *real* Alignment from sight.

He'd never known Darius actually existed . . . not until Operation Houdini pulled him and Gail off of Mesa. He'd known something *like* it had to exist, if only because his position on Mesa had required him to deal with and assimilate R&D which was obviously being conducted . . . somewhere else. But if there'd ever been something legitimately covered by the Alignment's iron "need to know" protocols, Darius's location, its organization, even its true function had to be it.

Now he'd learned a great deal about it—rather more than Gail, in fact. Most importantly, perhaps, he'd *also* learned of the existence of the star system called Galton, as well. He'd had to because of what he did for the Alignment.

The vast bulk of the Alignment's research and development, what Zach thought of as the "heavy lifting," was done not in Darius, but in Galton. Yet the very best of the researchers and engineers Houdini had snatched from Mesa had come to Darius, just as Zach had. At least twelve of the scientists he'd worked with back on Mesa, however, were in the Galton contingent, and Zach was certain that just as he'd known nothing about Darius—or Galton—before Houdini, none of them had learned a thing about Darius, even now.

Zach McBryde's function, what he was best at, was his ability to...enable research teams. He wasn't a researcher himself, and he was far too much of a generalist to grasp the true intricacies of any of the cutting-edge specializations which drove the scientific—and technological—frontiers ever outward. But what he did have, partly as a result of the McBryde genome's improvements, were a phenomenal memory; an ability to... mentally encapsulate the conceptual hearts of theories and hypotheses and evidence, to put "handles" on them; and an intuitive ability to recognize where those "handles" intersected. He couldn't really describe how it worked, even to himself, but that combination of abilities made him incredibly valuable, because specialists didn't speak one another's languages. They needed an interpreter—no, they needed a *matchmaker*, and that was Zach McBryde.

He was still doing that interpreting and making those matches, but the process had changed. Everything that any of "his" teams—the ones he was assigned to coordinate—produced came to him. Some of it came from people working right here in Darius, and that part of his daily routine was comfortingly the same. But even more came to him from Galton. From people with whom he no longer had—or had never had, in most cases—personal contact. That lack of contact, that inability to sit down with a cup of coffee and bounce ideas back and forth, made his job far harder, and he felt less effective. He also suspected that the memos he produced on the basis of the Galton datastream were thoroughly sanitized before his suggestions and observations went back to Galton. Because none of those people in Galton knew about Darius.

It was an incredibly inefficient way to use his talents, which were most valuable because they *increased* efficiency, but he'd come to understand why that was how things were done. Everything produced in Galton came to Darius, where it was evaluated and integrated into a database and research programs which both paralleled those of Galton and also headed in completely different directions. As just one example, the streak drive had been developed in Galton, but the spider drive—which he'd had no idea even existed before Houdini, although he suspected *Gail* had, given her own stratospheric area of expertise—had been developed in Darius and never shared with Galton. That was because only a tiny amount of traffic went to Galton from Darius. And much of what originated here and did go to Galton went only because Zach had tagged it as useful for one of the Galton programs he oversaw.

No one had told him why that was, and he didn't expect them to. But the problem with not explaining things to smart people was that they tended to keep mentally picking at the non-explanations.

And sometimes, they figured it out for themselves.

He still wondered how the traffic from Darius was inserted into the Galton effort once it got there. Given everything else he'd observed, it had to be done in a way which erased any hint that it had originated outside Galton, though. He knew it did, because he'd figured out at least one thing no one had told him.

Galton was expendable.

Zach didn't for a moment think anyone in Darius *wanted* Galton to be destroyed. His own knowledge of the system was extraordinarily limited, outside the programs he was dialed into, but it was obvious from some of the "sideband" information in the reports he saw that Galton's industrial base—and possibly its population base, as well, though he was less confident of that— were both far bigger than anything in Darius. Something that valuable *had* to be preserved.

Yet, ultimately, one of Galton's most vital functions—indeed, perhaps its *single* most vital function—was to die in Darius's stead if worse came to worst. It had to be that way, because Darius was the basket in which the Alignment had hidden away its most precious eggs. The best of its scientific thinkers. The true records of its genetic lines. And, especially, the highest echelon of its leadership. If Galton was the heart of the Alignment's presence off Mesa, Darius was its *brain*, but Galton didn't even know the brain existed. And so the Alignment could have its very heart cut out, yet survive.

And even without Galton, Darius's industrial base and research programs were more than sufficient to eventually regenerate everything Galton brought to the Alignment.

Zach McBryde had always known the Alignment thought in concentric terms, like the ancient Russian *matryoshka* dolls his mother had collected. Secret hidden within secret. Defense nested within defense. Yet the thought of a leadership that could conceive of an entire star system as an ultimately expendable deception chilled something deep inside him.

On the one hand, it made perfect sense. There was no conceivable way the Alignment would deliberately lead an enemy to Galton. It was far too valuable for that, if nothing else. Galton could only be threatened—far less "expended"—if the enemy had already discovered its existence and its whereabouts despite everything the Alignment could do to hide it. So building yet another fallback position behind Galton, and ensuring that there was no trail of breadcrumbs past Galton to Darius, was completely logical. No more than reasonable. Might even be called simple prudence.

But on the other hand...

Fanaticism, he thought. That was what chilled his heart. The fact that the movement to which he'd given his entire adult life was *fanatical* enough to think in those terms under *any* circumstances. To cold-bloodedly plan how best to use the deaths of millions—even billions—as an *acceptable* price if it preserved its core leadership and its purpose.

Because if it could think in those terms about an entire star system, then no matter how benevolent it might appear, no matter how comfortable it might make its adherents' lives here on Darius, it was equally well prepared to sacrifice any individual. Any *group* of individuals. If that suspicion, that awareness, had occurred to him once he came face-to-face with the realities of Houdini, what he'd learned about Galton since had absolutely confirmed it.

He wished it hadn't. That he'd never been allowed that peek behind the mask, that glimpse into the innermost chamber where decisions like that were made. But he had, and that meant Darius could never be the refuge he'd expected it to be in those long-ago, pre-Houdini days.

He'd wanted it to. He *still* wanted it to. He wanted to shake free of the secrecy which had been so much of his life for so long. Knowing that anyone he met was part of the cause to which he'd devoted his life since he was sixteen years old should have been a heady elixir. But that elixir had been bitter on his tongue, and not just because he'd learned about Galton. Indeed, once upon a time the realization of how the Alignment saw Galton, the recognition of its ability to think in such...heart-chillingly cold-blooded terms, wouldn't have bothered him. Oh, he would have regretted it, but it wouldn't have filled him with fear. No, *that* had required something else—something more. A sharpened mental vision. A heart that had learned to question all he'd ever believed about the Alignment.

As he gazed out over that magnificent cityscape, he tried to decide exactly where that quiet, persistent, mercilessly questioning voice had first been born.

Probably with Jack's death, he thought. He'd vehemently denied the possibility that Jack—*Jack!*—could have been a traitor. He'd known his brother too well to believe that for an instant. The very idea was ludicrous! But he wondered, now, if the reason he'd been so vehement, so absolutely certain, had been to convince *himself* of that even more than his superiors. Because he *had* known Jack, known his unshakable integrity. And if Jack could have turned "traitor"—if *Jack* could have blown up the Gamma Center, been part of the Green Pines Incident, killed so many of the men and women with whom he'd shared his devotion to their cause—then what had his brother discovered about the Alignment that Zach hadn't?

But his faith had weathered Jack's death, wounded yet still strong. After thirty plus years of commitment, of that burning sense of mission, it would have been astonishing if it hadn't. But then had come "Operation Houdini" and his forced extraction from Mesa. He'd been highly enough placed in the Alignment's hierarchy to know Houdini existed, just as he'd known something like Darius—or Galton—must exist. But they'd been only a remote fallback contingency he'd never expected to be used, and he'd never once considered what the Alignment's leaders might do to conceal Houdini's true purpose from its enemies. The possibility of such slaughter, so many deaths, had never even occurred to him. Not really. They should have, perhaps, yet they never had. Then again, he'd been an office nerd, what Jack had teasingly called a "tech weenie," and never a field agent. If he hadn't, if he'd had a little of Jack's experience, perhaps he would have known better, would have realized how murderous a beast something like Houdini must be... and the horrors he'd experienced after his abrupt removal from the only life he'd ever known would have been less shocking.

And maybe they wouldn't have, he told himself with ruthless honesty. He'd always known about many of those horrors, after all. Only intellectually, perhaps, but he'd known. Yet the knowledge had been abstract, accepted as unfortunate—even terrible—but unavoidable. Much as a civilian who'd never seen a battlefield might contemplate with equanimity the "collateral damage" that must inevitably accompany great causes and struggles.

Collateral damage.

That protective euphemism had been shattered for Zach aboard the slave ship *Prince Sundjata*, part of the Houdini pipeline that had eventually brought him and Gail to Darius Gamma. And what had shattered it—and Zachariah McBryde—was the question he'd asked his shipboard guide as he was escorted through an interlocking series of cargo bays. They were smaller than those of most freighters, yet they were fitted with enormous hatches that seemed oddly disproportionate to the holds they served.

So he'd asked about them.

And the crewman had told him.

"These? Well, sometimes we use the bays just as cargo holds. For dead cargo, I mean. But when we've got live cargo—" Zach had already learned that was the euphemism for slaves "—these are our safety valves in case we find ourselves being tracked by a Manty or Havenite warship."

The crewman had stopped and shaken his head.

"Those bastards—they catch you with live cargo, they'll likely just kill you on the spot." He'd used his chin to indicate the bay in which they stood. "This is where we dump the cargo. We flood their living quarters with a gas—strong stuff that'll drive anything ahead of it. They got nowhere to come but here, and then—" once again he'd used his chin to indicate the huge hatches "—pop goes the weasel. Out they go."

Then he'd turned and pointed to a series of tubes Zach had wondered about.

"Makes one hell of a mess. Puke everywhere, and there's always some that get mangled up on the way out. Those pipes'll flood the area with a high-pressure cleaning foam that blows everything out and leaves the bays bright and shiny. Spick-and-span, like nothing ever happened."

The man had shrugged, then resumed walking toward the far end of the bay once again.

"Doesn't always work, though. Does against the Sollies. They can't do a thing unless they can catch us with live cargo on board and prove we're carrying. No cargo, no harm, no fault. Some of these Manties, though—and Havenites are even worse, some of 'em—they'll just pitch us out of the same bays. All *they* care about is what they call the 'equipment clause.' They see this—" he waved at the bay again "—and they don't care whether or not they caught us with live cargo. Don't even bother stripping us out of our suits, those who're wearing one. What difference does it make if you're floating in vacuum half-naked or wearing a suit with air that'll run out in a few hours? Probably better to be half naked. At least for the cargo it's quick."

Zach had been on the verge of vomiting himself by the time they'd reached the exit. He'd had the image of a terrified child—a girl, maybe five years old—being flung out of the ship as the bay depressurized. By then, she'd have already emptied whatever little had been in her belly—her bowels, too, most likely. The vacuum would simply finish the business.

Maybe she'd have been held by the hand by an adult who died with her. It was the only small mercy Zach had been able to imagine.

And it had been all he could do to extend mercy to the crewman ahead of him. He'd struggled with the urge—the *need*—to smash the man's neck with his fist. Again and again and again... until all that remained of his vertebrae were splinters.

But he'd realized even then that that would have been sheer hypocrisy. Because, in the end, he—and Gail—were part of this, as well.

❖   ❖   ❖

Perhaps what he'd learned about Galton wouldn't have concerned him even now, if not for that moment aboard the slave ship. That instant in which God—or some greater power, at any rate—had reached out and rubbed not his nose, but his soul in the vileness with which the Alignment would compromise—would create and use—in the name of its lofty objective. Nobility of purpose, the splendor of the cause, were thin, cold comfort against that moment of transcendent reality.

And yet, as the weeks passed after they'd arrived in Leonard, he'd slowly come to realize that his...disenchantment had acquired another cause. One that went beyond the slave ship, beyond Galton. One that, in some ways, was even more powerful. It was certainly more frightening, since he'd always known he would never actually share the horrifying fate which had overtaken so many genetic slaves over the centuries. There was little chance that he or Gail would ever be directly brutalized by the Alignment. They might be executed, yes—it did happen, rarely. But the Alignment would do it quickly and painlessly. They'd probably never even realize it was happening to them. Nor was it remotely likely that they would be sacrificed as Galton might be, because they were in the innermost, safest *matryoshka* doll.

Yet there were other, deeper fears than mere death. Or even the icy fear of *Gail's* death. There was the dawning recognition that he and the woman he'd come to love weren't trapped in what was simply the galaxy's most gilded and inescapable cage. No, they were imprisoned at the heart of a great, darkly savage, beautiful, ruthless, and unstoppable beast. They were *part* of it... and there was no way out. No escape.

As he gazed out over the geometric glory of Leonard, he found himself considering once more—for the first time in sharp focus—his brother's last few weeks of life. What had he missed in those weeks? What had happened to Jack without his ever noticing? For himself, the breaking point had been that evacuation bay on *Prince Sundjata*, but what had it been for *Jack*?

He'd never know. He knew he would never know, and much as it grieved him, he'd discovered he could accept that. Because he did know *this*: his brother had found an escape. Not one that let him live, but an escape from the trap which had closed upon Zach. From the trap of being *part* of the beast. An escape, he knew now—knowing Jack as he had, seeing through eyes that were clear—in which Jack had struck back against that horror. He'd made his death *count*...because *his* brother would not have died any other way.

Fierce pride and satisfaction burned through him at the thought, and yet there was no way he could emulate Jack. Not on Darius Gamma. Death? Yes, that he could find. But redemption, the chance of actually accomplishing something, that was another challenge entirely.

He stood gazing out over the city for another moment, then turned away from the view and went back to his desk. There was still work to do, and he still had no answers.

And now he had Gail to think about, as well.

✦   ✦   ✦

The message light blinked from Gail's desktop com when she reached her office. She grimaced and pressed the acceptance key.

"Solange wishes to see you," a computer-generated voice said. "She awaits you in her office."

That was it. No explanation of why, and no one to ask, so Gail simply shrugged, headed back out of the door, and went down the long corridor to her supervisor's office.

The door was open when she got there, and she walked through it without knocking. She and Solange got along quite well.

"What's up, boss?" she asked.

The woman behind the desk was as diminutive as Gail was tall, although their complexions were very similar and they shared almost exactly the same eye and hair color. Like her, Solange was one of the Alignment's most capable military planners and logisticians.

Now she looked up at Gail's question and shook her head.

"The rumor's confirmed. You've either really pleased somebody, or really pissed them off. Not sure which." She gestured toward the screen on one corner of the desk. "Word was waiting when I got here this morning. You've been reassigned."

"Where? And why, for that matter?"

"The 'where' is TA-3. The 'why' is a question I'm nowhere nearly stupid enough to answer. Even try to think of an answer for."

Gail stared at her. The innocuous sounding "TA-3" was...

Well, not quite *notorious*, but awfully close. The "TA" part of it stood for Tactical Analysis. Nobody knew—nobody Gail knew knew, anyway—where the "3" came from, since there seemed to be no "1" or "2."

The only thing generally known about that department—division, section, whatever you called it—was that it handled the most highly classified military projects. The sort with "burn before reading" security classifications.

Which made the news exciting and...a little nerve-racking.

"Eek," she said.

✧   ✧   ✧

Gail tried not to stare too obviously as her uniformed escort led her into the huge, circular complex of offices that was apparently TA-3's headquarters. Office space was available in copious quantities in Leonard, but the Alignment was almost obsessive about fitting space to the actual need of whoever—or whatever—occupied it. Which meant...

They turned down a lengthy, curving corridor—one, she realized, that wrapped around the central core of the building. The outer wall, to her left, was composed entirely of one-way windows, while the one to her right was lined with closed doors. They walked at least fifty meters before they reached—eventually—one of those closed doors. There was no signage Gail could see, nothing to indicate what lay beyond that anonymous door, but her escort pressed his palm to a reader and the door slid open.

"Here you are," he told her, waving her through it, and she found herself in a large, tastefully furnished office.

The cheerful looking man who rose from his desk chair as she entered came as close to obese as any Alpha line she'd ever met. He just about *had* to be an Alpha line to hold a supervisory position here on Darius Gamma, she thought, as she extended her hand, but he was certainly the...plumpest one she'd ever encountered.

"I'm Gail Weiss," she said.

"Well, yeah," he replied as he gripped the proffered hand. "We're not likely to mistake someone's identity here. Besides, your reputation's preceded you."

"Reputation for what?"

She managed not to frown as she asked the question, and he grinned.

"Tactical wizardry," he said. "Of the variety you'd expect to get from a civilian, at least."

He turned toward an interior door, gesturing with his hand for her to follow.

"Come on. I'll introduce you to the team."

The *team* was clearly meant to be pronounced *Team*, she thought.

"I assume," he said, over his shoulder, "that you've already figured out that security on this project goes with terms like paramount, supreme, absolute—I believe 'drawn and quartered' is in there somewhere, too."

"Yes. Does 'security' include your name?"

The man stopped and turned around, his mouth slightly agape. Then he shook himself.

"Oh. Sorry. I forget stuff like that. I'm Antwone Carpinteria."

"And my new supervisor?"

"Not . . . exactly." He shook his head. "You'll find that TA-3 isn't much given to hierarchical arrangements." He headed for the interior door once more. "Just don't forget the drawn and quartered part. You can ignore the Iron Maiden, though, because it's off in a corner. But don't trip over the rack."

The passageway beyond the door was short . . . and opened into a chamber that explained the building's architecture. It, too, was circular, and it bordered on the gigantic. It had to be at least eighty or ninety meters in diameter, and one of the largest holo projectors she'd ever seen was mounted in the center of a ceiling at least twenty meters above the floor.

Two people awaited them, both in the maroon and green uniform of the Darius System Navy: a captain and a lieutenant commander. The captain was female, on the burly side, with very dark skin and blond hair cut rather long for a naval officer. The lieutenant commander—he seemed quite a bit older than his superior, oddly enough—was male, with the sort of unremarkable face and build that legend ascribed to top espionage agents.

Carpinteria waved a hand at them. "Captain Bernice Augenbraun. Lieutenant Commander Vergel Suarez." He jerked a short, pudgy thumb at Gail. "Gail Weiss. Civilian analyst."

Both officers nodded politely to her, and she nodded back. Then Carpinteria clapped his hands, and the grin was back on his face.

"And now, let's have the show," he said. "Back behind the lines, please."

He pointed to a twelve-centimeter-wide yellow line. It paralleled the chamber's walls, three meters out from them to enclose the holo display's area. He waited till they were all safely outside the hologram's display area, and then clapped his hands.

"*Avanti!*" he said, and the chamber was plunged instantly into darkness. But that darkness was the black-velvet background for a breathtakingly perfect hologram of a star system, and as her eyes adjusted to the dimness, she began discerning its details.

It was dominated, using the term loosely, by the orangey brilliance of what was clearly a K-class star. There were at least five planets, but only one of them, the fourth from the star, lay within the liquid-water zone and showed the cloud-swirled blue of a world with atmosphere. As if to compensate, there were two asteroid belts. She was pretty sure the outer one, which was exceptionally dense, lay outside the primary's hyper-limit, and the tiny fireflies of what were clearly resource extraction ships swarmed through it. Tiny as their icons might be, those ships were grossly out of scale, or she would never have seen them with her naked eye.

The outer belt might supply the raw materials, but the platforms which used them were much farther in-system, tethered to the gravitational anchor of the habitable planet and safely inside the hyper limit. There were at least a dozen artificial habitats, some of them downright huge, as well as a dense flock of what were clearly orbital refineries and an enormous bevy of orbital shipyards. Dense blocks of alphanumeric characters floated in the hologram, pegged to specific features. There were . . . a lot of them, and no doubt they contained tons of information, but most of them were too far away from her present viewpoint for her to read.

She had no idea where that system might be, but it was obviously a *major* industrial node.

"Welcome to . . . let's call it System Alpha," Carpinteria's voice said out of the murk to her left. "Your job is to help us figure out how to defend it against a massive attack. Unless we're wrong, if it has to be defended at all, the graserhead MDMs are going to be a key element in our tactics, and you're our leading expert on them."

Which was true, Gail reflected. She wasn't a physicist, but she *was* a topflight naval analyst, and she'd led the teams which had evolved tactical—and strategic—doctrine for the new graserheads. But why was Carpinteria talking about just the MDMs? Why not the torpedoes, as well? She could think of several stealth applications for *them* right off the top of her head. Were they . . . off the table, for some reason? If so, why? And what was "Alpha," and where—?

She shook that thought—*all* those thoughts—off. The less she knew about anything they didn't want to tell her about, the better. "You said 'massive,'" she said instead. "How massive?"

"Really, really, *really* massive, most likely," Carpinteria replied cheerily. "With everything the Grand Alliance has in its toolkit. On the other hand, you may spare no expense in its defense. Well, almost."

What the hell is going on? Gail wondered.

City of Old Chicago
Old Earth
Sol System

"WHERE ARE WE GOING?" CATHERINE MONTAIGNE ASKED.

She'd been whisked into the air car almost as soon as she'd landed at the O'Hare Shuttle Port. It was supposed to be taking her to deliver a speech on behalf of the Anti-Slavery League. She'd given a lot of those right here in Old Chicago, over the years, but they'd just flown past her normal landing platform. The one that led below the city's surface streets to give access to the capital's Old Quarter, since most of the Quarter was underground. In fact, it extended downward for more than a kilometer in some places.

"The Loop," as it was also known, was the Solarian League's most famous ghetto, and by far its largest one. It was home for millions of the capital's immigrants, who came from all over the League—especially from the poverty-stricken worlds of the Verge. Immigrants, both legal and illegal, could be found all over Old Terra, but by far the greatest, densest concentration of them was right here in the capital.

Other long settled and wealthy core worlds kept tighter restrictions on immigration than Old Terra, and especially on immigration from the Verge. But the human race's homeworld would have made that difficult, to say the least. It was the most polyglot planet in the human-settled galaxy. With so many family and other close ties to so many other worlds, it was simply impossible to regulate immigration all that tightly, and Old Terra was the destination of dreams, the planet with streets of gold ... especially for refugees fleeing the Protectorates and the Office of Frontier Security's "benevolent oversight."

175

"Soldier Field's back that way," Catherine half-protested now, looking over her shoulder at the rapidly receding landing platform.

"Your days of giving speeches in Soldier Field are over, girl," the woman sitting next to her in the rear seat said.

Her name was Fanantenanirainy, which combined her personal and surname after the custom of her homeworld of Antananarivo. She was every bit as imposing as her name, too. Her long, braided hair was about the same coffee color as her eyes and skin, and even sitting she was a head taller than Catherine. She probably weighed three times as much, too, and while some of that was fat, most of it was just her natural bulk.

Antananarivo, originally settled by people from Madagascar and Mauritius, was near enough to Sol to be considered a Core World, but it was clearly a second—or third—tier system, economically. Like many of Old Terra's immigrants, Fanantenanirainy's parents had moved back to the homeworld in search of brighter economic horizons when she was four T-years old. She'd lived here ever since and spent most of her adult life in Old Chicago, as a political activist engaged in the struggle against genetic slavery. In fact, she'd been the Anti-Slavery League's Sol System vice president for the past two decades.

Happily for all concerned, she answered to the name of "Fanny."

"We're headed to the Mandelbaum Amphitheater in Evanston," she continued. "But first..."

The air car began a shallow descent, sliding smoothly down the altitude lanes until it was no more than a hundred meters above a very broad surface avenue that ran more or less parallel to Lake Michigan. The thoroughfare still bore its ancient name of Lake Shore Drive, which was a bit absurd, two thousand years into the Diaspora. Over the last twenty centuries, the actual lakeshore had been pushed farther and farther to the east as the city expanded onto landfill. By now, Lake Shore Drive was on average four kilometers from the waterfront and never came closer to the lake than one kilometer.

"What in the—"

Cathy stared at the vid screen in the rear compartment, which gave her a better view of what lay ahead than she could have gotten looking through the windshield over the shoulders of the driver and the very large fellow in the passenger seat, whom no one had come right out and called her bodyguard.

"Why are all these people here?" she asked.

Lake Shore drive was bordered by very wide slidewalks and old-fashioned sidewalks—more like promenades, especially on the eastern side, nearer the lake—and they were packed. The huge crowd stretched as far ahead as she could see, and as she looked out the side window, she saw people perched on virtually every balcony of the towers that flanked the Drive.

"I will say it's always been one of your most attractive qualities, Cathy," Fanny told her with a grin. "You don't have the slightest interest in adulation or public acclaim." She gestured at the screen. "They turned out to greet *you*."

"It's freezing out there!" Cathy protested.

That statement might not have been totally factually accurate, but it came close, especially for the sensibilities of someone who'd been raised in Landing on Manticore itself. She felt sure it was at least ten whole degrees above the freezing temperature of water, but it was also late in an early April afternoon, sliding into evening in Old Chicago, at the bottom of a deeply shadowed ceramacrete canyon between the capital's enormous towers, and a brisk wind came whipping in off the lake.

"Freezing—nonsense!" Fanny said briskly. "It's a beautiful day. A little chilly, yes, but this is *Old Chicago*. You see what those people are wearing? They're called thermal jackets. They been around for more than two thousand years."

She shook her head at Cathy, then leaned forward.

"Turn on the exterior audio, Andy," she told the driver, and he fiddled with something on his panel. A moment later, Cathy winced as the roar of massed cheers flooded the air car.

"Turn it down!" she said, and Fanny chuckled again.

"You can turn it all the way off, Andy. I just wanted to give Little Miss Modesty a sense of what's happening, since she's obviously still mired in ancient history."

By now, they'd reached street-level, and the air car was in ground effect mode, thirty centimeters above the pavement as it skimmed along the Drive through the enormous crowd held back by barricades and a double line of police. Cathy was dumbfounded.

"I'd assumed that if I was met by any crowd except the regulars who came to hear me talk at Soldier Field—okay, that was a fair number of years back—that they'd be booing me as a Manticoran mass murderer."

Fanny's shrug was every bit as massive as she was.

"Most of these people are either immigrants or the children of immigrants, Cathy. The big majority come from the Verge—or their parents or grandparents did—and a significant fraction are former Manpower slaves, or at least related to ex-slaves. You think they give a damn how many Mesans got killed? Not very many of them believe the Mesan version of events to begin with, and those who do figure the bastards had it coming anyway. Of course—"

She pointed toward the west with the thumb.

"If we were driving down Michigan Avenue, you might get a different reception. But screw those people. They've had almost four months since Harrington came over the wall. Damned well time they got over it, but half of them are still hiding out in their fancy apartments. Especially today."

She swiveled ponderously in her seat to face Cathy as squarely as possible.

"I hope you've got your speech ready. There'll be somewhere north of a quarter million people in the amphitheater, and way, way more than that watching on video. We've got a system-wide hookup. Best estimate— What's it up to now, Yusuf?"

The bodyguard glanced down at his uni-link.

"A little more than three hundred and twenty million are already tuned in listening to the talking heads. That'll grow a lot, once the event actually starts and *she* goes live."

"Holy crap." Cathy's eyes were very wide.

"Like I said, I hope you've got your speech ready," Fanny said, and those eyes narrowed immediately.

"My speeches are *always* ready."

CNO's Office
Admiralty Building
City of Old Chicago
Sol System

WINSTON KINGSFORD LOOKED AWAY FROM THE HD TO HIS NEW Director—so new, in fact, that he hadn't actually been sworn in yet—of Naval Intelligence.

"Have you ever seen her speak before?" he asked, nodding his head toward the HD, where Cathy Montaigne had been speaking for almost twenty minutes, and Charles Gannon nodded.

"Quite a few times on recordings, and twice in person."

"You saw her in person? Where?"

"At Soldier Field—where else? She used to speak there quite often when she was living here in exile."

Kingsford shook his head in a gesture that bordered on disbelief.

"Chuck, I'm having a hard time picturing you underground, listening to a radical firebrand's speech in that location. Soldier Field's what... two hundred meters underground?"

"Not that far." Gannon shrugged. "More like a hundred, and it's not hard to find if you have a guide. And I had any number to choose from. No grad student in my field is worth a damn if he or she hasn't snuck into Soldier Field to hear radical speeches—not to mention sampling the coffees and teas and... other substances, whose precise nature I will glide over, in the multitude of shops in the Old Quarter. I didn't need guides anyway, since I spent several years as a grad student at the University of Chicago myself."

He looked down and plucked the sleeve of his jacket to highlight the elbow patches.

"After I became a respectable faculty member, though, I always wore one of these outfits when I ventured into the Loop."

"Protective coloration?" Kingsford smiled.

"Advertising, actually. No professor in my field's considered worth a damn by his best grad students if he doesn't make the occasional appearance himself. And Montaigne was always the biggest draw."

"I can see why." Kingsford looked back at the HD. "She's not at all what I expected."

"People—well, the proper class of people—are always surprised when they hear Montaigne speak. She has such a flamboyant political reputation that they expect some sort of shrill, over-the-top, haranguing rabble-rouser. Instead..."

He nodded toward the figure of the woman at the podium in the Mandelbaum Amphitheater.

"Instead, they get a calm, methodical presentation of a point of view that makes them uncomfortable, instead of scornful, because it's so carefully and thoroughly reasoned—and usually not something they want to hear."

"You sound like you admire her."

"Montaigne has integrity, and she places principles above whatever personal ambitions she may have. Well, to be fair, someone with her money doesn't have any reason for *that* kind of ambition, but you know the political animal even better than I do. Ninety percent of them are fueled entirely by ego and narcissism, and those are the furthest thing imaginable from *her* motivations. So, yes, I do admire her—respect might be a better word. Quite a bit, in fact, whatever differences I have with her. Which, by the way, aren't as many as you may think. I've agreed with her for decades—not years, Winston; *decades*—on the subject of genetic slavery and the vileness of Manpower Incorporated."

The CNO's expression wasn't exactly a scowl, but it came close.

"I don't doubt it. But that woman's consorted for those same decades—still does!—with terrorists." He made a downward waving gesture with his hand. "And please spare me the old saw about one person's terrorist being another person's freedom fighter. I grant you there's a lot of truth to it, but don't expect me to approve of their tactics. I can't think of any officer in the Solarian League Navy who ever snuck into the personal quarters of an undersecretary of the interior, cut his throat—and then removed the head of a statue and replaced it with the severed one."

"Ah, yes." Gannon smiled. "One of Jeremy X's more notorious

exploits. Would it be churlish of me to point out that the terrorists didn't simply leave Undersecretary Albescue's head behind, but his right hand, as well? Holding a chip that contained the undersecretary's lovingly recorded sexual exploits... prominent among them being the abuse of slave children."

"Albescue was a swine," Kingsford said in a disgusted tone. "That still doesn't mean—"

"Winston, leave off. You look at things like this from the standpoint of a man who spent his entire adult life as a naval officer. I came in as a rating, remember? From the view down there—and sure as hell from my later studies—I've developed a theory about this. To wit, the distinction between a proper soldier and a dirty rotten terrorist seems to be mostly a matter of the scale of the killing. If you smite your foe on an industrial scale—especially from a distance—you're a fine fellow. Do it up close and retail, and you're a vicious murderer. Now, I'll grant that there are terrorists and there are terrorists, and some of them don't give much of a good goddamn how many innocent bystanders they take out. After all, they're *terrorists*, right? They *want* their atrocities to be as visible, as striking, and as horrifying as physically possible. The bigger the damned body count the better! But the truth?" He looked Kingsford in the eye and shook his head. "The Audubon Ballroom was always a lot more careful about 'collateral damage' than the SLN, especially when we were supporting OFS, and you know it, Winston."

Kingsford *was* scowling now, and Gannon looked back at the woman speaking ten kilometers north of the CNO's office.

"You can fire me anytime you want, Admiral. But the way I see it, part of my job is to make you squirm a little from time to time."

"I forgot how good you are at it," Kingsford growled.

They sat in companionable silence for a couple of more minutes. Then Gannon shrugged.

"It makes you feel any better, I can pretty much guarantee there are plenty of people watching this who are squirming way more than you are."

"No—*really*?" The admiral chuckled. "Let's see... in alphabetical order, we could start with Senior—though very much not Permanent—Undersecretary of the Interior Aahlstrom. And end with—"

"The new chief financial officer of the Jessyk Combine?" Gannon suggested.

"Antoine Zuraaba? Good choice. More coffee?"

"Yes, please."

Kingsford poured from the old-fashioned carafe. Then he waited until they'd each taken a sip before he leaned back with a sigh.

"All right, out with it. You didn't ask me to watch this speech without a reason. You've either got a theory you want me to hear or—"

"Actually, it's a proposal."

"What I was afraid of." Kingsford sighed again. "So what is it?"

"I want your permission to get in touch with Montaigne—it will be done discreetly—and see if I can get her to agree for the Anti-Slavery League to start working—again, discreetly—with the Navy."

The admiral's eyes widened.

"Working with us on *what*?"

"Rooting out the slave trade—the whole apparatus involved with it, not just the slave ships and depots."

"But..." Kingsford's frown was one of puzzlement, not opposition. "I've been assuming—so have you—that whatever else it does or doesn't do, the Constitutional Convention's going to ban slavery outright, and no damn fooling around this time."

"Yes, it will. And then what? Winston, it's been officially illegal in the League for centuries. Have you noticed anyone actually enforcing that?"

"Well, the Navy—"

"All right." Gannon nodded. "I'll give you that. When a Navy ship actually encounters a slaver, with slaves on board, it seizes the ship and liberates the slaves." *And the* crews *of many of those slavers*, he did not add out loud, *quite often mysteriously disappear into the depths of space*. Which wasn't something people talked about very much.

"But how often does that really happen?" he continued in a more challenging tone. "And has the League *ever* signed off on the 'equipment clause'? Let me refresh your mind—it hasn't. It's right there in the Cherwell Convention, but the League has *never* enforced it. And any CO who dared try to was hounded right out of the Service. Manpower's bottom-feeding allies in OFS, the Interior Department—*and* the Navy, Winston—saw to that!"

He held Kingsford's eye until the CNO nodded, then shrugged.

"It probably wouldn't really have mattered if we *had* been allowed to apply the equipment clause, because slave ships are only the surface of the trade. If the last two or three hundred T-years have demonstrated anything where genetic slavery is concerned, it's that banning something is one thing. Actually *destroying* it is something else entirely, and especially when it's this deep an abscess. Genetic slavery—I'm talking about the whole business of it Winston; not just the ships and the depots, but the breeding facilities, the laboratories, the works—isn't just going to go poof because a bunch of politicians declare it to be poofed, even if they do really mean it this time. It's going to have to be *uprooted*—by force, more often than not."

"All right...I can see that." The admiral was still frowning. "But why the Navy? I'd think it was a police function. Aside from those slave ships, at least."

"And you'd be right," Gannon agreed. "Unfortunately, the police agency that ought to be doing it, especially in the Shell and the Verge, where it's most deeply encysted, used to be called the Office of Frontier Security. Which, you may recall, is in the process of disbandment as one of the Grand Alliance's surrender demands. Not that it'll make that much difference. Too much of OFS was in bed with the slavers to begin with."

"The Gendarmerie—"

"The Gendarmerie is undoubtedly going to wind up with final responsibility for this, and Attorney General Rorendaal hates the trade as much as I do." Gannon said. "She's going to push hard to convince Prime Minister Yon to officially instruct the Navy to begin applying the equipment clause. But as far as the Gendarmerie is concerned, Gaddis is up to his ass in alligators cleaning house right here on Old Terra. It's going to be a while before he's able to start culling out the bad apples in the Gendarmes who were assigned to work with OFS. Or on most of the Verge worlds, for that matter."

"We can't just start crosscutting jurisdictional lines," Kingsford objected. "The entire League's in a state of flux right now. Gaddis and I are agreed that the last thing we can afford right now is to even look like we're getting into some sort of turf war. Having the military and the police at odds—or even *looking* like they're at odds—isn't going to engender a lot of confidence in the Provisional Assembly *or* the Constitutional Convention."

"I'm not proposing anything of the sort," Gannon said patiently. "For this to work, it would have to be a cooperative effort with the Gendarmerie, as well. In fact, I've already, um, discussed certain hypothetical concerns with Brigadier Gaddis."

"You have, have you?" Kingsford eyed his ONI Director with distinct trepidation.

"Only hypothetically," Gannon replied reassuringly. "The thing is, genetic slavery is—technically, at least—already illegal in the League. That means the Gendarmerie is legally empowered to go after it. In fact, it has been for a long time. Slavery just hasn't been a priority, and the Gendarmes who wished it was have known they'd get zero support from their superiors if they diverted resources to it. Gaddis knows Attorney General Rorendaal will sign off on authorization to do just that. The problem is that, like I said, he's already got way too much on his plate. But he's informed me—hypothetically, of course—that he would be prepared to request the Navy's assistance. At which point, aside from assigning a few liaison personnel, he'd mostly concentrate on getting out of our way."

"But why *us*?" Kingsford asked. "The one thing I'm not is a cop, Chuck!"

"No, you're not a cop," Gannon agreed. "What you are, however, is the Chief of Naval operations, who happens to have at hand two of the three things you do need for the Navy to get started on the project right away."

"And those are?"

"First," Gannon held up a finger, "you've got an entire navy which may not be up to a war with the Grand Alliance, but is plenty strong enough to break up any criminal organization it encounters. Secondly," a second finger came up, "I can organize what amounts to an intelligence unit to guide the work right out of the Office of Naval Intelligence. We don't need outside approval for that, and it wouldn't be stepping on anyone's jurisdictional toes. For that matter, Brigadier Gaddis has agreed— hypothetically—that he might be able to lend me a few of his own brighter intelligence types to help out."

He paused to sip coffee.

"Those are the two things we've already got. What we still need are the assets that ONI's new intelligence unit—I'll call it the Frederick Douglass Bureau for the moment—will need to do its work. That means former slaves, first and foremost. And at least some of them will have to be former Ballroom members, because no one else—and I mean *no one*, Winston—knows where the slave trade is and how deeply it's hidden the way the Ballroom does. But they'll have to be people we can trust and be sure aren't rogue agents or just plain loose screws. And there's no one I can think of in a better position to provide us with agents like that—reliable ones—than Montaigne and the ASL."

Kingsford's frown had been fading, but now it came back.

"I can follow all that, but you still haven't explained why the Navy *should* do it. Oh, I'll grant that the slave trade is vile. That it's a cancer that corrupts and poisons everything it touches. Hell, I'll go further. *Somebody* needs to stomp on it, and stomp on it *hard*. But for Christ's sake, Chuck!"

He shook his head, his expression like iron.

"You know better than almost anybody how many *millions* of men and women the Navy just lost. But in case you haven't been thinking about that, let me put it into perspective for you. Our total casualties amount to almost thirty-two percent of Battle Fleet's prewar standing strength. *Thirty-two percent*, Chuck. There's not a single serving officer or rating who didn't lose *someone* they knew. And every one of our surviving capital ships is completely obsolete, every one of our surviving officers and ratings knows we got our clock cleaned every single time we went up against the Grand Alliance, and every single one of them knows we surrendered the capital system of the League—hell, the entire *League* itself—without firing a single shot at Harrington! You say Gaddis has his hands full repairing and rebuilding the Gendarmerie? What the hell do you think *I'm* doing? I've got way too much on my plate to be looking for additional missions!"

Gannon looked back at him levelly for several seconds. Then—

"Winston, the biggest thing—by far—that the Solarian League Navy has on its plate is rebuilding itself without doing it around a revanchist spinal cord. You're right about how brutally we got hammered. Mostly because of stupid fucking admirals and even stupider politicians who couldn't pour piss out of a boot, maybe, but you're right. We lost damned near a third of Battle Fleet's peacetime strength. And how many of the people we *didn't* lose, do you think, are happy about that? How many of them are sitting around thinking about the *next* time they go up against the

Grand Alliance...this time with matching tech? Hell, they'd be more than human if they weren't thinking exactly that!

"But we can't afford for them to think anything of the sort. You're just as worried about that as I am—we've talked about it Winston, a *lot*. We want the war with the Grand Alliance to be *over*. Done. Finished—for good and ever. The last thing we want is to just put it back on a shelf until the Navy's got the equipment to fire it back up and rip the human race apart all over again. This time on a scale I don't even want to think about!"

"Of course that's the last thing we want," Kingsford said just a bit testily. "That's why I'm about to sign off on Willis's force restructuring!"

It was Gannon's turn to nod.

Kingsford had handed Admiral Willis Jennings, his chief of staff, the unenviable task of reconsidering the Solarian League Navy's entire structure and organization—and how to fix its innumerable failures—in the wake of its devastating defeat. Jennings had approached his assignment with a ruthless pragmatism which had surprised even Kingsford, and the CNO knew as well as Gannon just how...unpopular some aspects of his chief of staff's proposed solutions were likely to be. Especially with the Navy's most entrenched bureaucrats.

Completely disbanding Battle Fleet would probably evoke the loudest screams...at least from Battle Fleet's existing hierarchy, Gannon thought. But Battle Fleet had to go. Jennings was absolutely on target with that. The SLN's formal division into Frontier Fleet, charged with executing the Navy's day-to-day duties and discharging its routine responsibilities, and Battle Fleet, charged with actually fighting any wars that came along, had been disastrous, Frontier Fleet had been badly enough tainted in the public's eyes (and its own, if the truth be known) by the way in which it had been sucked into supporting the Office of Frontier Security's corruption, but at least it had been steadily and fully engaged in *doing* things. Battle Fleet hadn't. It had been a black hole down which funding poured every fiscal year, but it hadn't had anyone to fight, and so it had stagnated. Its capital ships had served no function at all, except to fight battles, and the battles had never come.

Until, finally, they *did* come, and the stagnation and institutional arrogance which had encrusted Battle Fleet came home to roost like lethal barnacles. It had failed—utterly and abysmally—at the single function it had ever had, and it knew it. Whether or not it would ever be willing to admit its failure had been self-induced was something else, however, and Gannon's experience of human nature didn't make him particularly optimistic in that regard. In fact, he was convinced that Jennings—and Kingsford—were completely correct: if Battle Fleet continued to exist, it would inevitably become the host in which the revanchism all of them feared metastasized.

But as Jennings had pointed out in his preliminary report to Kingsford, the League didn't *need* Battle Fleet...and probably never had, really. Battle Fleet's function had been to be the threat, the unstoppable and invincible Juggernaut, which would dissuade any potential foe from even thinking about crossing swords with the League. That concept might once have made limited sense, at least earlier in the League's history. But the truth was that no star nation with a gram of sense would *want* to "cross swords" with something as large and powerful as the League had become over the T-centuries. Certainly the *Grand Alliance* hadn't wanted to. Its hand had been forced by the Mandarins' arrogance and stupidity...buttressed and fueled by Battle Fleet's own arrogance, stupidity, and *blindness*. A vastly smaller capital ship strength (assuming they'd been modern and effective capital ships, not obsolete deathtraps) would have deterred anyone smaller than the Grand Alliance quite handily, and without engendering the chauvinistic hubris which had been so central to Battle Fleet's institutional DNA.

Then there was the fact that the SLN had actually been *two* navies. Officers and ratings, but especially officers, had followed separate career tracks in either Frontier Fleet *or* Battle Fleet. Kingsford could have counted the number of officers, particularly senior flag officers, with experience in *both* Frontier Fleet and Battle Fleet on his fingers and toes...without taking off both shoes. There'd been lip service at the very top about cooperation and mutually supportive mission roles, but lip service was *all* it had been.

So what Jennings had proposed was that Battle Fleet simply be abolished and the Navy's total focus folded over into what had been Frontier Fleet. Frontier Fleet would also be abolished, as a separate organizational niche. Instead, there would simply be the Solarian League Navy, restructured to be what it should have been all along: a single, unified force and command structure serving the League's *actual* needs.

The abolition of both the Office of Frontier Security and its system of protectorates—there was a *lot* of abolishing going on, just at the moment, Gannon reflected—would simplify those needs enormously. It would also allow the Navy to step away from its distasteful role as OFS's enforcer when it came time to intimidate—or crush—opposition to Frontier Security and its cronies in the Protectorates. What would remain would be the problems OFS had been *intended* to address when it was first created: peacekeeping on the peripheries, search and rescue, enforcement of interstellar law, and the maintenance of an effective and *modern* combat capability sufficient to dissuade any realistic external threat to the League.

So every single existing Solarian ship-of-the-wall was destined for the breakers and reclamation. Battle Fleet's basing infrastructure would be hugely reduced—indeed, virtually eliminated—and what was retained would be repurposed to support a Navy whose largest unit, for the immediate future, would probably be a battlecruiser or a Solarian version of the Grand Alliance's LAC carriers, given how effective modern light attack craft would prove for most of the new SLN's probable requirements. Every existing battlecruiser—hell, every existing *heavy* cruiser—would probably be scrapped as well, really, because they were just as obsolete as the ships-of-the-wall had been in an era of multi-drive missiles and LACs, but that could be deferred, at least for a time. As Gannon had pointed out, obsolete or not, they were quite capable of dealing with anyone *short* of the Grand Alliance.

None of that could happen overnight, of course.

Gannon knew Kingsford was well aware that he couldn't afford to procrastinate. He had to move while the existing naval hierarchy's state of shock—and the Grand Alliance's... oversight—meant he could kick over rice bowls right and left. But at the same time, he also had to be aware of the consequences of the sudden and enormous reduction in personnel Jennings's recommendations necessarily entailed. A *lot* of officers—and enlisted personnel—were about to find themselves abruptly unemployed, and that would be particularly problematic in a League whose interstellar economy had been so badly damaged by the war with the Grand Alliance. And which was headed into an even worse shambles, in some ways, thanks to the sudden collapse of OFS and the trillions upon trillions of credits in assets so many transstellars had abruptly lost along with the Protectorates.

Of course, assuming he could convince whatever government emerged from the Constitutional Convention to fund it, the need to build so many replacement warships would provide a *major* impetus to at least one portion of that economy. As would the need to completely rebuild the Sol System's devastated—as in *obliterated*—industrial base. None of which could prevent the proposed changes from adding their own, not insignificant mite to the current miserable mess.

Despite that, Kingsford fully intended to make a start on his version of cleaning the Augean stable within the next T-month or two. Which undoubtedly explained his reluctance to take on additional missions just now.

"I'm perfectly well aware of how much you have on your plate, Winston," Gannon said now. "And, frankly, we're damned lucky Jennings has the moral integrity and brains—and *you* have the moral courage—to recognize just how bad the existing system had become and actually do something about it. In fact, that's the entire point, from the Navy's perspective, to what I'm suggesting. The need to refocus the Navy on something other than licking its wounds, resentment, and revenge is the whole point of Jennings's recommendations. Well, Frontier Fleet just lost seventy or eighty percent of its old missions, and the ones it still has are pretty much 'business as usual.' Nothing *there* to inspire men and women to embrace the total reorganization of their professional lives. But..."

He paused, eyebrows arched, and Kingsford nodded.

"Okay," he said. "I think I see where you're going with this now. Give the Navy an issue—an assignment that's an obvious break with that 'business as usual' past of yours—right away. One we can use as a focusing device, an illustration of what the Navy we need to build will be doing instead of sitting around thinking long and homicidal thoughts. And an assignment—"

"An assignment they'll feel proud of, instead of cynical about," Gannon finished for him. "Yes. Winston, that's what I'm proposing. To be honest, it won't be a big enough mission—or eat up enough time—to carry the full finding-our-way-again load for very long. But it *will* get us off on the right foot, and we can lean into the momentum it generates. But we can't do it without the help of the ASL, and, frankly, I'm fine with the fact that that requires us to rub elbows now and then with people like Jeremy X. Yes, he's ruthless, but he's not corrupt. People drawn to feathering their own nests at the public expense don't join organizations like the Audubon Ballroom. *They* tend to join organizations like Jessica Stein's Renaissance League." He made a dismissive gesture. "The League wouldn't have been much of an alternative to the ASL even when her father was running it. Today . . . ?"

"It's a bunch of stuffed shirts with its head up its collective ass. Good at collecting money and good at giving speeches—" Kingsford glanced at the now dark HD "—albeit, not as good as *that* one. Not so good at spending the money on anything except retreats and consultants' fees. Oh, and salary for the League's officers and administrators. What's that old saw about doing well by doing good?" He grimaced in disgust. "Even if Stein had any interest in actually doing something about slavery, they'd be about as effective for what you're talking about as toy poodles would be for hunting dogs."

"Worse than useless, in my opinion. Under Jessica's leadership, they've gotten awful cozy with the Renaissance Factor." It was Gannon's turn to grimace. "You know how I feel about them."

"You are one suspicious, distrustful man, Chuck. Always prone to see darkness everywhere you look. Did anyone ever tell you that?"

"Andrea, at least twice a week. But she's prejudiced, because she knows me so well. Look, I'm not claiming and never have that Mannerheim and the Renaissance Factor are agents of the devil. But underneath all that 'we're only organizing for mutual defense' they're every bit as ambitious as the people running the 'Mayan Autonomous Regional Sector.' The difference is that they're smarmy and a hell lot less open about it. No one can accuse Barregos and Rozsak of *that*."

"Not hardly." Kingsford snorted. "Not to mention that I'd much rather have Luis Rozsak and his people on my side in a battle than the Mannerheim Navy. They were magnificent in the Battle of Torch."

The CNO finished his cup of coffee.

"All right, Chuck. You have my permission to see what if anything you can get underway. But for the time being, this is just between you and me—maybe Gaddis—and the mice in the attic. Understood?"

Gannon's level gaze was back. "Fine. And Catherine Montaigne."

The gaze didn't waver, and Kingsford gritted his teeth.

"And whoever else you need," he said through those teeth. "Even—even—"

"It's all right, Winston." Gannon smiled. "You don't have to name any names beyond Montaigne. We have our understanding."

Tour D'Argent Restaurant
Seine Embankment
Phénix Paris
Old Terra
Sol System

"DID YOU WATCH THE SPEECH?"

"Yes. I had to make myself do it, but I did," Jessica Stein said across the glass a server had just refilled with wine. The head of the Renaissance Association took time to inhale the wine's fragrance. It was a Bordeaux whose cost didn't bear thinking upon. Fortunately, she didn't have to think about it, since it was being provided by her host, and he didn't have to think about it, either. Not really. Edward Tecuatl had been born into a wealthy Mannerheim family, not to mention the fact that he was the CEO of one of Mannerheim's major banks.

He was also a longtime supporter of the Renaissance Association, going back to when Jessica's father Hieronymus had founded it. After Hieronymus's assassination, Tecuatl had strongly supported Jessica's bid to replace her father as the head of the organization. Given that he was one of the League's two or three most generous donors, his opinion had carried a lot of weight. Enough that it might very well have been what ultimately tipped the balance in her favor.

Stein sipped the Bordeaux and smiled in pleasure, but the smile became a sneer as she set the glass on their table.

"The best I can say about Catherine Montaigne is that she's a bloody nuisance. She's been a thorn in our side for decades. I don't think anyone else can possibly have impeded the fight against genetic slavery more than she has, with her radical rhetoric—a lot of good *that* ever did!—and her association with the Audubon

Ballroom. She made it easy for the Mesans to smear all their opponents as terrorist sympathizers. Which—" the sneer became a scowl and her voice rose "—we most certainly were *not*."

"No," Tecuatl agreed. "Although Hieronymus was careful never to attack the Ballroom publicly. Not by name anyway."

Stein sniffed.

"My father could be softheaded sometimes. *I've* never hesitated to name names—including that of Jeremy X." She sat up a little, her shoulders stiff. "And damn the risk I took of being murdered by him myself."

"Let's be honest, Jessica," Tecuatl said in the same mild tone. "That wasn't much of a risk. Say whatever else you want about him, Jeremy X never struck at anyone just for being one of his many critics. You had to actually *do* something in support of genetic slavery, which was an accusation no one ever brought against the Renaissance Association or any of its members. Certainly not any of its leaders."

Stein sniffed again and waved one hand dismissively.

"Enough on that subject. Now that Montaigne's in the Sol System—and apparently plans to stay for a while—we need to step up our activities around the slavery issue at the Constitutional Convention, or the damned Anti-Slavery League will get all the publicity. Can we count on your support?"

"Of course." Tecuatl sipped from his own glass. "I can't say I feel as strongly about Montaigne as you do, but Mannerheim has always preferred your approach to that of the ASL."

❖   ❖   ❖

The rest of the dinner consisted mostly of the chit-chat of two people who'd been well acquainted, if not what anyone could call real friends, for many years. *Where's so-and-so these days* and *whatever came of that project, anyway*. It was pleasant for both of them, and the meal, of course, was superb—as one would only expect from a restaurant which claimed to trace its origins back to Ante Diaspora Paris.

That claim was fanciful, since the *Tour D'Argent* had gone out of business any number of times—once for almost four centuries—and had had more owners than anyone could remember. For that matter, the entire city of Paris had been obliterated in the Final War. The city of *Phénix Paris* had been rebuilt—magnificently—on the same site, rising from the ashes like the very phoenix with which it had become forever associated, but none of its original structures, including anything named *Tour D'Argent*, had survived the pair of megaton-range blasts which had levelled it. So the name was really just a name, now—one that kept getting resurrected because of its hallowed antiquity. But at least in its current reincarnation, the *Tour D'Argent* was back in the middle of a city on the River Seine. There'd been a stretch almost a thousand years back, shortly after the Final War and before *Phénix Paris*, when the restaurant that claimed the name had been located in Le Mans, of all places.

They went their separate ways, once dinner was done. Tecuatl had a permanently reserved suite in a nearby hotel—one equipped with very expensive and very secure communications equipment. Equipment he put to prompt use once he reached his suite.

"Yes?" a voice said.

"She's solid," he said, not bothering to identify himself. "No surprise there. But it never hurts to make sure." He laughed softly. "What was that term some ancient politician used? 'Useful idiot,' if I remember right."

May 1923 Post Diaspora

"Well, I'm not feeling all warm and squishy at the moment."

—Audrey O'Hanrahan

Amaguq Tower
City of Old Chicago
Old Earth
Sol System

AUDREY O'HANRAHAN SET HER HALF EMPTY COFFEE CUP ON THE small table, rose, and walked to the balcony's rail.

It was a breezy day, but at least April's late-season cold snaps were a thing of the past, and she enjoyed the way the breeze caressed her hair. She stood for several minutes, savoring the sensation and watching the always busy and sometimes frenetic traffic that poured through the huge city on so many different levels. And by so many different avenues and methods. Tubeways, air cars, slidewalks—she could even see a few genuine pedestrians here and there, along with what seemed like an army of joggers.

She didn't count the joggers as pedestrians. O'Hanrahan kept herself in excellent physical condition, but she did her exercising in private. There was no reason to inflect her sweat and grunts upon others, after all. She viewed public jogging as a mild form of narcissism.

When she'd first started coming to Old Chicago, before she'd acquired her apartment here in Amaguq Tower, she'd paid the upcharge to get rooms that overlooked Lake Michigan, since that was the view everyone recommended. And, indeed, it was always pleasant to gaze over the huge expanse of Old Earth's fourth largest lake, especially in summer when it was dotted with sailboats. And sometimes, it was spectacular—especially when one of the big storms rolled in.

But after a few visits, she'd started finding the view a bit boring. It was like visiting the Grand Canyon, which she'd also done... once. The first fifteen minutes were incredible; the next fifteen,

197

were...interesting. And after that... Well, before long even the most spectacular vista got pretty dull if it was completely static.

Lake Michigan was never completely static, of course, since there were always waves. But waves didn't begin to compete with the frenzy of human-generated urban traffic. So she'd saved some money by buying an apartment that overlooked the city itself when the time came for her to establish a permanent address in the capital. She had not, of course, saved the additional money she could have by buying an interior apartment, with no external balcony and no direct view at all. People could say whatever they wanted about smartwalls being "just as good" as a direct view, but Audrey O'Hanrahan wasn't one of them. And some hardships were unacceptable, especially given the income stream her site generated. The *O'Hanrahan Report* was the most widely watched investigative news site in much of the Solarian League, including here on Old Earth itself, with literally billions of subscribers. She'd worked hard to accomplish that. The assistance provided by her Alignment contacts had helped, of course, but most of it was the product of her own skill, her own talent, her own dogged, unyielding persistence, and her genuine passion for uncovering the truth.

Even if there were *certain* truths not even the *O'Hanrahan Report* could share.

That was the other reason she'd chosen Amaguq. According to the tower's website, it was named after Jacques Amaguq, a famous first century PD political leader from Old Terra's northern hemisphere, whose last name had meant "Father Wolf" in one of the ancient tongues of his ancestors. But O'Hanrahan had done a little extra research, and while all of that was true as far as it went, it struck her as utterly appropriate for her to find a home in a tower which was *also* named for the trickster god of the Inuit.

Normally, she would have spent at least a half-hour on her balcony, enough for two full cups of coffee. But today she cut it short after only ten minutes, before she'd finished even one. She had a script to write, and, as often happened, she'd discovered when she woke up that morning that the piece had mostly written itself while she was sleeping. So she wanted to get it recorded for posterity before she forgot anything.

For the vast majority of people, the verb "to write" actually meant to dictate to a voice recognition program. It usually meant that for O'Hanrahan, as well, but not when she had the luxury of a comfortable work environment and no deadline pressure. In those cases, she preferred to use old-fashioned methods. She was firmly convinced, whatever the neurologists said, that she thought better if her fingers were engaged as well as her brain. So, whenever possible, she used the keyboard.

She wasn't a complete throwback, however. She was quite happy with a virtual keyboard and harbored no need to damage her fingertips by beating them against hard, material keys. She'd once known a novelist who insisted upon using an archaic *mechanical* keyboard, and she'd wondered how much medical attention the silly woman required when she was finished with an entire book.

She settled at her desk, called up her keyboard, and began to type.

> *Catherine Montaigne's "spontaneous decision" to attend the galactic convention of the Anti-Slavery League in Old Chicago is a shrewd move. Not simply for her, but for the Manticoran government and the entire Grand Alliance. Of course, both the Star Empire and Montaigne herself will indignantly deny that her trip to Old Terra has any official sanction. It is, they will insist, no more than a private citizen's continuation of her long-standing commitment to and leadership role in the fight against genetic slavery.*
>
> *It is a shrewd move precisely because no one can effectively challenge that indignation. Catherine Montaigne does have an impeccable record, stretching back for decades, as one of the Anti-Slavery League's central leaders, and she is perhaps its best known and most eloquent public spokesperson. And although she is no longer an exile from the Star Empire and has even become politically respectable once more, neither she nor her Liberal Party are part of Prime Minister Grantville's Government. Indeed, officially they are still the "Loyal Opposition."*
>
> *Of course, that label can be misleading. It definitely is when it comes to Manticore's foreign policy. On those issues, the Liberals are now in practice part of an informal "grand coalition." While they continue their policy of disagreement with Grantville's Centrists on a number of*

domestic issues—issues Montaigne never hesitates to put forward—those issues are not central to the Star Empire's political life. Nor will they be, so long as the conflict with the Solarian League remains officially unsettled.

Which is what makes Montaigne's presence here in the Sol System particularly interesting. She has not presented any sort of ambassadorial credentials to the Provisional Government, and she is not here to attend the Constitutional Convention. Not officially, at least. And it's unlikely that she will personally attend any of its proceedings. But her mere presence on Old Terra reminds the population of the Sol System and the entire Solarian League that Manticore's track record in interactions with the independent star nations of the Fringe and even with the Frontier Security "protectorates" of the Verge is far better than the League's. That is true diplomatically, economically, and—most strikingly of all—in its handling of slavery and the slave trade, and much the same can be said for the Star Empire's one-time foe and now ally, the Republic of Haven.

To be blunt, the history of the Solarian League and genetic slavery stinks to high heaven. The League may well have outlawed the slave trade and the institution of genetic slavery itself, but that splendid official position is actually a fig leaf—and a threadbare one, at that. A longstanding, central feature of the general corruption of the League's officials and bureaucracies has been their studious avoidance of any investigation of the activities of any of the giant transstellar corporations doing business in the Solarian League. That same avoidance has applied to Manpower Incorporated and the transstellars associated with it . . . and to any effective enforcement of the laws against slavery and the slave trade. Our bureaucratic overlords' eyes were averted—but their palms were always outstretched.

It is not a popular position—not yet, at least—but in this reporter's opinion, the Grand Alliance's demand that the Solarian League summon a special convention and write a new Constitution that will prevent the reemergence of the politically unaccountable bureaucracy which gave us the Mandarins and their disastrous policies is not simply justified, but very much in the League's own interests. Lack

of accountability always engenders corruption. And cor-
ruption always engenders the abuse of power that allows
barbarisms like the genetic slave trade to flourish and,
in the flourishing, stain every citizen of the League with
blood guilt for one of the vilest institutions in the long,
dark history of human cruelty and corruption.

The central task of the Constitutional Convention will be
to prevent that corruption's regeneration, and this reporter is
confident that as a part of that task, its delegates will find
themselves compelled to grapple specifically with slavery and
the slave trade. I doubt if one could find a single delegate
to that convention who would say otherwise, and the vast
majority of them will be sincere in their determination. In
a very real sense, the slave trade—an execrable evil in its
own right—is also a focal point, a lens, the personification
of what that corruption allows. And, should any of the
convention delegates even consider not grappling specifically
with the slave trade, Catherine Montaigne's presence within
a few kilometers of their deliberations should certainly
stiffen their spines.

And so it ought to.

It is awkward, to put it mildly, to denounce the Grand
Alliance for its autocratic demand that we rewrite our most
fundamental law, or for its purported brutality during the
conquest of Mesa, when the people denouncing them belong
to a polity whose autocratic behavior and brutality toward
the immense populations of the Verge at the behest of giant
transstellars has been at least as bad. It seems...unlikely
that the Grand Alliance—or Catherine Montaigne—will
allow the Constitutional Convention or the League at large
to forget that, and well they should not.

Speaking of the Grand Alliance's purported brutality in
the Mesa System, this reporter has recently come into pos-
session of information which at the very least casts doubt
on Admiral Gold Peak's Tenth Fleet's responsibility for the
nuclear bombardment that blotted away millions of lives.
As the O'Hanrahan Report's listeners will be aware, I was
on Mesa at the time of that bombardment. And as those
same listeners will be aware, I have persistently questioned
the narrative of Manticoran and Havenite imperialism as

the driver of the war between the Grand Alliance and the Solarian League. Despite that, the initial evidence—or what seemed to be evidence—of the Grand Alliance's culpability in the Mesa Atrocity appeared overwhelming at the time. The new information which has come into my possession strongly counters that "evidence" of the Grand Alliance's responsibility, however. I intend to return to Mesa soon in order to investigate—

She paused. She hadn't actually made up her mind whether or not she was going to visit Mesa again, and her new "information" hadn't come from any Mesan source. What one of her many contacts within the Solarian military had actually provided to her was the analysis of the Mesa bombardment being advanced by Admiral Kingsford's new director of the Office of Naval Intelligence. The analysis was purely informal, with no official sanction or imprimatur, but given Dr. Gannon's apparent influence with the Chief of Naval Operations, it had to be taken very seriously.

And O'Hanrahan's problem was that she was almost certain Gannon was correct.

She'd never believed the Audubon Ballroom was responsible for the "terrorist" campaign which had preceded Tenth Fleet's arrival in Mesa. Her Alignment superiors wouldn't have sent her to cover it—wouldn't have known in advance that it was about to happen and would *need* to be covered—if the Alignment itself hadn't been involved. And, if she'd had any doubts about that, the way in which her Mesan itinerary had been shaped had resolved them. Besides, she had extensive contacts inside Mesa's intelligence agencies, which meant she'd known the Ballroom simply didn't have the resources in-system to carry out a campaign on that scale. A single incident like Green Pines... maybe. Her internal jury was still out on that one. She was willing to accept the possibility Ballroom terrorists might have been able to get their hands on one or two nuclear devices, and it was possible Green Pines *had* been their handiwork. Indeed, might well have provided the inspiration—and pretext—for the series of... copycat attacks she'd been sent to report.

But even accepting the possibility that the Ballroom had been involved in Green Pines, she'd never believed Gold Peak had ordered the nuclear strikes after her arrival. There'd been no logical reason for her to do it. The only theory anyone could give for why she *might* have ordered them was that the woman was a homicidal maniac. Or, at least, someone unable to control a ferocious temper under stress.

But nothing in the Manticoran admiral's history—O'Hanrahan had investigated her background—supported that notion. The woman who was Empress Elizabeth's first cousin, fourth in line for the Manticoran throne, wasn't going to murder millions of civilians and hand that sort of spiked club to the Grand Alliance's Solarian foes on a whim. And mere "stress" was... unlikely, to say the least, to change that. Besides, Gold Peak hadn't been *under* any stress. Her Tenth Fleet had already conquered Mesa. What was left of Mesa's government had been flat on its back, waving its paws in the air in abject submission. If there'd been a *less* stressful conquest of a star nation in the entire history of galactic warfare, O'Hanrahan had been unable to find it.

And if it hadn't been the Ballroom, and it hadn't been Tenth Fleet, that left only the Grand Alliance's explanation—that it had been O'Hanrahan's own Alignment. That explanation made far more sense than any other. So much sense that, in the end, O'Hanrahan had accepted it herself... privately of course.

She hadn't in the beginning, and not simply because she hadn't wanted to, for a lot of reasons, including the obscene death toll. She'd realized even then that that part of her response had been emotional, but it also hadn't been the only reason she'd rejected the entire notion. Just as in Gold Peak's case, she'd been unable to see any logical reason or motive for the Alignment. *Why* would it do something that savage?

She'd known for decades—had understood when she joined the Alignment as a teenager—that its leaders were capable of ruthlessness. But the leaders of every serious struggle in history had, of necessity, been ruthless. The Alignment's leaders were no different from dozens of examples she could have picked. The leaders of the democratic nations which had fought and defeated fascist tyrants a couple of centuries before the Diaspora, for example. They hadn't hesitated to subject their enemies to mass aerial bombardment—including incendiary raids and the very first use of nuclear weapons—that took more than two million lives at a time when there'd been little more than two *billion* humans in existence.

Once, there'd been no way to systematically address those problems. But that had ceased to be true centuries ago, given the steady development of genetic and biological science since the Diaspora, and that failure was no longer excusable. Limitations of the human genome were now enforced by nothing more than superstition, political misconduct, and cultural inertia. That was to say, by the very same factors which in the Ante Diaspora era had produced witch hunts, religious wars, pogroms—all manner of bestial conduct.

But while she could and did accept the ruthlessness that her cause at times found necessary, the operative word was *necessary*. The end, the objective—the *purpose*—must justify the ruthlessness. It must be worth the price that was paid, and it must never be paid *casually*. It must be justified morally, not simply pragmatically. And when the price was human lives, it must be paid only when there was no other option, no other coin by which the future could be purchased.

And the reason she'd found it so hard, initially, to accept the Alignment's responsibility for the nuclear strikes was that she'd been able to see no coherent motive. It had seemed like butchery for its own sake. Try though she might, she'd been unable to see any other motive—far less any other *justification*. That was something she'd never before seen from the leaders of her movement, and so she had been unable to believe that it had been them. Indeed, it might have been more accurate to say that she had *refused* to believe it had been them.

Until now.

No one had briefed her on any measures that might have been established to evacuate the Alignment's cadre from Mesa, yet she'd always understood—anyone in the Alignment's inner layers understood, simply by virtue of being very intelligent, if nothing else—that measures like that had to be in place. If there was one thing in which the Alignment believed, it was being prepared, and sooner or later it would almost inevitably be forced to evacuate Mesa. As an independent star nation, Mesa had never fallen under the protection of the Solarian League, and the misbehavior of its corporate leadership—especially Manpower's, although Manpower was scarcely alone—must eventually trigger nemesis. And if someone like, oh, the Grand Alliance, came along and conquered Mesa, the Alignment could never risk allowing its leadership to fall into the conquerors' hands. So, obviously, there must be a plan to extract that cadre safely and ahead of time.

And if Gannon was correct...if his theory that the retaliation had come so swiftly and powerfully that the Alignment had been caught off guard and only half prepared was accurate...

Even that couldn't explain or justify the Beowulf Strike, though.

The murder of over forty million civilians? Civilians who'd posed no threat to the evacuation of Mesa or to the Alignment itself. How in God's name did something like that fit into the Alignment's purpose and goals?

She didn't know the answers to those questions. What had happened on Mesa, yes. She could, now, accept that as the Alignment's handiwork. But Beowulf...that was hard. Indeed, she still didn't accept the Alignment's responsibility for that. The Grand Alliance might have assigned responsibility to the Alignment, and she could readily understand why it had, given everything else its members had endured. But the fact that the Alliance genuinely believed that didn't mean it was necessarily correct. God knew there were enough corrupt bureaucrats and transstellars with the reach to execute an atrocity like that because of their fury at Beowulf for supporting Manticore and the Grand Alliance from the outset. Indeed, she could have rattled off a list of over a dozen suspects, beginning with Volkhart Kalokainos at Kalokainos Shipping and extending through any one of the other shipping lines who'd suffered catastrophic losses as the Grand Alliance shut down the Solarian League's interstellar life's blood.

She suspected that one reason she found it so easy to construct that list was the very fact that she found it so impossible to construct an acceptable reason for the Alignment to have committed that atrocity. But that was no longer impossible where the *Mesa* Atrocity was concerned.

Yet she had to walk a very fine line here. On the one hand, maintaining—no, *enhancing*—her reputation as the galaxy's most reliable and incorruptible investigative reporter would be enormously beneficial to the Alignment, especially in the long run. On the other hand, how did she do that without persuading the galaxy that her Alignment was, indeed, an organization of savage mass murderers?

And little though she cared to admit it, even to herself, how did she do that when deep in the core of her own heart and soul she was still horrified by the sheer scale of what had happened on Mesa? However thoroughly she might grasp the pragmatic necessity of withdrawing their cadre to safety, how did the Alignment's leadership—how did any of the Alignment's members—square the moral balance of so many million deaths? Especially when she was still unable, desperately as she wanted to, to be *positive* her Alignment wasn't responsible for what had happened in Beowulf.

She sat, gazing at what she'd already written, for at least five minutes, then drew a deep breath.

She wasn't ready to tackle that particular problem. Not until she was certain in her own mind both of the accuracy of Gannon's analysis...and that she, Audrey O'Hanrahan, could accept that her Alignment had acted in accordance with its own purpose and standards. She wasn't certain of either of those, yet. And until she was...

She erased her final paragraph, deleted any mention of new information about Mesa, and finished with a short conclusion regarding Montaigne's likely behavior in the near future.

That done, she sent the piece off and headed for her bedroom to dress.

Delegates to the Constitutional Convention were still arriving from the Solarian League's more distant star systems. Size-wise, the League had much in common with a dinosaur, or perhaps an Old Earth blue whale. Even with hyper-bridges, it had taken literally months for even fast courier boats to reach some of those systems with news of the League's surrender. Then they'd had to select delegates—and hadn't *that* been a dogfight in some of them?—and then send the delegates back on the same months-long trip. It was actually remarkable that they'd been able to assemble enough of them for a quorum in "only" four months, and they still weren't prepared to start any serious constitution writing. They were, however, ready to at least approve—or reject, of course, politicians being politicians—the procedural guidelines the Provisional Government had proposed, and the Convention's first official session was scheduled for early afternoon. She wanted to be there when it convened. Actually, she wanted to get there *before* it convened in order to interview several of the more important delegates.

❖   ❖   ❖

Getting dressed was the source of some impatience and even more irritation.

When she'd returned to Old Chicago from Mesa, her handlers had informed her through one of their circuitous channels that they wanted her to employ the services of Whiting Security. They'd been quite emphatic about it.

Personally, she thought they were spooking at shadows. The Mesa-based transstellars she'd spent so many years infuriating had been routed, and with Attorney General Rorendaal and Simeon Gaddis breathing down their necks, the Solarian League's once-powerful bureaucracies had much greater worries than her. Oh, she probably still irritated the hell out of them, but they had far more pressing problems than her. With the Grand Alliance's intelligence agencies systematically dismantling the Mesan transstellars and Gaddis and Rorendaal turning over one rock after another, public exposés by one Audrey O'Hanrahan were far down their threat lists. She wasn't used to playing second-violin when it came to her work as an investigative journalist. But that was the way it was, at least for now, so it seemed . . . unlikely, to put it mildly, that anyone would waste resources on her assassination at a moment like this.

But her handlers had insisted. And while they issued such specific marching orders only rarely, they were very firm when they did—to the point of being obdurate.

So, good soldier that she was, she put on the protective garments Whiting had provided for her to wear whenever she went out in public.

That took a bit of time.

The "blazer" wasn't all that bad, actually. Not surprisingly, since it had to have cost a fortune. Its antiballistic smart fabric, guaranteed to stop anything short of heavy, military-grade pulser fire, was almost infinitely programmable for both color and cut. Loading the pattern for a tailored, single breasted jacket suitable for the day's cool temperatures and perfectly coordinated with her chosen pantsuit did take a little time, but it wasn't particularly difficult.

She could not say the same for the ridiculously elaborate contraption—why not just call it a chastity belt and be done with it?—she had to fit onto her abdomen underneath the "blazer." Adjusting *that* was aggravatingly awkward, to say the least. It was also uncomfortable.

And it made her look fat.

Eventually, though, she was equipped and sallied out of her apartment. To discover that her Whiting bodyguard had been standing right outside the door, waiting for her. For how long? She wondered, but she didn't ask.

She'd told the security service—rather firmly—that she did *not* need anyone guarding her apartment around the clock. They'd argued. She'd insisted. In the end, they'd given in...except that they hadn't. Instead, they'd "reached an understanding" with the tower's management to station someone permanently in the lift concourse for her floor. Officially, she didn't know anything about that, but she *was* one of the Solarian Leagues' star investigative reporters. On the other hand, she was under orders to use their services, so she couldn't kick them the hell out of her life. In fact, she couldn't even *argue* with them about it, because anyone who knew her knew she *wouldn't* have argued; she would just have fired them.

So they pretended they weren't watching her all night, and *she* pretended she didn't know they were doing it.

Sometimes she *hated* being a good soldier.

At least Michael Anderle, the bodyguard assigned for her close protection, had a sense of humor. And he might have been specifically ordered from Central Casting for the role of Intimidating Bodyguard. From his physical appearance and coloring, Anderle was of Samoan or some other Pacific island ancestry. He was also about two meters tall and must have weighed a hundred and sixty-five kilos, very little of which looked to be fat.

Well, if worse came to worst and she had a fainting spell, he could easily stuff her into a pocket and carry her home.

"I'm headed for League Plaza," she said, and he nodded.

"We have an air car waiting."

❖   ❖   ❖

O'Hanrahan would have been more inclined to call the large, heavily armored "air car" a pocket assault shuttle. But she refrained from wisecracks during the fifteen-minute flight to League Plaza. In her now-considerable experience with security services, she'd found that they had a sense of humor very like that of a sea urchin. That was to say, none at all.

The "Plaza" was actually an entire complex centered around Assembly Hall—a gorgeous, snowflake-shaped edifice of crystoplast, genuine marble, and polished alloy, set like a perfect, star-shaped gem into a spectacular park directly across League Avenue from George Benton Tower. It was far shorter than the tower—no more than sixty-five stories to the very top of its central spire—but it was perfectly integrated into the Plaza's landscaped grounds, statuary, walkways, and magnificent water features. And those landscaped grounds covered over fifteen square kilometers of *Old Chicago*, the most expensive real estate in the entire Solarian League.

Not even Audrey O'Hanrahan, who'd seen Assembly Hall more times than she could count, was immune to the Plaza's spectacular beauty. Built on what had been the western fringe of Old Chicago, following the Final War and the formal proclamation of the Solarian League, it had been intended from the outset as a fitting home for the capitol of the largest, wealthiest star nation in human history, and its designers had succeeded in their purpose. The Chamber of Stars at Assembly Hall's very heart was familiar to every Solarian schoolchild from HD and civics classes, but there was a difference between images, however spectacular, and the reality of thirteen centuries of governance. Of history. Of achievement and outreach.

Thirteen centuries which made what the League had eventually become even more contemptible, she thought, as the air car settled toward one of the Plaza's parking decks.

No, not contemptible. *Pathetic.*

She wondered how successful the Constitutional Convention would be in reclaiming the League's original soul. It was inevitable that it meet here, in the emblem of what the League had been and must become again, but its task was daunting. Of course, it was also—

"Got a problem, Michael," the driver said.

"What kind of problem?"

"Wave off from the parking deck." The driver tapped his earbud and shrugged. "Apparently some big muckety-muck just landed early and his security's squatting on our pad."

"Crap."

Anderle punched up a navigation app on his uni-link and scowled at it. Then it was his turn to shrug.

"Okay, if we can't land there, drop us at the Thurston-Holmes landing stage, instead."

"You got it."

The air car climbed slightly as it banked away, slotting into a different approach lane, and Anderle grimaced a bit apologetically at O'Hanrahan.

"Sorry about this, ma'am. I'm afraid we've got about a three-hundred-meter walk from the landing stage."

"I'm fairly sure I can hobble that far, even in my frail condition," she said dryly, and he snorted.

"Oh, I know." He'd been her bodyguard for more than a week now, which meant he knew just how briskly she would walk those three hundred meters. "It's just that it's all in the open and its sort of breezy out there today."

"Well, this *is* Old Chicago," she reminded him. She rather doubted that breeze had anything to do with his unhappiness, but she womanfully resisted the temptation to twit him about it. It was his job to worry about assassins, however silly it might be.

They disembarked, and the air car lifted away as they headed for the stairs to ground level. O'Hanrahan avoided the escalator and trotted briskly down the steps, confident that Anderle would have no problem keeping up with her. He might weigh three times what she did, but he was an athletic behemoth, and his strides were twice as long.

At the bottom of the stairs, she turned to her left, headed for the nearest slidewalk. It was about thirty meters away, and she reached into her pocket for her tablet and punched up the list of questions she intended to put to her prey once she had it properly cornered. She *probably* shouldn't think of her interviewees as "prey," she reminded herself, but she was pretty sure that was how they thought of themselves once she was finished with them. She certainly hoped it was, anyway!

Her lips twitched at the familiar thought as she scrolled through the questions. Now, should she start with—

A hydraulic-powered clamp closed on the back of her neck.

Her eyes flew wide as Anderle's hand drove her down to her knees—that *hurt*—and then flung her to the ground behind him. Impact drove the breath from her as she landed—hard—and the back of her head hit the ceramacrete. What the *hell*—?

Something whined. The sound was high-pitched and shrill, and for a moment, she couldn't place it. Then, as she stared up at Anderle's back, she saw his body being jolted by something—several times. Pulsers. That whine was *pulser fire!*

Her eyes flicked down, seeking its source, and saw a man and a woman advancing towards them. The man was in the lead, with a pulser in a two-handed grip. A pulser aimed at *her!*

The barrel looked as big as an old-fashioned drainpipe. Even as she thought that, a corner of her brain told her the thought was ridiculous. Pulser apertures were measured in a handful of millimeters. It couldn't possibly be as enormous as it looked!

But she had only a brief glimpse of it before Anderle went to one knee, interposing his huge body between her and the man trying to shoot her. Her bodyguard was jolted again, but now he was firing back. An instant later, she saw her would-be assailant stagger back into her field of vision. Blood pulsed from a wound in his chest—no, it was spilling down from his neck.

Behind him, the woman stepped to the side, looking for an angle from which *she* could shoot O'Hanrahan. Her pulser came up—

—and shot her accomplice in the back.

The man crumpled instantly as the wild shot took him down. O'Hanrahan had studied enough carnage in her journalistic career to know that sort of thing wasn't uncommon in close-quarter fights. But it wasn't going to save her, because the woman's nerves seemed to have settled. The pulser came to bear on O'Hanrahan, and an instant later, a hyper-velocity butcher knife sliced her right cheek apart. Blood flew everywhere, and her hand moved instinctively to cover the shredded flesh which had been her face.

Anderle tried to interpose himself again, but he'd been hit several times himself, and the damage slowed him. The woman fired again before he could shield O'Hanrahan.

She screamed as the first dart tore into her. Another hit her, and then a third, but all things considered, she was incredibly lucky. The killer's fire had gone wide again, ripping into O'Hanrahan's left leg. That was the good news. The bad news was that the darts came in at an acute angle, shredding flesh and shattering bone... and that the other woman was still shooting.

At that point, Audrey O'Hanrahan's world went mercifully black.

Oscar Cantrell Conference Room
Chamber of Stars
Old Chicago
Old Terra
Sol System

"AND WE'LL HAVE TO INCORPORATE A TIME LIMIT FOR REMARKS from the floor," Chong Chung-Ho said. "I don't expect that to be popular, but we'll simply have too many delegates for it to work any other way."

"Not popular will be putting it lightly, Chung-Ho," Jonathan Braunlich replied. "We're talking about writing an entirely new Constitution. A lot of our delegates are going to figure they have a right to have their comments—including their objections—on the record."

"Not to mention wanting their own time in the spotlight," Nasrin Khoshkam pointed out with a wry smile. "This is the political opportunity of a lifetime, and every one of our selfless fellow delegates will recognize that just as well as we do."

Chong snorted in amusement, but he also shook his head at her.

"Of course it is. But I don't think the Grand Alliance will be very happy if we waste a lot of time on nonessentials."

"Screw the Grand Alliance," Philippus Malherbe growled.

The delegate from Winepress possessed a personality that was naturally pugnacious, to say the very least, Chong reflected. And Winepress Transstellar, the biggest single corporation of his home system, had suffered catastrophic financial losses as a consequence of the Grand Alliance's commerce war against the League.

"The bastards may be able to dictate terms to us," Malherbe continued, "but I'll be damned if I spend time kissing their asses!"

212

"It's not about kissing anyone's ass, Philippus," Chong said. "It's about getting this Constitution written in some manageable length of time."

"Chung-Ho has a point. Whatever we do, it's going to take months, even after we assemble the entire Convention," Lidija Križanović, the Cooper System's senior delegate, put in. "I'm in favor of not keeping the entire League in limbo any longer than we have to, Philippus."

Chong nodded, both grateful for the support and irritated that what Križanović had just said was so obviously true. In some ways, it would be an enormous personal relief when they finally managed to assemble the entire Convention. At the moment, he was stuck with his position as Chairman of the Procedures Committee, and he could hardly wait to hand his current responsibilities off to the formally recognized chairman of the Convention.

Who, if he had his way, would be named anything but Chong Chung-Ho.

Malherbe glared at both of them. It would've been far simpler, or at least more efficient, to ease him off the committee. Unfortunately, Winepress lay only eighty-eight light-years from the Sol System, and it had gotten its Convention delegates selected with alacrity. Largely due, without doubt, to Winepress Transstellar's enormous in-system political clout. Winepress—both transstellar and system government, to the extent they were distinguishable from one another—was clearly determined to get its toe as firmly into the Convention's door as it could. Chong never doubted that Malherbe would have been just as big a pain on any of the other committees, but the Legislative Assembly had determined when it wrote the rules for delegate selection that seniority in the Convention would be determined by the date at which the various delegates presented their credentials in Old Chicago. And in fairness to Malherbe, Chong's native Theseus System was twelve light-years farther from Sol than Winepress, yet he'd arrived on Old Terra seventy-three hours before the Winepress delegation.

And it's probably better to have him over here than on the Rules Committee, Chong reflected. *Of course, they're having their own dogfights over there, aren't they?*

"Look," Braunlich said. "None of us is happy about having the Grand Alliance put a pulser to our heads to *make* us do this, Philippus. But, my God, man! Look at where the Mandarins got us." The Danube System delegate's expression was grim. "I hate how many people got killed, I hate all of the industrial and economic damage, but there hasn't been a real 'federal government' in T-centuries. There's been uncontrolled—and uncontrol*lable*—bureaucratic cronyism accountable to absolutely no one."

Malherbe's glare intensified. Winepress had done well for itself under that "bureaucratic cronyism," and he saw absolutely no reason why it should have been changed.

That was unfortunate, Chong thought, because whether or not the Convention was assembling under duress, Braunlich was right. This was something that should have been done long, long ago. At the latest, four or five T-centuries ago, about the time it became obvious that what its founders had envisioned as primarily a trade association with the *trappings* of a government had transitioned into an actual government without, unfortunately, the legislative oversight it required.

"I have to agree with Jonathan," Križanović said. "But whether he's right or not doesn't change the fact that the Grand Fleet isn't pulling out of the Sol System until we've got this thing written and ratified, Philippus. You may not like it. Hell, I may not like the fact that they've put 'a pulser to our heads'! But it's a little hard to see what else they could have done given the Mandarins' truly outstanding stupidity and ability to screw up by the numbers. Were they supposed to just let the League go on racking up the megadeaths?"

Her eyes were hard, touched with the fire of genuine anger. She and Malherbe had detested one another from the outset, and Chong hoped (without an enormous sense of optimism) that the personality clashes within his own committee didn't foreshadow what would happen once the entire Convention assembled.

"And I have to agree with Lidija's earlier point," he said now. "It's going to take T-months—*at least*—to write this damned thing even after we get a quorum in here and can actually begin drafting proposals. And the longer it takes, the longer the entire League is going to be in limbo, the longer the Grand Alliance is going to be in the Sol System, and the longer it'll be before we can start rebuilding the system infrastructure."

Malherbe looked even more wrathful, if that was possible, but he also jerked an angry nod.

"While I agree with you, obviously, Chung-Ho," Braunlich

said, "I think we need to be careful about what we propose when it comes to limiting floor time. The Rules Committee can cap each speaker's time, but I don't see a legitimate way to deny any delegate the right to speak from the floor."

"Most of the work's going to be done in committee," Križanović pointed out. "By the time it comes to the floor for a vote, the real nuts and bolts will already be pretty firmly in place, so by and large, anyone who speaks in debate on the floor is going to be speaking for or against committee decisions as draft items are presented. So maybe what we need to do is to restrict each system's delegation to a single speaker on the floor. Whoever they pick could speak for all of them, from a unified list of points to be made, within the time constraints set by the Rules Committee and the chairwoman. Wouldn't that tend to focus their comments? I'm thinking that they could designate a different speaker from the delegation whenever they wanted to, but they could only have one of them at a time during a 'working session.' When it's time to vote on final draft elements, we'd have to open it up a bit, of course, but even then—"

The conference room door opened abruptly, and Deepti Chandekar, one of the Landfall System's delegates, swept through it.

"Sorry I'm late," she said, and Chong's eyes narrowed. Chandekar was always a little on the flighty side, in his opinion. There was nothing wrong with her brain, and she'd already made several useful contributions to the Committee's work, but Landfall seemed to run to an excitable stereotype. This time, though, she seemed even more excited than usual.

"That's all right—" he began, but she cut him off.

"There's been a shooting!!"

The other committee members stiffened, looking at her in disbelief.

"Somebody just tried to murder Audrey O'Hanrahan right outside Assembly Hall!" she announced.

Ellery Hammett Hospital
City of Old Chicago
Old Terra
Sol System

SHE REMAINED UNCONSCIOUS FOR THE NEXT DAY OR SO WHILE her medical team went to work.

The facial wound was hideous but not life-threatening. Quick-heal could handle the damage readily enough, and while the reconstructive biosculpt might be extensive, it would also be routine. Regenerating the two teeth she'd lost would probably take longer than the surgery itself, unless she opted for prostheses, instead.

But her leg...

It had been hit by a total of four darts, and three of them had traveled lengthwise from just below her kneecap to a point just above midthigh. At their velocity, traveling on that trajectory, the result had been more than merely catastrophic. Her femur had been reduced to bone flakes, and the muscles around it had been totally destroyed.

There was no point trying to save a limb which had been that brutally damaged. All the doctors could do was amputate about twelve centimeters below the hip and prep her for regeneration.

✧   ✧   ✧

"Excuse me, Ms. O'Hanrahan," the private room's AI said, "but you have a visitor. If you're up to it, of course?"

O'Hanrahan looked up from her pad. She'd been conscious again for less than six hours, and she was still trying to catch up on what had happened to her. Personally, she didn't think much of the so-called newsies who'd covered the story. If *she'd* been reporting it, there'd have been a hell of a lot more details!

216

"Who is it?" she asked, her voice slurred by the immobilizing damage to her cheek.

"It's Hammond Whiting, Ms. O'Hanrahan," a human voice said before the AI could reply, and she frowned.

"Come in, Mr. Whiting," she invited, and a large, bluff, hearty-looking fellow stepped into the room.

"I came to personally apologize for letting this happen," he said. "There's no excuse for that, but in fairness to Anderle, it's *hard* to get weapons into League Plaza. Especially weapons like that." The owner and CEO of Whiting Security shook his head. "Good thing for you—and Anderle!—that they couldn't shoot straight, because both of them were using military-grade weapons. His body armor wasn't designed to handle that sort of firepower."

"How is he?" she asked quickly.

"He'll make it. He was in critical condition when they brought him in, but he responds really well to quick-heal." Whiting twitched a dour smile. "Good trait in a bodyguard. Be a while before he's back to work, though."

"Did they catch the woman?"

"No." Whiting shook his head. "No, she made a clean getaway. That part of it she didn't screw up, even if she did kill her own partner."

"Was she the one responsible for that? I think Michael shot him at least once."

"Yes, he did—twice. And either hit probably would've killed him. But the one that *did* kill him—almost instantly—came from his partner. *His* body armor wasn't that great to begin with, and her shot punched right through it. Blind bad luck, for him, where it hit, too. The dart cut his spinal cord and then perforated his heart. That's pretty much impossible to survive, even if you've got EMTs standing right there on the spot."

"Have they figured out who he was? Why he might have wanted me dead?"

"Who he was is fairly simple. His name was Avalon Huerta, and he had a police record as long as my arm. He'd never been convicted, but he was a suspect in three murders. All first-degree, all contract killings, the police think." Whiting shrugged. "A hired gun, in other words. If he'd survived, the police might have been able to get his employer's identity out of him. But probably not. Whoever it was has deep damned pockets, judging by the quality of the tech they were using—programmable nanotech to obscure their facial features and change their hair color, a full dermal appliqué that completely changed Huerta's complexion *and* masked any DNA traces he might have left behind. We assume his accomplice had the same tech, which is going to make it virtually impossible for anyone to ID her. The only reason the Old Chicago PD was able to ID Huerta was because it had his corpse to work with."

Whiting shook his head, his expression troubled.

"I'm not remotely prepared to suggest any names, Ms. O'Hanrahan, but whoever wants you dead is pretty clearly prepared to spend whatever it takes. And those kinds of people do their dirty work through cutouts. As sure as I'm standing here, Huerta never met with any of them—not directly—and with him dead and the woman vanished..." He shrugged again. "I'm afraid it's very unlikely we'll ever know who was behind it. Especially because—"

He hesitated, and she smiled more crookedly than the immobile state of her face alone could explain.

"Especially because the list of my enemies is longer than Huerta's police record," she finished for him.

"I'm afraid so." Whiting nodded, then grimaced as his unilink pinged. He looked down at it, then back at O'Hanrahan, with an apologetic expression.

"I really need to go deal with this," he said, lifting his wrist slightly. "But I wanted to see you as soon as I could. You're going to be in hospital for a while, Ms. O'Hanrahan. Regenerating a leg isn't something you do overnight. I've spoken with both the OCPD and the hospital administration, though, and we have a team in place to keep an eye on you. By the time you're able to leave, Anderle should be ready to resume his duties. Unless—" he cocked his head "—you'd rather I assign someone else to you? I can see where you might feel...let down, given where you ended up. He was supposed to keep you safe, after all."

He gestured at the bright, airy hospital room, and arched one eyebrow at her, but she shook her head quickly.

"He didn't keep me *intact*," she said, "but he did keep me *alive*—and at considerable cost to himself. From where I sit—or lie, at the moment—that's a pretty fair synonym for 'safe.' I'm fine with Michael as my bodyguard. In fact, I'd prefer it."

"Okay, then. Anderle it is."

Whiting nodded, then excused himself. To be honest, O'Hanrahan was glad to see him go. And not just because his energy level was exhausting as hell to an invalid.

She wondered if he'd been part of the plan. Probably not. He didn't seem all that intelligent.

But then, neither did Michael Anderle, and O'Hanrahan had no doubt he'd been at the very center of the plot. He had to have been. There was no way such a carefully orchestrated assassination attempt could have succeeded without him.

Could have *failed*, rather. She shook her head. The level of courage and fortitude required of Michael Anderle was breathtaking. He'd been willing to be severely injured himself—to come within a few millimeters of being killed. Or to *be* killed. Only a dedicated member of the Alignment would have agreed to that. The woman had to have been part of it, too, and O'Hanrahan felt confident Michael's armor had been unobtrusively enhanced. But Huerta wouldn't have been party to any of it, and any one of his shots might have been fatal, despite Michael's forewarning or any upgrades to his armor.

As Whiting had said, Huerta was just a hired gun. More precisely, he'd been just a hired patsy.

She smiled, slightly, derisively, wondering if any of the people who'd planned this had expected her to be fooled by the charade.

The woman who couldn't shoot straight.

To the contrary. That woman, whoever she was, had to be one of the Alignment's finest shots. Every dart she'd fired had been dead on target. The first one, killing her accomplice . . . that one had kept Anderle alive and made sure Huerta could never be interrogated.

Then, the shot that had ripped O'Hanrahan's own face open. She reached up, touched the bandages protecting the healing wound. If they'd been removed, her exposed face would be hideous—and she didn't doubt for a second that plenty of images of its original, gory horror had been captured by security cameras, passersby (there were *always* passersby with uni-link cameras), police forensic teams, and any newsy within five kilometers of the shooting. By now, they'd undoubtedly been distributed all over the Sol System—in fact, she'd seen some of them on her own pad before Whiting turned up—and were headed out to the rest of the galaxy. The more reputable sites wouldn't display them publicly, but there were tons of others that would put them up in an instant.

And then, after the face—the shots that had destroyed her left leg. She was certain just as many images of that shredded limb were also headed out to the galaxy at large.

Horrible, terrible wounds. Which—talk about blind luck—didn't actually threaten her life and wouldn't even significantly impede her activities as an investigative reporter. In fact, they'd probably enhance her ability to work, once she was sufficiently recovered. Fearless, intrepid Audrey O'Hanrahan—forced to limp around in a powered chair, poor thing. One of her legs destroyed, but her mind—both hands, too—still as good as ever while she proved no assassination attempt would cow *her*. Who could possibly *not* believe in the integrity of a reporter like that?!

She took a slow, deep breath and let it out just as slowly, forcing herself to exhale her anger with the breath.

Be a good soldier. She could hardly be philosophical about the Alignment's ruthlessness and then whine when that same ruthlessness was applied to her. As long as it was for a good purpose.

Which . . . she'd allow that it had been. Maybe not necessary, exactly. But there was no doubt in her mind that, after two previous attempts on her life—both of which she had escaped totally unharmed—this bloody near-murder would cement her reputation. There wasn't a door in the explored galaxy that would be closed to her, and no one would ever question the impartiality of her work or her conclusions.

Not in the Core, in the Shell, or in the Verge.

And not in the Grand Alliance.

Fearless, intrepid Audrey O'Hanrahan.

What the hell, why not? Her face would heal and be repaired, soon enough. And eventually, she'd have her leg back, too.

❖   ❖   ❖

O'Hanrahan's next visitor was a surprise.

"I won't stay long," Catherine Montaigne said.

The Manticoran crusader-cum-politician took a few seconds to study her, then shook her head.

"You look like shit," she pronounced. "You have my deepest sympathy—really you do. I just wanted to drop by for two reasons. First is to express my admiration for the work you've done.

We've never met, but I've been a fan of yours for years. Second, to indignantly deny that anyone would even suggest that my trip to Old Terra had any official sanction from the Star Empire's government and was anything other than an expression of my long-standing commitment to and leadership role in the fight against genetic slavery."

O'Hanrahan laughed. She tried to, anyway. It came out more like a croak.

"You saw my piece," she said, and Montaigne grinned.

"Oh, sure. I read or watch anything of yours I come across. As usual, your logic was impeccable. All wrong, mind you. But impeccable."

"Really?" O'Hanrahan studied her for a moment. Then—

"Give me a straight answer," she said abruptly. "Did Manticore do it?"

"How would I know?" Montaigne spread her hands. "I'm not in the Grantville Government, I'm not in the military, and I wasn't there when it happened. What I think, though, is that the charge is ridiculous. For any number of reasons. First, Manticore has no history of that kind of savagery. Not any of its administrations, even that swine High Ridge's, ever did anything like that. Second, neither has Michelle Henke—and I've known her personally since she was about four years old. Third, there was no reason to do it. Fourth, her entire staff and every one of her ship commanders would've had to acquiesce in the order, and all of her subordinates, throughout the entire fleet, would have to have kept their mouths shut afterward. Which is simply impossible. Manticoran officers are trained to refuse unlawful orders. If nothing else, at least one of them would have ratted her out. Fifth, she would have had to convince her *Havenite* subordinates to participate, and not even the *People's* Republic of Haven ever carried out a strike like that. It did some pretty awful things; orbital strikes on surrendered planets *wasn't* one of them, Sixth—"

She broke off.

"I could go on and on. But the final reason is the simplest of all. My boyfriend Anton Zilwicki is the shrewdest intelligence operator in the entire galaxy, and he tells me we didn't do it. That's good enough for me, leaving aside everything else."

"So you buy the Grand Alliance's theory that this 'Alignment' they talk about was responsible."

"How would I know?" Montaigne spread her hands again. "I'm not even the galaxy's most incompetent intelligence operator. What I do know is that my boyfriend—I did laud his talents in this area, right?—and his partner Victor Cachat, who is probably the second shrewdest intelligence operator in the whole galaxy, are the ones who came up with the theory in the first place. So, yes. I accept their opinion."

"But even if you assume this 'Alignment' exists, why would they have done it? Everything, I mean—not just the 'Mesan Massacre.'" O'Hanrahan waved one hand. "According to Duchess Harrington and the Grand Alliance, the Alignment was also behind the Yawata Strike *and* the Beowulf Strike, and I can't see any logical motive for that, either. Not for what happened at Beowulf, anyway."

"Why does it have to be logical?" Montaigne asked. "Whoever the Alignment is, the one thing that's sure and certain about them is that they're vicious bastards. Probably, they just got pissed because Michelle upset the applecart in Mesa and decided to murder forty-odd million people to get even with her."

"But—"

O'Hanrahan broke off. She didn't accept the Alignment's responsibility for the Beowulf Strike—she couldn't—but it suddenly occurred to her that there might be a way to thread the needle. The true danger to the Alignment wasn't the charge that it consisted of murderous savages. It was the possibility that others—like Charles Gannon—could figure out they'd gone into hiding and used the "Mesa Massacre" to cover their tracks. But if she started—very tentatively, at first—advancing the notion that something that *resembled* the "Alignment" the Grand Alliance talked about did indeed exist, and was in fact a pack of monsters—the sort of psychopaths capable of such wholesale slaughter...

It was worth thinking about.

But not now.

Fortunately, she didn't have to figure out how to get Montaigne to leave. The Manticoran was already heading for the door.

"I'll let you rest," she said. "Keep up the great work."

✧　　✧　　✧

Michael Anderle came to visit two days later.

She was surprised to see him in a counter-grav chair. Not

because his own injuries didn't warrant the device, but because she wondered where they'd found one large enough to fit him.

Her puzzlement must have registered with him, because he smiled and patted the armrest.

"It's mine. I had it made specially a few years back. This isn't the first time I've been shot up."

He folded his hands in his lap and gave her a solemn sort of look.

"I'm sorry I couldn't stop the whole thing cold. Being honest about it, I was caught a little off guard."

"Would you have been able to stop it if you *hadn't* been a little off guard?"

"Probably...not. The people who initiate a shootout always have the advantage. But I think I could have reduced your injuries, at least."

She shook her head.

"I'm not losing any sleep over it. What's done is done, and it would've been a hell of a lot worse if not for you. Don't think I'm unappreciative."

He nodded. But then a little smile, one that might have been called just a bit sly, crossed his face.

"One of the things I like about this chair, by the way, is that it's big enough for me to cart around some really good anti-surveillance gear," he told her.

"How good?"

"Well, *damned* good, actually."

"In that case—" she looked him in the eye "—how about we don't do that again?"

Anderle's smile widened, and it was now definitely sly.

"I told them you'd figure it out." He shook his head. "And you don't have to lose any sleep over that, either. Some things you only do once, because they'll only work once."

"Okay." It was her turn to nod.

"No hard feelings?"

"Well, I'm not feeling all warm and squishy at the moment. But...no. We're good."

Alexia Gabon Tower
City of Mendel
Mesa
Mesa System

KAYLA BARRETT HAD NO IDEA WHO ALEXIA GABON MIGHT HAVE been, although she suspected Gabon had been another of the historical heroines of the ASL, given that Collin McLeod Tower, the onetime headquarters of the Internal Security Directorate, had been renamed in her honor. That had offered fuel for a few nervous qualms as she rode the lift shaft to the tower's top floor. But the first thing she noticed when she was ushered into the office of the newly appointed director of the newly created Mesan Unified Magistral Police was the very comfortable looking arrangement of two armchairs and a divan in one corner of the spacious room.

The man sitting in one of the armchairs rose as she entered and gestured toward the other two pieces of furniture.

"Please," he said. "Have a seat wherever you'd like, Sergeant Barrett."

She felt the tension in her shoulders ease a little. Between the seating arrangement—this wasn't how a cop grilled somebody, as she knew from her own experience doing the grilling—and the use of her rank, she understood that the man who'd summoned her here was trying to put her at ease. The rank was nothing more than a polite fiction, of course, given that her previous outfit had been the Mesan Internal Security Directorate, to whom Collin McLeod Tower had once belonged. And which had recently been disbanded.

Disbanded with extreme prejudice, one might say.

She limped across the office. She no longer needed her crutches, despite the fact that she was one of those unfortunate souls who

224

responded poorly to the regeneration therapies, but the cane still came in handy. It took her a while to get there, but then she settled into the other armchair. They faced one another as the director resumed his own seat, and she took a moment to study the man.

The man being the now famous Saburo Lara, formerly Saburo X—one of Jeremy X's top subordinates. For someone from Barrett's background, this was a bit like meeting Satan would have been for someone from a Judeo-Christian background.

Well... like meeting Beelzebub or Moloch, anyway. Satan himself would be Jeremy X.

She couldn't say he wasn't what she'd expected, because she'd had no idea what to expect. She wouldn't have been completely astonished to discover that Director Saburo had cloven hooves, horns, and a tail.

But...

He didn't. She was sure about the horns, because his hair was close cropped and there was nowhere they could have been hidden. She was almost as sure about the feet, because she could see his shoes and she didn't think any kind of hooves could have fitted into them. The tail... maybe, but she didn't think it was likely.

First, because he seemed to be sitting completely at his ease in the armchair, which she'd think would be awkward for someone with a tail. Mostly, though, it was because he just plain didn't look like a devil. And didn't seem to be acting like one, either.

He was taller than she was, by perhaps eight centimeters. Given that she was only a hundred and seventy centimeters, that made him a bit shorter than the average male. Average Mesan full citizen male, that was. Slaves—former slaves—varied a lot when it came to height and weight.

His physique wasn't exactly stocky, but she suspected there was plenty of muscle hidden under the loose garments he favored. He'd probably looked pretty good in the new uniform of the MUMP, because the green would match his eyes and go well with his almost bronze skin color.

She wondered why he wasn't wearing that uniform. Was its absence a statement on his part? She felt herself relax a bit further at that possibility. Perhaps Saburo actually intended to run the MUMP as a police agency rather than a paramilitary organization like the MISD had been.

"How's it coming along?" he asked, nodding toward her right leg.

"Pretty well." She looked down at the supportive brace that swelled her pants leg. "The doctors seem satisfied with the progress, anyway. I can't say regeneration was a lot of fun, though. And the PT's almost worse."

"Done a bit of that myself, in my time," he told her with a nod, then cocked his head. "And what about the flashbacks? Are you still having them?"

"What—?" She stared at him in astonishment. "How do you know about that?" she demanded.

"I'm allowed to vet people within limits, and one of those limits includes basic information on their mental state, as long as I'm not prying into their personal lives. It was blindingly obvious even from the little your therapist was willing to tell me that you've got a bad case of post traumatic stress disorder. I got the feeling, although she wouldn't come right out and say it, that she's frustrated with you, too. PTSD *is* quite treatable, these days."

He leaned back and brought his clasped hands to rest on his chest as she half-glared at him.

"I know, because I needed treatment myself," he told her. "I didn't get it for years because of . . . let's call it my itinerant lifestyle. So I couldn't tell you how many times I had that flashback—that nightmare."

His expression remained calm, but it seemed to get a lot colder.

"The man I killed richly deserved it. He was one of Manpower's executives who handled what they called 'slave behavior.' I'm sure you're familiar with what that term entails?"

He held her gaze, his own eyes still mild but unyielding, until she nodded. She did know, and the difference between what someone like that did and torture was . . . completely nonexistent, really. He looked at her for another moment, then drew a deep breath and nodded in turn.

"I broke into his personal quarters and shot the piece of shit dead in his own bed," he resumed. "I didn't hurt his wife—she was lying right next to him—because she wasn't directly implicated in anything. It didn't bother me at all to listen to her screaming, though. I can tell you that. Music to my ears, really. But when I turned to leave, there was a little girl standing in the doorway."

He took another deep breath.

"I guess she was . . . five T-years old. The expression on her face, looking up at me . . ."

The next breath was deeper still.

"Let's just say it got fixed in my memory like it was cemented there. I have no idea how many times I saw that face afterward. Awake, asleep—it could come at any time. Usually accompanied by sweat and my heart pounding."

He unclasped his hands and lowered them back to his chair's armrests.

"So, Sergeant. What's *your* memory?"

She started to snarl that it was none of his damned business. But . . .

Something in that bronze face's matter-of-fact expression calmed her. The wisdom of explaining to one of the Audubon Ballroom's half-dozen most notorious assassins that the reason she had a severe case of PTSD was because she'd murdered a seccy woman after watching her fellow Misties butcher a bunch of seccy children in the cruelest way imaginable was . . . counterintuitive.

But . . .

She shrugged mentally. Someone with his background might be angry, but he wouldn't be shocked.

"It happened during the fight to seize Hancock Tower," she said. "Before the seccy bastards . . . uh, the opposition, dropped the floor on us, but we'd already taken a lot of casualties on the way in. And then we came across a dozen seccy schoolkids hiding inside a parking garage along with a couple of teachers." She took a deep breath of her own. "I was the sergeant in command. I ordered them to come out—which they did—and then . . . Then a couple of my troopers opened fire on them. They were using—"

Her face tightened.

"Neural disruptors?" he asked, and she nodded. He nodded, as well. "What you'd expect from Misties. A lot of them anyway." He gazed at her levelly. "Did you use a disruptor?"

"No." She shook her head. "I never liked the damned things. And I didn't kill any of the kids myself. I would've tried to stop it, in fact. But . . ."

"But it was all over in seconds."

"Yeah. Not more than a handful, at most. Seemed like it lasted forever, though."

"Always does, with disruptors. The killing takes no time at all, but the dying takes a lot longer."

She was silent. His gaze remained fixed on her as perhaps a dozen seconds trickled into eternity.

"There's something you're not telling me," he said then.

She sat silent for another long, still moment, then closed her eyes.

"One of the teachers was still alive. Kneeling right in front of me—too close for the troopers to use disruptors on her. She looked up at me—"

Her eyes opened, meeting his almost imploringly, but she could go no farther. She literally *couldn't.*

"So you shot her," Saburo said quietly. "Killed her."

Kayla nodded. His face blurred as the tears welled into her eyes, and for the thousandth time—who knew how many times it had really been?—she saw that other face again. The face she was pretty sure would be the last thing she saw in the final seconds of the day she died.

Saburo rose. He crossed to his desk, then came back and handed her a tissue before he resumed his seat.

"You need to see a trauma specialist," he said. "I can recommend several. That's not advice, by the way. That's an order. I don't need an assistant who's periodically disabled by PTSD."

"*Assistant?*" She'd been staring at the far wall, but now her eyes snapped back to him.

"Yes, assistant. That's why I summoned you here." He tilted his head slightly. "Didn't you wonder about that?"

"Some." She gave a little shrug. "But it didn't seem to matter to me, one way or another. That's because . . ." She shrugged again.

"Nothing seems to matter to you much, one way or another."

"No. Not any longer."

"Well, that's got to stop, too." He leaned forward, planting his elbows on his knees and relacing his fingers together. "We've got a very tough job ahead of us, ex-Sergeant Barrett. We've got to create a police force for Mesa that most of its citizens can regard with a reasonable amount of trust and confidence. That includes its former full citizens. For that, I need at least one of my top subordinates to be a former full citizen herself—*and* a former Misty. A former noncom, ideally. Someone who'd wielded authority but wasn't too prominent."

He un-laced his fingers, leaned back in his chair, and smiled widely.

"You're just about perfect—and you come highly recommended. In a grudging sort of way, but that's to be expected."

"Recommended?" She frowned. "By who?"

"The people who captured you. Who else? They got a pretty good look at you while you were a prisoner. And General Palane had some good words, too." His smile was quite thin, this time. "I wouldn't call them *kind* words, but she's not inclined to do that with anybody. They were still good. She's the one who first recommended you, in fact."

Kayla tried to wrap her mind around the idea that General Thandi Palane would have done anything like that. Her mind fell away, its limbs flailing helplessly. It was like trying to imagine an ancient dinosaur—a theropod, not a plant eater—doing anything other than devouring the landscape.

Palane was the most intimidating person Kayla had ever met. She'd never raised her voice once in Kayla's presence, or made any sort of threatening gesture, glare—anything. But then, Kayla didn't imagine a Tyrannosaurus rex had ever glared at anyone, either. Why bother—when you've got thirty-centimeter fangs and a bite force that would have petrified an Old Earth crocodile?

"So, what do you say?" Saburo asked.

Kayla discovered that she was having a hard time wrapping her mind around the entire situation. Her—working for *Saburo X*?

Fine. Saburo *Lara*. Big difference. How could she possibly explain it to—

Her mind stumbled. To her family? She didn't have one anymore, except for a few cousins she barely knew. And her mother, but they'd been estranged for years. The only ones she'd still been close to had been her brother and sister and their children. But they'd all been killed in the Blue Lagoon Park terrorist incident.

That was something her mind could latch onto.

"There's no way I'm agreeing unless you assign me to investigate what happened at Blue Lagoon Park," she said flatly.

There. That ought to put an end to the whole business. But Saburo surprised her yet again.

"That's what I was thinking myself," he said. "Not just Blue Lagoon, either. I want you involved in the investigations of *all* the terrorist incidents, starting with Green Pines and continuing through the wave of nuclear detonations after the liberation."

She thought about disputing the term "liberation," but the thought vanished almost as soon as it formed. First, it was a moot point now. Secondly, she understood exactly how someone like Saburo would see it that way. In some ways, she was starting to herself.

"Why?" she asked, instead.

"It's kind of the whole point. Especially in the short run. Look, we both know about my Ballroom background. Because of that, I *know* the Ballroom wasn't involved. But *you* don't, and a big percentage of the population of Mesa will never accept any explanation of those killings as the work of anyone except the Ballroom and the Grand Alliance—unless they have some reason to think the investigation wasn't purely partisan. And there's no better way to indicate it wasn't than to have an officer of the MUMP right in the middle of the inquiry who was—"

"First," he held up his thumb, "a full citizen at the time they happened.

"Second," his forefinger came up to join the thumb, "an ex-sergeant in the MISD.

"And, third," the middle finger came up, "someone who suffered the loss of most of her family in one of the killings."

He lowered his hand.

"And before you ask me how you can be sure I won't impede your investigation, the answer is that you can't—now. But you will be able to by the time you're done. That's not something you can be fooled about."

He was right about that. Which was what finally settled the issue for her. She *wanted* to find out who'd murdered her family. And if that took supping with the devil, so be it.

"All right," she said. "On one condition."

"What's that?"

"If we ever wind up eating together, don't complain if I insist on using a long spoon. A really long spoon."

"It's a deal. Although—" he chuckled "—I'm not sure anyone makes extra-long spoons."

"If I have to, I'll have it made special. So when do I start?"

"Right now, Lieutenant Barrett." He rose and extended a hand to help her out of the chair, but she ignored it. That was probably rude, but she'd look silly if she accepted a helping hand from the devil right after insisting on supping with a long spoon in his presence.

She managed well enough on her own. Judging from the small smile on Saburo's face, he wasn't offended, anyway.

She had a feeling that very few things would offend or anger her new boss. She also had a feeling that Saburo Lara was going to turn out to be a very *good* boss. Maybe the best she'd ever had. Which was the most unsettling feeling she'd had since she walked into the room.

"Do I need a uniform?" she asked, leaning on her cane.

"Fairly soon, yes. But not today. Today we're going to pay a very unofficial visit on some people whose affairs will be... intersecting with ours. Civilian clothes are the order of the day."

"What people?" she asked.

"You'll see."

Neue Rostock Tower
City of Mendel
Planet Mesa
Mesa System

"DAMN. THIS LOOKS LIKE HOME. EVEN BETTER, SOME WAYS!
Enkateshwara Tower wasn't actually *designed* to confuse people
and get them lost. It just seemed that way because of the clutter
everywhere. But this!" Daud ibn Mamoun al-Fanudahi nodded
at the door through which they'd just entered the room in Neue
Rostock tower. "*This* actually makes me feel right at home!"

"Ignore him," Natsuko Okiku said. The lieutenant colonel
headed toward the large, very modern conference table in the
center of the room. "He's got a fetish about being invisible to
bureaucrats and flag officers."

"That's not a fetish." Victor Cachat shook his head. "That's
just common sense."

"Does it matter where we sit?" Okiku asked.

"No," Anton Zilwicki said. He was on his way around the
table himself. "Just let me have the seat at that end—" he pointed
to the far end "—because it's got the main control console."

Cachat sat at the same end of the table, on the long side to
Zilwicki's left. Arianne McBryde sat down across from him. Irene
Teague sat next to her, and al-Fanudahi took the seat on the
opposite side. Major Tarkovsky took the one at the far end, facing Anton, even though there were still empty seats on the long
sides of the table. The Marine had the sort of personality that
automatically gravitated toward the far end of conference tables.

"Let me start by saying that this meeting is completely informal and unofficial." Zilwicki waved a hand at their surroundings.
"This conference room doesn't officially exist either, by the way.

232

It's shown on the tower's schematics as a linen closet"—he pointed over Tarkovsky's shoulder "—about fifteen meters that way."

"Oh, wow," al-Fanudahi murmured, looking more cheerful by the moment.

"Finally," Zilwicki continued "the suppressive anti-surveillance equipment in this room is top-of-the-line. I chose it and installed it myself. Nobody outside that door—" he pointed at the room's *only* door "—will hear anything we say in here. No one out there will be able to make records of any kind, and neither will anyone actually in the room."

"Why the secrecy?" Arianne frowned. "I'd think you'd want the records of an investigation like this to be available to the public."

"They will be, eventually," Cachat said. "The results of them, at least—and they'll be honest results. We have no intention of cooking the books, so to speak. But we also have to be able to talk to each other with complete candor, and you just can't do that when you know everything you're saying is being recorded for posterity."

"He's right about that, Ms. McBryde," Okiku said. "If nothing else, the confidentiality of sources and methods has to be maintained. In fact—"

"*In fact*," Tarkovsky interrupted her, "if I wasn't satisfied that was true, I'd get up and leave right now."

Arianne still looked uncertain, but she nodded in acquiescence.

"So where do we start?" Teague asked.

"We start—" Zilwicki broke off when a buzzer sounded from the doorway.

"What the hell?" he muttered, then gave Cachat an accusing glance as the Havenite came to his feet.

"I wasn't sure he'd show up. But, yes. I invited him."

By the time Cachat finished the sentence he was at the door. He opened it.

"Come in, Director," he said, stepping aside as Saburo Lara entered the room. "And this would be Kayla Barrett," he added as a woman followed Saburo. "Formerly a sergeant in the Mesan Internal Security Directorate."

"But now a lieutenant in the Mesan Unified Magistral Police," Saburo said. "Under whose jurisdiction, by the way, this meeting is taking place." He grinned. "Unofficially of course, but if anyone finds out, which is most unlikely"—he nodded toward

Zilwicki "—given who's running the counter surveillance, that's your cover. If it goes pear-shaped, you can blame me."

He'd walked around the table to an empty chair on its far side as he spoke. Now he pulled it out and sat. Moving more slowly on her cane, Barrett took the seat opposite him.

"In that case, I propose you chair this meeting," Zilwicki said.

"Seeing as how you're officially in charge of it, and all," Cachat chimed in. Al-Fanudahi didn't know the man, so he couldn't be certain, but his expression held a subtle suggestion of amusement. Cachat had blue eyes and blond hair and was extraordinarily handsome—far more than you'd expect from an intelligence officer. Al-Fanudahi wondered if any of that was due to biosculpt. Normally, that process would be applied the other way for someone in Cachat's line of work, where being too good-looking—and eye-catching—was a distinct handicap.

Either way, the Havenite's appearance suggested a streak of vanity that seemed at odds with his reputation.

Saburo glanced at Cachat, then shrugged.

"I suppose you're right. Very well. Let the meeting come to order. Now that that's done, Anton, you have the floor."

"I think we should start by hearing from everyone who has a theory about who's responsible for the mass killings on Mesa, beginning with the Green Pines Incident, as well as their motive." Zilwicki nodded toward Cachat. "Victor and I have one. Does anyone else?"

He looked around the table, his gaze stopping for a moment at each of the people who'd arrived from Old Terra.

"I don't know that I'd go so far as to call what we think a 'theory,'" al-Fanudahi said, "since there's nothing very definite about our conclusions yet. So why don't we start with yours?"

"All right." Zilwicki nodded. "What Victor and I think is behind all this is something that began six T-centuries ago—almost eight, if you go back to first causes. Because at the heart of it, it's about the Beowulf Code's position on the genetic improvement of humanity, and that position grew out of Old Earth's Final War. A lot of things came out of the Final War, but this... problem, in particular, grew out of something a bit farther down the road: the dispute between Leonard Detweiler and the Beowulf medical establishment over the manipulation of the human genome. 'Manipulation' is what the establishment called it; Detweiler's own term was 'enhancement,' and their disagreement was fundamental and bitter.

"The establishment was determined to preserve the prohibitions put in place by the Beowulf Code. *Detweiler's* view was that the Final War had happened—and the League had been founded—almost two hundred T-years before he was even born. Under the circumstances, he felt it was time to . . . re-examine those prohibitions. The establishment disagreed, and the dispute got increasingly public and increasingly virulent. When it couldn't be resolved, Detweiler and his adherents left Beowulf and settled here on Mesa.

"Detweiler made his views and intentions very clear at that time, and since he did, I think I can safely say that he would *not* have approved of the direction genetic science and engineering here on Mesa took after his death. But while the people who initially settled Mesa had a lot of financial resources, and a lot of scientific acumen, they were short on manpower. So Detweiler founded Manpower Incorporated to produce cloned colonists to provide the necessary labor force.

"Even before the move to Mesa, he'd been involved in 'enhancing' colonists for hostile environments. That had been standard, unchallenged practice before the Final War. *After* the war, and after the true horror of some of the genetically modified super soldiers had time to percolate, even that form of 'enhancement' was pretty much anathematized. Obviously, there were a lot of existing modification packages that were grandfathered in, but no *new* ones were entertained for quite some time.

"Detweiler thought that was even stupider than most of the establishment's concerns. In fact, he'd defied the general bias against the practice by providing that sort of enhancement—which wasn't, *quite*, illegal—even before he left Beowulf. So in addition to cloning workers for use right here in Mesa, he continued to offer enhancement for hostile environment colonies. In fact, for the next T-century or so, Mesa was effectively the *only* place in the galaxy where that capability was maintained and offered, and the Beowulf establishment wasn't happy about that. In fact, there's quite a bit of evidence to suggest that one reason Detweiler and the original iteration of Manpower were so aggressive about marketing their services was his bitterness about Beowulf's rejection. It was a way for him to put a thumb in the establishment's eye while simultaneously providing a service that—to be fair—the galaxy pretty much needed.

"But on Mesa, the clones—which, after all, had been manufactured specifically to provide a labor force—were regarded as indentured servants. That, too, was a violation of the Beowulf Code, and a considerably bigger one. Under the Code, clones are no different from any other human being in the eyes of the law. They have exactly the same legal rights, and the Code specifically prohibits their indentureship. There are several reasons for that, but the most fundamental is that since no clone has ever asked to be born, it is immoral, as well as illegal, to compel them to repay a debt they never chose to assume.

"Mesa saw things differently, and, again, I suspect it was Detweiler giving the Beowulf establishment the finger. I say that because, during his lifetime, he made damned sure Mesan clones weren't slaves. They were fully expected to earn their freedom over time and become Mesan citizens. Which almost all of them did, during Detweiler's day. Nor were they considered *second-class* citizens after they did. Not at first.

"But some of the other interests, especially the big transstellars that had really started to hit their stride a T-century or so after the creation of the League—which, after all, was envisioned more as a trade union than a true central government, at the time—were more concerned with bottom lines and less concerned about any niggling little moral issues. They, too, considered the colonists Detweiler and Manpower provided them as 'indentured servants'...officially. In fact, however, a steadily increasing number of them had no intention of allowing their 'servants'—or their servants' *children*—to earn or purchase their freedom."

His deep, rumbling voice paused for a moment, and he shook his head, his expression grim.

"That's how genetic slavery started. The shortcuts that led to shortened lifetimes, the development of specialized types like pleasure slaves, the view that they were somehow less than fully human—none of that happened while Detweiler was still alive and in charge. But even though that's clearly not what he ever intended, he and his supporters *were* the ones who enabled the monstrous cancer that's chewed up and spat out so many millions—*billions*, even trillions—of lives over the T-centuries.

"And after his death, things started to change pretty quickly.

The history gets murkier at this point, but there seems to have been a falling out among Detweiler's heirs, and the ones who came out on top started moving Manpower more directly toward what it eventually became. And as Manpower climbed ever farther into bed with the sort of transstellars who believed in slavery, Mesa became a haven for transstellar corporations. One that was especially attractive to the corporations most enamored of corruption as a profit driver. Over the next hundred T-years or so, genetic slavery emerged as a full-blown, galaxy-wide institution—even if the 'proper sorts' condemned it—and Mesa became the galaxy's most diversified headquarters for corrupt transstellars. Don't get me wrong. There are other star systems and even star nations out there that are effectively wholly owned 'company towns.' Technodyne of Yildun comes to mind, for example. But Mesa offered...an interface where corruption could always find other corruption when it needed it."

He stopped and looked at Arianne McBryde.

"Is that a fair summation?" he asked, and she nodded.

"Yes. But—"

"Give me a moment," he interrupted, holding up a hand, and turned back to the other people around the table.

"That development didn't go unchallenged," he told them. "A considerable number of Mesa's citizens—in particular, the descendants of the Detweiler heirs who wound up on the short end of the stick—took exception to Manpower's activities, as well as a number of the policies of Mesa's corporate government. When their protests were ignored, they founded an organization called the Alignment, which was devoted to genetic enhancement, yes—but all done within the constraints of law and on a purely voluntary basis. They specifically called for making Manpower's genetic slavery illegal."

He looked at Arianne again. She straightened a bit in her chair and nodded.

"Okay. I just wanted that included."

"But by that point," Zilwicki continued, "the transstellars who now effectively controlled Mesa were too powerful to dislodge. And they had no problem at all with Manpower's activities. First, because even that far back some of them were almost certainly owned by Manpower. Through cutouts of various kinds, of course, so the relationship wasn't visible."

"Jessyk," Tarkovsky grunted.

"Jessyk, almost certainly," Zilwicki agreed. "There were others, though, and Manpower had a financial interest even in most of those it didn't own. It was an incestuous relationship, with virtually all of the Mesan transstellars—and quite a few corporations officially headquartered in other star systems—joined at the hip.

"Given that, it didn't take long before a lot of political and other pressure was brought to bear on the Alignment. Those of its members and supporters who were known to the authorities weren't usually arrested, although some were, on specious charges that had nothing—officially—to do with their membership. For the most part, though, the penalties were economic. Careers stalled, contracts were canceled, people were reassigned to less prestigious or lower paying jobs, academic tenure was delayed or denied altogether. Younger members of Alignment families found their applications rejected by elite universities. That sort of thing."

"We didn't quit, though," Arianne said.

"No, some of you didn't. What happened was that the Alignment became a semi-underground organization. The repression was never harsh enough to force it into complete secrecy, with the cell system and the other security measures *totally* underground organizations require. But by four hundred T-years ago—at the latest—the Alignment had become all but invisible to most of Mesa's inhabitants."

He paused again and placed his hands flat on the table.

"And somewhere in that process—somewhere between five hundred and four hundred T-years ago—a new organization formed within the Alignment. The same sort of process has happened many times in history. A dissident group within a reformist political organization—which is what the original Alignment was, and most of its members continue to be today—becomes frustrated and dissatisfied with the slow pace of progress. In this case, no progress at all, because even after the Final War had receded into humanity's historical rearview mirror and the prohibition against enhancing colonists for hostile environments had disappeared, the Beowulf Code, accepted and followed—officially, at least—by virtually every human-settled star system, continued to prohibit targeted modification of the human genome for the *specific* purpose of genetic 'uplift.' In fact, it still does today.

"I don't think any of us are interested right now into getting into all the reasons for that, but from the perspective of the people

I know best in the Beowulf medical establishment, even today, the primary concern is one of human rights . . . and that concern has been exacerbated by genetic slavery. The prejudice—sometimes the *hatred*, to be honest—against genetic slaves is exactly what they fear in a society which is intentionally genetically stratified. They're afraid that if the human race . . . speciates into a spectrum of genetic types, genomes which can be clearly and scientifically differentiated from one another, eventually a qualitative judgment of which are 'superior' and which are 'inferior' will emerge. And, in the process, the fear of the 'other' which is at the root of every ugly human prejudice, just as it is against the genetic slaves, will reassert itself.

"To be honest, I don't know if that fear is valid. It exists today, however, and it *certainly* existed then. And because it did, and because of Beowulf's towering moral authority on genetic issues, even after two hundred T-years—*ten* generations in a pre-prolong galaxy—the Alignment's drive to improve humanity's genetic heritage was still stymied. Still effectively outlawed. Still something Alignment members could pursue only surreptitiously and in secrecy. And on top of that lack of progress on the reform front, which was the Alignment's primary motivation, there was Mesa's corporate prostitution.

"So what happens when a reform group is clearly making no progress or, at best, progressing only at a glacial rate?" Zilwicki shrugged. "The ones who grow most impatient start looking for a more *effective* means to their end. Which usually means they abandon any hope of evolutionary change and form a *revolutionary* organization. One that's prepared and willing to use violence to accomplish its goals.

"What was unusual about this formation—which *also* called itself 'the Alignment'—was that it never separated from the reformist organization that spawned it. Instead, the leaders of the new, revolutionary Alignment decided to remain within the original Alignment. That was for two reasons. First, it was the best place to hide from Mesa's authorities. But, secondly, the broader, reformist Alignment within which it operated provided the revolutionaries with most of their recruits."

He looked at Arianne.

"That's how your brothers would have been recruited," he said. She looked back, her face stiff, but said nothing.

"So far," Zilwicki resumed to the rest of the group, "there's nothing in this history that would explain the savagery of what the revolutionary wing of the Alignment became. Had they followed the same pattern that other groups like them have followed in history, they might have eventually succeeded or they might have eventually been crushed. But they wouldn't have become the monster they did become."

"So what happened?" Teague asked. She was obviously fascinated by Zilwicki's account, but remembered to add, "According to your theory, that is?"

"We're still working that out," he told her, "but it seems pretty clear that they got seduced by Manpower. They would undoubtedly have infiltrated it. The ranks of the Alignment—inner and outer both; or malign and benign, if you prefer—" he glanced at Arianne, whose face was still wooden "—would have been full of medical people, especially geneticists. Some of them would have gotten themselves hired by their enemy. Just to keep an eye on them, if nothing else. But then—"

"Of course!" Al-Fanudahi smacked the table. "Once they got drawn into the work, they would have recognized how valuable it could be for their own long-term purposes." He leaned back in his chair and stared at the wall opposite him. Not at anything in particular; just focusing his thoughts as he continued. "And once they started down that road, I'd be willing to bet that before long they saw ways they could manipulate Manpower and its associated transstellars in political terms. They started looking at the corporations they'd seen as enemies, as *tools*, instead."

"Tools for *what*?" Okiku sounded exasperated. "Hey, I'm just the thick-headed cop in the room. Spell it out in simple terms, Daud."

Cachat answered her before al-Fanudahi could.

"Tools—Anton and I call them 'levers'—they could use to pry open and then rip apart galactic society. Never forget that these people started as idealists. They had a *goal*. They weren't simply seeking power for its own sake. Improve the human race. Get past those blind, bigoted, sanctimonious, *stupid* Beowulfers and transform us from primitive hominids into something akin to demigods and goddesses. But to get there they had to clear a political path—the one dominated by those damned Beowulfers and their allies—as well as accumulating the necessary knowledge and skills. And in Manpower, they saw how to do both at the same time. No one else in the galaxy was conducting genetic experimentation as extensively—not to mention recklessly—as Manpower. The Alignment could learn a lot by being part of that. And no one else in the galaxy was laying the basis for the corruption of the Solarian League as effectively as Manpower and its crony transstellars, either."

"Yes, that's exactly what I was thinking." Al-Fanudahi looked back and forth between Cachat and Zilwicki. "If I can sum up, what you're suggesting is that there were three players involved, only one of whom was fully conscious of its game. The one *everyone* knew about was Manpower and its corrupt Mesan transstellar allies, who didn't give a damn about anything but money. Then, hidden beneath that surface, there was the broad—outer, benign, whatever you want to call it—Alignment that wanted to reform the Beowulf Code and embrace the advantages genetic engineering should have made possible. But neither of whom was aware of the *Malign* Alignment or the fact that it was using both of them for its own purposes."

"Exactly," Zilwicki said.

"Can we bring this back down to earth?" Saburo asked. "How does this tie into what we're supposed to be investigating, which are the mass killings that started with Green Pines?"

"I think that's obvious," al-Fanudahi said. He'd clearly kept thinking ahead. "Well . . . maybe not *obvious*. But I think it's clear enough. There's plenty of evidence—" he glanced around at his fellow Ghost Hunters "—we've come across it ourselves—that *someone* was working behind the scenes, first to instigate the war between Manticore and Haven, and then the one between the Solarian League and Manticore. Without knowing everything you've just told us, Captain Zilwicki, we couldn't figure out who the Other Guys—that's what we've been calling them—were or what they were after, but we knew they were there.

"I'm not prepared—yet—to say you've nailed it, but I think you're definitely building out a plausible theory to finally explain what the hell they want. And if there really was a revolutionary group dedicated to achieving its ends by any means necessary, and *if* those ends were obstructed because the Beowulf Code was generally supported by everyone else under the existing political order, that political order had to be changed. It had to be bulldozed out of the way, and the more completely that could be done—the more chaos and confusion the revolutionaries could engender—the less time anyone would have to worry about things like the Beowulf Code. So that's what they set out to do. They wanted the galaxy burned down, so to speak, but they also would have wanted the fire, the diversion, to last as long as possible."

He frowned more deeply for a moment, then grimaced and glanced at Zilwicki and Cachat with a suddenly sharper gaze.

"Of course that's what they'd want. And they'd take special pains to ensure that Beowulf's closest friends, the ones likely to be its strongest supporters, would *also* be...otherwise occupied. And who would those supporters have been, outside the League itself? The Star Kingdom of Manticore and the original Republic of Haven, that's who. So what did they do about that?" His mouth twisted. "They got behind existing factions, pushed to undermine the Republic's Constitution from within...and encouraged *it* to take out the Star Kingdom."

He paused again, gaze going distant as he contemplated the vistas opening before his mental eye, then shook himself back to the present.

"But it looks like the arrogant bastards were too smart for their own good. The Manticore-Haven war spun out of control. Both sides got damned good at fighting wars, but Manticore got even better—especially where applied tech was concerned—and then Theisman and Pritchart overthrew the People's Republic." He shook his head. "The way we all know they love working behind the scenes makes you wonder how much our Other Guys had to do with the High Ridge Government's stupidity and Pritchart's decision to go resume hostilities, doesn't it? But it must've seemed likely to them that Manticore would still win in the end, and the wars had driven Manticore and Beowulf even closer together in too many ways. So they launched the Yawata Strike to kneecap the Star Empire, figuring Haven would use the opportunity to finish taking down Manticore. Or at least stand aside when the Other Guys triggered off a war between the Solarian League and a militarily crippled Manticore. And if Haven did anything of the sort, that would poison—possibly permanently, but certainly in the short term—its relations with and support for Beowulf.

"But it all went wrong—and went wrong very quickly. Instead of a long, drawn out conflict between Manticore and the League that they could exploit, they got the Grand Alliance...and the Grand Alliance's war-fighting tech had improved so much that it handed the League its ass in very short order. Which means that instead of a house fire that lasts for decades and keeps everyone occupied, the new Grand Alliance—consisting of every single one of the opponents the Other Guys most feared—is free to come looking for them with blood in its eye."

He looked back and forth between Zilwicki and Cachat.

"That's basically your analysis, am I correct?"

"Pretty much right on the nose."

Something in Zilwicki's tone suggested he was both surprised and impressed by how quickly al-Fanudahi had put it together. That cheered the Solarian up quite a bit. He'd come into the meeting feeling like the dull kid in a room full of precocious ones. Manticorans and Havenites could be intimidating in more ways than just militarily.

"I still don't get it." Okiku sounded more than a *little* exasperated now. "So they're rotten, callous bastards and they've got a plan to overthrow the genetic order of the galaxy. I got that. But the mass killings, remember? What does this have to do with *that*?"

"I think I see where they're going, Natsuko." Irene Teague had been frowning since Zilwicki began his explanation, but now she leaned forward slightly in her chair. "What Daud and Captain Zilwicki and Officer Cachat are establishing—trying to, I should say—is that this 'Malign Alignment' suddenly discovered it had to get off Mesa much faster than it had ever expected. So they launched the killings to cover their tracks as they did so."

"Right on the nose again," Zilwicki agreed, but Teague was still frowning.

"I can see where that would explain a lot of it," she said. "Maybe even almost all of it. But it doesn't explain the Beowulf Strike. And, frankly, I don't see where Green Pines fits in."

Zilwicki and Cachat glanced at each other.

"It's time, I think," Cachat said, and Zilwicki nodded.

"The Beowulf Strike is one thing, and we know they were behind it, even if we don't understand why," he said. "But the reason you don't see how Green Pines fits in, Captain Teague, is that it doesn't. It's the one mass killing the Alignment—the Malign Alignment—wasn't responsible for."

"Then who was?" Tarkovsky asked from the far end of the table, and Zilwicki ran fingers through his hair.

"Well. I guess you could say *I* was. In a way."

"Oh, bullshit, Anton!" Cachat snapped in a rare lapse into profanity, and his hard gaze swept the table. "The one responsible for the Green Pines explosion was a man named David Pritchard. He was part of a small group of seccy revolutionaries Anton and I were working with when we were on Mesa. The *first* time we were on Mesa."

Teague's frown seemed fixed in place.

"Then why did Captain Zilwicki say *he* was responsible? In a way."

"The seccies had gotten their hands on two or three nuclear blasting charges." Cachat waved one hand. "Nothing fancy, just civilian construction devices. But they were wannabe revolutionaries, not experienced terrorists, so they hadn't realized the things had locator beacons. Those would have guided the authorities straight to them—and so to us. So Anton had to deactivate them."

"*What?!*" Arianne exclaimed.

"*You* provided seccy terrorists with usable nuclear weapons?" Kayla Barrett demanded, speaking for the first time.

But it was Bruce Tarkovsky who drew everyone's attention. He shot to his feet, slammed both hands on the table, and leaned forward over it.

"Are you telling me you *deactivated* the locator beacons on civilian nuclear devices?!" he demanded.

"Yes," Zilwicki said. "That's what I did."

The Marine stared at him for a second or two, then fell back into his chair.

"Jesus H Christ. I didn't think that was even *possible!*"

He bent his head slightly, peering at Zilwicki from under his brows, like an animal observing a nearby predator.

"You are one scary son-of-a-bitch, Zilwicki," he announced. Then, quite cheerfully. "I have *got* to hear this story. So tell us what happened."

✧   ✧   ✧

Zilwicki began by playing all the recordings he had of their contacts with Jack McBryde on the HD unit deployed from the center of the table. After the last one had finished, he looked around the table.

"Anybody have any questions?"

"I will have," al-Fanudahi said. "But I think it would make more sense to wait until you finish your presentation."

"Agreed," Tarkovsky said.

No one else said anything, but it was clear from their expressions that they felt the same way, so Zilwicki brought up a map of Green Pines, flanked by one of Mendel's suburbs and one of the areas surrounding the park. He spent another few moments highlighting several map locations in color, then cleared his throat.

"The red structure is Gamma Center. More precisely, it's Androcles Tower. Or, what *used* to be Androcles Tower, at least. It was primarily commercial space with only a couple of residential floors. Gamma Center itself was under the tower, even though its construction had been neatly erased from the Mendel Department of Buildings' database."

He shifted the bright arrow of his cursor to another location, this one outside the city limits of Green Pines.

"That's where Buenaventura Tower was located. It was an abandoned building in an industrial district. A very decayed industrial district. On a Saturday, which is when everything happened, the whole area would have been mostly deserted."

The cursor moved on to a highlighted structure close to Gamma Center.

"That's a sports stadium. It wasn't being used on the Saturday we made our escape from Mesa. And, finally—" the cursor moved again "—that's Pine Valley Park, where the Green Pines bomb actually detonated."

He paused long enough for his audience to orient itself geographically, then continued.

"Our plan was simple. Jack was supposed to leave Gamma Center and join Herlander Simões, and we'd smuggle both of them off-planet in a shielded crate on a freighter we'd been able to sneak past Mesan security. Assuming everything went smoothly, we'd be off-planet and out of the system before anyone realized he and Herlander weren't where they were supposed to be.

"At the same time, though, we set up a backup plan in case something went wrong, someone tumbled to our presence and what we were trying to do, and we had to make a hot extraction with people chasing us. If we had to pull out under those circumstances, we'd use one of the nuclear charges in Buenaventura

Tower and a second at the sports stadium as distractions while we made our escape. The explosions would be noisy, they'd attract all of the security forces' attention while we headed to the space-port, and while there would be a death toll, it would be minimal. And I think it's fair to point out that we were here on behalf of the Kingdom of Torch, which had declared a formal state of war against the Mesa System virtually the day it was founded. In fact, the Congo System was the *only* recognized belligerent involved even peripherally in Mesa's takedown. I'm not trying to pussyfoot around the fact that we knew our plan would kill citizens of Mesa; I'm simply saying that it was an act of war in a declared conflict and that our cover plan did its damnedest to hold those casualties to an absolute minimum.

"Unlike what Manpower tried, with the full backing of the Mesa System Government, to do to Torch when it sent the PNE to kill every living human on the planet."

His gaze circled the table, pinning every member of his audi-ence. Most of whom—with varying degrees of agreement—finally nodded.

"As it happened, something *did* go wrong with our extraction plan. We don't know what, and we probably never will. But when Jack realized we'd been made, somehow, he warned us in time to run. And when he realized he couldn't get out of Gamma Center and join us, he set off what was apparently an already installed nuclear device. One that amounted to a suicide bomb for the entire center. We presume the Alignment had installed it as part of their security measures."

He shook his head slightly.

"All of us who escaped owe our lives to Jack McBryde. He didn't just blow up Gamma Center. He also did something—don't ask us what it was, because we don't know—that obviously scrambled most of Mesa's security systems. We know, because he'd told Herlander, that he planned to do as much damage as possible to the Alignment's databases and computer support before he left, but this was more than anything he'd described to Herlander. Without knowing what access he had or how he used it, I can't say how he did it, but he got to the system government's systems, not just the Alignment's, and kicked the ever loving *hell* out of them. And what he did enabled our ship—the *Hali Sowle*—to leave the Mesa System unhindered. Nobody bothered us at all. We just . . . flew off."

"So that explains what happened to...Androcles Tower and the other one—Bonaventura," Okiku said. "But what happened at Pine Valley Park?"

"Once Jack blew up Gamma Center, there was no longer any point to detonating the nuclear device at the sports stadium. We blew Bonaventura Tower anyway, but not just as a distraction. We'd—I'd—hacked the local security cameras and planted a feed of Victor and me 'making our escape' through one of Bonaventura's underground access ways." He shrugged. "The camera I'd hacked was inside the explosion's primary destruction zone, so we figured anybody who'd figured out we were here and was looking for us would think we'd blown ourselves up with our own distraction. But there was no longer any point to setting off the second distraction in the sports stadium. Gamma Center had caused a hell of a lot more casualties and a hell of a lot more damage than the stadium bomb ever would have. The authorities were going to be totally focused on *it*, so blowing the stadium would only have inflicted property damage and a few more unnecessary civilian deaths. That and put David Pritchard at risk, since he was the one flying the air car that carried the stadium bomb.

"So we sent him a message calling it off. But he refused to obey. In fact, he lost it completely. He went into a fury. He condemned us for cowards, broke off all contact, and flew the air car into the center of the park, instead. From what we've been able to determine since, he must've set it off manually, killing himself at the same time."

"What in hell possessed you to put a lunatic like that in control of a nuclear device?" Tarkovsky demanded.

"I'm assuming," Saburo said, before either Zilwicki or Cachat could respond, "that it was because Pritchard was the only one of the seccies who could fly an air car. Am I right?"

"Pretty much," Cachat said. "Carl Hansen could probably have managed it, instead, but he was needed elsewhere." He gave Tarkovsky a cold look. "I take it you've never been involved in an operation where you weren't working with vetted and trained professional soldiers. Welcome to our world, Major. You use the people you've got as best you can. I knew—so did Anton—that Pritchard was wound pretty tightly. But there'd never been any indication he'd do something completely maniacal."

"Actually," Tarkovsky tipped back in his chair, meeting Cachat's gaze steadily, "I have a certain experience with...operatives who were neither vetted nor trained soldiers. Of course, I was trying to capture or *kill* them at the time. That doesn't mean I don't understand that necessity is the mother of improvisation, Officer Cachat."

"What difference does it make?" Okiku asked. "It happened. At least now we know *what* happened—and why."

"And knowing that clears up a lot of murkiness," Teague added. "Green Pines was always the one incident that didn't seem to fit any coherent pattern. Now we know that's because it *wasn't* coherent. Just an outburst of *incoherent* rage."

Al-Fanudahi's eyes were on Arianne McBryde. Her face was drawn, her lips tight, her eyes not focused on anything anyone else could see.

"Ms. McBryde," he said softly. She blinked and looked at him. "For what it's worth, based on what Captain Zilwicki's just told us, I deeply admire your brother. It couldn't have been easy for someone who'd devoted his entire life to a cause to break with it once he realized it had gone bad. That took courage, as well as morality. The same stark courage he showed at the end of his life. The whole human race owes him, if you want my opinion."

"I agree. Completely," Cachat said.

"And so do I," Zilwicki added.

Arianne stared at al-Fanudahi. It was obvious from her expression that the Solarian intelligence officer's statement had startled her. Her lips were opened.

Briefly. Then she closed her mouth, firmly, and nodded.

"Thank you," she said. "I appreciate that. This has been hard for me. Especially since from what Captain Zilwicki's told us, my other brother is still—" she thrust her chin forward, as if pointing to something in the distance "—out there somewhere."

"Which brings us back to the subject at hand," Tarkovsky said. "The Other Guys—what you call the Malign Alignment—are out there somewhere. But *where?*"

"Actually, that's—" Zilwicki began, only to cut himself off as the door buzzer sounded again. He glared at the closed door.

"What is this? A semi-secret meeting, or a party?" he demanded.

"It's got to be Yana," Cachat said. He was already halfway to the door...again. "She's the only other person I told we'd be here."

"Yana? Why would—?"

"Ask her yourself," Cachat said, stepping aside to let Yana Tretiakovna into the room.

The tall blonde had a long stride, and she wasn't given to diffidence. She crossed brusquely to the table and handed Zilwicki a chip.

"I figured you'd want to see this immediately," she said.

"What is it?" he asked.

"Dunno." Tretiakovna shrugged. "Information from Torch is all they told me. The courier boat got in less than half an hour ago."

She turned to go, but Cachat was still by the door, and he raised one hand to stop her.

"Stay, Yana," he said.

"Why?" There might have been just a hint of suspicion in her tone.

"We may need your input, for one thing. For another, if this new information leads to another expedition, we'd like to have you along."

The look she gave him was not a friendly one.

"The last time that happened you saddled me with tits the size of cantaloupes." She slapped the side of her chest. It was clearly a female chest, but her breasts were not especially prominent. "Now that I'm back to normal, I'd just as soon stay that way."

"I doubt any elaborate body sculpture would be required this time," Cachat said with a smile.

"Why not? You have no idea what's on that chip. For all I know, once you read it you'll want to turn me into...into—who *knows* what?"

"I promise."

Cachat was still smiling, and Tretiakovna sniffed.

"A promise from Victor Cachat is...is...well, pretty good, actually," she said. "All right."

Tarkovsky rose to offer her his chair. Her response was another sniff.

"I can stand, thank you," she said.

Zilwicki had inserted the chip into the console while she and Cachat were talking. He looked down at the small screen in front of him, reading quickly, then straightened abruptly in his chair.

"Anton?" Cachat said in the tone of a man who'd seen inspiration strike before.

"Everybody needs to see this," Zilwicki replied. "Well, actually, first everybody needs to see *this*."

He punched commands, loading imagery from the files he'd brought with him, and the maps disappeared from table's HD as something else replaced them.

"Those are diagrams of the new Cataphracts," Teague said.

"Yes." Zilwicki nodded. "This data's from Bo— From the Grand Alliance's primary R and D center. If you Solarians don't know where that is—and you damned well shouldn't—just curb your curiosity. Its name and location fall under 'need to know'... which you don't. Not now, anyway."

Teague only shrugged. Her attention was on the data display.

"They aren't exactly the same version," she said. "The differences don't amount to much, though. What's the significance?"

"The significance is in the star map and the chronological data," Zilwicki replied.

He expanded the time chart, then looked back and forth between the two Solarian naval officers.

"I don't get it," al-Fanudahi said with a frown.

"That's because you don't have all the information," Zilwicki said. "This came in from...that place a couple of weeks ago, so Victor and I have had some time to kick it around. The first thing is that these missiles represent two distinct Cataphract versions, as Captain Teague has already pointed out. *This* one—" one of the missile diagrams flashed "—is earlier in the development sequence than the other one."

He cocked an eyebrow at al-Fanudahi until the Solarian nodded.

"All right, *this*—" Zilwicki highlighted the timeline "—is a reconstruction of the timing for the delivery of these Cataphracts to two different fleets."

"I figured that much out," al-Fanudahi said. "So, one of them was Filareta's Second Fleet. Who's 'Attila'?"

"Attila is a reference to the fleet that attacked Congo," Cachat said.

"Ah?"

"Yes." Zilwicki nodded. "And 'Attila' is who got the later version of these two missiles."

Al-Fanudahi's frown deepened. He sat back in his chair, gazing at the star map and at the timeline for at least thirty seconds, and his hosts let him. Then he leaned forward again.

"Wait a minute. Attila had the *later* version?"

"Yep."

"But how is that possible?" Al-Fanudahi shook his head. "The only two places producing Cataphracts were the Sol System and Yildun. And the attack on Congo was—what? Eight T-months *before* Filareta crossed the Manticore hyper wall."

"Exactly." Zilwicki nodded. "Which, if you look at the rest of that timeline, clearly indicates that Attila received a more advanced model of the Cataphract than Filareta had . . . and got it before the SLN had received *any* of them. And there's no way a shipment from Sol or Yildun could have reached him before it reached Filareta. In fact, if you'll look at *this* entry—" he highlighted another date on the timeline "—it's unlikely that a shipment from Yildun or Sol could have reached Filareta before he headed for Manticore at all. It's not *quite* impossible, but they would have had to be in the delivery pipeline before Filareta's orders to attack Manticore had ever been cut."

Al-Fanudahi rubbed his chin thoughtfully. Then he nodded back to the Manticoran.

"The Other Guys, again," he said in tones of profound disgust.

"Absolutely, and this establishes a direct connection between the Malign Alignment and Technodyne," Zilwicki pointed out. "We always assumed there'd be one, given the extent of Technodyne's presence here in Mesa, but this pretty much confirms it. And given how widely separated Attila and Filareta were when they took delivery, the other thing this confirms is that there has to be at least one additional Cataphract-manufacturing facility. One that's not in the Sol System and isn't in Yildun. And probably—this is more speculative—one that was already producing Cataphracts before Technodyne got around to telling the Solarian League Navy the missile even existed."

Al-Fanudahi's eyes were very intent, and he looked across the table at Teague.

"It makes sense, Daud," she said. "And I don't like what it says about the industrial capability the Other Guys must have hidden away somewhere."

"We'd already realized they have to have an equivalent of . . . that place we're not going to tell you about," Zilwicki said with a shrug. "They had to build the ships they used in the Yawata Strike somewhere. We're not any happier about the fact that they've got their own shipyard complex somewhere than you are, Captain Teague. And it's almost certainly the same place they've located what has to be an unfortunately capable R and D capability, since they're also the only people we know of who've figured out how to pack a cruiser-grade graser into some sort of missile or drone. They used it against the Star Empire in the Yawata Strike, and then they used it again to clear the way when the SLN hit Beowulf, and it's dangerous as hell. But the really significant thing about this information is the way it establishes the direct connection between them and Technodyne."

He paused again, until all the Solarians had nodded.

"Now, as I say, Victor and I have known about this information"—he waved at the HD "—for a couple of weeks. But what we didn't know about was *this*."

He tapped a command, and the imagery from Bolthole shrank into one corner of the HD while the schematic of a single star system replaced it. It was labeled NZ-127-06, and the new imagery displayed it from multiple angles.

"What have we got, Anton?" Cachat asked.

"This is from Ruth," Zilwicki replied.

"Ruth who?" Tarkovsky asked.

"For the moment, let's just leave it at Ruth."

"That would be Ruth Winton, I imagine," al-Fanudahi said with a smile. "But it's just a wild guess on my part, you understand. You don't need to answer. Need to know, and I don't."

"There's an excess of brains in this room," Tretiakovna complained. "If it reaches critical mass, we'll all be incinerated by neuron radiation."

Teague had ignored the byplay as she studied the image carefully. Finally, she shook her head.

"There's nothing there," she said. "It's just a fairly typical red dwarf system. There's no indication of any settlements, even orbital habitats." She shook her head again.

"No, there isn't. But that's not really the point, Captain," Zilwicki said. "The point is that according to the information Ruth sent us, this is where 'Attila' picked up his Cataphracts."

"Really?" al-Fanudahi murmured.

"Exactly." Zilwicki nodded. "And, as you can see," he entered another command, and a star map blipped into the display with NZ-1207-06's position highlighted in red, "it's nowhere near Sol, Yildun, or Mesa."

"Which," al-Fanudahi said, gazing at the map, "suggests that it must be close to something *else*. Like possibly a—what did you call it, Irene? A secret manufacturing complex?"

Silence hovered as all of them looked at the star map and the bland schematic of the uninhabited system. Then Tarkovsky stirred in his chair.

"So now what?" he asked.

"Don't look at me," Tretiakovna said. "The last time I got involved with the dwarf—" she jerked her head at Zilwicki "—I got turned into a bimbo and lost an arm. And if there's anything in the universe more ridiculous than a one-armed bimbo, I can't imagine what it is."

"I can think of several possibilities," Cachat said.

"Like what?" she demanded suspiciously.

"I'm thinking. I'm thinking."

"Oh, hell." Tretiakovna looked at Tarkovsky and waved him away from the chair he'd abandoned. "Move. I'm going to need to sit down after all. Victor Cachat thinking is the stuff of nightmares."

✧   ✧   ✧

Several minutes passed in silence.

Cachat spent them in what one would have called a "brown study," if anyone other than Victor Cachat had been doing the studying. Given the man's nature and the intensity with which he developed plots and schemes, brown was far too warm and light a color to adequately describe what he was likely to be contemplating.

Zilwicki, Saburo, and Tretiakovna simply sat there with their chairs tipped back, watching him calmly. Barrett, who'd encountered Cachat during her captivity in Neue Rostock Tower, watched him with considerably greater trepidation. Arianne and the Solarians, unaccustomed to the patented Cachat Experience, looked at him, and then at one another with the expressions of guests who'd strayed into the wrong party and weren't quite sure what was happening.

Finally, Tretiakovna glanced at Zilwicki with one eyebrow raised. The Manticoran looked back, then checked his chrono just a bit conspicuously, and nodded.

"All right, Victor," she said. "Time's up! What's more ridiculous than a one-armed bimbo?"

Cachat's lips might—*might*—have twitched slightly, but he gave no other sign that he'd even heard her. Instead, he gazed down at the table for another several seconds before he looked up.

"The answer to your question," he told her, "is organizing an expedition to find out what happened in that star system, using some of the Attila ships captured at the Battle of Torch. And we need to do it with a reasonably powerful force. I'm figuring at least a cruiser and two or three destroyers."

Tretiakovna rolled her eyes. Daud al-Fanudahi frowned. Most of the others only looked confused, however, and Zilwicki smiled to himself.

Welcome to Victor's Wild Ride, he thought. *I'd call it Cachat's Folly if he hadn't pulled these schemes off way too many times.*

"What the hell are you talking about?" Tarkovsky demanded.

"I'd think it was obvious," Cachat replied, and nodded toward the red dwarf system on the display. "We need to investigate that system, but there won't be anything there to find by now."

"There won't?" Arianne frowned. "I'd think that large an operation would've had to leave *some* evidence behind."

Cachat looked at her the way a tutor might look at a valued but sometimes slow student who'd just given the wrong answer, but Zilwicki answered her before Cachat could.

"That's not very likely, Arianne," he said. "That's the reason they picked a random uninhabited system—well, not *entirely* random. It had to be in roughly the right place. But nobody lives there, so there wouldn't have been any witnesses. According to Ruth's research, they were delivered by freighters that didn't bother with any transponder codes. In the opinion of Attila's logistics people, they weren't any too modern or well-equipped with cargo-handling equipment, either. There was a lot of hand labor involved in getting the missiles transferred. Even so, it only took four or five hours, and then everybody left."

"Like I said." Tarkovsky sounded a bit exasperated. "What the hell are you talking about? What's the point of putting together a squadron to investigate nothing?"

Cachat looked at him, just a bit less benevolently than he had at Arianne, and shook his head.

"There won't be anything to find in *that* system, no. But with all due respect to Anton, they couldn't organize that big an operation without leaving witnesses behind. They just aren't in NZ-127-06. Given what Anton just said about 'hand labor' they had to find a labor force somewhere. And if Attila's people thought the freighters were less than modern, then it's unlikely they came directly from a star system capable of manufacturing the Cataphracts. *And* we all know how fond the Malign Alignment is of establishing cutouts and deniability. Attila never even suspected he was working with anyone besides Manpower, with under-the-table support from the Mesan government. He sure as hell never knew anything about the Malign Alignment. So, what do you think the odds are that they found another system—one that *is* inhabited—to transship the Cataphracts from their own freighters to the nice, deniable, unidentified tramps who actually delivered them to Attila?"

Tarkovsky's exasperation segued into thoughtfulness.

"Okay," he said after a moment. "You may—*may*—be onto something, but it's a big galaxy. How—"

"Hole in the Wall!" Irene Teague interrupted, she looked down at the table in front of her. "Does this have—?"

"Just a sec," Zilwicki said. He tapped the console in front of him, and a second, virtual control panel appeared on the tabletop in front of Teague.

She went to work, looking up at the HD while her fingers flew.

"If I remember correctly, Hole in the Wall isn't too far away from that system. And—"

The schematic of NZ-1207-06 disappeared and the star map showing NZ-1207-06's position expanded to take its place. Another star flashed as Teague highlighted it in red, and then the map moved up and to one side as the schematic of the newly located star system took center place. She zoomed in on the schematic, and an alphanumeric data block appeared with the system's astrographic data. The primary—catalogued as NZ-1207-12—was a G7, with six planets. The innermost planet, very close to the star, was much larger than Sol's Mercury but an equally worthless hunk of rock, and the two outermost were useless balls of ice. But the fourth was a gas giant inside the liquid water zone...barely, with a sizable family of moons. One of them was half again the size of Jupiter's Ganymede, with a diameter a thousand kilometers greater than that of Mars, which made it large enough to retain a breathable atmosphere. It didn't look any too hospitable—an initial impression that was confirmed as Teague highlighted its entry in the system's astrography data block and enlarged it. It was cold, with a very limited hydrosphere, and—not unexpectedly, given that only about thirty percent of its surface was covered in water—a lot of desert. But however unappealing it might be as a vacation spot, it was still within the bounds of habitability.

"There it is," she said. "Hole in the Wall."

"Which is . . . what?" Arianne asked, and Tarkovsky grunted.

"I've heard of it. A hangout for outlaws, basically."

"Oh, it's more than that," al-Fanudahi said. "In its own dis-reputable way, Hole in the Wall's quite famous. Well, notorious. It was founded—"

"Let's skip the history lesson, for the moment," Cachat said. "I've heard of it—although I don't think I ever heard exactly where it's located. I certainly didn't realize it was close to NZ-1207-06. But, yes, it's exactly the sort of place a joint operation between Technodyne and the Malign Alignment would've gone for ships and a workforce."

"Says here there's not much population," Saburo said, peering at the planetary data.

"It's more of a rendezvous point than any kind of industrial node," al-Fanudahi replied. "Oh, it's got some *light* industry in orbit, enough for some limited local manufacture of consumer goods and minor repairs and basic ship services, but nothing much more sophisticated than that. It does have some orbital warehousing and a rudimentary sort of port facilities, but only enough to handle the sorts of cargoes pirates like to fence with no questions asked. Its biggest—and most profitable—function is as a mail drop and . . . recruiting hall."

"Recruiting hall?" Arianne repeated.

"It's a place where the sort of people who might need the services of pirates or outlaws can post employment notices," al-Fanudahi said dryly. "And it's a handy, out-of-sight, out-of-mind rendezvous spot for shady sorts—like some of the less savory operatives of some of the less savory transstellars—to meet up with people their employers have retained. The kind of rendezvous where nobody asks any questions."

"Which is why I want to go in with a fairly small force," Cachat said. "There can't be any major military presence in the system; the people who live there are basically just pirates and smugglers. So nobody will have a fleet of superdreadnoughts, and I don't think they'd react very calmly if *we* showed up with one."

"Question." Tarkovsky clasped his hands behind his back, standing behind the chair he'd yielded to Tretiakovna, his expression now one of interest. "I'd like you to explain the logic of your proposal. Why send in a squadron at all? I mean, why worry about whether or not they'd react calmly? If we sent in a task group, instead, with a Marine expeditionary force aboard a couple of transports, we could just seize the facilities—as you just said, there's not going to be any major military muscle to stop us—and then sweat anyone in the system for information. And we'd have enough naval force to stop any ships from escaping. Why get fancy about it?" He smiled crookedly. "I'm just a simple Marine. I like keeping things simple. Mostly because the fewer hand grenades you're juggling, the less likely you are to drop one on your own foot and go boom."

"Actually, I prefer simple, too . . . when it'll work," Cachat told him with something much more like a smile. "But by the time any Marine force seized any installations—and I don't care whose Marines we're talking about, or how good they are—there wouldn't be any information left. The computers would all be slagged."

"There'd still be personnel we could interrogate," Tarkovsky pointed out. "Including the personnel who put the information into the computers before they were slagged, if you take my meaning."

"I think that's unlikely," Cachat said. "Oh, there might still be personnel we could interrogate—maybe. I'm not too optimistic about that you understand, but it's possible. What's *certain*, though, is that the ones who actually knew anything would all be dead."

"We could be in with very light casualties, on either side," Tarkovsky said. "We're pretty good at that sort of thing."

"Oh, I'm sure you could. And I mean that sincerely. But they'd still all be dead."

"But we—" Tarkovsky paused, his eyes widening. "What are you suggesting? Mass suicide?"

"It doesn't have to be *mass* suicide," Zilwicki said. "All you need is one fanatic willing to suicide and, in the process, commit mass *murder*. Let me show you something."

He called up another file, and the HD blanked, then displayed the image of a starship—a freighter—with a small naval vessel docked to it.

"What you're looking at is the slaver *Luigi Pirandello* being boarded by a Torch Navy pinnace. It was one of two slave ships at Balcescu Station when the Torches arrived. Both of them tried to run, but only one of them made it, and *Luigi Pirandello* wasn't able to reach the hyper limit before it was overhauled." Like a lot of professional naval officers, Anton Zilwicki refused to apply a personal pronoun to a slave ship. "We think it and the slaver that did escape the system—the *Prince Sundjata*—were both being used to transport some of the Malign Alignment cadre who'd fled Mesa before Tenth Fleet got here." He glanced at Arianne. "One of them was her brother Zach. We're ninety-nine percent sure he was aboard *Prince Sundjata*, though, so he would have made it out with the ship."

His eyes went back to the display.

"But once they realized they wouldn't be able to make their own escape, *Luigi Pirandello*'s crew surrendered, after being guaranteed that they wouldn't be executed so long as their slaves remained unharmed. The slavers evacuated in a pair of shuttles, leaving the slaves behind to be recovered by the Torches. But when the Navy pinnace came alongside—"

He tapped a key, unfreezing the image, and Irene Teague hissed audibly as the blinding glare of a nuclear detonation filled the display.

"The Torches' response came immediately," Zilwicki said dispassionately, and a new image appeared. It showed a pair of shuttles—and then, seconds later, the bright traces of projected missile vectors. Those vectors stretched swiftly across the display. They merged with the shuttles...and both shuttles died just as spectacularly as *Luigi Pirandello*.

"What happened?" Tarkovsky asked, his tone one of dispassionate professional curiosity.

"We don't know for certain," Cachat replied in the same sort of tone, "and while I don't blame the Torches one bit, they did pretty much ensure there were no survivors to interrogate. I'm sure if there had been any, they would have sung like little birds. At least half the Torches on those ships were ex-Ballroom." His blue eyes were cold with bleak confidence.

"Unfortunately, nobody got a chance to ask them," he continued. "The only thing that makes sense, though, is that an Alignment fanatic was still aboard the freighter and blew up the ship once the pinnace came alongside."

"Thus destroying all the evidence as well as striking one last blow at the enemy," al-Fanudahi said. "What you're suggesting is that if the people on Hole in the Wall knew anything important, could lead a hunting party to the Other Guys, someone like that would probably be present as well."

"And ready to do the same thing." Cachat nodded. "That's why we need to investigate without alerting anyone that either the Grand Alliance or the Solarian League—*any* reputable military force—is involved. That means putting together what amounts to a small pirate fleet. Except we don't have time—nor do I have the inclination—to go out and find real pirates. Besides, that would be silly when we've got ready-made crews at our disposal that would be a lot more disciplined and capable than freebooters."

"Excuse me?" Okiku was frowning again. "'Ready-made' crews?"

"Exactly...courtesy of Admiral Rozsak," Cachat told her with a thin smile.

"Wait a minute," al-Fanudahi said. "Admiral Rozsak? You're talking about the people—the...the People's Navy in Exile—who tried to *genocide* Torch?"

"I am." Cachat's smile was wider now. "Torch offered to send them all home to Nouveau Paris for trial, but President Pritchart had too many other things on her mind—and her plate—at the moment. And Admiral Rozsak didn't want them, because if Torch had handed them over to him, he would've had to put them on trial. They *had* tried to violate the Eridani Edict, after all. And if they'd testified in open court, it was much too likely that... certain aspects of his own ships' armament would have become part of the public record."

"You're saying he was already in bed with Manticore or Haven even then? That you people had supplied him with modern weapons *that* early?"

For some reason, there seemed to be very little surprise in al-Fanudahi's tone.

"Oh, no! Not Manticore or Haven." Cachat shook his head. "*Erewhon* provided him with modern weapons...and quite a few more ships than he ever admitted to Old Terra that he'd taken to the party."

"Ah." Al-Fanudahi nodded. "I'd wondered about the original chronology. MARS made it clear to the League when it seceded that it had them then. Far be it from me to suggest that they delivered that information as another minor fact for the Mandarins' to consider before they sent any punitive expeditions out to 'pacify' the Maya Sector, although I suppose that's *remotely* possible. But when they passed us that information, I went back and looked at Admiral Rozsak's report on Congo." He smiled broadly. "I *do* appreciate a well written bit of fiction. Thank you for clearing up what this one was designed to obscure."

"I doubt he'd mind your knowing now," Cachat replied with a tiny smile of his own. "In fact, knowing him, he's probably amused as hell by the thought of your realizing—finally—how long ago he and Governor Barregos started playing Old Chicago like a violin. And truth to tell, getting those ships out of Erewhon was the first overt step the two of them had taken."

"And it's a damn good thing he had them to take to Congo with him," Zilwicki said somberly.

"It is," Cachat agreed. "He and his people took horrific casualties, anyway, because nobody knew about Cataphracts at that point. He found out about them the hard way, and without matching weapons of his own..."

His voice trailed off, and silence hovered for a moment. Then he shrugged.

"But the relevant point right now is that since President Pritchart didn't want them, and Governor Barregos didn't want them, they've been parked on Torch—the Torches took a page from Cerberus and gave them their own island—ever since the battle."

"And why in hell would they want to come work for us now?" Tretiakovna asked, and Cachat looked at her.

"They've already been living on their island for the better part of two T-years," he pointed out. "How much longer do you think they'll be there?"

"How would I know?"

"You don't. Neither do I. Neither does *anybody*. For all they know, or we know, they may spend the rest of their lives marooned out there. It's not like anybody wants them, or like there's any incentive for anybody to find something better for them to do with their time. They can survive there just fine—they've been doing just that, ever since the attack—and there's no way they can escape. So the answer is probably that they'll spend the rest of their lives, or at least the next several decades, stuck out there. You really think we couldn't find enough volunteers for this expedition if they were given an incentive?"

"What incentive?"

"Freedom. And enough of a stake to allow them a fresh start."

"Some of those people are fanatics, Victor," Zilwicki pointed out. "I doubt they're the sort of fanatics who'd sign on just to get a chance to blow up their captors, but I've found over the years that fanatics can be...just a tad unreliable."

"I wouldn't know about that myself. I've never actually dealt with any fanatics, personally," Cachat said with an absolutely straight face, then raised an eyebrow as Tretiakovna experienced a sudden coughing fit.

"Oh, don't mind me!" she said, pounding her chest with one fist. "Must've been something I inhaled."

Somebody chuckled, and Cachat smiled. Then the brief humor disappeared.

"I'm not too worried about fanatics, Anton," he said. "By the time we could leave for Congo, Indy, Damien, and Fire Watch should be back."

"Fire Watch?" Tarkovsky asked.

"Damien's treecat," Zilwicki explained. "Although, to be fair, it would be equally accurate to say Damien is Fire Watch's *human*, you understand. And you're right, Victor. For that matter, there are at least three or four 'cats already on Torch. We should be able to vet our 'volunteers' for any lingering fanaticism."

"You're saying treecats really can read minds?" al-Fanudahi asked, interest kindling in his eyes.

"Not really. Not human minds, anyway. But they *can* read human emotions," Zilwicki replied. "They make damned good lie detectors. Or, in this case, fanatic detectors."

"Damn." Tarkovsky shook his head. "You don't think we could hire any of them to help Brigadier Gaddis out back in Old Chicago, do you?"

"'Fraid it doesn't work that way," Zilwicki told him with a smile.

"We'll need some people's commissioners, of course," Cachat said. Tarkovsky looked at him, and he shrugged. "Commissars."

"Oh, I know what they were," the Marine replied. "I'm just wondering where you're going to find them these days."

"I figure we can start with me and Yana. We can find some other people to use once we get to Torch. I'm sure some of the ex-Ballroom folks would be just delighted to help out. And I'll talk to Admiral Tourville before we leave. He can probably free up some of his people who'd be suitable for the expedition in one way or another. But, speaking of commissioners..."

He gazed at Tarkovsky with a look that could have been characterized as beady-eyed or simply Victorlike.

"What?" the Marine said suspiciously.

"I'm pretty sure *you'd* make a good commissioner," Cachat told him.

"You've got to be kidding," al-Fanudahi said.

"No," Tretiakovna said. "He isn't. When he gets like this, he's kind of like a black hole. He just sort of... *sucks* everyone in. And before you know it, he's got you dancing like puppets. Even people like me, who should damned well know better. Still—" she pursed her lips "—I've never been a commissar before. Should be interesting. Who knows? It might even be fun."

The Solarians and Mesans in the room stared at her.

"You have to make allowances," Saburo told them. "She used to be a Scrag. Those people have really peculiar notions of fun."

"So do a lot of Marines," Tarkovsky said. "Including me."

"Damn it, Bryce—be serious!" Okiku snapped.

"I am being serious." He rubbed his short-cropped hair. "The truth is Cachat's plan—well, plan-in-progress, maybe—actually makes sense to me. With a force that size, and with personnel whose dossiers will fit the story, we'd fit right in *and* be strong enough no one already in Hole in the Wall would be inclined to attack us. But not so strong they might not be willing to connect us with somebody who's strong enough not to worry about us."

He stopped rubbing his scalp and cocked his head at Cachat.

"You're proposing to pass us off as mercenaries, right? Renegades from a now collapsed counterrevolution who're looking for someone to put them on a payroll?"

"Exactly." Cachat nodded. "That's pretty much what the PNE was already, except they hadn't given up their political ambitions yet. Now?" He shook his head. "I'm sure there are still plenty of StateSec diehards on that island. But by now, a lot of those people will just be looking for a way out."

Tarkovsky nodded slowly, then stopped as he saw al-Fanudahi's expression.

"Relax, Daud!" he said with a chuckle. "I'm not suggesting you—or Irene—should be part of the expedition. I'm sure both of you would do more good staying here on Mesa and continuing your investigation.

"And I assume—" his gaze shifted to Zilwicki "—that you'll be staying on Mesa, as well, Captain?"

Zilwicki and Cachat looked at each other. After a second, Cachat shook his head slightly, and Zilwicki looked back at Tarkovsky.

"Yes, Major. I'll be staying here. At least for the time being."

"While Cachat and I go to Congo and see what we can work out. Or should I say work up?"

"Yes." Cachat nodded. "We'll leave as soon as I can talk to Admiral Tourville. That should give you time to make any preparations you need to."

"Plenty of time. By the way, Officer Cachat—"

"Call me Victor."

"Victor. I've never been a commissar—or a people's commissioner either. What are the main things I should aim for?"

"It's not really complicated. You just need to project an aura of authority backed up by subtle and subdued menace."

"Subtle and subdued?" al-Fanudahi murmured.

"Did you *say* something, Captain al-Fanudahi?" Tarkovsky inquired.

The menace was conspicuous. Subtle and subdued...not so much.

Speak Easy
Old Quarter
City of Old Chicago
Old Earth
Sol System

"I FEEL UTTERLY RIDICULOUS. HOW THE HELL DID I GET ROPED into this expedition?"

Catherine Montaigne spoke—groused, actually—loud enough to be heard by the very large woman who was less than a meter ahead of her. By mutual if unspoken agreement, Fanny was leading the way through the crowded passageways of Chicago's teeming ghetto. As slender as she was, Montaigne would have made little progress if she'd been in the forefront of their two-woman travel party.

"Expedition?" she repeated. "Say better, 'wild goose chase.'"

"Why would anyone chase a wild goose?" Fanny didn't bother to turn her head. With her booming voice it would have been completely unnecessary.

"How should I know?" Montaigne replied. "It's just an expression. Like 'in for a penny, in for a pound,' one of those saws whose exact meaning depends on terms that no longer have any content. What's a penny; what's a pound? And who cares, anyway? You know what it means just as well as I do."

She reached up to the mask on her face, fingering the well disguised controls. She was sorely tempted to turn the stupid thing off, but...

Fanny had insisted upon the need to wear the masks, even while she'd refused to explain why. Montaigne knew from experience that getting into a petty argument with the strong-willed vice president of the ASL wasn't worth the effort. It was like the

264

verbal equivalent of sumo wrestling...and she wasn't the one with the *avoirdupois*.

"We're here," Fanny announced, and stopped, suddenly enough Montaigne almost ran into (and bounced off of) her. The doorway before her bore no markings of any kind, aside from a small placard that read: SPEAK EASY.

"Oh, how quaint," Montaigne muttered. "Do I need to explain the connotations of that phrase, too?"

Fanny ignored her and waved a finger across a door buzzer whose aperture was so small only someone actively looking for it could have noticed it. A few seconds later, the door slid open to reveal a man who was larger even than Fanny. His clothing was subdued, but he might as well have carried a flashing sign that read: I AM THE BOUNCER. FEAR ME.

"Yes?" he asked.

"We're here for the waters," Fanny said.

"There are no waters in Casablanca."

"Surely we weren't misinformed."

"Welcome to Rick's Coffeehouse," the bouncer replied, and stepped aside, opening the door wide.

"It's *Café*, not Coffeehouse," Montaigne muttered as she entered. Like Victor Cachat, she was an aficionado of the so-called "films" of Ante Diaspora Earth. She darkly suspected that, unlike her, neither Fanny nor the bouncer had any idea of the provenance of their silly passwords and countersigns.

The door admitted them to a narrow corridor which led around a corner to another door, which—like the one they'd come through from the slidewalk—had neither handle nor other visible means of opening. There was no bouncer guarding it, but there was another small placard with the same inscription: SPEAK EASY.

"Easy," Fanny said, and the door slid silently open.

"Oh, for—!" Montaigne bit off the expletive and satisfied herself with an exasperated eye roll and a muttered "Can this *get* any cornier?"

At least this door let them into an actual room. A big room, filled with scattered tables and alcoves along the sides. The alcoves were shielded behind iridescent electronic privacy screens. Not so the tables—but everyone seated at them wore a mask like the ones Montaigne and Fanny had on.

Like them, at least, in terms of the electronics involved, which were not so much different—in purpose, at least—from the ones shielding the alcoves. But the masks' programming was more sophisticated than the alcove shields'. Each mask was not only different from any other, but also, in many cases, underwent constant transformations.

The person sitting at a table not far from them was a man, gauging by size, although one never knew. Fanny was considerably larger than him...or her. Probably a surer indication of the person's gender were the forms assumed by the mask he or she wore. The head of a creature that resembled a bear; then, the face of a man wearing a horned helmet; then, what seemed to be a supernova; and, finally, back to the quasi-bear head.

"Delusions of grandeur," Montaigne muttered. "Got to be a man."

That wasn't really fair. She'd known a number of women who'd suffered from similar delusions. But Montaigne wasn't in a very fair-minded mood at the moment. The escapade Fanny had talked her into was starting to get on her nerves.

"So where to now?" she asked, and Fanny raised her wrist to examine her uni-link. After studying it for a moment, she nodded toward an alcove close to the room's far right corner.

"That one," she said, and headed for it in her inimitable manner. Montaigne could never decide whether it reminded her of a small, fast-moving glacier or Newton's first law of motion. Either way, you would arrive where you were going.

As they neared the alcove, its privacy screen suddenly vanished. At least they wouldn't need another ridiculous password.

Four people sat at the table within. The one nearest the arch was male, judging by the apparel, which was the sort of jacket that mimicked antique fabrics all the way down to elbow patches. In Montaigne's experience, only men wore anything that impractical. If *she* needed protection from cold, she'd use a thermal jacket—and no modern clothing material was so flimsy as to require special protection for the joints.

Of course, protection wasn't the reason they were there, and she was all too well aware of what they actually proclaimed.

An academic. Wonderful.

She suppressed another muttered imprecation. She didn't get along well with academics, generally speaking. In fact, she could think of only half a dozen exceptions to that rule, like Web Du Havel.

But she decided to keep an open mind, at least for the moment, because at least the man's mask wasn't ridiculous. Her own mask was a utilitarian blank screen that showed nothing but her eyes. Fanny's was a bit more elaborate; also nothing but a screen, but using a subtle waterfall effect.

The seated man's mask, like his jacket, was very old-fashioned—the head of a long-beaked bird. That design was also archaic, Montaigne knew, going all the way back to masks worn by doctors in Ante Diaspora times to avoid infection by their patients.

Does this fine fellow think I'm contagious? Montaigne grinned at the thought as she slid into one of the two unoccupied chairs in the rather crowded alcove. The grin didn't show, of course, because of the mask. So it seemed there *were* some advantages to the ludicrous things.

Two of the other already-seated people were clearly women. The woman to the almost-certainly-an-academic's right wore clothing that wasn't flamboyant but fit her snugly enough to make her gender clear. She was full figured, on the stocky side, with the same sort of nondescript mask Montaigne wore, whose only purpose was to disguise her features. Her short-cropped black hair was swirled with gray, which piqued Montaigne's interest. That sort of mix was unusual for people who'd received prolong, and the fact that the other woman hadn't dyed it probably spoke well of her, in Montaigne's opinion. If *her* hair had been gray, she wouldn't have dyed it, either.

The second woman in the alcove was a bit taller, with fair hair. Her choice in clothing was more colorful—a pantsuit whose shade exactly matched the bright blue eyes showing in the slits of her mask—and she was considerably more slender.

The fourth and final member of the waiting quartet was even more clearly male. He was probably as tall as Fanny—it was hard to tell when he was seated—and he had extraordinarily broad shoulders. What she could see of his complexion was almost as dark as Michelle Henke's, and his short hair curled tightly against his scalp.

Fanny slid into the last remaining seat—a somewhat more strenuous task in her case, and one which left the alcove what might reasonably have been called "full"—and the privacy screen snapped back into place. Montaigne glared over her shoulder at it.

"Why all the damn secrecy?" she demanded irritably.

"A reasonable question," the man with the elbow patches replied, and his own mask vanished. The face thereby revealed was clean shaven, with brown hair, brown eyes, and a friendly smile. "The masks are just to avoid drawing attention to ourselves. If you came into this place without one, everybody would notice you."

"So what?"

"So, for reasons that I'll explain in a moment, I'd rather not be noticed, Lady Catherine."

"I'm not 'Lady' Catherine," she shot back testily. Despite his courtesy, she still felt cranky. "I gave up my titles years ago, when I decided I'd be more effective sitting in the House of Commons than as one more fringe lunatic peer. Too many damned gadflies in the Lords already. Why let them file *me* as another one? And who are *you*, while we're on the subject of names?"

"Chuck Gannon. Or Dr. Charles E. Gannon, to be formal. And while you may no longer be Lady Catherine in the Star Empire, we're on Old Terra. Here—anywhere in the Solarian League—you're still the Countess of the Tor."

"He's right about that," Fanny said. "It's part of your … what should I call it? 'Mythos' seems a little extravagant."

The woman to Gannon's right switched off her own mask, revealing an attractive, open sort of face, and smiled at Montaigne.

"I don't think it's extravagant at all, personally," she said. "My parents were enthusiastic on the subject of Lady Catherine, champion of the downtrodden and bane of the never-to-be-sufficiently damned Manpower Incorporated."

Montaigne stared at her, and the other woman smiled more broadly.

"I come from an abolitionist family. Caused me a bit of trouble at the Academy."

"More than a bit," Gannon corrected. "But I think general introductions are in order."

The last pair of masks disappeared, and he waved at the first woman.

"Liz here—Elizabeth Robbins, being formal again—is a rear admiral in the Solarian League Navy, and the 'Academy' she's referring to is the Naval Academy. Which does not hold nonconformists in high regard … a fact which probably explains why she's not *Vice* Admiral Robbins.

"Seated across from her, we have Lieutenant Colonel Weng

Zhing-hwan. She's currently the CO of the Gendarmerie's Intelligence Command's Operations Division, but she'll be moving up to command all of the Gendarmes' intelligence divisions shortly. And to my left is Major Jerzy Scarlatti, also of the Gendarmerie."

My, Montaigne thought, *what an ... eclectic crew.* Speaking of which—

"And you are ... what, besides a 'Dr. Charles E. Gannon'?"

"I'm the new Director of Naval Intelligence," he replied, and Montaigne frowned.

"Your name's somehow familiar, but that's not the reason."

"No?" Fanny gave a little grunt of amusement. "You probably heard it in connection with the Banerjee Award. He won it a few years back."

That was it. Montaigne felt her irritation begin to subside. The Banerjee was one of the few academic awards for which she had any respect. Unlike most, it wasn't given out for any specific piece of work. It was more along the lines of a "genius in general" award, and while Montaigne was just as skeptical about the term *genius* as she was about awards, she couldn't deny that the Banerjee had an impressive track record.

Predictably, as irritation faded, curiosity came to the fore.

"All right," she said. "So why did Fanny insist I come here with her? I'd been assuming she just wanted my moral support for whatever new scheme she'd cooked up. But now I'm beginning to wonder."

"'Cooked up'?" Fanny scowled slightly. "First of all, I don't 'scheme.' Secondly, if I did, I wouldn't be 'cooking' them. You may not have any respect for cuisine, but I do."

"No, it wasn't Ms. Fanantenanirainy I wanted to speak to," Gannon said. "It was you."

Montaigne was genuinely impressed. He'd managed to pronounce Fanny's full name flawlessly. One might even say he'd rattled it off. Clearly, a man of substance.

"I have a proposal to advance," he continued.

"So advance it, then."

"Perhaps we should order drinks, first," Fanny suggested.

✧   ✧   ✧

It took a while.

After Gannon finished, Montaigne stared down at the fancy, fluted container on the table in front of her. People still called them "glasses," even though only the fiendishly expensive ones were still made of that ancient material. The one thing modern glasses had in common with ancestors was their transparency. Presumably so that people could see the potion they'd ordered.

Hers was called a "Jupiter." Not being at all knowledgeable about the history of alcoholic beverages, Montaigne was unaware that her ancestors who'd drunk from actual glass containers would have been either astonished or appalled (or both) had they seen the liquid she'd ordered. It was arranged in alternating horizontal bands of various shades of orange, yellow, off-white, and beige which swirled about the globular "glass" in a rotation that took about ten seconds to complete. She disarranged the pattern briefly, each time she sipped from it, but only until it fell back into its proper order and motion.

As a centerpiece, the beverage boasted a large red spot that rotated with the rest.

Actually, she'd barely touched it, so far. Now she picked it up and swallowed about a third of it. As expected, it tasted great. Which it ought to, given what she'd been charged for it. The former Countess of the Tor seldom drank alcoholic beverages, but when she did, she saw no reason to stint. She was, after all, one of the wealthiest people alive.

"So what do you think?" Fanny asked, and Montaigne set down the glass and looked at her with what might have been called just a *trace* of suspicion.

"You put them up to this, didn't you?" she said.

Fanny placed a hand on her chest and did her best to look aggrieved. Her best was...not very good.

"Certainly not!" she said virtuously. "Although, I will admit that when Chuck raised the idea with me, I was quite taken by it." She gave Montaigne a look that combined accusation and defensiveness. Tried to, anyway. "I should think you would be, too."

Montaigne lifted her glass again while she considered the matter. It was more of a sip than a gulp, this time, but she took a lot longer at it. Then, finally, she shook her head.

"I admit I'm taken by the spirit of your proposal, Chuck. But you're going at it the wrong way."

"I'm all ears, as the saying goes."

"The problem should be obvious—to you, even more than me. Once there's any suggestion that the Solarian League Navy is consorting with terrorists—*Audubon Ballroom* terrorists, no less—you'll never hear the end of it. Every step you take will be dogged by reporters and politicians and the people paying them to dog you."

"I imagine that's actually something of an understatement," Colonel Weng said dryly. Montaigne glanced at her, and she shrugged. "I have to confess that as a 'spook,' I regard any op that strays into the open as a failure in fieldcraft. In this instance, though, my understanding is that we want to be as open as possible. After all," she looked at Gannon just a bit pointedly, "a lot of this, from our perspective, is as much about the Navy's redemption—in the public's eyes, as well as its own—as it is the actual suppression of the slave trade. Which means going public with it. And that means the newsies *are* going to get wind of it. We *want* them to. And when that happens, at least some of them are going to *hammer* any connection to the Ballroom. Aren't they, Dr. Gannon?"

Gannon made a face.

"I'll admit that's the Admiral's big reservation, certainly. I'm pretty sure I can finesse the issue, once it comes up." Something rather like a snort came from Weng's direction, and his lips twitched. "Still, I admit it will be tricky," he added.

"You don't need to finesse it," Montaigne said. "All you have to do is approach the problem from the side, so to speak."

"Unpack that a little, would you?"

"Sure." She took another sip, mostly to give herself a little time to think, then set the glass down. "You don't go anywhere near the Ballroom. Instead, you approach the government of the Congo System with a proposal to engage in joint military exercises. Specifically, antislavery patrols. You don't even have to wait for the Constitutional Convention to toughen up the existing laws, because they're already on the books, aren't they, Colonel?" She pointed an index finger at Weng, who nodded firmly. "Be pretty awkward for a politician—or even a scandal sheet—to give you a hard time because you've started to enforce the League's own laws."

Gannon leaned back and drank from his own glass.

"That's . . . certainly possible. It'd be very awkward if Torch were a member of the Grand Alliance, but it's not. Never has been."

"It was in spirit," Montaigne pointed out.

"So?" Gannon snorted. "The letter of the law can work both

ways. Especially now, if someone tries to make accusations against a nation of former slaves. The fact is that the majority of the Provisional Assembly, not just the Constitutional Convention delegates—and a pretty big majority—genuinely opposes slavery. And, let's face it, whether or not they want to admit it in public, just about all of them know that the League bureaucracies' 'sweetheart deals' with corrupt transstellars had an awful lot to do with why—and how—the League just got its ass kicked by the Grand Alliance. They're in no mood to let *that* kind of crap start back up again."

"That's our read over at the Gendarmerie, too," Weng said with another nod. "Some of us are more cynical than others about how long the current mood will last, you understand. Experience does not engender optimism in that regard. At the moment, though, that's exactly the vibe we're getting from our current political lords and masters."

"I agree," Fanny said. "And it's especially true of the Constitutional Convention. You haven't mingled with any of the delegates, Cathy, because...well, because you've got to remain diplomatic. You *are* part of the Grand Alliance. But I'm not, and I mix with them all the time."

"Excuse me." Rear Admiral Robbins spoke up for the first time since Gannon had made his proposal. "I don't have any problem with what you're suggesting, Countess—sorry, Cathy. But I'm not sure how it solves our problem of needing advisors—I'm being blunt here—from the Ballroom. We *will* need them, or we'll be blundering around at least half-blind."

Major Scarlatti chuckled.

According to Gannon's proposal—or the bare bones of it Montaigne had heard so far, at any rate—Scarlatti would be the Gendarmerie's point man, assuming this brainstorm got off the ground, and she wondered if one reason he'd been chosen was because he was so junior in rank to Robbins. Technically, the Navy would be operating under Department of Justice authority, which a stickler might argue meant a Gendarme should be in command. But because he was junior to Robbins, he'd be functioning as her *second* in command, not her CO.

It was obvious the two of them had a comfortable working relationship, but now Robbins raised an eyebrow at him, and he shook his head.

"Admiral, you haven't taken into account how many of the Torch Navy's personnel are former members of the Audubon Ballroom." He cocked an eyebrow of his own at Montaigne. "It has to be at least—what, ten percent, I'd think?"

"Closer to fifteen—or even twenty—from what Anton tells me," she replied. "Yes, there's quite a few of them. And several occupy command positions."

"I can work with that," Scarlatti said cheerfully. "As a matter of fact, I might know some of them."

"Excuse me?"

Both of Robbins's eyebrows were up now, and he chuckled again.

"Oh, yes." He gave Weng a sly, sideways smile. "Those horrible 'terrorists' and the Gendarmerie have occasionally—fairly frequently, actually—discovered that our interests were ... convergent, let's say. I'm sure that's happened even with the fine, upstanding officers of the Navy, upon occasion. I *know* it's happened with those paragons of virtue in the Royal *Manticoran* Navy, anyway."

The rear admiral snorted in acknowledgment and ran a hand through her short hair.

"I knew a lot of the Ballroom had 'come home' to Torch and ended up in the military," she said. "I hadn't realized it represented that big a percentage of their navy, though."

She sipped thoughtfully from her own drink. It was a purplish concoction that went by the name of "Manhattan." In honor of an ancient swindler, if Montaigne remembered her history correctly.

"All right." Robbins set the drink down and nodded. "That would work. But there's still a couple of problems."

"Problems?" Montaigne cocked her head quizzically. "What sort of problems?"

"Well, the first is getting there. It's about forty-six days from here to Congo, even by way of Manticore and Erewhon. It's a hell of a lot longer trip any other way, and the Solarian League Navy isn't exactly what one might call, ah, *welcome* in Grand Alliance Space just now. So my first question, Chuck, is whether or not we can afford to burn another seven T-weeks before we even get started?"

"Um." Gannon rubbed his upper lip, then shrugged. "I don't see why not. Obviously, we'd hoped to hit the ground running sooner than that, but Lady Catherine is right about where we should be going for the ... expertise we need. And we haven't announced any of this to the public—or the Navy at large—yet, either, so we're not under any heavy time pressure to produce results."

"Okay." Robbins nodded. "Second problem—that 'unwelcome' bit. You remember? The one where Duchess Harrington announced that any SLN ship found outside League space will be treated as a pirate and destroyed without being allowed to surrender? I've got this feeling that neither Beowulf nor Manticore have exactly shut down their system defenses. And I'd really, really hate to become a dead pirate instead of a live Solarian officer."

"Good point." Gannon nodded and cocked an eyebrow at Montaigne. "You wouldn't happen to know any prominent Manticoran political leaders who might be able to help us out here, would you?"

"I *hate* getting involved in the 'diplomatic' crap," Montaigne muttered. But then she grimaced and nodded. "I can have a word with Admiral L'anglais. Assuming she's willing to sign on—and I don't see why she wouldn't be—she can probably clear the road for you, at least as far as Manticore."

"Probably?" Robbins looked at her quizzically.

"Well, if she *can't* she'll at least tell me so."

"Well, assuming we get that far, that just leaves the last problem," Robbins said. "Introductions. I'll be turning up with my battlecruiser squadron and at least one destroyer squadron, plus a couple of support ships for logistics. Torch may not have been part of the Grand Alliance, but I'm guessing it does know about that whole 'piratical vessel' thing. I'd like to think they'd at least give us the opportunity to explain ourselves before they blew us out of space, but I'm not in favor of risking my people's lives finding out. And, member of the Grand Alliance or not, according to our reports there are frequently detachments of Alliance ships in Congo. For that matter, it's not all that long ago that Torch suffered an attempted genocide. I'm thinking the Torches aren't likely to respond well if we come over the wall uninvited, either."

"Oh, that's easy!" Fanny pointed at Montaigne. "Just have her lead the way in her yacht."

"*What?*"

Harrington House
Harrington City
Harrington Steading
Planet Grayson
Grayson System

HONOR ALEXANDER-HARRINGTON LOOKED UP AS SOMEONE KNOCKED lightly on the frame of her office door, then smiled at the brown-haired lieutenant commander standing in the doorway beside Corporal Joshua Atkins, her duty armsman, and shook her head.

"Waldemar. What an enormous surprise it is to see you again."

The casual observer might have been forgiven for detecting a certain irony in her tone, and Lieutenant Commander Tümmel smiled back at her.

"This time I was just in the neighborhood and thought I'd poke my head in, Your Grace."

"Now why do I find that difficult to believe?" she asked in a musing tone.

Her ex-flag lieutenant had been pressed into service by the Admiralty and Empress Elizabeth to play mailman to Honor here in Grayson. She appreciated the regular updates, but she'd made her position clear. She was *not* coming back to active duty.

Not anytime soon, anyway.

She pushed her counter-grav float chair back from her enormous, spotlessly neat, improbably well-organized desk and stood. The treecat who'd been napping on the perch behind her chair roused and bleeked a cheerful greeting of his own.

"I believe we can probably trust the Commander in my presence, Joshua," she said.

"Of course, My Lady," Atkins agreed, although she noticed he also shot Nimitz a rather pointed glance before withdrawing.

275

She hid a sigh. None of her armsmen were going to forget what had happened to Simon Mattingly... or Tim Meares, she thought sadly. But at least Joshua was willing to trust Nimitz to look after her if the nanotech assassins had somehow gotten to Waldemar.

Tümmel crossed the sunny office—she'd insisted on a skylight, mostly so that Nimitz would have real sunlight in which to nap, although it had required some reengineering to the Harrington House dome—and she held out her hand to him.

"Although I suspect you are here with a fell purpose, it's really good to see you," she said, smiling warmly as she gripped his hand.

"No, no 'fell purpose.'" He shook his head. "I do have some messages for you from the Admiralty and from Mount Royal, but Her Majesty specifically charged me to tell you that they are solely for your information and do not constitute what she called 'an attempt to inveigle you back to Manticore.' And, no, this time I wasn't sent specifically to deliver them. I'm actually on my way to Bolthole."

"Bolthole?" Honor arched an eyebrow. "Aren't you just a little off the shortest route from Manticore to Bolthole?"

"The shortest direct route, yes." He nodded. "But I'm picking up a half-dozen or so Grayson naval architects from Blackbird, and then I'm going on to Nouveau Paris to collect a couple of R and D types Admiral Foraker's specifically requested."

"*You're* picking up?"

"Well, yes," he said in an innocent tone. "Oh! Did I forget to tell you that they gave me *Gaswain* last week?"

"Really?" She gripped his hand harder, smiling with delight. "That's wonderful! And you darned well deserve it."

"I don't know about deserving, but I did sort of have to promise I wouldn't break her before they'd give me the keys," Tümmel replied with a huge smile of his own, and she laughed out loud.

HMS *Gaswain* was a *Roland*-class destroyer, a plum command for someone of his seniority, especially now that the war with the Solarian League was all but over. It wouldn't be *officially* over until the Constitutional Convention on Old Terra produced a constitution acceptable to the Grand Alliance and the new Solarian League signed the peace treaty. According to the other messages which had been sent to Grayson "solely for her information," however, that process was actually going fairly well. She wondered how Catherine Montaigne's presence on Old Terra was playing into that mix, but unlike many of her fellow aristocrats she liked—and admired—the bomb-throwing (figuratively speaking, of course) ex-Countess of the Tor. She expected any influence Montaigne exerted to be...lively, but she also expected it to be well thought out and effective.

It was going to take T-months yet, though. Anyone with a working brain knew that. Building an entire new star nation, especially one the size of the Solarian League, even after its substantial territorial losses, wasn't something that could—or should—be rushed. She vastly preferred for them to take the time to get it right.

But until they did, the navies of the Grand Alliance were basically in a holding pattern.

Most of Grand Fleet had returned to the Manticore System, leaving "only" three or four dozen pod superdreadnoughts and their attached elements in the Sol System under the command of Admiral Pascaline L'anglais. L'anglais had been Honor's Havenite second in command for Operation Nemesis, and she'd been just *delighted* to leave Pascaline to keep an eye on Old Terra and gently remind the Constitutional Convention that the Grand Alliance was looking over its shoulder. Politely, but firmly.

The collapse of the Frontier Security Protectorates was proving even messier than she'd feared, however. Too many OFS governors, infuriated by the loss of their cozy, corrupt, highly profitable personal empires, seemed to have decided to make the transition to self-rule as difficult as possible. Some had gone so far as to actually purge critical records on the grounds that their files contained classified information they couldn't let fall into non-League hands. Others had loaded every Gendarme in their systems of responsibility on transports, gone aboard themselves, and headed for the Core, leaving the local star system without any trained administrators, a local police force, trained traffic management personnel, or anything else they needed to create a stable government and economy of their own.

It *was* true that a higher percentage of governors than she'd hoped were actually trying to help the process move smoothly, or at least not making sure that it didn't. But the ones deliberately creating problems were being more bare-knuckled, petulant, and just downright vicious than she'd really anticipated.

And in the face of that rolling tide of potential disaster, the Grand Alliance found itself forced to be far more "hands-on" in managing those transitions than it had hoped would be the case. Which meant the Joint Chiefs had been forced to strip cruiser squadrons and destroyer flotillas from Grand Fleet—and anywhere else they could find them—to use for power projection and area control as they sent in administrators and technicians to help deal with the chaos. It was a tricky proposition, because it was absolutely essential that the Grand Alliance not look as if it was trying to acquire the sort of "influence" which would allow it to dominate and effectively control those theoretically independent star systems. In fact, the only thing more essential than avoiding the *appearance* of that was to avoid a situation in which it actually happened.

Which it could, Honor knew. And not because anyone wanted that. The trick was finding a way to stabilize the situation and provide the needed expertise in a way which kept the locals in command of their own, newly restored destinies.

She was just as happy she didn't have to do that.

She told herself that firmly. *Very* firmly.

"So, after you complete your chauffeur's duties, where are they sending you and *Gaswain*?" she asked. "Do you know yet?"

"We're assigned to DesFlot 62," Tümmel replied. "I don't know exactly what that's going to mean for *Gaswain*, but I know that they've broken at least three other flotillas up into divisions and assigned them to support our 'nation-building' efforts in the Fringe and Verge."

Honor grimaced mentally. She supposed there wasn't a better term for it, but the historian in her knew how often "nation-building" had turned out to be nothing of the sort. Not to mention blowing up in its practitioners' faces.

"How long are you in-system? Can you stay for dinner?"

"Oh, we're not leaving until tomorrow. Maybe not even until the day *after* tomorrow." Tümmel shook his head. "It's going to take at least another twelve, fourteen hours for my passengers to get themselves sorted out and ready to go. They didn't know they *were* going until I got here with their orders, actually." He grinned. "Gotta love the Navy, Your Grace!"

"If they can't take a joke, they shouldn't have joined," she told him solemnly, and he laughed out loud.

Although, she reflected, in some ways that particular bit of lower deck wisdom was less humorous than usual. Surprise movement orders were seldom welcome, and that was especially true for Blackbird right now. The devastating damage the Yawata Strike had dealt the shipyards orbiting Blackbird was far, far from repaired. The situation was enormously better than it had been, but the yards were up to no more than thirty percent of their pre-strike capacity, and that was being generous. And the people assigned to rebuild them had approached their task with a powerful sense of mission and almost religious—no, in some cases, it *was* religious—zeal.

"Well, at least that means we can feed you tonight. You'll bring your off-watch officers?"

"Of course, if they're invited...and if there's enough room. If we won't be imposing."

"Waldemar, how many times did you visit Harrington House when you were my flag lieutenant?"

"Uh...a bunch?" he ventured.

"Maybe even twice that many," she said. "You do remember how big the state dining room is, don't you?"

"Well, yes, Your Grace. But, um, I thought you didn't like using it. I seem to recall your calling the process 'de-mothballing the mausoleum.'"

"Yes, I did," she said in a judicious sort of tone. "However, at the moment there are a few extra mouths to feed. Me, Earl White Haven, Nimitz, a total of—let me see...nine treecats, my mom and dad, Faith and James, Raoul and Katherine, Lindsey, a dozen or so armsmen, Sandra Thurston, Admiral Brigham, Admiral Yu, Austin, Bethany, Rebecca, Constance, Honor Mayhew, Reverend Sullivan—"

She paused as he raised both hands in laughing surrender.

"As you can see," she said sweetly, "including a half-dozen officers—heck, including your entire *ship's company*—wouldn't actually add a lot to the crowd."

"Is it really that bad every night, Your Grace?" he asked, still laughing.

"No, not *every* night," she acknowledged. "But most nights we do have quite a crowd sitting down to eat." Her smile faded. "I think part of it is that they want me—well, the kids and me, and Hamish—to know they love us. That they're here for us. So even when they drive me craziest," her smile brightened, "I'm actually sort of touched."

"I can understand that," he said, and the empathic sense she shared with the treecats told her he really did.

The one-two punch of the Yawata Strike and Beowulf Strike had cost too many people too much, but it had hit Honor and her family especially hard. Tümmel knew that if anyone did. He knew virtually her entire family on Sphinx had died in the Yawata Strike, and he knew Emily Alexander-Harrington had died in her arms, believing their husband was dead in Beowulf. That Honor had *known* Hamish was dead, when she hypered out to Sol to execute Operation Nemesis and bring the war to a close. And so Tümmel knew, better than most, how close to the ragged edge she'd come, how horribly she'd been wounded, before Hamish was miraculously restored to her.

And, yes, he understood exactly why the people who loved her—the surviving members of her extended family and her steaders—were determined to prove to her that she was not, and never would be, alone.

Of course, she'd already known that, she thought as she turned to open her arms, and Nimitz jumped into them, then swarmed around to her shoulder. She felt his mind-glow touching hers, fusing with it, and the assurance of his love flowed through her like the sunlight pouring through the skylight.

"Yes, well," she said, turning back to Tümmel. "I'll just tell Mistress Thorn we'll have a few *extra* extra mouths tonight. She'll be thrilled. She actually *likes* cooking for a Marine company or two!"

✧　　✧　　✧

"Are you okay, sweetheart?" Hamish Alexander-Harrington's low-pitched voice was almost lost in the background murmur of conversations, the sounds of tableware.

"Fine—fine!" Honor replied, but both of the treecats perched in highchairs beside their people gave her the sort of look they gave James or Faith when they *swore* they had no idea who might have raided the cookie jar.

Hamish glanced at them, then gave Honor a very old-fashioned look of his own.

"Traitors!" she muttered at their furry minions.

"What is it?" Hamish asked, and she sighed.

"Morning sickness." She poked moodily at the delicious pot roast on her plate. The pot roast she just *couldn't* make herself choke down. "Or, maybe *evening* sickness, I guess."

"Again?" His tone was carefully neutral, and she smiled a bit crookedly at him as she tasted his mind-glow. Genuine concern, mixed with at least a trace of amusement and a sense of wariness, predominated.

"Yes." She set down her fork, picked up her goblet, and sipped.

She'd never been all that fond of fruit juices before her pregnancy. She'd never disliked them, but they hadn't been high on her list of favorite beverages. Now, however, the combination of pomegranate and blackberry juice had proven itself as something her occasionally picky stomach could tolerate.

Picky stomach, she thought. *That* was something someone with the Meyerdahl mods seldom experienced. They were usually too preoccupied with stoking their active metabolisms for pickiness. Well, except for broccoli, of course. Now, though . . . not so much.

"I thought this was supposed to ease up after the first trimester," Hamish said as she put the goblet down. He picked up the carafe and poured more juice into it, his blue eyes amused, compassionate, and touched with that little edge of concern. "In fact, I'm pretty sure that's exactly what Dr. Frazier said was going to happen."

"She said that was what *usually* happened," Honor replied. "And I figured she was probably right in my case, given how easy all of Mom's pregnancies have been." She looked down the table to where Allison Harrington was laughing delightedly at something one of Tümmel's officers had just said. "Heck, *Mom* was never morning sick at all. There are times I am sorely tempted to strangle her."

Nimitz laughed, and his hands flashed.

"No, I don't think I *am* joking," she told him as she read his signs. Then the flickering fingers slowed, and her expression softened.

"You're right—you're right!" she said. "I still wouldn't miss it for the world. But that doesn't mean it's all a bed of roses," she added, smiling into Hamish's eyes.

"I always figured a bed of roses would be full of thorns, anyway," he told her.

"Of course it would—especially if it belonged to us!" Honor chuckled, pressing one palm to the gently swelling dome of her belly. "I don't believe we've ever done *anything* the easy way, have we?"

"Well...let me see..." He sat back in his chair, rubbing his chin with a studious expression. He stayed that way for at least fifteen or twenty seconds, then shook his head solemnly. "Nope. Can't think of a thing."

"Neither can I, but—" she reached for his wrist, placed his hand on that gentle swelling, and smiled into his eyes "—I wouldn't have missed *any* of it for the world. You know that, right?"

"Oh, I think you can assume the answer to that question is yes." He leaned close to kiss her gently on the cheek. "Nothing worth doing comes *easy*," he told her as he settled back.

"No, but I wouldn't object if it at least came without the nausea," she said a bit tartly, and it was his turn to chuckle.

"Well, I sort of wondered if this was going to happen. You seemed a little peckish at lunch. So—"

He looked past her as a swinging door opened and Mistress Sue Thorn, Honor's redoubtable housekeeper and cook, came through it. Honor had no idea how he might have signaled Mistress Thorn. On the other hand, she wouldn't put it past him to have enlisted James MacGuiness's assistance. She looked down the table to her right, to where MacGuiness sat beside Honor Mayhew, and the man who had once been her steward and was now her majordomo, keeper, and right hand, looked back at her blandly.

Yes, she thought, sampling his mind-glow. Hamish *had* drafted him for the "How Do We Feed Honor Tonight" conspiracy. She hadn't noticed him reaching for his uni-link, but her suspicions hadn't been engaged...then.

Mistress Thorn reached her, set down the tray she'd carried, and laid one hand lightly on Honor's shoulder.

"The Earl told me you might be...a little off your feed again tonight, My Lady," she said, squeezing gently. "So I made this."

She lifted the cover from the tray, and Honor smiled as she saw the honey-glazed tapioca. Tapioca had been one of her favorite desserts from childhood. More to the point, it was something she'd discovered she could get down—and keep there—no matter how bad the morning sickness was. Well, usually, anyway. There'd been that *one* time...

She blotted that particular memory from her mind and reached for her spoon.

"Bless you, Sue!" she said.

"Not like it's got everything you need," Mistress Thorn told her. "But if it goes down smooth, that's enough for now. Besides, that's what supplements are for." She squeezed again. "You just tell me if there's anything else you think you can eat. We'll get it for you."

"I know you will." Honor blinked momentarily misty eyes as she reached up to cover the hand on her shoulder. "I know you will." She glanced around the table, realized how many of the people around it—the people she loved—were looking back at her, and her smile trembled just a bit as she turned her head to look back up at her housekeeper.

"I know you will," Honor Alexander-Harrington repeated softly.

Capital Spaceport
City of Mendel
Planet Mesa
Mesa System

"DON'T BOTHER TO UNPACK." CACHAT WAS WAITING ON THE concourse when Damien Harahap and Indiana Graham disembarked from the shuttle. "We're leaving in a couple of hours."

He jabbed a thumb at another shuttle, parked on an adjacent pad.

"Just go ahead and take your bags to *that* one," he told them. "We'll be going aboard as soon as everyone gets here."

Indy and Harahap looked at each other, then back at Cachat and the large fellow in the uniform of a Solarian Marine major standing next to him.

"'Everyone' being—?" Indy asked.

"This is Bryce Tarkovsky. He'll be going with this. I'll explain later. We'll have plenty of time on the trip to Congo. Right now, I suggest you stow your gear and then grab something to eat."

"I can recommend the diner on Concourse G," Tarkovsky said. "Provided you like Vietnamese cuisine with a heavy dose of Basque, at least. Don't ask the chef to explain it. I made that mistake, and I haven't recovered yet. But it tastes good."

"Vietnamese/Basque?" Harahap smiled. "Just what I've always daydreamed about. Will you be joining us?"

"He will," Cachat said, nodding toward Tarkovsky. "I won't. I'm having lunch with Thandi. I don't know when I'll see her again."

Indy and Harahap looked at each other again. The treecat on Harahap's shoulder shook his head in a resigned gesture he'd learned from his two-foot. Then all three of them looked back at Cachat.

"Am I correct in assuming Indy and I are in that same 'don't know when we'll see X again' situation?" Harahap asked.

"Yes. You are."

Cachat nodded, and Harahap and Indy looked at each other again.

"The only one I'm close to, other than you," Harahap said, reaching up to touch Fire Watch's ears, "is this guy."

Fire Watch bleeked.

"And he's coming with us," Harahap added. "How about you?"

"Not anybody in range." Indy shrugged. "My folks and Mackenzie, but they're back in Seraphim. And...uh...well. There's maybe someone else, but I can't reach her in two hours, either."

Harahap nodded, then turned back to Cachat.

"Lucky you," he said brightly.

June 1923 Post Diaspora

"Oh, if your heart's bleeding for them *now*, just wait."

—Anton Zilwicki

Smooth and Wrinkled Club
Jordan Parker Pavilion
City of Mendel
Planet Mesa
Mesa System

SO THIS IS HOW THE OTHER HALF LIVES, KAYLA BARRETT THOUGHT
as she followed Arianne McBryde through the corridors and
airy rooms of the Smooth and Wrinkled Club. The S&W, as
Arianne referred to it, was a private club whose membership
was by invitation only. It occupied an entire level of the Jordan
Parker Pavilion, a modest little ten-floor structure set amid the
water features of the Jordan Parker Greenbelt, near the heart of
Mendel. A building that short, on such astronomically valuable
real estate, was about as ostentatious a statement of conspicuous
consumption as it was possible to make.

And the sheer luxury of the pavilion's interior only emphasized that point.

One thing she already knew about the S&W was that it cost an
arm and a leg to join...although not, apparently, for everyone. She'd
done a discreet investigation of the McBryde family's finances. They
were certainly in a comfortable position, but there was no indication they were especially wealthy. It was possible the cost of a club
membership had been waived or at least reduced in their case, and
if so, the reason was almost certain to have been their affiliation
with the Alignment. On the other hand, the S&W had been around
a long time, and more than a few of its memberships had been
passed between generations. It was entirely possible the McBrydes
were grandfathered in from one of those earlier generations.

Which, again, might well be because of that Alignment affiliation.

The Smooth and Wrinkled Club's premises were certainly large enough for a clandestine subset of its membership to operate quietly—and without any public notice—from within it. So far, Barrett had seen three meetings taking place in various meeting and conference rooms they'd passed—and that was only counting the ones who'd left their doors open. There'd been any number of *closed* doors, with no way to tell whether the rooms on the far side were empty or in use.

"Well, this is about as upper crust as it gets," a voice muttered behind her.

She was pretty sure Daud al-Fanudahi was talking to himself, not her. One thing she'd already gathered was that the Solarian wasn't what one might call a huge fan of ruling elites, whether they were Solarian or Mesan. She suspected that it had quite a bit to do with how many millions of people the Solly elite had managed to get killed. Nor had what he'd learned so far about the Alignment been designed to make him any fonder of the Sollies' Mesan counterparts.

He was obviously very good at his job, however, and Barrett was confident that was why Arianne McBryde had wanted him for the Solarian representative to this meeting. She hadn't provided much detail as to what the meeting was for and who would be attending, but it had all the earmarks of a gathering to persuade people of something. And that "something" couldn't be anything other than what Barrett had come to think of as the WOG issue: Who are the Other Guys?

Her thoughts had distracted her from her immediate surroundings, and she half-stumbled as an awkwardly placed side table forced her to shift to her weak side. She caught herself on her cane before her bad leg could buckle, but she also felt a hand under her elbow as she brought herself fully back upright.

"You okay?" al-Fanudahi asked.

"Sure." She flashed him a crooked smile. "The damned leg's getting stronger all the time. That's what my therapist keeps telling me, anyway." She shrugged. "But I could wish I wasn't one of the people who regenerate so slowly."

"Better than *not* regenerating," he told her. "One of my cousins?" He shook his head. "Can't regenerate at all. Lost an arm in a grav ski accident when he was only about...what? Thirteen T-years old? Went through three prostheses before he finished his last growth spurt."

"Well, at least I managed to avoid that. I will say, though, that I've developed an entirely different perspective on the term 'obstacle course.'"

"I imagine you have." He chuckled. "I have to say, I'm just as happy I've managed to avoid ever being—"

He broke off whatever he'd been about to say as Arianne came to a halt at a very fancy and ornate-looking door. The old-fashioned wooden panel bore the words *Yardley Room*, inlaid in ornately flowing script that looked like genuine, antique gold leaf. Below that, a more modern electronic display added: "Private Meeting. By Invitation Only."

If Arianne had announced their arrival somehow, Barrett detected no sign of it. But the door was already opening—inward, as if it were on hinges of some sort. Speaking of "old-fashioned" . . . Would they squeak? she wondered, hoping they would.

No such luck, though. The mechanism might be anachronistic, but the technology underlying it wouldn't be.

The person who'd opened the door didn't look antique, certainly. From her indefinable poise, Barrett was sure the woman was well into her fourth or fifth decade, although her rather . . . gaudy fashion choices suggested someone considerably younger than that.

"Nice to see you again, Arianne," the woman said, and waved a hand toward the room beyond. "Come in. Everyone's here already."

As she stepped into the room, Barrett saw that it shared the antique flavor that appeared to be the hallmark of the Smooth and Wrinkled Club. It was large and high-ceilinged, with what certainly looked like a floor of genuine hardwood sprinkled with armchairs that looked like overstuffed monsters from a pre-technic age. She rather doubted they actually were, however, and three of them were already occupied, by two men and a woman. The woman who'd let them in walked past them to drop gracefully into one of the vacant chairs.

That left five empty ones. Arianna walked to the one that more or less faced the foursome who projected an aura of "the audience" and seated herself. Barrett chose one a bit to the side. Al-Fanudahi gave her a hand as she settled into it, then crossed to a chair of his own, to Arianne's right.

As Barrett had guessed, the armchair was extremely comfortable, adjusting almost instantly to her shape and preferred posture. It might look like an antique, but it definitely wasn't one.

"Hello, Arianne." It was the man on the far left of their audience. He was slender to the point of looking a bit skeletal, with blond hair, light skin, and eyes that were very pale blue. "Do the introductions, would you?"

"This is Captain Daud Ibn Mamoun al-Fanudahi of the Solarian League Navy," Arianne said, waving her right hand at him. "He's with the Office of ONI's Operational Analysis. He arrived in Mesa just recently as part of a Solarian investigative team."

"Investigating what, exactly?" asked the woman who'd let them in.

"I'm part of an informal group within the Solarian government—mostly from the Navy, but we include some Gendarmes—who have been investigating all the incidents the Grand Alliance claims are the work of what they call 'the Alignment,'" al-Fanudahi replied. "That includes—"

"You can go into the details later, Captain," the blond-haired man interrupted with a small, courteous smile. "Let's finish the introductions first."

"Of course." Arianne waved her other hand at Barrett. "This is Lieutenant Kayla Barrett, from the Mesan Unitary Magistral Police. Before she was recruited for that, she was a sergeant in the Internal Security Directorate."

The spokesman's eyes widened. So did those of both of the women in his group. The other man, however, only nodded slightly.

"She's one of Director Saburo Lara's closest subordinates," Arianne continued, and, despite herself, Barrett snorted a laugh.

"I'm his only 'close subordinate,' for the moment," she explained when the others looked at her. "The Mumps are very much a work in progress."

"The 'Mumps'?" the man who hadn't yet spoken asked. "I'm Gebhardt Juarez, by the way. Call me 'Geb.'"

"'Mumps' is the slang term for the Mesan Unified Magistral Police," Barrett replied.

"You've *already* got a nickname?" Juarez sounded surprised, and Barrett smiled.

"Sure. Saburo saw to that right away. It's the reason he hung that clumsy excuse for a name on us. He says the *hoi polloi*—that's an old term—"

"Yes, I know what it means."

"Well, Saburo says they're bound to develop a nickname for

the cops before long, and he wanted to make sure it was the right sort of nickname. Somewhat disrespectful—that's a given, he says—but not one that projects too much in the way of over-bearing authority or menace."

All four of the people they'd come to meet stared at her. Then Juarez nodded again.

"I'd heard he was shrewd."

"Oh, yes. He's *that*, for sure," Barrett agreed.

"And he doesn't have a problem with your being a former 'Misty'?" the woman sitting next to Juarez asked.

She didn't look any older than the woman who'd admitted them to the meeting room—or than Barrett herself, for that matter—but she was much more conservatively dressed. Now she pointed at Juarez with a thumb.

"I'm Geb's cousin. My name's Janice Delgado."

"No, he doesn't have a problem," Barrett replied. "In fact that's one of the reasons he enlisted me. He wants enough people in the Mumps who come out of the old security services to keep the full—former full—citizens from getting too twitchy."

"Shrewd indeed," Juarez said. "What do you think of him?"

Barrett thought about that for a moment.

"Well...I have mixed feelings about Saburo," she said. "And it's a peculiar mix. On the one hand, he's scary as hell."

"Threatening?" Delgado asked with a frown.

"No, not at all. He seems completely relaxed and easy-going, pretty much all the time. That's what I find scary. I pulled up his file—which he's made no attempt to hide, by the way. It's partial as hell, of course, but what we did know about him..."

She paused again, pursing her lips, like a woman trying to decide whether or not she liked the taste she'd just sampled.

"There's something really scary about a really scary person who makes no effort at all to seem scary," she said finally, and Juarez nodded yet again.

"Yes, that I can believe. What else strikes you about him?"

"He's extremely capable—that's already obvious. And...well, the truth is I'm starting to like him. He's a damn good boss, that's for sure. Way better than any I ever had in the Misties."

Juarez considered that, then looked at al-Fanudahi.

"You say you've been investigating this so-called 'Alignment' for some time, Captain. But not officially, I take it."

"Not until very recently. Before that—"

"Do I take it that 'before that' refers to the change in the Solarian League's...ah, 'management,' let's call it?"

"Yes." Al-Fanudahi nodded. "Before that, we just referred to ourselves as the Ghost Hunters."

"And did you find any ghosts?" Juarez asked with a smile.

"Oh, yes. By now, we've compiled a lot of evidence that there is indeed some...malignant force at work. Among other things, over forty highly placed Navy officers and civilian bureaucrats have keeled over and died of 'natural causes' when we took them into custody. You wouldn't believe how varied those 'natural causes' have been. But the fact that they all dropped dead as soon as they realized they were under arrest is pretty compelling evidence that whoever's been playing us has been doing it for a long, long time. And that they're ruthless as hell."

"So you agree with the Grand Alliance's claim that what they call 'the Alignment' is responsible for all these mass murders?" It was the man who'd started the conversation but still hadn't been identified. When al-Fanudahi looked at him, he added: "I am Kevin Olonga. The one—the only—member of our group here who has an official status that's relevant. I sit on the recently convened General Board of the Provisional Government. The *very* provisional Provisional Government."

"And may I ask who all the *rest* of you represent?"

"Us?" The man gestured towards his three companions. "Well, what we represent—and Arianne—is what *we* call the Alignment. Which is one reason we're curious about whether or not you agree with the Grand Alliance."

The Solarian rubbed the back of his neck thoughtfully.

"I suppose the answer is yes...and no. We agree with them that *somebody* is up to no good. For our part, we just called whoever it is the Other Guys. But we haven't officially signed on—yet—to their theory of the Alignment."

"Yet?"

"I think the odds are that we will in the end," al-Fanudahi said. "They have a coherent theory that hangs together and fits all the evidence we've been able to accumulate. So, many of the Ghost Hunters—most of us by now, including me—are strongly inclined in that direction. For that matter, we just got copied on an analysis Director Gannon—he's the new head of ONI—commissioned. I haven't had an opportunity to really go through the underlying data yet, but in general, its conclusions agree very closely with the ones Captain Zilwicki's reached independently. But as far as who they are and why they're doing what they're doing, we're keeping an open mind until we've had a better opportunity to test their theory. Trying to, at any rate.

"But I should also say," he added, raising one hand in a warding gesture, "that we don't think—and neither does the Grand Alliance, by the way—that *your* Alignment is responsible for any of the killings."

"Well, that's a start, anyway." Olonga leaned back in his chair.

"So what do you want from us, Captain?" Delgado asked.

"Your cooperation and assistance. We'd like you to be involved in the investigation. Among other things, the more we can learn about you and your organization's history, the better the fix on where what the GA is calling the Malign Alignment split from the rest of you. And, frankly, with the perspective we can bring to it, you may actually be able to identify more of the Malign Alignment's cadre for us than you think you can."

"Arianne?" Delgado looked at the younger woman. "What do you think?"

"I agree with them, and I think that's exactly what we should do," Arianne replied firmly. "In fact, I've already been doing it, as an individual. Now I think we should do it as an organization, too. If for no other reason than to clear our name."

"A nice thought, but I'm afraid that's a lost cause by now." Olonga shook his head. "Oh, I agree that we need to clear *ourselves*, but that name's hopelessly tainted now. We need a new one."

All three of his companions frowned at that, but not Arianne.

"He's right," she said firmly. "So I propose we call ourselves the Engagement. We need to come out of the shadows and engage with the rest of the human race—which is what we should have done T-centuries ago."

Singlaub Tower
and
Alexia Gabon Tower
City of Mendel
Planet Mesa
Mesa System

THE LIFT DOORS OPENED ON HER FLOOR, AND KAYLA BARRETT
stepped through them.

Singlaub Tower was primarily residential, but every tenth floor
was zoned commercial around the central lift banks, and Barrett normally enjoyed the bustle and flow of the tower's residents
as they patronized the shopping malls, boutiques, small shops,
restaurants, and food courts.

This time, though, she stopped a dozen steps into the concourse. She shifted her posture, balancing her weight on her good
leg and transferring the cane to her left hand.

That freed up her gun hand.

She didn't draw her pulser, because so far as she could tell,
none of the people with cups of coffee sitting around the food
court table just outside the lift were armed. That didn't mean
they weren't, though. All three of them, like her, had been sergeants in the Mesan Internal Security Directorate. And all of
them—just as she had then and was now—were in the habit of
carrying concealed backup weapons.

"Are we looking at a problem here?" she asked.

Two of the people seated at the table frowned at her. The
third—the older of the two men in the group—just chuckled
and shook his head.

"Well, that much about you hasn't changed," he said. "Damn,
Kayla. What trauma in your life made you so distrustful?"

"It started with being born, which nobody warned me was about to upset my happy state of unconsciousness. And it went downhill from there. What do you want, Jake?"

"We want to talk to you, Kayla," the lone woman of the group replied. "About—"

She glanced at her companions and sucked in a breath, like someone contemplating a leap from a risky height.

"We need jobs," she said. "And about the only thing we have any skills at is police work."

"Is that what we used to do, Sandra? You'd get an argument about that from a lot of people, and just about any seccy. Uniformed goons, is what I remember us mostly being."

The younger man, Esteban Burkhanov, scowled at her. But the older one, Jake Abrams, only shrugged.

"I expect you're right," he said. "But we did do some actual police work, and part of the reason we got along with each other is because none of us liked the rough stuff and we tried to keep it down as much as we could."

That was true enough, Barrett thought, although you didn't want to examine the statement too closely. "Keeping down the rough stuff" looked a lot different depending upon the end of it from which you looked at it. Still, she felt herself relaxing.

"If you want to talk, let's go to my apartment. The furniture's more comfortable, we'll have some privacy, and there's better stuff than coffee to drink."

❖   ❖   ❖

"You sure about this?" she asked, once everyone was comfortably scattered around her living room with drinks in hand.

Sandra Tuminello and Burkhanov had beers, but Abrams had opted for coffee, after all. Barrett had decided to follow Abrams's example. Now she took a sip, then set the cup down. It was still too hot.

"Look," she said. "For me, it's pretty easy. I don't have any family left, and I never had all that many friends to start with. By now, half of them are scattered to the winds—or dead, for all I know. But unless things have changed, all three of you still have close ties. If you join the Mumps, you'll probably lose half your family and friends."

"I won't," Tuminello said. "Not family, anyway." Which was probably true, Barrett reflected; the Tuminello family was extended and close knit. "And whatever friends I lose—" Tuminello shrugged and swallowed beer. "Fuck 'em. The way I see it, they weren't really friends to begin with."

"How I feel, too," Burkhanov said. "My dad'll never forgive me, but we haven't gotten along in years anyway."

Abrams only sipped coffee with a sphinxlike lack of expression, and Barrett shrugged. She'd given them the obligatory cautionary statement. Whatever happened from here, they couldn't say she hadn't warned them.

"So tell us, Kayla," Tuminello said. "What's it like?"

"The job? Hard to tell, so far. We're still getting organized."

"I meant working for a—" Tuminello's lips tightened.

"Ballroom terrorist?" Barrett said dryly. "Slavering baby-killer?"

"I'm serious, Kayla."

"So am I. That's how other people—people all of you know—are going to describe him when they demand to know how you could possibly work for someone like *him*. If you can't handle that, you need to drop the whole idea. Now."

"What's he like?" Abrams asked. "This Saburo guy."

Barrett considered that, for a few seconds, then shrugged.

"I guarantee he's not what you'll expect. The man is deadlier than anyone else you'll probably ever meet. Don't think for a moment that he isn't. But now...I think he's just focused on creating a new Mesa."

Abrams pursed his lips, then nodded.

"I can see that happening. So will you recommend us to him?"

"I'll recommend you and Sandra, sure. Esteban—" Barrett gave the younger man a thoughtful look. "I'll recommend you, too...but I'll also warn Saburo that you've got a short fuse."

"What the hell?" Burkhanov jolted upright, spilling beer in the process. "Listen, you goddamn—"

"Congratulations," Abrams said dryly. "You just proved her point."

"You do have a quick temper, Esteban," Tuminello chimed in. "It's gotten you in trouble before."

Burkhanov slouched down in his chair, glowering. Abrams kept an eye on him for a few seconds, and then looked back at Barrett.

"We might be able to sweeten the deal," he said.

"*Might*," Tuminello stressed. She waggled her hand in a gesture of uncertainty. "We're not completely sure of it, though."

"Sure of what?"

Abrams and Tuminello looked at each other. Then Abrams looked back at Barrett.

"We think we know—*may* know, but there's a pretty damned good chance we're right—where Regan Snyder and François McGillicuddy are hiding out."

Barrett jerked straight up in her chair. Regan Snyder was—had been, rather—a member of Mesa's governing General Board, as well as Manpower's Vice President of Operations. McGillicuddy had been Mesa's Director of Security. No former members of Mesa's ruling elite—except for Bentley Howell, the head of Internal Security, who'd called down the huge KEW strike on Hancock Tower—were more wanted by the authorities.

Wanted *alive*. Saburo had stressed that to her when they'd discussed the issue.

"We want public trials, Kayla," he said. "Not just corpses. Put the swine in the dock, try them—fairly, I'm not talking about a kangaroo court—convict them, and then lock them away for the rest of their stinking existence. That's one nice thing about prolong. A life sentence without parole goes on for a long, long time."

"What's a kangaroo court?" she'd asked.

"What slaves and seccies used to get. They named them after an animal back on Old Terra that hopped around, which is what some judges would do. Hop—you're guilty—hop—you're guilty—hop—get out of my way, I haven't got time to look at the evidence."

"Oh."

She'd felt a little guilty, then. The truth was that the Internal Security she'd once belonged to often hadn't even bothered with a summary court. Just shoot them and be done with it...

She jerked her mind back to the present.

"Where are they?" she asked, and her three guests looked back and forth, obviously hesitant.

"Oh, for God's sake. Cut it out. Trust me, I know the man fairly well by now—Saburo's not going to haggle with you. You deal with him in good faith, and he'll do the same for you. That doesn't mean he'll hire you, but it does mean he'll consider it honestly. So, I'm asking again—where are Snyder and McGillicuddy?"

To her surprise, it was Burkhanov who provided the answer. Maybe he was trying to make up for his earlier belligerence.

"We think they're holed up in Jessyk's headquarters."

"*Jessyk?*" Barrett shook her head. "Their headquarters are deserted. And Hibson's MMA swept it before they locked the entire floor down. Its offices weren't demolished the way Manpower's were, but they did get swept for warm bodies. Not that they found anyone stupid enough to be hanging around after what happened to Manpower. Too many seccies and slaves knew who hauled 'cargo' for the bastards."

The number of *ley du fuga* killings when Manpower's headquarters were overrun, right after Tenth Fleet arrived in-system, had been...large. As in damned near total. A handful of clerical workers and the seccy maintenance staff had been spared. For the rest, not so much. It was a testimony to the arrogance of that transstellar that it apparently hadn't dawned on most of its executives that their immunity from punishment had just evaporated. Which meant there'd still been a lot of them on-site when the seccy and slave mob stormed it.

"Yeah, but I doubt the GA search teams were even thinking in terms of secret hideouts behind the bookcases or whatever," Tuminello said. "Like you say, they were looking for warm bodies that wanted to stay that way. People who *wanted* to be taken into custody, if that was how they got out alive. Who had time to go around tapping on walls?"

She's got a point, Barrett thought. *Probably. But she's sure as hell right about how full the teams' hands were, at least.*

Yes, it made sense. If Jessyk had constructed well-designed hideaways as a precaution—in which case they would have demonstrated a lot more intelligent foresight than Manpower—fugitives could have found shelter there. Assuming, of course, that they'd gotten there quickly enough, knew the shelters existed, and had pull with Jessyk officials...all of which was true of Snyder and McGillicuddy.

She thought about that a moment longer, then stood.

"Let's go," she said.

❖   ❖   ❖

Saburo held this audience in more formal style, seated behind his desk with Barrett and her three companions' straight-backed chairs lined up in a row in front of him.

"How sure are you that Snyder and McGillicuddy are there, and why?" he asked.

He had his elbows propped on his chair's armrests and his hands clasped below his chin, with his forefingers making a steeple at his lips. It was a more thoughtful sort of pose than Barrett had ever seen him use. She suspected he was doing it mostly to calm the nerves of the three ex-Misties, who had no experience dealing with him. For them, a face-to-face meeting with a top striker of the Audubon Ballroom had to be unsettling, to say the least.

"Esteban and I got drunk a while back with a couple of Misties we used to work with," Abrams replied. "One of them let slip that they'd escorted Snyder and McGillicuddy into the Jessyk complex in Nakatomi Tower the day the shit hit—the day the Grand Alliance arrived. His partner got pissed at him and told him to keep his mouth shut. Then she told us to forget what he'd said, because it was nonsense. She added some vague threats on top of that. Then the two of them got to quarreling."

"Which they do a lot," Burkhanov added. "How the hell they've managed to stay together as long as they have is a mystery to everybody."

"The point being that it's not very likely they remember much if anything of what was said that night," Abrams said. "They were a lot more plastered than we were. We wound up having to help them get home."

Saburo tapped his lips with his fingertips a few times.

"All right, that's a pretty good indication that Snyder and McGillicuddy went into Jessyk's headquarters that day. But what makes you assume they stayed there?"

"Where else would they go?" Tuminello asked. "And more important—why?"

She glanced at her two partners, drew a deep breath, and held it for a couple of seconds.

"Look, Mr. Saburo," she let out then, in something of a rush, "I don't think you probably understand—"

"It's just plain Saburo," he interrupted. "If you were going to use a surname, it would have to be Lara, and—" he smiled thinly "—Mr. Lara? I'd never hear the end of that from her ghost."

He unclasped his hands and waved for her to go on.

"Protocol lesson's over. Keep talking."

She drew another deep breath.

"What I mean to say is that you don't—well, I don't think you do—understand just how panicked and scared the full citizens were. Still are."

"*Former* full citizens, Sandra," Abrams corrected with a little wince.

"Don't worry about that right now." Saburo smiled again, more broadly. "If you come to work for the Mumps, you'll have to learn the correct terminology, and pretty quickly. But that's for another day. Keep talking, Ms. Tuminello."

"The thing is, both Snyder and McGillicuddy were very well known and pretty instantly recognizable."

"Especially that snotty bitch," Burkhanov said. "She belonged to one of the New Lodges. Those are—"

"I know what they are. So she'd have plenty of piercings and tattoos, which aren't that easy to get rid of without time and a lot of quick-heal."

"She was tall and very good-looking, too," Tuminello added. "Much as I hate to say it."

Saburo cocked his head at her.

"I take it you weren't fond of her?"

"I can't say I really knew her, except by reputation. Which stank." Tuminello shrugged. "But the one time I actually ran into her, she lived up to it."

"McGillicuddy wasn't as striking looking," Abrams said. "But he was extremely well known. He would have been recognized by almost any full citizen. *Former* full citizen."

"That *is* something of a mouthful," Saburo said with a genuine chuckle. "I'd replace it with a nickname, but the only one I'd been able to think of so far is *fofucit*, which is just asking for a fight."

He said it with an absolutely straight face, and all four of the ex-Misties laughed. And then all of them—aside from Barrett, looked simultaneously aghast and...well, a little intrigued. Barrett remembered the feeling. Saburo was not what you'd expect from a denizen of the underworld.

"But I get your point," he continued. "Both of them would have had a hard time moving around without being spotted. And neither of them had a lot of fans, and it didn't take long for word to get out that there was a hefty reward for anyone who turned them in. Which is still in place, by the way. So if you're right about this, the three of you will be coming into quite a bit of money. Enough to live on—"

"For a little over seven years, split three ways," Abrams said. "We already figured it out."

Saburo nodded and looked at him with a quizzically raised eyebrow.

"That sounds about right. Which leads me to my next question. That being so, why do you still want jobs?"

"Well..." Abrams glanced at the other three, then turned back to Saburo. "We can't guarantee our info. We think it's good, but no one can know one way or the other until it's checked out, and if it turns out we were wrong, we still need work. And—I'm speaking for myself, now—when I heard you'd hired Kayla—" he twitched his head at Barrett "—I started wondering if you'd hire *me*. I know how much she hated some of the crap the Misties did. If she'd found a way to step away from that whole pile of shit—and the people who'd thought it was a good idea—and do something *positive* with her life...

"I'm no saint, Saburo. I may have hated some of what 'the job' required, but I went along to get along. Never thought I could have changed it, but I never *tried* to, either, aside from doing what I could to hold down the freelance rough shit. When I heard Kayla was trying to do something *right*, something that might make up for even a little of what all four of us had done, been part of... Well, I wanted in. I'd really like it if I could start looking into the mirror in the morning."

He fell silent, his expression more than a little abashed, and Saburo sat back to contemplate him for several thoughtful seconds of silence. Then he looked at Tuminello and Burkhanov.

"And you two?" he asked.

"I never thought it out the way Jake has," Tuminello said after a moment. "But now that he's put it into words, yeah. Yeah, I think that *is* a big part of what's been going on in my own head, even if I never looked right at it. I mean, I'm a hell of a lot better looking than he is," she quirked a fleeting smile at Abrams, then looked back at Saburo, "but I've been kind of avoiding mirrors, too."

Saburo nodded and moved his gaze to Burkhanov, who shrugged a bit irritably.

"Hey, I'm okay with mirrors," he said. "Doesn't mean I liked everything the Misties did, though. I'm not looking for any kind of redemption, here. But I'm not much of one for sitting on my ass drinking beer and getting fat, and at least this is something I know I can do. Do *right*, I mean, not the way the Misties did it. And if I can help make some of *that* stuff right, then, yeah. I'm down for it. What the hell else am I gonna do?"

He met Saburo's eyes levelly, and the ex-Ballroom striker smiled very slightly, then nodded.

"All right," he said. "I'll hire all of you for the Mumps, partly because of what you just said, but—being honest, here—mostly because you come with Kayla's recommendation. I may find other reasons down the road to be glad I did, but for right now, that's the biggie. She wouldn't have brought you here without checking with me first if she had any major reservations."

"Fair warning, boss. Esteban has something of a temper."

Saburo gave the young man no more than a glance.

"Learn to control it. And whatever you do, don't lose your temper with me." The flat affect with which he said that made it all the more menacing, and then he held up a cautioning finger. "But—you'll all be on probation for a while."

"Yeah, sure." Abrams nodded. "That's a given."

"All right, then." Saburo stood. "Let's get the ball rolling."

The people sitting in front of his desk came to their feet. Quickly, except for Barrett, thanks to her bad leg.

Tuminello looked a little startled.

"Uh, Mister—ah, Saburo. None of us brought any of our gear with us."

This time, he bestowed an actual grin on her.

"You think I'm dumb enough to launch a tactical assault with a team that's never trained together? No, no—and it's not just you. The Mumps are still getting organized. We don't have *any* tactical assault teams yet. That means I'd have to call on either Drescher or the Grand Alliance to provide troops, and the day it's a good idea to use soldiers or Marines for police work is the day we've reached the heat death of the universe."

He headed for the door.

"No, we're starting somewhere else. Before you start even thinking about a tactical op, you need to know the terrain, what you're sending your people into. And I think I know *just* the fellow to help us figure that out."

Hugo de Vries Tower
City of Mendel
Planet Mesa
Mesa System

"THIS IS THE FIRST TIME YOU'VE BEEN HERE, ISN'T IT?" ANTON Zilwicki said as he pointed to a conference table five meters or so from what he chose to call his workstation. Which, Kayla Barrett thought, was about as appropriate as calling a luxury yacht a dinghy.

"Have a seat," he continued. "I'll stay at my workstation, but I can project anything interesting I find over to you."

Zilwicki's version of "taking his seat"—at least as far as his workstation was concerned—reminded Barrett of someone fitting themselves into the cockpit of some sort of transatmospheric racer. *Ordinary* mortals required only a virtual keyboard to search for data. Not him, though.

Granted, he *was* famous, at least in certain quarters, for this sort of thing.

"Yes," Saburo said, settling into one of the chairs. "Last time I saw you at work, you were still in Neue Rostock."

"They've got too much rebuilding still to do. Workmen and repair bots everywhere. Makes maintaining any sort of real security almost impossible. This place—" he waved a hand "—used to be a data center for Domestic Intelligence Analysis. Since they don't exist anymore, I figured they didn't need all the space and equipment gathering dust in here anymore, either."

"So you commandeered it."

"I didn't 'commandeer' anything. I signed for it," Zilwicki told him, and Saburo smiled.

"And what was it you signed, if I may ask?"

"A document. I'm sure it's been recorded somewhere. Arianne might know what happened to it." He pointed at a door in the wall to his right. "She's in there, if you want to ask her." He shrugged and turned back to his console. "Give me some time. This'll take a while."

He didn't resurface for almost an hour, and when he did, it was only to shift to another workstation. He entered commands, and a hologram appeared above the table-mounted projector.

"Can you come in here?" he said into his headset, then looked at the visitors. "I think it'd be a good idea to involve Arianne in this."

He waved at the hologram in front of them.

"This is an actual schematic—an *official* schematic—of Jessyk's headquarters complex. It doesn't show any secret chambers, but it's obvious where they are. If you look here and here—" he highlighted the sections he was referring to "—and then match what's shown against the official blueprints for the *tower*, not just their floors, on file with Building Safety and Permitting..."

Anther hologram came up, with more highlighting.

"...you can easily see that there's way too much unused space, according to the tower's plans. Sooo, one of them is lying to us."

Arianne McBryde entered the room while Saburo, Barrett, and the three new Mump recruits were studying the display. Anton waved at her, and she crossed to take a seat at a secondary terminal at the head of the conference table.

"It's not very detailed, Anton," Saburo said. "We're going to need more precise information before we can raid the facility."

"Don't teach your grandfather how to suck eggs. And before you ask, I have no idea where that expression comes from. I just know what it means."

"Which is... what?"

"Which is that it's stupid to work yourself to death trying to decipher schematics that were deliberately designed to be inscrutable, when a quick and simple analysis of other, way more scrutable data, can uncover the architect who produced the original plans in the first place. Well, archi*tects*, I should say. It could be any one of these three people."

The schematic disappeared, replaced by the images and dossiers of three architects. One was male, and the other two were female.

"As I say, it *could* be any one of the three," Zilwicki said, "but it's pretty much got to be this one." He highlighted the image of one of the women. "At least an eighty percent probability, I'd say."

"Why do you think—?" Saburo broke off. "Never mind. I'll take your word for it. So where do we find her?"

"Why go look for her at all? I've already found her address. Why don't we just screen her and tell her we'd like to talk to her. Here."

"She might run for it."

"Not likely," Arianne said. "Look at her record. This is hardly the profile of someone who takes risks. Everything in her life, it looks like she's done by the book. Besides . . . give me a moment."

Her hands moved across the virtual keyboard. Less than fifteen seconds later, the image of a door in a residential tower appeared in the hologram. It opened onto a pleasantly airy but not overly huge access corridor with only two slidewalks.

"That's her front door," Arianne said. "It's where she's lived since she got out of college. You're seeing it courtesy of the security cams in her tower's public areas. Aside from the fire escape, which is alarmed, it's the only way out of her apartment. So we'll know when she steps through the door. If we really want to, and if Saburo knows a convenient judge—which I'm sure he does—we can activate the emergency locator function on her uni-link without alerting her, which would let us track her anywhere on the planet, at least until she took it off. But there are a *lot* of security cameras in that tower, not to mention covering every public access way in the city. If Anton and I working together can't track her using those cameras—or cheating, and using her uni-link, if we have to—I will eat one of my new shoes."

She reached down and worked at a foot for a moment, then held up a very stylish blue shoe.

"This one, just in case I lose. It's my right shoe, and my left foot is the bigger one."

"I've got her com combination," Zilwicki said. "Here we go."

✧   ✧   ✧

Arianne was never in any danger of having to engage in papoutsisphagy, which was just as well, since unlike leather, the substances used to make modern footwear were quite impervious to boiling water.

The architect reached the south entrance of Hugo de Vries Tower about as quickly as was humanly possible. Sandra Tuminello was waiting and ushered her up the lifts to Zilwicki's lair on its eighty-seventh floor. She was visibly nervous as she came in.

"I'm Lillian Hartmann," she blurted almost before she crossed the threshold. "What's this all about?"

Zilwicki, who'd already risen, gestured politely at the conference table.

"Please, Ms. Hartmann. Have a seat. We need to show you something."

She sank warily into one of the unoccupied chairs, then stiffened as he brought the hologram back to life.

"I believe you recognize these, don't you?" His tone was just as courteous as before, but her expression had turned hostile... or perhaps *defensive* would have been a better description.

"I haven't done anything wrong! There's nothing illegal about anything I designed."

"I'm sure there isn't," Saburo said. "In fact, I'm quite sure everything is up to code—and then some, probably. But while what you *designed* may be legal, the fact that no one ever got around to providing a record of it to Building Safety and Permitting violates several statutes. I'm not guessing about that, by the way. We looked it up."

Hartmann opened her mouth, but he raised his hand before she could speak.

"Ms. Hartmann, we're not interested in pressing charges over that. I'm simply pointing out to you that we could. What we *want* are the people who we think are hiding in those secret areas you designed—" he pointed to the hologram "—and whatever help you can give us in figuring out how to arrest them without killing anybody. Or injuring them, if possible."

Hartmann settled back in her chair. Her expression remained tight, but hostility had begun shifting toward simple anxiety.

"You won't be able to break in quickly or easily," she said. "And there's no way you can do it without setting off alarms."

"What about gas?" Zilwicki asked. "Could we inject some sort of knockout gas into its air supply?"

"That won't work." Hartmann shook her head. "My clients were adamant about security. We built in detectors that will spot anything—*any* substance, even if the detectors can't analyze it—that doesn't match Mesa's standard atmospheric composition— oxygen, nitrogen, carbon dioxide, stuff like that. And if they *do* detect anything from outside that mix, they shut down the entire air system's intakes and call for human supervision to decide if the stuff is toxic. And if there aren't any human supervisors—or if there are and they tell it to—it operates on recycled air for as long as possible. Which is measured in days, even if they're at maximum possible occupancy, not hours or minutes. I can't remember how many, exactly, but it's close to a week."

Zilwicki frowned.

"Not very promising," Saburo said. "I really don't want to try blasting our way in, though."

"Power," Barrett said. Everyone looked at her, but she was looking at Zilwicki. "Are their offices still connected to the power grid?"

"Yes," Zilwicki said. "And that's a thought. If we turned off the electricity, they'd have to come out sooner or later. Especially if *we* shut down the external air intakes at the same time their air-conditioning goes down and seal them up with only the air inside their hideout."

"That would take at least a week," Hartmann said. "Their internal standalone power system is guaranteed for that long."

"Damn," Barrett muttered. She was too deeply sunk in thought to notice the speculative glance Saburo gave her before he turned his attention back to Hartmann.

"You said it shuts down the external air intakes and goes to recycled air if it detects something that shouldn't be there?" he asked.

"That's right."

"Where's the internal ducting? Can we get to it without setting off the system's alarms?"

"Um." Hartmann frowned, gazing absently at the schematics and blueprints while she thought.

"You *might* be able to, actually," she said finally. "It wouldn't be easy. But I couldn't entirely avoid service crawlways. I mean, I could wall off the *internal* crawlways and access shafts, but I had to work around the...public service access. The part that shows up on the official blueprints."

"And?" Zilwicki prompted.

"And the circulating fans back up against one of the public shafts, and they can't shut down the internal fans without making the place uninhabitable pretty quickly. I inserted a ten-centimeter scab of armor between the fans and the wall of the shaft, but if you drilled through, you could inject your gas directly into the fans."

"Ah!" Saburo smiled. "I take it that it didn't occur to you to plant vibration alarms in your armor?"

"Actually, it did." Hartmann managed a smile of her own. "You'd have to use laser drills or something like that. And there's still a chance you'd set them off when you started injecting the gas. But—"

She shrugged.

"Sounds like that might be the way in," Zilwicki said.

"Ultimately, we know we can wait them out, no matter what," Arianne pointed out, and Saburo nodded.

"The problem is that we don't know if either of them would suicide, given time and opportunity," he said. "Frankly, I could live with that. But the bigger problem is that if we 'wait them out,' they'll have time to destroy records. And to be honest, much as I would love to see these...people in a courtroom, I want their data even worse."

"Here's a thought," Barrett said slowly. All eyes turned to her, and she raised an eyebrow at Hartmann. "You've got detectors and alarms on what goes *into* the complex. What about what comes *out* of it?"

"Out?"

"That's a pretty big area," Barrett pointed out, waving at the display. "I'm willing to bet you that Snyder and McGillicuddy aren't sitting there all by themselves playing two-hand Hearts. So there's probably quite a few other people in there with them. And what do people produce?"

"This is going...where?" Saburo asked, although his sudden smile suggested to Barrett that he already knew his question's answer.

"They produce shit," she said. "And that has to go somewhere. So, are they connected to the tower's sewerage systems? And if there *are* connections, are there alarms on them?"

"Uh, they're connected. And—" Hartmann looked a bit chagrined "—it never even occurred to me to put alarms on the outgoing plumbing."

"Oh, my!" Zilwicki smiled. "Talk about poetic justice! And, frankly, it wouldn't matter if the pipes had alarms, unless you'd also found a way to shut them down against a lot of back pressure."

"There *are* automatic flow blockers in the system," Hartmann pointed out. "That's standard, and in most towers, there's enough height for straight gravity flow to produce some pretty significant pressure, so the one-way valves are . . . robust, I guess you'd say."

"Doesn't matter, especially if we can get in close enough to where they connect to the central plumbing stack," Zilwicki replied. "I'll guarantee you that we can pump enough pressure into the system below them to produce the mother of all blowbacks."

His smile grew even broader as he contemplated exploding urinals and toilet-born geysers.

"That's true," Saburo agreed with a matching smile. "On the other hand, generating that much pressure is going to take a lot of gas. I know it'll have a fair volume to disperse into, but to be effective enough fast enough, it'll need to be pretty powerful stuff. The kind of stuff that can kill people in sufficient concentration."

"Oh, no." It was Arianne's turn to smile. "I've got something a lot better than knockout gas." It was her turn to become the focus of all eyes, and her smile got broader . . . and acquired an edge of vengefulness. "What we need is something specifically designed to enable people to keep moving—moving fast—not make them unconscious. Hold on."

She called up something on her terminal, and then leaned back as a complex chemical formula appeared on screen. The name under it was multi-multi-syllabic, and Saburo shook his head.

"Arianne, I'm just a country boy. I have no idea what that is."

"Yes, you do. That's the gas slavers use to drive slaves into the expulsion bays when they need to jettison what they call 'the cargo.'" Arianne's eyes were hard as she, too, gazed at the screen. "It won't knock anyone out, and it won't kill anybody directly. They need the slaves to be able to move. But it effectively incapacitates everyone caught in it. They can't fight—they can't even think. They just have to get *away*."

"And how do *you* know about this stuff?" Saburo's tone had dropped and his expression bordered on hostile.

"It's her specialty, Saburo," Zilwicki answered for her. "Settle down. She's a top-drawer chemist and the Alignment—okay, the *Engagement*—spent centuries studying Manpower. And not because they *approved* of the bastards."

"Oh. Right." Saburo inhaled. "Sorry, Arianne."

"Don't worry about it." Arianne's smile turned downright

savage. "I do think it's about as...appropriate as karma gets, though. Of course, you *will* have at least one problem: finding combat suits impenetrable enough to protect *you* against that stuff. After all, you'll be charging through it yourself to find your quarry and arrest them. If I were you, I'd make sure the suits were puke-proof, too. Depending on how many people are in there, you're going to run into a *lot* of vomit."

The only adjective for the light in her eyes was beatific.

✧   ✧   ✧

"So you're good with the plans you've already got?" Saburo asked. Barrett and the other newly fledged Mumps had returned to Alexia Gabon while he remained behind to nail down the final details with Zilwicki. "I'm sure you've got access to even better data on the building than I do, but this is one I really don't want to screw up on."

"I haven't actually pulled up the plumbing schematic yet," Zilwicki replied, "but I can't foresee any problems there. And Hartman's going to send us her personal files of the original blueprints. We're good."

"Good." Saburo showed his teeth in a brief smile. "I *want* these people."

"We all do," Zilwicki agreed, and Saburo nodded and headed for the door.

He stepped through it and paused. Arianne McBryde was waiting in the corridor, her arms crossed and her expression stiff.

"I was kind of upset by that, Saburo," she said. "I thought by now...I don't know. I guess I thought—or hoped, anyway—that you wouldn't still have me lumped in with"—she uncrossed her arms and waved one hand in a broad gesture—"them."

By *them* she meant the thirty percent of Mesa's population who'd been the only real citizens before the Grand Alliance's arrival. She and her family certainly weren't in the upper reaches of that class, and they'd never been involved in genetic slavery or the slave trade, but they were part of it.

Saburo sighed.

"I really am sorry, Arianne. But what happened—the reason I reacted that way—was actually the opposite of what you think. By now, I *do* have a very high opinion of you. So I was caught off guard and... Well, some attitudes are deeply ingrained and can flare out if your brain short-circuits a little. Please don't take it as anything other than that. Really. Please don't."

She stared at him for a moment. Then her shoulders relaxed.

"Okay," she said, and smiled.

He smiled back and continued down the corridor, and she watched him go until he rounded the corner. She tried not to be obvious about it, but she really enjoyed watching the man move. Saburo had a natural grace and athleticism that...

She sighed herself and returned to the conference room. Zilwicki was back at his workstation.

"You've known Saburo for quite some time, haven't you?" she asked, and he looked up.

"Not as long as Victor has—certainly not as long as Jeremy. But, yes. It's been a while now. Why?"

"I was just wondering...I know he and Lara were very close. Is he still..."

She felt like a damned fool, and that was something she wasn't accustomed to. Arianne prided herself on her self-control, and now she was fumbling around like a halfwit.

"Grieving for her?" Zilwicki filled in. "Sure. You never stop grieving for someone you loved that much. It's been almost nineteen T-years since my wife Helen died, and I'm still grieving for her. Not a day goes by that I don't get a little jolted by something that reminds me of her." His massive shoulders made the motion that was his equivalent of a shrug. "But life goes on for most people. Mine did."

"How about Saburo?" she asked, and Zilwicki chuckled.

"You know, Arianne, in my experience, the best way to find out how someone feels is to ask *them*."

General Board Boardroom
Madison Grant Tower
City of Mendel
Planet Mesa
Mesa System

THE MEMBERS OF THE PROVISIONAL GOVERNMENT OF MESA LOOKED up as Saburo Lara, Kayla Barrett, and Anton Zilwicki walked into their meeting room. Susan Hibson, Cynthia Lecter, and General Drescher were already present, and Drescher nodded to Saburo and Zilwicki as they crossed to the conference table. Electronic placards with their names gleamed from the tabletop in front of two empty chairs. Barrett took a seat of her own, behind Saburo.

"Welcome, gentlemen... and lady," Jackson Chicherin said. He still wasn't certain how he'd ended up Chairman of the Provisional Government. Although, to be fair, he hadn't. The CEO of the new government had acquired a new title as part of the conscious effort to break with Mesa's tainted past. Which hadn't prevented his astonishment when neither the Grand Alliance nor the seccy bosses had insisted on putting someone like Jorgen Dusek into that role.

"Thank you for fitting us into your schedule on short notice, Mister President," Saburo replied. "I asked for this meeting because we need to bring you up to speed on what happened three days ago in Nakatomi Tower."

"The raid that finally caught up with Snyder and McGillicuddy?" Dusek asked with unmistakable satisfaction. "Did you really use slave gas to—pardon the expression—flush the bastards out?"

"We did." Saburo smiled. "In fact, that's one of the things we wanted to brief you all on. Kayla here—" he pointed a thumb over his shoulder "—had to sit it out, because of her leg. I was there,

314

though, and I can tell you that no verbal report could possibly do justice to what actually happened. Fortunately, however, we don't need to rely on that."

"You don't?" Brianna Pearson asked.

"No. They were...rather preoccupied, and despite whatever forethought they showed in building their hideaway in the first place, once it was built, they were sloppier about their internal security arrangements than they might've been. Apparently, they assumed that anyone who wanted to arrest them would have to come in hard, which would give them time to slag their records. That didn't happen. Which means we got all of them, including the internal security camera footage of what happened during the raid itself. Anton?"

He glanced at Zilwicki, who'd quietly inserted a data chip into his terminal at the table while the Mesan Unified Magistral Police's director spoke. Now the Manticoran entered a command, and the conference room HD unit activated.

"This is the security cams' imagery from the raid," he said, looking around at the Provisional Government's members. "And I should add, in case you hadn't already heard, that Fran Selig was hiding in there, too."

"She was?" Drescher asked.

Selig hadn't been quite as sought after as Snyder and McGillicuddy. As the former CO of the Office of Public Safety, she'd come close, but although she'd technically been Howell's boss, she'd never been as highly visible and profoundly hated as he. Where Howell had enjoyed being flamboyant, Selig was a savvy and seasoned bureaucrat, who'd understood the benefits of a certain amount of anonymity. That said, she was still the former commanding officer of the OPS, which had automatically placed her on the Ten Most Wanted list.

"Yes." Saburo nodded. "We hadn't had any reason to think she was, until we actually raided the place, though. Let us show you."

He nodded to Zilwicki again, and the HD unit came alive with an overhead view of a meeting in what appeared to be a communal mess hall. Not that "meeting" was precisely the right term for the social interaction taking place. "Screaming match" would have been a better one. Even with the volume turned far, far down, that much was obvious. Snyder and McGillicuddy were clearly the two principal combatants, but each was backed by several subordinates or lackeys, none of whom seemed shy about adding their voices to the bedlam.

And bedlam it was, too.

"What the hell were they fighting about?" Dusek asked.

"I'd say a pretty severe case of what used to be called 'cabin fever,'" Zilwicki replied. "McGillicuddy was pissed at Snyder because she was the one who suggested using their hideout, since she was a crony of big shots in Jessyk and figured it was the best hiding place around. Of course, neither of them had expected that they'd be stuck in it for months, which is why he was so ticked. He didn't see them getting out anytime soon, and he and his people were going more than a little stir crazy. I think Snyder was, too, but her position—let's call it that, for the moment—was that he was a moron who hadn't had an alternative refuge to suggest, anyway, so why didn't he shut up. Selig was over there in the corner, just watching. I think she was actually more amused than anything else. The others were basically weighing in on the same points as Snyder and McGillicuddy. None of them had found their little hideaway very useful, except as a place to hide, but they couldn't get out, and sooner or later they knew they'd have to."

"My heart bleeds for them," the seccy boss said sardonically.

"Oh, if your heart's bleeding for them *now*, just wait," Zilwicki said, and the view shifted to a large, tile-floored restroom fitted with plumbing appliances which would have been recognizable to any denizen of Ante Diaspora Old Earth.

"There were two communal heads off the mess hall," Zilwicki said. "One on each side. With, as you can see, multiple urinals and stalls in both of them. Ten...nine...eight...seven...six...five...four...three...two...one—"

KABOOOOOM!

Clouds of water erupted upward from each toilet, and three of the urinals literally blew off the wall as the back pressure exploded through the plumbing. The tile floor cracked as the flying urinals smashed down and skidded across it, and ongoing geysers of water blew upward from the toilet bowls in dancing plumes of spray.

"That's the gas pressure," Zilwicki said, zeroing in on one of the geysers. "And here we go."

The view returned to the mess hall. Half the verbal combatants had jerked to their feet. All of them were now staring at the restroom arches. And as the Provisional Government watched, expressions changed—abruptly. Astonishment, confusion, and fear were abruptly replaced by something else: sudden, acute, total nausea.

Within five seconds, all of them were staggering and projectile vomiting.

More explosions came from someplace in the distance, and alarms wailed in warning. But no one in that mess hall paid any attention to the security system's alerts. They had other things on their minds. Like being somewhere else as the solid wall of stench rolled over them from the restrooms. Unfortunately for them, there was only one exit... which was almost instantly jammed by far too many people trying to force their way through at the same time.

And vomiting onto one another.

A lot.

Zilwicki switched the view to the corridor outside the exit. Even with the jam up, people had begun popping out of the mess hall. At least one was ejected by the pressure behind her and landed with the limpness of unconsciousness, probably from the effects of the jam up. Those who were still mobile split, staggering in both directions along the corridor. It was blindingly obvious none of them had been able to formulate a coherent plan of action. They weren't running *to* anything; they were simply running away from the mess hall, too nauseated and stricken to do anything but seek an escape route.

Any escape route.

Unfortunately for them, the gas was clearly pursuing them. And while they might—*might*—have outdistanced it eventually (presuming their flight path didn't intersect any other of their hidden retreat's restrooms), it didn't matter.

The first members of the assault force appeared, heading down the corridor from the breaches they'd blown. And—in another bitterly appropriate irony—they were equipped with the stun wands slavers routinely used on their "cargo"... when they weren't using neural whips, anyway. Stun wands were a less agonizing experience than a neural whip, but they were more than unpleasant enough to be going on with.

In this instance, however, the fugitives truly didn't seem to mind. That was probably because unconsciousness was so much more pleasant than the convulsive retching and other loss of bodily function associated with the gas.

The attackers weren't particularly gentle about the way they wielded their high-tech nightsticks, but they were certainly efficient. And as soon as anyone was unconscious, he or she was easy enough to haul out.

It didn't take very long.

"Oh, *shit*—you should pardon the expression!" Dusek hadn't been able to stop laughing from the instant the toilets blew up. Now he wiped his eyes, shook his head, and looked across at Barrett.

"This was *your* idea, Lieutenant?" he demanded.

"It was, uh . . . a joint effort, Sir," she replied, and it no longer struck her as even remotely odd to call a seccy "Sir." What did surprise her, just a bit, was how much she liked the change.

"Kayla came up with the . . . vector," Saburo said. "It was Arianne McBryde who came up with the gas."

"Why am I not surprised?" President Chicherin, who'd known Arianne since she was a schoolgirl, asked rhetorically. Unlike the ex-seccies in the room, he'd managed not to laugh, but it had been a very near run thing, and his eyes gleamed.

"Well, whoever came up with it, I'm impressed," Dusek said. "Delighted with the outcome, of course, but—let's be honest here—I'm even more delighted by the nature of their . . . comeuppance."

"So am I," Susan Hibson said. "Although, in my case it's partly because you did such a neat job. Aside from the post-op clean up, of course." She grimaced. "I don't imagine that was very pleasant. But you made an absolute clean sweep—for certain values of 'clean'—without a single serious casualty. On either side." She shook her head. "That's impressive."

"I thought so, too," Saburo agreed.

He gazed at the frozen images in the HD for a few more moments, then turned his attention back to the others seated around the table.

"As I said, I wanted to bring you up to speed on what happened in Nakatomi. What I should've said, though, was that I want to bring you up to speed on what we found in Nakatomi when we got into their secure data files. What we turned up goes beyond the purview of the Mesan Unified Magistral Police.

Jessyk—and Manpower—were not only sloppy in their procedures for purging their files, but their cybersecurity was...not up to Captain Zilwicki's weight, let's say."

His tone now bore a distinct resemblance to the satisfied rumble of a large cat—tiger, lion, something in that size range— about to dine on the prey it had brought down.

"What we now have in our possession is proof of something everyone has known was true but which had been kept fuzzy enough to prevent really firm action. That is, the fact that Jessyk is wholly a creature of Manpower. The official ownership records are tortuous almost beyond belief, but Anton here was able to unravel them."

"You mean for the first time *ever*?" Captain Lecter asked. She was frowning. "I would've thought..."

"No, Captain." Saburo shook his head. "Like I said, the reality of the relationship between the two of them has been understood for a long time. I have to say that very few ever realized just how intimate that relationship actually was, or that Jessyk was effectively a wholly owned subsidiary, but just about everyone knew the relationship *existed*. The problem was that no one was ever able to *prove* it. Now we can."

"And what we'd like to propose," Zilwicki said, "is a coordinated assault to bring Jessyk down—completely. Dismantle it, strip it of all its properties, and convict and imprison as many of its top officials as possible. That's already happening to Manpower, although—" he sniffed "—the Sollies are being sloppy and inefficient about it even in Manpower's case. Partly that's because nobody in the League was actively enforcing its own anti-slavery laws, so their investigators and prosecutors are having to make it up as they go along. And at least some of the Gendarmes involved are more concerned with helping their accomplices get away than they are with arresting them and winding up incriminated themselves. But it's also been because..."

He cleared his throat.

"Also because nobody was all that concerned over maintaining the fussy legal fine points immediately after the surrender. The Grand Alliance wasn't in a position to do anything about it yet, and sure as hell no slave or seccy on Mesa worried one damned bit about it. They had other things in mind."

Saburo grunted.

"That's one way to put it. For all practical purposes, what happened to Manpower's senior hierarchy—hell, *most* of its hierarchy—here on Mesa was a mass lynching. And it didn't stop just with the senior executives and their staffs. What the mob didn't smash with hammers, it set fire to." He shrugged. "That was probably inevitable, but it only made any sort of *galaxy-wide* purge of Manpower even more difficult, because we lost so many potential witnesses and so many records. But with the data we've turned up now, we can not only destroy Jessyk, but finish uprooting Manpower, as well."

"That'll be easy enough to do here in Mesa," General Drescher said. "But Jessyk wasn't as concentrated here as Manpower. Most of its operations and facilities were—still are—in the Solarian League."

Zilwicki and Saburo nodded, almost in unison.

"Exactly," Zilwicki said. "And their facilities are even more widely distributed than most other transstellars'. Partly that's because they're a shipping line—they have to have an entire network of port facilities, management nodes, all that sort of thing. Based on what we know now—well, can *prove* now; we actually knew it a long time ago—a lot of that dispersal is also part of their security arrangements. They're so spread out that no one could possibly shut down all of their central nodes simultaneously. It would have to be a rolling operation, which would give at least some of their personnel time to purge records and haul ass before they could be grabbed.

"All of which means we need to send a delegation to Old Terra with everything we've collected and a plan of action we want to propose to the Solarian authorities. Even with the Sollies, we can't roll them up *simultaneously*, but we could come a hell of a lot closer to that with their backing."

The people sitting around the conference table looked at each other.

"Who exactly is the 'we' you're talking about?" Dusek asked after a moment.

"The nuts and bolts of it will be done by the same people who took down Jessyk," Zilwicki said. He pointed a thumb at himself, followed by a finger at Saburo. "Him and me, to start with. Some other people, especially the Solarian investigators who've been here for a while now. The delegation itself would be headed up by me, Captain al-Fanudahi of the Solarian League

Navy, and Lieutenant Colonel Okiku of the Gendarmerie. Saburo would be a nice add, if his, ah, checkered past wouldn't be a problem for the Sollies. But we obviously don't have the authority to do that. For that, we need—" He swirled his finger around in a circle. "All of you."

"Okay," Dusek said. "I vote 'yes.'"

Every other seccy boss's "yes" vote followed immediately. So did Jackson Chicherin's. Within a few seconds, they'd been joined by Thandi Palane, Jeremy X, Lakshmi X, and Kevin Olonga.

That left just one holdout.

"Look," Brianna Pearson sighed, "I don't know whether or not I'm still working for Technodyne. I haven't heard anything from them one way or the other. Which I figure probably means I've been fired. But I still retain a certain . . . institutional loyalty, let's call it, to the company. Not to everyone in current management positions, not to the people who have almost certainly cut me adrift. Hell, not even to the shareholders, in a lot of ways, even if most of them are honest investors. But to the company itself. To the people who work for it, who depend on it. And what I'm concerned about is where all this might lead.

"I don't care about Jessyk. I sure as hell don't care about Manpower. But whatever the rest of you think, and whatever criticisms I may have myself, I don't think you can lump every transstellar into the same category as Manpower and Jessyk."

"What are you worried about, Ms. Pearson?" Jeremy asked. "That we just might be starting a general purge with no limits?" He smiled rather wickedly. "A new Red Terror, spanning light-years instead of the pitiful area of Ancient France?"

She looked at him.

"Yes." There was no smile on her face. "That's exactly what I'm worried about."

"Well, you needn't be. Mind you, in my more cheerless and morose moments, I might contemplate the notion. It does have its charms. But—"

He rolled his eyes and raised his hands in melancholy resignation.

"Sadly, my Queen would strongly disapprove, and beneath that sweet façade lurks the soul of a tyrant." His expression became at least marginally more serious. "She'd never agree to it."

"Neither would I," Thandi Palane said in a much firmer, less whimsical tone. "I won't tell you not to worry about it, because it's something any sensible person should at least think about. But I don't know anyone and—" she pointed at Dusek "—I doubt he does, either, who equates Technodyne and Manpower."

"No, I don't," Dusek agreed. "Which doesn't mean I don't know plenty of people—starting with me—who have a low opinion of Technodyne and just about every other transstellar I can think of. Certainly any of them who had seats on the old General Board. But that's not the same thing as Manpower and their Jessyk flunky."

"That's good," Pearson said, but she was still unsmiling. "But tell me this—what happens to everyone who works for Jessyk, or for some purely local, one-system company that *depends* on Jessyk, if we just go in and totally destroy the corporation? There are ripple effects from something like that, and the ripples don't magically stop with the guilty."

She looked around the meeting room, her eyes dark.

"I know that to some extent my view on this has to be suspect. I'm trying to keep that in mind from my side, too, because I've spent so long looking at transstellars from inside the managers' suites. And maybe it's just second nature for us plutocrats to find moral justifications to keep ourselves and our cronies in business. But that doesn't make anything I just said about ripples untrue."

Several people looked at least a bit more thoughtful, and silence lingered for a moment. Then Cynthia Lecter broke it.

"I can't speak for Admiral Gold Peak without reporting all this back to her first, of course. And if she were here herself, I'm sure she'd say this is legitimately a decision for the Provisional Government, not her or even the Grand Alliance. But speaking for *myself*, I think Ms. Pearson's raised a valid point."

"I agree . . . and disagree," Susan Hibson said. All eyes turned to the diminutive general, and she shrugged. "Jessyk has to go, at least under its current management. That's a given, just as it's a given that Manpower has to go, root and branch, no matter *how* many 'legitimate' jobs go with it. And Captain Zilwicki has a really good point about how dispersed Jessyk's operations are and the need—from a purely intel viewpoint, at the very least—to hit as many of them as physically possible as close to simultaneously as possible, without giving the cockroaches we want time to scatter. But the fact that we take the company down doesn't mean it has to *stay* taken down."

"Meaning ... what, General?" Person asked, gazing at her intently.

"Jessyk has millions—probably hundreds of millions—of employees," Hibson replied, "and if anyone knows what that means to an economy and the people who make it up, a Manticoran does. The entire Star Kingdom was *built* on interstellar trade and the corporations that make it work. The Crown never let any of our homegrown transstellars get as ... out of hand as the Sollies' did, but we've seen a *lot* of what goes on inside the Solarian versions. And I will guarantee you that only a small percentage of the millions of people working for Jessyk are actively involved in its 'dirty' operations.

"It can't be any other way in a transstellar that size that's managed to keep its dark side so well concealed that not even *Solly* courts were eventually forced to go after it. We tend to forget that no matter how corrupt the League got on a *federal* level and in terms of its foreign policy, there have always been dozens of Core World systems that *weren't* corrupt—like Beowulf and Hypatia, to name just two. Jessyk had to stay 'legit' enough to keep the AGs in those systems from going after them on a purely local level. They could get away with some pretty rough stuff, granted, and their footprint in Beowulf is a lot smaller than in some other systems I could name, but they couldn't allow the kind of stuff they did with and for Manpower to become part of their general operations."

"That's true enough," Zilwicki allowed. "They'd have to be compartmentalized to prop up even the pretense that they weren't a wholly owned subsidiary of Manpower. What we've found so far looking at their records strongly suggests they've got an 'Operational Division' that's deep in bed with Manpower, and it looks like their legitimate operations are seeded with individual managers and execs who handle anything 'black' that comes through their star systems without involving the other locals. But the overwhelming majority of their employees are probably never involved with anything that's actually criminal. Well, beyond some purely local smuggling and customs evasion. Mind you, most of those same employees have to know about their employer's ... unsavory reputation. But that's hardly the same thing as directly participating in a criminal enterprise."

"Exactly." Hibson nodded. "So in response to Ms. Pearson's

concerns," she nodded to the Mesan across the table, "I suggest two things. First, that we make it clear from the get-go that we're after the bad actors, not the entire transstellar. That we—we being Mesa, the grand Alliance, and the Sollies, assuming they sign on—plan to prosecute actual criminal actions to the maximum, which will certainly result in lengthy prison time for convicted individuals and may well result in some hefty corporate fines and penalties, but we have no intention of prosecuting anyone else. And, second, that we set up a conservatorship under court supervision to take over and manage Jessyk's operations during the course of our investigation and any prosecutions resulting from it. And we make it clear from the outset that at the end of the day, that conservatorship will oversee a transition back to private management once Jessyk's corporate house has been thoroughly cleaned. Or, at the very least, a phased breakup of Jessyk's transstellar operations into smaller, more locally owned units that will continue to operate."

"That . . . might allay my worst concerns," Pearson said after a few moments of thought. "It would be a step in the right direction, at least. And it would also address another concern I think we need to bear in mind. The League's interstellar economy is still in what you could call a chaotic state thanks to the war, and that's leaking over onto quite a few of the intra-system economies at this point. Not as much as the woman in the street might expect—however enormous interstellar trade is in absolute terms, it still represents a fairly modest percentage of most developed systems' economies—but more than is healthy. And a lot of the less diversified systems—like Montana, which depends so heavily on its beef exports—are getting hit a hell of a lot harder. I really don't think we need to be making that any worse by eliminating one of the largest shipping concerns in the galaxy."

"Another thing that's true enough." Zilwicki nodded. "Jessyk couldn't have gotten as big as it is if there weren't a genuine need for the services it provides. Which means not only that just yanking them out from under the economy would be a bad thing, but also that it should survive pretty well, even if it does it under a new name or as a group of smaller, independent corporations, post-takedown. The need will still be there to support its operations."

"I think General Hibson's suggestions are very sound," Olonga said.

"I tend to agree," Palane said, looking at her Manticoran colleague approvingly. Then she looked back around the table. "Of course, the devil will be in the details. Hitting them hard enough to take down the people we really want while keeping the rest of the corporation alive will be tricky. I think we can probably do it, but I'd be lying if I said I was *sure* we can."

"I know." Pearson looked far less unhappy than she had a few minutes earlier. Which was not to say her expression was even remotely cheerful.

"It would be best if we had a unanimous vote that the delegation could report to the Sollies' provisional government, Brianna," Jackson Chicherin, the only other person present who'd also been on the former regime's General Board, told her almost gently.

She looked at him, then sighed again.

"I know," she repeated. "I just wish I weren't still as . . . nervous about where this could end up. But I'll vote 'yes,' too."

"All right, then!" Dusek said. "Anton, Saburo—you've got the go-ahead. Go forth and smite Jessyk."

L'Ouverture Station
Torch Planetary Orbit
Congo System

RUTH WINTON SWIVELED IN HER CHAIR AS SOMEONE KNOCKED softly on the frame of her open door. Ensign William Howe stood there, with a slightly wary expression.

"Sorry to bother you, but..."

His voice trailed off, and Ruth felt a bit guilty. She knew she had a reputation for being a tad abrupt—well, more than a tad, maybe—when people distracted her while she was concentrating on something. But in this instance, she was actually grateful for the interruption. In the absence of anything interesting to analyze—or anywhere to go, or anything to do, or anything that wasn't intensely *boring*—she'd been reduced to playing Galaxy Conquest on her computer. Admittedly, the magnificent system with which she'd been provided made Galaxy Conquest rather more interesting and challenging than it might have been otherwise. But she was on her third round of conquest as Minette the Merciless.

Which meant even that was approaching the dread territory of boredom.

"Come in, Bill." She gestured to a nearby chair. "Sit down. What's up?"

"Well..." He sat in the indicated chair. "I'm sorry to bother you, Your Highness, but—"

"Oh, for God's sake! How many times do I have to tell you to leave off the damn royal protocol? I answer to 'Ruth' just fine."

Then she felt guilty again. He was only trying to be polite, and the fact that she was bored and had been cooped up on the station *forever* was no excuse for snapping at him. Even if she

326

did wish people wouldn't waste her time and theirs with point-less formalities.

"Sorry," she said with genuine contrition. "I didn't mean to snap at you. And for the record, by the way, the proper appellation if you really feel the need to go all formal is 'Your Grace.' 'Your Highness' is reserved for royal scions in the line of succession." She flashed him a smile and he smiled back. "So what's up?"

"We were trying to track down the cause of a malfunctioning—oh, never mind." Howe waved a hand. "It's complicated, and not really relevant. Anyway, we found something in one of the PNE ship's computers that . . . Well, it's kind of weird, really."

"Weird how?"

"Weird in that we have absolutely no idea what it is, what it's for, or why it's there at all. It's clearly an executable of some sort, but it doesn't seem to *do* anything. As far as we can tell, it isn't attached to anything, and it doesn't show up in any of the manuals or operations guides."

"Really?" She swiveled back to her computer, banishing Minette the Merciless's all-conquering armada to a saved file. "Which ship?"

"The *Toussaint*. But she's not in active service yet, so she may be in your records under her old name—the PNES *Cerberus*."

Ruth nodded. It didn't take her long to find the ship and log into its central computer net.

"Show me what you're talking about," she invited, pushing back in her float chair to let Howe reach her keyboard.

He slid his own chair into the space she'd freed, and she watched as he started working his way through the net. Howe was very good at his job, despite his junior rank, yet he began to frown in obvious perplexity. He paused long enough to check something on his uni-link, then went back to the keyboard. But his frown only deepened, and, finally, he sat back and shook his head.

"Okay, now that really *is* weird," he said. "I don't see any sign of it, Your Gr—uh, Ruth. It ought to be right here." He indicated the currently displayed file directory. "This is the Communication suite, and I checked my notes to be sure I'm looking in the right place." He tapped his uni-link. "And according to them, it ought to be right between these two. But it's not showing."

"Really?" Ruth beamed. It probably wasn't anything earth shattering, but what Howe called "weird" might at least be *interesting* to track down. "Let me back in there."

The ensign stood and moved aside, and Ruth studied the screen, then opened one of her personally designed search programs. It found nothing, and she cracked her knuckles in delight and delved deeper into her cybernetic bag of tricks. It took her the better part of fifteen minutes, but finally—

"*There* the little bugger is!" she announced finally. The new entry on the directory blinked exactly where Howe had said it should be, but she frowned as she contemplated it. It was marked as a corrupted and deleted file. "Or I think it is, anyway. Take a look."

"That's the right file designation," Howe said, after a moment. "But it's not deleted. Not according to any of *Toussaint's* terminals, anyway. Well, maybe *any* of her terminals is a little extreme, but I know we've found it on at least three of them."

"Okay, I think calling that 'weird' is probably justified," Ruth said, studying the deleted file's history. "It looks like it was entered as part of a much larger package of upgrades. But our mystery program was also deleted—according to what I'm seeing here, at any rate—within a couple of minutes. Almost like the original upload was just an accident."

She rubbed the tip of her nose.

"What do we know about the rest of the upgrade package, Bill?"

"Mostly it's just routine cybernetics stuff for communications and the sensor suite." Howe shrugged. "The PNE's software was... pretty basic, in a lot of ways. They got a lot of upgrades—hardware, not just software—as part of their deal with Manpower. This set of mods—" he indicated the files on Ruth's display "—were added in the same overhaul when they replaced *Toussaint's* point defense clusters' on-mount sensors and upgraded the sensor suites' processors."

"So Manpower provided the files?" Ruth asked thoughtfully.

Howe straightened and looked down at her.

"I have a nasty, suspicious mind," she explained.

"I guess you could say Manpower provided *all* of their upgrades," he said. "I mean, it was all done by their contractors. But they were all third-party outfits. Manpower didn't do any of the work directly—so far as we know, none of the software came direct from Manpower, and none of the overhaul work was done in Mesa, either—if that's what you mean."

"And there's no documentation—no indication at all—on what it's supposed to do?"

"No. And we haven't poked at it too much, either. Like I say, it's clearly an executable. Until we have at least some idea of what it does, nobody's real crazy about executing it."

"Good." Ruth nodded vigorously. "Fiddling around with military programs we don't understand strikes me as a really bad idea."

"That's what we thought, too," Howe agreed with a crooked smile.

"All right, you said it's displayed as not deleted on at least three of *Toussaint*'s terminals?" Ruth asked, and he nodded. "Okay, point me at one of the ones you know it was displayed on."

"Try Com Seven. That's the first place I saw it."

"Okay, Communications...Seven." Ruth's fingers flew as she remoted into the indicated workstation aboard the battlecruiser. And then she sat back with another, deeper frown.

"Bill—"

"I see it." Howe's voice was as perplexed as his expression. "I swear it was there when I looked for it aboard ship, though!"

"Well, it's not there now." Ruth indicated the file directory, where the mystery file showed exactly the same deletion history as in the directory she'd accessed direct from *L'Ouverture Station*.

"Hang on a sec."

Howe activated his uni-link's com.

"Com Regis," he told it, and waited a couple of seconds.

"Regis, Bill," he said then. "Pull up that directory and tell me if that file is still there." He listened to his earbud for a moment, then snorted. "No, I *didn't* 'accidentally delete it.' Quit giving me a hard time and go look." He waited another minute or so, then grimaced. "Okay, thanks."

He looked back down at Ruth.

"It may show as deleted here, but the terminals on *Toussaint* still show it as a current file."

"Really?" Ruth beamed. "Hallelujah!" She pushed her chair back and stood with the air of a woman freed from prison. "I have *got* to see this for myself. Let's go!"

✧   ✧   ✧

An hour later, Ruth sat glowering at a display aboard TRNS *Toussaint*.

The directory before her did, indeed, list the elusive file as current, and she'd spent the last twenty minutes prodding very cautiously at it. In the process, she'd discovered that the executable in question was actually running in the background. But apparently one of the things it was doing as it ran was to lock out any access to any terminal not physically aboard ship. And it was clearly sufficiently sophisticated to recognize a remote access attempt through one of the shipboard terminals.

"Somebody went to one hell of a lot of trouble to hide this thing," she said. "And that makes me really, really nervous."

"You and me both, Your Grace," Captain Maurice X said. Maurice, *Toussaint*'s designated CO, had met her at the boarding tube. Now he stood looking over her right shoulder while Cynthia X looked over the left one. "I really do not like the thought of something Manpower thought would be a good 'surprise' to tuck away in my ship's gizzards."

"Me neither." Ruth glowered some more, then she brightened.

"Me neither," she repeated, in a much more cheerful tone, and Cynthia looked at her with a certain degree of trepidation.

"I know that tone," Cynthia said.

"Well, if none of *us* know what it is, we should talk to somebody who may," Ruth said brightly.

"And that would be . . . ?"

"Who do you think? The previous owners!"

"You expect the PNE to cooperate with us about something like this?"

"Well, not all of them." Ruth slid her chair back and stood. "But I expect we could find somebody willing to cooperate. After all, they've got to be almost as bored as I am!"

❖   ❖   ❖

"No," the man on Ruth's com screen said. He didn't sound especially discourteous, but he *did* sound very firm. "I'm afraid that's out of the question."

"But all I really want—"

"I'm sorry, Ms. Winton," as the CO of the People's Navy in Exile's POWs, Santander Konidis was not the sort to use any "elitist titles" in addressing his captors, "but we're still under discipline out here, and we're still prisoners of war. Under the Deneb Accords, we're under no obligation to assist our captors."

"But all I'm asking is—"

"All you're asking is for us to help you restore captured ships to service," Konidis pointed out. "Which is specifically prohibited under the Deneb Accords." He shook his head. "Under the circumstances, I'm not going to even let you ask them."

Ruth glowered at him and considered pointing out that the Deneb Accords didn't apply to genocidal butchers out to destroy an entire planetary population.

She didn't, though. First, because that it would almost certainly be . . . counterproductive. Second, because—technically—the PNE *was* protected by the Deneb Accords, because they hadn't actually *carried out* any acts of genocide. And third, because, in fairness, Konidis, as Adrian Luff's successor in command, was the one who'd decided they weren't going to. Of course, Luis Rozsak's task force had blown the hell out of Adrian Luff's task force before he reached that decision—all fourteen of his battle-cruisers had been destroyed before they could come into attack range of Torch. And although the force under Rozsak's direct command had been crippled in the process, he'd left ample fire-power in Torch orbit to take out Konidis's remaining cruisers and destroyers. But the fact remained that he could have completed his original mission, if he'd been willing to risk almost certain destruction.

More to the point, he'd made the decision not to before anyone in the PNE knew the defenders orbiting Torch were there.

"What if I came out to the island?" Ruth asked. "Are you saying you'd *forbid* anyone to meet with me—or cooperate with us—if they voluntarily chose to do it?"

"Probably." Konidis shrugged. "Of course, we *are* POWs. What I can and can't do physically may not be the same as what I can and can't do legally."

Then why don't you just bow to the inevitable and go ahead and let me talk to them now *instead of being a pain in the neck over it?* Ruth wondered. *It's not like it's going to make any difference in the end, is it?*

"Well, then—" she began out loud.

"I don't think that would play very well with your bodyguards," Cynthia said from beside her. Ruth looked up at her, and the pint-sized ex-Ballroom killer shrugged. "For all we know, there are still some genuine fanatics down there. No offense, Citizen Commodore," she didn't sound especially serious about that, "but I doubt you can honestly say that every single one of your people is definitively *not* a fanatic."

"I don't think anybody could say that definitively," Konidis said with another shrug.

"But—"

"You could *probably* overrule them on this," Cynthia said. "You are, effectively, the head of Torch Intelligence, at least while Captain Zilwicki's away. But most of your bodyguards are genuinely attached to you. You'd have to *really* overrule them, and do you want to put that kind of strain on your relationship with them?"

Ruth glared at her. The worst of it was that Cynthia had a point. By the same token, she actually was willing to "strain" her relationship with her bodyguards—even Captain Razeen Montgomery, who commanded the entire detachment—if that was what it took. Because Cynthia was also right about who she was and her place in Torch's intelligence establishment. She understood that she shouldn't—and, to the best of her keepers' ability, *wouldn't*—be exposed to avoidable risk. But when she decided a risk wasn't avoidable if she was going to do her job properly, then—

"Excuse me," a voice said from the compartment's doorway, and Ruth and Cynthia both turned their faces toward the newcomer.

"Yes?" Ruth said. "What is it, Nandi?"

"I thought you'd like to know a ship from Mesa made its alpha translation about ten minutes ago. It's twenty-four light-minutes out. At five hundred and fifty gees, it should be in Torch orbit in four and a half hours."

"Really?" Ruth frowned. They weren't expecting anyone to return from Mesa this soon, but God knew plans changed without notice, especially on an interstellar scale. "Did they say why they're here? Or, for that matter, who's aboard?"

The Congo System had been equipped with the Grand Alliance's FTL communications capabilities, so there'd been plenty of time for messages to pass back and forth, despite the range.

"Nothing yet on *why*." Nandi X shrugged. "And Agent Cachat didn't say who else was on board, either."

"Victor?" Ruth's eyes lit. "*Victor Cachat* is on board?"

"Yep." Nandi nodded, and Ruth chortled.

"I foresee a sudden antidote to any of Razeen's complaints!" she said.

"You mean—?" Even Cynthia was chuckling now.

"Oh, yeah!" Ruth said gleefully. "You really think Razeen is going say 'no' when I've got *Black Victor* in my corner?!"

❖ ❖ ❖

"I don't think that's a very good idea," Captain Razeen Montgomery said.

He was a tallish man with dark hair and dark eyes who, despite his very different coloring, reminded Ruth—painfully, sometimes—of Lieutenant Ahmed Griggs, the commander of the security team which had died protecting her in Erewhon. The fact that Griggs had been Montgomery's cousin, and that Montgomery had specifically volunteered to accompany her to Congo as the commander of the security team her Aunt Elizabeth had insisted on detaching from the Queen's Own Regiment to protect her did nothing to deaden that memory... or the pain that went with it. But it was an old and familiar pain, now. One that troubled her dreams more than she might have wished, but seldom intruded into the front of her brain.

Empress Elizabeth had never said so in so many words, but Ruth knew that even now, her aunt hadn't forgiven Victor Cachat's decision to let her security team die to further his own mission objectives. Elizabeth understood that he'd been under no obligation to protect a member of the royal family of the star nation with which his own had been at war for the better part of two decades. So her... disinclination to forgive wasn't remotely personal. Yet she'd made it quietly—but inflexibly—clear that her niece would be allowed to become part of the Torch intelligence establishment only if she was protected by a security detail whose loyalty was to *her*, not to Torch or anyone else in the galaxy.

Thus, Razeen Montgomery. Who was not in the least intimidated by "Black Victor" where his professional—and personal—responsibilities were concerned. Which was not to say that he was impervious to "Black Victor's" accomplishments and general aura.

Now he looked Cachat calmly in the eye, awaiting his response.

"Why not?" the Havenite asked in a reasonable tone. He and Montgomery understood one another. In fact, he rather respected the Manticoran. And sympathized with him, too. "Razeen" meant "calm" or perhaps "composed" in one of Old Terra's languages, and Lord only knew Montgomery needed all the composure he could get dealing with his sometimes rambunctious charge.

"Because it's an unnecessary threat environment," Montgomery replied. "We have com contact with the island. There's no need to expose the Princess to a potential physical threat. And don't tell me there isn't one, because we don't know that. We can be pretty sure there aren't any pulsers or tribarrels down there, but they were issued tools, including vibro blade machetes. God only knows what else they could've cobbled up to go with that. And it's not as if anyone's done anything to sort out potential fanatics among the POWs." He shook his head. "I couldn't even begin to put together a threat file."

The micrometric change in Cachat's expression was the equivalent of someone else's unwilling frown, because Montgomery had a point. The decision to simply leave the PNE prisoners to stew in their own juices had a lot to recommend it. Or, rather, it *had* had a lot to recommend it when juice-stewing was all they'd been doing. But it wouldn't have been that difficult for the Torches to at least start sorting out which of them were diehard fanatics, still loyal to the "ideals" of the Committee of Public Safety, and which were sane.

Unfortunately, the Torches had had other things on their minds... and weren't especially motivated to expend a lot of time or effort on people who'd been sent to their star system to kill them all.

"I understand what you're saying, Razeen," he said, after a moment. "And you probably have a point, at least from a royal bodyguard's perspective. But Ruth—" he deliberately didn't use her Manticoran title "—has a damned good point of her own. She *is* the senior member of the Torch intelligence establishment in-system, and this *is* something we need to get to the bottom of."

"I'm just not comfortable taking her out there with nothing but me and the rest of the detail." Montgomery's expression was polite, but stubborn. "Especially, when, as I say, there's no reason *anyone* has to physically visit the island in the first place."

"Oh, you're wrong about that." Cachat smiled very slightly. "As it happens, *I* have to 'physically visit the island.' I've got a... proposition to lay before Citizen Commodore Konidis and his people. One, now that I think of it, that might actually help produce the cooperation Ruth needs to chase down her computer gremlin, as well."

"*You're* going to the island?" Montgomery asked.

"Yes, I am. And a certain amount of... potential intimidation wouldn't come amiss for the purpose of my visit."

"Really?" Montgomery had actually begun to smile. "'Potential intimidation,' you say?"

"A certain amount," Cachat repeated, and Montgomery's smile broadened. What Victor Cachat thought of as "a certain amount of intimidation" was the equivalent of someone else's cold-blooded terror.

"Well," he said judiciously, "if you're going to be there personally, with whatever you deem an appropriate force level, and if I'm allowed to bring a full six-man team for site security, then I suppose I might be able to see my way to signing off on the expedition. Against my better judgment, you understand, but—"

He raised both hands, palms upward...just before Ruth squealed in delight and hit him with a bear hug.

Lincoln Island
Azure Ocean
Planet Torch
Congo System

OFFICIALLY, THE ISLAND WAS CALLED LINCOLN, AFTER ONE OF Old Terra's greatest abolitionist political leaders. In practice, it went by several names. The two most common were "Despair Island" or "Where the Bastards Are Island," depending on whether one asked the island's inhabitants...or the people who'd overseen their involuntary emigration to it.

At the moment, Victor Cachat, Ruth, Cynthia, Bryce Tarkovsky, and six members of Ruth's protective detail stood in a largish pavilion on the island's designated landing ground. The crews of Cachat's two assault shuttles had erected the pavilion after landing. Then the platoon of Torch Marines had deployed to the perimeter of the landing ground and the shuttles had gone airborne once more. Now they and a quartet of sting ships circled watchfully overhead.

"Potential intimidation," indeed, Ruth thought. *The man does have a way about him.*

Citizen Commodore Santander Konidis looked very much alone as the sole individual present in the uniform of the defunct People's Republic of Haven's equally defunct State Security. Ruth was a little surprised by how spruce Konidis looked. There wasn't any reason he shouldn't have. The POWs had fabric printers that could produce whatever clothing—or uniforms—they needed, and the royal government wasn't *too* stingy about supplying them with raw materials for them. But it said something for the man's internal discipline that he could have served as a recruiting poster after so long stuck on Lincoln.

336

"So, I understand you're still in command, Citizen Commodore."

There might have been just a carefully metered edge of skepticism in Cachat's tone, and Konidis frowned.

"Why wouldn't I be? This is a military unit, and I'm the ranking officer."

Cachat gave him an impassive, thoughtful look. Ruth had seen it before. It wasn't intimidating, exactly—certainly not by Victor Cachat values of intimidation. But she understood why it tended to unsettle people. It said *I see through your prattle with the clarity of a god.*

And it spoke especially loudly to anyone whose conscience bore even an infinitesimal stain of guilt.

Konidis's lips tightened, and he looked away for a moment.

"There *is* a group of dissidents," he acknowledged. "They've set themselves up on the northern peninsula of the island. We don't have much to do with them any longer. But—" his eyes came back to Cachat and met that basilisk gaze levelly "—most of our people are still under discipline."

"Good." Cachat nodded. "That'll help." He made a small dismissive gesture. "We'll just leave the northern riffraff out of it."

"Out of what? What exactly are you here for?"

"Think of it as . . . a recruiting trip," Cachat said.

"*Recruiting* trip?" Konidis repeated, and Cachat allowed himself a slight smile, then gestured toward a conference table in the pavilion. It was big enough, with enough chairs, to seat half a dozen people.

"Why don't we sit?" he invited. "This will take a while."

❖   ❖   ❖

In fact, it took the better part of two hours to lay out Cachat's proposal and set it in context. About halfway through, Konidis had summoned two of his subordinates—Citizen Captain Jarmila Soubry and Citizen Commander Jacob Trevithick—to hear him out. They flanked the citizen commodore at the conference table, and when Cachat finished, he looked back and forth between them, then back at Cachat.

"Why do you think you can trust us? By 'us,' I mean whichever of our people might agree to participate. Which I certainly won't."

He gave his head a quick jerk. It wasn't so much a headshake indicating disagreement as the gesture of someone tossing off an unwanted burden.

"I *can't* participate in something like this. Most of our people won't be able to even if they want to, because you'll only have room for—what do you figure? Fifteen percent, at most, of them?"

"About that, yes," Cachat replied, and Konidis nodded.

"Well, there it is. I'm the commanding officer here. That means I owe it to my people to stay with them. I'd be shirking my duty if I didn't."

He looked back to Soubry and Trevithick.

"But that doesn't apply to either one of you—and I think you should both do it. Accept the offer."

Trevithick's expression didn't change. Soubry opened her mouth as if to protest, but no words came out.

"Jarmila, face it," Konidis said. "Staying on this island is a death sentence, and we all know it. Sure, we've all got prolong, so we could last an entire century or two. But so what? This—" he swept an arm at the island beyond the pavilion "—isn't a *life*.

"And you." He transferred his gaze to Trevithick. "You've got a wife and two kids out there."

"Somewhere." Trevithick grimaced. "Maybe. It's been more than two T-years since Linda's had any news of me. She probably thinks I died in the battle. For all I know, she's got a new boyfriend or husband."

"Don't you want to find out?"

The burly, dark-haired citizen commander looked down at the hands clasped on the table in front of him.

"Yes," he said.

"So this is your chance," Konidis told him. "Like I say, take it."

Trevithick went on looking at his hands, but Soubry gave Cachat a suspicious look.

"How do we know they'll keep their end the of the bargain?" she asked, blue eyes wary.

"This is Victor Cachat you're talking to," Ruth spoke up. "If Victor says he'll do something, he will. The man can be an assho—not a nice person. And he can be ruthless as hell. But if he gives you his word, he'll keep it. If only because of how valuable it is for someone in his position to have—and deserve—a reputation for keeping promises."

"And just who are you?" Soubry asked.

"Ruth Winton. Yes, from *that* Winton family. We've got a pretty good reputation for keeping *our* word, too, and I'll add my promise to Victor's."

"To get back to your original question, Citizen Commodore," Cachat said, "I have four reasons I think I can trust you to complete the mission without betraying us. The first and crudest is that I'm a very difficult person to betray. There are some advantages to having been trained by Oscar Saint-Just, and I was one of his top subordinates. Of the troubleshooting variety, you understand. I never spent more than two months in StateSec's HQ in Nouveau Paris after I graduated from the Academy."

He shifted his gaze to the two less senior officers.

"If any of you want to improve your backstabbing skills, find a top predator somewhere else. Don't try it on me."

His tone was completely dispassionate. Almost as if he were bored.

"The second reason is that I won't be operating alone. I'll be in command of the expedition, but we'll have enough 'people's commissioners' to oversee the crews of every ship we bring along. None of them are people anyone in his or her right mind will take lightly.

"He's one of them." He pointed a finger at the man seated to his right. "Major Bryce Tarkovsky, of the Solarian Marines. You'll be meeting some of the others shortly. Most of them were provided by Admiral Tourville. I believe you're probably familiar with his reputation.

"The third reason is that the people we select will have a major incentive to cooperate. Once the mission is over, if they've conducted themselves properly, they not only get their freedom but enough of a stake to let them leave Torch and resettle somewhere else. They get their lives back. Whereas if they try to betray us, even if they succeed—which is highly unlikely—they're just back on the run again."

He paused. After a few seconds, Trevithick frowned.

"You said there were four reasons. What's the last one?"

"You'll be meeting them shortly. You have two days to talk it over and come to a decision." He made a little circular motion with his finger. "That's two days for the three of you and whichever other officers you choose to involve in the discussion. If the decision's positive, I'll give you another three days—four, if you need them, but I think three should be enough—to talk it over with your noncoms and enlisted."

He paused again to allow the three PNE officers to think it

over. After perhaps ten seconds and another exchange of glances, Konidis nodded.

"Agreed," he said. "Are we done?"

"Not quite. We have a technical problem we'd like your assistance with. There's something peculiar about the programming of your warships. Your former warships—some of which are the ones we'll be using for the operation." Cachat tilted his head at Ruth. "We need a few of your best cyber people to work with Ruth to figure out what the problem is."

"That's your field, Jarmila," Konidis said to Soubry, and the auburn-haired citizen captain nodded.

"Give me an hour or so to round up the people I need. If it'll take even that long. It's not as if—" her lips twisted into a sour smile "—anyone in the settlement has much of anywhere to wander off to."

"Then we're done for the moment." Cachat rose. "Let me introduce you to some of the people waiting outside."

✧   ✧   ✧

The first person they encountered after leaving the pavilion was a tall, powerful looking blonde.

"Here's one of your commissioners," Cachat said. "Yana Tretiakovna. And here are a couple of others." Two more people came from around the side of the pavilion. "The one on the left is Indiana Graham," he said.

But all three of the PNE officers' eyes were fixed on Indy's companion. Or rather, on his *companion's* companion, who rode his human's shoulder.

"That's a treecat."

There was more than a trace of protest in Trevithick's tone, and Cachat glanced at him. The dispassionate, almost bored expression was back.

"What part of 'I am a very difficult person to betray' are you having the most trouble with, Citizen Commander?"

TRNS *Toussaint*
Torch Planetary Orbit
Congo System

"THIS IS TRULY WEIRD." CITIZEN CAPTAIN SOUBRY LEANED BACK in her chair on the heavy cruiser's bridge and looked at the man seated beside her. "Any brilliant ideas, Gabriel?"

"Not a clue, Citizen Captain," the young citizen lieutenant replied. "It's clearly an executable, and it's clearly running now. Not using a lot of memory, though. And aside from whatever's telling it to hide from us, it doesn't seem to be doing much of anything, either."

"Maybe not," Ruth Winton said slowly.

Soubry and Citizen Lieutenant Gabriel Chapuis had the captain's and XO's stations on *Toussaint*'s bridge while she had the tactical officer's. Now the two Havenites swiveled their chairs to look at her.

"I don't think I like that tone of voice...Princess." Soubry obviously had some lingering issues with the elitist title, but "Citizen Princess" would have gone beyond silly-sounding to stupid. And she wasn't prepared yet to use a simple "Ruth." But the three of them had been working together for a day and a half now, and she'd developed a profound respect for Ruth's capabilities.

"Well, I just found another one," Ruth told her.

"Another one?" Soubry repeated. She and Chapuis looked at one another, then back at Ruth.

"Yeah, and—hold on. Here's *another* one!"

Soubry climbed out of her chair and walked across to stand at Ruth's shoulder. When she did, she realized the younger woman had her personal minicomp up and running at her elbow. The tac officer's display was in split-screen mode, showing two different directories, each of them with a single highlighted file header.

341

"Why didn't we see those before?" the citizen captain asked.

"Because I'm an idiot," Ruth replied with a wry smile. "I had a belated brainstorm. I've got this—" she tapped the minicomp "—networked to *L'Ouverture*. From there, it's linked to this terminal." She tapped the tac officer's station. "But I've also got a direct, partitioned feed from the terminal direct to the minicomp. So our 'I'm not here' executable is reading the link from *L'Ouverture* to *Toussaint* as an attempt to access remotely and hiding from it. But the minicomp can also see what's actually showing on the tac terminal because of the partitioned feed, and I've got the two of them running comparative search programs. They're both looking for files that show as current on *Toussaint*'s internal systems but the minicomp can't see looking in from *L'Ouverture*."

Soubry nodded with a touch of chagrin. They'd been focused on searching *Toussaint*'s computers from the shipboard access points because they knew they couldn't see an accurate picture of the current directories—and deletion histories—from the space station. Ruth's approach hadn't occurred to her. Maybe she just wasn't devious enough?

"So, what else—"

"Whoops. Here's *another* one," Ruth said as the tactical officer's display split into thirds and another highlighted file blinked.

"This is frigging ridiculous," Soubry growled. "Okay, so what we have now is one executable in the sensor and communication suite. Another one—" she leaned closer to Ruth's split screen display "—in the *logistics* software. That's weird. And then a third in the tactical software. But this one . . ."

She frowned as Citizen Lieutenant Chapuis walked across the bridge to join the two women.

"That's the Engineering net," he said.

"So we've got Communications, Logistics, Tactical, *and* Engineering," Soubry said.

"Yep. But the only one currently running in background is the one in Communications," Ruth said. "And look at this. The file size on the two in Engineering and Logistics is almost twice as big as either of the others."

"Any thoughts about that one, Gabriel?" Soubry asked.

"No, Citizen Captain."

Chapuis shook his head, and Soubry's frown deepened. The citizen lieutenant was young—well, he was at least five T-years older than Ruth Winton, but, then, Ruth was a mere child, as far as Soubry was concerned—but he was very smart and very good. That was why she'd recruited him for this.

"I think we have to assume that all of these are linked, though," he continued. "And I don't like the size of this one." He tapped the Engineering directory with a fingertip. "I don't know enough about Engineering to know how *much* I shouldn't like it, but I've got a really bad feeling about this, Citizen Captain."

"So do I." Soubry spent another twenty seconds frowning, then shrugged. "We need to get Giselle Montcalm up here to look at this."

"Who's that?" Ruth asked.

"She's probably the best Engineering noncom we've got," Soubry replied. "She'd have been an officer back before—well, before . . . you know—if not for a couple of black marks in her file. But she knows the ins and outs of Engineering better than any commissioned officer on that damned island. She might be able to make sense of this. Citizen Lieutenant Chapuis can track her down in the compound."

"Have at it, then," Ruth said.

She swiveled her chair to face Indy Graham, who'd been amusing himself at the communications officer's station with his own Galaxy Conquest campaign. Ruth had managed to dissuade Razeen Montgomery from posting an armed-to-the-teeth representative of the Queen's Own to keep an eye on the two Peeps only because Fire Watch had cleared both of them of deception. But it had been a very near thing, and she'd prevailed in the end only by agreeing to take Indy along, instead.

"Go with him, would you, Indy?" she asked. "That way we know no busybody will busybody him."

"I'll leave as soon as someone from your detachment gets here."

"That's not—" Ruth began, then paused as he gave her The Look. He was right. Razeen Montgomery would hit the deckhead if Indy left her "unprotected" with a pair of StateSec holdouts, no matter what the treecats had said about them.

"Fine," she said instead, just a bit huffily, and watched Indy talking into his com.

Ten minutes later, Corporal Andrea Merino arrived from *L'Ouverture*. She took up a watchful stance which didn't even try to be unobtrusive just inside the hatch and regarded the two Peeps with a cool and dispassionate eye.

Indy grinned, gestured for Chapuis to precede him, and followed him out.

"This will take a while," Ruth said into the somewhat awkward silence. "But Captain Maurice has the galley up and running. Anyone want something to eat?"

Field Pavilion
Lincoln Island
Azure Ocean
Planet Torch
Congo System

BRYCE TARKOVSKY USHERED ANOTHER CANDIDATE INTO THE FIELD pavilion. It was a very bare-bones sort of command building, with little in the way of furnishings, much less luxuries. But it did well enough for Cachat's purposes.

He sat on one side of the conference table, facing an empty chair on the other. The only things on the table were a tablet and a stylus.

"Have a seat." He gestured toward the chair across from him, then glanced at the tablet. "You're a missile tech, name of Petro Calais. Is that correct?"

"Yes . . . Sir," Calais said as he took the indicated seat. Tarkovsky sauntered across to the coffee urn on a side table and drew himself a cup.

"You don't call me 'sir,'" Cachat said. "You don't do it here, because I'm not—yet, anyway—in your chain of command. And, frankly, you sound awkward as hell saying it. What's more important is that if you do go on the expedition, you'll refer to me as Citizen Commodore. Assuming we have any personal interaction, which is unlikely. We probably won't even be on the same ship."

"Yes, Si—" Calais paused, looking a bit confused. "Uh, what *do* I call you here, then?"

"Why call me anything? A few minutes from now, we may be complete strangers again. Look over there."

He pointed over Calais's right shoulder. The PNE missile technician twisted in his chair to look behind him, then froze.

345

"Ever seen one before?" Cachat asked. "If not, that's a genuine Sphinx treecat."

Fire Watch sprawled comfortably on the portable perch Damien Harahap had set up on the back of his own camp chair for him. Now he yawned widely, as he'd done for every PNE candidate. A treecat's yawn was...impressive. Their fangs might not be all that *long*, but there were a lot of them and they were very, very, *very* sharp.

Harahap didn't even look up from the book reader in his lap.

After a few seconds, Calais turned back around to Cachat. His face seemed a bit paler, although it was hard to be sure, given his dark complexion.

"You've heard they can read minds, right?"

Calais nodded.

"Well, that's nonsense. Treecats are empaths, not telepaths. They can't read your thoughts, but they can detect your emotions. So, if you lie to me at any point during this interview, the treecat will let me know. His name's Fire Watch, by the way. But don't let that bother you, because nobody's going to execute you just because you lie. Not me, not the treecat, not anybody."

Cachat nodded back the way Calais had come.

"You just go back out into the compound and spend the rest of your life on this island, staring at the ocean but not swimming on account of the marine life. With prolong— How old are you now?"

"Forty-six."

"Then you'll have at least two T-centuries of being a beachcomber to look forward to."

"And what happens if I don't lie but you still don't want me for this—whatever you're doing that you're hunting volunteers for?" the PNE officer demanded. He didn't—quite—glare at Cachat, and the Havenite leaned back in his chair, drumming the fingers of his left hand on the table.

"Good question—to which I don't know the answer. Yet. Put yourself in our shoes. What would you do with a bunch of prisoners who'd set out to exterminate you?"

Calais stared at him for a few seconds. Then the hostility faded from his eyes, and he chuckled. It was a harsh-sanding chuckle, but still a chuckle.

"Hell, Whatever-You-Call-Yourself, I would've shot all of you right off."

"Don't think there weren't a lot of people on this side who advocated exactly that." Cachat grinned. "But we decided not to. That road usually leads to ugly destinations. I know, I used to be an officer in StateSec myself."

He looked back down at the tablet.

"Now, let's get to business. What we want you to do is serve in a naval squadron that's going to investigate a star system where unsavory people are likely to be found. What you'll be doing is exactly what you've been trained to do and have experience doing. Nor will we be asking you to do anything that might tax your intellect. You'll be posing as pretty much exactly what you are: a PNE missile tech who's given up trying to restore the former regime in the Republic and is now working as a mercenary."

He looked up, stylus poised over the tablet.

"What's your reaction to that proposal?"

Calais looked out the open side of the pavilion at the emptiness of the landing area. And, beyond that, to the tropical foliage of the island. And, through gaps in the foliage, to the ocean in which no one quite dared to swim. Then he looked back at Cachat.

"Sure, I'll do it. Beats the alternative hands down."

"No regrets? No lingering loyalty to the old regime?"

"Regrets? Some, I suppose. But they're fading. And I know damned well now that the 'old regime' isn't coming back. Hell, I guess I really knew that even before we hypered out for Congo. Now I just want to get a life back. They told me you'd set me up with enough to do that, once the mission's over."

"Yes, we will."

"I can go anywhere I want?"

"As long as wherever that is will let you in." Cachat shrugged. "You won't be able to stay here on Torch, assuming you wanted to. And I doubt Haven will let you go home again. I haven't been able to discuss it with anyone in the government, but Admiral Tourville believes you'd be allowed to go back long enough to find whatever family you have and take them with you to somewhere else. Assuming they agree to go."

It was Calais's turn to shrug. "For me, that's a moot point."

Cachat glanced at Fire Watch. The treecat yawned again. Harahap kept reading. He looked back at Calais.

"All right. Welcome to Epsilon Squadron."

Calais stood and gave Cachat a stiff little nod.

"At your orders, Citizen Commodore," he said, and Cachat smiled.

"I knew you'd be a smart fellow. The name's Beaumont, by the way."

TRNS *Toussaint*
Torch Planetary Orbit
Congo System

"MARY, MOTHER OF GOD," CITIZEN PETTY OFFICER GISELLE MONT-
calm whispered.

"That's why you never made senior chief, Giselle," Citizen
Captain Soubry said. "You know how Pierre and Saint-Just felt
about religious superstition."

"They're dead," the noncom replied, and jabbed a finger at
the display in front of her. "And we'd be, too, if this had ever
gone off."

"What are you talking about?" Any trace of levity had vanished from Soubry's expression.

Montcalm had been aboard *Toussaint* for almost eighteen
hours. She'd spent most of that time disassembling—very, very
carefully—the Engineering Department's software.

"I'm saying I just blew up the damned ship, Ma'am," Montcalm said. She was clearly one of the members of the PNE who'd
washed her hands of restoring the revolution. "Or I would have,
if the bottle had been online."

The petty officer turned her head to give Ruth a nod.

"Taking the fusion plants off-line before you let me start
fooling around was a really, really good idea, Ma'am. Because
there was some kind of tripwire on that file. When I got close
enough to it, it executed itself." She frowned. "I'm not sure if
it detected me or if that first damned file—the one we already
knew was running—spotted me and ordered it to execute. But I
know what it did."

"What?" Soubry asked sharply.

"It turned off the fusion mag bottles...without turning off
349

the feed or the grav compression field." Montcalm switched her gaze from Ruth to the citizen captain. "The technical term for what would've happened when it did that—if the plant had still been online, even at standby load—is 'BOOM,' Ma'am." She shook her head. "I always wondered what Foraker did to Citizen Rear Admiral Heemskerk at Lovat. I don't *know* this is how she did it, but..."

"A suicide option?" Soubry shook her head. "No way. I was *Anshar*'s CO. I'd've known about it if we'd set up something like this!"

"If *you'd* set up something like this, yes," Ruth said, her eyes on Montcalm's display.

"But... in that case, who...?"

"Your employer, who else?" Ruth finished for her.

"She's right, Ma'am," Montcalm said. "That program didn't get there by accident, and it didn't install itself. Somebody had to put it there, and I can't believe anyone in *Cerberus*'s crew would've done it. There are a lot less complicated ways to commit suicide than—" she jabbed a finger at her display "—this. And if it wasn't us, then it had to be the contractors who handled the overhauls and upgrades."

"Suicide's out, anyway," Ruth said. "It wouldn't have been done just to this ship. I'll bet that if we looked—*when* we look, because we're sure as hell going to—we'll find the same programs tucked away on every surviving ship in your fleet."

"She's almost certainly right, Citizen Captain," Citizen Lieutenant Chapuis said. "We've found too many 'what-the-hell-is-that' program files for it to be a coincidence."

"I'm willing to bet the ones in the Logistics and Tactical software are tied into the magazines," Ruth said thoughtfully. "Which probably means it's a good thing the Navy offloaded all your warheads when they put *Cerberus* into its parking orbit. If the one in Engineering tripped and we didn't blow up, they probably tried—or would've tried, if they'd had any warheads—to blow the mags, as well."

"And the other one?" Soubry regarded Ruth with a certain dreadful fascination, and the young woman shrugged.

"If the PO is right, it's the master, coordinating program. The one that keeps an eye out for anyone who pokes too deeply at the kill files. And—" Ruth's gaze sharpened "—probably the one that listened for the execute order."

"And that makes sense, too," Chapuis said grimly. "It's in the sensors and communications systems. The perfect place to listen."

Soubry looked back and forth between them, her face pale. But then her expression changed and her face turned brick red, instead.

"*Milliken*," she hissed.

"Who's Milliken?" Ruth asked.

"Commander Jessica Milliken, Mesan System Navy." Soubry hammered each word out. "She and her boss, Captain Maddock, were the watchdogs—call them commissioners, if you want—the Mesans assigned to us. Hell, *Manpower* assigned—we all knew who we were *really* working for! Maddock was killed in the battle."

She glared at the display, then looked back at Ruth.

"We need to find that bitch and haul her up here. Now!"

"I think that's a very good idea," Ruth said, and looked over her shoulder. "Indy?"

"Jessica Milliken, commander in the Mesan System Navy," Indy repeated. "Got it. They're the ones with the black-and-gray uniforms, right?"

"That's them," Soubry said. Those two words sounded forged, too.

"Where am I likely to find her?"

"She'll be somewhere in the compound. Ask any one of our own officers."

"I will, but first—"

"I already commed Razeen," Ruth sighed, waving her uni-link, "and Andrea will be—"

Corporal Merino appeared, and Indy chuckled.

"You're learning, Your Grace," he told her, then nodded to Merino and headed for the hatch himself.

"At the risk of repeating myself, this will take a while," Ruth said. "Anybody hungry again?"

Lincoln Island
Azure Ocean
Planet Torch
Congo System

"YES?"

The blond-haired woman who'd opened the roughly built cabin's door was on the petite side, and her black tunic and charcoal-gray trousers didn't match the uniforms of the other POWs. She shared her quarters with three other female officers, and their cabin hadn't been hard to find.

"Jessica Milliken?"

"Yes," she said again, in a more cautious tone.

"Come with me."

"What for?" she demanded, her expression wavering between indignant and anxious.

"Because you're a POW, and I told you to," Indy replied. "Next question?"

"But—"

Indy raised one eyebrow—it was a mannerism he'd borrowed from Harahap, seasoned with more than a dash of Cachat—and Milliken cut off her protest.

"All right." She looked back over her shoulder. "Josette, I've got to go," she called. "I'm not sure when I'll be back."

An indistinct voice from inside the cabin said something Indy couldn't quite hear, and Milliken stepped outside and closed the door behind her.

"Let's go," she said resignedly.

It was a fifteen-minute walk back to the landing field and the Navy pinnace which had transported Indy down from *Toussaint*. The Torch Royal Marine lieutenant whose platoon was responsible for the field's security while Cachat conducted his interviews greeted Indy when they arrived.

"Found her, I see."

"Yep." Indy nodded and glanced at the pavilion. "Is Victor free?"

"No." The Lieutenant shook his head. "Just started interviewing another candidate. I can interrupt him, if you want."

"Don't bother." Indy shook his head. "When you get a chance, tell him I'm taking this one—" he twitched his head at Milliken "—up to *Toussaint* to talk to Ruth and Citizen Captain Soubry, but it's not time-critical. Certainly not important enough to interrupt him."

"You've got it." The lieutenant nodded and watched Indy and his...companion board the pinnace. Then the sleek trans-atmospheric craft rose on its counter-grav. It pointed its nose heavenward, its turbines wailed suddenly louder, and it flashed away from the island, climbing steeply.

✧   ✧   ✧

Victor Cachat stood, stretched, and walked to the pavilion's entrance as his latest interviewee—this time, one who'd failed to attain Fire Watch's seal of approval—stalked moodily away. The Havenite inhaled deeply. He really hated "office work." Not because he failed to appreciate its importance, and not because he didn't do it well. But he was always most at home in the field. In his opinion, it was grossly unfair of Anton Zilwicki to opine that he'd been born expressly to juggle hand grenades, but there was no denying that he performed at his best under pressure.

Bryce Tarkovsky joined him, and they stood gazing out across the island. It was really a pretty nice place, Cachat thought. Assuming one could visit it and then leave again. When its shores became the boundaries of one's universe, however...

No wonder the POWs were so eager to get off it.

"Excuse me, Officer Cachat."

It was the Marine platoon sergeant, and Cachat nodded to him. "What is it, Simon?"

"The Lieutenant told me to tell you Indy was here."

"Really?" Cachat looked around. "Where?"

"Sorry." The sergeant grimaced. "What I meant is that he *was* here, but he's headed back up to *Toussaint* with that officer he came to collect."

"Which officer?" Cachat frowned ever so slightly.

"The one he came to get to help Ruth figure out whatever it is she's trying to figure out." The sergeant shrugged. "I didn't catch the name. But she wasn't in Peep uniform. Black tunic and gray pants."

"Black—?" Cachat's eyes narrowed suddenly. "She was in *Mesan* uniform?"

"I guess so." The sergeant shrugged again. "Far as I know, I've never seen a Mesan Navy uniform before."

"Hell and damnation!"

"Victor?" Tarkovsky asked sharply. That sort of outburst was...very un-Cachat.

"We need to get up there, Bryce. *Now.* Hopefully—"

Cachat's jaw tightened and he shook his head.

"We're done for today. Come on!"

TRNS *Toussaint*
Torch Planetary Orbit
Congo System

"ADMIT IT, DAMN YOU!"

Citizen Captain Soubry loomed over the short, slender PNE officer. It looked like she was on the verge of punching Milliken, which, given the difference in their sizes, would have produced rather dramatic consequences. Which would be unfortunate. They needed the Mesan conscious and in reasonably sound condition if they were going to interrogate her, and Ruth sent an appealing glance at Indy Graham.

So far, Milliken hadn't confessed anything. But that was, perhaps, because Soubry hadn't given her an opening to say anything at all. The citizen captain was obviously...unhappy at the thought that she and all of her fellow officers and enlisted personnel had been sent off aboard booby-trapped ships their "employer" could blot out with a simple com code any time it chose. She'd been cursing and threatening Milliken nonstop since the Mesan had been brought onto the bridge.

Indy stepped forward in response to Ruth's silent appeal and placed a restraining hand on Soubry's shoulder. Very lightly—he wasn't trying to physically restrain her, just give her a cautioning touch.

"Citizen Captain, may I make a suggestion?"

"*What?!*" Soubry shifted her glare to him. It didn't fade much.

Indy simply looked at her. He didn't say a word while he did it, but he didn't need to. There was a reason Captain Montgomery had signed off on allowing him to provide Ruth's security. Not many people had led the successful rebellion of an entire planet or fought their way room-to-room across its capital city against

355

heavy odds. And equally few had understudied Damien Harahap while they did it.

Indiana Graham was a nice young man...and a very deadly one.

Something of that showed in his calm eyes, and Soubry's nostrils flared. Then she closed her own eyes and made her jaw unclench.

"What?" she repeated in a noticeably less belligerent voice.

"This doesn't seem very productive," he said in the same calm, pleasant tone. "On the other hand, one of the galaxy's primo interrogators is on Torch right now. In fact, by now I'm sure he's been informed of what this is all about and he's probably on his way here. So why don't we just wait until he arrives?"

"Who the hell you talking about?"

"Oh, Lord," Ruth said, and Soubry's glare shifted to her.

"You know who he's talking about."

"Yes, I do." Ruth leaned back—slumped back, really—in her chair and puffed out her cheeks. "He's talking about Victor Cachat—the guy who told you he was a hard man to betray. And he's hard to lie to, too." She looked at Milliken. "Especially if you want to stay alive. His methods are...ah..."

"Rigorous," Indy supplied.

Ruth's com buzzed, and Indy smiled crookedly.

"Now, I wonder who *that* is?" he mused.

❖   ❖   ❖

Cachat stepped onto the bridge twenty-odd minutes later, with Bryce Tarkovsky at his heels.

Courtesy of a somewhat terse com conversation with Ruth, he was fully up to speed, and he stalked straight over to Milliken, seated in the assistant tactical officer's chair. She was even shorter seated, and he was even taller than Soubry, which put the Mesan at a distinct disadvantage. Still, she rallied as best she could.

"This whole thing is outrageous. I'm an officer in the Mesan System Navy. I should be treated with at least a modicum of respect."

"What you are," Cachat said "is a member of the Mesan Alignment. And while I'm sure your story is interesting—we'll get to that soon enough—what really has me intrigued is something else."

He bent forward and planted his hands on his knees, bringing his face down to twenty-five centimeters from hers.

"Why are you still alive?"

❖   ❖   ❖

Someone gasped behind him, and Cachat lifted his head and looked over his shoulder. Ruth Winton stood two meters away, her eyes huge and one hand covering her mouth. When he glanced to the left, he saw Indy with an equally tight expression.

"Oh, give me a br—"

He sighed and stood up straight.

"I wasn't wondering why none of you had executed her." He turned back to look down on Milliken once more. Her mouth was open as she stared up at him. "What I *am* wondering is why she hasn't committed suicide yet. Or—this is more likely—why her automatic suicide protocols haven't done it for her."

"*Damn*," Tarkovsky hissed. "I didn't even think of that."

"Not too surprising." Cachat shrugged. "She's been a prisoner in enemy hands for almost two T-years, and it hasn't killed her yet. And unlike you, I knew we'd captured a Mesan officer along with the PNE. I *hadn't* asked myself why she was still alive, either, because I didn't know about the suicide protocols when she was captured, and I'm afraid she'd been out-of-sight, out-of-mind until Sergeant Simon reminded me. I *did* think about it, after that. In fact, I spent most of our trip up trying to figure out how we might outsmart the protocols. But then I realized she *had* been a prisoner, and—if that hadn't been enough—she'd just been told she was going up to *Toussaint*, and why, and her nanotech still hadn't killed her."

He stopped there, studying Milliken for a moment. For her part, she looked away. Apparently she found something of absorbing interest in a completely normal—and blank—tactical display.

"You know what I'm talking about, don't you, Commander Milliken?" he said. "But I'm willing to bet you've never seen it actually happen. Trust me, it's startling. One moment you're talking to someone who seems perfectly healthy and alert, and the next moment they've fallen over dead. It's not uncommon for them to have a startled look on their faces."

He glanced at Tarkovsky.

"Was that your experience, too?"

"Yes. Yes, it was. Your description's dead accurate."

It was possible—remotely—that Tarkovsky had placed a certain, slight emphasis on the word "dead," and Cachat turned back to Milliken.

"So why weren't *you* given the protocols? Or perhaps you

were, but they weren't activated. We—the Grand Alliance, that is—still haven't figured out exactly how the nanotech works, although we can detect its presence after the fact now, sometimes. At a guess..."

"It'd be harder to set a suicide trigger with a combat officer, Victor," Tarkovsky said. "I've read your people's reconstruction of what happened aboard Filareta's flagship at Manticore, and I think they're probably right. The 'Other Guys' got to someone—probably his ops officer—and planted the equivalent of one of their assassination commands. But carrying out a specific command that's programmed into the nanotech that physically takes over its target is way different from how any suicide package would have to work. Unless that nanotech is a lot more sophisticated, more capable of differentiating between fear and stress reactions than I'd think is possible, a naval battle already has so many of what you might call 'risk factors'—really severe ones—baked into it that they'd be in danger of having officers drop dead at their posts."

"Yes, that's what I was thinking." Cachat frowned. "And the Alignment probably doesn't worry much about the risk, anyway, because an active-duty combat officer—" he glanced back down at Milliken "—which is what she was, isn't really in much danger of being interrogated. If her side wins the battle, she's free and clear. If they lose—"

He shrugged.

"People on the losing side of a naval battle tend not to survive, and if they do, and if they *are* captured, the odds that anyone would think of doing the kind of interrogation we'll be doing are extremely low."

He settled into the tac officer's chair which Ruth had abandoned. That put him about a meter and a half from Milliken, and the grin he bestowed upon her would have done any treecat proud.

"You've never experienced that kind of interrogation, Commander Milliken." He raised one hand, as if warding something off. "Oh, you don't need to be afraid of torture. That's for amateurs."

"You can't—"

"Yes, I can, Commander." Cachat cut off her attempt at resistance. "Have you considered just how isolated and powerless you are? You're a captured officer, purportedly of a Mesan Navy that no longer exists—since the Mesan government it served no longer exists—while actually being a member of a secret organization, that theoretically has *never* existed and certainly isn't covered by the Deneb Accords, and when captured, you were a participant in an attempted Eridani Edict violation, which definitely voids the Accords. You have no legal standing, you belong to no political or military body which can or has any desire to help you, and you are the captive of people who have complete power over you . . . and every conceivable reason to wish you ill."

He paused for a moment to let her digest that.

"So don't tell me what I can and can't do. It's both silly and undignified. You'll be on the next available ship to Mesa on a voyage whose end you will really not be looking forward to, and for extraordinarily good reasons. Two in particular: a man named Anton Zilwicki, and another who now goes by the name of Saburo Lara. His previous surname had only one letter. The one he uses now is the name of the woman he loved . . . who was murdered by your Alignment."

He paused again, for a considerably longer moment. The silence lingered. Then—

"You'll talk," he said.

"Ah, Mr. Cachat." Soubry cleared her throat. "Don't be in too great a hurry to ship her off-planet. We may need her help to defuse these sabotage programs."

Victor glanced at her, and then back at Milliken.

"I'd be very surprised if she knows anything about those programs beyond the fact that they exist and what they do. Am I right, Commander Milliken?"

But Milliken was only staring at the blank tactical display again. Her face was drawn, pale—and completely devoid of expression. She looked like an exhausted mouse, trapped under the cat's paw and no longer even trying to struggle.

Soubry blew out a frustrated, wordless expulsion of air.

"Great," she added, once that was done.

"Actually," Ruth said, "I don't think we really need her. It'll be a little bit of a pain, but I think we've got this, now that we know—or we're pretty sure we know—what they do and how they do it."

"Excuse me?" Soubry gave her a skeptical sort of look.

"Sure." Ruth shrugged. "Petty Officer Montcalm didn't blow us up when the program tripped because the fusion plants were off-line. And if the Logistics and Tactical programs *were* supposed to blow us up the old-fashioned way if the Engineering program failed, they couldn't, because the magazines were empty. Well, the magazines are empty aboard all of the ships that haven't been put back into commission again. And the ships that *are* in commission can offload all of their missiles and warheads. Then we go aboard each of them, one at a time, and with the fusion bottles down, we rip these things out by the roots. No need for finesse if the hardware conditions they rely on aren't there, anymore."

"That should actually work," Soubry said. "Of course, first—"

Cachat ignored the rest as Chapuis and Montcalm clustered around Ruth and Soubry and started in on the incomprehensible naval details.

He turned to Bryce Tarkovsky and Indy Graham, instead.

"We're not needed here any longer, and I need to get back down to the planet. Would the two of you do me the favor of escorting Commander Milliken back aboard *L'Ouverture* and finding her a nice, secure, *locked* cabin?"

"Sure." Indy went over to Milliken and said, rather gently, "Get up, please."

It took two or three seconds, but then the Mesan officer looked up at him.

"Get up, please," he repeated.

She did, and Indy guided her toward the hatch by an elbow. Tarkovsky loomed right behind them. It was painfully obvious she had no intention of putting up any resistance, but Cachat followed them, too. He'd be of no use on the bridge, and his shuttle was docked next to Indy's pinnace.

Indy glanced over his shoulder at him.

"I think I can handle this, boss."

"If you're still using reactionary salutations like 'Boss,' I need to keep an eye on you anyway." The smile that followed held some actual humor. "You never know where treason will rear its furry little head."

"Treason is a mammal?"

"You didn't know that already?"

Field Pavilion
Lincoln Island
Azure Ocean
Planet Torch
Congo System

THERE WAS NO SIGN EITHER HARAHAP OR FIRE WATCH HAD moved at all while Cachat was gone. Fire Watch only twitched an ear at them as Tarkovsky took his usual place by the entrance and Cachat crossed to the conference table and sat down.

"We should have time for two more interviews today, after all," he said. "Bryce, would you please usher in the next candidate?"

The woman who came in wore the uniform of a chief petty officer. According to her file, she was fifty-two T-years old, but she looked like a pre-prolong twenty-year-old. Third-generation prolong, then.

"Magdalena Frazier?" he asked.

"I usually go by Maggie," she replied a bit carefully.

"Maggie, then." He indicated the char across from him. "Have a seat."

He waited until she was settled, then leaned back slightly.

"Has it been explained to you what—"

❖   ❖   ❖

That interview went smoothly. The next one didn't. Five minutes into Cachat's conversation with the next applicant, Fire Watch raised his head and came alert on his perch.

"You're lying about something, Citizen Lieutenant Granger," Cachat said. "I don't know what it is, but I don't care, because it doesn't matter. The mere fact of the lying is enough to disqualify you." He pointed a finger at the entrance. "Leave, please."

The beefy citizen lieutenant bristled and came to his feet.

361

"Listen, you—" He leaned toward Cachat belligerently, then jerked upright with an undignified squeal as Bryce Tarkovsky twisted his right wrist up to touch the back of his neck. The Marine made sure they had good contact by wrapping the fingers of his free hand in Granger's rather unkempt hair and pulling his head back.

The citizen lieutenant tried to wrench free—briefly. Tarkovsky was even beefier than he was...and unlike Granger, none of Tarkovsky's beef was fat. He turned the PNE officer by his two painful purchase points and frog marched him toward the pavilion entrance.

It was possible that the velocity with which the citizen lieutenant left of the pavilion might have owed something to the toe of Tarkovsky's boot.

Fire Watch settled back down with an amused bleek, and Cachat shook his head.

"Well, given how short *that* interview was," he said as Tarkovsky walked back to his place, dusting his palms together with an undeniably smug expression, "I think we can squeeze in one more."

"Slave driver," Harahap said, without ever looking up from his book reader.

LaGrange Point B
L'Ouverture Station
Congo System

MINETTE THE MERCILESS LAUNCHED HER INVINCIBLE FLEET AGAINST the armada of the wicked Grahamian Empire and tried not to snarl.

It was difficult.

Figuring out how the Trojan Horse programs worked, and how to defeat them, had been interesting. And she was pleased that her proposed solution for deactivating them seemed to be working smoothly. But now that it was, she was back in durance vile, chained to her computer, locked in her lonely tower aboard a space station which had been falsely named for one of humanity's great liberators. Trapped at the heart of its battle steel web.

And bored to tears once more.

They hadn't let her actually help disarm any of the booby-traps, of course. It had been her solution, and it had worked, but there'd always been the possibility that it might not, and God forbid a princess of Manticore should get blown up in the line of duty. Never mind that several members of the Winton family had suffered that fate over the T-centuries. For reasons that defied her comprehension, it was acceptable for that to happen to upright military personnel, but not to sinister spooks like herself.

Cynthia X had tried to explain the conundrum to her.

"The issue isn't death, Your Grace," she'd said, using the title with malice aforethought. "It's capture. The likelihood of that happening to a Winton in uniform aboard a warship is slight. The likelihood of that happening to a Winton skulking in the shadows in enemy territory is anything but."

"Really?" Ruth had regarded her scornfully. "Then Aunt Michelle didn't get herself captured by Javier Giscard at the Battle of Solon?"

"That was different," Cynthia had said.

"Oh, it was *hugely* different! After all, she's fourth in line for the throne... and I'm not in the succession at all! I *totally* see why it would be far worse if the bad guys captured *me*."

"Okay, I'll give you that, but—"

"I don't want to hear it. 'We can't risk having you taken as a hostage again.' Except it *wasn't* me; it was Berry."

"Because they thought she was you."

Ruth had ignored that. She'd thought of it as not dignifying it with a response.

"Damn it, I want to *do* something," she'd said instead. "And not—" she waved at her elaborate workstation "—*that.*"

Not that her protests had done her any good, of course. And the fact that all the people so determined to protect her actually *liked* her only made it worse. Especially since so many of them, like Razeen Montgomery, weren't above guilt-tripping her into submission.

Damn the man!

Minette the Merciless glared at the computer display and ordered her fleet to take no prisoners.

❖   ❖   ❖

And then, to the princess's amazement, Victor Cachat, that most unlikely of paladins, came to her rescue yet again.

"What are you doing here?" Ruth asked him after he sat down in one of the chairs in her cubicle. That was the term she used. It was actually quite a spacious and attractively designed and decorated suite. For a cell, anyway.

"Do I need to leave?" Cynthia asked from where she'd been seated at the suite's second computer terminal. "Is this a 'need to know' thing?"

Cachat shook his head.

"It is. But I interpret that phrase as I choose. And I can see circumstances that could very well make you a useful addition to the mission."

"Mission?" Ruth came instantly alert, sitting up in her chair. "What mission?"

"The one I'm about to propose to you, assuming we get to carry it out, after all." He spread his hands in a cautioning gesture. "I don't know how my original plans are likely to be impacted after the Sollies get here, but I'd be surprised if they didn't have at least some effect. Not enough to abort the mission, though. Most likely, anyway. But it could happen."

Ruth nodded. No one knew exactly *why* a Solarian League Navy light task group was on its way to Congo, but they knew that its passage had been okayed by the Grand Alliance, that it should be arriving shortly, and that some sort of intelligence-sharing operation appeared to be in the cards. It was fortunate the Alliance squadron of podnoughts that were sent to deliver the heads-up—and bolster Congo's defenses, just in case—had arrived when it did, because Cachat had been on the brink of hypering out for Hole-in-the-Wall.

"Unless there is a significant change," he continued now, "what I have in mind would get you out of Congo and off Torch. Before you get cranky about it, though, I'll tell you right off that there's no significant danger for you in it. Which I've been told you seem to crave, for reasons that defy comprehension, given that you're not an imbecile."

"Told? Told by *who*?"

"Who *didn't* tell me?" Cachat snorted, and pointed at Cynthia. "Her, for one. Razeen Montgomery—hell, your entire security detachment—for another . . . oh, *dozen* or so. Then there was Lieutenant Howe. Indy. Damien. *Fire Watch*. Bryce Tarkovsky tells me you've even griped to him about it."

"Okay, so I'm surrounded by rat finks. What's the mission? Fair warning, Victor! You and Anton Zilwicki are supposed to be training me to be a real *espionage agent*, not—" she waved her hand at her terminal "—a glorified clerk."

"What I have in mind for you may well be the most critical mission the Grand Alliance has at this moment. For the first time since Simões defected, we've captured, alive and with no suicide protocols—no activated ones, at least—a known member of the Alignment. Not the Benign Alignment we've uncovered back in Mesa. The real, undisputed, *Malign* Alignment. You know who I'm talking about."

"Milliken."

"Exactly. If we can turn her—and I think we have a very good chance of doing so—we may gain a tremendous asset."

"*Turn* her?" Cynthia sat up straight in her own chair. "Hell, Victor—just *shoot* her. I volunteer!"

The look he gave her was pure, trademark Cachat exasperation.

"I've piled up enough Alignment corpses already. So have you—I've read your dossier."

"You *spied* on me?" Cynthia's eyes narrowed.

"Of course I did. That's what I am, remember—a spy."

"You're supposed to do that to the *enemy*."

"Who needs to be identified, which is why I spied on you. If it makes you feel better, my verdict was 'Nope, she's one of ours.'"

"You bastard."

Cachat ignored that and returned his attention to Ruth.

"The key to turning an enemy agent is to provide them with someone on your side they come to trust. That's what I want you to do. Get her to trust you."

"*What?*" Ruth's mouth fell open and her eyes widened.

"You heard me."

"You're insane! I can't think of anyone less capable of making friends with a fucking monster—which is what she is—than I'd be."

"I can." Cynthia raised her hand. "Me."

Cachat shook his head.

"You didn't pay attention. I didn't say you had to make friends with her. What I said was that you had to get her to trust you."

"What's the difference?" Ruth asked with a frown.

Cachat reached up and ran fingers through his long, curly, quite striking blond hair. Then almost snatched the hand back. That was a habit he'd gotten into since his nanotech physical transformation, and *not* one of which he approved. He'd been too busy to go through the rather lengthy process of restoring his natural face and form, which he wanted to do as soon as possible. So did Thandi. She found his current astonishingly good looks almost repellent. (Not quite, but she did insist on turning off the lights.)

He lowered his hand rather firmly to his right knee.

"Try putting yourself in Milliken's place. I meant every word I said to her. She's as helpless and alone as anyone can be. She has no one to help her, no one she can trust, nowhere to go, and no knowledge of what will happen to her in the next minute, much less the next day or week or year."

He let that sink in for a moment.

"I don't doubt that she has physical courage—most combat officers usually have that, in one degree or another. But that sort of courage is all wrong for her situation. What she needs now is the sort of resilience and endurance that a good spy possesses.

The sort of courage it takes to keep silent and accept dying in darkness, with your body pitched into an unknown grave, is a very different kind of courage than what you need in open combat. I have it—a great deal of it—but she'll have very little."

He stopped again, and looked at Cynthia.

"You understand what I'm saying, don't you?"

"Yes," she said, a bit reluctantly. "When you—someone like me or Saburo, I mean—go out on a strike, you're usually on your own. No one will know what happened to you if you don't come back, except the scorpions who killed you. Medals, honors, pride in your unit, public remembrance—none of that will ever come *your* way."

Victor nodded and returned his gaze to Ruth.

"If it will make you feel any better about this, not everyone who belongs to the Alignment—even the *Malign* Alignment—really is the 'fucking monster' you called her. I'm not saying she isn't, because I don't know. For what it's worth, Fire Watch doesn't think she's what he calls 'an evildoer,' and you might want to remember what Jack McBryde did at the very end of his life. So it's possible she isn't. On the other hand, you know I'm about the farthest thing from a Pollyanna, and I'm totally willing for her to be just as much a monster as you think she is right now, if we can still turn her. And I don't care whether we turn her because she thinks it's the best deal she'll get, the way she gets off with her life, or because she sees the light and comes over to the side of goodness and right.

"I don't care because it doesn't matter. What matters is the opportunity she offers."

"But what makes you think I'm the one to make her 'trust me?' What am I supposed to offer her?"

"You're not supposed to offer her a damned thing." Cachat shook his head. "You're supposed to be the person she trusts, the person whose judgment she turns to, when someone *else* makes her an offer. And almost all of the things that make you think you couldn't do this job are exactly the things that make your success possible. Milliken wouldn't trust a quick smile and a friendly demeanor for a second. She's not stupid. But the truth is that behind that opinionated, occasionally brilliant, cantankerous not-so-easy-to-get-along-with-when-you-don't-get-your-own-way prima donna you can turn on at need, you're actually a friendly soul, who cares about the people around her, who doesn't go out of her way to hurt people, and who's—I'm sorry, but it's true—a pretty piss-poor liar."

"Gee, thanks, Victor."

"Black Victor, remember?" He smiled. "You said it yourself: he's an asshole, but you can trust him. That's the kind of trust that can turn an agent. Not trust that you're really her friend, but trust that if you say you'll try to help her find a new place in the universe—especially if she's started figuring out what her *old* place in the universe was really like—you won't let her down. It doesn't matter whether she thinks you're helping her because you like her, because you feel sympathy for her, or just because your cold-blooded judgment says it's the most valuable thing you can do for your side. What *matters* is that when you say you'll do it, she believes you will. And the truth is, Ruth, that if you tell her that, you *won't* let her down. It's not in you. I think hereditary, aristocratic forms of government are one of the stupidest innovations humanity ever came up with, but I've seen your family in action. It's not in *any* of you."

Ruth looked at him silently, her eyes dark, and the silence lingered. After a moment, she glanced at Cynthia, and the Ballroom assassin nodded back to her.

"You really think I can do this?" she asked Cachat finally.

"Have I been suggesting for the last—oh, fifteen minutes—that someone *else* can do it?"

"Well, no...."

"Then there you are." Cachat snorted. "You are one *stubborn* young woman, did you know that?"

"Razeen's said something about that every once in a while, I think."

"Damn straight he has. But look at it this way. At least it'll get you out of—" it was his turn to wave at her computer station "—this assignment."

That was the clincher.

"Okay, I'll do it. Cynthia and Bill Howe can handle this end plenty well enough. But—" Her eyes narrowed again. "Since when do you have the authority to get my assignment changed?"

"I wouldn't worry about that. After all, I'm Black Victor, aren't I?"

July 1923 Post Diaspora

"Probably the one thing Pierre and Saint-Just got completely right was fumigating the bureaucracy with extreme prejudice."

—Victor Cachat

TRNS *Rei Amador*
and
L'Ouverture Station
Torch Planetary Orbit
Congo System

THE BRIEFING ROOM HATCH OPENED, AND INDIANA GRAHAM stuck his head in.

"Just got a heads up from Vice Admiral Correia, Victor—I mean, Citizen Commodore Beaumont." The suspicious might have viewed the grin which accompanied his self-correction as a tad insincere, but his tone was serious. "It looks like the Sollies are here."

"Oh?" Cachat looked up from the conference table's display of the star map he'd been perusing with Jarmila Soubry, Jacob Trevithick, and Bryce Tarkovsky "They're early."

"Only a day or so," Tarkovsky pointed out. "And like Correia told us when he got here, Robbins's movement schedule wasn't absolutely confirmed when he left Manticore."

"True. I could wish they'd told him at least a little more about what this is all about, though." Cachat's tone was a bit sour. "It's not like we don't have enough going on already."

"No, it's not," Tarkovsky agreed. "On the other hand, it must've taken something pretty compelling to convince the Grand Alliance to let a Solarian task group transit both Beowulf and Manticore to get here." His tone had turned rather more somber than Cachat's had been.

That "convincing" had undoubtedly been especially difficult where Beowulf was concerned, given the forty-three million Beowulfers who'd died in the course of a Solarian attack on their star system. But the Star Empire of Manticore—for that matter, the Grand Alliance in general—was not what one might call a great

371

admirer of the SLN, either. Tarkovsky understood the reasons for that only too well, despite the cooperation and genuine friendships he'd formed with Cachat and a lot of those same Manticorans over the past few months. It was more than a little humiliating to be forced to ask permission to send Solarian naval vessels outside the League's own systems, and he would have been more than human if a part of him hadn't resented the hell out of that. But he had to admit that the Grand Alliance had actually imposed far less stringent terms than it might have, considering the ample grounds for hatred the Solarian League and its navy had given its members. Of course, that was more true for Battle Fleet than for Frontier Fleet, from whence their current visitors sprang.

"Did Admiral Correia give us an ETA, Indy?" Cachat asked.

"A bit over three hours." Indy shrugged. "I think he said they're eight light-minutes out and pulling about four hundred gravities of acceleration."

"Sounds about right," Soubry said, then snorted. "Only about seventy percent of their max accel, though. You think maybe they're being just a tiny bit...circumspect?"

"With an entire squadron of Grand Alliance podnoughts sitting on the planet? Oh, and let's not forget their *escorts*," Trevithick said. "*I'd* damned straight be 'circumspect' as hell, at least until I was sure the message approving my visit had gotten here before I did!"

Even Cachat smiled a bit at that. The Grand Alliance might have approved transit for the Solarian task group, but they'd used Vice Admiral Lawrence Correia as a convincing argument to discourage any possible Solly lunacy after it arrived. Personally, Cachat didn't think there was a chance in hell of any "lunacy" getting past Grand Fleet, Empress Elizabeth, or the treecats who'd undoubtedly personally vetted the Solarian CO before she was allowed to continue her journey.

He *did* approve of thoroughness, however.

"Well, if we've got three hours, why don't we finish our discussion before our...guests arrive?" he said.

✧   ✧   ✧

"Ruth!"

Berry Zilwicki charged across the *L'Ouverture* concourse, much to the chagrin—but not at all to the surprise—of the waiting security detail.

The detail of exactly three, including her Secretary of the Posterior, did not express that chagrin, however. They had learned from sad experience how little patience their monarch had with the notion that she needed protecting.

Despite an assassination attempt which had come terrifyingly close to success little more than two T-years ago.

Fortunately for the peace of mind of the pair of Torch Marines who had "just happened to" be on the concourse when Queen Berry "just happened to" arrive, Ruth Winton was, as always, accompanied by two members of her own security detachment. And while Berry might pooh-pooh the notion that *she* needed bodyguards, she was quite prepared to insist that her friend Ruth be protected at all times. Ruth had occasionally mentioned that minor inconsistency to her.

With absolutely no effect.

Now the two young women wrapped their arms around each other in enthusiastic greeting under the watchful gaze of their long-suffering protectors.

Berry let Ruth go, only to wrap her arms around Hugh Arai. Well, as far around him as she could reach, at any rate. Some might have remarked upon the fact that she had greeted Ruth first, but watching her now, any unbiased observer would have been forced to conclude that she had fully internalized her stepmother's notions of propriety, especially where the object of her affections was concerned.

A point which was brought fully home when Ruth whistled and began clapping.

Berry and Arai parted with a last, lingering kiss, and the queen looked down her nose at her best friend.

"There was something you wanted to say?"

"I was going to tell you two to get a room," Ruth replied with a grin. "But then I remembered you have an entire palace full of rooms down on the planet. So, why don't we get the pair of you down where you can greet Hugh properly, without the inhibition imposed by his shy and retiring—not to say repressed—nature?"

"That sounds like a very good idea," Berry agreed, tucking one arm possessively through Arai's. "Don't you think so, Hugh?"

"I'm too tongue-tied with embarrassment to reply," Arai told her with a slow smile.

"Well, we'll just have to work on that. Come on—the landing shuttle's waiting!"

"Uh, excuse me, Your Mousety?" Web Du Havel said.

"Yes?" Berry looked over her shoulder at her prime minister, who had followed her rather more sedately into the concourse.

"I realize some things are more important than others, but don't you think there are a few introductions that need to be made first?"

"Of course there are. But that's why you're here."

"I beg your pardon?" Du Havel raised an eyebrow, and Berry made an airy hand-waving gesture she'd *also* learned from Cathy Montaigne.

"That's a ministerial level sort of thing," she said with a grin. "Besides, it's the kind of sneaky stuff someone like you really likes. While *I*—" she leaned her head against a large, solid, conveniently placed shoulder "—prefer, um, something else."

✧   ✧   ✧

"So, *here* you are, Victor," Web Du Havel said thirty minutes or so later.

"And where did you expect me to be?" Cachat swiveled his chair to face the briefing room hatch without climbing out of it. His planning session with Soubry, Trevithick, and Tarkovsky had run longer than expected, as such things tended to do.

"Oh, I suppose I thought you might accompanied joined Ruth across to *L'Ouverture* to welcome us home," Du Havel replied a bit quizzically.

"I'll see all of you tonight—well, tomorrow probably—at the shindig Ruth's been planning for the last week," Cachat pointed out in a dry tone. "Besides, it would have been more than my life was worth to get between Hugh and Berry."

"He was that eager to see her, was he?"

"Who the hell was talking about *Hugh*? We both know Berry."

"Good point." Du Havel nodded with a broad grin. "On the other hand, now that I've tracked you down, I have a couple of people to introduce. It's what Berry refers to as a 'ministerial level sort of thing.'"

"Show them in."

Cachat waved his left hand in an inviting gesture as his right forefinger hit the button that blanked the star system schematic he and the others had been studying. Then he pushed his chair back from the briefing room table and stood.

Two people in Solarian uniform followed Du Havel through

the open hatch. The first, a woman, wore that of a Solarian League Navy rear admiral, and the other wore that of a Solarian Gendarme. A major in his case.

"Victor Cachat, let me introduce Rear Admiral Elizabeth Robbins and Major Jerzy Scarlatti. Admiral, Major—the famous secret agent, Victor Cachat."

Major Scarlatti's lips twitched as Cachat rolled his eyes ever so slightly at the word "famous." Rear Admiral Robbins's expression was admirably grave as she extended her hand.

"Officer Cachat," she said. "I hope you won't take this wrongly, but I've heard a great deal about you."

"There seems to be a lot of that going around," Cachat replied as he shook her hand.

"Pleased to meet you," Scarlatti said, holding out his hand, in turn. "I have to say, though, that you don't match the imagery in our files."

"You have imagery of me in your files?" Cachat frowned.

"Well, there were the visual records from your file when you were assigned to the PRH's embassy in Old Chicago. And that incident with the Scrags *under* Old Chicago," Scarlatti pointed out. "And then there was that episode in Erewhon. *Lots* of pictures from that one. And then—"

"I get the point." Cachat shook his head in disgust and ran one hand's fingers through his blond hair. "I have got to get back to something closer to normal, but if I'm on every news service's wallpaper..." He looked at Tarkovsky. "And why didn't you and your friends mention anything about my notoriety in the League?"

"We didn't want to hurt your feelings," the Marine said, and nodded to Scarlatti. "Good to see you, Jerzy. It's been a while."

"Gotten drunk in any good bars lately?" Scarlatti asked with a smile.

"That entire incident was only part of my cover story," Tarkovsky replied.

"*Sure* it was." Scarlatti agreed with a noticeable lack of sincerity, and Tarkovsky snorted.

"Speaking of cover stories, Admiral," Cachat said, turning back to Robbins. "Would you mind telling us why you're here?"

"They didn't already tell you?" Du Havel sounded surprised.

"And why would you assume they'd tell us anything?" Cachat asked. "I can understand why seeing Admiral Correia's squadron in orbit might have led someone who was less familiar with how information flow actually works in the Grand Alliance to the erroneous conclusion that we *had* been told. Unfortunately—"

He shrugged, and Du Havel grimaced.

"I'm sorry about that," he said with genuine contrition. "There's a reason to keep a tight lid on this one, but not tight enough for *that*."

"Actually, the problem may have been at our end," Robbins said with a grimace of her own, and looked at Cachat apologetically. "The security concern, I mean. We really, really don't want any word of what we're up to to leak where any embedded apparatchiks whose loyalty might be questionable could hear of it, so we pasted a great big 'need to know' label on it. That may have splashed onto what your people were willing to tell you."

"Apparatchiks?" Cachat snorted. "Trust me, I'm familiar with the breed. Although, the Legislaturalists did have a rather different variety of them in Nouveau Paris. Once upon a time. Probably the one thing Pierre and Saint-Just got completely right was fumigating the bureaucracy with extreme prejudice."

"In fairness, not *all* of ours were corrupt, Officer Cachat," Robbins said earnestly. "Why, I estimate that at least—oh, *six percent* of them weren't."

"That many?" Cachat's snort was an actual laugh this time.

"I think the Admiral's probably being overgenerous," Scarlatti said. "On the other hand, it wasn't just the apparatchiks that had us worried about leaks. It was everything else—all the silliness and confusion in Old Chicago right now. I guess that's probably pretty much inevitable when something as big as the Solarian League is undergoing a massive transformation, but it doesn't exactly inspire a hard-working spook with confidence about keeping secrets."

"I can imagine." Cachat shook his head. "Even the best politicians are still politicians, and I've never met one who could keep his or her mouth shut unless they knew they'd be shot at dawn if they let something leak. And then there are those 'apparatchiks' of yours. They're given to aggressively loose lips under the best of circumstances, even when corruption isn't their primary motivation. And you're dealing with apparatchiks *multiplied* by politicians!"

"And lobbyists—don't forget them. I figure they have an

exponential effect." Scarlatti made a face. "I've never been sure if the reason Biblical Egypt wasn't struck by lobbyists instead of locusts in the eighth plague was because lobbyists didn't exist yet, or because God was being merciful."

"Oh, that was clearly an example of divine mercy." Cachat smiled and waved toward the briefing room conference table. "But now that we've been introduced—oh, wait. Admiral, Major, these are Citizen Captain Soubry and Citizen Commander Trevithick, recently of the People's Navy in Exile and currently members of what we're calling Beaumont's Irregulars. For now, at least."

"I'd wondered about those uniforms," Scarlatti said, reaching out to shake hands. "I didn't want to risk seeming rude by asking, but it does seem, um, a little odd, given what we understood about the Battle of Congo back home."

"The citizen captain and citizen commander are working with me on a little project," Cachat said. "Which leads to another question," he added, resuming his own seat as Scarlatti, Robbins, and Du Havel settled into chairs. "I'm not concerned about their loyalty at the moment, but they won't always be working with me. So, is their presence going to be a problem for that 'need to know' label of yours?"

The two Solarians looked at one another for a moment, then Robbins shrugged and turned back to Cachat.

"The outcome of what we need to discuss is going to become public knowledge—*very* public knowledge, really—eventually. We just don't want word of it getting to the wrong ears before we're ready to bring the hammer down. May I assume that the citizen captain and citizen commander will be occupied on this joint project of yours for at least the next three or four T-months?"

"Frankly, I'll be surprised if we're done that soon."

"Then I don't see any reason not to let them stay. In fact, forgive me if I'm stepping on any sore toes here, but it's my understanding that Manpower was actually pretty deeply involved in the attack on Congo?"

Robbins looked back and forth between Soubry and Trevithick, and the citizen captain scowled.

"All the squadron and division commanders pretended it wasn't," she said, "but, yeah. Manpower was involved up to its stinking neck. And the truth is, all of us really knew it, whether or not we wanted to admit it." She looked down at the tabletop.

"And we didn't. We didn't want to admit how far down into the muck we'd crawled. We were telling ourselves a lot of lies about then."

"If it makes you feel any better, Citizen Captain," Robbins voice was oddly gentle, "I'm Frontier Fleet. Or I was, anyway. The Battle Fleet-versus-Frontier Fleet distinction is going away pretty soon. And Frontier Fleet's spent a long time doing an awful lot of absolutely shitty things for the kinds of people Frontier Security hung out with. Believe me, your people don't have any monopoly on not wanting to admit the muck they've wallowed in."

Soubry looked up. Their eyes met, and then, finally, the ex-Peep nodded.

Silence lingered for a moment, but then Cachat tipped back in his chair.

"Well," he said in a deliberately lighter tone, "if everyone's staying, why don't you and the Major bring us up to speed, Admiral?"

❖   ❖   ❖

"Okay," Cachat said forty-five minutes later. "I think I've got a handle on what your Director Gannon has in mind. I'm not sure I agree with him and Admiral Kingsford as to the effect it will have, but it's certainly worth trying. Not to mention totally worth doing on its own merits. And it might just tie in with something that we—" a wave of his right hand took in Tarkovsky and the pair of ex-Havenites "—have been working on. Oh, and his—" an index finger jabbed specifically at Tarkovsky "—'Ghost Hunter' buddies, too."

"'Ghost Hunters'?" Scarlatti repeated, looking at Tarkovsky.

"Just a little nickname we bestowed upon ourselves when we were the only members of the entire Solarian intelligence community smart enough to pour piss out of a boot and figured out there really was *something* out there, whether we called it the Alignment or not," Tarkovsky told him.

"And 'we' would be who, exactly?"

"Actually," Tarkovsky's voice turned more serious, "it was Brigadier Gaddis who gave a half dozen conspiracy theorists the support we needed to prove at least some of what was really going on."

"So you were part of the people who helped put that whole... well, we can't call it a coup, so let's call it a 'takedown,' instead, together?"

"A part." Tarkovsky nodded. "And the Brigadier sent us out to Mesa to help Victor and Anton Zilwicki beat the bushes."

"Why do I have the feeling that this operation—*potential* operation—is about to find itself going in a lot of different directions at once?" Robbins asked.

"Not in so many directions, I think, as much as towards so many different *objectives*," Cachat replied. "But you're right that there are a lot of wheels in motion. Or will be, anyway. Which tells me that we need to bring a few—and when I say a few, I mean quite a lot, actually—other people in on this."

"Who are we talking about here?" Scarlatti asked.

"Pretty much everybody." Cachat shrugged. "Me, Queen Berry—her prime minister's obviously already up to his ears in it." He nodded his head in Du Havel's direction. "Then there's you and the Admiral, and any of her staff she wants to bring in. And the former Haven StateSec fanatics and would-be mass murderers—" the head tilted in Soubry's and Trevithick's direction "—I've been assembling into my own squadron for a purpose that I think—I've just started thinking, I warn you—will intersect with your aims."

Robbins might have looked just a bit cross-eyed.

"And...does a kitchen sink figure in anywhere?" she asked, and Cachat grinned.

"A fellow antiquarian, I see! No, there's no antique drainage unit. But I *can* toss in a reformed Scrag and a fellow with a shady past and a treecat."

Scarlatti laughed, and Robbins raised an eyebrow at him.

"I was just thinking that anyone 'Black Victor'—and, yes, we had *that* in our files, too, Officer Cachat—thinks has a 'shady past' has *got* to be interesting as hell."

"Oh, really?" Cachat smiled at him. "As a matter of fact, I think it's entirely possible you already know him."

"Say what?"

"Well, most of his shady past was done wearing a uniform very much like *that* one," Cachat said, pointing at Scarlatti's own Gendarmerie uniform. "As a part of which, he did some work for Mesa, Manpower and a stack of dirty transstellars—loaned out by his own Gendarmerie superiors, you understand, not freelancing on his own time. Until the insurrection he was fomenting in the Talbott Sector went belly-up at a place called Monica, at least, at which point one—or more—of his employers tried to kill him. The assassination attempt worked out poorly—for the assassins—but he was clearly blown. So, following that minor unpleasantness, he spent some time working directly for the Alignment-slash-Other Guys. He didn't know who they were or exactly what they wanted, you understand, but it was that 'any port in a storm' sort of thing that happens to people in our business from time to time. He was pretty damned effective for them, too, until he orchestrated a successful rebellion against the Frontier Security-backed oligarchs in the Seraphim System, got caught in the fighting himself, and fell into Manticoran hands. They wanted to discuss his activities in Talbott with him, so he was shipped off to the Star Kingdom to have his brain vacuumed. Only then the treecat who was supposed to rip his throat out if he tried to betray or mislead the Manties decided to adopt him, instead. Which is why he's now working for the Star Empire. Oh, and with us."

Robbins's eyes were definitely crossed now, and Scarlatti shook his head.

"Okay, now I *really* have to meet this guy!" he said.

"Well, let me get on the com, and I'll see what I can do to... facilitate that."

❖   ❖   ❖

It turned out to be a little more complicated than that.

Some of the people they would need were still on Lincoln Island, others were on *L'Ouverture*, and still others were aboard *Obdurate*, Robbins's flagship. It was also shading into late evening in Port-au-Prince, the planetary capital. Queen Berry was about to sit down to an intimate little dinner in her private suite and had exactly zero intention of putting a toe outside it until morning—*late* morning.

Under the circumstances, she declared, bearing in mind the number of warm bodies involved and all the places they needed to be gathered from—and the fact that in Jeremy X's absence, she had no minister of war, which meant she would need her Secretary of the Posterior's advice—there was no point scheduling the meeting before tomorrow afternoon at the earliest, and they might as well hold the discussion in a central location. For which, she nominated the newly constructed Rodential Palace in Port-au-Prince.

Admiral Robbins was looking cross-eyed again as Cachat broke the connection.

"Your Mousety, the Secretary of the Posterior—and now, a Rodential Palace?"

"Should I assume Queen Berry didn't travel from Old Earth aboard *Obdurate*, Admiral?" Cachat asked with a gleam.

"We invited her to, of course. My feelings weren't too crushed when the invitation was—politely, mind you—declined by her security detail. But, no. I'm afraid I didn't have the opportunity to get to know her. Obviously, I should have." Robbins shook her head. "Why do I feel like I've wondered into an ancient fairytale?"

"Which one?" Cachat smiled. "*Alice in Wonderland*?"

"That's the one I'm hoping for—which is a scary enough thought, where 'off with her head' is concerned. Given that the alternatives that spring to mind are the stories of the Brothers Grimm and Edgar Allen Poe, however..."

Cachat laughed.

"You don't need to worry about those, Admiral—or *Alice in Wonderland*, for that matter. The Queen of Torch isn't anything like the Red Queen or the Queen of Hearts. The truth is, she dotes on whimsy, and the only head *she* wants lopped off is social pretense's."

"So I gather." Robbins shook her head again, this time with a smile of her own. "I'm really looking forward to watching her in action."

Rodential Palace
City of Port-au-Prince
Planet Torch
Congo System

"OUT OF IDLE CURIOSITY, YOUR MOUSETY," ELIZABETH ROBBINS said, looking around the comfortably furnished meeting room, "why did you name this the 'royal ambience chamber'?"

"Oh. Well, the name's not actually given to this particular room—or to any of them, really. It follows me around. Ambience refers to surroundings, so whichever room I'm in at the moment, that's the royal ambience chamber."

Robbins was tempted to ask if that included the bathroom, but she decided discretion was the better part of valor. She was getting a sense of Torch's monarch, and the answer was almost certainly "yes."

"This is the first time I've ever actually been in this particular room," Berry said, looking around it herself. "This really is a brand-new palace." She frowned, slightly. "I didn't want a palace at all, to begin with. But these two—" her forefinger indicated Web Du Havel and Hugh Arai "—insisted, and I caved in to them. Web's the Prime Minister, so I figured I should give his opinion some weight. And Hugh threatened to tickle me if I didn't."

"They did a good job of it, though." She leaned back in her chair. "I especially like the cartoons on the walls instead of royal portraits. But we should get down to business."

Her eyes narrowed and she directed her sharpened gaze upon Cachat.

"So, why'd you want us all here, Officer Cachat? Yana tells me you've been thinking ever since we got here, which has her terrified. Me, too."

382

Cachat shifted in his seat.

"How did I get this ridiculous reputation, anyway?" he demanded.

"Cold, hard, bitter experience," Arai promptly replied, but Du Havel shook his head.

"That's not fair. Cold and hard, I'll accept. Bitter, no." He moved his head in a little circle. "Victor Cachat's scheming and plotting is the only reason we have this planet. Don't forget that. I certainly haven't. That said..."

He looked at Cachat, his own eyes so narrow he was almost squinting. "So, what's your scheme this time, Officer Cachat—and don't bother telling me you haven't cooked one up."

"I wouldn't call it a 'scheme.' More in the nature of an operational plan with a few variable elements. The core remains the same—we use the *Rei Amador* and three light cruisers to become a mercenary force of former PNE cadre, and we've come to Hole-in-the-Wall hunting employment."

"Excuse me," Robbins said, "but I do have a question before we dive into that."

"You want to know how rousting Hole-in-the-Wall is going to get you any closer to suppressing the slave trade?" Cachat said. She nodded, and he shrugged. "The short answer is, that it isn't. Not immediately, at any rate. But if we're right about the connection between Manpower—and probably the Alignment—and Hole-in-the-Wall, and if we can get our hands on proof of that, it would probably provide a wedge into some of the activities Manpower most wants to hide. If you want to take down the slave trade, the best way to do that isn't running around hitting junction ports or depots that will probably be empty by the time you get there anyway. The *best* way to do it is to get inside their hierarchy by grabbing exactly the sort of data we're hoping to get our hands on.

"And the truth is, that we don't need your entire task group for what I have in mind. A division of battlecruisers, maybe half your destroyers, are about all I'm likely to need in Hole-in-the-Wall. That means the rest of your ships can embark the 'advisors' you came out here to get and head back for more... conventional hunting." He gave her a razor of a smile. "I happen to know—I asked around—that some of the ex-Ballroom types are ready to share the database they put together back when they were still nasty terrorists instead of heroic patriots. Oddly enough, they seem to have kept it up to date with exactly the sort of information those nasty terrorists would have been looking for if they hadn't become heroic patriots. I expect you'll find plenty of useful information there, and at least some of them would be willing to come along in person. In fact, it's my impression that you'd probably need armed guards to *keep* them from coming along."

"Hot damn!" Scarlatti rubbed his hands together. "I *knew* this was gonna be fun!"

"Were you and Bryce separated at birth or something?" Indy Graham asked. Scarlatti looked at him, and the young Seraphimian raised both hands. "Just asking."

"*Anyway*," Cachat said, "what I'm looking at at this point is for the portion of TG 437 I'm hoping Admiral Robbins will be willing to loan us to accompany us to Hole-in-the-Wall. But when we make our alpha translation, *they* stay in hyper just outside the limit, until the *next* addition to my plan tells them it's time to come join us."

"Next addition?" Hugh Arai repeated with a certain dread fascination.

"That would be the *Hali Sowle*, which will be masquerading as a freighter attached to the Beaumont's Irregulars. The one loaded with the latest in Solarian military equipment."

"Solly equipment?" Indy asked in a tone of mild interest.

"Exactly." Cachat turned to face Robbins directly. "You'll have to provide us with that equipment, but you should have enough spares between the ships of your task group. We don't actually need an entire freighter load of it. We just need some genuine hardware we can show as samples to induce the powers that be in Hole-in-the-Wall to cooperate. I'm pretty sure we'll be able to get it all back for you, as well. Most of it, anyway."

Robbins's expression was a mix of intrigued interest and *you-have-got-to-be-kidding*. But all she said was, "Keep going."

"Meantime—" Cachat nodded to Ruth "—Ruth and several of her associates will have come with us. She'll remain aboard the *Rei Amador*—that was the compromise I had to make with Captain Montcalm before he'd agree to let her come along at all—while those associates I mentioned actually land on Hole-in-the-Wall. Ruth tells me she'll be able to work with her aides at a remote distance to penetrate whatever IT systems might be present and start... draining their data."

"It'd be easier if I could land myself." Ruth sounded more than a bit disgruntled. "But since Razeen decided to get all pig-headed about it, we'll have to do it this way."

"But *can* it be done?" Robbins asked. "I'll grant you that criminals and pirates are probably pretty sloppy with their IT security, but even so—"

"We're not actually interested in data we could hack from pirates," Ruth said, shaking her head. "Oh, we'll take anything like that we find. But we've got bigger fish to fry. Victor's pretty sure—so am I—that unless all of our speculations are off-base, the Alignment has people in Hole-in-the-Wall. It's *their* data we want."

Robbins opened her mouth again, but Ruth held up one hand.

"Hear me out, please. Yes, *those* people's cybersecurity will be a monster to crack. But it's not impossible, under the right circumstances. We really need two things, one is access to Hole-in-the-Wall's public datanet, and the other is a way to identify the Alignment's people once we get there. Victor's plan to dicker over our 'stolen' Solarian hardware should by us all the time I need to break into the public com net's servers. From there, I should be able to branch out and at least identify everyone connected to it. Victor is also pretty sure that we can narrow possible suspects for the Alignment connection. They'll have some sort of cover, obviously, but we can be fairly sure it's not just one guy working in a bar somewhere. There are only so many kinds of covers that could provide them with the access they need, and it will probably be a business front of some sort.

"Once I'm into the public net, I can analyze business traffic and I should be able to eliminate down to at most one or two possible alignment covers."

"And then?" Robbins asked.

"And then I very cautiously probe their security. One thing probably true is that their security will be better than anyone else on the planet has. So if I find something like that, we're getting close. And while I don't want to sound immodest or anything—" there might have been a hint of insincerity in Ruth's tone "—I doubt it will be able to keep me out. So, hopefully, I'll be able to gain access to their system without their knowing I'm there.

"Given the encryption I expect, I probably won't be able to *read* very much of what I find right away, but I'll steal everything I can get and we'll crunch away at it later. In a best-case scenario, we get everything they've got. In a not-best-case scenario, they've got a standalone in there somewhere I can't reach without physical access." She shrugged. "Either way, we've got more than we had before."

"I'd really like for us to be able to break their encryption," Victor put in, "and I think Ruth might be a bit overly pessimistic about whether or not she—or she and Anton together—will be able to. But whether we can read it or not, *analyzing* it could very well tell us a lot. Who are they talking to in Hole-in-the-Wall? How much message traffic do they have? How important is Hole-in-the-Wall to coordinating their actions in the region? You can tell a *lot* just from *who* someone's communicating with, and identifying their other contacts gives you more potential penetration points that you might come at them from. And one thing I really want to get out of this is a better read their emergency response procedures."

"And exactly how do you propose to do that?"

"That's where you come in, Admiral," Cachat said. "What we need to do is give them something that's a significant threat to their operational security. But it has to be the right sort. We don't want something that induces panic, because if that happens, whatever suicide protocols are in place will almost certainly activate. That would be confirmation that the people who just died were part of the Alignment, but it wouldn't tell us very much about their SOP. What we need is one they can see coming but protracted enough for them to think 'Hey, this might become a problem, we'd better erase the dangerous stuff and go to Condition Cover Your Ass' but not 'Oh, shit! Press the button and we all die!' If we can find out what they do under Condition Cover Your Ass will have a lot better insight when it comes to taking down any other Alignment nodes we can identify."

"And my people provide the threat?"

"Exactly." Cachat nodded. "When the *Hali Sowle*—probably, at least; it might be a different ship—comes back across the alpha wall, that's when the ships you've detached to support us make *their* alpha translation. They come over the wall in pursuit of those dreadful mercenaries blaring '*stop, thief!*' That will almost certainly panic the outright pirates and criminals—the sort who *really* don't want to discuss their operations with the Solarian League Navy—into making a run for it in whatever ships they have in-system. But the Alignment and Manpower people should have steadier nerves than that. Unless we miss our guess, they'll be more in the service end of the system's infrastructure. Not the sort to get their own hands bloody. I think they'll figure the SLN is unlikely to just chuck *them* out an airlock if it gets its hands on them and that they'll be back in business again as soon as your people take themselves across the hyper wall headed home. So they'll probably activate Cover Your Ass, which will give us our opportunity to observe exactly what that is. Most likely, they'll figure they have time to do a controlled data wipe and every reason to want to preserve their hardware—and, for that matter, anything on their systems that wouldn't lead us to the Alignment—for future use, so if circumstances suggest it would be worthwhile, we can get physical access to their servers and see what Ruth can figure out from tearing them down molecule by molecule."

"It's entirely possible none of this will work out the way we've envisioned," Ruth chimed in. "I may set off an alarm on my way in and provoke the panic reaction we're trying to avoid, in which case we get nothing and don't even get that peek at their emergency reaction plans. For that matter, they may not react the way we're projecting when your ships turn up and just go ahead and kill themselves then. But we might succeed at least partially, and if we don't, we're no worse off than we were."

"Unless they catch your ground party in the act," Scarlatti pointed out with the air of a man who'd seen black bag ops go wrong in his time. "It could get dicey, then."

"It could," Cachat agreed. "On the other hand, if the operation's blown, we just greet your ships happily—and very publicly, on every frequency we can reach. At which point the powers-that-be will suddenly find themselves looking not at four long-in-the-tooth mercenary cruisers, but two Solarian battlecruisers and a half-dozen destroyers. They might be willing to go toe-to-toe with a force our size, but when they see your ships coming, the only thing they'll be thinking about is how to get the hell out of the system."

There was silence for a few seconds, while everyone in the ambience chamber considered what they'd heard.

"You'll forgive me if I say it sounds...tricky. Especially your part, Princess," Tarkovsky said finally.

"It is, and it isn't," Ruth replied. "My part, I mean. It would be better if I had direct access, without the kinds of delay remote access imposes. And the fact that certain parties insist that I stay on the ship, in orbit, is going to lengthen that delay just because of light-speed limitations. But if we can get my remote equipment close enough, it won't be appreciably harder to break into any Alignment front's system from the *Rei Amador* than it would be if I were right there on the planet."

"Not for the right person, anyway," Citizen Captain Soubry put in. She shook her head. "I've worked with the Princess, Colonel—I mean Citizen Commissioner." She grimaced. "I'm no slouch when it comes to hardware, and Jacob's no slouch when it comes to software, but neither of us is in the Princess's league on either end. It's not even a matter of experience, really. It's more a matter of having the right feel—the touch. Breaking security on a system like this will take a combination of brute force techniques and subtlety. Maybe the word I'm really looking for is intuition. Some people just have that a kind of second sense that lets them anticipate, puts them ahead of the curve." She shook her head again. "Princess Ruth has it, and I don't. Never will, either, because it's not something you can learn. It's a gift you're given."

"Cybernetics aren't my comfort zone, either," Cachat said, "but I don't think you're wrong, Jarmila. It's basically what Anton's said to me. A lot of people who ought to know consider him to be the best in the galaxy at what he does. Personally, he thinks he's in the top one or two percent. He's told me often enough that no matter how good you may think you are, or how good you may really be, on any given day, there's someone out there who's better. It's like any other field of human endeavor: by the time you get into that top two or three percentage points, there's not really that much to choose between the people in it. But Anton's also told me he believes Ruth comes very close to being his equal. In fact, in some ways, he thinks she's already his superior. That the only thing holding her back—a little—is that the Manticoran royal family and their security people are too cautious about her safety for her to get as much in-the-field, hands-on experience as she should. As a spook-in-training, not a royal princess, of course."

"Which is exactly what *I* keep telling them!" Ruth said.

Silence filled the room again for half a minute or so. Then—

"Well—"

The single word came almost simultaneously from Du Havel, Berry, Arai, and Admiral Robbins. They all stopped speaking—again, almost simultaneously—and looked at each other.

"Personally," Scarlatti said, "I think it sounds...workable. Not foolproof, by any means, but if you show me a field op that's foolproof, I'll show you one whose planning is overly cautious. I say they've got a good shot at pulling it off, Admiral. And, like Officer Cachat says, we can spare them the ships he's asking for without compromising our own mission stance. I'd suggest Commodore Rabellini's division, since I know she's had a certain, um, degree of experience supporting black ops."

"You do, do you?" Robbins said dryly. "I thought you two seemed to know each other pretty well."

"What can I say, Ma'am?" Scarlatti held out his hands. "Birds of a feather."

"Of course."

Robbins drummed lightly on the table while she considered Cachat's plan. It fell well outside anything Director Gannon or Admiral Kingsford had authorized, but Gannon *had* emphasized the League's urgent need to begin building bridges with the Grand Alliance. And if the Congo System wasn't *technically* part of the Grand Alliance, everyone knew...

"Sounds good to me," Rear Admiral Elizabeth Robbins announced.

Tactical Analysis 3
City of Leonard
Planet Darius Gamma
Darius System

GAIL WEISS STOOD BESIDE HER BOSS AND WATCHED INTENTLY AS the evolution they'd designed unfolded in the now familiar confines of what Antwone Carpinteria had called System Alpha.

That familiarity bothered her, because it was atypical, to say the least, of the analyses upon which she'd worked back home on Mesa. Not the evolution itself, but the unchanging astrographic real estate. It was far more common, in her experience, for developing operational and tactical concepts to be tested in a variety of different environments. Once an operational approach had been worked out to a satisfactory conclusion given one star system's astrography, the most common approach—indeed, the almost invariable approach—was to begin trying the same approach given different tactical considerations. Which normally meant given different "terrain" in which to game it out.

Not so in Alpha's case. Or perhaps it would be more accurate to say that they weren't approaching the problem from the perspective of refining operational doctrine at all. What they were doing was designing different defensive scenarios for a single star system, for a single battle. And that strongly suggested to her that System Alpha truly existed somewhere...and lay in the path of a cataclysmic assault.

She had no idea where Alpha was, of course. She found that ominous, too. In fact, she found a lot about this assignment ominous.

She watched the attacking Grand Alliance fleet drive into the teeth of Alpha's defenses and wished yet again that she'd been allowed to use the graser torpedoes. The spider drive was slower than any impeller-drive missile, but it was also incredibly long-ranged, extraordinarily powerful, and virtually undetectable. If she'd been allowed to deploy a few thousand torpedoes on the attacker's probable approach vectors, they could have wreaked havoc on the capital ships and LAC carriers that never saw them coming. And they could strike their targets well before the attacker reached her own range of Alpha System's vital organs. No one had explained to her why she *couldn't* employ them, but it was self-evident to her that if her superiors had regarded Alpha's survival as truly vital, they would have released the torpedoes to her.

Not that it would have made much difference in the end.

And that, she had realized, was what bothered her the most.

This entire effort, everything she, Carpinteria, and their team had put together over the past months, was an exercise in futility. The plain, ugly truth was that no single star system could successfully defend itself against the kind of massive, sophisticated firepower which was the Grand Alliance's signature. It simply couldn't be done. Fixed defenses, however powerful, were ultimately doomed against anyone with that sort of long-ranged, stand-off capability and deep enough magazines. The Grand Alliance could generate salvos that were tens of thousands of missiles strong, and they could fire them from outside a star system's hyper-limit, then vanish across the alpha wall before any return fire reached them. And if someone fired, say, fifty thousand missiles at a target—especially a *fixed* target, like, say, orbital industrial platforms and habitats—whose passive and active defenses stopped ninety percent of the incoming laser heads, that meant *five thousand* were getting through. And five thousand of the Grand Alliance's current generation MDM laser heads would gut the biggest conceivable orbital structure.

That was why she most wanted the torpedoes. They had ample endurance to reach any attacker from inside the hyper-limit, and fleets didn't dodge weapons they didn't know were coming. At the very least, a sufficiently massive wave of torpedoes had the potential to inflict enough damage to compel the attackers to ... reevaluate their own approach. Yet even that would be—*could be*—only a stay of execution. Because the next time the attackers *would* know about the torpedoes. They would drop across the wall, acquire their targets, dump their shoals of missiles, and then promptly disappear back into hyper, counting on the Mark 23-E's sophisticated AI to manage that torrent of destruction. It might—probably would—increase the final civilian death toll, because not even the Mark 23-E could be expected to differentiate between targets based on possible numbers of inhabitants rather than their electronic signatures and industrial potential. For that matter, relying solely on the AI's discretion and judgment would almost have to increase the odds of a catastrophic kinetic strike on the planet by a rogue missile that had missed its intended target. Indeed, that consideration might be the one thing that precluded the GA from adopting that approach. Gail didn't know the actual mass of the Grand Alliance's Mark 23, but she did know its maximum velocity from rest, and even if its mass was as low as fifty tons, something traveling at eighty percent of lightspeed would pack twenty-five percent more energy than the worst-case estimate for the Chicxulub Impactor that ended Old Earth's Cretaceous period. She didn't want to think about a fleet commander willing to risk something like that, but if they'd taken massive casualties in an earlier attack, the temptation would have to be there. And it would certainly be an *effective* tactic. One for which Gail could see no winning counter even *with* the torpedoes.

She watched the Grand Alliance decelerating towards a point just outside the Alpha System's 15.4 LM hyper-limit. On its last approach, she and Carpinteria had allowed the attackers to pass within eight light-minutes of the massive superjovian of Alpha VI on their way towards the star system's enormous outer asteroid belt. Assuming they arrived on a least-time course for Alpha IV, the system's habitable planet, that was a not unreasonable supposition, since VI was just past conjunction from IV.

Although it was clear that the belt was heavily exploited, all of the refinery platforms were well inside the hyper-limit. Not only that, Alpha V, which *also* lay inside the limit, was another gas giant, if of a lesser stature than VI. That was where all of Alpha's atmospheric mining facilities were located, which meant there was nothing worth attacking—and thus nothing worth *defending*—outside the limit... or anywhere near Alpha VI.

That was the reason Gail had hidden the next best thing to a hundred thousand missile pods and their coordinating fire control platforms in VI's family of moons, with only a single heavily stealthed control ship to manage them.

That had been one of her more successful ploys. The attackers' losses had been just short of catastrophic, and the computer judging the exercise's outcome had ruled that they'd withdrawn to lick their wounds. Of course, that didn't mean they wouldn't come back both wiser and more wary. The only problem was that navies which had learned so many painful lessons after the last quarter T-century of bloodletting were unlikely to come that close to any celestial body that offered a handy gravitic anchorage for nasty surprises. They *might*, but only if their sensor platforms had swept the volume of space in question without finding anything, and despite the Alignment's superb stealth systems, the Grand Alliance's Ghost Rider reconnaissance drones were only too likely to spot *something* if that many pods were concealed in that relatively small a volume.

Given that probability, Gail knew she couldn't recommend stacking all of their defensive eggs in that small a basket. Besides, if they were deployed around Alpha VI, they *wouldn't* be deployed to cover any other volume, and there was no unwritten law that said an attacker *had* to come anywhere near the gas giant. That didn't exactly fill her with confidence in the deployment plan. And neither did the fact that, like every other tactic she'd been able to generate, her victory had been ultimately futile. The Grand Alliance *would* be back again, assuming Alpha was remotely as important as it appeared to be, and all she'd really accomplished was to kill thirty or forty thousand Grand Alliance spacers.

Which brought her right back to the question of what they'd do on their second attack run if the first one had been heavily bloodied.

The current juggernaut of attackers decelerated to zero relative to the system primary in the enormous holographic plot and began deploying their shoals of missile pods. And as they did, the heavily stealthed destroyer hiding with the defensive pods Gail and Carpinteria had deployed along the innermost edge of the outer asteroid belt for *this* simulation fired their familiar hundred thousand-strong salvo.

The scenario assumed the attackers had been smart enough to make their approach with their hyper generators at readiness. Given who the attackers were, any other approach simply wasn't going to happen, but even with that start an *Invictus*-class super-dreadnought required four and a half minutes to translate back into hyper. That was the missiles' time window, and Gail had been forced to spread them around the inner edge of the belt in an arc she hoped would give her the best coverage. There was no way to be certain of any attacker's precise approach vector, since even a least-time approach depended on a host of factors it was impossible to predict with absolute accuracy. The exact point at which the attacker crossed the alpha wall, how quickly she could orient her task force in normal-space to begin her attack run, what deployment approach she'd chosen for her own missiles...

No one could precisely predict how all of those factors might interact. A general volume in which they would attempt to place themselves before launching against the inner system could be defined, based on the known parameters of their own weapon systems, but it was necessarily amorphous. It could be refined—marginally—if the defenders knew who the opposing commander was and had the opportunity to analyze her record, assuming she had one. But even under the best of circumstances, an attacker determined to be difficult could always choose a less-than-optimum launch point specifically to avoid ambushes.

That became a problem because of flight times.

Just as Gail had been denied the graser torpedoes, she'd also been denied the Ninurta, the Alignment's latest anti-ship missile. The ones she'd been allowed instead were basically improved versions of the Solarian League's Cataphracts, considerably inferior to the Ninurta, especially in terms of drive endurance. Although they were larger and more destructive, with better targeting systems and better defensive EW than anything which had been provided to the SLN, their acceleration rate and endurance were identical to the last flight Cataphract. Which meant that they had a maximum effective acceleration time of 255 seconds. In that timeframe, they could travel 33.8 light-seconds. She could inject a ballistic phase at 180 seconds, and it could last as long as she chose, but velocity at that point would be only 84,176 KPS, so even allowing for a superdreadnought's translation time, that bought her only another 126,000 kilometers of attack range within her available window. Thirty-four light-seconds was an enormous reach by pre-multidrive missile standards, but the best deployment pattern she'd been able to devise meant that a maximum of "only" forty-five thousand of her total launch would be able to attack at any specific point within the roughly defined volume.

The computers had determined the actual approach vector, and she and Carpinteria watched as the missile storm drove in on the attackers. Forty-five thousand laserheads would have annihilated any Solarian—or Mesan Alignment—fleet that size, but the Grand Alliance was a very different proposition.

Gail knew far more about its defense systems' critical parameters than the Solarian League Navy had known before it crossed swords with the Grand Alliance, thanks to the Alignment's previous penetration of the Star Empire of Manticore and Republic of Haven. She still knew far less than she wished she did, though, because their spies had been able to obtain only limited information on the actual hardware. And their continuing penetration of the Solarian League had been unable to fill in the blanks, because no Solarian fleet had survived long enough to report that sort of information. Well, the survivors of the attack on Hypatia had, but even they had never gotten a really good look at the Manticorans' defenses, given the range at which the engagement had been fought.

Still, she did have a solid grasp of the fundamentals of the Allies' defensive doctrine, and the attackers in her simulation had applied all of them. Shoals of light attack craft, configured for missile defense, swerved to intercept the incoming tide of destruction. Torrents of counter-missiles erupted into its path, and her attack birds melted like snowflakes in bright sunlight.

The simulation flashed with brilliant pinpricks as her salvo's tattered survivors reached attack range, stabbing at the invaders with not only the clusters of X-rays the Grand Alliance had no doubt expected but also with the far more dangerous graser warheads mated to the Alpha System's MDMs.

They destroyed two battlecruisers, six destroyers, and thirty-seven LACs.

That was all.

And that assumed she'd made sufficient allowance for the Grand Alliance's Lorelei decoys and the other electronic warfare systems.

The attackers absorbed their losses without so much as a hiccup and finished deploying their own pods. Then *they* launched, and eighty-five thousand MDMs streaked toward the inner system. The range to the primary was fifteen and a half light-minutes, but the range to Alpha IV—and all of its orbital infrastructure, plus the handful of warships Alpha System could muster in its defense—was only a bit over *nine* light-minutes. Given what they did know about the Mark 23's parameters, that required a 6.5-minute ballistic phase at eighty percent of light-speed. Fifteen and a half minutes after launch, the display glared with a brighter and more terrible fury than her defensive salvo had produced.

The defending starships fired in desperate defense. But Alpha System's naval strength amounted to less than sixty superdreadnoughts, less than a quarter of them pod-layers. Against that hurricane, seeded with what they did know about the Grand Alliance's penetration aids, all they truly contributed were additional, even more fragile targets.

The defenses did rather better this time than they had against the last attack Gail had launched upon them. They stopped almost sixty percent of the incoming fire, but the damage was still catastrophic. And a second attack salvo, almost as large as the first, was only five minutes on its heels. Just long enough for FTL control links with the Grand Alliance's bandwidth to report back and for the launching ships to update targeting queues.

That second savage hammer crashed down, targeted this time on the orbital platforms which had revealed the fact that they were armed. Gail had assumed the Grand Alliance was here to capture the system, not simply to destroy it, so very little of that fire was wasted on industrial platforms, orbital shipyards, or the orbital habitats that had shown no armament. Instead, it tore the armored fortresses apart and, as an afterthought, polished off the half-dozen surviving defensive warships. Most of the fortresses simply died, but—as usually happened because of its sheer size—the fortress designated as Alpha Prime, the central command and control nexus of the entire star system, survived. For certain values of "survived," at any rate. It was reduced to an air-bleeding wreck, shattered and broken, but still there.

And then, once again, it was over.

"That...sucks," she said to Carpinteria.

"Not our highest score, no," he agreed, and Gail turned to face him. The two of them were outside anyone else's earshot, although she certainly wasn't going to assume they were out of the *surveillance systems*' earshot. But just this once...

"This is pointless, Antwone," she said quietly.

"No," he disagreed, still looking into the display. "No, it's not."

"But we can't win. Not in the end." She, too, looked at the glaring icons indicating dead and dying orbital infrastructure. "Even if we drive them off once, they can always come back again. And again. And nothing we—or, Alpha System, at least—have can compensate for their range and missile-defense advantages."

Carpinteria turned to look at her. Both of them knew what she'd meant.

"We still can't give them the torpedoes," he told her. "But we've been cleared to use graser-armed Hastas."

"We have?" Gail's ears perked up. "Just how are we going to pull that one off?"

The Hasta had been produced by Technodyne as an emergency counterweight for the MDM. It was slow and pathetically short-ranged compared to the Alignment's spider drive torpedoes, but it was almost as stealthy, because it was basically a weaponized impeller-drive reconnaissance drone. That meant it could carry only a very light missile, however, since reconnaissance drones were stuffed full of the systems required for their designed mission. Which meant the Solarian version couldn't possibly accommodate something the size of a graser torpedo warhead.

"It's actually what you might think of as a Hasta upgrade," Carpinteria told her. "Upgraded impellers, better stealth than the basic Solly recon drone, and up-sized to accommodate the graserhead."

"And do I get unlimited numbers of *them*, too?" Gail demanded. The tactician at her core felt the first real enthusiasm she'd been able to muster for weeks as the possibilities unrolled before her.

"No," Carpinteria told her in a tone of mild regret. "As of now, you can assume they have about a thousand already available. They'll be increasing that number, but for the purposes of our simulations—" he met her eyes levelly "—we have to assume the birds are coming off a new assembly line that's currently producing about a thousand a week. They'll be phasing in additional production, and in a couple of months, that will jump to around five thousand a week. And a month or so after that, production will be about *twelve* thousand a week. They'll max out at that point."

"Damn."

Gail turned back to the wreckage which had once been a star system. Enough of Carpinteria's "Hasta upgrades" might have allowed her to implement some of the graser torpedo scenarios she'd played around with on her own time. But she needed them in far larger numbers to make that tactic truly effective, because their lower speed and paltry endurance meant she couldn't emplace enough of them to saturate the possible attack points. Even if she assumed a six-month production window, she'd have only a little over two hundred thousand to work with. That would let her hurt the attackers a hell of a lot worse than anything she could do without them, but it wouldn't be decisive.

And why the hell should their simulation assume the defenders would cap production at only twelve thousand? Given Alpha System's self-evident industrial capacity, and their ability to ramp production up by twelve hundred percent in only three months, why stop there? Why not—?

She stopped herself. Those were the sorts of questions she couldn't afford to ask anyone. Including herself. But—

"That'll help a lot," she said. "I can begin building scenarios around these Hasta upgrades of yours, and if we can get enough of them—I mean, if the simulation's parameters *assign* us enough of them—we can make Alpha a lot tougher, harder target. But they still can't win in the end. So why don't they—"

"Be careful, Gail," Carpinteria said softly. "You're treading on thin ice."

Why? she wondered. That was the question she wanted to scream at him. *Why is "Alpha System" going to mount a defense at all? It can't win, even with these new Hastas. All it can do is make the cost increasingly horrific for the Manties and their friends, which will only make them more vengeful. It will certainly push aside any effort on their part to minimize Alpha's casualties, and that will get thousands, probably millions, of the system's defenders and civilians killed. It's stupid! The only way Alpha "wins" this battle, in any sense of the verb, is to never fight it!*

"A security issue?" she asked instead. "We both have high clearances."

"The term 'security' is like a polygon," he replied. "It has many sides."

She chuckled. The sound was soft, but its tone wasn't.

"A decagon, at the very least," she said.

"More like an apeirogon," he replied with a chuckle of his own.

"Now, that's one I've never heard of."

"An apeirogon is a degenerate polygon of infinitely many sides. Welcome to Security."

He turned to face her fully.

"The level of someone's security refers only to their readiness and willingness to keep silent. But it's not telepathy. Security is never telepathy—and the people who oversee it are very aware of that. So they watch for other things, as well. Things that might give them insight into what the watchee is actually thinking. Or, more importantly, feeling."

"Well, they can't be too surprised if we're feeling a little futile after months of losing this battle!" Gail said in a deliberately brighter tone. "I'd like to win it, at least once."

Carpinteria turned back to the display as the Grand Alliance's fleet accelerated toward the shattered inner system. Then he tapped the control that killed it, and the two of them stood in the dimness, alone with their thoughts...and Security's listening electronic ear.

"Yes," he said quietly, softly. "I'd like to win it at least once, too. But we won't." He looked at her in the darkness, his voice even softer. "That's not what this is about."

Xanadu Restaurant
Roosevelt Gardens
City of Leonard
Planet Darius Gamma
Darius System

THE XANADU WAS ONE OF ZACH AND GAIL'S FAVORITE RESTAU-
rants, for a lot of reasons. One was that they both liked the cuisine,
which was a fusion of Old Terran Chinese and Middle Eastern.
Another was the garden seating, especially just at or right after
sundown, when the glow-roses, bioluminescent flowers native to
Darius, came to soft, gorgeous life in the surrounding Roosevelt
Gardens. And yet another was the waterfall at the center of the
outdoor seating. Most of Xanadu's patrons loved the light show
focused on the waterfall, the way the lights reacted in never-
repeating, impossible to predict patterns keyed to whatever the
restaurant's current background music might be.

Zach and Gail liked all of those things, but what they liked
most about it was privacy. The sound and light show would can-
cel out most routine surveillance. It wouldn't deter sophisticated
equipment, or prevent someone from miking the table itself, but
Zach wasn't worried—not much, anyway—by that possibility.
His own work brought him regularly into contact with security,
which meant he understood its conundrums better than most
people did. Not simply because of his own experience with it,
but because of Jack, as well.

The critical weakness of what one might call "preventative
surveillance" was data overload. Zach was pretty sure that had
been true since the priests of Sumer hired too many snitches,
each and every one of whom had a vested interest in exaggerat-
ing the importance of the information he brought in.

Modern AI could go a long way toward automating intelligence analyses, but the underlying dynamic remained. The problem was that eventually a human being, not a computer, had to make a decision based on the data he or she was given—data which, as a rule, he or she had played little or no role in collecting, which left him or her with precious little guidance for evaluating its reliability.

He remembered how Jack had summarized it for him.

So Spy A gets paid and promoted based on how much data she turns over, and Analyst B gets paid and promoted based on how many options and recommendations he advances based on too much data that he didn't have enough time to properly assess, and then Security Hotshot C—that's me, by the way—has to make a decision in too little time based on too much crap all of which has been at least partly degraded. I admit, the pay's pretty good, and you get promoted regularly. Aside from that, it sort of sucks.

Garbage in, garbage out.

The simplest way to keep the problem from getting out of hand, Jack had explained to him, was to just not collect too much data to begin with. And to never forget that human beings were *going* to grouse, no matter what. They were going to complain about their bosses over lunch with fellow workers. They were going to whine over their pay. They were going to have bad days when they complained about *everything* associated with their jobs. It was *going* to happen, and smart security forces had to allow for that and let it go. If you had a reason to think a given subject was actually a security risk and not *just* grousing, then fine: devote some major resources to spying on him. Otherwise, just make sure the population as a whole has enough cause for paranoia to make the grousers think twice before they start taking their own grousing seriously.

"So, why did we come here tonight?" he asked Gail quietly after they'd entered their drink and appetizer orders on the table's terminal. "I thought we were coming Friday?"

"We both like the food," she replied. "Is there a reason we can't make an extra visit?"

"Of course not," he agreed, but he also regarded her thoughtfully across the table, and, after a moment, she sighed.

"You're entirely too good at reading me, Zach," she said, reaching across to touch the side of his face.

"Hey, I'm a people person! Remember? That's why I'm so good at my job."

"What you are," she said with a gurgle of grateful laughter, "is an idiot. *My* idiot. But—" her eyes darkened "—your 'people sense' *is* reading me again. It's . . . work."

"Oh?"

"Yes. I can't tell you much, even if I knew everything that's really going on, but it's getting to me." Her eyes were darker than before. "I don't think I'm doing the best job in the world of dealing with it, either. In fact, I'm feeling more and more depressed, and I don't want my mental state—or anything else—to . . . splash on you without any warning."

She did not, he noticed, mention what that "anything else" might be. Or suggest that perhaps she could discuss her depression—or the reasons for it—with one of the counselors their superiors were so happy to provide.

"Ah?" He cocked his head and took her hand in his own. "How much of it *can* you tell me?"

"Well . . ."

She paused as the genuine, human waiter arrived with their drinks and pot sticker and hummus appetizers. They smiled up at him, but then he left and Gail took a healthy sip of her drink. She sat, hands folded together around the glass on the table, and gazed down into it.

"It's just . . . just this tactical project they've got me working on," she said slowly. "No matter what I do, the defenders keep losing. And the casualties are heavy, every time." She looked up at him. "Truth is, I don't think there's anything anyone could do, given the scenario's parameters, that would let them win. But the parameters specify that they never surrender, no matter how hopeless it is. And it's the same star system every time. I guess . . . I guess the problem is that I'm getting really tired of watching the same system ripped apart again and again. I mean, Antwone and I have run—what? Forty different simulations now? Something like that. And I know it's just a simulation for a generic tactical evaluation, but—" her eyes met his across the table "—I really wish they'd at least let me change system templates. Watching it happen over and over again to the same system is just getting to me."

No, Zach thought. *It's not "getting to you" because it's a simulation. It's getting to you because you don't think it's a "generic tactical evaluation" at all, love. And that's a dangerous thing for you to be thinking.*

"That kind of thing doesn't happen over in my shop," he said, and his gaze met hers. She saw the receipt of her unspoken message in his eyes, and her shoulders seemed to relax ever so slightly. "But we do do simulations, and sometimes it's hard to remember they're computer-generated. You can get way too invested in them. So I can see where watching even a fictitious bunch of defenders getting reamed over and over again, no matter what you do, would have to be at least a little depressing."

"Yeah." She nodded and took another sip. "I guess part of it is just that I really like to win. That's why I got into this in the first place. Well, that and it was 'suggested' to me by my advisors right out of high school. And I'm pretty sure one reason it bugs me is that I can see ways I could alter the starting parameters, using tech that's already available to the defenders, even if they aren't us, that could considerably change the outcome. I don't know that it'd let me win, but it would at least give my—what was it you called it? my 'fictitious bunch of defenders'?—a lot better chance of not *losing*."

"Hey, lady! If what you do was easy, they'd probably let someone like me do it!"

He grinned at her, and, as he'd hoped, it won him a chuckle, and he was relieved to see her body language relax further. It wasn't as if he'd had to walk her back from the brink of a cliff, or anything, but hopefully the knowledge that he understood—and sympathized—would help her keep a handle on things. Because the last thing either of them needed was for her to be called in to speak to one of those counselors their superiors were always so ready to provide.

"Oh my God!" She shook her head. "The mere thought of *you* running a tactical analysis is enough to chill the blood! As a tactician, you'd make a really good brick mason."

"I don't know a thing about laying bricks!" he protested.

"That's my point," she said dryly, and punched up the tabletop menu. "I think I'm feeling like steamed vermicelli rolls and fried shrimp with pistachios. What about you?"

"Me?" He glanced down at his own menu display. "I think maybe General Abdallah's chicken with yellow rice."

"Sounds like a winner," Gail agreed and began tapping in their order.

Zach sat back and watched her with a smile, but behind the smile, a trace of fear lingered. He was pretty sure he knew why all of her simulations were running in the same star nation. And he was afraid he knew why the defenders never surrendered. But if the Alignment's leadership was genuinely preparing to sacrifice Galton, it posed a deadly threat to the woman he loved. He was confident they hadn't told her anything at all about the system she was defending, aside from the physical characteristics she had to know to plan the simulations. But if they'd been so fanatical about making certain no one in Darius even knew Galton existed, about hiding any connection between the two star systems, then Gail would represent a potentially dangerous loose end where their strategy was concerned. A potential loose end in a strategy they simply could not afford to see fail.

And Operation Houdini had shown *exactly* how the Mesan Alignment snipped loose ends.

TNS *Rei Amador*
Torch System

RUTH WINTON STOPPED IN THE PASSAGEWAY. THE PAIR OF QUEEN'S
Own bodyguards stopped as well, a few meters behind her, and
Ruth jabbed a finger at one of the cabin doors.

"All right, this is where you'll be staying," she told Jessica
Milliken. "There'll always be someone standing guard here, so
don't get any wild ideas. And *this*—" she pointed to the next
door "—is where I'll be staying. For my sins, I've been assigned
to be your watchdog. Sort of."

Cachat had decided to move all of his newly recruited personnel aboard ship and begin the shaking-down process while
they waited for the Solarian delegation's arrival. The move had
included Ruth and Milliken because, he'd said, Ruth might as
well start shaking down with *her* mission—which happened to be
Jessica Milliken—and living in close quarters aboard ship would
make that easier.

Now the former Mesa System Navy officer looked from one
door to the other with no expression.

"Why am I on this ship at all?" she asked. "I assumed I'd be
getting sent to either Mesa or Old Terra."

"Which you *should* be, damn it!" Ruth glared at her, and then
at the door. "I told Victor this was stupid. The idiot wants me to
'turn' you. Yeah, that's what he calls it, as if you are some kind
of vehicle instead of a monster."

Somewhere in the back of her mind, even Ruth-in-high-
dudgeon knew that was a pretty stupid statement out of someone
whose own ambition was to become an espionage agent. But
Ruth-in-high-dudgeon wasn't what anyone, including herself,
would call a paragon of serene wisdom. Despite that, no trace of

expression crossed Milliken's face. The Alignment agent gave no indication of what she thought about Ruth's comment. Instead, she reached out and opened the door to her quarters.

"It's not locked," she said. "Will it be, once I'm inside?"

Ruth hadn't even thought about that, mired as she'd been in high dudgeon, and she looked at her guards a bit helplessly. From their expressions, it was clear Milliken had spoken loudly enough for them to hear.

"What's the answer, Andrea?" she asked.

"I don't know," Corporal Merino said with a shrug. "All I know is that Captain Montcalm's set up his watch bill to put one of us out here in the passage permanently. I've got the first watch; Jorge here will relieve me in four hours. Nobody said anything to us about her." Merino twitched her head at Milliken. "Except that she's not supposed to go wandering around on her own."

"Wonderful." Ruth jabbed her finger at the door again. "Just go in there, Milliken, and stay until someone comes to get you. Which will probably be me, the way things are going, since I seem to have pissed off the goddesses of the galaxy."

She gave the ex-commander another glare, then stalked through the adjacent door into her own cabin.

❖   ❖   ❖

Ruth was in a much better mood an hour later. First, because when she left her cabin, Milliken was nowhere to be seen, a state of affairs which Ruth considered ideal. Secondly, because a few minutes later she got to say "Permission to come onto the bridge?" which she thought was delightful. Third, and finally, because permission was given.

Under the circumstances, the fact that Cachat was also on the bridge was only a minor annoyance. Until he glanced at her.

"Where's Milliken?" he asked, immediately upping her annoyance to a less minor quotient.

She saw no reason to dignify that with a reply, and Cachat shook his head and went back to studying whatever he'd called up on the tac officer's display.

"Don't forget you have more than one assignment, Your Highness," he said. The *Your Highness* was his way of indicating disapproval. "A superspy has to be able to walk and chew gum at the same time."

"Chewing gum is a disgusting habit," she told him. "It's unsanitary. I don't have any interest at all in chewing it."

"I'm not encouraging you to *do* it. I'm simply pointing out that you need to be *able* to do it. Which brings us back to Milliken."

Ruth tried to remember why she'd wanted to come onto the bridge in the first place.

City of Leonard
Planet Darius Gamma
Darius System

THE ANTI-SURVEILLANCE SYSTEMS IN THE SMALL ROOM THAT appeared on no blueprints anywhere in the City of Leonard offered far better security than Xanadu's waterfall. None of the two men and three women seated around the table at its center were really delighted to be here, and all of them had exercised excruciating care in making their way to it. They'd never seen any sign that anyone even suspected their activities, but Alignment Security was very good at hiding its hand until the time came to strike. And, unfortunately, there was no such thing as genuinely secure electronic communications. Not in the Darius System. Conversations "under four eyes," as the Erewhonese might have put it, in places where they could be at least reasonably confident there were no electronic eavesdroppers, was the norm for their own organization's leadership cadre, however little they might like risking face-to-face contact.

They had three more "nonexistent" meeting rooms scattered around Leonard, courtesy of one of their founders in the City Engineer's office. They rotated between locations in a computer-generated random pattern designed to prevent Security's surveillance algorithms from tagging them in the same place without a very good reason for being there.

And it still worried the hell out of them.

They had quite a few things to discuss, and they moved through them quickly. None of them wanted to spend any more time huddling about clandestinely than they had to, and all of them felt a sense of relief as they reached the last point on their current agenda.

"So, have we made a decision about her?" one of the men asked.

"Not a final one, no." One of the women shook her head. "But it's starting to look like she might be a risk worth taking. Him, too, for that matter."

"That's your view," one of the other women said. "All right, it's also ultimately your *decision*, I suppose. But, personally, I think we'd be moving too fast just with her. Much less with *him*!" She shook her own head. "I don't like shooting blind on this sort of thing, and whatever may or may not be true about her, we don't have anyone close enough to him for an evaluation!"

"No, but at the moment at least, they come as a pair. And she's getting close to the point where someone's likely to activate her suicide protocols just to be on the safe side," the second man said. "So far, I think I'm the only one on the team to recognize the degree to which this whole exercise is getting to her, but that's likely to change if anybody decides she's figured out about Galton and started feeling disaffected."

"I understand that, Antwone," the first woman said. "Really, I do. But even if they activate them, I don't see them putting them into autonomous mode. Not when there's no indication that the Grand Alliance has actually figured out even where *Galton* is, far less Darius."

"No," Antwone Carpinteria acknowledged, his expression bitter. "I'm pretty sure that—for now, at least—they'll settle for just arming them in remote command mode. The instant they *do* think Darius may have been located, they'll push the button and kill her, just to be safe. Hell, they'll do it if she's still alive when they decide it's time for them to go public on their own! She's a loose end now, just like me, and she's not going to just forget the simulation that the defense couldn't possibly win. And she's smarter than hell. I'm pretty sure she's figured out exactly why the defense will never be able to win...and will never surrender without one hell of a fight."

"I don't doubt it," the woman said, her expression sympathetic. "And I can see that you like her, a lot. Trust me, that's a point in her favor, too, because—I wouldn't want you to get a swelled head or anything—but your 'people sense' is pretty damned good. You're right about what's bound to happen to her in the end, if we don't intervene, too."

She looked at the man seated to Carpinteria's left.

"Can you activate the Janus protocols?"

"Maybe." He rubbed his chin. "She got run back through the entire vetting process when they assigned her to Antwone's merry crew, so I had an excuse to review her file. She's due for her next regular medical in about three months, and she's already scheduled for another nanite function test as part of it. You understand that I may not be the technician assigned to her for that, though?"

"Please." She grimaced at him. "You expect to be fired between then and now? You're the one who makes the assignments in the first place."

"True, but a lot can happen between now and her appointment. I might have an accident. I *might* get fired, although I admit that's unlikely. The possibility of getting reassigned so I don't get to go hands-on anymore is a bigger one. And I might be on vacation. In fact, I think I am, according to the rotation."

"You approve vacation times, too," she pointed out. "And you have a reputation as a good boss. I'm pretty sure you can find somebody you could trade vacation time with because they really need time off for something else, good, compassionate soul that you are."

"True," he said, the word a bit drawn out. "In fact, I can think of a couple of possibilities. But—"

"And the horse might learn to sing. Relax, will you? I'll take the chance. I'm not taking unnecessary risks with this one."

"I thought you just said you thought it was worth taking a chance."

"It is—which is why I don't want to take any unnecessary ones. I'm not worried about the risk to *us*. We've done it often enough that I'm confident we can do it again. What I *don't* want to risk is losing *her*."

August 1923 Post Diaspora

"It's a lot easier to analyze military intelligence data than it is to predict which way politicians—even honest ones—are going to jump, Kayla. In fact, I think it's probably harder for us Solarians to predict how the *honest* ones will react, because we've had so little experience with them at the federal level."

—Captain Daud al-Fanudahi,
Solarian League Navy

Anti-Slavery League Headquarters
Arnold Logan Tower
City of Old Chicago
Planet of Old Earth
Sol System

"I'M SORRY, BUT CATHY ISN'T ON THE PLANET. SHE'S NOT EVEN in the solar system." Fanny, one of the ASL's vice presidents, looked down on Anton Zilwicki with a sympathetic expression.

Looked way down. So far down that Kayla Barrett had to stifle a smile as she watched the interchange. To go with the dwarf-king width of his shoulders, Zilwicki was almost as short as a dwarf. Well, that was an exaggeration. The man was on the stubby side, true, but he was still about a hundred and sixty-five centimeters tall, well within the range of normal human males. Mostly, it was the sheer bulk of the woman from Antananarivo that produced the effect. She was close to two hundred centimeters tall and must have weighed somewhere in the vicinity of a hundred and twenty-five kilos.

Zilwicki scowled. Well, again, "scowled" was an exaggeration, produced by the same dwarf-king aura. Barrett thought he was just frustrated for the completely commonplace reason that his girlfriend was unexpectedly absent.

"Where'd she go?" he asked.

"At the moment, she's probably in Cyclops. Her itinerary covered at least three of the inner Core systems: Kenichi, Heimdall, Cyclops, and Lusitania, for sure. And possibly Eris, if she has enough time."

"When will she be back?"

"Within the month, certainly. Probably sooner. The Constitutional Convention's working sessions are starting to gather steam.

She wanted to give them a chance to get themselves organized 'without me underfoot,' but she's not going to stay away long."

"Thanks, Fanny." Zilwicki nodded, then turned away to face Barrett and Jake Abrams. "Guess we'll have to look for lodgings elsewhere. I propose—"

"I'm sure Cathy wouldn't object if you used her quarters," Fanny put in from over his shoulder, and he turned back around.

"How would I get in? And *please* don't tell me she isn't following my advice on security."

"Well..."

"Great." Zilwicki rolled his eyes. "And what half-baked, so-called protection agency is she using, instead? Slumbering Sentries, LLC?"

"Well..."

"She isn't using *any*?"

"She had a service—I don't recall the name of the company, if I ever knew it—but she let them go for the time being. Just while she was gone. She didn't see any point spending money to protect someone who wasn't there anyway."

Zilwicki clapped the back of his neck. Barrett thought that was probably a substitute for pulling out his hair.

"Jesus Christ on a crutch! So now she'll have to spend twice as much money having her quarters swept when she gets back. And since when did Cathy become a miser? The woman's not exactly a spendthrift, but sometimes you have to squint to see the difference."

Fanny gave him an exasperated look.

"Anton, you of all people should know how much Cathy resents having to spend any attention at all on her own security."

"Yeah, sure. And maybe in her next life she can choose charity for waifs and urchins for a hobby instead of pissing off powerful and malevolent corporations and government agencies."

"The fight against genetic slavery is not a 'hobby,' Anton!"

He started to snarl something in response, but clamped his jaw shut, instead.

"No, it isn't," he said after a moment. "Which is exactly why—Never mind. What's done is done. But I'm still looking for our own quarters because *I* don't want to have to pay to have hers swept for bugs and booby-traps. We'll deal with that when she gets back. Thanks, Fanny."

That last was perhaps a bit curt, but she only nodded in response.

"Let's go, folks," he said. "I know a good hotel. The prices are even reasonable, for Old Chicago values of 'reasonable.'"

Barrett wasn't worried about that, anyway, because she wasn't going to be picking up the tab.

George Benton Tower
City of Old Chicago
Old Earth
Sol System

THE NEXT FEW DAYS WERE UNEVENTFUL, AT LEAST FOR BARRETT and Abrams. Zilwicki, al-Fanudahi, and Okiku vanished every day, only to return to their hotel closemouthed about where they'd been and why. So the two ex-Misties spent their time sightseeing. Neither had ever been to the Sol System, and Old Chicago probably had more sights to see than any other megalopolis in the human-inhabited portion of the galaxy, so it wasn't hard to find plenty of things to do.

It was a pleasant a few days. Although she'd known Abrams, at least professionally, during their days with the Internal Security Directorate, Barrett had never suspected what an excellent traveling companion he could prove. He was curious without being excitable and phlegmatic in the face of the confusions and frustrations tourists inevitably encountered. And he had a nice, dry sense of humor, to go with it.

Yet all good things came to an end, and on the fifth day after their arrival, they had to go back to work. To her surprise, she discovered that she and Abrams were included in the delegation that would meet with Brigadier Gaddis, the Solarian Gendarmerie's CO.

"Why us?" she asked al-Fanudahi as they climbed out of the taxi at the League Plaza landing stage. "Jake and I are just the hired hands."

"I'm not sure. At a guess—"

"They want to see the dancing bears," Colonel Okiku interjected.

"Huh?" That came from Abrams, and al-Fanudahi smiled.

416

"That's a crude way of putting it—shame on you, Natsuko!—but I'd say she's right."

"Can somebody translate that into proletarian, please?" Barrett shook her head. "I know what a bear is, but I've never seen one, and I didn't know they can dance."

They'd reached the enormous, frescoed portals of the League Plaza entry to George Benton Tower while they were speaking, and she had to wait for a reply while Okiku negotiated their way past the security guards.

"Bears can dance, in a manner of speaking," the colonel said as they started across the enormous lobby. "But it's not something you'd see them doing in a zoo or in the wild. What I meant by the wisecrack is that they know you're both former Misties, and I'm pretty sure they want your opinion on who was responsible for the nuclear strikes."

Abrams frowned as he tried to sort through the logic, but it was already clear to Barrett. She felt some anger rising, and tried to damp it down.

"And me in particular, right?" She nodded toward Abrams. "He didn't lose anybody besides a cousin."

"I hadn't seen in years, anyway," Abrams added. The frown was gone. "Okay, now I get it."

He looked at Barrett, then glanced at al-Fanudahi.

"How do you know what we're going to say?" he asked.

"We don't." The captain shrugged. "You'll say whatever you think, and we'll go from there."

It was odd, but al-Fanudahi's simple statement was what finally crystallized Barrett's thinking on the subject. Odd—and vastly relieving. She realized for the first time just how much tension she'd felt. It wasn't easy to work with people, some of whom you thought might be mass murderers, and simultaneously feel your respect and liking for them grow by the day.

"What *I'm* wondering is why the Brigadier told us to come *here*," al-Fanudahi said as they reached the lift bank and he tapped the call screen. "I'd have thought we'd meet him at JISDC HQ over in Smith."

"That's where Joint Intelligence called home before we left for Mesa," Okiku said. He raised an eyebrow at her, and she shrugged. "Maybe they moved while we were gone. There's been a lot of reorganizing going on, if you hadn't noticed, Daud."

"I don't think—" Al-Fanudahi broke off as the lift door opened. "I guess we'll find out soon enough," he said with a shrug and waved the others into the lift.

The trip to their first transfer stop seemed to be taking considerably longer than Barrett had expected, but only until she glanced up at the flashing floor indicator. Al-Fanudahi saw her eyes widen slightly, and chuckled.

"It's an express shaft," he said. "There's not a lot of residential space in Benton. Only twenty floors or so, really—just enough for the core staff to be close to work. The rest of it's all given over to support functions for the government. So at least two shafts in each bank are express instead of breaking at the concourses. It can still take a while, but at least we don't have to stop and transfer every seventy floors the way most towers here in Old Chicago do."

Barrett's eyes went a little wider still. This entire enormous tower—Benton was probably a good two hundred floors taller than anything back home in Mendel—was basically nothing but government *office space*? Somehow, that brought home the sheer enormity of the Solarian League in a way not even Old Chicago—not even Assembly Hall, itself—had been able to.

There was no more sense of motion in this lift shaft than in any other modern, grav-plate lift, yet she still felt a sense of soaring ever upward, until the floor indicator finally stopped flashing. They were on the 809th floor, and she forced herself not to shake her head as she realized Benton was even taller than she'd thought. That many floors meant they were at least three kilometers above ground level.

The door opened. A uniformed Gendarmerie major was waiting for them.

"This way, please," he said.

❖   ❖   ❖

Four people, in addition to Brigadier Gaddis, waited in the conference room into which they were led. All of them were introduced to the new arrivals, but none of the names really meant anything to Barrett. Except one. Bozhidara Abadjieva was the Foreign Minister of the Solarian League, at least in the Provisional Government. From the little Barrett had picked up, it seemed likely that Prime Minister Yon's government would be retained after the new Constitution was finally completed.

Well, she supposed some people might call it the Ranta Government, given the fact that Marjut Ranta, who had been the senior Assembly delegate from Ridnitšohkka, had been confirmed as the Provisional Government's acting President. But the Solarian League's president had always been—theoretically, at least—the head of state, not of government. Under the letter of the old constitution, the prime minister had headed the government. It was unfortunate that the letter of the Constitution had been so thoroughly ignored.

It wasn't being ignored anymore, even if everyone knew its days were numbered, but current reports indicated that the Constitutional Convention would almost certainly retain a parliamentary, cabinet-style government at the end of the day. No doubt there would have to be new elections once the Constitution was written and ratified, but Yon and his colleagues seemed to have done a pretty good job under very trying circumstances over the past six or seven T-months. None of them seemed in any danger of losing his or her seat in whatever the legislative branch was ultimately called, so all of them ought to be available for ministry service after those elections. In light of that, it seemed unlikely—to Barrett, at least—that the League would want to change horses under the new dispensation.

Assuming of course that Yon Sung-Jin and his colleagues were willing to go on serving.

Abadjieva took charge of the meeting as soon as Gaddis finished the introductions.

"We'll get to the Jessyk issue later. But I want to start by asking the two officers in the—the 'Mumps,' is it?—who *they* think is responsible for the mass killings on Mesa immediately after the Grand Alliance seized control of the system."

She paused, very briefly. Just long enough to give both Barrett and Abrams a direct look.

Barrett and Abrams glanced at each other. He gave her a little nod.

"I don't know who did it," she said then. "What I'm sure by now, though, is that it *wasn't* the Grand Alliance, and it wasn't the Audubon Ballroom."

"Why?"

"As far as the Grand Alliance is concerned, it just doesn't make any sense. They already had control of the system. The

Navy had surrendered, and so had the General Board. The only thing a nuclear bombardment could really have accomplished would have been to make people on Mesa hate them—it sure wasn't going to make anyone any gladder to see them! And even if there *had* been some way it might have made some kind of tactical military sense, it still doesn't ring true. It's not just that they didn't have to do it or that it would've been a stupid thing for them to have done. It's that neither the Manties nor the Havenites have any history of that kind of indiscriminate killing. Ever. As for the Ballroom—"

She hesitated. She was tempted to glance at Abrams again, but she didn't. He'd react to what she was about to say however he chose.

"There are two reasons I don't think the Ballroom did it, either. And by now, I've investigated the issue myself. Pretty thoroughly, I assure you. First, they simply didn't have the resources in-system to do it. We'd have known if they did, trust me. We might not have been able to stop all of the incidents, but we would have known if the Ballroom had been able to build that kind of presence, with that kind of firepower. But, secondly, even if we might somehow have missed something like that, I've gotten to know the person who was in charge of Ballroom operations on Mesa. He's my new boss, in fact. He tells me they had nothing to do with it, and I believe him."

"Why?" Abadjieva repeated.

What part of "I've gotten to know the person" went over your head? Barrett wondered. But she didn't say that out loud.

"It's just not the way the man's mind works," she said instead, with a shrug. "Or the way Jeremy X, his boss back then, thinks, either. These people are killers, for sure. Deadly ones. But there's no history of the Ballroom engaging in indiscriminate murder. The Ballroom's victims were *targets*. They weren't selected at random."

Abadjieva frowned, tapping her lips with a thoughtful forefinger while she did just that.

"That sounds like a very fine line, to me," she said finally, in a less than approving tone.

"Not to me, it doesn't," one of the other women at the table said. Barrett couldn't remember her name—Sayavong, maybe?—but she did remember that she was connected with one of the Solarian intelligence services. Or had been, at any rate.

"Lieutenant Barrett has a point," she went on. "A pretty good one, actually. There's a big difference between 'indiscriminate murder' and targeted assassinations. One of my jobs over in Gendarmerie Intelligence Command was to recruit and train people analogous to what the Ballroom called 'strikers.'"

"Assassins, you mean," Abadjieva said, still frowning.

"Sometimes." The other woman nodded. "Especially when somebody in Interior tasked us to support OFS." She grimaced as if recalling a bad taste. "But mostly, yes. It's more complicated than that, but for our purposes here, I'll accept the term. My point is that for something like that, you need people who are *focused*. Trigger-happy thugs are worse than useless."

She turned to Barrett directly.

"You sound pretty confident about that judgment," she said. "Are you? And is it really *your* judgment? Not just the party line?"

Barrett started to reply, but before she could, Abrams preempted her.

"Anybody who knows Kayla Barrett trusts her honesty," he said. "And in case you didn't already know, she lost almost her entire family in one of the terrorist incidents that preceded the nuclear strikes. The ones the system government—even our own bosses in MISD—claimed were Ballroom attacks. Which means that her boss today—who's my boss now, too, by the way—would have been directly responsible for killing her brother, sister, sister-in-law, two nieces, and a nephew. Do you really think she'd still be working for him if she thought he was guilty?"

There was something very like scorn in his eyes as he looked at the seated Solarians. Then he shook his head.

"I don't think the GA or the Ballroom did it, either. Like Kayla says, it doesn't make any sense, and it doesn't match their historical track record. No. It was somebody else. Who, I don't know." He twitched his head at al-Fanudahi. "He and his people call them 'the Other Guys.' The Grand Alliance is more specific, except not even they can pin down the identity of this 'Alignment.' But whoever it was, they're out there somewhere. And we need to find them before they do it again."

Abadjieva considered him for a moment, her eyes dispassionate, then turned at that basilisk gaze on Simeon Gaddis.

"Brigadier?"

"In my opinion, Lieutenant Barrett is almost certainly correct,"

Gaddis replied without hesitation. "Admittedly, some of her reasoning is probably a bit subjective. But my own people's analysis strongly suggests—"

The discussion continued for quite some time, with al-Fanudahi and Zilwicki carrying the weight for the delegation from Mesa. Their arguments were far more detailed and sophisticated than Barrett's or Abrams's had been. But it seemed clear to Barrett that the two of them had shifted what might be called the center of gravity on the issue.

Finally—the woman was nothing, if not persistent—Abadjieva ended the discussion.

"All right, I'm satisfied," she said. "I know the Brigadier already agreed with Lieutenant Barrett and Sergeant Abrams. What about the rest of you, now that we've had a chance to hear their presentation?"

She looked around the conference table, and all three of her fellows nodded. She looked at them a moment longer, then nodded back.

"It's too late to take up the Jessyk question today," she said. "We'll do it tomorrow, starting at nine o'clock."

Silversmith Hotel
The Loop
City of Old Chicago
Old Earth
Sol System

ANTON ZILWICKI STAYED BEHIND TO CONTINUE THE DISCUSSION
with al-Fanudahi, Okiku, and Gaddis, so Barrett and Abrams
returned to the hotel on their own. Finding their way was a
bit daunting, and not just because of Old Chicago's immensity.
It was fortunate that they'd had several days of sightseeing to
reduce some of the intimidation factor, but not even that was
truly adequate preparation for the Loop.

Barrett had felt more than a little uneasy when it turned out
that the hotel Zilwicki preferred was located a hundred meters
or so underground in the galaxy's most famous—or infamous—
ghetto. The Loop reminded her of a far less embittered seccy
district, in a lot of ways, probably because so many of its inhabitants were immigrants, very few of whom held any fondness for
any transstellar, including a liberal sample of ex-slaves who had
ample reason to hate *anyone* from Mesa. For the first day or so,
she'd imagined that they—especially the ex-slaves—were seeing
her in her old MISD uniform, which had created a certain itch-
ing sensation between her shoulder blades. But she'd gotten over
that, and discovered that she really liked the yeasty ferment that
seemed to power the Loop's bubbling energy.

According to its brochures, the Silversmith Hotel predated the
Diaspora. Not the same buildings, of course. But it maintained
that there had been *a* Silversmith Hotel in the same location
for close to three millennia, and nothing she'd been able to find
disproved its claim.

In its current iteration, the Silversmith was a comfortable, reasonably priced, ever so slightly down-at-the-heels haven, and its aura of welcoming, lower-class respectability made her feel much more at home than one of the grander hotels located in one of the city's towers might have.

They took the lift—barely five floors, this time—to their floor and stepped out of it into the hallway to their rooms. By now, Barrett carried her cane more out of habit than anything else, and the two of them walked down the carpeted hall in companionable silence.

Abrams's room was closer to the lift than hers, and he unlocked the door. Then he hesitated for a moment.

"Want to come in for a drink?" he asked.

As it happened, Barrett had been pondering the same question. She and Abrams had been coworkers on Mesa, and gotten along well, but they'd never been in the same unit. She'd known him, but she'd discovered that that wasn't the same as actually *knowing* him. On the other hand, she really liked what she'd seen since he'd joined her in the Mumps, and especially on this trip. And she'd been alone for a long time now. It was actually still less than a year since she'd lost her family and her leg, yet it seemed much, much longer.

There was a theory, she knew, that claimed Hell wasn't the cauldron of flame most people thought of. That it was a frozen place, instead. An endless expanse of ice, stretching to eternity. She couldn't attest to the theory's accuracy, but she knew now from personal experience just how long being emotionally frozen could seem.

"Sure," she said.

Adam Smoltz Conference Room
George Benton Tower
City of Old Chicago
Old Earth
Sol System

"I'VE GOT TO SAY I'M A LITTLE TICKED OFF." KAYLA BARRETT told Jake Abrams as they watched the people in the large conference room take their seats. "Yesterday, they sent just *one* cabinet minister to make a decision about their attitude toward the murder of millions of Mesans. Today?"

She used her chin to point to the table at the center of the room. There were at least a couple of dozen staffers and witnesses seated in neat rows of comfortable chairs facing that table, and Brigadier Gaddis and Natsuko Okiku sat directly in front of it. They were flanked by two empty chairs, facing the seven people who sat at the table itself.

"Today, they send the entire Cabinet just to decide whether they're going to approve what amounts to a police operation that probably won't kill more than a handful of people, if any."

She'd spoken softly enough that her words couldn't have carried more than a meter or two. But al-Fanudahi was close enough to hear them, and he paused beside her on his way to join Gaddis and Okiku.

"Don't take it personally," he said, also speaking softly. "First of all, yesterday was actually good news. Abadjieva was there as the Cabinet's official representative because she's the Foreign Minister, but the reason Prime Minister Yon didn't send anyone else with her is that the Cabinet was already leaning strongly toward the opinion that the Grand Alliance wasn't responsible. These people—" it was his turn to point at the table with his

425

chin "—may be politicians, but they're very smart ones, and they recognize a nonsense theory when they see one.

"But today's a different ballgame, Kayla. A decision to come down hard—'hard' as in outright destruction—on one of the galaxy's dozen wealthiest and most powerful transstellars has huge political implications. Especially when the transstellar in question isn't even incorporated in the League."

"I don't see the big deal," she said. "Who cares where it's incorporated? Or how wealthy it is? Nobody seemed to care when we took Manpower down!"

"Even at its peak, Manpower was always seen as an outlaw corporation, here in the League," al-Fanudahi replied. "Sure, it was paying off a lot of Solarian bureaucrats, Gendarmes—even a lot more Navy officers than I'd like to admit—but it was still engaged in a trade that was illegal under Solarian law. So nobody could afford to weep any public tears for it, no matter what they felt. Trust me, there are more than a few career apparatchiks who were *really* unhappy to see Manpower go down. They just weren't stupid enough to show it.

"But the League wasn't involved in taking down Manpower as a corporation. Even Gannon and Kingsford's decision to finally begin enforcing the laws against the slave trade was directed only at actual criminal operations—slave ships, individuals working in depots where slaves were traded or transshipped, that sort of thing—and not after Manpower as a corporate entity."

"What?" She looked up at him from her chair. "Why not?"

"Because the League doesn't have jurisdiction over Manpower as a corporation," al-Fanudahi said patiently. "We could fine the corporation for illegal operations that occurred inside our borders. We could arrest its personnel and try to convict them for violating our domestic law, if they did it inside our borders. We could even shut down its Solarian operations and refuse to allow it to do business in the League at all, although it probably could have spun out the court challenges to that kind of action for years. But we couldn't simply go after it and force its complete shutdown because it was a *Mesan* corporation, not a Solarian one.

"And the same thing is true for Jessyk. It does an enormous amount of business in the League, it has to be licensed, bonded, and insured in the League, and it's obligated to observe League law in its operations here. But it's not headquartered here, not a Solarian corporation or organized under Solarian law. And unlike Manpower, Jessyk will be able to find a *lot* of Solarians willing to stand up and raise Hell over any onslaught against it. Why not? It's operated openly, and as far as anyone can prove, legally, in the League for T-centuries, and it employs millions of Solarian citizens, every single one of whom will see an attack on it as an attack on his or her livelihood."

"But we can prove that it's really been part of Manpower from the beginning, and that it's been violating Solly law—against the slave trade, if nothing else—for T-centuries, no matter what it looked like. So what's the big deal? Oh," she waved an irritable hand, "so it's a Mesan corporation, not a Solarian one. Well, it's the Mesan government asking for Solly help to deal with a rogue criminal operation!"

"It's the *provisional* Mesan government asking the *provisional* Solarian government to help deal with an *allegedly* rogue criminal operation, when both of the governments in question are due to be superseded sometime very soon now by permanent governments elected under brand-new constitutions, both of which are being written at the demand of and under the supervision of the Grand Alliance...who happen to be the people who invaded and conquered both governments' territory."

He looked down at her quizzically, and she grimaced.

"Oh, okay, maybe it's not as simple as I thought it was," she half-growled. "But do all of those adjectives and adverbs of yours mean they're likely to say no?"

"How would I know?" He chuckled at the look she gave him, but he also shook his head. "It's a lot easier to analyze military intelligence data than it is to predict which way politicians— even honest ones—are going to jump, Kayla. In fact, I think it's probably harder for us Solarians to predict how the *honest* ones will react, because we've had so little experience with them at the federal level.

"One thing they're all going to be aware of is that agreeing to help Mesa and the Grand Alliance—don't forget the Grand Alliance bit, because a hell of a lot of Solarians are going to notice it, I promise you—will send an unmistakable message to everyone in the League, from the executive boards of Technodyne and Kalokainos to a janitorial engineer on some backwater planet in the Verge. Exactly what that message will—"

"Let's come to order, please," a deep male voice said, and al-Fanudahi and Barrett both looked back at the conference table. The voice belonged to a dark-haired, dark-eyed man of slightly less than average height.

"Prime Minister Yon," al-Fanudahi murmured, pitching his voice even lower as silence descended almost instantly upon the conference room.

"Brigadier Gaddis," Yon continued, turning towards the Gendarme, "please begin by presenting the conclusions you've come to and the reasoning behind them."

Who is "you"? Barrett wondered. The Gendarmerie was included, obviously, but she was pretty sure a lot more people had been involved in the deliberations which had produced the conclusions Gaddis was about to present.

"Are you one of those you's?" she murmured to al-Fanudahi, and he smiled.

"I'm not sure you have a need to know who the you's are. But, yes. I'm one of them."

He gave her a wink and trotted down the aisle to join Gaddis and Okiku.

✧   ✧   ✧

Gaddis presented an overall, broad-strokes summary of the conclusions "his" investigation had reached. Al-Fanudahi and Okiku followed up with a more detailed presentation of the evidence.

The Cabinet was clearly focused on five points. First, could it be *proven* that Jessyk was actually and *legally* Manpower's creature? Second, could it be *proven* that Jessyk was actually guilty of a systematic pattern of law-breaking? Third, did the Provisional Government of Mesa have the legal standing to request the Provisional Government of the Solarian League to assist in a joint investigation and takedown of a transstellar whose operations spanned both governments' borders? Fourth, just what would be involved in the aforesaid takedown? And, fifth, were the Solarian League's police agencies and military prepared to conduct joint operations with the Grand Alliance which had destroyed or captured well over a thousand Solarian capital ships, killed millions of Solarian military personnel...and completely demolished the industrial infrastructure of the Sol System itself?

As the hearing proceeded, it became obvious that the answer to the first question was a resounding yes. The blind fronts and paper entities erected to obscure Manpower's ownership of a ninety percent stake in Jessyk were even more involved than the arcane smokescreens of most transstellars. Unfortunately for Jessyk and Manpower, Mesa and the Grand Alliance had acquired Jessyk's own *internal* records, the key that deciphered all the obscuration, in the Nakatomi Tower raid.

The answer to the second question was a slightly less resounding yes. The Nakatomi data was more strongly focused on the corporate level and what might be called the hierarchical spine of the two transstellars' relationship. *Operational* data was scarcer and less obvious, but enough could be teased out to confirm Jessyk's active involvement in the transportation of genetic slaves, smuggling, illicit weapons sales, and a dozen lesser infractions, all punishable under existing Solarian law.

The answer to the third question was...probably. No one could doubt that both of the "provisional" bodies involved were, and had been for some months, discharging the responsibilities and duties of the governments of their respective star nations. The League's provisional government had a somewhat stronger imprimatur than the Mesan Provisional Government, given that the Assembly had selected its members whereas its Mesan cousin's members had been directly appointed by the occupiers, but no other entity was in a position to speak for either Mesa or the League. There was a very real possibility that whatever sanctions were imposed on Jessyk would be contested in court because of the "provisional" in front of both governments' names. Hu Sunghyon, the Interior Minister, seemed particularly worried about that possibility, but Attorney General Rorendaal was able to answer most of his concerns. There *would* be litigation, she agreed, but the last half millennium provided plenty of case law and precedents to support their actions.

The answer to the fourth question was...problematical. Jessyk might be a Mesan corporation, but Mesa was a single star system. Despite the enormous influence Jessyk had wielded within the Mesa System and on the old Mesan General Board, at least eighty-five percent of all of its operations were conducted in *Solarian* space. And, as Brianna Pearson had pointed out immediately after the Nakatomi raid, the Solarian interstellar economy was already on life support. Not only that, but what had happened to the Sol System's deep-space infrastructure required mammoth amounts of merchant shipping to provide the goods its own demolished industry no longer could. The last thing any Solarian government, be it ever so "provisional," wanted to do was to kick one of that interstellar economy's major props out from under it. Chris Holderbaum, who'd inherited the Treasury from Agatá Wodoslawski, and Takahara Mikazuki, who'd inherited Commerce from Omosupe Quartermain, were especially concerned about that. With, Barrett was forced to concede, good cause. In the end, however, both of them—Takahara rather more happily than Holderbaum—appeared willing to sign off, at least provisionally (there was that adverb again), on the approach Susan Hibson had proposed, although it was evident there were going to be a lot of devils in that particular set of details before all was said and done.

But that brought up the *fifth* question.

"Look," Prime Minister Yon said, finally, after forty-five minutes or so of increasingly...energetic debate, "let's all agree that this is going to be what they used to call a 'hot potato' no matter how we approach it. My sense, though, is that we're pretty much in agreement that it *needs* to be approached. Is that fair?"

He looked around the table at his colleagues. Abadjieva and Rorendaal nodded immediately. Interior Minister Hu followed, a bit more begrudgingly. Holderbaum glowered at the prime minister for a moment, but then he, too, nodded. That left Takahara, and Minister of Defense Solange Dembélé.

"Mikazuki?" Yon said.

"I agree that the entire situation is...unfortunate," Takahara said, then grimaced. "That's not the right word at all, is it?" she said. "I don't know what the right word *is*, though. I'm still deeply concerned over the possible repercussions for our shipping industry, even with the conservatorship approach. Not just in terms of Jessyk and the possible loss of its carrying capacity, if it goes down, but also in terms of the confidence of other transstellars. If people decide we're handing out bull's-eyes to paste on transstellars' backs for past actions, what happens to investor confidence? For that matter, what happens to the confidence of the transstellars themselves, especially after the hits so many of them have taken in the Protectorates? I'm...I'm just not sure this is the best time to be doing it."

"I agree with you, in a lot of ways, Mika," Holderbaum said.

"But if we're going to clean out all the crap that landed us in our current mess, we have to start somewhere." He shrugged. "This looks like a good place, symbolically, as well as pragmatically. And if we have to do it, I'm inclined to think it would be better to do as much of it as we can *now*, when we can...can get all the bad taste done as quickly as possible."

Takahara looked at him for a long moment, and then—manifestly unhappily—she nodded.

That left only Dembélé, and the prime minister cocked his head at her.

"I have...some reservations," the defense minister said. "Mostly, it's a matter of mission creep for the Navy. We've got a lot on our hands right now, and I've already signed off on Kingsford's and Gannon's plan to go after the slave trade. I don't have any problem with whacking any of Jessyk's people or operations we run over in the process of finally enforcing our own domestic laws against genetic slavery. In fact, it's been overdue for as long as most of us have been alive.

"But that's a matter of domestic law—*our* domestic law. And while Brigadier Gaddis and his people have been very careful to present this as a Solarian issue, it's not. Not really. It's a *Mesan* issue...and the Grand Alliance's." Dembélé's eyes hardened. "I'm not sure we should be opening this can of worms at all, and if we decide we do have to, I question the priority and the timing."

Barrett frowned. There was something else behind the defense minister's arguments. She could feel it.

"Wonder who she lost to the GA?" Abruzzi murmured in her ear, and her own eyes narrowed.

"You may be onto something," she replied, equally quietly. "On the other hand, I'm pretty sure a *lot* of Sollies would prefer to tell the Grand Alliance to piss up a rope, whatever it was asking for."

"I think the consensus is that we *do* need to deal with this, Solange," Yon said after a moment.

"If that's your judgment, and the rest of the Cabinet agrees with you, then I'll certainly abide by the 'consensus.'" Dembélé didn't sound very happy, but she nodded. "That still doesn't say we need to do it *now*, though. Or that we need to do it in conjunction with the Grand Alliance," she added.

"I prefer to look at it as acting in conjunction with Mesa," Abadjieva said. "And, frankly, Solange, we need all the good press we can get in that regard. You know as well as I do how much of the galaxy resented the hell out of Solarian demands for 'cooperation' with *our* requirements. Go back and look at how many of the League's 'joint operations' and 'bilateral cooperation agreements' actually benefited anyone except the League over the last T-century or so. Trust me, that point's been made to *me* pretty firmly over the last six T-months. If nothing else, this represents an opportunity for us to respond to someone else's request for assistance. We could really use that in the court of public opinion."

"And, with all due respect," Rorendaal said, "we don't have an unlimited time window here. At the moment, we don't *think* Jessyk knows the Mesan authorities captured their records. But what I know for an absolute fact is that the fact that they did is going to leak. I don't know where, and I don't know how soon, but it's going to. At which point the opportunity to act on the intelligence, on the evidence, is likely to evaporate."

Dembélé scowled, but she also nodded unwillingly.

"So we're essentially in agreement that it's appropriate and reasonable for us to cooperate with Mesa," the prime minister said. "Which means that the real issue, what's really standing in the way of a decision, is whether or not it's appropriate and reasonable for us to cooperate with the *Grand Alliance*, at the same time."

He looked around at his colleagues' faces again and snorted.

"We're scheduled to adjourn in about another thirty minutes," he said, "and I don't think forcing this through to a premature conclusion would be very beneficial. So, I'm going to go ahead and adjourn now. All of us need to think about this between now and tomorrow morning, when we reconvene. I'd like to have a definitive answer—and the reasoning behind it—from each of you at that time. Agreed?"

This time, everyone nodded, and he smiled a bit tartly.

"In that case, we stand adjourned," he said simply.

❖   ❖   ❖

As she headed toward the exit, Barrett reflected upon the fact that no one had asked her or Abruzzi a direct question. In fact, they'd been completely ignored, as far as she could see. Which was perfectly fine with her, but—

"I wonder why they told us to come at all," she said quietly to Abrams, and he looked at her with a twisty sort of smile.

"At a guess, Gaddis and his people wanted to prove that 'yes, the bears are here. Would you like to see them dance?'" he said. "And nobody did, because the interesting thing about dancing bears is that they can do it at all."

Kayla snorted. She'd discovered that one of the things he liked about him was the sardonic lens through which he viewed the universe.

"Why did you join the Misties?" she asked abruptly, and he shrugged.

"Family tradition, going back four generations. And I couldn't think of anything else I wanted to do when I got out of school. You?"

"Me?" There was no humor in her chuckle. "I picked the wrong boyfriend when I was young and stupid. I expressed an interest in doing security work. He told me I didn't have what it took to become a Misty. So I called him on his dare, told him what he could do with his opinions, and signed up the next day."

"That was pretty stupid."

"No." She shook her head. "Joining the Misties was the minor stupidity. The Big Stupid was that I broke up with the bum first, *before* I signed up. So what was the use of proving he was wrong at that point?"

"Hang on a second," a voice said from behind them, and they looked back to see al-Fanudahi catching up with them. "You two don't need to come to any of the other meetings," he said.

"Like I said," Abrams muttered. "Nobody actually wants to see the bears dance."

"Precisely," al-Fanudahi agreed with a smile.

"So what do we do instead? Besides just sitting around, I mean? Not that I figure Old Terra's run out of tourist attractions. All we've seen so far is Old Chicago, and this is, after all, the home planet of the human race."

"I want to see Angkor Wat," Barrett said. "I saw a picture of it when I was a little kid."

"'Fraid not." Al-Fanudahi shook his head. "You're going back to Mesa with me. Ship leaves the day after tomorrow."

Now that she thought about it, it occurred to Barrett that the chain of command was fuzzy, when it came to her and Jake in the Sol System. "Fuzzy" as in completely unclear. Or even nonexistent.

"Who says we are?" she demanded.

"The Ones Who Command Bears to Dance," al-Fanudahi replied with a grin. "Whose identity, you don't need to know."

❖   ❖   ❖

"Welcome aboard the *Avra Barbidi*," the uniformed young woman seated at the arrivals desk said as Barrett and Abrams stepped out of the boarding tube and into the passenger ship's main airlock. "On behalf of Kalokainos Shipping, we appreciate your decision to travel with us—" she looked down at a touch screen in her desktop as the airlock's sensors picked up the ID codes from their uni-links "—Lieutenant Barrett and Sergeant Abrams. You're traveling separately, correct?"

Barrett blinked mentally. She hadn't thought about that. But this was a commercial passenger ship, not a military one where berths were assigned by the powers-that-be, which meant—

"No," she said. "We don't need separate cabins. One stateroom will do."

She ignored Abrams. If he wanted to object, that was up to him. Instead, she bestowed a smile on the boarding officer, who was frowning a bit. Probably because the nature of her job led her to dislike surprises—changes of any kind really. In fact, she looked like she was going to be stubborn about it. But—

"I'm frugal," Barrett explained, before she could object.

The young woman looked at her for a moment, then shrugged.

"I can arrange that," she said.

"Thank you," Barrett said brightly.

Abrams, on the other hand, said nothing at all. That was another thing Barrett liked about him: he knew when to shut up.

September 1923 Post Diaspora

"God help me, that almost makes sense."

—Fleet Admiral Winston Seth Kingsford,
Solarian League Navy

Howard Clinkscales Memorial Hospital
Harrington City
Harrington Steading
Planet Grayson
Grayson System

"REALLY, MOTHER! DON'T YOU THINK THIS IS A LITTLE EXCES-sive?" Lady Dame Honor Alexander-Harrington demanded.

"What?" Allison Harrington looked up at her much taller daughter from the hospital bed. "I have no idea what you're talking about," she said in a tone which might have been described as "severe innocence."

"I know you and Daddy insist on doing things without artificial assistance," Honor said. "If I *didn't* know that, however, I would assume that you were stacking the deck instead of rolling the dice."

"You got that dreadful turn of phrase from your Uncle Jacques, didn't you?" Allison glowered at her. "It's from all that time you spend with the SCA, isn't it?"

"No, I didn't, and quit changing the subject!" Honor's stern tone was sadly undermined by the bubble of amusement in its depths.

"I'm not changing the subject," Allison protested. "I'm simply focusing attention where it ought to be, given your undutiful attitude, young lady!"

"I am neither young, anymore, nor a lady, except technically," Honor replied. "And I want to know about this twins thing of yours. Are you *sure* you and Daddy didn't get Illescue's help this time?"

"Honor *Stephanie* Alexander-Harrington! You know we're *monogamous*! And even if we weren't, Franz Illescue is the *last* man I'd—!"

437

That was as far as she got before Honor collapsed—carefully—into the bedside chair in helpless giggles.

Allison beamed at her, and Honor laid one hand on her own profoundly pregnant abdomen as she fought the giggles woman-fully under control.

"Oh, Mother! That was underhanded!"

"I have no idea what you could possibly be talking about," Allison said serenely. "Now stop giggling—it makes you sound like a twelve-year-old—and come over here to kiss your brothers."

The aforementioned giggles threatened to slip their leash once again, but Honor Alexander-Harrington was made of sterner stuff and brought them firmly to heel. Then she pushed up out of her chair once more and crossed to bend over her mother's bed and the tiny, red-faced infants on either side of her. Allison's arms held the small, blanket-wrapped, peacefully sleeping baby boys close, and despite their badinage, her eyes were misty as she looked up at her daughter.

"They're beautiful, Mother," Honor said softly, bending to press her lips to each tiny forehead in turn.

"And you've known for months they were going to be twins," her mother pointed out. "I don't see why you seem to be so surprised at this late date."

"I'm not 'surprised.' I'm . . . perplexed." Honor straightened, touched the side of her mother's face gently, then settled back into the chair once more. "I don't quite understand this effusion of twins, is all. I mean, wasn't I satisfactory? Is there some reason you feel obligated to produce paired siblings this way?"

"You were eminently satisfactory," Allison said in a softer tone. "Although, if I'm going to be completely honest, I sometimes do regret that we didn't give you any sibs when you were younger. We should have."

"Nonsense." Honor reached across to squeeze her mother's shoulder. "I did just fine, and I suppose you and Daddy weren't the *worst* parents in the explored galaxy." She shrugged. "I just figured that maybe the two of you were a teeny bit slow just at first there, so you restricted yourself to practicing on just one of me until you were confident you'd gotten it right."

Had anyone else entered the room at that moment, they would have known exactly whom Honor had inherited her giggles from, and Honor grinned in triumph.

"Well, thank goodness we had Nimitz to help," Allison said, getting her own mirth under control and looking at the treecat stretched across the back of Honor's chair. "That was one of the most important lessons we learned, actually. Always involve the treecats in raising kids!"

It was Nimitz's turn to bleek in laughter, and mother and daughter watched his hands flash signs.

"It did *not* take your *entire* clan to keep me out of trouble, Stinker!" Honor protested, but Allison nodded enthusiastically.

"Did, too! And that's why we're so happy the 'cats have been helping us raise Faith and James."

"Well, I admit it takes every treecat we can find to ride herd on those two, but that's because they aren't as demure, obedient, and conscientious as *I* was as a child."

"Dear, if you're going to say things like that, could you possibly step out into the hall? I'd hate for the babies to be incinerated when the lightning strikes."

"Mother!"

"Well, I don't want to hurt your *feelings* or anything, but telling whoppers like that?" Allison shook her head mournfully. "I see I have, indeed, failed you in some ways as a parent."

"No." Honor squeezed her shoulder again. "No, Mother. That's one thing you and Father never did. And I hope Hamish and I do half as well with Raoul and Katherine as you did. And with Andrew Judah Wesley."

She rested her other hand on the dome of her belly, feeling the child within her stir and tasting his unborn mind-glow, shifting dreamily as he dozed his way towards birth.

"You've decided on the names, then?" Allison asked gently.

"Yes." Honor blinked misty eyes. "We've lost so many we could have named him for. We were leaning toward Howard, but you and Daddy already saw to it that we'll never forget him. Or Michael." She smiled down sadly at Howard Simon Harrington and his brother, Michael Jeremiah. So many friends to miss and mourn, she thought. So many lives to remember and celebrate. "We thought about Benjamin, too," she said. "Hamish suggested that. But, I just..."

Her voice trailed off, and Allison loosened her embrace of Michael Jeremiah and reached up to touch Honor's wrist in understanding. It was irrational, of course, but she did understand the almost instinctive fear that if Honor and Hamish named their son for Benjamin Mayhew the Fates would take him from them the way they had taken *Michael* Mayhew and so many others.

"Well, we do seem to be coming up with quite a few rather Biblical names," she said in a determinedly lighter tone.

"Grayson has that effect," Honor replied. "And we could do worse! Hamish actually suggested Algernon Aloysius Alexander-Harrington, on the basis that a 'triple-A' name was only appropriate for *our* offspring. That was when I told him making jokes like that to a pregnant woman constituted a basis for justifiable homicide."

"Love, I admit it *ought* to be justifiable homicide," Allison said with a laugh. "I don't think it *is*, though."

"It is under Harrington Steading's laws," Honor replied. "*Now*, anyway!"

"I think that was an *excellent* addition to your jurisprudence, Dear."

"So do I." Honor smiled, then shook her head.

"What?" Allison asked.

"It's just that I forget how *tiny* they are." Honor touched Michael Jeremiah's pouting, rosebud lips. "How small and fragile. Raoul and Katherine are four now, and Faith and James are *ten*! It just doesn't seem possible they were ever that tiny."

"Children grow up, Sweetheart. I remember my mother telling me I'd have two weeks with you."

"Two weeks?"

"Two weeks." Allison nodded. "Because, she said, that was how long it was going to seem when I looked back. I'd have two weeks with you, so I needed to make every day of those two weeks count. I didn't always see eye-to-eye with your grandmother, Honor, but she got that one right. In my mind, in my heart, you're still the little girl running madly around the greenhouse, getting into mischief. And looking so damned *cute* no one could stay mad with you, whatever you did. I am so unspeakably proud of the woman you've grown into, of the strong, wonderful person you've become. But in my heart, I still hug that little girl every single night."

"Well, if I turned out well, it's because of who raised me," Honor said softly. "And I'm pretty darned proud of you and Daddy, too. But I don't want it to have been just 'two weeks' with Raoul and Katherine."

She touched her stomach again, and her mother smiled a bittersweet smile.

"I'm afraid there's not much we can do about that," she said. "But in about three months, you'll start that clock ticking again with Andrew, won't you?"

"Yes, I will." Honor smiled back at her. "And you know what? I *will* make every single one of those days count."

CNO's Office
Admiralty Building
City of Old Chicago
Sol System

"SO, NOW THAT ROBBINS IS BACK, WHAT DO YOU THINK ABOUT Torch?" Winston Kingsford asked, and raised a cautioning finger at Charles Gannon. "And I'm giving you fair warning. 'It's interesting' won't satisfy me."

"Well, it *is* interesting. Not quite what I expected, though—in some ways, not at all what I expected." Gannon grimaced. "If I'd been able to take my finger off the pulse here in Old Chicago long enough to tag along, I'd be able to give you my firsthand impressions. But Robbins and Scarlatti recorded most of their actual sessions with Queen Berry's government and with Cachat. With the Torches' full approval, mind you," he added as Kingsford's eyebrows arched. "In fact, it was the Queen's suggestion. She wanted to be certain we understood exactly what they'd had to say. And, to be honest, there were some... call them 'sideband' elements to those conversations. Plus Robbins's report on her personal impressions, of course."

"So share them."

Gannon gazed at something only he could see, lips pursed as he paused to gather his thoughts. Then he refocused on Kingsford, his eyes once again sharp.

"What comes to your mind when you hear the phrase 'a state founded by a successful slave revolt'?" he asked.

"Haiti," Kingsford replied immediately. "I'll admit, though, that's probably because of Samantha." He shrugged. "Somewhere around sixty percent of her genetic material traces back through the ancient Caribbean islands. A lot of it is Haitian. To be honest, I didn't know much about Haiti or L'Ouverture before we met."

"Samantha could be the reason it pops to mind for you, but
442

I'm willing to bet that *most* people would answer the question with 'Haiti'—assuming they knew any ancient history to begin with."

Kingsford's yeoman arrived with the coffee service and poured. Gannon nodded his thanks, then paused to take a sip before he set the cup down.

"And what does the term 'ancient Haiti' bring to mind?" he continued.

"Poverty. Grinding poverty, at that. Quite a bit of brutality, too. Slavery's not an ideal environment for teaching people a civilized way to deal with one another."

"Well, Torch is about as different from that as you can imagine. To begin with, it's a very wealthy planet."

"Pharmaceuticals," Kingsford said.

"That's just the start of it. The planet and the rest of the system have quite a few other resources, but it's fair to say that the biggest one is obviously pharmaceuticals. And the new regime's first major economic decision was to nationalize the industry. Pharmaceuticals are owned by the government, lock, stock, and barrel."

"Really?" Kingsford frowned. "I had the impression Torch had a rather freewheeling economy. Lots of entrepreneurship."

"It does—except for pharmaceuticals. And when I say 'pharmaceuticals,' I'm referring to the manufacturing core of the industry. There are plenty of private enterprises involved in the harvesting, sale, and distribution of pharmaceuticals, as well as on the research and development end. But what Du Havel succeeded in doing by nationalizing the manufacture of pharmaceuticals right off was to avoid the 'resource curse.'"

"Which is...? I'm not familiar with that term."

"It goes back to ancient history on Old Earth—but you see it today all over the Verge, too. Sometimes they call it the poverty paradox. Why do so many nations with a great natural resource—fossil fuels were the main one, back on Old Earth, but there were others—wind up being poorer than nations *without* one? The answer is that such a concentrated and easily monopolized source of wealth also makes it easy for a government to make a sweetheart deal with powerful and wealthy corporations, often foreign corporations. There were instances in which that didn't happen, but that was usually true only if the nation already had well established, representative government and a diversified economy when the natural resource was discovered."

"And how often did *that* happen?"

"About as often as it happened in the Protectorates." Gannon shrugged. "Back before the Diaspora, the region they called the Middle East was a poster child for how it didn't happen. An enormous percentage of the world's known oil reserves were found under the sand that belonged to people who'd never heard of representative government. Hell, the oil was first discovered while the region was still controlled by imperialist European powers!

"But later, significant oil reserves were found in the North Sea, off Alaska, and in Western Canada. In those cases, the nation states involved were already well-established representative governments and already had healthy, *diversified* economies. They could adjust to their newfound treasure trove, and *their* governments were transparent enough to make it impossible to cut 'sweetheart deals' with the local elites. But where those conditions didn't—or don't—apply, most of the nation's wealth gets siphoned off by those wealthy, usually foreign, corporations. Plenty of it goes to enrich the native elite, though, so they go along with the racket, the population as a whole doesn't have the power to *stop* them from going along with it, and so that population as a whole stays mired in poverty."

"All right." Kingsford nodded. "I can see that. But what I *don't* see is how making such a resource the monopoly of the government would solve that problem."

"By itself, it wouldn't. But remember what I said about representative government. Torch may be a monarchy, but it's one that's responsive to its citizens. Nationalizing the resource makes the government directly responsible for the industry. It has to answer for what happens. It can't just shrug it off by claiming it's the corporations' doing."

"And you're saying that in Torch's case, who it would answer to are a bunch of ex-slaves who have what you might call limited experience in self-government?" Kingsford said skeptically.

"Exactly." Gannon waved a hand. "For the moment, just trust me on this one. Next time you run into Web Du Havel, ask him to explain it to you. Brace yourself, though. Web is probably the galaxy's leading expert on the subject. Actually, on the *subjects*, plural. He has very strong opinions on how government is supposed to work, and what he's succeeded in doing by nationalizing the production of pharmaceuticals is to control its growth and spread out the wealth it generates. There's plenty of room for private enterprise, but there's also no poverty and no huge income inequality or wealth disparity. Housing, education, healthcare—all of that is readily and cheaply available. Which also means that Torch's politics lack the harshness poverty brings with it."

"All right." Kingsford nodded. "I'll take your word for it. But we do have business to conduct, you know. So tell me what came of your project to have the Navy start working with Torch to uproot slavery."

"Well... There's been something of a change in plans."

"Why does that phrase 'change in plans' fill me with dread?" Kingsford inquired pleasantly.

"Well, it's like this. Robbins and Scarlatti arrived on schedule, but they didn't really expect to find Victor Cachat in residence." Gannon shrugged. "From what I've been able to determine, plans tend to change any time Cachat is in the vicinity. So—"

❖   ❖   ❖

"I expect my flag officers to exercise initiative," Kingsford said, twenty-odd minutes later. "This may be just a bit *more* initiative than I'm comfortable with." He eyed Gannon quizzically. "I don't see where involving a Solarian task group in one of Cachat's schemes— the man's notorious for them—advances our interests. It seems only indirectly tied to the slavery issue. If it's even tied to it at all."

"Admiral, if the GA's theory about the Alignment is accurate, this may lead us to the heart of it. But leaving that aside—"

"I *knew* it." Kingsford scowled. "I *knew* you had something up your sleeve. You're almost as bad as Cachat, when it comes to scheming!"

"I'm hurt." Gannon's aggrieved expression might actually have fooled someone who didn't know him.

"The hell you are. Out with it, Chuck."

Gannon considered for a moment, then shrugged.

"I wouldn't call it a scheme, actually. 'Scheme' implies a plan of action. What I have is more in the way of an assessment."

"Which is what?"

"Which is two things, actually. One of them is immediate, what you might call 'tactical,' but the other is more long-term. Strategic."

"So, tell me about tactical."

"So the data Torch has shared with Robbins, and the ex-Ballroom intelligence types who came home with her, all point to a much deeper relationship between Manpower and some of our more 'legitimate' transstellars than we thought. We're still looking at how deep it goes with some of them, but if the Torches' information is as accurate as I think it is, we may actually have a smoking gun where Jessyk is concerned."

"Really?" Kingsford tipped back in his chair. "I didn't expect that," he said, then snorted. "I *should* have. It just hadn't really occurred to me that we'd get that kind of evidence. Is this something we need to be turning over to Gaddis and his crew before they bring the hammer down on Jessyk?"

"That's why I called it 'immediate,'" Gannon said. "I've already given Simeon a heads up, and we'll be briefing him over at JISDC tomorrow morning. I'm not sure how this is going to impact our original plans for hunting down the slavery infrastructure, but I don't see how it could hurt. Certainly not from the perspective of finding a positive mission objective for the Fleet. I don't think I can make any actual recommendations until I've had a chance to talk it over with him—and probably with Zilwicki and the other representatives from Mesa—but I'm pretty sure it'll make a lot of sense to fold the two missions together after I have."

"All right." Kingsford nodded. "I imagine that makes sense, as long as we don't end up buried in some sort of mission creep." He grimaced. "We saw too much of that kind of crap with Frontier Security."

He sat thinking for a moment, then shrugged.

"Sufficient unto the day, for that one," he said then. "Trot out this 'strategic' assessment of yours."

"All right. It's my assessment that the Solarian League should bend over backwards—do whatever it can—to develop the best possible long-term relationship with Torch," Gannon said flatly.

"Why?" Kingsford held up his hand. "I'm not necessarily against the idea, but I'd like to hear some rationale that goes beyond 'people should be nice to each other.'"

"Actually, that's not a bad reason, when you come down to it. If you look at the past few T-centuries of the League's history and try to describe it, 'being nice to people' is *not* the descriptor that leaps to mind. Quite the opposite, in fact. Plunder and loot under the guise of saccharine necessity is more like it. I'll grant you that Frontier Security started out with all sorts of wonderful intentions . . . which lasted just long enough for the people *running* Frontier Security to realize how rich they could get."

"I wish I could argue the point," Kingsford said with a grimace, "but I can't. Go on."

"At times like this—I can cite historical precedents—a smart nation realizes that it's time to make amends. For its own self-respect, even more than for outside approval. And if you're going to do it, try to do it well. By which I mean, take on projects that have a good chance of success—and success that's highly visible, both for your own citizens and for everyone else. To be honest, the domestic consequences are even more important. Self-perception, the way a star nation sees itself—how it *wants* to see itself—shapes its policies, and that shapes the health of its political system. The last thing any star nation in the League's current position needs is to have its own people thinking that the new Constitution is no more than 'business as usual' under a new fig leaf."

He paused to drink coffee, then continued.

"Enter Torch. You have combined under one roof a nation of the most oppressed and brutalized people in the galaxy, an objective situation in the form of the planet's natural resources, and one of the best political leaderships to be found anywhere."

He drained the rest of the cup and set it aside.

"Web Du Havel is something of a political genius, in my opinion. He's not just one of the best informed, most knowledgeable experts in the fields of both history and political science. He's also one of the handful of academics in history who are superb when it comes to applying that knowledge to real life. Most of them are abysmal at the trade.

"That probably includes me." He grinned. "Happily, I work entirely through an intermediary—that would be you—rather than trying to deal with the unwashed and unruly masses myself. But it's not just Du Havel. Jeremy X could be considered a political mastermind in his own right."

"Jeremy?" Kingsford frowned again. "I don't see where the man's done much of anything since the Torches rebelled against Mesa."

"Which is precisely my point. If you're a government, especially a legitimate government, you don't *want* someone like Jeremy X to do much of anything."

Kingsford's expression was puzzled, and Gannon snorted.

"Come on, Winston. You, of all people, should be familiar with the concept of a 'fleet in being.'"

Kingsford's puzzlement turned into a scowl.

"I'm a goddamned admiral. Of course I'm familiar with the concept!"

"Well, think of Jeremy X the same way. He's Torch's homicidal maniac in being. By doing nothing, he plays a major role in maintaining stability, since no one in his right mind wants to provoke him into *stopping* doing nothing."

Kingsford chewed on his lower lip for a moment, then nodded.

"Okay," he said a bit grudgingly. "I see your point."

"Those two aren't the only ones. Not by a long shot. Queen Berry is a pure treasure. Thandi Palane has managed in an incredibly short time to give a barely-out-of-the-crib star nation a serious military presence and reputation. It's still a *tiny* military, but it's got some friends who are all grown up, and nobody in its own weight class wants to get on its wrong side. And, finally, Torch is playing a central role in re-creating Mesa as a real star nation. And the process is reciprocal, because people from the Alignment—the benign one, I mean; not the nasty bastards—are starting to show up on Torch, offering their assistance with genetic and medical problems. Put it all together, and what have you got?"

He didn't wait for Kingsford's replied.

"What you've got is one of the most exciting and promising political situations anywhere in the galaxy. It's only one star system, so nobody expects it to shake the rest of the galaxy by the scruff of its neck, but anybody who's paying attention knows that it's just starting out. Thirty years ago, nobody had ever heard of *Grayson*, either. You think anybody in his right mind wants to piss off Benjamin Mayhew at this point? And don't think people aren't already taking notice! Believe it or not, tourism is starting to become a significant factor in Torch's economy. The League would be foolish not to do everything in its power—its very considerable power, let's not forget—to help things along."

"All right, all right." Kingsford held up both hands. "I've still got my doubts—might be better to call them reservations—but I'm willing to go along with your scheme for a while."

"It is *not* a scheme. I think of it as a stratagem in being."

Kingsford lowered his hands to his head and started rubbing his temples.

"God help me, that almost makes sense."

Alexia Gabon Tower
City of Mendel
Planet Mesa
Mesa System

"HE'S NOT IN THE OFFICE, LIEUTENANT BARRETT." SABURO'S SEC-retary pointed to the door and then looped his finger to the right, indicating which direction to go once she and Jake Abrams were back in the corridor. "He's in room 355-H, swearing in some new recruits."

Barrett looked at the door, hesitating.

"Don't worry, Lieutenant. By the time you get there, he should be done. He's not one to drag out protocol, you know," the sec-retary said, and Barrett chuckled.

"That's putting it mildly. Thanks, Fred."

She headed for the door, with Abrams following, and turned right. They walked rather slowly, but it still didn't take long to get to room 355-H.

Barrett wasn't familiar with the recruit at the open door, "guarding" it only in the most perfunctory sense of the term, but he saw her lordly lieutenant's insignia and stepped aside so she and Abrams could enter. The room on the other side of it was the size of a small assembly hall, and they parked themselves against the wall, next to the door. About thirty people sat in chairs, facing a lectern in the front, where Saburo was coming to the end of the proceedings.

"—remember that. It's the one thing that will get you fired—" he snapped his fingers "—that fast."

He paused to let those words sink in, and his voice had that same flat effect Barrett had heard before when he was making what amounted to a threat. The menace lurking beneath the words was all the greater for the fact that it was given no verbal emphasis.

449

"You can ask questions about anything else with no repercussions. But where a fellow officer in the Mumps comes from—their genetic background, class origin, previous employment, anything having to do with their personal past—that's off limits. If someone wants to volunteer the information that's fine. But you don't ask. Speculate all you want, alone or with friends. Just. Don't. Ask."

He paused for another beat, then gestured toward Sandra Tuminello, whose uniform now sported a sergeant's stripes.

"Sergeant Tuminello will now administer the oath of office."

He waved for Tuminello to replace him behind the lectern, then moved down the central aisle toward Barrett and Abrams. Tuminello began intoning the oath as he waved them both back out into the corridor with him.

"Congratulations," he said, once they'd moved away from the door. "Daud tells me you did a great job on Old Terra."

"We didn't really do all that much," Abrams said.

"Sometimes not doing much is what it takes to do a good job. But that won't be true of your next assignment."

"Which is what?" Barrett asked.

"Patience." Saburo raised his hand. By now they'd reached the lift shafts, and he summoned a car. "I need to introduce you to some people."

✧ ✧ ✧

The room they finally followed him into was twenty-seven floors down. Size-wise, it fell between Saburo's office area and the much larger room they'd just left—a middling sized conference room, dominated by a big oval-shaped table surrounded by a dozen chairs, seven of which were occupied. Four of the people already there were women whom Barrett had never met. One was a boy, who looked to be just entering his teenage years, and one was an adult male. Barrett estimated that one of the women was well into what an earlier era had called "middle age," although it was always hard to tell with people and prolong. The other women, as well as the man, were quite a bit younger. Somewhere around Barrett's own age, or even younger.

There was one other woman at the table, whom Barrett knew already—Arianne McBryde.

Saburo took the chair at one end of the table, next to Arianne. He gestured for Barrett and Abrams to take whatever open seats they chose, and once everyone was seated, he clasped his hands and placed them on the table.

"I just gave a batch of new recruits my standard bloodcurdling speech promising to fire them in a heartbeat—probably
after having them drawn and quartered—if they committed the
cardinal sin of prying into the backgrounds of other Mumps."
He smiled a wide and sardonic smile. "Which prohibition I am
now about to violate myself, because the assignment you've all
volunteered for—well, all but Justine—" he raised one hand and
pointed to the older woman "—requires you to know each other's
background. So, here's my brief introduction."

He hadn't lowered the finger pointing at the older woman.

"Justine's last name is Jackson, and she's one of Jurgen Dusek's
aides. She'll be coordinating what you do with him, and, through
him, with all the seccy bosses in Mendel who need to be involved."

The finger shifted to the woman sitting next to Jackson.

"This is Cary Condor, and next to her is Stephanie Moriarity.
They were members of the seccy resistance prior to Tenth Fleet's
arrival, although neither was technically part of the Audubon
Ballroom."

Condor waggled her fingers.

"Think of us as Ballroom sympathizers and occasional aiders-
and-abettors," she said, and Saburo snorted before he pointed at
the boy.

"This is Hasrul, who still won't provide his last name. He's
a seccy from Lower Radomsko who provided Victor Cachat and
Thandi Palane with information and some other assistance after
their arrival on Mesa. He's agreed to keep doing that for us. For
those of you who may be familiar with Ante Diaspora detective
stories, you can think of him as the leader of our version of the
Baker Street Irregulars."

Lower Radomsko. Barrett had a bad feeling about where this
was headed. She was tempted to ask Saburo exactly when she
and Jake had "volunteered" for any assignment having to do with
the worst crime district on the planet. But she kept it to herself,
since she knew the only response would be the same sardonic
expression her dirty rotten bum of a boss still had on his face.

Saburo's finger moved on to the male adult and the redhaired
woman sitting next to him. The man was quite large; the woman
quite small.

"The big fellow is someone I've known for a long time. I
asked him to come help us here and he agreed. His name is

Supakrit—Ah, what surname did you pick when you dropped the 'X'? I forgot to ask."

"I just picked hers, after we got married." The man pointed with his thumb to the woman next to him. "It seemed the simplest way to go. So I'm now Supakrit Takahashi."

"That *should* be Takahashi Supakrit," the woman said. "But he's a stubborn bastard. I'm Ayako."

Despite her name and insistence that the surname should come first, Ayako didn't look like someone with East Asian ancestry. Except for the red hair, she looked like someone whose forerunners had lived in South America's Altiplano.

"Supakrit," Saburo continued, "was once a Ballroom striker—"

"A long, long time ago," Supakrit said with a smile.

"—before he became a lieutenant in the Royal Torch Marines, specializing in close quarters assault."

"Which is where he met me," Ayako said. "I was one of the Manpower slaves he and his people liberated from a slave ship."

She stuck out her tongue, displaying the Manpower genetic marker. The gesture had a defiant feel.

"Arianne McBryde is a former full citizen of Mesa, and a long-standing and prominent member of the Engagement," Saburo said. "She's been working closely with me and . . . some other people since we got here. She's become one of our top analysts. Finally—"

He nodded towards Barrett and Abrams.

"This is Lieutenant Kayla Barrett and Sergeant Jake Abrams. As you can see from their uniforms, they're both members of the Mesan Unified Magistral Police. And both of them were formally sergeants in the Mesan Internal Security Directorate."

Most of the people sitting at the table stiffened abruptly. Saburo swept them with a quick glance.

"Stand down, damn it." It came out in very close to an outright growl. "What's most important about them is that they both have my full trust and confidence."

After a moment, the postures eased—well, except for Hasrul's. *He* was eyeing the door as if estimating his chance of making a quick getaway.

"And I'll leave you to it." Saburo rose from the table. "The assignment—most of you already know this, and the rest of you have probably guessed by now—is to figure out how we're going to clean up Lower Radomsko. More than that: what sort of administration can we develop that would work there? It's the worst district, but it's not the only one that doesn't have much in the way of law and order—and that's only going to become more of a problem as the sixty percent of our population who used to be slaves start creating their own districts."

He looked around the room again.

"I'd like a proposed plan of action—first draft of one, anyway—on my desk no later than three days from now."

✧   ✧   ✧

Several hours later, Saburo's secretary ushered Arianne into his office. Saburo glanced at the time.

"Three-thirty," he said. "I wouldn't have thought you'd be finished for the day yet."

"No, they're still going strong." Arianne shook her head. "But for what they're discussing now, I'm not much use. And there's something...Well, we're both so busy we don't see much of each other these days, Saburo. And..."

She was clearly fumbling with something. Saburo got up and moved from his desk to the conversational nook he'd created in one corner.

"Have a seat," he said settling into one of the armchairs. "What's on your mind?"

Arianne settled into the facing armchair.

"I want...Can I ask you a personal question?"

He opened his hand by way of invitation.

"I can't promise I'll answer until I heard what it is, but you can certainly ask," he said, and she drew a deep breath. Then—

"When did Lara die?"

She almost blurted the words, and Saburo stared at her for a moment. Then he looked out the window next to him for several seconds.

"About two and a half years ago."

"How long were you together?" she asked, and his lips twisted in a wry smile.

"Less time than it's been since she died. She had quite an impact on me, starting with the way we met."

"Which was how?" Arianne cocked her head, her eyes intent.

"In the middle of a military operation, when I was still in the Ballroom. Lara and another Scrag—they were both in Thandi

Palane's Amazon unit—took the lead in breaking into the objective. I followed with some other Ballroom people, but by the time we got inside, it was all over. My only contribution was to intimidate the targets that were still alive and conscious by giving them the Ballroom tongue salute."

He stuck out his tongue to show the Manpower genetic marker.

"I didn't have much use for Scrags at the time—still don't, as a rule—but I complimented Lara on a job well done. She told me to stick out my tongue again. I did; she said she could deal with that, and asked me if I had a current girlfriend. I said I didn't, and she said—her exact words, I've never forgotten them—'You do now.' And then she announced that I was her new boyfriend because the one she'd had wasn't going to live out the day on account of she'd kill the swine if no one else did."

Arianne giggled. She tried not to—she really *tried*—but she couldn't help it.

"You're *kidding*. What did you say?" she asked, and he grinned.

"I didn't say a damned thing. I was too...What's the word? Discombobulated, I guess. She said I could have a little time to get used to the idea, but not too long. On account of she was horny. I thought she was crazy. But..." He shrugged. "It turned out she wasn't."

He frowned. Not angrily, just in puzzlement.

"Where are you going with this, Arianne?" he asked, and she drew another deep breath. A considerably deeper one.

"I asked about Lara because...I don't know. I felt a little like a vulture or something. I knew how much you cared for her. I just didn't know how much time you'd had to grieve."

She spent a few seconds looking out the same window.

"I'm discombobulated myself right now. I'm completely out of my depth, Saburo. Nothing in my life's experience has...has..."

She turned her head back and looked him directly in the eye.

"How does someone like me ask a former member of the Audubon Ballroom—top officer, in fact, except I don't think that's the right term—if you'd like to go on a date with me?"

"Uh."

The frown vanished. Saburo leaned back in his chair, hands gripping the armrests. His own expression was now blank.

"Uh..."

"Look, I'm not dumb," she said. "I'm very attracted to you,

but I know perfectly well that just because I feel that way doesn't mean the feeling is reciprocated." She shook her head. "If that's the case, just say so. I'm a big girl. You don't have to figure out how to wrap it in a sugar pill. Just—"

He waved his hand as if batting something away.

"That's not an issue, Arianne. That's really not an issue. The fact is, I've thought about it myself. But I just . . . put the thought aside."

The wry smile was back, and he shook his head.

"How does someone like *me* ask—?"

He broke off with a shrug, and Arianne nodded.

"The thing is, Saburo, I've never known anyone like you. But for the first time in my life, these past few months, I don't hate my home planet anymore. I can't say I'm proud of it—not yet, anyway—but I *am* pleased and proud with what we're doing, and I don't feel like my life is aimless. I want to deepen that as much as I can.

"Okay." She stood. "That's enough to get started. Let me know when you'd like to talk some more. Any time."

She headed for the door. Then stopped abruptly and turned.

"I really mean it: any time. My code is 56YH344, then 443. Yeah, I know it's primitive. My brain just doesn't run in those channels. Can you remember that?"

"56YH344, then 443. I have a good memory. I won't forget."

A moment later, she was gone.

The door closed behind her and Saburo got to his feet and went to the window. He stayed there for quite a while.

Hadcliffe Residential Tower
City of Mendal
Planet Mesa
Mesa System

THE DOORBELL CHIMED.

Arianne looked up from her tablet and glanced at the time. She'd found it a little harder than usual to concentrate on her reading, and she was a bit surprised to discover she'd been home for almost six hours.

The bell chimed again, and she set her tablet aside, climbed out of her chair, and headed for the door. When she reached it, though, she stopped and smiled.

"Use the code," she said loudly.

The door opened a second later, and her smile grew very wide as Saburo stepped through it.

"You do now," she said, and opened her arms.

✧   ✧   ✧

Arianne was already dressed and moving by the time Saburo woke up the next morning. She poked her head into the bedroom.

"You want some breakfast? The Robo chef makes a really good one—actually, a bunch of them. I was going to have scrambled eggs and bacon. What would you like?"

He sat up. "The eggs sound good. But I don't like bacon, so you can skip that."

Her eyes widened.

"You don't like *bacon*?"

"No, never have."

"Wow." She made a face. "So I had sex with an alien last night. Okay, I guess I can live with that." She headed back toward the kitchen. "On the bright side, we won't have to be concerned about reproductive issues."

456

October 1923 Post Diaspora

"I've discovered that simply knowing there's a 'cat 'getting inside their heads' tends to rattle people into giving away a lot more than they ever would have under other circumstances."

—Damien Harahap,
Solarian League Gendarmerie, ret.

Joint Intelligence Sharing and Distribution Command Center
Smith Tower
City of Old Chicago
Old Earth
Sol System

SIMEON GADDIS LOOKED UP FROM HIS CONVERSATION WITH ANTON Zilwicki as the Gendarmerie sergeant opened the conference room door.

"Admiral Robbins is here, Sir," she announced, and Gaddis nodded.

"Well, send her in, Sergeant!" he replied, and stood as the sturdily built naval officer stepped through the door, followed by two men and a woman in the green tunics and brown trousers of the Royal Torch Marines.

"Admiral," he said in greeting.

"Brigadier."

Robbins crossed to her host and extended her hand. Technically, she was senior to the other officer, but everyone knew Simeon Gaddis should have been at least a major general. In fact, he carried that as an acting rank now, as the Gendarmerie's commanding officer (although he still preferred to be addressed as "Brigadier"), and it would be made permanent sometime soon. All official promotions remained frozen until the new Constitution was ratified and a permanent government was seated, at which time Gaddis would receive the rank he so amply deserved.

Besides, no matter who was technically senior, this was effectively his operation. Well, his and that of his—and her, for that matter—rather unlikely allies. Speaking of which—

"Allow me to introduce Queen Berry's representatives." She

459

turned to the trio of Torches with a slightly wicked smile. "This is Colonel X, Captain Sharpe, and Captain X."

"I see." Gaddis's lips twitched.

"It's even worse than Liz is implying, Brigadier," Colonel X said, reaching out to shake hands in turn. "If we'd realized we'd be dealing with a batch of Solarians, Lucia here"—the tall, powerfully built colonel indicated the petite, red-haired female captain on his right "—would have hung onto her Ballroom surname. Then we'd *all* have been 'X's."

"I have to admit it's crossed my mind that it has to be a bit confusing," Gaddis said as he gripped the colonel's hand.

"That's the reason most of us use our first names, even when we hang a rank title in front of it," the Torch acknowledged. "Probably a leftover from our less reputable Ballroom days, too. My first name is Ronglu, by the way."

His eyes met Gaddis's, but the brigadier's expression never even flickered.

"I'm sure your people and mine have crossed swords more than once, Colonel," he said. "That's what happens when someone kills Solarian citizens . . . even the ones who obviously had it coming. I can't say I was one of the Ballroom's greatest admirers, but I never thought you were a vicious pack of rabid murderers. It wasn't something those bastards like MacArtney wanted to hear, but the Gendarmerie always knew we could rely on *sanctioned* Ballroom hits to be carefully targeted, with as little collateral damage as possible."

He did not, Ronglu observed, mention that a Ballroom striker named Ronglu X had graced the Solarian Gendarmerie's "most wanted" list for almost twenty years prior to the creation of the Kingdom of Torch.

"I won't pretend that was out of the goodness of our hearts, Brigadier," he said. "But it's always a good thing when smart tactics and the right thing to do can reinforce each other."

"Trust me." Gaddis grimaced. "Too many gendarmes out in the Protectorates were involved in crap almost as bloody as anything the Ballroom ever did, for reasons a hell of a lot worse."

Ronglu nodded, then released Gaddis's hand and gestured at his fellow Torches.

"Captain Sharpe can probably get along with your using her surname, if you're more comfortable with that. But I imagine you'll probably want to call Captain X by his first name—Nganga."

"Believe me, if you're comfortable with that, *we're* comfortable with it," Gaddis said, shaking hands with both captains in turn.

At 185 centimeters, even Ronglu was ten centimeters shorter than the brigadier. *Most* people were shorter than Simeon Gaddis, actually. But Lucia Sharpe had obviously been designed as a pleasure slave. She was petite, slender, and barely four centimeters taller than Natsuko Okiku. That made her the next best thing to forty centimeters shorter than Gaddis, and her eyes were so dark they looked black. No, they *were* black, he realized as he got a better look at them. So black the pupils were literally indistinguishable from the irises, which created a stark contrast with her flame-red hair. One her Manpower designers had clearly intended her to have.

Nganga X was taller than she was, about midway between her and Ronglu, with fair hair and green eyes. But if his coloring was less exotic than Sharpe's, his modified genotype was at least equally obvious as he and Gaddis shook hands. He was the first person Gaddis had ever met with two opposable thumbs on each hand. It made shaking hands an interesting experience.

"I understand you've mislaid one of my majors, Admiral?" the brigadier said now as he released Nganga's hand and waved the newcomers towards the chairs around the conference table at the center of the room.

"I wouldn't say I'd *mislaid* him, exactly." Robbins shook her head. "It's more a case of his falling into bad company."

"That's one way to describe Bryce, Ma'am," Daud al-Fanudahi said.

"That was my impression," Robbins agreed, and smiled at Lieutenant Colonel Weng. "On the other hand, I didn't feel entirely comfortable sending Commodore Rabellini off with Agent Cachat—and Major Tarkovsky, for that matter—without at least a little adult supervision from the Gendarmerie."

"I'm not certain the word 'adult' belongs in the same sentence with Jerzy Scarlatti. Or Bryce Tarkovsky," Weng Zhing-hwan said dryly.

"Probably not," Robbins acknowledged as she took the chair at the foot of the table, facing Gaddis down its length. The three Torches sat to her left, across from the other members of Operation Rat Catcher's planners.

"Admiral, Colonel Ronglu," Gaddis said after everyone was

seated, "allow me to introduce you and your team to the other participants in our current endeavor. Colonel Weng is the new CO of the Gendarmerie's Intelligence Command. That just came through last week, in fact. Colonel Okiku and Captain al-Fanudahi are part of the team Director Gannon and I very quietly sent to Mesa to liaise with the Grand Alliance's investigation of what they call the Alignment and we've just been calling the 'Other Guys.' Mr. Harahap, recently retired from the Gendarmerie, and Mr. Graham, of the Seraphim System, are part of that same joint investigation, and the Star Empire has decided to lend them to us for our current endeavor. And that brings us to Captain Zilwicki, who's currently wearing rather more hats than the rest of us. As I understand it, he represents the Provisional Government of Mesa, the Grand Alliance in general and Empress Elizabeth in particular, the Anti-Slavery League, and—last but not least—your own Kingdom of Torch and the Audubon Ballroom, although we don't talk about that last one very much."

"Well, if you're going to kill as many birds as possible with a single stone, you might as well make it a hefty one." Ronglu smiled and nodded. "Good to see you, Anton."

"And you," Zilwicki rumbled back. "All three of you, actually. Even Lucia."

"You only pick on me because I'm cute," Lucia said.

"No, I pick on you because you get along entirely too well with Cathy."

"I notice you only say that when she's not around."

"Do I *look* stupid, woman?"

"Well, now that you bring it up . . ."

She let her voice trail off, and Gaddis cleared his throat. He'd suspected that herding this particular batch of cats was likely to prove challenging.

"Sorry, Brigadier."

Zilwicki didn't actually *sound* all that sorry, and Gaddis's lips twitched, but he only shook his head.

"A good, comfortable working relationship is a thing to be treasured, Anton. On the other hand, we really do need to get this up and moving. At least from the planning end. Before we dive too deeply into the weeds, though, let me sketch out the parameters for all involved as we see them right now.

"First and foremost, Prime Minister Yon has authorized Rat

Catcher. Attorney General Rorendaal and Admiral Kingsford have tasked me to plan the operation. Admiral Robbins will command the Navy side of Rat Catcher, and Colonel Okiku will be my deputy for the Gendarmerie. Colonel Weng and Captain Zilwicki will coordinate intelligence from all of the star nations and alliances—the *many* star nations and alliances—involved in making this work. If it becomes necessary to liaise with any independent star nations, Foreign Minister Abadjieva will provide us with representatives from her ministry. We don't anticipate that happening at this time, but it's a possibility we may have to bear in mind. And, I should also point out, Rat Catcher has been cleared with the Grand Alliance, which has formally signed off on the operation but agrees that since its targets are located almost entirely in Solarian space, the League Navy and Gendarmerie are the proper agencies to execute it."

He paused, looking around the conference table, and nodded in satisfaction at the serious expressions that looked back at him.

"Despite the multinational aspects of this operation," he continued after a moment, "this is primarily a domestic *police* operation. It is obviously related to but separate from the Navy's operations directed solely at taking out the garbage where the slave trade and the entire institution of genetic slavery are concerned. In addition, since one of our primary objectives is to secure intelligence and as many detailed records as possible, we need to stay as far under the radar as we can until we pounce. Officially, the League wants any records of Jessyk's involvement with Manpower as part of our takedown of the slavery infrastructure and because any participation by Jessyk in the transport of slaves was a criminal act for which the corporation can be legally charged. *Un*officially, we want them because we hope they'll lead us closer to the Other Guys and, especially, provide proof that they at least exist. In either case, if they see us coming, those records are certain to be destroyed, and we don't want that to happen.

"Anton, Daud, and I have already done some preliminary work in that regard, and we'll be sharing our thoughts with you to get your input, Admiral. Right now, what we're looking at is assembling Gendarmerie strike forces for each of our target systems. Thanks to the war against the GA, we still have a lot of idled freighters, and Treasury Minister Holderbaum has authorized us to requisition as many of them as we need. We plan to load our strike forces aboard them to insert our people into the target star systems without alerting anyone—and that includes local system governments or our own gendarmes—that we're en route. The Navy will provide each freighter with a light escort and a Marine transport with backup manpower, but they won't cross the hyper wall into our target star systems unless we need the additional firepower. It doesn't seem likely that we will, but it's always better to have a bigger stick than you need rather than the reverse.

"We'll have all of the needed paperwork and authorization, but for this to work, we'll have to execute the equivalent of 'no-knock' warrants. And, frankly, even so, we're likely to lose a lot of the records we're after. On the other hand, we're *un*likely to lose very many of the *people* we're after."

Colonel Weng raised one hand, and Gaddis nodded to her.

"People are better than nothing, Sir," she said. "If they *are* working for the Other Guys, a lot of them are likely to drop dead when we take them into custody, though."

"Understood." Gaddis grimaced. "We've come to the conclusion—admittedly, it may represent a little wishful thinking on our part—that they can't program *everybody* to die on cue. If this relationship's been around as long as the Mesan records indicate it has, there has to be at least some leakage between the people who actually know *why* things happen and the ones who only know *what* things happen. We can do a lot with enough bits and pieces like that."

"I agree, Sir. I'd really rather have the raw data, though. Assuming the bad guys keep accurate records, the data's a lot less likely to lie to us."

"That's a given, Zhing-hwan," Gaddis acknowledged. "In this instance, though, we'll have certain advantages, including one that was only confirmed yesterday. Perhaps you'd care to expand upon that for the benefit of the group at large, Mr. Harahap?"

"Of course, Sir," Harahap acknowledged, then looked across the table at Robbins and the Torches as he rubbed the ears of the treecat sitting upright in a human-style chair beside him. "As Brigadier Gaddis mentioned earlier—and as Colonel Weng already knows—I spent many years in the Gendarmerie," he told the newcomers. "I've been through some career changes recently, however, which is how I ended up in the service of the Star Empire. And adopted by Fire Watch here."

The treecat buzzed an undeniably complacent purr and pushed his head against the caressing palm.

"Along the way, I've learned some interesting things about the 'cats," Harahap continued. "Among other things, I learned that, despite any wild rumors to the contrary, they are *not* mind readers. They are, however, highly intelligent. Their minds don't work quite the way human minds do, but that doesn't mean they aren't just as smart as we are, and they've recently acquired the ability to communicate fluently with us. And while they can't read minds, they *can* read emotions. Which means they can tell when someone is lying. Since we're all going to be good, law-abiding representatives of the Solarian League, there are limits to how hard we could sweat anyone we took into custody," his tone added an unspoken *this time, at least,* his audience noticed. "But I've discovered that simply knowing there's a 'cat 'getting inside their heads' tends to rattle people into giving away a lot more than they ever would have under other circumstances. And the treecats and the Star Empire have agreed to provide us with at least one 'cat-human team for each of our strike forces."

"That's true," Zilwicki rumbled. "And, speaking as a Manticoran, I would very, very strongly urge those strike forces to take good care of the 'cats. Trust me. Letting something unfortunate happen to one of them would *not* be a good thing for Solarian-Manticoran relations."

"That's probably fair," Harahap agreed. "On the other hand, treecats are very...direct souls. They're likely to want to get closer to the sharp end than might strictly be good for them, and the 'cats back home understand that. And, of course, they'll all be armed themselves."

"I've worked with 'cats back on Torch," Captain Lucia said. "Is it true Duchess Harrington's had pulsers made for them?"

Fire Watch raised his right true-hand, thumb and third finger spread. He nodded it up and down, and Lucia chuckled.

"Outstanding!"

"The point," Gaddis said, "is that we'll have the treecats available to at least sort through any Jessyk personnel we get our hands on. I don't anticipate the need for them to go storming in pulsers blazing, however. And—" he bent a stern gaze on Fire Watch "—I'd better not *hear* about anything like that, either."

The treecat looked back at him with the innocent expression of one in whose mouth celery would not melt.

"Now," the brigadier continued, turning back to the two-foots around the table, "that's the basic profile of the operation. The actual targets and the order in which we go after them will depend on the data Mesa captured in the Jessyk takedown, but I understand our friends from Congo have some additional information that will bear on our target selection?"

"We do," Ronglu said. "But I think we should probably let Anton tell us which systems he thinks should come first on the list."

"There are about twenty-five total locations we need to hit," Zilwicki said. "Most of them are fairly minor facilities, by Jessyk's standards, and we're unlikely to need an enormous amount of manpower to take those down. Eight of them are big enough to require serious strike forces, however. Two of those are far enough out into the Verge that we're planning on delegating them to the Grand Alliance. The other six are actually located in the Core, however. In fact, all of them are within a hundred and fifty light-years of Sol, and, frankly, those are the ones we need to hit first. Given the distance between star systems—it's a two-month voyage from Sol, one way, to some of them for a freighter—we don't have to worry about perfect synchronization, but we do need to hit them all in the same fairly tight window of time.

"In order of proximity to Sol, we're talking about Danube, Warner, Dickerson, Sadako, Van Gogh, and Rondeau. From the Jessyk records, Dickerson is especially important, given how deeply Technodyne seems to have been in bed with the Alignment."

"That all sounds reasonable from where we sit," Ronglu said. "For that matter, except for Sadako, all of them were already on the Ballroom's list because of their connection to Manpower and the trade. And I understand why you're especially interested in Dickerson and the Yildun connection. But I think you might want to move Warner up to a higher priority, as well."

"Really?" Zilwicki cocked his head. "Why?"

"Because you're looking for the Alignment, and there's something wonky about Warner," Captain Nganga said. "We don't know exactly what or why, but Manpower's moved a hell of a lot of Manpower 'special cargo' through that system over the years."

"How much is 'a hell of a lot,' Nganga?" Zilwicki asked.

"In the last ten or twenty T-years?" Nganga shrugged. "Not much at all. It was still an active route, right up to when the

GA hit Mesa, but by that time it was a lot less active than most of the other routes. Probably no more than a slaver a T-year or so, and most of those were headed for a handful of really shady Solly transstellars' operations in the Fringe. But going back longer than that? Lucia here pulled our records on every known slave ship and its history when Admiral Robbins turned up in Congo, and when we got here and found out about the possibility of a direct link to the Alignment—and especially about those wild-ass theories about secret bases built up centuries ago—she did a deep dive into the older ones. And guess what? Between 1681 and 1707, Jessyk sent a lot of known slave ships through Warner. We obviously can't confirm that there were slaves aboard them every time they went through, but we're talking about some of the bigger slavers. The kind that can carry upwards of three or four thousand slaves in a single run. According to the number of trips we've been able to confirm, they made at least fifty-three runs through Warner between 1681 and 1707, and there damned well may have been more. Maybe even a *lot* more. That's *at least* somewhere between a hundred and sixty thousand and a quarter million slaves in a single twenty-six T-year span, and there weren't one hell of a lot of settled star systems out that way two hundred and fifty T-years ago. Certainly not ones in which that many slaves could have been sold without leaving one hell of a footprint. But despite that, we haven't been able to account for where a single one of them ultimately ended up. After 1707, the tempo started tapering off pretty abruptly, and by 1730 or so, we were down to no more than a slaver or so a year passing through Warner."

Everyone on the other side of the table was gazing at him very intently, and he shrugged.

"If somebody who believed in genetic slavery was involved in building a secret base somewhere, and if they needed an initial labor force really quickly, until they could build up a self-sustaining population of workers, where do *you* think they'd get it?"

Chamber of Stars
Old Chicago
Old Terra
Solar System

CATHY MONTAIGNE SIPPED MORE BEER, SET THE GLASS ON THE small side table beside her armchair in the observation room, and leaned back to watch the delegates to the Constitutional Convention. At the moment, the wrangling involved a point of order which Montaigne didn't really understand because: a) it was obscure; b) the League didn't follow the exact same rules of order that the Manticoran Parliament followed—most such rules of order were the descendants of someone named Robert, but two millennia of evolution had produced a lot of variations—and c) she didn't really care anyway (see point "a").

Besides, it was all an illusion. She wasn't actually gazing down at the proceedings taking place in the League's majestic legislative chamber. The real Chamber of Stars—the one made of molecules—was one hundred twenty-six meters above her head. More precisely, it was one hundred twenty meters above the elevation of her head, because it was also offset horizontally six hundred meters to the southwest. For security reasons, the area directly below the Chamber was reserved for government officials.

She was underground. What she was actually looking "down" at was the virtual version of the structure, the one composed entirely of electrons. (Maybe some hadrons, too; Montaigne's grasp of physics got fuzzy at the edges.) When the Chamber of Stars was designed and built, many centuries earlier, the architects' concerns had been more aesthetic than practical. And it clearly hadn't occurred to them that people liked to come and personally visit the places where their governments make decisions.

Unfortunately, the Chamber couldn't be easily expanded once construction was finished because of its geometric design. Under considerable pressure from the public (and especially politicians), the architects and builders did grudgingly add a ring of gallery boxes above the uppermost fourteenth ring of delegate seating, but that was nowhere near enough to accommodate the crowds of tourists that soon began to visit the capitol.

So, eventually, the subterranean accommodations were added. That didn't satisfy the purists and snobs, but it suited the great majority of visitors just fine. People had become accustomed to an existence that was to a considerable degree virtual, rather than "real," even before the Diaspora got underway.

Montaigne preferred it this way, herself. She occasionally observed the proceedings from the vantage point of one of the larger delegations' boxes on the Chamber's seating rings. Guests were sometimes invited by one delegation or another. But those boxes tended to be crowded, there was often little in the way of privacy, and even less in the way of ease and comfort to hold quiet discussions—which was usually the reason she was there to begin with.

"Down in the basement," as it was called, the practical realities were much superior. She could use the public accommodations, which were free on a first-come, first-served basis, or she could watch the proceedings in a private lounge as spacious and comfortable as she chose to rent or lease, which gave her as much privacy as she needed.

She normally attended in the quite sizable lounge leased by the Anti-Slavery League. But, given that today's discussions were mostly focused on issues of specific concern to the Star Empire, the lounge in which she currently resided was the one which had been reserved by the Manticoran government.

"So, how are things going?" McCauley Sinclair—sometimes called "Mack the Knife"—was a short fellow, who'd arrived in the lounge no more than ten minutes ago. He was also one of the central leaders of the Star Empire's Liberal Party.

"Cathy's grouchy." Monica Acevski, seated to Montaigne's right, had very dark hair, cut rather short, a very light complexion, and blue gray eyes. She was about as slender as Montaigne and just about the same height. Had they all been standing, Sinclair would have been the shortest person in the room by a good fifteen centimeters.

He really was very short. But no one had called McCauley Sinclair a "shrimp" since he was eleven years old. He'd been suspended from school for a week after the ensuing fight. It had taken longer than that for the bruises to fade on the face and person of the incautious lad who had issued the taunt.

"What she grouchy about now, Monica?" he asked, and Montaigne sat up indignantly.

"What do you mean by 'now,' damn it?" she demanded.

"Face it, Cathy," Akanyang Moseki, the fourth and last person in the lounge, said. He'd just finished pouring himself a drink at the well-stocked wet bar and was returning to his own seat. "You get indignant pretty regularly."

He slid into his seat.

"In answer to your question, McCauley, she's irritated because people from some of the Shell systems—"

"Some?" Montaigne interrupted. "How about 'at least a dozen'?"

"Like I said—some—which is what 'at least a dozen' out of several hundred systems constitute." Moseki swallowed a fair portion of his glass's contents. "Anyway, they keep approaching Cathy privately to see if there's any possibility the Grand Alliance—or just the Star Empire—might be willing to enter a defensive alliance with them."

"Ah." Sinclair nodded. "Let me guess. A very narrowly defined and highly contingent defensive alliance. Call it an insurance policy in the event that the reconstruction of the Solarian League goes pear-shaped."

"Exactly." Moseki nodded. "They're a wee bit nervous. For which you can hardly blame them, given the history of the League."

"So why the indignation, Cathy?" Sinclair looked at her. "It's hardly surprising. In fact, it was predictable. If you want to feel sorry for someone, feel sorry for our compatriots who do hold power. They're getting hit up on the same subject constantly."

He looked around the lounge.

"Speaking of which, where are they? We Liberals don't usually have this lounge all to ourselves."

"They're meeting with the delegation from Lima," Moseki said. "They should be back shortly."

"Of course it's predictable," Montaigne said. "But why are they asking *me*? As I keep telling them, I'm not in the Government. Parliament, yes; Cabinet, no. Enough of these idiots have parliamentary governments of their own that they damned well ought to understand the distinction!"

"They do. And so what?" Sinclair looked at her quizzically. "You're not in the Grantville Government, so, it's true you have no *formal* position in it. You are, however, the Opposition Leader, since we're the only party—well, the only legitimate party—that isn't currently part of the government. Which means you're almost always brought into the discussion when something important happens or is under consideration."

Montaigne's expression acquired what might be called a pickled look.

"Fine. I'm consulted. I'm still not the one who makes policy."

"No, not now," he conceded. "But you are someone whose opinions are taken into consideration—quite seriously—when policy is decided upon, and they make sure they keep you updated on whatever policy is. For that matter, it's entirely possible that someday you'll *be* the Government."

Montaigne's expression got still more pickled, and Sinclair glanced at Acevski and Moseki.

"Is she *still* pretending she'll always be a member of the Opposition?"

"Pretty much," Acevski said. "She's got no excuse, either. I was there—right there in the conference room of the hotel, no more than two kilometers from here—when Web Du Havel gave her a brilliant hour-long exposition on the political dynamics of a democratic society. Not that long ago, either."

"It was all theory and conjecture," Montaigne protested, and Sinclair made a sound somewhere between a snort of derision and a sigh of exasperation.

"Yeah—and all of it supported by nothing more than a mere two millennia of experience," he said. "If I remember right, it's what Du Havel calls the flatness problem in political science. Why do all democratic societies maintain a close equilibrium of political viewpoints unless some sort of powerful force deforms the situation?"

"Like the domination of the League's bureaucracy," Acevski put in. "That may have taken almost a millennium to develop, and it damned well resulted in what no honest observer could call a 'democratic' government, at least at the Federal level. I imagine you could call that a 'powerful force.' But Du Havel's right: in the absence of something like that, the natural pattern *is* for major political parties to come in and out of power—swap power, you can call it—almost like a metronome. A sixty percent majority is considered a landslide, and more than that is extremely rare. More than two thirds is almost unheard of. The pattern can be frozen for a bit, usually by a war or some other major crisis, but once the crisis is over, the balance gets restored. In a lot of ways, it's how democratic government breathes."

She, Sinclair, and Moseki all bestowed a gaze of reproof upon Montaigne. There was a lot of affection in it, but it was still a gaze of reproof.

"Cathy, face it," Moseki said. "Whether you like it or not, sooner or later the electorate of the Star Empire's going to decide they've had enough of the current government, especially since peacetime conditions seem at hand. And when that happens, there's only one realistic alternative, given the implosion of both the Progressives and the Conservatives. That's us—the Liberal Party."

"Bullshit," Montaigne replied. Moseki blinked, then opened her mouth again, but Montaigne continued before she could interrupt.

"Bullshit I said, and bullshit I meant. Oh, not Web's analysis of how the process works. I'm way too smart to argue with him about that. But it's not going to happen anytime soon in Manticore, and I expect he knows that as well as I do. Hell, people! Aside from the half dozen peers the Conservatives still have, and the even smaller number of Old Liberal peers who refused to sign on with us, we're the only party that's *not* part of the Grantville Government. And the only reason *we* aren't is because I insisted that there had to be an Opposition willing and able to speak up to remind Willie Alexander that he, too, is mortal."

She more than half-glared at her companions, and they were forced to nod in agreement. That was, indeed, the only reason the Liberals hadn't joined the coalition government William Alexander, Baron Grantville, had formed after the ignominious collapse of the disastrous High Ridge Government, barely three T-years ago. And the truth was, that Grantville had formed his coalition only because he'd chosen to, as a statement of national unity in the wake of High Ridge's corruption, ambition, and rank stupidity. In fact, his own Centrists held an outright majority of almost eighty percent in the House of Commons and a twenty-seven-seat majority in the Lords. Given that the seats the Centrist *didn't* hold were split between four other parties, that the Crown Loyalists—who were essentially an auxiliary wing of the Centrists—held another eleven seats in the Lords, and that Montaigne's Liberals—as distinct from the handful of Old Liberals who'd been unable to stomach Montaigne's brand of politics, despite their own willingness to wallow in the public trough along with High Ridge—held sixty percent of the Commons seats Grantville's supporters didn't...

The Centrists held an overwhelmingly dominant position. Not only could they have governed without any other party, had they chosen to, but they had overseen the successful recovery from High Ridge's disastrous military policies; overseen the annexation of the Talbott Sector and the creation of the Star *Empire* of Manticore as an expansion of the old Star Kingdom; weathered the Yawata Strike; ended the decades-long war with the Republic of Haven; formed the Grand Alliance *alongside* the Republic of Haven; uncovered the existence of the Mesan Alignment and its covert manipulation of the entire human-settled galaxy; conquered the Mesa System and dealt genetic slavery its deathblow; and, as a sort of encore, defeated the Solarian League, the largest, wealthiest, and most powerful star nation ever to exist, so utterly and completely that the Grand Alliance's capital ships were still in orbit around Old Terra...and the League's millennia old constitution was in the process of a complete rewrite.

The other members of Grantville's "coalition" had strongly supported his policies—for that matter, so had Montaigne's Liberals—and rightly shared in the victor's glow at the end of the day. With that chain of successes to its credit, however, the Centrist Party's hold on political power seemed destined to last for quite a while.

"Does anybody really think there's a chance in hell that Grantville's going to lose his majority anytime soon?" Montaigne demanded, half-glaring at the others.

"Well...no," Sinclair said finally. "It's going to happen *eventually*, though. Du Havel's right about that, and you know he is."

"Fine." If she'd been standing and wearing an old-fashioned gown, Montaigne would have flounced at him. "Eventually. Fifteen, twenty T-years from now. Maybe. If he gets a sudden attack of the stupids and manages to screw some pooch I can't even imagine right now."

"Okay, twenty T-years from now," Acevski said. "It's still going to happen. And since we *are* the Opposition, and since you *are* regularly briefed by the Government as the Constitution requires, when 'eventually' gets here, guess who's going to become prime minister."

"This is all speculation," Montaigne shot back, although the pickled look was back. "And even if it happens, that doesn't mean *I'm* the one who becomes prime minister. I may be the official Opposition Leader right now, but I'm only *one* of our party's leadership cadre. All of *you* are in that group, too, Monica, and I've always thought—I think all of us do—that you're much more suited for that post than I am. For the sake of all that is or isn't holy, the last time *I* held an executive position was—was—

"I can't remember when it was! Maybe never!"

She threw up her hands, but Acevski shook her head.

"Hair-splitting, Cathy. Oh, I'll grant you that you haven't held an official executive position in the Government. You have a staff, you have an official role as a privileged advisor to the Government, and while I realize that you delegate every single thing you possibly can to someone else, you are also—officially—the executive head of our party. So, I'm not so sure that 'I never held an executive position' argument is going to hold up.

"Now, I admit that I think I'd make a—well, 'better' isn't the right adjective, but certainly a more *proficient* prime minister than you. So would Akanyang and two or three others back home on Manticore. But that's not what the Liberal Party needs when it comes time for someone to replace the current regime in Landing. What we need is the leader who restored *integrity* to the Party. Who created and led the Opposition that can ultimately provide the alternative Web's 'power-swap' metronome requires, when the tick comes due. And he's right about that, you know. There *has* to be an alternative to the party or group of parties currently in power, or else we lose the ability to accommodate that inevitable—and natural—swing that's fundamental to representative government. In a very real sense, that's our *job*—our function—and when it finally comes time for us to do that job, the only possible choice for prime minister will be the person who made it possible for us to do it.

"You."

Montaigne looked from Acevski to the two men sharing the lounge with them, and saw agreement looking back at her.

"Don't *worry* so much, Cathy!" Sinclair told her with a grin. "Like you say, it's going to be years before Willie screws up badly enough to require replacement. I mean, personally, I'm counting the days, but I'm just as happy we all have prolong, given how many of them I'll have to count. That said, though, we really do need to formalize the Shadow Cabinet when we get back to Manticore, and there's no way in God's universe that anyone is letting you off the hook, Madam Shadow Prime Minister."

Montaigne's shudder was not entirely assumed.

"Mack's right," Moseki said encouragingly. "But you're right about how long it's going to take. And here's another bright side you can look on."

His grin was even wider than Sinclair's. "Given your natural ineptitude for the position of prime minister, you're bound to fumble something within a couple of years badly enough to get voted out of office. But by then, you'll have completed resurrecting the Liberals as a legitimate governing party."

"Thank you very much for that vote of confidence," Montaigne said sourly.

The lounge door opened and three people came through it.

"So, how'd the meeting go?" Moseki asked in greeting. "Or is it 'need to know' only?"

"Hardly that," the woman in the lead replied. Her name was Janet Bradford, and she was the Foreign Ministry's Deputy Assistant Secretary for Political-Military Affairs, Foreign Secretary Carmichael's senior delegate to the Constitutional Convention. "Ask James," she continued as she made a beeline for the bar. "I need a drink."

"No, it's not 'need to know,'" James Gutierrez told Moseki with a smile. "They just wanted to make sure the Grand Alliance wouldn't get twitchy at the idea that they're pushing to create a new major branch of government for the League."

"Ah," Sinclair said. "Are they still calling it by that weird name, James?"

"Ombudsman?" Gutierrez asked, and Sinclair nodded. "I admit it's weird sounding, at least to us. Derives from old Swedish, I think. But, no, they've dropped that one in favor of either General Inspectorate or the Office of the General Inspector. No matter what they may wind up with, the idea's to create a branch of government whose responsibility is to investigate complaints about misbehavior or corruption by the executive or legislative branches by citizens or under bodies of government."

"Not the judiciary?" Acevski asked. "I'd think—"

"Oh, now, that's where it gets interesting, Monica!" Janice Kolisnychenko, the third person who'd just entered the lounge laughed aloud. "So far as we can see, any delegate who has any connection to the judiciary branch is adamantly opposed to allowing general inspectors—ombudsmen, tooth fairies, anybody—to have the power to investigate judges, much less discipline them."

"Well, sure!" Acevski agreed with a laugh of her own.

"I think it's a good idea, myself," Cathy said. "There's simply no way the day-to-day operations of a polity as huge as the Solarian League—even if it loses half its systems, which it won't—can be effectively overseen by a legislative branch. And the judiciary can't, either, because in the nature of things, the wheels of justice turn way too slowly. And letting the executive branch supervise *and* regulate itself is a recipe for disaster. Give it a few centuries, and you've got the Mandarins running the show again."

By the time she'd finished, the three representatives of the Grantville Government had found seats of their own.

"Well, I can see that," Acevski acknowledged. "But at the same time, I don't see why it has to be an entirely separate branch. I think *it's* going to need some supervision of its own to keep it from turning into the tail that wags the dog. So if it was placed inside the judicial branch, for instance, but the *legislative* branch named its members and their tenures were limited to no more than—"

The discussion waxed vigorous, and McAuley Sinclair watched, saying very little himself. Montaigne, on the other hand, showed no hesitation about expressing her own opinions. In fact, Bradford and the others deliberately invited them. Most of them were quite well thought out, too, whether the Star Empire's official delegates entirely agreed with them or not.

Sinclair smiled quietly and bestowed a silent blessing on the recognized leader of his party. Montaigne had faults, like anyone, but she'd been able to restore the unofficial but essential ingredient to the healthy functioning of democracies. Manticore's political parties—those that mattered, anyway—were back to being opponents, not enemies. Most of the time, they got along reasonably well, and they could usually unite around a common cause when they really needed to.

He did have to suppress another grin, though. When the time came, as it inevitably would—unless Montaigne fell seriously ill or had a bad accident of some kind—they'd have to drag her kicking and screaming to Mount Royal Palace to accept Empress Elizabeth's request that she form a new government.

But, as Montaigne herself had pointed out, that was a problem for the future. Right now, they had to do what they could to help most of humanity get back on a sound political footing of its own.

Lower Radomsko District
City of Mendel
Planet Mesa
Mesa System

"IT'S A REAL WARREN IN THERE, SABURO," ARIANNE SAID, STUDY-ing the screens in front of her. "We've been able to infiltrate surveillance into less than forty percent of the corridors." She tried to control the anxiety in her voice, but she had a feeling she hadn't succeeded.

Not fully, for sure.

"Don't worry about it," Saburo's voice said over her earbud. "What we can see inside the gang's hideaways is less important than what *they* can see of us coming toward them."

That makes no sense at all! Arianne managed to not blurt out that exasperated thought.

"This isn't a military operation, Arianne. We're dealing with gangsters, not soldiers. Once they realize what we're bringing down on them, most of them will surrender without a fight. Probably not all of them—Marković almost certainly won't, and some of his closest aides won't either. But that'll just be a mop-ping up operation."

Again, she had to figuratively bite her tongue. *"And when have you ever seen a mop?"* was what she wanted to ask him.

She knew what a mop was. Like brooms, they were still in existence as low-tech substitutes for proper cleaning bots, although she'd never personally used one. Not that either of them had anything at all to do with what was about to happen.

The here-and-now translation of the ancient term "mopping up operation" was that Saburo was about to wander into a maze in Mendel's most crime-ridden and violent district, in the hope

478

that he could spot and shoot psychopaths who'd been murdering people since they were toddlers—well, not quite that young—before *they* shot *him*.

"You're the Chief of the whole damn Mesan Unified Magistral Police," she muttered to herself. "Which connotation of the word 'delegate' do you fail to understand?"

But, he wouldn't. Delegate, that was. Maybe in the future he would. But this was the Mumps' first major assault operation—the raid on Jessyk's secret headquarters didn't count—and Saburo insisted on leading it himself.

Speaking of ancient expressions, she wondered how far back *stomach tied in knots* went. *Arianne* was in no danger—the command center gave her total access to the Mumps' surveillance and command channels without ever venturing into the field—but Saburo was out there with no protection other than body armor. Sure, it was good body armor. Arianne knew exactly how the stuff was made, and what it was made of. But in the race between weapons and armor, weapons had a nasty way of coming out ahead.

❖   ❖   ❖

"Yeah, so what?" Branko Marković demanded.

The big gang leader stood on the stage at the front of what had been a school auditorium before the Radomsko Diabły had appropriated the Nadzieja Borowiecka Secondary School as its headquarters. It hadn't been much of a school, but it had been outfitted with security cameras, some of which even still worked, and he hefted a military-grade pulse rifle as he squinted at the screen that showed the approach corridor.

"We chewed up the Misties and Safeties, didn't we?" he snarled. "That's all these sorry-ass Mumps are—except by now half of them don't even have *that* much experience in a real fight."

Adam Zhang stood at the back of the auditorium, where Marković couldn't see him, and looked at the woman standing beside him. He shook his head; she rolled her eyes. Celeste Bianchi was a screwball in a lot of ways—Zhang had once made the mistake of getting sexually involved with her—but she wasn't stupid. She knew as well as he did how ridiculous the gang leader's braggadocio was.

First, it wasn't true that *they* had "chewed up the Misties and Safeties." There'd been very little fighting in Lower Radomsko during the seccy insurrection, because the Mesan authorities had concentrated on the really powerful bosses in districts like Neue Rostock and Hancock. But leaving that aside—

A woman standing near the stage verbalized what Zhang was worried about.

"Boss, some of those units out there—the ones with the really heavy equipment—are *Torch Army*. They're keeping Drescher's people out of this entirely. Those are *Thandi Palane*'s troops, damn it! Half of 'em were in the Ballroom once. Even if we fight them off—fat chance of that happening—I do *not* want to piss off every damn ex-slave on the planet. Just give it up."

"You gutless bitch," the gang leader sneered at her, and pointed at the auditorium's exit. "You want to surrender, go ahead. Enjoy the rest of your life in prison. Me, I figure if nothing else those of us with a backbone can make an escape."

He swiveled around and glared at the small crowd.

"Who's with me?" he growled, and three of his closest people—Paulie, Chad, and Branko's girlfriend Aisha—signaled their allegiance.

About what Zhang had expected. Between them, those three had the collective intelligence of one of Mesa's rodent analogues.

No, less. By now, any self-respecting guyle or longmole would have scurried at least two hundred meters from here.

"Let's go," he said softly to Celeste. "Prison beats dead."

The two of them were out of the auditorium and headed down the corridor a few seconds later, with others following them. *Not* into the corridor that had been shown on the security screen. It was conceivable—not likely, but possible—that they could make an escape going in the opposite direction. It was much more likely they'd have to surrender to the Mumps, but at least they wouldn't be dealing with units primed for immediate combat. Surrendering to the Misties had always been a dicey proposition. Zhang had no great confidence that the Mumps who'd replaced them would be any less trigger-happy.

✧   ✧   ✧

"We want a minimum number of casualties, people," Saburo said. "And as many arrests as possible. That's why I told Supakrit to keep his Torch unit back. Thandi Palane trained them, and she comes out of the Solarian Marines, whose idea of arresting somebody is shredding them with a tribarrel."

"Not such a bad idea, you ask me," Abrams muttered. He'd muted his mic before he said it, though, so Barrett was the only one who heard, and she shook her head at him with a smile. Not that she completely disagreed. She understood why Saburo wanted this operation conducted this way, but it was bound to increase the risk factor.

There was no point arguing about it, though. They'd already done that, and although Saburo had listened to them, he'd had no trouble demonstrating his grasp of the old axiom that the boss might sometimes be wrong, but he was always the boss.

"I know we're taking more risks right now," he'd said. "But you need to look at this with an eye to the future. As long as criminals think they're as likely to get killed trying to give themselves up as they'd be if they kept fighting, they'll fight to the end. We need to prove to people—everybody on the planet—that the Mumps are a police force, not a reincarnation of the MISD or the OPS."

Then he'd grinned.

"Hey, I'll be the one in front, so what are you worried about? If anybody gets ambushed, it'll be me, right?"

Some of the Mumps' newer recruits had wondered about that. The heads of police forces didn't normally lead arrest operations. Most of them were of the opinion that he was doing this only to enhance his prestige, but Barrett knew the truth.

The real reason Saburo was taking point was because he figured that was the best way to keep *all* the casualties to a minimum. She could only hope his self-confidence wasn't misplaced.

They'd find out soon.

❖   ❖   ❖

By the time Zhang and Celeste got to the exit from the school's basement that he hoped would be unguarded, half a dozen more gang members had joined them.

"Who stayed with Branko?" he asked.

"Besides the three lumpkins who'd jump into a volcano if he told them it was safe?" Kell Haglish shook his head. "Nobody, so far as I know. You think we can get out this way?"

Zhang shrugged. "I figure it's worth a try. Let's go. No point waiting."

He led the way out into the covered alley beyond. He couldn't see anyone, looking in either direction, which was probably a bad sign. Normally, that alley was filled with street vendors hawking their wares, but now all of them had closed and locked up their booths and disappeared.

Which way to go? North, he decided.

They'd moved possibly twenty meters when four of the closed-up booths suddenly seemed to explode and people in body armor came out of them. They wore the new Mumps uniform, although Zhang couldn't see very much of them under the body armor. Those uniforms looked weird to someone like him, who was accustomed to the black and dark blue uniforms the Misties and Safeties had favored.

Who the hell wore emerald-green uniforms with ocher stripes and lampasses down the trousers?

But however comedic the uniforms might look, there was nothing humorous about the weapons pointing at them. Pulse rifles, flechette guns—Christ, one of them had a fucking tribarrel.

Zhang stood very still. Then, slowly and carefully, he raised his hands.

So did everyone with him.

❖   ❖   ❖

"If I'm reading the sensors right—they're pretty hashed up, though—I think someone's approaching you from that alley at two o'clock."

Arianne stifled the curses she felt like issuing. (Issuing? Say better, screaming.) The problem—one of the many problems—with conducting operations in the warrens of Lower Radomsko was the level of electronic background radiation. Didn't *anybody* there know about shielding? Short of direct visual observation, it was hard to interpret what she was seeing on her displays.

Saburo made his way toward the alley mouth, moving quickly, almost running. Just before he got there, though, he apparently spotted something she hadn't noticed and made a quick leap across the corridor and crouched down behind some sort of obstruction. Arianne couldn't make it out, but it seemed to give him at least some cover.

She hoped he'd stay there. She almost said something to that effect, but stopped herself when she realized how absurd it would be for someone who'd led her sheltered life to tell an experienced assassin how to do his work.

Her last serious boyfriend—she'd lived with the guy for sixteen years—had been a civil engineer. He'd slipped once on the job and broken his leg: the fibula, the small bone in the lower leg, not the femur or the tibia. It had been quite a to-do—a veritable calamity.

"Tuminello for Saburo." The voice came in on a secure channel, and Arianne shunted it to Saburo's com.

"Go," he said.

"We've captured the group that tried to escape through the market alley. You should know that all but one of them were wearing some kind of body armor."

"How good was it?"

"What you'd expect from gangsters and Lower Radomsko. Cruddy."

"Did they have gorgets?"

"Hold on. I'll check."

"No," Tuminello said after a moment. "None of them did."

"What I figured. Unless they're well-designed and well-made—which means expensive—gorgets are literally a pain in the neck. Okay, thanks."

Arianne looked at the Torch Army sergeant Supakrit Takahashi had assigned to the control room staff.

"What's a gorget?" she asked, and he raised his hand to his throat.

"Neck armor. I've used them. Even the well-made ones aren't comfortable. Between that and the expense, Saburo's figuring they won't be using them. So he plans to go for the sniper's triangle. Hell of a shot with a pistol, though."

Arianne looked back at the displays just in time to spot what looked like movement in the alley. That came from an acoustic sensor, though, not direct visual detection.

"I think they're coming out, Sa—!"

People burst out of the alley before she could finish his name. Four of them—all firing their weapons already!

"Saburo, look out! They—"

But Saburo had already sprung up from his crouch. His pulser was up, held two-handed, and—and—

Four bodies hit the ceramacrete. It had all happened in...

Three seconds? Maybe less.

"Holy shit," the Torch sergeant muttered.

❖　　❖　　❖

"Eight shots," the medical examiner told Barrett and a small group of Mumps later. "Double-tapped all of them. Don't know why he bothered, though. Every shot except one was almost instantly fatal."

The ME tapped his throat above the sternum.

"Two of them, including the guy with the mill-spec pulse rifle, got it right in the jugular notch. Severed their spines, among other things—all of them gruesome. The other two were turned a little away from him, so he shot one in the carotid, and severed it completely."

The man was obviously one of those medical examiners who took a macabre interest in his profession.

"The last asshole—now, *there* it gets interesting. Apparently, because of the angle of fire, your boss didn't have a neck shot. So his first dart went in just below the chest armor—by less than a centimeter—and struck the guy's hip. That turned him just enough so the second dart hit the jugular notch. Lucky shot? I wouldn't bet on it."

He snorted a laugh.

"I recommend not getting into a gunfight with him. Challenge him to spades, instead. Or tiddlywinks."

❖   ❖   ❖

"That went about as well as we could've hoped for," General Drescher said, and Thandi Palane nodded.

"I'm thinking there's really no reason I need to stay on Mesa any longer," she said. "Although it'd probably be a good idea for me to leave Captain Supakrit and his unit here, at least for a while."

"I'd appreciate it," Drescher said. "I really don't want to use the Mesan Army to deal with civil disturbance. And Admiral Henke doesn't have any desire for her ground forces to do anything beyond occasionally show themselves in public and look impressive. But between the reputation the Mumps are starting to build and, in a pinch, a company of Torch Army troops, I think we're in pretty good shape."

❖   ❖   ❖

Late that night—very late; Arianne's anxiety had fueled a lot of passion—she raised herself on one elbow and looked down at Saburo.

"Would you like to meet my family?"

He thought about it for a moment.

"How are they going to feel about that?"

"I don't know. Well, my father will probably be okay. It's harder to know with my mother, and damn near impossible with my older sister."

Saburo thought about it a bit more.

"What's the worst that happens? We get shown to the door and they tell you never to darken it again?"

"Uh . . . Well, I don't think that'll happen. But, yeah. The worst that happens is that my family and I part company."

"You've already lost both of your brothers, Arianne. Since the risk is all yours, it's entirely your call."

She didn't have to think about it. She'd already done that—for several hours.

"Yes, I want them to meet you. I need to know," she said, and he smiled, then.

"You're such a daredevil."

November 1923 Post Diaspora

"I cannot *believe* your timing, Honor Stephanie Alexander-Harrington! Your father and I are both doctors, HCM has the best obstetrics and neonatal departments on the entire planet, we monitor every *step* of this pregnancy, and you do *this!*"

—Allison Harrington

Tortuga Tower
Tortuga by the Sea
Sultan III
Hole-in-the-Wall System

"—TOLD THAT WORTHLESS SON-OF-A-BITCH THAT IF HE *EVER*—"

"Commodore, we have a situation."

Abelard Ishtu broke off as a short, stocky woman with hair in stripes of green and pink came into the lounge. Her stride was brisk, her expression was sour, and her tone expressed some urgency. Not really anxiety, and certainly not panic, but—

"Huh?" Ishtu blinked at her, his mouth the next best thing to agape. "What do you mean—'situation'? What situation?"

"'What situation,'" she mimicked. "How about you lay off the khat when you're supposed to be on duty? The 'situation' in which somewhere between three and five of what are probably warships just came across the alpha wall."

The commodore levered himself angrily out of his chair, using the armrests. Once he was on his feet, he needed a couple of seconds to find his balance. In fact, he staggered a little and had to brace one hand on the table.

"Watch your mouth, Knežević! Don't forget who's in command here."

The expressions of his table companions, two men and a woman, became the blank faces people take on when others have a quarrel that doesn't involve them. For her part, Knežević shook her head—a gesture that signified exasperation, more than anything else. Abelard Ishtu wasn't actually a bad sort, as Hole-in-the-Wall commodores went, but he wasn't the one you wanted in charge if a problem arose. Knežević would have been happier if Ursula Mason had been this month's commodore, even if she disliked the woman. At least she was capable and didn't spend half her waking hours in a khat-chewing haze.

"They're thirty light-seconds outside the limit," she told him with more than an edge of disdain. "That puts them just under nine light-minutes from us. So you've got about ten minutes to get yourself together. Unless you want *me* to handle it, of course?"

She turned and went back through the door to the control tower without waiting for an answer. It was less than two minutes' walk to the communications center. Even a stumblebum like Ishtu ought to be able to get his ass to the com before any signal from the newcomers could reach Tortuga Tower. And it wasn't like it would be that much of a loss if he couldn't.

Besides, even if they came straight to Hole-in-the-Wall, it would take them over three and a half hours to make the trip.

The short lift shaft deposited her on the tower's top floor, and as she usually did, she took a moment to admire the vista. Whoever had designed Hole-in-the-Wall's control center, he or she had apparently been a history buff with a romantic streak. The tower's name should have been a clue in that direction, but so had the fact that there was a "tower" at all. There was no reason to stick the control center on a planet's surface, instead of in a logical orbital station, to begin with. And if it was going to be a ground base, there was no reason it had to be a tower. Certainly not one with wraparound windows stuck in the middle of a pinhead-sized "city" on a teeny-tiny bay named "Tortuga Bay" for the sole reason of calling the city in question "Tortuga by the Sea." In her opinion, that had been a long, long way to go for a name.

But the tower's windows did make for a superb view.

Hole-in-the-Wall, more formally known as Sultan III, was on the edge of human habitability. Back on Old Earth, its terrain would have been characterized as a high desert, but it would be more accurate to call it a high desert on steroids. The moon's diameter was less than eight thousand kilometers—about sixty percent of Old Earth's—with gravity to match. The atmosphere was very thin, not that much denser than the one found in Mount Everest's notorious "death zone." Most people used atmosphere masks and supplemental oxygen any time they ventured out onto the surface. For that matter, *everyone* used them if they were going to be outdoors for more than an hour or two or exert themselves—and the only people who'd do *that* were those who'd become acclimatized to Hole-in-the-Wall for at least a year.

But if Hole-in-the-Wall's surface was dreary, its sky certainly wasn't. The gas giant it orbited, aptly named Sultan, was huge—half again the mass of the Sol System's Jupiter. Like Jupiter, it had distinct and well-defined cloud bands, but the color pattern was quite different: mostly shades of green, yellow and blue. Its prominent set of rings was less spectacular than Saturn's, but was still striking. And it had even more large moons than Jupiter: no fewer than six of them were as big or bigger than Europa. Two of them—Hole-in-the-Wall and Jackstraw, otherwise known as Sultan VI—were larger even than Ganymede, although only Hole-in-the-Wall had a significant atmosphere.

Only two things made Hole-in-the-Wall habitable (with some modest shelter). Sultan's eleven-light-minute orbital radius lay inside the primary's liquid water zone—right on its outer edge, perhaps, but still inside it. And Sultan's magnetosphere was much weaker than Jupiter's, because it had no moon analogous to Io to eject gas into space and provide Sultan with the large plasmid torus of Jupiter, while the gas giant's rotation was much slower than Jupiter's: thirty-nine hours, instead of ten. So Sultan's magnetosphere was sufficiently strong to protect the planet and its satellites from the radiation of their G-7 star, yet lacked the sheer fury of Jupiter's.

Knežević's moment of sightseeing was brief. Commodore Ishtu stalked, still a bit unsteadily, out of the lift less than a minute behind her, much sooner than she'd expected.

"All right, damn it," he said. "Give me what you've got on this 'situation' of yours."

"He's the com officer." Knežević pointed at Maurice Belknap. "Ask him."

The term "com officer" was a courtesy on her part. Hole-in-the-Wall's rank structure was fluid and informal. Even the title of "commodore" was mostly an honorary one. Every month the title rotated from one to another of the long-established ship's captains whose vessels currently orbited the moon. In Belknap's case, "communications officer" also covered responsibility for the system's rudimentary traffic control and supervision of its equally rudimentary sensor satellites.

Like the ancient pirates of the Caribbean, Hole-in-the-Wall's outlaw inhabitants' attitude toward authority and defined hierarchies was exceedingly democratic. Sometimes, to the point of anarchy.

"Still no signal from them," Belknap said, "but it's definitely four ships, and one of them's quite a bit bigger than the others. Assuming they're warships—which I think is a pretty safe assumption, since they're pulling about three hundred and fifty gravities—we're probably looking at a heavy cruiser and either three light cruisers or three big destroyers. My bet's on the light cruisers, though."

Ishtu started gnawing his lower lip. Knežević knew what he was pondering. A flotilla of a heavy cruiser and three lights wasn't powerful enough to defeat the vessels orbiting Hole-in-the-Wall. But it could give them a serious fight which, at the very least, would produce a lot more casualties—and damage—than any outlaw or pirate crew wanted to suffer.

A greeting on the friendly side seemed in order, then. Friendly, but . . . firm.

✧   ✧   ✧

"We've got an incoming signal," Belknap announced, eight minutes later.

"Put it up," Ishtu said, settling into his own command chair.

"Gotcha."

The image of an auburn-haired woman with sky-blue eyes appeared on the master display. Unlike many of Hole-in-the-Wall's visitors, she was in uniform, although Ishtu couldn't immediately place whose it was.

"Tortuga Tower, I am Citizen Captain Soubry, commanding officer of the heavy cruiser *Turenne*," the woman said. "*Turenne* is accompanied by the light cruisers *Murat*, *Massena*, and *Davout*, under the command of Citizen Commodore Beaumont."

Citizen commodore? Ishtu thought. *Crap! That's whose uniform she's wearing! Are there really lunatics out there who don't know the People's Republic of Haven's deader than last Thursday's fish?*

And if there are, then why—?

"We're just here with some stuff to sell and to look for suitable work," Soubry continued, smiling ever so slightly, as if she'd read his mind.

Ishtu relaxed in his chair, and the tension in the control tower eased considerably at the evidence that they weren't dealing with anyone's regular naval units after all.

"Welcome to Hole-in-the-Wall, Citizen Captain," the commodore responded. "Meaning no offense, but until we've gotten to know each other better, we'd appreciate it if the *Turenne* and two of your light cruisers parked in orbit around Hole-in-the-Wall VI. One of your light cruisers can come on in to Hole-in-the-Wall."

He sat back to wait out the twenty-minute round trip light-speed lag. Then Soubry nodded.

"Sounds reasonable. Will do. We'll be in touch."

The screen blanked, and Ishtu climbed out of his chair.

"Always nice to deal with gentlemen," he announced, then cocked an eye at Knežević. "And ladies, of course."

TRNS *Rei Amador*
Hole-in-the-Wall System

"ANY LAST-MINUTE THOUGHTS?" VICTOR CACHAT ASKED.

"No." Ruth Winton's reply came without hesitation.

They'd hoped she'd be able to work from her customized computer station aboard *Rei Amador,* but they'd also realized going in that Hole-in-the-Wall was likely to be just a little leery of allowing an unknown heavy cruiser—or the rest of its squadron—into a parking orbit around their moon before they'd had time to check out its bona fides.

"Everything I'm likely to need is already aboard the shuttle," she continued. "Bill, Cynthia, and I—*and* Andrea—" she added, looking over her shoulder at Corporal Merino "—are ready to transfer to whichever light cruiser you choose. I can work from there just as well as I could have if they'd allowed *Rei Amador* into orbit. As long as Bill and Cynthia can get their end of the equipment down to the shuttle pad."

Her last sentence ended on a slightly rising note, and Cachat shrugged.

"I'd be very surprised if they won't let us put a shuttle down. Wouldn't be very hospitable of them." He smiled thinly. "All right. Let's get this show on the road."

"You going with them, 'Citizen Commodore Beaumont'?" Yana asked.

"Of course."

"Are you sure that's wise, Citizen Commodore?" Soubry asked. "I doubt they'd be too surprised if you sent your flag captain down to make the initial contact."

"We're dealing with outlaws and pirates," Cachat disagreed. "They'll insist on having a face-to-face meeting with whoever's in command of our outfit sooner or later."

"That's how Scrags would do it, too." Yana smiled thinly. "The still uncivilized ones, I mean."

"Exactly." Cachat shrugged. "We might as well get it out of the way early."

Soubry was clearly still a little unhappy.

"I don't expect any trouble, Citizen Captain," Cachat told her. "That old saw about honor among thieves actually has some truth to it. When there's no legal authority to rely on or appeal to, a code of honor becomes essential. It does get broken, but not often—because whoever gets a reputation for doing so usually winds up in a world of hurt very quickly."

Ruth thought the likelihood of anyone in charge of Hole-in-the-Wall choosing to double-cross Victor Cachat was minimal. First, because when he wanted to, she knew no one who could project cold menace as well as he could. And, secondly...

She had to stifle a laugh. Well, sort of a laugh.

The Victor Cachat standing on *Rei Amador*'s bridge was unrecognizable, even to someone who'd known him as long as she had. She knew he would have preferred spending the weeks-long voyage from the Congo System to Hole-in-the-Wall getting rid of the way-too-handsome appearance his last nanotech transformation had created. Both he and Thandi wanted his old, "real" appearance back.

Unfortunately, creating his current genetic disguise had been a lot more complicated than mere biosculpt or a simple, skin-deep applique. It had, in fact, required cutting edge bio tech available only on Beowulf, and no one else—certainly not anyone on Torch—had the equipment or the requisite skills and experience to have reversed it. Besides, whether he liked it or not, Cachat's normal appearance had become far too well known, so reclaiming it might not have been the wisest possible move for Citizen Commodore Beaumont.

On the other hand, it was at least possible that his glamour boy look had also become known. Despite his best efforts, he'd been plastered all over the public boards in Mesa following the system's conquest. That was anathema for any intelligence operative, but at least he'd been able to console himself with the thought that he'd be jettisoning his new image sometime very soon. And then, inevitably, "sometime very soon" had kept creeping farther and farther away from him. It was unlikely, to say the least, that footage from Mesa had reached the authorities here in Hole-in-the-Wall. On the other hand, if there truly was a connection to the Alignment out here, the odds that its personnel had been briefed on events in Mesa, complete with recorded video of a revoltingly handsome Victor Cachat, were much higher.

He'd solved the problem in his usual manner. Directly, you could call it. Some would have said "brutally."

He'd resolved the pretty boy issue by having his nose broken. The ship's doctor had made sure it healed poorly, with a thick, heavy bridge. A few touches of simple biosculpt had widened his jaws and beetled his brow. Then he'd grown a thick, short beard, dyed it black, and shaved his head, eradicating any trace of the blond dazzler.

And finally—the *pièce de résistance*—he'd taken advantage of the fact that Torch had several very accomplished tattoo artists. He'd had his entire skull and face covered with tattoos modeled on ancient Maori designs. He'd done the same with his right shoulder and chest, and down his right arm to the wrist, as well.

"That's kind of cute," Yana had said when she saw the end result. "Sort of. Don't know how Thandi's going to like it, though."

Bryce Tarkovsky's reaction had been even simpler: "You are one crazy bastard."

Ruth had been more worried.

"You can get rid of all that, can't you?" she'd asked. "Because I think Yana's right. Thandi's *not* going to like it."

"Of course I can get rid of it. It takes a while, and I'm told some of it can be painful."

Ruth had managed to stifle her immediate *oh, goody!* response. She liked Cachat a lot. She really did! But some part of her still held a grudge over the way he'd declined to stop the Masadan fanatics who'd killed her security detail aboard the *Wages of Sin*.

"Gee, I'm sorry about that," she'd said, instead, and Cachat had smiled.

"No, you're not."

Amherst Imports and Exports
Tortuga by the Sea
Sultan III
Hole-in-the-Wall System

"SO, IS ANY OF THIS SOMETHING WE SHOULD BE CONCERNED about?" Hormuzd Kham asked.

"Probably not," Eileen Patel replied, "Unless we're interested in the fact that they say they're looking for work?"

Patel had relayed the message from Maeva Knežević, informing them of the new arrivals in the system. Knežević wasn't part of the Alignment herself—she had no idea it even existed—but she was one of the many people who served the Alignment as informers, in one manner or another.

Now Kham tipped back in his chair in the Alignment's extremely unofficial headquarters on Hole-in-the-Wall, to consider what she'd just said. Officially, the small building belonged to Amherst Imports and Exports, which served as something of a double-blind. Something like a third of all businesses on Hole-in-the-Wall were agents and brokers of one kind or another involved in interstellar trade, so Amherst fitted right in. And since posing as a trade agent was a traditional dodge for criminal enterprises, going back to Ante Diaspora times, anyone who got suspicious would simply assume they were garden-variety criminals.

And, in fairness, the primary reason the Alignment maintained an ongoing presence on Hole-in-the-Wall was, in part, because it truly was involved in interstellar trade. As a rule, the Alignment employed perfectly legal and above-board enterprises for that purpose—using the terms loosely, for the Jessyk Combine and a few others. But there were occasions when less savory and respectable operatives were useful. At those times, Hole-in-the-Wall and its analogues elsewhere came in handy.

It was a two-edged sword, though. The Alignment was always on the lookout for new players in the game. It was relaxing to use long-established proxies, but doing so carried its own risks, and it was always good to have extra options. Familiarity didn't necessarily breed contempt, but it did tend to breed carelessness. Field agents for the Alignment had a saying that went back centuries: *The road to hell is paved with routine.*

The trick was to find initial jobs that tested a possible new agent without risking anything. Those weren't always easy to come up with.

Kham swiveled his chair to face the woman working at a corner console.

"We got anything suitable, Roberta?"

"Not really." Roberta Bailey shook her head without looking away from her display. "At least, that's my opinion. You're the boss, though, so it's your call. The one and only thing I've got at the moment is that the Sarretti System's having an upsurge in piracy and could use some help squashing it."

Kham gave a little snort.

"Where *is* Frontier Fleet when you need it?" he asked with a smile. "One of those little consequences the 'Grand Alliance' doesn't seem to have considered."

"Frontier Fleet's at least still in existence," Patel pointed out. "It's even fairly intact, compared to what happened to Battle Fleet."

"Sure. But there's that bit about 'any Solarian League Navy ship outside Solarian space' being considered a pirate and destroyed on sight," Kham pointed out.

"The evidence is that the Alliance's being more reasonable about that, given how the Constitutional Convention's coming along," Bailey put in. "But even assuming they'd be prepared to make an exception in Sarretti's case, it gets a little tricky. The pirates must have inside information, because the ships they're targeting are ones carrying cargo Those-I-Shall-Not-Name in Sarretti don't want the authorities looking at. That's the only reason it got flagged to us."

"In other words," Patel said, taking a seat at another desk, "the smugglers are getting robbed, and it's awkward to call in Sheriff Doright." She shook her head. "Nobody in Sarretti knows who we really are, but we've run at least half a dozen ops through there. Personally, I think something like this has too many loose ends dangling around to risk using newbies we don't know anything about. But like Roberta said, it's your call, Hormuzd."

"I agree with you," Kham said. "And if this really is another batch of PNE orphans, it's probably just as well to stay clear of them. Eileen, tell Knežević we don't have a dog in this fight. So to speak."

"It's not a dog fight—not yet, anyway. Just some dogs sniffing each other's asses." Patel sniffed. "And we're not inclined to join them. I'll let her know."

"How about security?" Bailey still hadn't looked away from her display. "Any orders for the *Hudson*?"

The *Hudson* was the Alignment's current courier ship, in low orbit around Hole-in-the-Wall. In the event of serious trouble, her instructions were clear and simple: *get out of the system.* The plebeian-looking little freighter boasted a military-grade inertial compensator and impeller nodes, which would give her a lot of extra acceleration when it was time to run, but she wouldn't have much time to dawdle if she truly had to run for it, even so. Anyone headed in-system would have a significant overtake velocity, and if the anyone in question was a warship of the Grand Alliance, its acceleration rate would be quite a bit higher even than *Hudson*'s. Against a Solly warship, on the other hand, she might well be the one with the acceleration advantage.

If there was time for the personnel stationed on the surface to shuttle out to *Hudson* before she had to leave orbit, that would be nice—but not essential. In the T-century since the Alignment had established itself on Hole-in-the-Wall, it had unobtrusively fortified its base. The bunkers below the office building were equipped with an independent energy source and hardened against any bombardment short of a major KEW strike. It was also stocked with enough provisions to enable the handful of agents left behind to survive for more than a T-year.

And if worse came to worst, these were trained and experienced field agents. They'd commit suicide; or, if any of them shied away from that, their nanotech protocols would do it for them.

"I don't think *Hudson* needs any special orders." Kham shrugged. "Just tell them to be alert."

"Great." Bailey rolled her eyes. "I'm the one who gets to tell them to do what they're going to do anyway, so I'm the one who gets snarled at. Wish *I* were a boss."

Kham just grinned.

TRNS *Rei Amador*
Hole-in-the-Wall System

"ARE YOU SURE YOU'RE NOT FORGETTING ANYTHING?" CACHAT asked as Ruth headed for the inboard end of the docking tube to the shuttle which would transport them to the light cruiser *Davout*. In point of fact, that cruiser's name was TRNS *Bulavin*, but it was unlikely that pirates—even pirates who'd once regarded themselves as the keepers of the Havenite Revolution—would name its ships for the leaders of slave and serf rebellions.

"No," Ruth replied. "Everything Bill and Cynthia will need is already on the shuttle, and I've got everything I need right here." She patted the satchel slung over one shoulder.

"Are you *sure* you're not forgetting something?" Cachat repeated. He looked around the boat bay and then lifted the palm of his hand to indicate something about 150 centimeters from the deck. "I'm thinking of an object about this tall. It's hard to miss, since it's got two legs and walks around on its own."

"For God's sake, Victor! You seriously expect me to bring Milliken along on this mission?"

"Why shouldn't you?" he inquired, and Ruth tried not to grind her teeth.

"How about we start with security concerns?" she shot back.

"What security concerns? We're not going to allow any personnel from Hole-in-the-Wall to board the *Davout*. Or the shuttle, for that matter, although that's irrelevant, since neither you nor Milliken will be aboard it. I assume—I think this is safe enough—that neither you nor Citizen Captain Trevithick will be allowing Milliken to use the ship's communication equipment. That leaves her trying to compromise our mission by shouting a warning to the bandits from Hole-in-the-Wall, which will have to pass through a

500

light cruiser's armored hull and the vacuum of space to reach their ears. Barring a sudden transformation of the laws of nature, that seems unlikely to be successful."

"Very funny! What if—What if—?"

Ruth tried to think of a hypothetical situation in which Milliken could pose a genuine security risk.

She tried hard.

And . . . came up short.

There were times she really, really didn't like Victor Cachat at all.

"All right, fine," she almost hissed. "I suppose you expect me to go track her down, too?"

"Oh, there's no need for that. I sent a rating already. She should be arriving—"

He turned his head at the sound of a slight commotion from the boat bay's entry hatch.

"Now," he said.

Tortuga Tower
Tortuga by the Sea
Sultan III
Hole-in-the-Wall System

"THEY'VE GONE INTO ORBIT AROUND JETHRO," MAURICE BELKNAP said. "And one of the light cruisers is headed in-system."

Commodore Ishtu started gnawing his lower lip again.

"Did the heavy cruiser transfer anyone to the light cruiser before it left Jethro?"

"Excuse me?" Belknap rolled his eyes. "For fuck's sake, Abe! Jethro's more than two light-hours away at the moment! If you want to know what two ships are sending back and forth that far away, then you'd better stick a satellite or two in Jethro orbit."

"What's the big deal, anyway, Commodore?" Maeva Knežević asked. Belknap was one of Ishtu's khat-addict buddies, so he could get away with calling Ishtu "Abe." If Knežević tried it, she'd only kick off another spat. "Of course they transferred someone. According to Soubry, their CO was on the flagship, but if there's any serious dickering to do, he'll be the one doing it. We told them to send in one of the lights. They're doing that. And that means he has to be aboard it at this point."

Ishtu didn't reply for a few seconds. Then he released his well-chewed lip and puffed out his cheeks.

"Yeah, I guess. All right, let me know when they're an hour out from Hole-in-the-Wall orbit."

He turned and left the control center.

"When does Mason rotate into the commodore's slot?" Knežević asked no one in particular.

Belknap ignored her. He and she didn't like each other much.

502

But Kelly Dudek, the woman running the weather console turned her head and looked at the digital clock on the wall.

"Eleven days, fourteen hours, and eight minutes," she said. "But who's counting?"

Dudek was really good at math, and had even less use for Ishtu than Knežević did.

TRNS *Bulavin*
Hole-in-the-Wall System

"THE FIRST THING WE HAVE TO DO—AND DO IT FAST—IS TO figure out if there actually are any Alignment forces on the moon or in orbit around it." Ruth glanced over at Cachat, who was engaged in a discussion with Trevithick. "Victor—Citizen Commodore Beaumont—" she rolled her eyes "—thinks they probably have both: a base somewhere on the surface, probably in that town by the bay they call Tortuga, and a courier ship in orbit.

"*But—*" she held up a cautionary finger "—don't assume it'll look like a dispatch boat. It probably won't, according to Victor." The hell with all the Beaumonts, she decided. If she wasn't getting down to the damned planet, she'd call him whatever she liked! "He thinks it's more likely to be a small freighter that's been modified or special-built with mil-spec impeller nodes and a mil-spec inertial compensator," she continued. "A thoroughbred in mule's clothing, in other words."

"What's a thoroughbred?" Cynthia asked.

"A thoroughbred is a kind of racing horse."

To everyone's surprise, the answer came from Milliken. The Alignment officer sat at the same table as the rest of them. Ruth had insisted on that as a sort of thumbing of the nose at Cachat. *You insist I drag this creature with me everywhere? Fine. She can sit on my lap.*

"Uh...a horse is—" Milliken continued a bit awkwardly as all eyes turned to her.

"I know what the hell a horse is!" Cynthia snapped, and Bill Howe smiled.

"I even rode one once," he said. "It wasn't doing any racing, though. Just a steady walk. I was still scared I'd fall off it. It's

504

unsettling to ride a vehicle that has a mind and will of its own. But to get back to the subject at hand, how do we distinguish an Alignment signal from anyone else's, Ruth?

"According to the other Andrea," he pointed a thumb at Citizen Petty Officer Andrea Cinq-Mars, the ex-PNE rating manning the light cruiser's com station, as distinct from Corporal Andrea *Merino*, standing behind Ruth's chair, "these Hole-in-the-Wall idiots don't maintain much in the way of message discipline. 'Seems like they babble nonstop,' is the way she put it."

Ruth ran her fingers through her hair, and, for perhaps the hundredth time in the last month, reminded herself to get it cut.

"We probably won't be able to identify them in the hot take," she said. "Not unless Victor can figure out a way to keep our shuttle on-planet for a lot longer than we can count on. But that's okay... sort of. We're going to be looking for two things. One is pattern analysis. If there's anybody on the planet who *isn't* 'babbling nonstop' it's probably the people we're looking for. They'll have some kind of front or cover set up, and it will be communicating as much as anyone else in what passes for a 'legitimate business community' out here, but probably only with other businesses. They won't have all of the sideband communications and calls flying around that the locals do. So we'll look for installations maintaining only a few links. If we assume—"

She paused briefly, then shrugged.

"We're going to assume we're dealing with one surface base, probably covered as some sort of local business or freight agent, and a single smallish ship in orbit. If we don't see an obvious courier boat, then they have to be using a 'freighter,' just like Victor expects. And, frankly, there aren't going to be that many freighters in orbit around a place like Hole-in-the-Wall, either. So first, we locate any freighters in orbit that aren't obviously attached to one of the mercenary outfits passing through. Then we look for any of them maintaining a com link with one—just one—station on the surface. Then we try to separate out the surface stations that are only talking to other commercial stations. If we find one of those, and it's maintaining a link to one of the freighters, that'll be a pretty good indication we've found who we're looking for."

"If they're using a whisker laser link to their freighter, your chance of spotting it is pretty close to nil," a voice pointed out, and everyone looked at the speaker, because, once again, it was Milliken. "That's what I'd do," she continued with a shrug. "Assuming I wanted to keep the fact that I was talking to my ship a secret, anyway. Unless you can figure out how to put someone—or a disguised sensor drone or something—physically between the ship and the ground station, you'd never be able to detect it."

They all stared at her, and she grimaced.

"Look, whatever else you think of me, I *am* a naval officer. I'm pretty familiar with how starships *talk* to each other, and if you want to go completely covert, you set up a com laser on the planet and track the freighter whenever it crosses your sky on its current orbit. There's practically zero chance of anyone off the planet picking up your traffic, and at this piddling a range, any com laser from the ship to the surface would be tight enough to drop into a receiver bucket no more than a meter or so across. So there's not much damn chance of anybody down there accidentally eavesdropping on the ship's end of the conversation, either."

Ruth realized her mouth was slightly agape. She shut it firmly.

"That's what I was about to say," she said. "Which sort of brought me to the next point on my agenda. Data collection."

Milliken looked at her for a moment, then nodded.

"I wondered why you'd built so much bandwidth into the shuttle end of this," she said. "You're going to try to tap in and scoop up *everything*, aren't you? Then you're going to store it all so you can work on breaking it at your leisure."

Ruth stared at her.

Someone needs to shoot this woman, she thought. She'd had no idea Milliken was this perceptive. In all the time she'd known her, the Alignment officer had seemed practically brain-dead.

Well, yeah. Of course she has. She's been scared to death. That thought was followed by: *Huh, maybe Victor knows what he's doing, after all.*

What the hell, give it a try.

"That's right," she said. She hesitated for another moment, but only long enough to remind herself of Cachat's sarcasm about Milliken as a security risk.

"We're actually going to come at this in several ways." She looked around her intently listening minions. "The truth is that Commander Milliken's right about com lasers. On the other hand, any Alignment people on Hole-in-the-Wall are obviously here on a long-term basis, and as Bill just pointed out courtesy of the other Andrea, Hole-in-the-Wallers in general are sloppy as hell about their communications. So, while the people we're looking for almost certainly will minimize their com traffic and the number of people they're speaking to, they won't want to go about it with any paranoia-level security that would cause local eyebrows to rise if anyone noticed. So, they'll be using the local datanet, just like everybody else. They'll have really good encryption, which will probably be effectively unbreakable, but they'll be talking to relatively few other people.

"Now, there's not going to be a whole lot of message traffic for them to hide in. Hole-in-the-Wall's just not that big. So, Bill and Cynthia are going to hack into the net once they get down. We're going to turn the shuttle into a ground station, because they probably do take more precautions against somebody in orbit—especially somebody in orbit like us, that isn't a regular here—than they do against signals originating from the ground. Once you're into the net, I'll take over from *Bulavin*... using one of those com lasers. I'll be going for local mail and com network handling, and if I can get in—and if their security protocols are as sucky as I expect they are—I'll steal everything."

"Which you still won't be able to read, because, like you say, encryption is cheap and really, really hard to break," Milliken said, gazing back at her with narrowed eyes. "But if you get away with it, you'll have com records going back *months* to play with from a pattern analysis viewpoint."

"No, we won't be able to read them immediately. But like you pointed out earlier, we'll have plenty of time for me to play with it," Ruth replied. "And with all due modesty—" Cynthia made a sound remarkably like a not-so-smothered snort "—I'm pretty good at this kind of thing."

"But something about that still bugs me," Howe said. Ruth made a "go ahead" gesture, and he shrugged. "We know—" he gave Milliken an unfriendly glance "—*all* of us know, just how maniacal the Alignment is about security. I understand encryption is hard to break and that they can't afford to be too obviously secretive, but I find it hard to believe they'd risk really sensitive material on any kind of public channel."

Ruth started to reply, but then had another *what the hell* moment and looked at Milliken, instead.

"What do you think the answer to that is? Might be?" she asked.

Milliken returned her stare for a few seconds. Then she looked away and sighed softly. To Ruth, it sounded like one of those *in for a penny, in for a pound* sighs. (And she made another vow to track down the origins of that weird old saw.)

"I'm sure—and, yes, I'm speaking from a certain degree of personal experience—that whenever any Alignment base here in Hole-in-the-Wall needs to send a really sensitive communication to their ship, they use a com laser," Milliken said. "And, frankly, that's the only place they'd be likely to be sending anything *really* sensitive. But an even safer way, if you're not under any time pressure—and the way *I'd* send just about anything truly sensitive to someone else in a settlement as small as Tortuga—is to use a courier carrying a chip."

"Then what are the odds of our getting anything useful out of all of this?" Cynthia demanded.

Ruth began to answer, but Milliken cut her off.

"The princess isn't looking for the critical smoking gun. Not at this point," she said. "Oh, if there *is* one and it gets scooped up in her datamining operation, I'm sure it won't break her heart." The Alignment officer quirked a bittersweet smile. "And the truth is, that getting her hands on their routine traffic would probably be useful as hell, because *unless* they regard a message as really, really sensitive, they probably are using the public channels and relying on that encryption of theirs. So if she can scoop all that up, and *if* she can break the encryption, your people can probably learn one hell of a lot about how the Alignment runs its outposts in a place like this.

"But what she's really looking for at this point is finding the people who *own* the smoking gun—isn't that right, Princess?"

She looked challengingly at Ruth, and Ruth surprised herself with a desert-dry smile of her own.

"That's exactly right." She nodded. "Once we've figured out where to find the people we're looking for—the ones who own that 'smoking gun' the commander's talking about—I'll be able to give them special attention. That's where this software—" she patted the satchel sitting beside her chair "—comes in. As we've just established, they almost certainly have a portal to the public net. Unless their security's a lot better than I expect it is—I expect it to be really, really *good*, you understand; but, again with all due modesty, they probably didn't design it with Anton or me in mind—I should be able to use that to access their private servers. It's possible that they maintain a complete air gap between anything connected to the net and the computers with their really critical data, but we won't know that until we try. And if I do find something like that, then we've identified a potential target for a customized Victor Cachat black bag operation. Or, failing that, an old-fashioned 'kick-in-the-door' approach when Commodore Rabellini gets here with her Marines. Our chances of getting in before they slag everything would be...poor, especially with an open smash-and-grab operation, but they wouldn't be zero."

Cynthia and Howe were both nodding.

And so, Ruth Winton noticed, was Jessica Milliken.

Captains' Lounge
Tortuga by the Sea
Sultan III
Hole-in-the-Wall System

"YOU'VE GOT *CATAPHRACTS*?"

Commodore Ishtu sounded more accusing than questioning. Clearly, he was skeptical of Cachat's claim to have the Solarian League's newest and most effective shipkiller missiles.

"I do." Cachat nodded. "And I've got a pipeline to more of them. Which is why I have several hundred available for supply."

"And you're carrying 'several hundred' excess Cataphracts aboard your cruisers?"

Ishtu's tone remained barely short of outright sarcasm, and Cachat gave him a cold stare that lasted for several seconds. A Cachat "look of menace" would have been intimidating on the face of a child. Sitting on what looked like the face of an ancient tattooed barbarian warrior, it was enough to cause Ishtu to step back a pace.

"Are you trying to be abrasive?" Cachat asked. "Of course we're not carrying that many missiles in the cruisers. And I wouldn't be selling you anything out of our own magazines, anyway! That's why we brought a freighter with us."

"Where is it?"

"On the other side of the alpha wall, where else?" Cachat replied in an *I'm-speaking-very-slowly-so-even-an-idiot-like-you-can-understand-me* tone, and Ishtu flushed. "I'm not about to risk something as slow as a freighter until I know who and what I'm dealing with here." He shrugged. "If it looks like I've got a buyer, I send one of the other cruisers back across the wall to fetch it."

The Captains' Lounge had filled with Hole-in-the-Wallers when

510

word of Citizen Commodore Beaumont's arrival spread. Several of the captains who rotated through the commodore's position were present, and Ursula Mason gave the current commodore a disapproving look.

"Will you cut it out, Ishtu? You may not know how to conduct a business deal, but I do."

"So do I," Ivan Kraus said. He commanded three of the ships in orbit, including an ex-Andermani battlecruiser. Cachat wondered how he'd gotten his hands on her, although the vessel was long past its prime and wouldn't have been a match for any modern battlecruiser. Still, by pirate standards, it was pretty impressive. "And I would definitely be interested in getting my hands on some Cataphracts," Kraus continued. "*If*, that is, you've also got pods for them. None of my ships have tubes big enough to handle a Cataphract."

"I've not only got the pods, but they're last-generation—well, next-to-last-gen—with onboard impellers. Cuts the throw weight by one bird per pod, but makes it a lot easier to recover them for reuse."

"Okay, then!" Mason slapped her hands together. "Call in your freighter. We can make whatever security arrangements you'd be comfortable with."

TRNS *Bulavin*'s Shuttle
Tortuga by the Sea Spaceport
Sultan III
and
TRNS *Bulavin*'s CIC
Hole-in-the-Wall System

"ALL RIGHT, YOUR GRACE. WE'RE IN."

Ruth Winton straightened in her comfortable chair in *Bulavin*'s CIC as Bill Howe announced success from the light cruiser's grounded shuttle. A second or so later, the blank display in front of her blinked to life, and data began pouring across it as a waterfall display crawled upward.

"Good work, Bill!" she said, watching the treasure trove of messages flow into *Bulavin*'s memory. She began tapping in commands, reaching through the portal Howe and Cynthia had opened to trace the local datanet's architecture.

Locating the disguised courier ship shouldn't be particularly difficult. Assuming there *was* a courier ship, of course. Orbital traffic in Hole-in-the-Wall was sparse, at the best of times, and there were only a couple it could be. And—

Aha!

She smiled as she found one of the targets she'd sought and insinuated a custom-tailored spyware program into it. It wasn't particularly difficult. These people were even sloppier about their security than she'd expected. Although, to be fair, most of the ships in orbit around the moon probably had better internal security than Tortuga by the Sea's public net. And, also to be fair, her current target probably wouldn't have been considered especially sensitive—or valuable—by anyone on the moon. For that matter, the "system authorities" didn't much worry about keeping it rigorously updated, although she was confident her team could winnow out the information they needed.

"All right," she said over her shoulder to Citizen Lieutenant Chapuis. "I'm into what passes for the system traffic control database. Start your analysis."

"On it, Princess," the ex-Havenite acknowledged, taking over the feed, and Ruth returned to her own analysis, watching as a schematic of Tortuga's com links and data usage grew steadily on one of her secondary displays.

"It looks like *Hudson*'s been parked here for at least a couple of months," Chapuis said. "This time, at least. From the traffic records, it looks like she's a regular."

"'A regular'?" Jennifer Milliken said from where she sat in an out-of-the-way corner. "They have *regulars* out here?"

"Apparently," Chapuis replied a bit shortly. He was less actively hostile towards Milliken than many of the ex-PNE officers who'd learned about the self-destruct software in their ships' computers, but that didn't mean he was especially fond of her.

"Expand on that," Ruth said, turning her chair to face him.

"Well, it looks like there are at least a couple of ships that make regular or semiregular runs through Hole-in-the-Wall," Chapuis said, watching the information still flowing across his own display. "Like *Hudson*, they're all small—tramps that probably couldn't make a living competing with the big freighters in a legitimate star system. Makes sense, I guess. I mean, the system *is* a rendezvous point for smugglers and pirates, as well as mercenaries. If they're fencing stolen goods here, the odds are that they're relatively small-bulk but high-value items, and someone has to be picking them up to dispose of elsewhere. Looks like that's what *Hudson*'s been doing."

"That's interesting," Ruth murmured. Milliken looked a question at her, and—somewhat to her own surprise—Ruth found herself expanding on her observation.

"According to this," she waved a hand at the schematic on her display, "*Hudson* doesn't have a single active com link to the surface. Not through the city's servers, anyway. They're not even tied into the port master's advisory channel. So it doesn't sound like they're actively trolling for cargo at the moment."

Milliken nodded, and Ruth nibbled her lip for a moment.

"Cynthia," she said.

"Yes?" Cynthia X replied from the shuttle.

"See if you can get into the port cargo master's files. You should be able to do that from down there without anybody noticing you. Find out how often *Hudson*'s loaded cargo. In fact, pull a list of every cargo she's ever loaded here in Hole-in-the-Wall."

"On it," Cynthia replied laconically.

"You're thinking that if she's the courier ship, she has to occasionally go off and do courier things," Milliken said.

"Well, somebody has to maintain communications between these people and their—*your*—bosses, doesn't she?" Ruth shot back. Milliken winced slightly at the emphasis she'd put on "your," but she also nodded. "It'll be interesting to see just how 'regularly' she disappears and reappears," Ruth continued. "Might give us an idea about how important this node is to the Alignment. How much communication is flowing through it. And if *Hudson* is the courier we've been looking for, and if she has some sort of schedule to keep, then she can't absolutely rely on a 'legitimate' pirate turning up with a cargo when she needs one. So it's likely that at least every so often her bosses here in Hole-in-the-Wall have to arrange for her to find one at the appropriate time."

"Probably." Milliken nodded again, and her tone was odd, Ruth thought. Almost, but not quite, *satisfied*, perhaps.

"These people really *are* sloppy," Cynthia said over the com. She sounded both pleased and disgusted. "Cargo master's records are inbound to your terminal, Ruth."

"Thanks!"

Ruth left her autonomous systems to play with the expanding chart of Hole-in-the-Wall's communications network while she dove into the fresh information. She entered a brief series of queries, then leaned back with a thoughtful frown.

Most of *Hudson*'s cargoes were, indeed, small in bulk and high—relatively, at least—in value. Her captain had picked up about forty percent of the freight she'd carried by bidding on consignments to dispose of elsewhere. For most of the rest, *Hudson* had been chartered to deliver cargo to specific parties in other star systems by someone in Tortuga. And—

A chime sounded as one of the search parameters she'd entered came up, and her frown turned into a gleeful grin.

"Bingo!" she announced. "We have a match!"

"What sort of match?" Cynthia asked.

"Well, we have here a freighter with no active com links to the planet or to the cargo master," Ruth replied. "And we have a cargo agency in Tortuga which has zero non-business com links to anyone else on the moon. No entertainment links, no personal coms, nothing. But the same agency—it's called Amherst Imports and Exports—has chartered *Hudson* several times. In fact, Amherst's provided almost a third of the ship's charters."

"How many other cargo or trade agencies are there?" Chapuis asked.

"Seven," Cynthia replied from the shuttle.

"So a third of her charters come from one of *eight* agencies," Milliken murmured. She was obviously speaking to herself, but Ruth nodded vigorously.

"And none of the other seven match the 'We don't talk to nobody except on business' profile, either! And it looks like Amherst *has* downloaded quite a bit of 'public link' com traffic to her whenever they've chartered her." She chortled. "Like I say, bingo!"

"What the hell is a 'bingo,' anyway?" Cynthia asked. "People keep using that expression, but I've never heard anyone explain what it is or what it means."

"The theory I heard once—fair warning: the guy I heard it from was a know-it-all blowhard," Howe said, "is that a bingo was a now-extinct Old Terran marsupial that hopped in and out of burrows which made it hard to hunt. The custom was that if you'd managed to bring one down, you shouted 'bingo'!"

Cynthia squinted at him, and he shrugged.

"Hey, that's the story I heard. I can't say I have a lot of faith in it."

Captains' Lounge
Tortuga by the Sea
Sultan III
Hole-in-the-Wall System

"OKAY," THE DUTY COM OFFICER ANNOUNCED OVER THE LINK TO Tortuga Tower. It was a woman whose name Cachat hadn't been given, not Belknap. "*Massena*'s come back over the wall, and there's a ship with it. At their current acceleration, they're about four hours out from Jethro. And from the acceleration numbers, it does look like a freighter—probably somewhere around four million tons."

Cachat looked at Ursula Mason across the small table and rolled his eyes ever so slightly.

"You expected exactly what else?" he asked. "A squadron of superdreadnoughts?" He snorted. "You think I'm in the habit of arranging sneak attacks when I'm sitting all alone in the captains' lounge of the port I plan to attack?"

"Of course we didn't expect some kind of double-cross," Mason replied. "On the other hand, I'm sure you can understand why we like to be *certain* about things like that."

"I suppose," Cachat conceded, and Mason smiled.

In fact, the atmosphere in the captains' lounge had just improved noticeably. It hadn't been hostile prior to that, but it was obvious that the lounge's occupants found the arrival of a freighter big enough to carry the promised missiles reassuring.

Despite that, Cachat found the company of a couple of dozen pirates and outlaws...somewhat irritating. They weren't a pleasant group of people. The amount of bickering that went on between them wasn't astonishing, but it circled that territory. In fact, it was a little amazing that Hole-in-the-Wall had managed to stay in continuous operation for so long.

Probably, now that he thought about it, because pirates and

outlaws also tended to be lazy, and fighting civil wars required some serious energy.

"Once the *Hali Sowle* goes into orbit around Jethro, you can send someone out to look over the merchandise." A thin smile crossed Cachat's face. Thanks to the tattoos circling his mouth, it looked more like a rictus than what any sensible person would call a smile. "A bit of warning, though. The old harridan who owns and captains that ship has a foul temper and uses language that's even fouler."

"Why don't we head out now?" Mason proposed. "This operation's already taking forever."

Cachat said nothing. It was absurd for Mason to complain about "taking forever." She knew as well as anyone how long it took ships to get from Point A to Point B. Besides, the security arrangements which sent *Hali Sowle* to Jethro instead of Sultan III had been set up by Hole-in-the-Wall. He'd helped push the idea, as subtly as possible, but the decision had been Ishtu's, and Mason knew it. But that kind of cross-grained, surly abrasiveness was just Mason's personality at work. She could give Ganny Butry a run for her money in the foul temper department, without having any of Ganny's sense of humor. But the main reason he didn't say anything wasn't to avoid a quarrel. In fact, it was the same reason he hadn't complained about the security stipulations Ishtu had made. He didn't want to draw any further attention to the fact that the process *was*, in fact, taking longer than it should have.

That was deliberate, of course. He wanted to give Ruth and her minions as much time as possible to hack into Amherst Imports and Exports, now that they'd identified their target. Although "hack" wasn't really the verb to describe what they were doing. *Slowly, carefully, and oh-so-delicately infiltrate* would have been closer to the mark.

Happily, the pirate captains in the lounge started bickering over which of them would get first crack at the prized Cataphracts.

Mason was at the center of it.

TRNS *Bulavin*'s Shuttle
Tortuga by the Sea Spaceport
Sultan III
and
TRNS *Bulavin*'s CIC
Hole-in-the-Wall System

"HOW'S IT COMING?" CACHAT ASKED, LEANING OVER HOWE'S shoulder for a closer look at his display. Which was . . . completely incomprehensible to him.

"Pretty well," Ruth said over the com link to *Bulavin*'s shuttle. "It's slow going, but we knew it would be from the get-go. We've vacuumed up all of the public net's message files, although we're not even close to cracking the encryption on most of them so far. We'll have time to work on them later, of course, and we've collected the com history, as well, so we'll know what was sent to whom and when. We've got the cargo master's files—and the encrypt on them is a joke—and Cynthia's just finished download-ing all of the available records on ship movements from Tortuga Tower." She grimaced at Cachat from the small bulkhead-mounted com display. "Their so-called 'traffic control files' are an even bigger joke than the encryption on the cargo master's files, if not for the same reasons. The problem is that they can't tell us as much as I'd like because they're so damned incomplete."

"Really?" Cachat straightened. "I thought you'd been able to confirm *Hudson*'s movements."

"We have," Howe put in. "They keep better track—for the records, at least—of freighters than they do of the other ships visiting the system."

"They probably conveniently 'lose' a lot of records like that," Cachat said dryly. "People who associate with places like Hole-in-the-Wall don't like leaving footprints if they can help it."

518

"I'd say that was probably the reason for their sucky record keeping," Ruth agreed.

"I take it the reason it's going slow is Amherst's security systems?"

"You take it correctly," Ruth said. "If I hadn't been pretty convinced already that we'd IDed the Alignment's snake nest here in Hole-in-the-Wall, I would be now. It's kind of neat, in a sneaky sort of way."

"What sneaky sort of way would that be?" Cachat asked with the wariness of a man intimately familiar of the sort of sneakiness Ruth Winton found "kind of neat."

"Well, we always figured that anybody working for the Alignment would have better security than the rest of the sloppy local stumblebums. And Amherst does. But the only reason I know that is because first I had to go through a security fence that was only about forty or fifty percent better than the local datanet's admittedly low bar. Because I was already pretty sure we'd found the Alignment, though, I treated it like it was actually first-rate security and sort of eased my way through it. Which was fortunate, because it let me through into a completely legitimate-looking computer net that was really a hacker trap. Everything going in and out of Amherst's real servers goes through an entirely separate server, and the security between that separate server and their real computers is about a *thousand* percent better than the local datanet's."

"Can you get through it without being detected?"

Ruth glared at him from the com.

"That's two separate questions, Victor. *Of course* I can 'get through it.'" She sniffed. "That's what I *do*. But this is good enough that I can't *guarantee* I'll get through undetected. And, of course, if I *am* detected, then they'll know we're on to them and slag their files."

"How much longer do you think you'll need?" Cachat raised one hand in a placating—for him, anyway—gesture before she could snap at him. "I know you're an artiste and that you'll serve no hack before it's time, Ruth. But I do need some kind of timeframe, because the natives are getting restless. I need to know how much longer I have to stall them before I call in the Sollies."

"Um." Ruth tugged on a lock of hair. "Okay, I'm about ready

to try sliding through their inner security fence. I'm guessing, looking at where we are right now, that I'll either be through it clean or get detected sometime in the next... thirty-five or forty minutes. What I won't know until I get through it is whether or not the clever bastards have *another* level of security waiting inside this one. Frankly, I'm inclined to doubt that. But it's certainly possible, given how careful they've been, that they have a standalone secure server in there which sends their really sensitive message traffic directly to their courier ship via laser."

"Can you determine whether or not they do?" Cachat asked.

"Not definitively," Ruth admitted. "I can probably find some pretty strong evidence one way or the other *if* I get into their 'public' servers, but not hard and fast proof."

"Well, we can have Rabellini back into n-space in forty-five minutes, outside." Cachat scratched his black beard. "I'll wait until you can be more definitive about what you're up against, but, frankly, the sooner we can call him in the better. In terms of our relations with the Sollies, at least."

"Why so?" Ruth arched her eyebrows.

"Because we can't keep stalling half a dozen pirate chiefs much longer by holding a bidding war before we have to sell *somebody* some Cataphracts. They're already getting cranky. Of course, they're always pretty cranky by nature."

"I don't— Oh."

"Yeah." Cachat snorted. "Pirates may be cranky by nature, but the Solarian Navy will get pretty cranky itself if it discovers we actually *did* sell a bunch of Cataphracts to outlaws—who have since departed Hole-in-the-Wall with them."

"Let me see what I can do, then," Ruth said, and turned back to her computer.

❖   ❖   ❖

"—and, sooner or later, even Ganny's not going to get them to bid any higher."

Victor Cachat was tipped back in the shuttle's pilot's couch, conducting a perfectly legitimate—for certain values of "legitimate"—conversation with Citizen Commander Trevithick aboard *Bulavin*. It was precisely the sort of conversation a pirate commodore ought to be having, and he was careful to conduct it through the planetary communications net. His encryption was far better than anything on Hole-in-the-Wall—short of Amherst

Imports and Exports, at least—but that didn't mean it couldn't be broken. And the real reason for the conversation was to let the local riffraff know he was in communication with his ship . . . and that he wasn't using any sneaky, secretive whisker lasers to do it.

"I don't know, Citizen Commodore," Trevithick said dutifully. "If I had to bet, I'd bet on Ganny!"

"Which is why I'm completely content to let her handle that end of it," Cachat replied with a smile. "On the other hand—"

"Bingo!" a voice said over his earbug. "Bingo! We're in!"

"—all good things come to an end, and I think we're getting there pretty rapidly," he continued without so much as an eyeblink. Then he shrugged. "Anyway, I think we'll have a sale or three sometime pretty soon. They'll probably let us bring *Hali Sowle* into orbit here to make delivery, but they may insist on picking them up out at Jethro. So pass that on to Citizen Captain Soubry and the rest of the squadron, please."

"Of course, Citizen Commodore."

"Beaumont, clear."

Cachat cut the link, rose, and walked back to the passenger compartment.

"Congratulations," he said, but Ruth grimaced at him from the com screen.

"We're in, and there isn't another security fence. We're downloading everything from their 'public persona' server right now. But I was right. They do have another one in there that's physically separated from the rest of the system."

"You found your evidence?"

"Pretty much." She rubbed her forehead for a moment. "The main thing is what I'm *not* finding, actually," she said then. "I've got quite a few messages from Amherst to Hudson, but only what looks like routine crap. I can't prove that, because we can't read their encryption, but every single message I'm finding goes through the public net. We've pretty much established—or at least strongly inferred—that they have a secure link to Hudson that they're using for something. And if the something isn't on the servers that are connected to the net, then they have to be on one that isn't." She shrugged. "That means they have another one in there somewhere, and if I was using a second server, then I'd make damned sure it was completely air-gapped, physically isolated from anything else on the planet or in the star system.

It wouldn't make a lot of sense to *not* air-gap their real commo data, under the circumstances. And if that's what they've done, we can't get into it from here. We'd have to have physical access from on the premises."

"Which we're about as likely to get as I am to be adopted as your aunt's heir," Cachat said dryly. "Before they can wipe their records, I mean."

"Oh, I think it's actually even less likely than Aunt Elizabeth's deciding to adopt you," Ruth said, even more dryly. "But we definitely aren't going to be able to touch it remotely."

"Then I suppose it's time we were little more direct," Cachat said calmly, and looked at the screen beside Ruth's, which showed Trevithick over the same covert link. "Pass the word to *Crixus*, Citizen Commander. And then keep a really close eye on our friend *Hudson*."

"Right away," Trevithick responded.

"I know you can't get into their standalone servers, Ruth," Cachat continued, turning back to her, "but keep an eye on those 'public persona' servers. Let me know if you see any sign they're scrubbing those."

"Gotcha," she replied, then sat back in her chair and ran her fingers through her hair again.

One way or the other, they were in the endgame, she reflected. TRNS *Crixus* was the Torch Navy frigate which had ridden across the alpha wall tractored to *Hali Sowle*'s hull. That meant she'd arrived without any betraying hyper footprint of her own...and that she could quietly sneak back across into hyper-space, where Commodore Rabellini and her SLN squadron were waiting.

Ruth started to climb out of her chair, then paused as one of *Bulavin*'s junior officers cleared his throat beside her. He looked like he'd been there for a while, she thought. Had he been waiting for her to come up for air?

"Yes?" she said.

"I looked it up for you, Princess. It turns out 'bingo' was an ancient ceremony—mostly a religious one, apparently—where people assembled the right numbers in some sort of order as quickly as possible. If you could manage it faster than anyone else, you called 'bingo!' and got rewarded."

"Rewarded with what? Eternal life?"

**Tortuga Tower
Tortuga by the Sea
Sultan III
and
TRNS *Rei Amador*
Jethro Orbit
Hole-in-the-Wall System**

"I'M GETTING SICK OF THIS!" URSULA MASON SNARLED. "BAD enough you insisted on a bidding war instead of just offering a straight up price—"

"What?" the woman on Mason's display interrupted. "I came all the way in from Jethro to *Davout* just to avoid that stupid four-hour com loop after *you* insisted all of our ships had to stay safely away from Hole-in-the-Wall. I could be sitting there on my own bridge, drinking coffee, instead of listening to your horseshit complaints!" She shook her head in disgust. "A donate-to-charity denizen of Hole-in-the-Wall is upset that I'm trying to get the best price for my goods? That's rich. Next I'll be hearing fish complain that water is wet!"

"Damn you, Butry! This has gone on long enough. Start selling or—"

"Captain!" the communications officer of the watch interrupted. "Captain! I've got a major hyper footprint! There's at least—" She studied her displays. "At least a dozen ships just made translation!"

She watched the displays for several more seconds, then turned to look at Mason, and her face was tight with anxiety.

"Ma'am, I don't have any kind of light-speed confirmation yet, but from the wedge strengths and acceleration curves, I think four of them are battlecruisers."

"*Battlecruisers?*" Mason strode over to look at the displays for herself.

"Battlecruisers," she muttered.

The only battlecruiser already in Hole-in-the-Wall was the flagship of Ivan Kraus's three-ship "squadron." But that battlecruiser was antiquated. Maybe not a museum candidate—yet—but getting close. Mason was pretty sure—no, she was dead certain—that the battlecruisers which had just come over the wall weren't antiquated at all. The good news was that they were more likely Solarian than Grand Alliance, judging from the acceleration rates. But even a quartet of Sollies would shred anything that went up against them.

"Time to go," she hissed. "Now!"

She wheeled away, headed for the tower entrance and the shuttle to her own orbiting ship, but she paused briefly beside the communications officer.

"Send it out on the all-ships channel. Anybody who wants to run had better start making tracks."

And that was her good deed for the day. Now it was time to run.

✧   ✧   ✧

Unlike Hole-in-the-Wall's regular residents, Jarmila Soubry had known what was coming. She'd also held *Rei Amador*'s impeller nodes at full readiness ever since their arrival in-system, despite the additional wear and tear that inflicted. That meant it took her ship and her two light cruiser consorts less than five minutes to bring up their wedges...and their sidewalls came with them. That was, perhaps, an unfriendly thing to do in the midst of polite company. (Well, fairly polite.) But when the company consisted of criminals with a long history of violence, she made no apologies about it.

Fortunately—for it—the single pirate cruiser sharing Jethro's distant parking orbit with "Citizen Commodore Beaumont's" ships chose not to make an issue of it. It was too busy bringing up its own wedge to worry about anything like that. Soubry considered calling on it to surrender, but that was only an auto reflex of the naval officer she'd been. A good pirate would be more concerned about running herself than breaking the kneecaps of any fellow pirates. Besides, the poor bastards weren't going anywhere unless the Sollies let her. Unlike *Rei Amador* and her smaller sisters, the pirate cruiser had shut down her nodes completely when she went into orbit. She was looking at a minimum of forty minutes to get them activated, and if the incoming Sollies were really interested in catching her, she was as good as caught.

The situation around Sultan III, on the other hand, seemed likely to be more interesting.

"Send a signal to Commodore Rabellini," she told her com officer. "I know they've got our transponders on file, but...better safe than sorry."

Amherst Importers and Exporters
Tortuga by the Sea
Sultan III
and
TRNS *Bulavin*
Sultan III Orbit
Hole-in-the-Wall System

"DO WE HAVE ENOUGH TIME?" HORMUZD KHAM'S TONE WAS INTENT but calm. Alignment operatives at his level weren't given to panic.

"No." Eileen Patel had been working the numbers. "They're coming in with too much initial velocity for even *Hudson* to outrun."

"Wonderful." Kham grimaced. On the other hand, that geometry had never been unlikely, if they really had to run. He looked at the woman at the com station. "Roberta?"

"I don't think they're here for us," she said. "They seem to be really, really pissed off with Citizen Commodore Beaumont, actually."

"Do they?"

"Yeah, when you strip it down, what they're really saying is 'Stop, thieves! Resistance is futile!'" She snorted. "I think they want their Cataphracts back."

"And we're caught in the middle of it." Kham puffed his cheeks for a moment, then shrugged.

"Okay, standard protocols," he said. "Roberta, make sure the secure server's dumped to *Hudson*. Eileen, you make sure we're not leaving anything incriminating in the warehouse. I don't think we are, but double check. I'd hate to lose it, but better to blow it if we have to than to leave any breadcrumbs. When Roberta's completed the upload, slag all the computers. Meanwhile—" he pushed his chair back "—I'll be prepping the shuttle."

✧　　✧　　✧

"Annnd . . . we're down," Ruth announced as her covert link to the Amherst servers went dead.

"They're prepping their shuttle, too," *Bulavin*'s tactical officer announced.

"Pity." Cachat pursed his lips. "A part of me hoped they'd be confident enough the Sollies were after us, not simple honest merchant traders like themselves, to try riding it out in place. At least that way we might've gotten some Alignment operatives to play with." He shrugged. "Of course, unlike Milliken, they'd've been dead by the time we got our hands on them. And we've already lost their secret files."

"I'm sure they uploaded all of them to *Hudson*," Ruth pointed out.

"And if we grabbed her, her files would be gone—or her fusion bottle would blow—before we got a single kilobyte out of their computers," Cachat replied, but although his tone was resigned, it was also philosophical. "And it's unlikely we've got anything really sensitive in the data you were able to vacuum up, Ruth. But that's the way intelligence ops go. Spectacular successes are spectacular precisely because they happen so rarely. Most of them go a lot more like this, with partial success, at best. But you got one hell of a lot of data. I wouldn't be surprised if, between you and Anton, you were able to get at least a few nuggets out of it, but we always knew it might work out this way. And even in a worst-case scenario, we know a lot more than we did about their operations in general and in Hole-in-the-Wall, in particular. I'm pretty sure this has been a valuable node for them, and since we aren't planning on burning it to the ground, they may just decide to come back again. Which would mean we'd know where to find them, wouldn't it?"

He smiled unpleasantly.

❖   ❖   ❖

"Well, this sucks," Hormuzd Kham said philosophically as he stepped onto *Hudson*'s command deck.

Given the possibility that customs inspectors might get a look at the ship's interior, it was just about as bare-bones as one might have expected out of a slightly down-at-the-heels tramp freighter. Or it looked that way, at any rate. Behind the façade of worn, well-used consoles in need of replacement were sensors, instrumentation, and an engineering plant that were all state-of-the-art and perfectly maintained.

"Shuttle's secured, Sir," *Hudson*'s captain said as Patel and Bailey followed Kham onto the command deck.

"All right," Kham replied. "In that case, let's get out of Dodge."

"Yes, sir!" the captain said, and *Hudson*—whose nodes were *always* hot, if anyone had thought to check—brought up her wedge and accelerated smoothly out of Sultan III orbit. Under the circumstances, she settled for the sedate acceleration one might have expected from the sort of freighter she looked like. After all, the last thing she wanted was to draw extra attention to herself.

"I've always wondered," Roberta Bailey said, watching the astrogation display. "What *is* Dodge? And why would people want to leave it in a hurry?"

"You should study more history," Kham told her. "Dodge was a town on Ante Diaspora Old Terra. It was the terminus for regular cattle drives—men on horseback who manually forced beasts weighing more than half a ton across hundreds of miles of wilderness to be slaughtered. All of the 'cowboys' were armed with primitive gunpowder weapons, and they were a pretty rowdy crowd. Sometimes gunfights would erupt—once they reached Dodge, they'd typically get drunk—and the less bellicose types would say 'Let's get out of Dodge.'"

Patel laughed.

"He's pulling your leg, Roberta."

"No kidding." Bailey scowled. "How gullible do I look, Hormuzd?"

✧   ✧   ✧

"There they go," Ruth murmured to herself as she watched the repeater display that showed *Hudson* scudding away from Sultan III.

The freighter wasn't alone, although she'd clearly been the readiest of the ragtag ships orbiting Hole-in-the-Wall. The next fastest fugitive was at least thirty minutes behind her, and each of them had picked a different direction in which to run. None of them had the base velocity or acceleration to stay away from the Solarian warships, so obviously they were hoping that with only so many platforms available, the Solarian CO would choose to run down someone *else*.

Bulavin wasn't even trying to run, of course. Neither had it made any move to interfere with *Hudson*'s departure. If he couldn't get his hands on its secure servers, Cachat wanted the

Alignment to escape Hole-in-the-Wall secure in the knowledge that none of their information had been compromised.

Especially because it might have been.

"God, I love being a spy," Ruth said, leaning back in her own chair in her personal quarters. "And they *finally* let me do it."

Of course, as Cachat had already pointed out, the odds were that she hadn't been a *successful* spy. Or, at least, not a *totally* successful one. She did wish there'd been a way to get into that secure server of Amherst's. Still, they'd stolen a lot of material. Whether any of it was truly useful was more than she could say, and whether or not they'd ever be able to access it remained an open question. She thought they could crunch their way through the encryption in the end. She and Anton Zilwicki had really good computers and even better software. But maybe this whole adventure would turn out to have been pointless. Well, except for at least temporarily scouring clean a notorious nest of ruthless and bloodthirsty pirates and outlaws, of course.

But that wasn't Ruth's line of work.

She was a *spy*.

"It's too bad we don't get to wear fancy uniforms with lots of stripes and ribbons on them," she told herself. "But... Well, granted, that would be sort of self-defeating."

Café Bilbao
Hadcliffe Residential Tower
City of Mendel
Planet Mesa
Mesa System

THOMAS MCBRYDE FINISHED HIS CUP OF TEA AND SET IT BACK down on the small table in the café's back corner.

"May I make a suggestion, Arianne?"

"Of course, Dad."

He pursed his lips, clasped his hands together in front of his chest, and spent a moment looking at her.

"Let me preface this by saying that if you think my suggestion would offend—even irritate—your friend, then we'll forget I made it."

"Dad," Arianne smiled, "there really aren't many things in the universe, so far as I've been able to tell, that offend Saburo. And he handles irritation by...well, not suppressing it, exactly, but—"

She took a sip from her own cup, giving herself time to think about how to say what she was about to say. But her father beat her to it.

"I imagine," he said with a small smile, "that someone with his body count can put irritation in perspective."

Arianne smothered a laugh and set down her cup.

"Well, I suppose that's one way to put it. I was going to just say he's very even-tempered—which he really is, by the way. It's one of the things I like about him. I don't know how well you remember my former boyfriend—"

"Kenneth? Rather well—possibly because I found him a bit irritating. Dear God, that man could turn any mishap into a catastrophe."

Thomas rolled his eyes, and this time, Arianne did laugh.

"Couldn't he? Anyway, don't worry about offending or irritating Saburo. I may or may not agree to your suggestion, since I don't know what it is yet, but it'll be something we can gauge on its own merits."

"All right, then. What I suggest is that instead of bringing Saburo over to have dinner with us—or inviting us to your place—start by allowing your mother and sister to encounter him in a setting with more people, so they can observe rather than having to engage him directly. And make it a setting that allows them to see him through the eyes of the people who actually work with him every day."

"Like...what?" Arianne asked with a slight frown.

"Like a celebration of the Mumps, specifically. More generally, a celebration of the progress Mesa's made over the past several months in creating a new society. Invite some key people from the Mumps—obviously, that would include Saburo—along with some people from the administration you think would be helpful. And, of course, some people from the Engagement. That, along with the fact that we're also your family, would be enough to get us into the affair."

Arianne's frown deepened.

"I'm...not...I'm not sure what would be gained."

"Arianne, *think*. You're too close to this. Leaving aside the personal relationship you've developed with the man, you've been working alongside Saburo for months. He's become what you might call a complete human being to you. But what does your mother or sister know about him? Nothing, except that he's a notorious ballroom terrorist—call him a 'striker,' if you prefer—and the concept of 'Ballroom striker' is just an abstraction to them. If you do it the way I'm suggesting, they get to encounter him in a broader context and can interact with him—or not—however they choose. Whereas, if you plunk him straight down next to them at a dinner table, you'll be jamming them into a corner."

She thought about it. Put that way, she could see his point. But there was something that made her bridle—

"Dad, how come *you* aren't having a problem with this?" she asked, and he chuckled.

"You've been in existence for almost half a century and haven't figured out that people are different?" He shrugged. "It's probably due to our varied experience. Your mother's an artist.

That makes her sensitive to what I'll call the human condition, but it doesn't give her much exposure to it, beyond what she's encountered in her own life."

"Fair enough. But you and JoAnne are both educators, and if anything, I think JoAnne is likely to have more trouble accepting Saburo than anyone else in the family."

"'Educator' is too broad a term." Thomas shook his head. "JoAnne is a *teacher*. And the kids she teaches are, and always have been, full citizens. I'm an administrator, and quite a bit of my work—you might be surprised how much—required me to deal with the education of slaves."

She reached down, but her cup was empty. She preferred coffee, though, and she'd already had two cups. That was her limit for the day. Anymore and she'd get jittery.

"Slaves," she repeated. "What about seccies?"

"Seccies were on their own. Whatever educational systems they had, they had to create and maintain themselves. For the most part, that was handled by the criminal syndicates and religious denominations. But slaves weren't allowed any self-organization at all, so their education had to be provided by the Mesan authorities." She was still staring at him, and he shook his head again. "Arianne, whatever else Mesa was—and still is—it's a highly advanced technical society. Illiterate and ignorant slaves are simply of no use."

He sighed and stared down into his empty cup for a moment, as if he were reading tea leaves—except there weren't any.

"I've understood for a long time just how hideous a society we created here—though not for us, of course. I'm supposed to look down on someone like Saburo because he's a killer? At least he committed his killings on a retail scale—and he chose his targets carefully, and for good reasons. We were just indiscriminate mass murderers. Our entire society here in Mesa was built around an institution that murdered millions and tortured millions more in the name of 'training,' that manufactured human beings and then regarded them as inferior, expendable property.

"I know that wasn't what the Engagement wanted, but we couldn't help being a part of it, even if it was only because of our inability to bring an end to the nightmare. But it doesn't stop there, you know. If even half of what the Grand Alliance is telling us about their 'Malign Alignment,' we were also party, even if it was at one remove, to an organization which used genetic slavery for its own purposes and then engineered wars that killed more millions, all of it justified by the supreme goal of uplifting the human race—and never mind if it was done on the corpses and crushed lives of real, actual people."

"Dad, that's not really fair to us."

"As individuals? No, it isn't. But nobody is *just* an individual, Arianne. Every one of us is also a member of a society, and carries that responsibility as well. And that doesn't change simply because the society places extreme limits on the options an individual might have. Yes, very tight limits were placed on us—those of us full citizens on Mesa who disapproved of what Mesa had become. So what? Even tighter limits were placed on someone like Saburo—or Jeremy X, for that matter."

He broke off to order another cup of tea from the auto server. Then he looked back across the table at her.

"My point is simply that if people are going to accept the constraints under which they were placed—and forgive their own sins because of those constraints—then it behooves them to extend that courtesy to others, as well. I'm not going to condemn a man like Saburo for his past choices, since I find it quite easy to understand why he made them. I don't think I would've made the same choices myself, but—" he smiled "—if I'd had his hand-to-eye coordination, I might have. Who knows? But what really matters are the choices that he—all of us—make *now*. And from what you've told me—and I've spoken to other people about him, after I realized the two of you were in a personal relationship—Saburo's choices seem to have been very impressive."

The new cup of tea emerged from the auto server, and Thomas reached for. He took a sip, set the cup down, and smiled again, more widely.

"Mind you, I can't say I ever had hopes that someday you'd pick a cold-blooded assassin, with what my knowledgeable associates tell me is a well-nigh incredible track record, for a boyfriend." He lifted the cup and what might almost have been called a salute. "But I can handle it."

For a moment, Arianne was tempted to tell her father the whole truth about what had happened to her brothers. But...

No. Not yet.

The problem wasn't Jack's fate—her father had accepted his

oldest son's death long since—but that of her other brother. Zach might not even be alive, but if he was, he was apparently still loyal to the "Malign Alignment." Eventually, she'd have to tell the rest of her family what had happened to Jack and Zach, but she shied away from doing so until there was more clarity on exactly what Zach was bound up with.

Of course, there was a very good chance they'd never have the answer to that question. But until she was sure that was true, she just couldn't bring herself to inflict still more grief on her parents and her sister JoAnne.

So she turned her mind to another subject. Her dad wanted her to organize some sort of *different setting*. What could that extraordinarily all-encompassing term be translated into?

"A formal ball?" she thought out loud. "Maybe at the Bristol Hotel? On the plus side, I'm willing to bet Saburo's a terrific dancer."

"I don't know that you need anything that elaborate."

"You're probably right. So...?"

"Make it a reception at the Smooth and Wrinkled Club. They have rooms that would be big enough."

"They're pretty exclusive, Dad," she pointed out with a frown.

"I have some influence over there. And raise it with Jackson Chicherin. He's a long-standing member of the club, and he's probably got more clout than anybody else these days, at least in those circles. I'd bet he'd have some good advice on who to invite and how to organize it, too."

She thought he was probably right—and she knew Chicherin and got along with him pretty well.

"Okay."

Decorations, though...

She burst into a giggle.

"What's so funny?"

"Ah... never mind, Dad."

Hanging Saburo's silhouette targets on the reception room's walls was contraindicated. And they didn't actually look all that impressive, anyway. His shots were so closely grouped in the center that it looked as if he'd just fired one shot from a really big gun. And nobody who hadn't witnessed it personally would find the range at which he'd fired them plausible.

Floral arrangements, ninny.

Harrington House Infirmary
Harrington City
Harrington Steading
Planet Grayson
Grayson System

"I CANNOT *BELIEVE* YOUR TIMING, HONOR STEPHANIE ALEXANDER-Harrington! Your father and I are both doctors, HCM has the best obstetrics and neonatal departments on the entire planet, we monitor every *step* of this pregnancy, and you do *this!*"

"Not—"

Honor broke off to pant hard, squeezing her husband's hand in her artificial left hand and pressing her right hand to her rippling abdomen as the fresh contraction hit. Her mother laid her own small, cool hand on her forehead, and Honor treasured the comfort of that touch almost as much as the love that filled Allison's mind-glow.

She rather wished there was less worry in that mind-glow at the moment, though.

Nimitz lay curled on the foot of her bed while Samantha stretched along the back of Hamish's chair, both of them pouring their own love and support into her. She was pretty sure she would have been a lot more worried, maybe even frightened, without that link. None of this was supposed to be happening yet, and she pursed her lips, panting as the contraction rolled through her and she tasted her unborn son's mind-glow. He was...unhappy, she thought, which was hardly surprising given the way his universe was shaking about him, and she felt the 'cats reaching out to him, as well, soothing his unformed fears.

"Not...not my idea," she got out in a more natural voice as the contraction eased. "I was being good!"

535

"'Good' has always been a relative term where you're concerned, dear," Allison said severely.

"No, I was!" Honor insisted. "It wasn't my fault!"

Nimitz sat up straight on the bed, hands flashing, and Allison frowned as she read them.

<She's right,> those hands said. <It was Swimmer.>

"Swimmer?" Allison repeated.

She looked sharply at her daughter as Honor started panting again.

"She was on the stairs." Hamish sounded more resigned than worried. Unfortunately for him, Honor could taste the emotions behind his determinedly calm tone. "She didn't see Swimmer and he apparently didn't see her. He ran right between her feet, and—!"

He broke off and shrugged, and Allison shook her head. She smiled down at Honor, then took her hand from her forehead as she moved closer to the bed to examine the diagnostic readouts. No one simply looking at her would have noticed the way her tight shoulders relaxed, but even through the contractions of premature labor, Honor could taste the vast relief that flowed through her emotions as those readouts registered.

A relief which made Honor feel enormously better, if the truth be told. She knew the situation was under control. She *knew* that, whatever it felt like. But at the moment her own emotions were barely on speaking terms with her forebrain.

"She was headed down to her office," Hamish said. "Swimmer came scooting up them. You know how bouncy all the kittens are!"

Alfred Harrington stepped up beside Allison. He tucked an arm around his wife while he, too, studied the readouts, then smiled down at Honor.

"Swimmer, was it?" he said in the resigned tone of a two-leg who'd had far more experience with treekittens than most. "Well, I suppose 'bouncy' is *one* way to put it. Personally, I'm in favor of something just a tad stronger, though. He's even worse than Jason was!"

<No one is worse than Wanderer,> Samantha signed from the back of Hamish's chair, and Alfred laughed.

Jason, the firstborn of Nimitz and Samantha's first litter, was thirteen T-years old, which was only the late stage of childhood among treecats. 'Cats matured physically by the time they were ten or eleven T-years, although all of them—and especially the males—still had quite a bit of "filling out" to do at that point. But there was a difference between physical maturity and adulthood. A treecat's age could be estimated pretty closely from its tail, which showed rings rather like those of an Old Terran raccoon. Unlike a raccoon, however, a treecat was born with no rings or bands. Instead, they developed as the 'cat aged, at the rate of one every three Sphinxian planetary years, or just over fifteen and a half T-years. The appearance of the first ring marked the end of kittenhood, in the treecats' eyes, but 'kittens weren't considered *adults* by their elders until the second ring appeared.

In Jason's case, it seemed unlikely they'd consider him an "adult" until he produced his *third* ring, however. Wanderer, his treecat name, had been assigned when he'd been less than a T-year old as a recognition of his propensity to do just that—wander. As in wander *away* from his parents and wander *into* trouble.

Which he still did at the drop of a celery stick.

"Maybe not more bouncy, but I think he's even more headstrong," Alfred said, and Samantha considered that for a moment. Then she held out both true-hands, palm up, and touched her right true-hand to her muzzle in the sign for "maybe," and Honor surprised herself with a somewhat breathless giggle as she tasted Samantha's resigned agreement.

Swimmer was from Artemis and Hood's first litter. He was also less than two T-years old, and he took after his father—whose treecat name was Sleek Fisher—rather strongly. The Harrington House staff had become accustomed to finding him swimming strongly around Honor's Olympic-sized pool, which was why his two-leg name was Poseidon, and he was noted for the reckless abandon with which he raced through the world about him.

"Not really his fault, either," Honor got out now, as the contraction released her. "And if I wasn't so pregnant, I'd've been able to avoid him."

"Sure you would have." Hamish was clearly less inclined to make allowances for Swimmer's tender years, and she smiled fleetingly as she tasted his fond exasperation. Honor had maintained a modified version of her normal workout schedule, but as her pregnancy had progressed, she'd had to cut back on it. And it was certainly true that she was less agile than she had been. But still—

"The good thing," Hamish continued, looking across the bed

at Allison and Alfred, "is that Spencer was right there. He caught her before she could go all the way down, but not even he could keep her from landing on both knees—hard. And by the time we got her back on her feet and down the damned stairs, her water had broken and it was pretty obvious Andrew had decided to put in his appearance earlier than scheduled. So we got her into the infirmary here rather than trying to get her to the hospital."

"And she's going to be fine," Dr. Ambrose McWhirter said, stepping back into the room. It was a rather large room, actually, but it seemed to be getting a bit crowded from where Honor lay. "We've been monitoring all along, so we already knew the baby's lungs are fine. Yes, he's over a month early, but that's only because of the prolong involved. In a lot of ways, we've just been marking time till your due date, really; neither he nor you took any actual harm from the fall, My Lady; and thanks to both Doctors Harrington, Howard Clinkscales has the best neonatal unit on the planet. So if he wants to sneak into the world a few weeks early, that's fine by me. Although—" he looked at Honor and his Grayson accent seemed a bit more pronounced than usual "—this is *not* the approved way to induce labor, My Lady."

"I know! I know! But Hamish and I don't do anything the easy—"

Honor broke off, panting again, and McWhirter checked his chrono.

"All right," he announced. "Obviously this young man's even more impatient than I'd expected. I realize that at the moment we have something of a plethora of physicians, but I think Lady Harrington and I need a little room in which to work. So if you'd all just step back? No, not you, My Lord." He shook his head at Hamish. "You stay right where you are and hold onto that hand. And I don't suppose there's much point asking the treecats to leave?"

"No," Honor told him just a bit breathlessly.

"What I expected." McWhirter shook his head again and made shooing motions at the room's occupants. "In that case, surplus two-foots in that corner," he pointed, "and treecats on the perches over there."

He pointed again, and waited until Honor's family—two-foots and treecats alike—had obeyed the imperious gesture, then smiled warmly at his patient.

"And now, My Lady, I suppose you and I had better get to work. Although—" his eyes twinkled at her "—I expect you'll find the division of labor, you should pardon the expression, just a bit unfair."

✧   ✧   ✧

"Not too shabby, sweetheart," Allison said, some hours later. Honor had been moved back to her own bed, and her mother sat beside it, holding her newest grandchild in her arms as she smiled at her daughter. "Not too shabby, at all. Although, you clearly have a few things to figure out about doing it the old-fashioned way. Falling down a staircase six weeks before your due date is usually frowned on."

"No? Really?" The actual delivery had been an easy one. That was what both Ambrose McWhirter and her parents told her, anyway. Odd that an "easy delivery" could leave her feeling so exhausted. Of course, the run up *to* it had been anything *but* easy. "You know, I don't think anybody ever told me that part. Thank you!"

"It's what a mother's here for," Allison told her, bending to press a mothwing kiss on Andrew Judah Wesley Alexander-Harrington's forehead, while Nimitz crooned a soft laugh from where he lay stretched along the bed's carved headboard. The sleeping baby paid it no heed, and Honor's lips trembled ever so slightly.

I will not *get all misty-eyed*, she told herself firmly. *I'm sure it's just exhaustion from the delivery. Yeah*, sure *it is!*

Exhausted or not, sore or not, she'd never felt a deeper, more abiding joy in her life. Except—

"I wish Emily were here," she said softly. She reached out, laying one hand on her son's tiny, tiny chest, drinking in his slumbering mind-glow, feeling his heartbeat against her palm.

"I know you do." Allison's voice was equally soft. "And I do, too. But she really *is*, you know. She's here in your heart and mine, and in Hamish's. And in Andrew, too." She blinked misty eyes of her own. "For that matter, I'm sure she's been watching both of you all the way through this pregnancy."

"I hope so," Honor said. "I mean, it was hers, too."

"Yes, it was." Allison smiled at her. "And now, young lady, I think you've had a busy enough day. Why don't you take a nap?"

"I will, but there's one thing we still have to do."

"Honor—"

"Sorry, Mom." Honor's lips quirked in a weary smile. "It's the law."

"Stupid damned patriarchal, fossilized, outdated—!"

"Oh, behave yourself!" Honor said. "Mind you, I think you have a point, but when the law was written, there weren't any female steadholders. I'm pretty sure I could get Benjamin to grant an extension while I rested up, but I'm not going to. Which doesn't mean I won't lean on him a little to get the law modified for the future."

Allison looked rebellious, but then she sighed.

"All right. All right! At least I had a chance to get you up here and get you settled, first. But you listen to me, Honor. You'd *better* get this changed before my next grandchild arrives, or else you'd better handle the pregnancy the same way you did with Raoul. Or at least not scare me the way you did this time!"

"I'll work on that—all of it," Honor promised. "But for now..."

Allison nodded and climbed out of her chair. She handed the drowsing baby to Honor and saw him settled in the crook of her right arm, then crossed to the bedroom door and opened it.

"All right, people. Get in here!"

It was not the most gracious invitation Honor had ever heard, but at least it was obeyed with a certain alacrity, and Allison stood aside as Alfred, Hamish, Benjamin Mayhew, Austen Clinkscales, Reverend Jeremiah Sullivan, Spencer Hawke, and Jefferson McClure stepped past her into the spacious bedroom. Samantha rode Hamish's shoulder as he crossed to her bedside and took her left hand.

"I believe we're all here now," Honor said.

"It *is* something of a dog-and-pony show, isn't it?" the Protector of Grayson said. "You know, we really could have waited to do this tomorrow, Honor. Or even the next day."

Something suspiciously like a snort sounded from Allison Harrington's direction, but Honor ignored it.

"No, this is important," she said, and looked at Reverend Sullivan. "Reverend?"

Sullivan looked at her for a moment, then raised his right hand.

"O Creator and Tester of us all, look down upon this most worthy daughter and be with her and with her son both this day and forever more. Amen."

"Thank you." Honor's eyes were soft. She might not be a

formal communicant of the Church of Humanity Unchained, but her respect for it was profound. She gazed at him for another moment, then moved her eyes to Clinkscales.

"This is my son," she said, speaking to them all, "Andrew Judah Wesley Alexander-Harrington. Flesh of my flesh, bone of my bone, heir of heart and life, of power and title. I declare him before you all as my witnesses and God's."

"He is your son," her regent replied, and bowed deeply. Genetically, Andrew wasn't her son, of course. But that didn't matter to her, and it had *never* mattered to the law—or the church—of Grayson. He *was* her son, third in the succession of Harrington Steading, and her eyes moved from Clinkscales to Jefferson McClure.

"This is my son," she told the man who'd been Emily Alexander-Harrington's personal armsman, who'd been there the day Emily died in Honor's arms, the very day Andrew's zygote had been fertilized, "and I name you guardian and protector. I give his life into your keeping. Fail not in this trust."

"I recognize him," McClure said, "and I know him. I take his life into my keeping, flesh of your flesh, bone of your bone. Before God, Maker and Tester of us all; before His Son, Who died to intercede for us all; and before the Holy Comforter, I will stand before him in the Test of life and at his back in battle. I will protect and guard his life with my own. His honor is my honor, his heritage is mine to guard, and I will fail not in this trust, though it cost me my life."

His steady voice wavered ever so slightly as he finished the ancient formula, the oath that made him Andrew's protector and guardian, and Honor's eyes burned as she remembered another voice, the voice of another Grayson named Andrew, swearing that same oath the day Raoul was born. A Grayson who'd honored that oath at the cost of his own life...and who she'd known would never have done anything else when that horrible moment came.

She'd had to think neither long nor hard before she knew who must become Andrew Alexander-Harrington's personal armsman, and she hoped—oh, how she hoped!—that Emily was watching this, too.

She drew her hand out of Hamish's comforting grip and unwrapped her son's blanket. Andrew stirred, eyes opening but unfocused, as she worked one tiny hand free and McClure extended his own open hand. She placed Andrew's palm against the palm of the man who'd sworn to die—as Andrew LaFollet had died—in her son's defense and looked deep into that man's eyes.

"I accept your oath in his name," she said, as she'd said to Andrew LaFollet. "You are my son's sword and his shield. His steps are yours to watch and guard, to ward and instruct."

McClure bowed deeply, and she bent her own head in acknowledgment. Then she tucked that small, delicate hand back inside the blanket, wrapped it tightly, and held her son—and Emily's—in her arms.

It was done, she thought. It was done.

"Thank you all for coming," she said. "But for right now—" she turned her head and smiled wearily at Hamish "—I think Andrew and I could use a nap."

"Can't imagine why," Hamish said with a smile, bending to brush a kiss across her forehead and touch their son's cheek gently.

"All right, clear the room!" Allison commanded.

"You're always so . . . subtle about these things," Alfred told her with a chuckle, and she gave him a swat.

"All of you go away and let them rest!"

The laughing severity in Allison's voice couldn't have fooled any of them, Honor thought. It certainly hadn't fooled her, and she tasted her mother's own memory of the day of Raoul's birth.

And of the day Andrew LaFollet had died saving her life along with her grandson's.

The bedroom emptied. Even Hamish left, although Samantha remained, and Honor lay back on the pillows, aware—now that Andrew's formal, legal recognition had been accomplished—of the fatigue the need to accomplish that had held at bay. She blinked drowsily as her mother came quietly back to the chair beside her bed, and felt the treecats wrapping their love about her and Andrew like yet another blanket.

"And now," Allison said softly, "about that nap?"

"About that nap, Mama," Honor agreed softly as her mother's mind-glow wrapped itself about her, as well. "It seems like a very good idea," she murmured.

"There, now. Aren't you the clever one?"

Allison smiled and cleared her throat gently.

"Lulla-lulla-lullaby," she sang, and Honor smiled at the ancient, familiar words from her own long-ago nursery.

"Thank you, Mama," she murmured, and Allison stroked her forehead again.

> "Hush, little baby. Don't say a word.
> Papa's gonna buy you a mocking bird,
> And if that mocking bird don't sing
> Papa's gonna buy you a diamond ring..."

The soft, soft voice followed Honor Alexander-Harrington down into the deep, sweet sleep her day deserved.

December 1923 Post Diaspora

"First, we're the good guys, not the bad guys. Secondly, I doubt very much that *you're* one of the bad guys, either. So there's no need for any unpleasantness, as far as I'm concerned. How do *you* feel about that?"

—Captain Anton Ziliwcki

Jessyk Station
Warner Terminus
Warner-Mannerheim Hyper Bridge
Warner System

"I GUESS IT'S GOOD TO SEE TRAFFIC STARTING TO PICK UP AGAIN," Morris Gwaltney observed. The traffic manager sipped coffee as he stood at Susannah Gulo's shoulder, looking at her display. He had the morning shift this month, and he did like his caffeine. "Be nice if the damned Manties would just get out of the frigging way and let things go back to normal!"

"I don't think you can blame all of this on the Grand Alliance," Gulo replied. She sat back and reached for her own coffee cup. She was Gwaltney's senior controller, and the Jessyk Combine promoted a relaxed work environment, especially here in Warner. Which didn't keep her from watching her board with an eagle eye.

Besides, Gwaltney made really, really good coffee.

"They never shut *us* down here in Warner, for example," she added.

"Who's talking about the 'Grand Alliance'?" Gwaltney demanded. "Everybody knows it was the Manties calling the shots for the 'Alliance's' trade war policies! And they're still doing their damnedest to choke every other carrier while the choking's good." He sipped more coffee, his expression moody. "They can say whatever the hell they want, Sue, but they're riding this as far as they can, and you know it!"

Gulo shrugged. She liked Gwaltney a lot, but he had a personal thing about Manticore. She'd never figured out what it was, but it went beyond the envy most people in the freight-hauling business cherished for the advantages the Manticoran Wormhole Junction had bestowed upon the Star Kingdom of Manticore. Personally, Gulo didn't doubt that there were Manticoran shipping lines who were, indeed, "riding this" as far as they could, but unlike Gwaltney, she found it hard to blame them. First there'd been the sneak attack by parties unknown—Susannah Gulo found it difficult to believe in the "Mesan Alignment," because in real life, conspiracies just didn't last for centuries without springing leaks—which had devastated their home star system's industry. Then there was the damage their own merchant marine had suffered when the Grand Alliance virtually shut down the Solarian League's interstellar commerce. After that double whammy, probably as many as twenty-five or thirty percent of the Manticoran lines had gone under. No doubt the survivors needed every credit they could scrape up.

The Grand Alliance in general, and the Star Empire of Manticore in particular, couldn't be blind to that consideration, but they also couldn't be blind to the resentment festering in the Solarian League's shipping industry. Or among any of the transstellars who relied on interstellar markets they could no longer reach in Solarian-flagged hulls. They'd have had to be a lot stupider than Manties had ever been before to not realize it was fence-mending time. For that matter, from everything Gulo had seen coming out of the Constitutional Convention on Old Terra—admittedly, these days, any news from the Sol System was over a month old by the time it reached them here in Warner—the Grand Alliance was being as reasonable as the people who'd conquered the most powerful star nation in human history could be. It seemed pretty obvious to her that they were doing everything they could to tamp down any inevitable Solarian revanchism, anyway.

She doubted anyone could have gotten Morris Gwaltney to admit anything of the sort, of course.

"Well," she said out loud, "I agree it's nice to see one of our own ships passing through."

"Yeah." Gwaltney nodded, but he also scowled.

"What now?" Gulo asked.

"What?" Gwaltney looked down at her, then shrugged with an edge of apology. "Sorry. Didn't mean to grump all over you, Sue! I was just thinking it would be nice to know when Corporate's going to get around to telling us how the company's been affected by what's happening in Mesa. Or that Harris would tell the peasants like you and me something, at least!"

Jacqueline Harris was Director of Operations for the Jessyk

Combine's terminus operations here in Warner. As such, she was the senior Jessyk executive in the star system, and given Jessyk Station's importance to the combine, that made her a pretty big fish in the Jessyk pond.

In some ways, Warner and the Manticore Binary System had a bit in common. They each had a wormhole and they each had multiple habitable planets. In Warner's case, Jacob, Warner III, was chilly, and its thirty-one-degree axial inclination made for severe seasonal climate variations. Wilhelm—Warner IV—was over two and a half light-minutes farther from the system's G9 primary, which made it even chillier, and on the undersized side, barely half the size of Old Terra and with only about sixty percent of the ancestral home world's gravity. But even a small habitable planet was a largish thing, and between them, Jacob and Wilhelm provided plenty of places for people to live. In Jacob's case, they clustered around the equator, where the seasonal variations were as minimal as they got. Wilhelm's axial tilt, on the other hand, was barely half that of Old Terra's, which meant its seasonal variations were far milder, and despite its even lower average temperature—a good four degrees cooler than Old Terra's—its population was spread over a much broader percentage of its surface.

But the sad truth was that Warner had been shortchanged in the galactic sweepstakes compared to Manticore. Manticore had *three* habitable worlds, all of them—except, perhaps, Sphinx—warmer than Warner's two. It had three extraordinarily rich asteroid belts to sustain its deep-space industry, compared to Warner's single depressingly average belt. And *Manticore*'s wormhole was a junction, with no fewer than *seven* termini that covered a preposterous volume. Any one of those termini, except possibly the one to the Lynx System, saw almost as much traffic as passed through Warner in a given year, even with Mannerheim and the rest of the Renaissance Factor at the other end of its warp bridge. So even though Warner had been the very first wormhole ever discovered, the next best thing to six hundred T-years ago, the Warner System had never come close to matching Manticore as a shipping, banking, and communications hub.

"Actually, I doubt the director's keeping secrets," Gulo said now. "If she'd heard anything, I'm pretty sure she'd have passed it on to us. And if all of this is frustrating to you and me, it's got to be even worse for her!"

"You think?" Gwaltney snorted. "But you're probably right. I'll bet she's ready to start reading tea leaves by now." He shook his head. "What do *you* think's headed our way?"

"Probably nothing good," she conceded. "Not in the short term, at least. On the other hand, Jessyk's too damned big to just go down the tubes. We'd take too many other people and jobs with us and *somebody*'s got to carry the freight. My guess?" It was her turn to shrug. "There's going to be some major 'housecleaning,' and probably quite a few indictments in the executive suite. For that matter, I wouldn't be all that surprised to see the entire company taken over by someone else—someone in the League, probably, not in Mesa—and given a complete facelift. Maybe even broken up into smaller, independent operations. I'd rather not see that happen, but I'll be honest with you, Morris—I'd be just tickled to cut the entire Mesa connection." She waved her coffee cup. "I know Jessyk's been based in Mesa for T-centuries, ever since it was founded. But tell me you haven't been unhappy about working for someone that friendly with the goddamned genetic slavers!"

Gwaltney grimaced, but he also nodded again.

"I guess some good can come out of just about anything," he acknowledged.

❖   ❖   ❖

"I don't suppose *Marzipan*'s got any messages from anywhere interesting for us?" Jacqueline Harris grumbled.

She was a very tall, very thin woman, but there was nothing fragile about her. She had a genetically modified heavy-worlder's musculature and the metabolism—and appetite—to go with it. It wasn't at all uncommon for her to nibble away during conference calls or even personal face-to-face meetings with her subordinates here in her office. This time, though, she poked moodily at the omelet on her plate as she glowered at Mîrhem Alîkar, her assistant director. Alîkar was a good five centimeters shorter than his boss, dark complected and dark-haired to her platinum blond, and considerably bulkier. In fact, he bordered on marginally obese.

"She hasn't told us about it if she does," he said now, leaning back in his chair on the other side of her desk. "The fact that she's here at all is probably good news, though."

Harris nodded a bit glumly. Jessyk's corporate operations had shifted to its Sol System sector headquarters, the biggest ganglion of its nervous system outside Mesa itself, when Mesa went down, but it was evident that the Solarians weren't a lot happier with the Mesan transstellars than the Grand Alliance was. As far as she could tell, they hadn't reached the stage of cutting off their Jessyk nose to spite their Solarian face, but they were keeping a lot closer eye on Jessyk's operations than they ever had under the old government. Not too surprising, probably, given how many "special friends" almost all the transstellars had lost in Old Chicago when the Mandarins went down. But she'd anticipated—at least initially—that things would get a lot closer to back to normal, especially after all these months, than they had.

Unfortunately, both the Solarian Provisional Government and the Constitutional Convention seemed focused on keeping things from *ever* getting "back to normal" where the transstellar business community was concerned.

And in the meantime, Jessyk was operating pretty much on autopilot. Nobody was setting any new policies, at any rate. And they probably wouldn't be, at least until the new Constitution was ratified and—hopefully!—the Solarian regulatory agencies eased their death grip on the corporation's windpipe.

At least we can be confident the Manties and their friends didn't get hold of Central's classified database, she thought. *If they had, we'd have damned well heard about it by now!*

That wasn't something she could discuss with Alîkar, but it was something that had worried her—a lot—when the initial reports of mobs storming Manpower's and Jessyk's home offices in Mesa reached Warner. She had no idea of everything that might have been in those classified records, but she knew there'd been enough to make plenty of problems for the corporation. Especially if the Sollies were serious about erasing every trace of the genetic slave trade.

But it would seem the Sollies—and the Manties, damn them— were finally allowing at least some of Jessyk's ships back into operation. There still wasn't all that much for anyone to be hauling around, since the Manties continued to occupy so many of the critical wormhole junctions, but the interstellar economy was beginning to pick up again. And the newly organized Renaissance Factor which had coalesced around the Republic of Mannerheim and its neighbors was one of the healthier nodes of that reviving commerce. It was unfortunate, if scarcely surprising, given what had happened in Mesa, that virtually all of the freight passing through Warner these days was in non-Jessyk freighters, but *Marzipan*'s arrival was a heartening sign that that might be about to change.

"How far out is she?" Harris asked now, and Alîkar checked his uni-link.

"Another forty minutes or so," he said. "And she may have something to hand-deliver, now that I think about it."

"Really?" Harris quirked an eyebrow.

"She's requested docking space at Able One," Alîkar replied, and Harris frowned thoughtfully.

Jessyk Station was actually a sort of shorthand, or at least a collective noun, for the seven separate platforms the transstellar maintained out here at the Warner Wormhole Terminus. In fact, Jessyk was the most heavily represented of all of the shipping lines doing business in Warner, but Able One was the administrative hub of the combine's operations here. It did receive, warehouse, and transfer cargo, but that was no longer its primary function. So Alîkar might well have a point.

And there are message chips, and then there are message *chips,* Harris thought, and anticipation tingled through her. As far as Alîkar knew they were out of touch only with their corporate masters. He didn't need to know about the other people who might be sending one Jacqueline Harris sensitive communications.

"Well, I guess we'll find out in forty minutes or so," she said, and speared a bite of omelet with her fork with more enthusiasm.

✧   ✧   ✧

"*Marzipan* is coming up for the parking queue on Able One, Morris," Susanna Gulo reported. "Can I tell them to go ahead and let her dock?"

"Yeah, we're cool," Gwaltney said, looking up from his own console. "I'm not sure where the glitch was, but their paperwork's coming through now."

He rolled his eyes, and Gulo chuckled. Traffic managers hated delays in paperwork transmission, but they were a fact of life. Management might try to schedule shipments sufficiently in advance to forewarn their cargo agents about what was inbound, but they had about as much luck in that regard as the fabled Ante Diaspora king who'd tried to stop the tide from coming in. Most of the time, the first thing an orbital or deep-space warehouse knew about what they'd have to accommodate this time around came with an incoming freighter's bill of lading and transshipment orders. And "glitches" in transmitting that information to the people responsible for managing it were far more common than they ought to have been.

"Says here they only have about four hundred ISCs for us." The Interstellar Shipping Container was the standardized base unit of interstellar commerce. "Call it six hundred thousand tons. But they've got another couple of dozen ISCs of pressure-sensitive cargo they'd prefer to transship by tube, and they've got a dozen replacement crews for the cargo tugs, too."

"Well, hallelujah!" Gulo pumped a fist. "Kondraty's going to be glad to hear that!"

Kondraty Akdag managed Jessyk Station's fleet of tugs, and his crews were seriously understrength at the moment. The prolonged downturn in interstellar commerce had idled better than two thirds of his tugs, and most of the personnel who'd manned them had been laid off. Harris probably hadn't wanted to do that, but she hadn't had much choice under the combine's established SOP and she'd been unable to get authorization to modify that SOP in the wake of Mesa's conquest. The people who'd been laid off had, understandably, taken other work, wherever they could find it. Those of them who weren't from out-system and hadn't simply decided to return to their home star systems and families, at any rate. Now that trade had started picking up again, Akdag's remaining tugs were grossly overworked.

"Yeah, he definitely is," Gwaltney agreed. "But since they've got the pressure sensitive stuff and a personnel transfer they're asking for a direct mooring so they can transfer via tube rather than cross loading everything."

"Um." Gulo punched up a side display and considered it for a handful of seconds. "No problem," she said then. "I can put them on Able One's Tube Four. If that'll work for their cargo, anyway. I'm thinking that if they're bringing us replacement personnel, the newbies're gonna have to go through Admin and quarters assignment, so that's probably the logical place to put them."

"Should be okay for the cargo," Gwaltney replied. "Looks like most of it's exotic pets, of all damned things. From the dimensions in the download, they should be able to get all of it into the axial cargo tubes and down to controlled environment holding."

"Tube Four it is, then," Gulo declared, and keyed her com.

"*Marzipan*, Traffic Control," she said, and the Station's communications AI plugged her directly into the freighter.

"Hello, Control," a voice said in her earbug. "Should I assume you have that docking clearance for us?"

"You should, indeed, *Marzipan*. You are cleared to Cargo Tube Four on the Able One platform for personnel and cargo of. Freight Management will contact you on Channel Three for vacuum-certified cross load. I am sending you confirming vector commands now, and then I'll be transferring you to Able One Approach Control. They'll take you the rest of the way in, and I'm sure the tugs will be standing by if you need them."

"I'll pass the word to the Skipper, Traffic Control, but I don't think we're going to need the tugs. In fact, she's a little... touchy about suggestions that she can't dock her own ship if she needs to."

"Really?" Gulo looked over her shoulder and rolled her eyes at Gwaltney. "She does realize we're here to help if she needs us, though?"

"I'm sure she does, but to be honest, she probably won't need you. Just between you and me, she's *almost* as good as she thinks she is."

"Should I take it that she's not on the bridge right this moment listening to your end of the conversation?" Gulo inquired with a smile.

"Since I'm neither stupid nor suicidal, you may indeed assume that," the voice in her ear told her with a chuckle. "*Marzipan*, clear."

❖   ❖   ❖

"Damn, she *is* good," Kondraty Akdag muttered as the six-million-ton freighter just kissed the midships cargo tube with the delicacy of an Old Earth hummingbird. The stupendous ship was well clear of Able One itself—fully extended, the flexible cargo tube was the better part of a half kilometer in length—but he'd been more than a little nervous watching *Marzipan*'s approach. Even a minor slip had major consequences when a ship that size docked with a freight platform that massed right on thirty million tons. Exclusive of the vast, open-to-vacuum storage platforms at the ends of their own individual cargo booms, of course.

But the freighter's mistress after God had played her ship's reaction thrusters with the skill of a concert pianist. Thank goodness.

"Good seal," the cargo technician standing beside Akdag at the inbound end of the cavernous tube said.

The manager nodded in acknowledgment. Tube Four was fifty meters in diameter, and no one wanted to take any chances opening the tube airlocks until they knew for damn sure the docking collar at the outboard end had sealed properly to *Marzipan*'s hull.

"Cracking the outboard lock now," the cargo tech continued, still watching her readouts carefully. "Pressure looks good," she said after a moment.

"In that case, open her up and let's get this show on the road," Mbuso Gambushe said. The Able One duty-watch freight foreman actually looked a great deal like his Ndebele ancestors, and he gazed down at his personal minicomp as he spoke. "It says here your incoming people have all been precleared by Medical," he told Akdag, and looked back up. "You've got quarters assigned?"

"Sort of." Akdag shrugged. "Nobody told me they were coming, either. Housekeeping's spinning up a couple of extra pods, but it'll be another two or three hours before anybody can move into them. I figured I'd take them down to Admin and give them the five-credit virtual tour of the Station while we waited."

"Works for me," Gambushe said, and nodded to the tech. "Tell them to come on down!"

Akdag moved to the center of the inboard end of the tube and gazed down its lighted length as the inboard airlock cycled open. The people swimming the tube's microgravity toward him were tiny with distance, initially, but that changed as they got closer. And then the first man reached the grab bar, swung out of the tube into the cargo bay's standard single gravity, and moved forward to clear the landing area behind him.

"Howdy," he rumbled in a subterranean bass that went almost inevitably with his incredibly broad shoulders and powerful musculature. The newcomer wasn't actually short, Akdag realized; he just looked that way because he had so much...heft. "Which one of you's Akdag?"

"That would be me," Akdag said, holding out his hand.

"Pleased to meet you. I'm Umebayashi."

"Already figured that out," Akdag said dryly, and Umebayashi chuckled.

"Guess I'm not exactly the hardest guy to recognize from his personnel file imagery," he acknowledged, gripping Akdag's hand with carefully metered force. "My friends call me Mitsukuni."

"And I don't suppose too many people are *un*friendly where somebody built like you is concerned," Akdag said.

"Well, no. But mostly because I'm such a friendly sort myself," Umebayashi said with a deadpan expression, and Akdag laughed.

"I expect we'll get along just fine," he said, and jerked a thumb at the forty or so other men and women who'd swung out of the boat bay and assembled themselves, more or less, behind Umebayashi, the senior skipper of the newly arrived crews. "This everybody?"

"We've got a couple of guys running behind." Umebayashi shrugged. "Always something to screw up a personnel transfer."

"We need to wait for them?"

"Nah." Umebayashi shook his head. "It's just last-minute paperwork screw ups. Not their fault, not *Marzipan*'s fault—just one of those things. You know how it goes."

"Tell me about it. Well, if they're going to be a while, why don't I get the rest of your people down to the Admin chow hall? I figured coffee and donuts might dull the pain of the mandatory briefing in."

"Kondraty, I see you are a man of great wisdom." A shovellike hand smacked Akdag lightly on the shoulder. "I think this is the beginning of a beautiful friendship!"

"When Mitsukuni's orphans get here, can you download the platform schematic to their uni-links, Mbuso? And highlight the route to the main dining hall?"

"Not a problem, Kondraty," Gambushe said with a wave, his attention on the first of the cargo flats already floating down the tube towards him.

"In that case, Mitsukuni, step this way."

✧   ✧   ✧

The trip to the dining hall didn't take long. Able One wasn't the largest of Jessyk Station's platforms, but it was big enough for slidewalks, which delivered the largish group to the central lift shafts. There were enough of them to require a couple of trips once they hit the lifts, and Akdag stood on the raised stage at one end of the spacious compartment, chatting with Umebayashi while they waited for the second round to arrive.

"First time in Warner?" he asked.

"First time," Umebayashi confirmed, and gave him a quizzical look. "I didn't get the background brief on the system, just on the Station. I guess they figured I could get the rest of the information on my own." He rolled his eyes. "Gotta love the way the suits look after us working stiffs. But I have to say, this star system's planet names are even weirder than most!"

"Well, maybe," Akdag acknowledged. "I mean Mumblety-Peg's got some pretty strange names. But I'll give you weird for Warner. The ship that surveyed the system was from a German-speaking system, and its captain was obviously a bit of a romantic. And probably a degree or two off-plumb. Anyway, he named the two habitable planets for a pair of Old Earth brothers who collected fairytales, and then he named everything else in the system for characters out of the stories they'd collected. So you get things like Aschenputtel for Warner I and Rotkäppchen for Warner VI."

"I'm not familiar with those characters," Umebayashi said, hauling a minicomp out of his pocket and tapping the display.

"Sure you are!" Akdag grinned. "Aschenputtel is Cinderella, and Rotkäppchen is Little Red Riding Hood. The guy obviously had a sense of humor, since Rotkäppchen's 'only' about two thirds the size of Old Jupiter!"

"I think you're right about his sense of humor," Umebayashi said, then looked up from his minicomp's display. "And I hope *you've* got a sense of humor, Kondraty."

"What?" Akdag's eyebrows rose, because there was something odd about Umebayashi's tone.

The other man didn't reply. Instead, he looked over his shoulder at a much younger fellow.

"Cameras are down, Indy," he said.

"All right!"

The young man had set his personal carry-on bag on the table in front of him and opened it. Now he reached in and brought out a military-grade pulser.

"Hey! What—?!"

Akdag's blurted question was interrupted as "Indy" tossed a *second* pulser towards Umebayashi . . . who caught it neatly without seeming to actually look at it at all.

Akdag, on the other hand, looked at it very closely. That tended to happen when someone aimed a pulser directly between his eyes.

"Now, don't get excited, Kondraty." Umebayashi's tone was calm, almost soothing. "First, we're the good guys, not the *bad* guys. Secondly, I doubt very much that *you're* one of the bad guys, either. So there's no need for any unpleasantness, as far as I'm concerned. How do *you* feel about that?"

Akdag swallowed hard. More pulsers were turning up—lots of pulsers—all around the dining room, along with what looked like stun rods and tanglers, and he stood very still as another of Umebayashi's people, a diminutive Oriental woman, stepped up onto the stage, careful to stay out from between Umebayashi's pulser and Akdag, and calmly relieved him of his uni-link.

"Oh, just this minute I'm feeling like the most pleasant guy you know," he told Umebayashi fervently.

"Good! Then why don't you just go with Natsuko here and have a seat."

✧   ✧   ✧

"That's weird," Abigail Sorokin muttered. She frowned and tapped a brief series of queries into her terminal, then looked over her shoulder.

"Director, we've got a sensor outage."

"What kind of 'outage'?" Christian Espina, Jessyk Station's Security Director, crossed Security Central to Corporal Sorokin's station. Espina had a comfortable, well-furnished office with every imaginable communication device about ten meters down the passageway from Central, but he was seldom in it if he could help it.

"They don't know, sir," Sorokin replied, and pointed an index finger at her display as Espina arrived at her shoulder. "See?" She tapped the flashing red line on the schematic. "That's the feed from the Executive Suite."

"*Just* the Executive Suite?" Espina's eyes narrowed and his tone sharpened, but Sorokin shook her head.

"No, sir. It's some kind of rolling interruption. Looks like some sort of bug got into the servers, frankly. Look! The Executive Suite's back up, and we've just lost the link to Operations."

"That *is* weird," Espina acknowledged. "And I don't like it. Report it to Maintenance."

"I already did, sir. They've got a tech on his way up here now."

"Good!" Espina encouraged his people to take initiative, and he was glad Sorokin had in this case. As he watched, Operations' security cams came back up, but the ones covering Engineering went down. None of them were staying down long enough to seriously interrupt their coverage, but there was no guarantee that wouldn't change. The sooner Maintenance got in here and found the gremlin behind it, the better!

The compartment hatch slid open and an extraordinarily broad-shouldered man stepped through it with a toolkit in his left hand and a satchel over his right shoulder.

"Understand we have a problem," he rumbled in a voice as extraordinarily deep as his shoulders were wide.

"That's one way to put it," Espina acknowledged. "It's not that bad, but—"

He broke off as a short, slender Oriental woman and a remarkably ordinary-looking man with brown hair, came through the hatch. Espina's eyes flicked to them, then back to the first tech... whose right hand had just produced a long-barreled pulser from that satchel over his shoulder.

"My name's Zilwicki," he rumbled pleasantly. "*Captain* Zilwicki, and I'm afraid I'm responsible for the little glitch your systems have been experiencing. You people really needed better security." He shrugged. "But now, I'd appreciate it if everyone would just stand up, hold your hands where we can see them, and move away from your consoles. And before any of you get any ideas about punching panic buttons, at the moment, all of your hardwired lines are down. Like I said, you needed better security. So why don't you just go ahead and skip the bit where you try to do something heroic and somebody gets hurt?"

"What the hell is this?!" Espina snapped.

"What this is, Director," the teenaged-looking woman who'd followed Captain Zilwicki into the compartment said, "is a raid." Espina's eyes snapped back to her, and she drew a very familiar looking badge from the pocket of her utility coveralls. "My name's Okiku—*Colonel* Okiku, Solarian Gendarmerie—and all of you are under arrest." She smiled pleasantly as four more men stepped into the compartment. "For most of you, it will be a brief experience which we'll try to make no more unpleasant than we must."

Espina's eyes narrowed again. Then they widened suddenly, and both hands went to his temples as his knees buckled.

✧   ✧   ✧

The door chime sounded, and Jacqueline Harris looked up from the paperwork *Marzipan* had uploaded to Jessyk Station and quirked an eyebrow. She didn't have anything on her calendar at the moment, and it was unusual for Sheldon Jackson, her secretary, to ring for admittance if he needed to talk to her. On the other hand, an interruption wouldn't be totally unwelcome. She'd wanted to hear from corporate headquarters in the Sol System, and she reminded herself of her mother's advice: "Be careful what you wish for. You may get it."

The sheer quantity of it was bad enough, although that was hardly surprising after so many months of virtual silence. But it could have been expressly designed to anchor her to her desk while she dealt with the queries, requests, and God knew what else that had been sent along. The fact that Corporate wanted all of its boxes checked and lines filled out before *Marzipan* headed for her next destination only made it worse.

The door chimed again, softly—politely—and she chuckled, then pressed the admittance stud.

The panel slid aside, and Harris shot to her feet as a total stranger—the most remarkably unremarkable-looking fellow she'd ever seen in her life—stepped through it...with a pulser in his hand.

"Who the hell are you?!" she snapped.

"I hate to intrude this way," he said, "but—" he gestured with the barrel of the pulser "—could you please step away from the desk?"

Her toe came down on the floor-mounted alarm button under her desk, but nothing happened.

"I'm afraid most of the station's systems are under our control," the ordinary-looking man told her. She stared at him for a moment, then stepped away from the desk.

"I asked you who the hell you are!"

"The name is Harahap," he said. "Damien Harahap. And I'm with the Solarian Gendarmerie."

"The *Gendarmerie*?" She glared at him. "What the fuck are you doing in *my* office with a *pulser* if you're a gendarme?"

"I'm not actually *a* gendarme anymore," he told her as two more strangers followed him into her office. "Although I am *with* the Gendarmes at the moment. And I'm afraid the Gendarmerie is taking over Jessyk Station until we sort out a few minor concerns that have been raised back in Old Chicago."

"What sort of 'concerns'?" she demanded.

"We'll get to that," Harahap assured her. "But first, we have to finish tidying up some loose ends. So, if you'll just step this way?"

"Loose ends," she repeated in a much softer voice.

"Exactly." His own eyes had narrowed. "If everything's on the up-and-up out here, we'll be out of your hair in no more than a couple of days."

"Oh, I think you'll be out of *my* hair sooner than that," she told him with an off-center smile, and picked the small, antique paperweight off her desk. "Catch!"

She tossed it at him underhand, far too slowly for something that light to even leave a bruise. It should still have distracted him, but to her surprise, his eyes didn't even flick to it. He simply stepped to one side, with a fluid speed that was astonishing. It sailed right past him, and the pulser in his hand never wavered.

But that was all right. Moving the paperweight was only the first stage. It armed the system. What *triggered* the system was something else entirely.

Her right rear molar crunched as she bit down on it three times in rapid, carefully timed succession, and her eyes rolled up. Then she hit the floor in a limp, boneless sprawl, and the standalone air-gapped server tucked away in a corner of her bedroom, two decks below her office, exploded.

January 1924 Post Diaspora

"You know perfectly well that it's not going to be a 'pleasure' talking to me, Brigadier, but you're willing to pretend. Like I said, a true gentleman."

—Audrey O'Hanrahan

Joint Intelligence Sharing and Distribution Command Center
and
Brigadier Simeon Gaddis's Office
Smith Tower
City of Old Chicago
Old Earth
Sol System

"WELL, RONGLU, FOR WHAT IT'S WORTH, YOUR PEOPLE WERE obviously right about Warner."

Daud al-Fanudahi's delight—if any—seemed remarkably restrained. It was difficult to blame him under the circumstances.

"We strive to please, Captain," Ronglu X replied. "Sometimes we're more successful than others."

"I hate negative confirming evidence," Weng Zhing-hwan said, with a restraint that more than matched al-Fanudahi's.

"It wasn't *all* negative evidence," Anton Zilwicki rumbled.

"No?" Al-Fanudahi looked at him. "So, correct me if I'm wrong, but this *was* the only Jessyk installation you raided where more than a single person dropped dead, wasn't it? And also the only one where your teams—including, I might add, a certain champion-level hacker of my acquaintance—lost a complete standalone computer which undoubtedly contained the information which would have explained to us why five—not two, not three, not even four, but *five*—senior Jessyk employees fell over dead when they found out they'd been busted?" He snorted sourly. "I'd say that's a pretty conclusive indication we'd found a link to the Alignment, but there's not a single scrap of actual *evidence* that we did."

"Fair's fair, Daud," Natsuko Okiku said. "Anton was inside their systems. He had total penetration of their entire network. But

Harris's computer wasn't just air-gapped from the main servers. The only connection to it was a hardwired line that ran from a terminal in her desk which was *also* completely physically isolated from the main servers. The only way into it was from her desk, so of course he couldn't keep her from demolishing it. Personally, I find it interesting that they blew it the hell up instead of just slagging the files or telling the mollycircs to reconfigure into a blank state. Whatever was on it, they weren't taking *any* chances of someone else getting her hands on it."

"And," Damien Harahap put in, "the postmortem on Harris found a tiny blood oxygen monitor in one of her teeth, linked to a transmitter. It looks like she armed the self-destruct system when she threw that paperweight at me, but it also looks like the system was probably rigged to wipe itself anyway if the monitor's transmitter told it she was dead. Whether or not it would have blown up under those circumstances, I don't know, but it looks to me like she was making doubly sure of something that almost certainly would've happened no matter what after she 'dropped dead,' as Daud so charmingly put it."

"All that's true," Charles Gannon acknowledged. "But Colonel Weng and Captain al-Fanudahi still have a point. From the *Navy's* perspective, Rat Catcher was a resounding success. We've turned up plenty of evidence that Jessyk and Manpower were Siamese twins. In fact, we captured the combine's records almost entirely intact everywhere but right here in Sol. And even here, only one guy keeled over when we raided their Ganymede offices and our search teams didn't find any completely isolated computer systems, which would seem to indicate there were only dirty little *corporate* secrets hidden away in the files that got wiped. Admiral Kingsford and Admiral Robbins are just delighted to have targets for their Wilberforce cleaning teams, and the Attorney General's office has everything it needs to *nail* these bastards for their collusion in the slave trade. In fact, we've got evidence of at least five additional criminal enterprises, any one of which would be enough to justify the dissolution of the corporation. For that matter, we got plenty of *that* kind of evidence in Warner! But all of that only makes the huge, sucking hole where Harris's personal server used to be hurt even more."

"Before we just throw in the towel," Zilwicki said mildly, "let's take a close look at what we *did* get from Warner."

"Such as?" It would have been unfair to call Brigadier Gaddis's tone skeptical, but he did sound like someone who suspected someone else of searching desperately for a less-dark side so that he could gaze upon it and call it bright.

"Well, among other things, we got their entire historical archive," Zilwicki pointed out.

"And?" Gaddis prompted.

"And, Brigadier," Lucia Sharpe said, "those records confirm every report we had of slavers transiting the Warner wormhole. In fact, we found twenty-four additional transits by known slavers we hadn't previously realized were in the Warner queue. That brought our total up to seventy-seven, and we got better reads on their tonnage and life-support from the records. Assuming each of them was carrying a ninety-percent capacity load of slaves outbound, that's about three hundred sixty thousand slaves, not two hundred and fifty."

More than one jaw at that conference table clenched at the thought of that many purpose-built human beings being shipped off like so many spare parts.

"I'm not sure knowing the scale is going to make me feel much better, Captain Lucia," Weng said.

"No, it won't," Zilwicki agreed grimly. "But of those seventy-seven transits, seventy-four of the slavers came back through Warner on the return voyage. Only three of them didn't, which means that only three of them either went on to a different destination from the others, or else stayed in their destination system, for some reason."

"Really?" Gannon tipped back in his chair.

"Really," Zilwicki confirmed. "And those same records indicate that the ships in question all passed through Warner to the Mannerheim end of the bridge. I thought that was interesting, so Damien, Indy, and I made a hop through to Mannerheim, ourselves. In a splendid dispatch boat that's almost as fancy as Cathy's idea of a yacht and homeported on Jessyk Station. By the oddest coincidence, it happened to be crewed by its regular Jessyk crew, with Damien and Fire Watch—" the treecat stretched across the back of Harahap's chair stroked his whiskers with a panache d'Artagnan himself might have envied "—keeping an eye on them to make sure they didn't even think about doing something we wouldn't like. And because I was aboard Director

Harris's personal yacht, Mannerheim Wormhole Astro Control had no problem at all letting me log into their records of Jessyk-registered ships who'd used the wormhole. They probably didn't realize that when they let me into the current files, they were also letting me into their archives, and I saw no reason to worry them about any possible flaws I might have detected in their cybersecurity. In fairness to their security people, the files in question *are* public record, not the sort anyone would worry about wiping to conceal secret knowledge. In fact, I could've just asked for them, if I hadn't wanted to keep any reports that we'd looked at them from getting back to the Alignment.

"What I found, though, was that not a single one of our known slavers headed away from the Mannerheim terminus on exactly the same vector. I don't think anyone's going to believe there were seventy-seven different slave-buying star systems, all of them unknown to the Ballroom, convenient to Mannerheim. Which means the only reason to head out on different bearings was to be damned sure they concealed the actual bearing to their destination. Wherever those slavers were headed, they were making it impossible for their ship captains to get lazy and save a few hours or days in transit by heading out on a least-time course to wherever they were going. That's the kind of paranoid precaution we've come to associate with the Alignment, and the fact that they were taking it here is further confirmation that whatever else it may have been, the Warner-Mannerheim Bridge is looking more and more like the gateway to wherever the Alignment set up housekeeping outside the Mesa System."

"Do you think Mannerheim might have more useful information for us?" Gaddis asked.

"Almost certainly not... unfortunately." Zilwicki shrugged. "None of the slavers went anywhere near Mannerheim—well, no nearer than the terminus—and I doubt anyone in the Mannerheim System government could shed any light on where they *went* after they crossed the alpha wall outbound. For that matter, there *wasn't* a Mannerheim government at the time these slavers started passing through. The bridge was pretty much lost in the wilderness when it was discovered, and the first colony wasn't planted in Mannerheim for seventy-odd T-years after that. Its population was only up to around eighty thousand or so by the time our known slavers started using Warner, and the

Mannerheim Association, the predecessor of the present republic, wasn't organized until fifty T-years or so after the last of them had passed through."

"Agreed." Gannon nodded. "But I have the strangest suspicion that you're heading somewhere beyond that, Captain," he said slowly.

"Well, as you may have heard, I'm a fellow who likes to crunch numbers. So I did. And as a consequence, based on the hyper speeds we know the ships in question could make, I can tell you that their actual destination system lies somewhere between a minimum of two hundred and a maximum of two hundred and fifty-three light-years of Mannerheim. The inner limit's more problematic, of course, because they could always have extended their layover time when they got where they were going, and at least some of them obviously did. The maximum is a hard number, though—the farthest they could physically travel in the time available."

"That's still a rather large volume," Gaddis pointed out dryly, and Zilwicki nodded.

"I'm aware of that. But we can make some assumptions, I think. First, I suspect we have to be looking for a system with at least one habitable planet, not one where everyone's living aboard orbital habitats. If they were going to base everyone in deep space, there were a hell of a lot of obscure places to build habitats that are a hell of a lot more convenient to Mesa than anything out Warner or Mannerheim's way. Another reason to think that is that the Mannerheim archives also suggest that maybe a dozen heavy construction ships came through from Warner during the same general interval but never arrived at any known destination. That much industrial capacity would be a plenty big kernel for an infrastructure built around a planet with breathable atmosphere. It wouldn't have been anywhere near enough to build the orbital platforms to support three hundred and fifty thousand slaves, though. So I think we can begin by eliminating any star system that *doesn't* have habitable planets."

"Okay." Gaddis nodded, his expression intent.

"Secondly," Zilwicki continued, "while I'm not prepared to state this anything remotely like unequivocally, I suspect that their destination system *may* lie somewhere to galactic north of Mannerheim."

"Why?" Gannon asked.

"Because virtually all the ships that headed out on southern vectors took longer to make their runs. Only by a tiny amount— not more than a day or two, at most—so it's not obvious until you look very carefully at the numbers. It's a pretty consistent differential, but I have to admit that I'm speculating kind of wildly at this point." The massive Manticoran shrugged again. "Maybe it's only because of how desperate we are for clues, but I think it's worth keeping in mind."

"Okay, I agree we can add that to the 'interesting conjecture' file," Gannon said. "I don't think we can legitimately call it anything more than that at this point, though."

"I concur." Zilwicki nodded. "And I don't want that 'conjecture' to bias us when we start looking at evidence. But it does suggest to me that that's the direction we should concentrate on at least initially."

"Probably." Gaddis nodded back to him. "In the meantime, though—"

A com chimed, and Anton glanced down at his uni-link. It took him well over a minute to read the entire text, and he was a very fast reader. Finally, he looked up again.

"It would seem Black Victor and his crew of cutthroats have just returned from Hole-in-the-Wall," he announced.

"Really?" Harahap chuckled and Fire Watch bleeked a laugh of his own. "That's not bad timing!"

"No, it's not," Zilwicki agreed. "It doesn't look like we're getting the payoff we hoped for from the operation, though."

"No?" Weng Zhing-hwan looked at him, and he shrugged.

"Oh, Ruth's along, and she did her usual bang-up job. We've got tons of material from the Hole-in-the-Wall servers, including the entire public communications log for what was almost certainly an Alignment front. And before they left, they made damn sure they had everything from Hole-in-the-Wall's records, including ship movements, cargo manifests, names and places, going back over the T-century and a half there's *been* a Hole-in-the-Wall. Mind you, they're not the best records anyone ever kept, but they've got them. Unfortunately, they haven't been able to break the encrypt on the captured message traffic—yet, at least; maybe Ruth and I can make some progress working on that together—and physical investigation of the Alignment front's premises confirms that there was a complete standalone server core that was thoroughly slagged before the occupants pulled out." He shrugged. "They didn't blow this one up, at least, but there was zero recoverable data when they got done. That's almost certainly where anything we really wanted was hidden, so unless there's something really strange in the records they did manage to pull out, it looks like Victor's op was a dry hole."

"How long before they make Old Earth orbit?" al-Fanudahi asked.

"They're still twenty-five light-minutes out. That's why he sent a text instead of comming. So from *Rei Amador*'s current velocity, a little under six hours."

"In that case, I suggest we adjourn," Gaddis said. "We can reconvene once Agent Cachat and Princess Ruth join us and we can get a better look at the information—or non-information— from Hole-in-the-Wall."

"Makes sense to me," Gannon agreed, and his smile was almost seraphic. "I'd just as soon head back over to the Admiralty and spend the intervening moments gloating over what the Navy's going to do to the slave trade's infrastructure now."

✧   ✧   ✧

"Excuse me, Brigadier, but there's someone here who'd like to speak to you," Sergeant Major Sumit Roychaudhuri said from Simeon Gaddis's desktop com.

"I'm rather busy at the moment, Sumit," Gaddis replied after a moment. "Does this person have an appointment of which I'm simply unaware?"

"I know you're busy, Sir," an unruffled Roychaudhuri replied. The sergeant major was the senior noncom on Gaddis's personal staff, and he and the brigadier-who-should-have-been-a-major-general went back a long way. "And, no, she doesn't have an appointment. However, she *has* convinced me it would probably be a good idea for you to find out why she's here."

"And does the mystery lady have a name?" Gaddis prompted.

"Why, yes, Sir. Her name is O'Hanrahan. Audrey O'Hanrahan."

✧   ✧   ✧

"Ms. O'Hanrahan," Gaddis said, rising behind his desk to greet his unexpected guest. "To what do I owe the pleasure?"

"A true gentleman," O'Hanrahan said with a smile as she crossed the office to him, trailed by her massively-built bodyguard.

The fellow was one of the few people Gaddis had ever seen who could have given Anton Zilwicki a run for his money in the sheer muscular bulk department. He'd also been deprived of no less than four lethal weapons before Roychaudhuri passed him into Gaddis's presence.

"I beg your pardon?" the brigadier said now.

"You know perfectly well that it's not going to be a 'pleasure' talking to me, Brigadier, but you're willing to pretend. Like I said, a true gentleman."

"I don't *think* I've done anything that should have me worrying about any corruption exposés. In fact, my conscience is as clean as new fallen snow. Well," Gaddis considered that for a moment. "Maybe second-day snow, now that I think about it."

"Oh, I'm not here about any teeny-tiny trace of moral turpitude on your part," O'Hanrahan assured him as she shook his hand and settled into the indicated comfortable chair.

Her bodyguard moved to stand behind her, and Gaddis noted the aura of personal, as well as professional, closeness they radiated. He knew from the thumbnail brief Roychaudhuri had fed him before admitting O'Hanrahan to his office that Michael Anderle had been her bodyguard the day someone nearly killed her less than three kilometers from Smith Tower. He'd been hurt pretty badly himself, apparently, but neither of them looked much the worse for wear now. O'Hanrahan *might* have limped just a tiny bit on her way into the office. If so, that was the only sign of the complete loss of her left leg.

"Not even a *trace* of turpitude?" Gaddis inquired dryly. "I don't know whether to feel relieved or slighted."

"If you really want me to dig up something on you, Brigadier, I'm sure I can," the galaxy's leading muckraker assured him with a chuckle. "I mean, there's at least one tiny skeleton in almost anyone's closet. And you *have* been a Gendarme for a long time."

"True." Gaddis nodded. "So, considering everything, I've decided to settle for relieved in that respect and ask why else this meeting might be less than thoroughly pleasant?"

"Because I've become aware of a joint operation between the Solarian League, the provisional Mesan government, the Grand Alliance, and the Kingdom of Torch," O'Hanrahan told him in a tone which was suddenly considerably less humorous. "That struck me as a rather odd clutch of allies, given recent galactic history, so I did a little digging, and it turns out that the operation—whatever it is—appears to be coordinated through your office, with input from Director Gannon, Captain Anton Zilwicki, and, according to my latest information, Agent Victor Cachat of the Republic of Haven. With, I might add, input from the Audubon Ballroom, which is still a proscribed terrorist organization in the League, if I remember correctly."

Gaddis smiled at her.

It wasn't easy.

"Now, I have to say that discovering all of that piqued my curiosity," O'Hanrahan continued. "But aside from confirming that whatever the operation is it actually exists and does appear to involve all of the entities I listed above, your security has actually held. I'm impressed by that. It's not often that I hit anyone's security fence and just bounce."

"I can believe that," he said with complete sincerity. "Dare I ask why you've brought all of this to my attention? Rather than that of your subscribers, that is?"

"I can think of only two objectives, two targets, that might have brought that particular group together at this point in time." O'Hanrahan's expression and tone had become dead serious. "One, especially given the Ballroom's involvement, would be Admiral Kingsford's Operation Wilberforce, and speaking as a human being with a functional conscience, I am totally in favor of eradicating every single trace of the genetic slave trade. But the other possibility, the one I find much more intriguing as a journalist, is that this collection of recent enemies is seeking to confirm—or permanently disprove—the existence of the Manties' and Havenites' 'Mesan Alignment.' In fact, what I strongly suspect, is that all of you have already *accepted* the Alignment's existence and that you're trying to hunt it down, wherever it's hiding."

"Really?"

"Really," she said. "As it happens, I've come to share the Grand Alliance's suspicions about the existence of this Alignment of theirs. I'm not convinced they've accurately identified it or all of its motives, but there has to be something out there orchestrating all this mayhem, bloodshed, and destruction. And if there is, it has to be found and it has to be stopped. I'm as totally onboard with that mission as I am with Operation Wilberforce's. But I'm also a journalist."

"And this means...?" Gaddis asked in the tone of a man who already suspected the answer.

"And this means I want *in*, Brigadier," she said flatly. "Up until I started hearing quiet whispers about what you people have been up to, I was focused on the Constitutional Convention. But the final draft's in—and looks damned good, by the way—and everyone involved in writing it has signed off on it. It's just a matter of getting authorization for all of the other delegates to formally ratify it in their home systems' names, and I'd be astonished if that takes more than another T-month or so. But that's a done deal, now. I'd say any more scoops are highly unlikely to come out of the Convention. Not only that, there are plenty of reporters and services covering that story. After all, it's the biggest one in the galaxy right now, isn't it?

"But this..." She shook her head. "Unless I miss my guess, Brigadier, or unless the people involved suddenly prove a lot less competent than they've always been in the past, your people are going to prove the 'Alignment' exists and, with just a little luck, you're going to drag it out into the sunlight. And I want to be there when that happens. I want to cover it from the inside."

"And if we don't let you, you'll go public with what you already know?"

"No." She sat back in her chair. "No quid pro quo's, Brigadier. If I'm right about what you people are doing, it's way too important for me to go around joggling elbows or upsetting apple carts. So, no. Whatever happens, I'll sit on everything I know at least until someone else breaks the story. At that point, I'll go public with every detail I've been able to dig up working on my own, but until then, you have my word that I won't publish a single syllable about this."

It was Gaddis's turn to sit back as he realized she meant every word of it.

"That's... a surprising concession from a journalist in your position," he said slowly. "Or maybe not. I've often suspected that there were times you've sat on stories because you knew breaking them prematurely could have...unfortunate consequences, let's say."

"I hope you haven't shared that suspicion with anyone else." O'Hanrahan smiled tartly. "A certain reputation as a blunt object can be really useful when it comes to beating information out of people with secrets to hide."

"No, I haven't shared it."

He swung his chair gently from side to side while he thought. Then he shrugged.

"All right, Ms. O'Hanrahan. This isn't my decision. It's my *operation*, but I'm not in a position to authorize letting you inside. Having said that, I think it would actually be a good idea."

"Do you?" She arched an eyebrow.

"In several ways, actually," he said. "One is that you have a reputation for honest reporting, so if we do find something and you report it, verify what we've found and how we found it, that will mean something to the man or woman-in-the-street. And God knows the entire subject of the Alignment is touchy enough we're going to need all of the support we can get to convince the galaxy at large that it might truly exist. Another is that a reporter with your contacts and experience might actually have some helpful perspectives to share with us while we dig away at this thing, and we can use all of those we can get, too. And yet another is that no one could have read or viewed the pieces you've done on corrupt transstellars in general and the genetic slave trade in particular without recognizing a genuine sense of outrage. If we find what we've come to suspect we're going to find, I expect the outrage you'll feel when we do will dwarf anything any of those transstellars have ever done. Including Manpower. And I expect that outrage will come through clearly when you report at the end of the day."

She looked back at him without speaking, but he thought he saw at least a trace of surprise in her eyes.

"So," he stood behind his desk, "I'll kick this up the chain of command, with my recommendation that you be admitted to the secret. And if this leads where it might well lead, I'll also recommend that you be embedded with our people for the actual takedown. I can't promise the politicians will agree with me, but I'll certainly give it my best shot."

Garnet Room
Smooth and Wrinkled Club
Jordan Parker Pavilion
City of Mendel
Planet Mesa
Mesa System

"A SETTING WITH PEOPLE," ARIANNE MUTTERED, AS SHE TRIED
to push her way through the crowd without actually injuring
anyone. "A setting that allows them to see him through the eyes
of the people who actually work with him every day."

Of whom there weren't all that many in the whole room, at
least as a percentage of the attendees. The very large ballroom,
to be precise. The program hadn't even started, and already it
was standing room only for most people. She could only hope
her father had managed to get her mother and sister—plus an
aunt, two uncles, and at last count five cousins—seated at their
assigned table before the mob poured in.

What Arianne had intended to be a fairly modest gathering
of fewer than fifty people had turned into an extravaganza. No
one was even pretending any longer that she was the person
organizing the event. That role had been taken over by Janice
Delgado, one of the movers and shakers in what had been known
for centuries as the Alignment but had now changed its name
to the Engagement.

Arianne's annoyance was petty, and she knew it. She herself
had been the one who proposed the name "Engagement," and she
knew the affair's expansion was tremendously positive. Essentially,
the Engagement had decided to use the celebration of the Mumps
as its own coming out party. Although the fruits of that wouldn't
be immediately evident, in the long run the transformation of
the Engagement from a secret organization into one playing an

open and active role in both Mesan and galactic affairs would be profound.

Still... it was annoying to have to force her way through a ballroom that was coming to resemble the proverbial can of sardines.

Finally, she spotted the table she was looking for. It was toward the front of the ballroom, close to the speakers' podium but a bit off to one side.

Her father spotted her at the same time, stood up, and gave her a hand wave. That was fortunate, because a second later the table vanished from view again, and the only remaining sign of its location was her father's hand rising above the mob.

When she reached the table, she was relieved to see that there were several seats still available. She hadn't been worried about herself, but...

She climbed indecorously up on the seat of her chair and searched the room. It didn't take long for her to find the two people for whom she was looking. One nice thing about the emerald uniforms Saburo had ordered for the Mumps was that they were easy to spot almost anywhere—which was the reason for the color, of course. The Safeties and the Misties had favored very dark uniforms, black into deep blue, because they imparted a certain aura of menace. Saburo wanted the exact opposite image for the new police force.

True, some people were starting to call them the "Greenies" as well as the Mumps, but he was indifferent to that issue.

"They can call us the Leprechauns, for all I care," he'd told Arianne. "The key thing is that there's no suggestion of a secret police and—this will take some time, of course—that people stop being afraid of us."

"Kayla! Jake!" she called out, waving her hand. "Over here!"

The two of them looked toward her; then made their way toward the table with expressions of deep relief. When they arrived, Arianne made the necessary introductions, and they took their seats.

Just in time—the podium had now filled up, and Janice started the proceedings. That meant speeches, of course, by various dignitaries, a high percentage of whom were members of the Engagement. But the speeches were all reasonably short; even coherent, for the most part.

That was followed by questions from the press, which was the portion of the event that made Arianne a bit nervous.

And for good reason, as it turned out.

"Here comes trouble," Barrett murmured, twitching her head toward the section of floor reserved for newsies.

Arianne followed the indicated direction and saw that a columnist from the *Citizen Sentinel* had just stood up. That was a new outlet, one oriented toward the former full citizens. More precisely, toward the most disgruntled of that class of people. The *Citizen Sentinel* skirted the edge of being openly hostile to the new dispensation.

And to make things worse, the columnist was Gail Velasquez, possibly the most belligerent of the lot.

"Don't *call* on her," Barrett murmured. "Just don't call on her."

But there was no chance of that happening. Janice Delgado had a lot more experience dealing with the press than Kayla Barrett, and she knew that if she avoided calling on Vasquez she'd just give the woman more prominence. *They refused to call on me because—!* was a lot more likely to be repeated and given more publicity by other outlets than whatever her question might be.

"Yes, Ms. Vasquez?"

"I couldn't help noticing that the chief of the new police force hasn't spoken. Is that because this Saburo person doesn't want attention drawn to his history as a terrorist?"

Arianne's lips tightened. Barrett hissed in a little breath, but Abrams, sitting next to her, only smiled.

"She's *toast*," he said.

Saburo had been seated toward one end of the podium. Now he rose and crossed to stand at the speaker's lectern. There was no need for him to do so for technical reasons, of course. The entire stage was miked for sound, so he could have been heard perfectly well from where he'd sat. But Saburo had his own well-honed knowledge of how to handle a public confrontation.

He gave Vasquez the flat, expressionless stare that was so intimidating, for reasons Arianne had never really understood. Abrams said it was because it reminded people of the dispassionate way an apex predator gauged whether a possible meal was worth the effort.

"There's an old quip," Saburo said after a moment. "'That word you keep using'—'terrorist,' in your case—'I do not think it means what you think it means.' To begin with, it's so broad it has no clear meaning in any context. Applied to the context of the world I come from, it's gibberish."

He leaned forward just a bit.

"*Who* did I 'terrorize'? That's the question you need to answer before you ask me any others. There were only three classes of people who ever needed to fear me, or Jeremy X, or any other of the Ballroom's strikers.

"Officials of Manpower Incorporated." He held up a thumb. "Public officials who aided and abetted Manpower." A forefinger. "Or people brutal enough and stupid enough to think working as their thugs and henchmen was a smart idea." A middle finger.

He held his hand there for a slow three-count, then lowered it.

"Nobody else ever had any reason to feel terror on account of our existence and activities. I'm sure many did, but I'm no more responsible for their irrationality than I am for someone else's fear of heights or fear of chopsticks." He grinned, rather savagely. "Oh, yes. That fear exists. It's called consecotaelophobia."

Laughter rippled around the room. Echoed by dozens of people, it was quite loud.

"I never had any illusions—neither did Jeremy X or Donald X or Lakshmi X or any other Ballroom striker—that our tactics of assassination had any chance of defeating Manpower and its allies in military terms. That wasn't the tactic's purpose. Its purpose was cruder and simpler: to maintain as best we could the self-respect of Manpower's victims.

"Our goal wasn't to *terrorize* anyone. It was to exact vengeance. It was to make clear to the human race, and especially to that portion of it whom Manpower had condemned to genetic slavery, that we were *not* slaves. We were people—and if you harm people, they will harm you in return. The harm may be greatly disproportionate. It certainly was in our case. Manpower brutalized far more of us, and often in worse ways than we ever did in return. But there's another old quip that applies here, one that every kid with spunk learns early in life when he or she encounters bullies. 'You may get a meal, but I'll damn well get a sandwich.' The kid may—usually does—walk away from that fight battered and bruised, but they retain their self-respect. And without self-respect, you have nothing. You're lost. Completely lost."

He inhaled a slow, deep breath.

"But here's what you need to understand. Vengeance is the weapon of the weak. It's not the tool of the strong. And today, those of us whose genetic heritage was misused by Manpower and its creatures are *strong*. We are no longer weak. We have our own nation, on the planet of Torch. And we now also have a position of great power on Mesa, the planet where we were first abused and brutalized—not unilateral power, because we share it with others, including all of you in this room—but it's still great power."

"So we've given up vengeance." He spread his hands wide. "We no longer need it, because our self-respect is now assured. And that being the case, to continue to exact vengeance would simply diminish us."

He left the lectern and headed back to his seat. Before he'd taken two steps, Barrett and Abrams were on their feet, clapping their applause. Before he'd gotten halfway back to his seat, every Mump in the room—there were about twenty—was doing the same or rising to their feet to join in. By the time he sat back down, many other members of the audience were doing the same. And before another five seconds had passed, most of the crowd had joined in.

From what Arianne could see looking around, every member of the Engagement was contributing to the applause. She was immensely pleased—and proud—to say the least.

Apparently, Vasquez had no further questions.

✧   ✧   ✧

A bit later, as the food was being served, Thomas McBryde looked across the table at Arianne.

"I have to say I'm genuinely impressed," he said. "I hadn't realized how much respect—allegiance also, I think—your fellow had gained from the members of his police force."

Arianne opened her mouth, but Abrams beat her to it.

"Saburo was already getting there anyway. You just can't work with the man *without* coming to respect him. But it was the raid in Lower Radomsko that really solidified it."

"I'll say!" Barrett barked a little laugh. "First of all, a sizable percentage of the Mumps are ex-Misties, like me and Jake. At a rough guess, I'd say it's almost twenty-five percent." She glanced around the room. "Besides us, there are at least five who came today."

"*That* many?" Thomas asked, and Abrams shrugged.

"Kayla and I weren't the only ones who didn't like a lot of how the Misties operated."

"After the raid," Barrett said, "we joked with each other, trying to imagine Bentley Howell personally leading an assault on one of Lower Radomsko's most vicious gangs." She barked another, sharper laugh. "Fat chance of that ever happening!"

"It wasn't just that," Abrams added. "We'd all heard tales about Audubon Ballroom terrorists, of course. We figured they were just bullshit tall tales, and if we ever did run into one of their so-called strikers, we'd set the punks straight."

He shook his head.

"Then we saw the real thing. In action. None of us had ever seen anything like it. And the funny thing is, that made all of us feel good. The toughest, baddest, most dangerous outlaw you could imagine was now our boss."

"Nice guy, too," Barrett said. "Of course, you don't want to cross him. Really, really, really don't want to do that—but who's counting? It's actually pretty hard to piss Saburo off."

Arianne's mother and sister had been listening to the conversation. Now Christina McBryde rose to her feet.

"Okay, it's time. Get up, JoAnne. You're coming with me."

JoAnne seemed to hesitate.

"Get. Up," her mother repeated.

❖   ❖   ❖

They were back a few minutes later.

"Saburo will come over for dinner this coming Wednesday," Christina announced. "I figure we'll serve some kind of Italian food, since he doesn't suffer from—what did he call it, JoAnne?"

"Zymarikaphobia," JoAnne replied. "It means 'fear of pasta.'" She gave Arianne a sideways look. "Your boyfriend has an interesting vocabulary."

"I'm impressed you remembered it."

JoAnne shrugged.

"I'm a schoolteacher. Kids say the darndest things."

February 1924 Post Diaspora

"I can read your emotions about as easily as a treecat. So, in answer to your question, Elizabeth, I don't *think* you're after something; I *know* you are."

—Honor Harrington

Mount Royal Palace
City of Landing
Planet Manticore
Manticore Binary System

"ALL RIGHT, ELIZABETH. WHAT ARE YOU *REALLY* AFTER?"

Very few people in the galaxy would have used that tone with Empress Elizabeth of Manticore. It was neither disrespectful nor defiant. But it was...testy. And the look that came along with it was the one a governess bestowed upon a child she couldn't *prove* had been up to no good.

Yet.

"What makes you think I'm 'after' anything, except for the formal christening of my newest godson?" Elizabeth asked mildly.

"Because one doesn't normally send a writ of summons to a peer of the realm for a christening."

Honor Alexander-Harrington stood at the foot of the private Mount Royal shuttle pad, brown hair stirring on a Landing City breeze, with Andrew Judah Wesley Alexander-Harrington in a soft-structured carrier across her chest. Raoul and Katherine stood behind her, Katherine holding Lindsey Phillips's hand while Raoul held his father's. Nimitz had consented to ride Clifford McGraw's shoulder to spare Honor the additional weight, but Samantha perched upright on Hamish's.

And, of course, a veritable passel of armsmen stood alertly behind them.

"A writ of summons," Honor continued, "is the sort of thing one sends when one wants to make certain the peer in question can't just send her regrets and remind one that she informed one that she intended to stay home and be a mother for a while. Besides, I don't imagine you've forgotten I can read

585

your emotions about as easily as a treecat. So, in answer to your question, Elizabeth, I don't *think* you're after something; I *know* you are."

"And hello to you, too, Hamish," the Empress said, smiling past Honor at the Earl of White Haven. "How nice to see you."

"And to see you," Hamish Alexander-Harrington replied politely. "What are you after?"

"I am cut to the quick," Elizabeth told him. She seemed remarkably placid about it, though.

"I might point out that unlike the mother of my children, I'd already promised you and Willie I'd return to the Admiralty this month," Hamish said. "And Honor was already planning to relocate to White Haven with the kids. You didn't have to yank us back three weeks early. Unless—" his blue eyes narrowed "—you're planning on extorting something from us. And I can already tell you that you don't get me back as First Lord if you intend to extort something out of Honor."

"So apparently you both think I arrived on yesterday's produce shuttle?" There was a hint of acerbity in Elizabeth's tone this time. "I said I understood when Honor...handed in her resignation. I did, and I still do. For that matter, I also understand that if there are two people in the entire Star Empire who are stubborner than *I* am, I'm looking at them. There are, however, circumstances which can change someone's plans and intentions. And, no, I'm not talking about my changing *my* plans or intentions."

It was Honor's eyes' turn to narrow. Elizabeth's tone had become entirely serious, and so had the emotions behind it.

"What is it, Elizabeth?" One of Honor's hands cupped the back of Andrew's head, and her own tone matched the Empress's.

"I'd really rather not discuss state secrets on a shuttle pad, if you don't mind." Elizabeth smiled tartly. "I know your entire crew just got here, Honor. Did your mother and father go on to Harrington House?"

"They did." Honor nodded. "Hamish and I—well, and our 'entire crew'—came straight here."

"Thank you for that," Elizabeth said softly. "If you like, one of Ellen's people can escort Ms. Phillips and the big kids—" she smiled warmly at three-year-old Raoul and Katherine "—on to Saint Michael's Tower while we do the adult-talk. Justin and Joanna are already at the tower, and Roger and Riva are flying home from a ribbon-cutting expedition as we speak. All of them will want to see you for dinner. And your mom and dad are invited, too, of course!"

"That should work fine," Honor said, nodding to Colonel Ellen Shemais, the head of Elizabeth's personal security detail. "I don't know if Mother and Father will want to eat at the Palace tonight, but Hamish and I certainly want to see Justin and the kids. And to show off Andrew Judah."

"And rightly so." Elizabeth smiled broadly. "I wouldn't want this to go to your heads, but you and Hamish do good work."

Honor nodded again, then turned to Lindsey and her older children.

And their armsmen, of course.

"You guys go on to the tower," she said, bending to ruffle Raoul and Katherine's hair. "We'll be along as soon as Her Majesty turns us loose."

The look she gave Elizabeth held more than a hint of challenge, but the Empress only smiled again and nodded.

"Of course, Your Grace," Lindsey said, taking Raoul's hand from Hamish. Then she, the older children, and their bodyguards followed one of Shemais's sergeants towards the ground cars waiting to one side of the shuttle pad.

Honor waved to them as they went, and then turned back to the Empress.

"And now, about that 'adult-talk' of yours, Elizabeth?" she said.

❖   ❖   ❖

Honor was scarcely surprised to see two of the people who rose respectfully as she, Nimitz, Hamish, Samantha, and Andrew Judah followed Elizabeth into the high-security briefing room buried deep in Mount Royal Palace's basement. The other four were unexpected, however.

Nimitz had leapt down from McGraw's shoulder when the sergeant peeled off to stand post outside the briefing room door. Now he flowed across the floor and hopped up into one of the unoccupied chairs around the enormous conference table. Samantha waited for Hamish to lift her properly from his shoulder, then settled into the same chair as her mate. The two of them leaned together as Honor and Hamish found chairs of their own, and Spencer Hawke and Tobias Stimson stepped back against the briefing room's wall.

No one even considered suggesting that either armsman should "wait outside," any more than someone might have been sufficiently imprudent to suggest the same thing to Shemais.

The Honorable Charles O'Daley, one of the two people whose presence had come as no surprise, had been confirmed as Barton Salgado's official replacement to head the Special Intelligence Service over ten T-months ago. The other, Vice Admiral Joanna Saleta, had been promoted from rear admiral and named as Patricia Givens's successor as Second Space Lord, which made her the director of the office of the Office of Naval Intelligence, O'Daley's uniformed equivalent. Given the flavor of Elizabeth's emotions, Honor had expected to find those two involved. But she'd had no idea the other four—well, five, actually, counting Fire Watch—were even in-system.

Of course, spies tended to come and go under the radar. And it wasn't as if *she'd* been in the Manticore Binary System for the last T-year or so, either.

"Since we all know each other, I think we can dispense with formal introductions," Elizabeth said as she headed for her own chair at the head of the table.

"I'd say that was probably fair," Honor conceded, and Hamish chuckled.

"Maybe not formal introductions," Anton Zilwicki rumbled, crossing to shake hands with Honor and Hamish in turn. "I do want the opportunity to meet the newest member of the ever-growing Alexander-Harrington clan, though," he added with a smile, touching Andrew's cheek with an immensely gentle fingertip. "It's been a while since Helen was this tiny."

Andrew Judah reached out, clutching at his finger with both tiny hands, and he chuckled softly.

"Trust me, we can give you all the baby time you could possibly desire!" Hamish shook his head. "We left for Grayson with four kids, counting Faith and James. We came back with *seven*."

"But at least this one didn't get the Meyerdahl mods," Honor reminded him with a smile, then looked at the others. "You cannot begin to imagine how much easier it is to deal with a four-and-a-half-month-old's feedings when he *doesn't* have the Meyerdahl metabolism! Speaking of which, a certain young man is going to demand that Mommy feed him sometime pretty soon now, anyway."

"Which is another excellent reason we should probably be moving right along," Elizabeth observed. "Find chairs, everyone."

She waited until everyone was settled, then looked down the length of the table to where Honor sat at its far end.

"Captain Zilwicki, Agent Cachat, and Mr. Harahap and Mr. Graham brought me some very interesting information, Honor," she said, and despite any possible whimsy in her words, her tone—and emotions—were as deadly serious as Honor had ever tasted them. The last time she'd tasted such an unyielding focus in Elizabeth's mind-glow had been in the wake of the Beowulf Strike. But this wasn't the grieving, half-stunned, furious, brutally determined aura she'd tasted that day. Of course, her own emotions might have made Elizabeth's seem even grimmer after Beowulf.

But this mind-glow, now that Elizabeth had allowed her inner focus to return to whatever reason had led her to summon Honor home, was neither stunned nor grieving. Indeed, it was... exultant. And yet it was also harder and more focused than a battle steel blade.

"While we've been waiting for the League to ratify its new constitution, these gentlemen and certain of their friends have found a way to stay busy," Elizabeth continued. "Along the way, they've discovered a lot more than any of us had expected about events in Mesa and the nature of the Alignment."

Honor nodded. She might have been off in Grayson on inactive duty and maternity leave, but she was still a fleet admiral, a duchess, *and* a steadholder, whose brother-in-law happened to be Prime Minister and whose husband also just happened to be the First Lord of Admiralty, although he'd taken family leave time, as well. For that matter, she was one of the people who'd been consulted about the practicality of any cooperative venture involving the Solarian League and the Audubon Ballroom. As such, she and Hamish had been kept up to speed on events in Mesa and elsewhere. And that meant—

"Should I assume," she asked in a careful tone, her flesh-and-blood arm wrapped around Andrew Judah as she leaned back in her chair, "that Anton and Agent Cachat are back from their hunting expeditions?"

"You should, indeed," Elizabeth told her, and nodded to Zilwicki. "Captain, why don't we start with what you found—and didn't—in Rat Catcher, and then Agent Cachat can update us on what happened at Hole-in-the-Wall?"

"Of course, Your Majesty." Zilwicki gave the Empress a respectful, seated half-bow across the table, then turned to Honor and Hamish. "Director O'Daley and Vice Admiral Saleta have already been briefed on this, Your Grace," he said, and she and Hamish nodded in understanding.

"Well," he continued, "I'm afraid the truth is that even though the Warner-Mannerheim Bridge turns out to have been just as important as we'd hoped it might, we failed to acquire a single megabyte of any 'secret records' the Alignment might have maintained on Jessyk Station. And the evidence is pretty strong that they had quite a bit of data stored there."

He shrugged, and Honor's eyes narrowed as she tasted his emotions. For someone who'd just confessed the failure of a major intelligence operation's overriding primary objective, he seemed to feel remarkably satisfied.

"What we found," he continued, "was that—"

❖   ❖   ❖

"So," Zilwicki wrapped up the better part of fifteen minutes later, "we did get some leads from Rat Catcher, but not the sort of leads we'd hoped for. We're confident we've confirmed the Alignment's existence—again—and that it was probably as deeply embedded in Jessyk as it was in Manpower. Assuming, of course, that we want to stipulate there was any distinction between those two transstellars. But aside from a possible distance from Mannerheim to wherever all those slaves were bound, we didn't come away with a *lot* more information than we had before we ever went to Warner."

"Maybe not," Hamish said, "but confirming the additional shipments of slaves—and the construction ships—was probably worth the entire expedition. It's a lot closer than we ever had before to a smoking gun we could show the rest of the galaxy. And while I'd have to concede that being able to place the Alignment's equivalent of Bolthole within a five hundred-light-year sphere doesn't get us any closer to actually finding it, it does at least give us a place to start looking for other clues."

"Indeed it does, Milord," Zilwicki acknowledged. "But that's where Victor—and Ruth—come in."

"Where *is* Ruth?" Honor smiled crookedly. "I wouldn't have

thought you could have pried her away from something like this with a tractor beam!"

"Ah, but she already knows everything we're telling you," Elizabeth pointed out. "More to the point, you're overlooking the countervailing pressure of being summoned to a command-performance family dinner with her father, her mother, and half a dozen of the other women who escaped from Masada with Judith."

Honor looked at her quizzically, and Elizabeth's smile turned into something more somber.

"This month is the twenty-fifth anniversary of their escape. Or, rather, of all of them becoming naturalized citizens of Manticore," she said. "We didn't know exactly when you and Hamish were going to get here from Grayson when they scheduled the reunion, and Ruth is with her mom and all of those 'godmothers' of hers at the moment."

"I see." Honor inhaled deeply. "I can understand that entirely."

"So can I," Zilwicki agreed, although Honor noted that Victor Cachat seemed less impressed by the emotional freight. "But the point is what she and Victor turned up. Victor?"

"At first," Cachat said, "we didn't think we'd gotten anything truly significant, either. But when we got back to Old Chicago and started comparing notes with Anton, Damien, and the Ghost Hunters, we realized something interesting. We still haven't broken the encryption on any of the Alignment messages we acquired from the Tortuga servers. Between them, Ruth and Anton have broken a lot of *other* people's traffic, but not the Alignment's. What we have managed, however, is to date all of the messages that we uploaded and also to do a thorough analysis on the shipping records we brought back with us.

"It turns out that the Alignment used a pair of courier ships, not just one. The ship that was on station when we arrived was the *Hudson*, which looked an awful lot like your typical, slightly rundown, smallish tramp freighter. The other ship they used was named *Teacup*, of all damned things, and looked just about as beaten-up as *Hudson*.

"Nothing too surprising about any of that," he said with a shrug. "But we were able to correlate dates on message traffic with the arrivals and departures of the couriers. And some of that traffic *didn't* go via their private whisker laser. I doubt that anything that didn't had any operational significance. In fact, I think Anton and Ruth are probably correct that most of it was personal correspondence to people 'back home.' There are a few of what we're fairly sure were 'cover' shipping orders, as well, but we're inclined to think a lot of it was generated solely so that there'd be detectable communications between them and the ships."

"But why—?" Honor began, then cut herself off. "Alignment paranoia in action again," she said with a grimace. "A legitimate business would communicate with its freight carriers using public channels. So to be sure they looked legitimate, they did the same thing *in addition* to whatever secret messages they were sending back and forth over their private link."

"That's exactly what we think a lot of it was, Duchess," Cachat agreed. "But in this case, we also think their paranoia turned around and bit them."

"Why?" Honor gazed at him intently, and he smiled ever so slightly.

"Because the timestamps on that correspondence give us what is probably a fairly tight number for the round-trip voyage time between Hole-in-the-Wall and whatever command node Amherst Importers and Exporters was talking to."

Honor's eyes widened and she glanced quickly at Hamish, whose expression was as intent as her own.

"By itself, that was interesting but not particularly galaxy-shaking," Zilwicki said. "But when we took those numbers and adjusted for the possibility—the probability, really, I suppose—that the couriers were equipped with the 'streak drive' Herlander Simões has told us about, we were able to calculate a bubble around Hole-in-the-Wall that was about five hundred and ten light-years across. One that we knew held at least one Alignment node. And the interesting thing was that when we drew that sphere around Hole-in-the-Wall, and another sphere, five hundred light-years across, around Mannerheim, they intersected. In fact, their shared volume falls in a region of space where there are relatively few stars. Or, at least, stars that could have habitable planets."

"Really?" Honor murmured, brown eyes glowing, and Zilwicki nodded.

"We can't be positive," he rumbled, "but it looks very much as if the destination all those slaves shipped through Warner and Mannerheim went to is also the node to which Amherst reported from Hole-in-the-Wall. And if it is, then we may just know where the Alignment's Bolthole is."

"Charlie and I have considered their data carefully, Your Grace," Vice Admiral Saleta put in. "We approached it as skeptically as we could, but it looks solid to us. Their conclusions based on it are more speculative, of course, but it strikes us as *smart* speculation. In fact, we're in agreement that Captain Zilwicki, Agent Cachat, and their friends are onto something here, so we had my people run an analysis of the astrography in the overlap zone. Agent Cachat's right that there aren't a lot of stars in it, and in our own minds we've narrowed the possibilities down to no more than three—possibly four—potential candidates."

"Unfortunately, we haven't confirmed that," Elizabeth said, "because—"

"Because their sensor platforms would have picked up the hyper footprint of whoever you sent to check," Honor said, and the Empress nodded.

"We *are* going to confirm it, though," she assured Honor in a voice of Gryphon granite. "And when we have, we're going to send a fleet with enough firepower to...deal with anything we find there. I've already talked to Tom and Eloise, and we've begun assembling the fleet. Given the drawdown, our deployments since the Sollies surrendered, and how much of Grand Fleet's still been hanging about in the Sol System, we're looking at another two, maybe even three months to assemble the kind of force we have in mind. And once we have, we'll need someone to command it."

She looked deeply into Honor's blazing eyes.

"You wouldn't happen to know where we might find such a commander, would you?"

**Admiralty House
City of Landing
Planet of Manticore
Manticore Binary System**

HONOR ALEXANDER-HARRINGTON LOOKED UP FROM A QUIET conversation with Captain (senior grade) Andrea Jaruwalski as Rear Admiral Garlan Thwaites entered the briefing room. He crossed to the table at the center of the room and braced to attention.

He was a tallish man, about a centimeter or so shorter than Honor herself, with brown hair and brown eyes, and although no one could have told it from his expression, his mind-glow tasted rather puzzled about the reason he was here. She tasted an increase in his speculation as he took in her own presence (he'd *expected* to report to Vice Admiral Marcos Antoniadou, who'd replaced Lucian Cortez as Fifth Space Lord, and she was in Grayson attire, not uniform), with Spencer Hawke standing behind her chair and Jefferson McClure, standing with Hawke to keep an eye on the bassinet beside her. But—

"Your Grace," was all he said.

"Admiral Thwaites," she replied, smiling at his composed reaction, and waved at the empty chair on the other side of the of the table. "Please, have a seat. I promise this will all make sense after a bit."

"I assumed it would, Your Grace." Thwaites smiled back. "I have to confess, right this minute I can't imagine a reason *why* it will, though."

"I'm not surprised," Honor told him as he took the indicated chair.

"First, I apologize for being out of uniform myself," she said then. "I'm scheduled for a dinner with the Prime Minister and the Andermani ambassador as soon as we're done here, and for reasons that I think will become clear, we'd prefer for no one to be associating me with any command duties at the moment. Which is one of the reasons I got Admiral Antoniadou to loan me his briefing room. Officially, I'm only visiting Admiralty House for a general intelligence update. Which is also, frankly, one of the reasons—if not the most important one in my personal opinion—for this young man's presence." She touched the baby sleeping in the bassinet gently. "Serving flag officers don't normally take their babies to work with them, so, hopefully, Andrew here will serve his very first function as a servant of the Crown by helping to divert any suspicion about the reasons for my visit."

"I'm sure he'll look back on the moment with a sense of deep pride, Your Grace," Thwaites said with a twinkle. "And, of course, I'm positive that's the *only* reason you brought him with you."

"Well, perhaps not the only reason," Honor conceded.

"Trust me, I've got three of my own, Your Grace." Thwaites smiled at her. "I wasn't a flag officer when even the youngest was born, but if I *could* have taken any of them to work with me..."

"We have three, now, too. And I'm going to hate leaving them behind."

"You're going back on active duty, Your Grace?" Thwaites seemed surprised, and Honor snorted.

"I am, indeed. At least temporarily. Her Majesty's found the one bait that could lure me away from Andrew and his sibs. And that's why you're here. Because we need you and your people for a rather specialized reconnaissance mission."

Thwaites's eyes narrowed, and Honor understood why.

Garlan Thwaites commanded the Royal Manticoran Navy's Survey Command. Survey Command was one of the Navy's smaller commands, but during peacetime—which no one in the RMN had experienced for the last few decades—it was also one of its more active forces. It was specifically responsible for updating star charts and astrographic databases, looking for undiscovered wormholes, and pushing outward from places like the Talbott Quadrant to survey additional star systems around the periphery of known space, which was more than enough to keep its ships and crews busy. In wartime, it became what Allison Harrington referred to as the Navy's "redheaded stepchild." It wasn't that Survey's mission became less important; it was simply that the Navy's war-fighting functions had become vastly *more* important.

"We have a problem, Admiral," she told him. "We have a general volume of space—a rather large one—in which we *think* there's a heavily industrialized and almost certainly heavily fortified star system. We need to confirm or deny its presence, and we need to do it without anyone in the star system knowing that we have."

Those eyes were *very* narrow and intent now, and she sat back in her chair to let him think about it for a moment, because she wanted to see what he came up with from what she'd already told him. Nimitz flowed down into her lap from the back of her chair so she could do something useful—such as petting him—while she waited, and she glanced at Jaruwalski, who was smiling faintly as she, too, watched Thwaites working through what Honor had said.

Honor was glad she had Andrea back, although the captain had seemed surprised to be offered the chief of staff's slot. Despite her recent promotion, she was still a bit junior for the position, especially with the drawdown of the Navy's strength and the number of officers who'd been sent to half-pay simply because there were no longer commands for them. But there'd never been any question in Honor's mind who she wanted, since she *couldn't* have Mercedes Brigham back.

Brigham had finally accepted a long overdue promotion of her own, to vice admiral in her case, in the Grayson Space Navy. In fact, she'd relieved Alfredo Yu as the commanding officer of the Protector's Own, and Honor knew how delighted the Graysons were to have her back. Mercedes Brigham had been special to Grayson, ever since HMS *Madrigal* died covering the Grayson Navy's escape in the First Battle of Yeltsin, and Honor was perfectly aware that the only reason Brigham had declined to pick up her admiral's stars so long had been her determination to remain her own chief of staff. She would miss Mercedes, but she was delighted the older woman had finally taken the incredibly well-deserved promotion the Graysons had wanted her to accept for so long.

So Jaruwalski had stepped up to the chief of staff's position, and Honor had enticed Dame Megan Petersen, Baroness Arngrim, into the ops officer's slot in her place. She knew Peterson had deeply regretted giving up HMS *Arngrim* when the Admiralty jumped her directly to captain in well-earned recognition of her superb performance at the Battle of Hypatia, but she'd become too senior for a destroyer CO—even if the destroyer in question was a *Roland*. No doubt she'd cheered herself up with the not so minor consolation prize that it allowed her to stay home on Manticore while her fiancé rehabbed at the Bassingford Medical Center. She'd been slated as a tactical instructor at Saganami Island until a cruiser command came open, and Honor suspected that she'd be excellent in the classroom, but she needed an operations officer with a touch of audacity, and that described Megan Petersen perfectly.

There were other new faces on her staff, of course. In fact, there were more new than old. It couldn't have been any other way, after so many months. Lieutenant Commander Brock Justinian had replaced Waldemar Tümmel as her flag lieutenant. He'd been one of Honor's star students when she'd taught at Saganami, and his rapid promotion to lieutenant commander confirmed all of the good things she'd thought about him at the time. George Reynolds was still her intelligence officer, but Commander Lang Yazhu had replaced Theophile Kgari at astrogation and Lieutenant Commander Ona Eriquez had replaced Harper Brantley at communications. Commander Angela Clayton of the GSN was back, as her official liaison to High Admiral Alfredo Yu, who'd replaced Judah Yanakov after his death in Beowulf, and Clayton had taken back her second "hat" as Honor's logistics officer. The final new addition to her staff was Lieutenant Kondrad Chudzik, her public information officer, although there would be precious little for a PIO to do for the next few months, if things went the way they were supposed to.

But at least she was getting back *Imperator* as her flagship, and Captain Rafe Cardones still commanded her. Which wouldn't have been the case in another seven or eight T-months, when *Rear Admiral* Cardones handed the superdreadnought's keys to his successor and assumed the well-earned command of a division of battlecruisers.

A sudden bright spike in Thwaites's emotions and the expression on his face told her he'd had long enough to digest what she'd told him.

"Should I assume from your expression that you have a suspicion or two about what I have in mind, Admiral Thwaites?" she asked a bit whimsically.

"I can only think of one possibility, actually, Your Grace," he replied slowly, cautiously. "I'm sort of afraid to let myself believe in it, though. Have we actually found the *Alignment*?"

Honor wasn't surprised he'd made the connection. Everything

in his record said he was a highly intelligent officer who'd specialized in survey work because of a driving need to see what was on the other side of any hill.

"That's exactly what we think—hope—we've done," she said. "For obvious reasons this is about as classified as things come. And one of the many reasons Nimitz is here—" she rubbed the treecat's ears "—was to sample your emotions when you figured that out." There was no need to explain that she hadn't really needed Nimitz for that. "We know the Alignment infiltrated our command structure. We *think* we've plugged all the leaks, largely with the 'cats' assistance, but we can't be certain about that yet. So there will be a 'cat in the vicinity whenever anyone gets told about this."

"I think that's an excellent idea, Your Grace."

"I thought you would. But the reason you and I are meeting right now is that we'll need at least a month or two to assemble the forces to deal with these people. And we *will* deal with them." Battle steel glinted in her brown eyes. "And I don't propose to waste that time. Since it's going to take that long anyway, I intend for your people to confirm our target for us and bring back any information you can."

"I can see why you called it 'a rather specialized reconnaissance mission,' Your Grace."

"Operationally, it should actually be fairly straightforward." Honor sat forward, folding her hands on the table in front of her. "The devil will be in the details, of course."

Thwaites nodded.

"Admiral Saleta's people have narrowed the probable targets down to three or four star systems. We're going to assume that the Alignment's sensor technology at least equals our own, and we could pick up a hyper footprint within about two and a half light-weeks of Manticore. So, what I intend to ask you to do is to dispatch one of your survey ships—we'll send along a couple of battlecruisers or *Saganamis* to ride herd on them—to each of those stars. They'll come out of hyper *three* light-weeks from their destinations and carry out detailed visual and passive sensor observations. If this really is what we're looking for, there's no way they could conceal a high-tech presence on the level they'll have to have. If you detect that kind of presence, your escorts will accelerate up to about forty percent of light-speed and launch Ghost Rider drones on ballistic courses. They'll stay well out of the inner system, but they should have the reach to give us pretty good reads on what we're looking at. Your survey ship will complete all the observations it can make from its original position, and then return directly to Manticore while the escorts will duck back into hyper and micro-jump to the far side of the system. They'll make their alpha translation three light-weeks out, then move in to about one light-week to meet and recover their drones. At point-four cee, that will take the next best thing to ten weeks, but by way of the Terre Haute terminus, it's only about seventeen or eighteen days to any of our target systems. So, presumably, your survey ships can get in, spend a week or so making observations, and still be back to base in about six weeks. That will let us begin preliminary planning at this end. Then your escorts should be back to base with the take from the Ghost Riders about two months after that. That's what I have in mind, anyway. Does it sound workable from your end?"

"The logistics of it sound fine, Your Grace," Thwaites said thoughtfully. "You're talking about at least three months before you've got the intel, though."

"As long as security holds, we've got time to burn," Honor pointed out. "We'll use your visual observations as the hot take for our preliminary planning, so we'll be in a position to plug-in any additional data from the recon drones. And we'll be able to take however long we need to evaluate it. As I said, we're looking at a minimum of two months, and more probably three, just to assemble the fleet."

"That's true."

Thwaites nodded, then snorted in amusement. Honor raised an eyebrow at him, and he shook his head.

"I was just thinking, Your Grace. This isn't exactly the sort of thing Survey trains for. Usually, the Navy's at least got a pretty good idea what star system it's going to attack, and we don't worry a lot about making our alpha translation so far out no one can even see our footprints! This will be a novel experience for my people."

"And an important one," Honor said quietly. "Maybe the most important one since we and the Havenites started shooting at each other at Hancock Station. If we're right, if we really have found the Alignment, then this time we're going after the people who are almost certainly responsible for every single person we've killed since then. And, especially, the people behind the Yawata Strike and the Beowulf Strike. I *want* those people, Admiral."

She looked him in the eye, and her own eyes were dark, colder than the depths of space.

"I want them very badly, indeed... and you're going to give them to me."

March 1924 Post Diaspora

"My God. So the Manties have been right all along?"
—Audrey O'Hanrahan

Der Bierkeller **Restaurant**
City of Old Chicago
Old Terra
Sol System

AUDREY O'HANRAHAN BLINKED AS A WOMAN SHE'D NEVER MET
before stepped into the privacy-screened alcove in her favorite
restaurant and sat down across the table from her without Michael
Anderle so much as twitching.

"You can call me Phoebe," the woman told her.

"And why should I want to call you anything?" O'Hanrahan
asked a bit tartly.

"Because we got your message," "call me Phoebe" replied
calmly, and it was a good thing O'Hanrahan routinely used *Der
Bierkeller*'s privacy screening services. "You were right to be
concerned, but it isn't us."

"Excuse me?"

"I said it isn't us. Or we're pretty sure it isn't, anyway."

"'*Pretty* sure,'" O'Hanrahan repeated, and woman shrugged,
but there was something almost like sadness in her eyes.

"We can't be certain . . . yet. But everything you've been able to
tell us so far, and I realize it's only bits and pieces, says it's probably
not us. But that's one of the reasons I'm here. We never intended
to bring you this far inside, at least before we went public, but it
turns out we're not going to be going public as soon as we thought
we were, and you need to know what's happening here."

O'Hanrahan considered pretending she didn't know what the
other woman was talking about, but the temptation was brief.
And there was a reason she'd sent the whispers she was hearing
up the line to her superiors. So instead of wasting time on evasion, she sat back and cocked her head, instead.

"So I assume you've come down the chain to explain things to me?"

"To explain *some* things to you, not all." Phoebe shrugged again. "I'm here to tell you everything we can without further compromising our security. Well, that's not entirely accurate. I'm here to tell you everything our superiors think you have to know, not necessarily everything I *could* tell you. Fair enough?"

"I won't pretend the reporter in me won't be tempted to dig for more." O'Hanrahan smiled tightly. "But I understand the ground rules. And I know better than to push a source beyond what she's willing to give up."

"That's good." Phoebe reached across the table and helped herself to one of O'Hanrahan's bratwurst bites. She chewed it appreciatively, then sat back on the other side of the table with a serious expression.

"The stories you've been doing, the slant you've been giving them—separating whatever the Manties have been calling the Alignment from the benign organization they'd actually found on Mesa—worried us a little when you first began," she said. "But then we saw where you were going, and we realized you're even smarter than we'd thought. Which, by the way, is a pretty profound compliment, given how smart we already *knew* you were. What we weren't certain of was whether you actually believed what you were writing. Did you truly think there was another . . . organization out there in the stars that was behind all the chaos and bloodshed? Or did you think we really had done it and you were only working on a cover for us? Trying to give us a fig leaf to pretend we were as nonviolent as the people on Mesa when we went public, even though we'd been responsible for every single one of those deaths? Although, it didn't actually matter which it was, in a lot of ways. Because you were a lot more accurate than you might believe."

"I was?" O'Hanrahan's expression sharpened.

"I'm afraid so." Phoebe shook her head, and the sadness in her eyes was more evident. "There really are two Alignments, Audrey. Depending on how you want to look at it, what you and I belong to is either the original Alignment or a rebellious offshoot of it. I prefer to think it's the former, since we're the ones who have adhered to the original vision of Leonard Detweiler. He never envisioned, never would have *contemplated*, all the bloodshed and destruction that's been unleashed on the galaxy!

He wanted us to be proactive, yes, and he wanted us to shape events whenever and wherever we could. Infiltrate governments, acquire the means to defend ourselves if we needed to once we went public, embed ourselves in academia and politics and the media to steer the narrative when the day finally came? Yes, he understood why we'd need to do *all* of that. But attacks that killed millions? Setting the Solarian League and the Grand Alliance at one another's throats? We knew the others were getting desperate, but we *never* anticipated anything like that!"

"What 'others'?" O'Hanrahan demanded.

"The other Alignment," Phoebe replied. "Oh, not the one the Grand Alliance uncovered on Mesa. We had close ties to that Alignment, you understand, but almost all of them were shattered by the other Alignment's actions." She grimaced, like a woman who'd just bitten into something spoiled. "They called it 'Operation Houdini,' you know. They visualized it as some sort of game with smoke and mirrors that would cover the evacuation of *their* people from Mesa. And they killed one hell of a lot of *our* people in the process. Not only that, the Alignment still remaining on Mesa is distrustful enough now—for damned good reason—that it'll be decades, at least, before we dare to reestablish communications with anyone in the star system."

"My God," O'Hanrahan murmured. "So the Manties have been right all along?"

"Yes, and no." Phoebe shook her head. "Yes, there's something that calls itself the Mesan Alignment that was responsible for the Yawata Strike, the Beowulf Strike, the war between the Grand Alliance and the Solarian League. For that matter, we *think* it was behind the overthrow of the original Republic of Haven and the creation of the People's Republic, because it was afraid the Republic would go right on growing and be a major barrier to their plans when they finally came into the open and *forced* genetic uplift on the rest of the human race. That's what the entire war between the Grand Alliance and the League was all about, Audrey. They wanted to destroy the entire Solarian League and simultaneously cripple the Manticorans and Havenites, who have always at least agreed on how much they hated genetic slavery. They wanted that, no matter how many millions of lives it cost, because the entire objective was to kick the foundation out from under anything which could have opposed them."

O'Hanrahan looked at her, and the delicious meal she'd been eating was suddenly heavy in her stomach. She'd always known the entrenched opposition to Leonard Detweiler's vision would have to be overcome, and she'd always known that sometimes violence would be necessary, just as she'd recognized that the Alignment's leadership couldn't shirk the ruthlessness its cause required. She'd even realized the death toll could be horrendous. And she hadn't had a problem with that—although, she thought now, she certainly *should* have—as long as that glorious vision was served. As long as the deaths were a *necessary* part of advancing the cause to which she'd dedicated her life. She would have regretted every single one of them, yet she could have *accepted* them. But if what this woman was telling her now was true...

"We realized—or, rather, our predecessors realized—long ago that the Alignment was losing its way," Phoebe continued. "That's when we split from them. The Grand Alliance is right, there *is* a star system out there that's home to the people who've caused all of this suffering and death. But there's another one, that we've hidden even from that 'Alignment.' One where there's no enslaved labor force. One that's continuing Leonard Detweiler's dream. We can't know for certain at this point whether Gaddis and the others are on our trail or that other Alignment's. Under the circumstances, we strongly suspect they've followed links from Mesa, through 'Operation Houdini' and other evidence, which don't lead to *us*, since we had nothing to do with Houdini. If it *is* us they've found, we'll have no choice but to surrender and hope they believe us when we try to prove we're not the ones they're looking for, and it should help—some—that we can tell them exactly where the people they're really looking for live. If they've found the *other* Alignment, I can guarantee you no one will be doing any surrendering. And, to be totally honest, no one in our Alignment will shed any tears for those monsters.

"But all of this has set back our plans to 'go public' by decades, if not longer." Her expression turned bitter. "One way or the other, the Grand Alliance and the League are going to drag the Alignment into the open. If they've found us, we're going to be tarred with the same brush as the people who actually did all of this. We may be able to convince them we had nothing to do with it, but, frankly, the odds don't look very good. If they've found the other Alignment, what they'll find in its records when they take it down will absolutely validate every horrible thing they've said about the Mesan Alignment. It will prove the Alignment was just as vile and just as megalomaniacal as they ever thought it was.

"And if that happens, we'll have to stay in hiding long enough, continue working surreptitiously enough, for the perfectly legitimate horror the galaxy will feel to begin to dissipate. If we step into the open tomorrow and tell everyone 'It wasn't us!' who do you think will believe us? Especially—" Phoebe broke eye contact at last, looking away, and her shoulders slumped ever so slightly "—since we've taken advantage of some of the things the other Alignment's done over the years. We couldn't stop them without revealing our own existence to the rest of the galaxy," she looked back at O'Hanrahan, "and since we couldn't, we factored their actions—their *atrocities*, more often than I care to think about— into our own strategies. Took advantage of them when we could, tried to mitigate them without giving away our own existence if we thought there was a way. That's why we've flagged stories to you that actually helped push the others' agenda, like the ones you wrote about what happened at New Tuscany. We knew they were protecting their foothold in Mesa, although we thought New Tuscany was only a move to pressure the Manties, that they figured Manticore would back down from the threat of a direct confrontation with the League and pull in their horns in Talbott. And we were fine with that, because protecting *their* people on Mesa also protected *our* people there. We didn't realize—then— that what they really wanted all along was outright war between the League and the Star Empire!"

She laid her hands on the table, looked down at their backs for several seconds, then raised her eyes to O'Hanrahan's again.

"We'll be a long time forgiving ourselves for that," she said softly. "We knew they were fanatics. We don't have as much penetration into their leadership as we did once, but we knew that. What we didn't realize was that they'd gotten even more desperate—or just *impatient*, perhaps. And we thought they were too smart to make a boneheaded mistake like that! My God, weren't they paying attention to the wars between Manticore and Haven?! *We* sure as hell were, and anyone with half a brain should have realized—"

She broke off with a frustrated wave of both hands and leaned back in her chair once more.

"Anyway, by the time we realized where they were headed, it was too late to stop them. All we could do by that point was play defense, try to minimize the damage. To the galaxy at large, where we could, but if I'm going to be honest, our true focus was on preserving the real Detweiler Plan. That's the reason we sent you to Mesa during Operation Houdini and made sure you had the access to question the Ballroom's involvement. We needed your perspective on it, needed you to personally cover it. Both because we wanted the truth to come out but also so that if the time came, you'd have the moral standing to help prepare public opinion for our emergence into the light.

"But, especially after the Beowulf Strike, we don't see that happening anytime soon. And the truth is that that's our fault, in a lot of ways. We knew about Houdini. We didn't know its full depth, we didn't know how much destruction it was going to do or how many people they were prepared to kill, and we didn't know Admiral Henke would be blamed for it, but we knew a plan existed. We knew it would be put into effect if it looked like Mesa was likely to be conquered. And we didn't say a word about it. We hesitated. We *dithered*. We tried to decide how we could warn people without pointing a finger straight at ourselves, and while we were vacillating, they put Houdini into effect. How could we expect anyone—not just in the Grand Alliance, but in *Mesa*—to forget that or forgive us for it?"

"I think you could be wrong about that," O'Hanrahan said quietly. "I mean, the discovery of the 'Benign Alignment'—the 'Engagement,' they're calling it now—on Mesa has gone down a lot more quietly than I would have expected. Look at the way people are responding to my stories about the difference between it and the people you're talking about. It's being accepted as a legitimate movement, Phoebe. We might be, too, if we can prove it wasn't us, either."

"Personally, I think you might be right," Phoebe said. "But the people who make the actual decisions aren't going to take a chance on that unless they absolutely have to. Not after so many T-centuries in the shadows, so many lives committed to the Detweiler Plan. If they have to, if they're given no choice, they'll all hope like hell you're right about that and do their best, but *unless* they have to, they aren't going to risk everything on a single throw of the dice."

O'Hanrahan frowned, but she also nodded. She was on the outside, looking in. She couldn't possibly know all the variables the Alignment's—*her* Alignment's—leaders had to balance. And bitterly disappointing though it was to discover that they all might have been able to step into the light and now couldn't, she felt a vast, bright bubble of joy—of gratitude—welling through her. No wonder she'd been unable to understand everything the Alignment had done, all the murder and bloodshed and devastation. It hadn't been *her* Alignment at all!

"So what do you want me to do?"

"We want you to go on doing exactly what you've already done. We want you to tell Gaddis every single thing you've learned, and we want you to ask him to let you inside."

"I already have," O'Hanrahan confessed. Phoebe's eyes narrowed, and the reporter shrugged. "I was worried, afraid they'd really found us—*you*, I suppose—and getting inside was the only way I could see to get more information."

"I can see that," the other woman said slowly. "How did he react?"

"Positively, I think. In fact, better than I expected. I'd hoped to get access to the story, maybe far enough before the fact for anything I learned to be useful, but at least to put me into a position to ... shape the narrative, if worse came to worst. I haven't heard back from him yet, but he's told me he's going to ask the Powers That Be if he can actually embed me in the operation."

"That's outstanding!" Phoebe beamed at her. "Anything you can learn that might tell us whether it's us or the other Alignment they've found would be incredibly valuable, of course. But you're absolutely right that getting you that far inside will give us our best shot at 'shaping the narrative' when the truth comes out, and that may well be even more important, in the long run. You'd be someone the galaxy recognizes as an honest, authoritative voice coming down on our evil twins just as hard as they deserve. But it may ultimately be even more valuable if that same honest, authoritative voice continues to hammer home the distinction between what they've found hiding in the stars and what they found on Mesa. To point out that it's possible to share Detweiler's dream without turning into vicious murderers."

"To set the stage if our Alignment does decide to step into the light," O'Hanrahan said.

"Exactly. And if you're right there, covering the story from the inside from the moment they discover the awful, dark side of our legacy, you'll have far more credibility when that time comes. I don't know if there's any real likelihood of that happening, for all the reasons I've already given you plus some that, frankly, you don't need to know about at this point. But if it does happen, we'll need all of the support structure we can find, and we want you to be one of the pillars for that structure."

"Of course," O'Hanrahan said quietly.

HMS *Alistair McKeon*
Flagship CruRon 96
and
HMS *Exploratrice*
Survey Squadron 6

"SO, WHAT DID WE DO TO DRAW THE DEAD END?" LIEUTENANT Xander Riley complained over his morning cup of coffee.

"Dead end?" Commander Miloslav Brož, HMS *Alistair McKeon*'s executive officer, raised both sandy brown eyebrows at the ship's communications officer. "What makes you so certain we've drawn 'the dead end,' Xander?"

"I don't know, Sir." Riley took a disgusted sip and lowered the cup. "Maybe the survey report?"

Brož gazed at him thoughtfully, then leaned back, holding his own coffee cup in both hands, and looked around the breakfast table.

"Would anyone else care to expound upon this mystery for our junior lieutenant's edification?" he inquired mildly.

At thirty T-years, Riley was very young for a full lieutenant in a prolong society, and something suspiciously like a chuckle came from Lieutenant Commander Eskildsen, the heavy cruiser's diminutive tactical officer. But then she looked sternly at the XO.

"Don't pick on Xander," she said in a scolding tone. "He can't help how young he is."

"Oh, thank you, Ma'am!" If Riley's ego had been crushed by Brož's comment, he showed remarkably little sign of it.

"You're very welcome," she said soothingly. "But, in answer to your question," her tone grew considerably more serious, "we didn't draw the dead end, Xander. In fact, according to a little birdie I know in *Quentin Saint-James*, we got the assignment specifically because of that survey report."

611

Brož grinned. It wasn't exactly common knowledge, but Eskildsen and Lieutenant Commander Mateusz Ødegaard, Rear Admiral Terekhov's staff intelligence officer, were a couple. There was no way Ødegaard would have shared classified information with her, but none of the information about their destination star system was classified. Which Riley could have discovered for himself if he'd only looked in the right places. And then made the proper connections between the bits and pieces of information, at least.

Clearly, he hadn't, because his expression was puzzled, and Eskildsen shook her head.

"Xander, the people we're looking for—if they exist—have been hiding out here for somewhere around two and a half centuries," she said. "When was the Qaisrani survey report filed?"

"I don't know, exactly," Riley replied.

"*I* do." Lieutenant Mikhal Velychko, *McKeon*'s astrogator, raised his hand.

"Well, of course *you* do," Riley said.

"Kindly inform our junior lieutenant, Misha," Brož said.

"1664," Velychko said, and Riley's eyes widened.

"Ah! The light dawns!" Eskildsen said teasingly.

"Seriously," Brož sat forward again, and his tone was much less teasing, "we know these people have been around a long time, Xander. And we know they plan ahead and that they're sneaky as hell. So, if you were a bunch of fanatical 'genetic supermen' looking for a star system to call your own—one you didn't want anyone else ever finding out about—how would you go about hiding it?"

"Altering a survey report in the Survey Archive would be awfully hard, Sir," Riley pointed out, and Brož nodded.

The Solarian League's Survey Archive contained every survey report filed since the League's founding. There might have been a few predating the League's creation which had never found their ways into the Archive, but there couldn't have been very many. And the Archive was scrupulously maintained and backed up in multiple secure locations. Getting to all of them would have been a significant challenge, even if the general corruption of the League's bureaucracies had applied to it, and it hadn't.

"You're right, it would have been hard to *alter* a survey report," the XO agreed. "But it wouldn't have been all that difficult to file a *false* report in the first place. Out here on the ass-end of nowhere, especially back then?" He grimaced. "Wouldn't be that hard to bribe some hardscrabble survey crew to falsify its findings if you saw a way to make use of them."

"No, I can see that," Riley said slowly.

"And that same little birdie of mine in *Quentin Saint-James* tells me the survey ship that filed the report in question was lost to 'hazards of astrogation' only a couple of T-years later." Eskildsen's expression was very serious now. "That's one of the main reasons ONI flagged the system in the first place."

Riley nodded. "Hazards of astrogation" was the blanket term for "we don't have a clue what happened to them." And while far too many ships' disappearances came under that heading, it *was* interesting that the ship which had surveyed ACR-1773-16 was among them.

"Okay," he said in a much more satisfied tone. He sipped coffee. "Okay."

❖   ❖   ❖

"Alpha translation in one minute, Sir," Lieutenant Dreyfus announced.

"Thank you, Elspeth," Commodore Prescott Tremaine replied, exactly as if he hadn't already known that, and Dreyfus smiled. Both of them knew it was her job to tell him anyway.

"Just reminding you, Sir," she said, and Tremaine chuckled as the rest of his staff grinned.

Their amusement was a welcome break in the electric tension which had built steadily as the final minutes till their destination slipped away into eternity, and Tremaine smiled back at his staff astrogator. Then he returned his attention to the flag bridge plot with a familiar sense of gratitude for the fact that he'd managed to hang onto his entire original staff, despite the RMN's general shuffling of personnel. That was largely because CruRon 96 had been part of Tenth Fleet, and Tenth Fleet had been recalled from Mesa barely four T-months ago, following the ratification of the star system's new constitution.

That ratification hadn't been a given, especially in light of the number of ex-seccies and ex-slaves being allowed to vote for the first time in their lives, but the draft constitution had passed with a clear majority. One of very nearly eighty percent, in fact. The fact that it had been required to pass muster with the Grand Alliance, whose charter members had always been the galaxy's most serious star nations where enforcement of the Cherwell Convention against genetic slavery was concerned, had probably been a factor. A lot of people thought so, anyway. Tremaine suspected that the careful thought all of those ex-seccies and ex-slaves had given to it, their recognition that it represented a genuine tectonic shift in their power over their own lives, had been an even bigger one. It was entirely too easy for casual observers to equate those who had been disenfranchised for their entire lives with someone ignorant and uninformed about political realities.

It looked to him as if the new Mesan Republic stood a far better chance of not simply surviving but healing—gradually, not overnight, but *healing*—the ugly scars and hatreds of T-centuries of oppression and brutality than he'd truly believed was possible, going in. Only time would tell, of course, but if he'd been a betting man...

Whatever ultimately happened in Mesa, the need for Tenth Fleet to remain on station until the Grand Alliance formally recognized the new Republic had protected its units against both the drawdown and the general redeployment to cover at least some of the hottest of the Fringe's newborn hotspots. That redeployment had fallen most heavily on the Navy's lighter units, its cruisers and destroyers, and quite a few other cruiser squadrons had been broken up into divisions and parceled out for picket and flag-showing duty.

"Thirty seconds," Dreyfus said, and the digital time display ticked steadily down until—

"Translation," she announced, and *Alistair McKeon*, her division mate *Madelyn Huffman*, and HMS *Exploratrice*, dropped smoothly out of hyper into normal-space, three light-weeks from the star listed as ACR-1773-16. It was a very low-speed translation, dropping all three ships back into phase with the rest of the universe at an effectively zero velocity relative to the star.

Tremaine tipped back in his command chair and glanced at his electronic warfare officer with a raised eyebrow.

"Don't look at me, Sir!" WO5 Sir Horace Harkness said. "This here's not my bailiwick."

"But you *always* know what's going on," Tremaine said. "That's one of the foundations of my universe!"

"*Sure* it is. You just keep telling yourself that, Sir. In this case, though, I got nothing."

"My childlike faith has been shattered."

Tremaine shook his head mournfully, and Harkness snorted. Several other people on the flag bridge shared fresh grins. The commodore and Harkness went back a long way, and "childlike faith" was *not* the best way to describe their relationship. Faith, yes; childlike, not so much. There were, in fact, those on Tremaine's staff who suspected that Sir Horace's legendary skills at... manipulating personnel assignments, not to mention electronic data, had had something to do with *Alistair McKeon* drawing her present assignment. Of course, he *said* he was reformed, but...

"Excuse me, Sir," Lieutenant MacDonald said. "Incoming signal from *Exploratrice*."

"Put it through, Stilson," Tremaine told the com officer, and turned back to face the main display as a very dark-skinned commander appeared upon it.

"Commander Nelson," Tremaine greeted him.

"Commodore," the commander replied.

Ryder Nelson was a career survey officer, with multiple degrees in astrography and astrophysics. He was a compact, square-shouldered man who managed to simultaneously project the aura of a tough, competent naval officer and of the sort of academic still referred to, in some quarters, as a "nerd." And the reason he could do that was that he was both of those things. The mood Tremaine normally associated with him was one of thoughtful, almost detached calm, but Nelson's brown eyes were anything but detached at the moment.

"I have a preliminary report for you," he continued, and inhaled deeply. "We've got it, Commodore! It's El Dorado!"

✧　　✧　　✧

"Lieutenant Salinas is right, Sir," Commander Francine Klusener, Tremaine's chief of staff, said with a respectful nod at the briefing room's bulkhead com display that showed Commander Nelson aboard *Exploratrice*.

Stephen Salinas was the survey ship's astrogator, which in Survey Command, meant he had almost as many degrees as Nelson himself, including a doctorate in astrophysics. In this case, however, that particular qualification was secondary to his observations and conclusions.

"We've got multiple—as in literally hundreds—of high-energy sources in the star system," Klusener continued, her drawling, aristocratic accent more clipped than usual. "We've got a habitable planet, where the survey report says there isn't one. And we've got visual confirmation of dozens of orbital habitats, what have to be industrial platforms, and God knows what else." She shrugged. "I suppose it's remotely possible two supersecret organizations could have spent the last couple of T-centuries building hidden high-tech redoubts, but I'm inclined to doubt it."

"No, really?" Tremaine said dryly, and Nelson chuckled from the display.

"I'm sure Stephen will be relieved to hear that you concur with him, Francine," *Exploratrice*'s CO said. "I'll try to keep it from going to his head."

"Good," Tremaine said with a smile, but then he sobered. "I know we've only been here twelve hours, but do the two of you think you have as much data as you're likely to pull in from this range?"

"I'm an astrophysicist, Commodore," Nelson said. "Given my druthers, I'd sit right here for another week, because there are always more details to ferret out. In this case, though, I'd say we've definitely got what we came for. The truth is that we're not going to get any better observational data without micro jumping around to the other side of the system. I'm sure the computers will be able to tease more out of the raw data, but there's really no point, because Francine's right. This has *got* to be El Dorado, and that means getting more details is up to your people."

"I agree." Tremaine straightened in his chair. "In that case, Ryder, we'll bid you adieu. Godspeed back to Manticore."

"Thank you, Commodore." Nelson smiled fiercely. "There are a lot of people back home waiting for this."

"Then don't keep them waiting. We'll be along in a few weeks with the follow-up data."

"Yes, Sir. Nelson, clear."

The display blanked, and Tremaine turned to Klusener and Captain Mary-Lynne Selleck, *Alistair McKeon*'s CO.

"All right," he said. "Time to get us up to speed and deploy those drones."

April 1924 Post Diaspora

"Star systems are sort of hard to pack
up and carry away with you."

—Fleet Admiral Lady Dame Honor Alexander-Harrington,
Duchess and Steadholder Harrington

Harrington House
City of Landing
Planet of Manticore
Manticore Binary System

AUDREY O'HANRAHAN FOLLOWED HER GUIDE THROUGH THE COM-
fortably furnished mansion and tried not to feel too obviously
nervous about the green-uniformed bodyguard following her. The
fellow couldn't have been more courteous, but his polite demeanor
had been unflinching when he suggested that Michael Anderle
wait for her in the Harrington Guard's ready room.

It had been the sort of "suggestion" it was impossible to decline.

Now the man who'd greeted her when she arrived on Harrington House's doorstep stopped and knocked once on the frame
of an open double door.

"Yes, Mac?" a soprano voice said.

"Ms. O'Hanrahan is here, Ma'am."

"Well, by all means show her in."

James MacGuiness stepped aside and swept a half-bow, and
O'Hanrahan inhaled surreptitiously as she stepped past him. At
the moment, she really wished Michael was present to loom pro-
tectively over her, but she fully understood why Honor Alexander-
Harrington's armsmen would never allow an unknown bodyguard
past them with a weapon.

Although, from everything she'd been able to discover about
Alexander-Harrington, she could probably look after herself just
fine if someone did get by them.

She stepped through the door into a large, graciously appointed
library with a broad skylight. The woman she'd come to meet
stood in the doorway of another room on the library's far side—an
office, with enormous windows that looked out over the sparkling

expanse of Jason Bay. O'Hanrahan had expected her to be in uniform, but she wasn't, and the reporter recognized the Grayson influences in her elegantly tailored gown.

"It's a pleasure to meet you, Ms. O'Hanrahan," Duchess Harrington said, extending her hand. "I've been an admirer of your work for a long time. Even—" she smiled a bit tartly "—when it wasn't exactly flattering to the Grand Alliance."

"I always try to be as honest as I can, Your Grace," O'Hanrahan said, and it was true, within certain limits. In fact, she intended to *never* lie to this woman. Assuming her background research was as accurate as it usually was, that would come under the heading of a *very* bad idea. Which wasn't to say that she could tell Harrington the full truth, for obvious reasons.

"I know you do, which is why I've admired your work even when I didn't agree with your conclusions," Harrington told her. "Please," she released O'Hanrahan's hand to wave at a conversational group of armchairs. "Have a seat."

"Thank you."

O'Hanrahan sat and watched the cream-and-gray treecat leap lightly up to stretch along the back of Harrington's facing chair. It was the first time she'd actually seen a treecat in the flesh, and she was struck by how sinuously graceful it was. And as it butted its head affectionately against the back of Harrington's neck before it settled, O'Hanrahan could see why the unwary might think of it as a fluffy, adorable pet rather than the deadly protector her research told her it was.

Another of Harrington's armsmen stood quietly to one side, eyes watchful, and O'Hanrahan glanced at him.

"I'm afraid Simon won't allow me to run around unsupervised, even here at home," Harrington said with another fleeting smile. "It's been a while since the last time anyone tried to assassinate me, but Grayson armsmen have long memories."

"From everything I've been able to discover, that's probably a good thing," O'Hanrahan replied.

"I imagine personal experience has something to do with your view on the subject," Harrington said. "After all, the last attempt to kill you was a lot more recent than anything that's happened to me. Lately, at least." She grimaced. "I trust you're fully recovered?"

"I am, thank you. And you're right, being shot on the streets of Old Chicago does tend to give someone a rather different appreciation for bodyguards and the problems we make for them. Or the ones they make for *us*, for that matter. Michael—Michael Anderle, *my* bodyguard—doesn't really approve of my meeting with shady, anonymous contacts. I understand his thinking, especially since the authorities still don't have any idea who was behind it, but that kind of caution puts a bit of a crimp in a muckraker's professional life. It's been difficult to hammer out a workable compromise."

And that, too, was nothing but the truth, she thought. Anderle took his responsibility to protect her dead seriously. He *didn't* like some of the odd places her profession took her, and, she suspected, part of that concern, at least lately, stemmed from the stories she'd been posting—especially since her conversation with Phoebe—pointing an accusatory finger at the "other" Alignment. Those stories were likely to be more than mildly irritating to them, and they'd proven they weren't shy about using murder, even on an industrial scale, to swat irritations.

"I can see where that might be true." Harrington's eyes gleamed with what certainly looked like genuine amusement, and O'Hanrahan felt herself relax—slightly, at least.

"I invited you here to discuss the ground rules," Harrington said then. "I understand exactly why General Gaddis and Prime Minister Yon want you along, and frankly, I'm delighted they do. Certainly everyone on the Grand Alliance's side will value an unbiased Solarian viewpoint on whatever we discover about the Alignment."

O'Hanrahan's nerves tingled at the word "Alignment," and Harrington's eyes narrowed ever so slightly. O'Hanrahan noticed the change and grimaced.

"Forgive me, Your Grace," she said, "but according to some of the research I've done, your friend there—" she pointed at the treecat "—isn't the only empath in the room." Harrington's eyes narrowed a bit more. "I don't know exactly how closely held that particular fact is, but I *am* a reporter, and I do try to do my research. And I have to tell you that knowing you can read my emotions makes me...a little nervous. And a bit uncomfortable, really."

"I can understand that," Harrington replied after a moment. "In fact, that's one reason we haven't gone out of our way to publicize the 'cats' abilities, or—obviously—my own. But you're right. I can 'taste' your emotions. Unfortunately, it's not an ability I can turn on or off. It's just . . . *there*. I assure you, though, that I don't go around eavesdropping on people's feelings any more than I can help. And please remember that emotions are *all* I can read. I can't read your thoughts—for that matter, Nimitz couldn't. Admittedly, the fact that we can tell what someone is feeling makes it very hard to lie to us." There might, O'Hanrahan thought, have been an edge of warning in that. "But neither he nor I can tell what you're actually *thinking* at any given moment. So if you can, try to just think of me as someone who's exceptionally good at reading expressions and body language."

"That's what I told myself to do." O'Hanrahan smiled crookedly. "But I've just discovered that that's easier to tell myself than to actually do. And, I hope you'll forgive me for saying this, but I've also just decided that I never want to play poker with you, Your Grace!"

"I'm not surprised. My husband feels the same way, actually." Harrington chuckled, but her answering smile was sympathetic. "Just understand that by now I've become so accustomed to the 'background noise' of other people's emotions that unless I make a conscious effort to focus in on a given individual, it's very difficult for me to actually 'hear' anything. And also, understand that I'm fairly sure anyone in your position, even the galaxy's premier muckraker, has to feel a little . . . anxious when she ventures into what was enemy territory only a year or so ago. I'm not going to hold any unavoidable nervousness on your part against you."

O'Hanrahan nodded. She was relieved to know Harrington was prepared to make allowances for a League-based reporter coming face to face with an empath. Anyone would feel at least some reservations about that, but reporters had more secrets and sources to protect than most. Of course, some of them had even more of those secrets and sources than others, and she spared a silent prayer of thanks for Phoebe. Thanks to her revelations, O'Hanrahan had no reservations at all about helping drag the "other" Alignment out into the daylight and clubbing it to death. In fact, she hoped Harrington "tasted" her burning determination to do just that.

"I'll try to bear that in mind," she said out loud.

"Good." Harrington nodded back to her, then leaned back in her chair and reached up to caress the treecat's ears with one hand.

"I have to confess to a certain curiosity of my own," she said. "One of my closest friends here in the Star Kingdom, Stacy Hauptman, is deeply involved in the Star Empire's—well, the Old Star Kingdom's—news services. As a consequence, I have some idea of how you 'newsies' work, but General Gaddis and his associates thought their security on this one was pretty tight. So may I ask how you became aware of Operation Rat Catcher?" O'Hanrahan's nerves tightened, and Harrington shook her head quickly. "I'm not trying to catch anyone out, here. It's just that the Alignment is far more thoroughly wired into events just about everywhere than I could wish, and I'm wondering whether or not *it* may have caught some of the same clues."

"I'd be extraordinarily surprised if anyone else could have learned about Rat Catcher the same way I did," O'Hanrahan replied after a moment. "I won't say it's flatly impossible, but the truth is that I've spent decades building a network of sources I can trust because they trust me. And—" she showed a brief flash of tooth "—because they know damned well I'll burn them at the stake, figuratively speaking, if they try to play me. I hope you'll forgive me if I'm not prepared to tell you who they are?" She looked at the duchess levelly. "I don't *think* any of them actually violated any laws, but even if they did, I owe them confidentiality. Like I said, they trust me, and I won't violate that trust."

"Of course you won't. And I wouldn't ask you to," Harrington replied.

"Thank you," O'Hanrahan said with quiet sincerity, because those people *did* trust her, and they deserved her protection in return.

"It's possible somebody else—including this Alignment of yours—could have built an equally extensive network, I'm sure," she continued, "but I had to combine bits and pieces from over a dozen sources before I began figuring out what Brigadier—well, I guess *General* Gaddis, now—was involved in."

All of which, O'Hanrahan thought gratefully, was true. Harrington still looked a bit bothered, though.

"Your Grace," she said, "I probably couldn't tell you now, myself, exactly how this first came to my attention. I have friends and sources in the Navy, in the Justice Department, in the Gendarmes, in the Anti-Slavery League, even a few I'm pretty sure are part of the *Ballroom*. As nearly as I can piece it together, Director Gannon over at ONI started the ball rolling, in some ways, with his brainstorm—which I thoroughly approve of, by the way—about eradicating every trace of genetic slavery's infrastructure. I found out he was talking to Cathy Montaigne, which suggested both the Anti-Slavery League and, quite possibly, the Ballroom would be involved. And then one of my sources on Mesa told me there were rumors that sensitive records had been 'acquired' when the Mumps hit the secret Jessyk headquarters in Mendel. And then, other sources in the Provisional Government, the Constitutional Convention, and what's left of the Department of the Interior told me a delegation from Mesa—and the Grand Alliance—was meeting with representatives of the Prime Minister to authorize some sort of clandestine op. And after that, Captain Zilwicki, who's probably the galaxy's most well known 'secret agent,' disappeared for a couple of months, only to reappear and then promptly vanish back into General Gaddis's lair."

She shrugged with a wry smile that was completely genuine.

"Exactly how all of those bits and pieces combined in my newsy's hindbrain to suggest that your people might be on the track of what you call the Alignment is more than I could tell you," she said honestly. "And, I'm afraid, whether anyone else could have made the same connections, or had access to the same clues, is also more than I could tell you."

"I'm afraid I understand *that*, too," Harrington said.

She sat for a moment, frowning slightly in thought. Then she gave her head a little toss and refocused on O'Hanrahan.

"Obviously, I hope no one else—or none of the bad guys, at least—*have* made the same connections. On the other hand, if we're right, if we really have found their secret hideaway in the stars, there's probably not a lot they could do with the information, anyway. Certainly not in the short term. Star systems—" she smiled thinly "—are sort of hard to pack up and carry away with you."

"That's true, but that's not the only thing you're thinking about," O'Hanrahan said slowly. "You're also thinking about that old aphorism. The one about being forewarned and being forearmed. You're worried that if they realize you're coming, you'll lose the advantage of surprise and find them waiting for you with everything they've got."

"I am." Harrington nodded again, this time with more than

a trace of respect. "That's exactly what I'm thinking about. Well, that and the fact that these people seem to be really good about destroying their sensitive records whenever they have half an opportunity."

"I can see where that would be frustrating, but if you've really found their 'secret hideaway,' how much good would that do them?"

"Hopefully, none. But if we've discovered anything about the Alignment, it's that it could have given Hydra lessons about growing secondary heads. Even if we lop this one off, there's no saying we'll have gotten every bit of the tumor."

"No, I suppose there's not," O'Hanrahan agreed, slowly, hoping that Harrington would put her sudden spike of anxiety down to an equally sudden realization on her part that the duchess might be right.

"I may be worrying unnecessarily." Harrington sounded almost as if she was trying to reassure her. "And even if they destroy a lot of their records, it's unlikely they could destroy enough to hide something like that from us. If we're right about the size of their installation, and how long they've been working on it, there'd have to be enough human beings in the system to give us some clue if there were any significant secondary headquarters."

"That's probably true," O'Hanrahan said thoughtfully.

"Well," Harrington's voice turned brisker, "about those ground rules I mentioned. Here's the way I see this working. You'll be aboard *Imperator*, my flagship. I'll introduce you to my staff, and you'll have access to them. They'll be instructed to answer all of your questions as fully and completely as they can, although I'm sure you'll understand that any answer they give you may be affected by considerations of purely military security. Lieutenant Chudzik is my staff public information officer, and he'll answer any background questions you may have, but your primary contact—the person specifically responsible for seeing to it that you're kept fully informed and of keeping *me* aware of any needs you may have—will be Lieutenant Commander Justinian, Brock Justinian, my flag lieutenant. In addition, Lieutenant Commander Eriquez, my staff communications officer, will see to it that any inquiries you might have for someone outside *Imperator* get priority. Brock and Simon here—" she waved a graceful hand at the uniformed armsman standing behind her "—will be responsible for arranging transport if you want to interview anyone aboard one of the other ships of the fleet or get a closer, hands-on look at some particular aspect of our operations. From your track record, I expect you'd probably be willing to run more risks with your personal safety than we are, but don't expect me to overrule them if they tell me they think something's too risky. It would probably be inadvisable, let's say, to let something happen to the Solarian League's most widely known muckraking newsy."

"That's actually rather more than I'd hoped for, Your Grace," O'Hanrahan said truthfully. "On the other hand, in keeping with my reporter's God-given responsibility to push the envelope, may I assume I'll be allowed down on to whatever planet or aboard whatever habitats your ships ultimately secure?"

"Within limits," Harrington told her. "After the fact, once we're reasonably confident about the security environment, you should have complete access. After all, we want you there to get out the truth of anything we find. But, again, no one's going to let you get too near the sharp end until we can be fairly confident nothing like what happened to you in Old Chicago will happen again."

She looked at O'Hanrahan levelly, and the reporter shrugged.

"I can live with that," she said.

May 1924 Post Diaspora

"This isn't another star nation we're fighting. Not this time. This is a *cancer*, and we're going to cut it out and cauterize the wound. Whatever it takes, we will *do* it."

—Admiral Honor Alexander-Harrington,
Steadholder and Duchess Harrington

HMS *Imperator*
San Martin Planetary Orbit
Trevor's Star System

"ATTENTION ON DECK!"

The men and women seated around the large briefing table rose as she stepped into the compartment. She paused, briefly, just inside the door to survey the gathering of flag officers and their senior staff, then strode across to her own place at the head of the table, accompanied by Admiral Mark Sarnow, who'd been summoned home from Silesia to replace Sir Thomas Caparelli as First Space Lord. Captain Andrea Jaruwalski moved to stand behind the chair to Honor's right, and Captain Petersen moved behind the chair beside Jaruwalski's.

She and Sarnow seated themselves, Nimitz leapt up to curl across the back of her chair, and she looked around the table one more time.

"Be seated, ladies and gentlemen," she said, then, and all of them settled back into their chairs.

She took a moment to contemplate all of the years of experience, all the proven capability, seated at that table. Any one of those flag officers could have commanded Grand Fleet. Indeed, at least one of them had. This was the Grand Alliance's first team, the men and women she would have requested above all others. Oh, there were one or two—all right, at least a dozen!—others she wished could have been here, could have held command for this operation. But much as she might have wanted to include them, there was not a single officer at that table who she would have replaced.

Not one of them.

She smiled briefly, fleetingly, at that thought, and reflected once again on the perversity of human nature. None of them knew exactly what they were about to run their heads into. No one knew how many of the people sitting around this table might die in the next few weeks, yet all of them knew from bitter, personal experience that it could happen. That it had happened, far too often, for all of them over the last two and a half decades of bloody warfare. And yet, when they must prepare themselves to venture back into the furnace, they wanted their friends, the men and women they knew and trusted, at their sides. Wanted that even though they knew they risked losing yet more of those friends, more pieces of their souls.

And I'm just as bad as any of them, she thought, savoring the mind-glows of her task force and task group commanders. She tasted more than a little trepidation in some of those mind-glows, but no hesitation, no doubts.

Admiral Pascaline L'anglais, her senior task force commander, sat at the table's far end, flanked by Admiral Lester Tourville and Vice Admiral Jennifer Bellefeuille, her task group commanders. High Admiral Alfredo Yu, commanding Task Force Three, sat to L'anglais's right, between Admiral Mercedes Brigham and Admiral Michal Lukáč, his task group commanders. Admiral Chien-lu von Rabenstrange, commanding Task Force Four, sat between Admiral Grauer Berg and Admiral Grünes Dorf, facing Yu. And to Honor's right, just beyond Megan Petersen, sat Admiral Michelle Henke, the CO of Task Force One, the one woman above all others Honor Alexander-Harrington wanted at her side for this operation, flanked by Admiral Alice Truman and Admiral Allen Higgins.

She allowed herself another moment of that awareness before she turned her head to look at Sarnow.

"I believe you wanted to tell us something, Admiral?" she said, and saw the memory in his green eyes. The memory of another day in a star system called Hancock. She would never stop missing Thomas Caparelli's bedrock, unflinching determination, yet there was something incredibly fitting about Sarnow's presence here today. He and she had fired the first shots of the long war against the People's Republic together. Now he was here on the eve of the final campaign against the people who had engineered that war.

"Actually, Your Grace," he said, "I do. It's official." It was his turn to survey Honor's COs. "You hyper out Tuesday."

Honor tasted the way nerves tightened throughout the compartment. None of them were surprised. In fact, what Sarnow had just told them was undoubtedly among the most superfluous things anyone had ever said.

Except that the fact that he'd said the words made it official.

"Thank you, Sir Mark," she said quietly, and every eye returned to her, waiting. In most senses, everything she was about to say was just as superfluous as anything Sarnow had said. But the boxes had to be checked. Besides, this meeting was much less about planning or intelligence analysis than it was about mutual recognition. About seeing one another face-to-face, in person, one last time before they set out.

And that was why Sarnow was here, as well. To hear what she said, measure her senior commanders' confidence, share his own with them, and lend his own—and the Admiralty's—final imprimatur to their operation.

"Thanks to *Exploratrice* and Commodore Tremaine," she continued, "we've been able to do more planning than I'd really anticipated, given the pains the Alignment's taken to cover its tracks."

More than one of her officers smiled nastily as they, too, contemplated the data Scotty Tremaine's recon drones had brought back. They would all have liked more—they were professional naval officers, who knew they could never have too much information, that reconnaissance was often the difference between who lived and who died—but they had immeasurably greater detail than *Exploratrice*'s initial observations had provided.

Not all of it was *good* news, of course.

They knew, for example, that the system which had been dubbed "El Dorado" had over thirty orbital fortresses, the smallest of them as large as the fortresses covering the Manticoran Wormhole Junction. They knew there were at least fifty superdreadnoughts to support those fortresses, although the drones, confined to the outer reaches of the star system in the name of stealthiness, had been unable to tell them how many—if any—of them were pod-laying designs. Those same drones had observed what looked like exercises by multiple squadrons of LACs, and they'd also detected at least one clump of missile pods. That had been purely fortuitous—and statistically improbable—because the drone in question had passed close enough to spot them visually.

Which raised the question of exactly what missile pods were doing that far out-system.

One thing they could be certain of was that there had to be thousands of pods the drones *hadn't* detected.

They also knew they were looking at a system that was even more heavily industrialized than they'd anticipated. The drones had confirmed *Exploratrice*'s initial estimate: there were almost a dozen massive industrial platforms, served by an entire fleet of asteroid extraction ships and orbital smelters, spaced around the outermost asteroid belt, while gas-mining tankers shuttled back and forth between the inner system and El Dorado-V, the inner of the system's two gas giants, which lay just inside the system's hyper-limit.

Under the circumstances, they were fortunate El Dorado wasn't fortified even more heavily, and all of them knew it. Unfortunately, there were still all too many things they *didn't* know.

"We all know we're traveling light, in some ways, compared to the fleet we sent to Sol, even with Admiral von Rabenstrange's task force," Honor continued, and shrugged. That was inevitable, given the way the Grand Alliance had already begun drawing down its wartime fleets. "But we'll have a solid core of heavy hitters—" in fact, they would have over two hundred pod superdreadnoughts and almost eighty CLACs, not counting the Fleet Train and its escorts "—with all the firepower we need to look after ourselves in any fleet engagement. And if we need them, there are five hundred thousand-plus Mark Seventeens aboard the Feet Train's colliers. Fifty million or so Mark Twenty-Threes ought to be more than enough, but trust me—if it turns out we're still overly optimistic about how strongly fortified El Dorado is, I have no intention of committing to an attack straight into it. We'll have ample strength to blockade the system and picket its hyper-limit, and if we're right, if this is really the core of the onion, they don't have anywhere else to go. If El Dorado's too strong for us to attack out of our immediate resources, we'll nail its door shut and keep it that way while we whistle up a fleet strong enough to take *any* objective, even if we have to build the ships we need from scratch."

She let her eyes circle the table once more.

"We've discussed all of the planning we can and can't do," she continued. "Personally, I think Admiral Saleta and Admiral Trenis are correct when they suggest that it was actually the Alignment, fronting through Technodyne, who provided the SLN with the Cataphract. We can't *prove* that, especially since Yildun is one of the systems which has declined to ratify the new Constitution, which means even our friends in the League aren't in a position to lean on Technodyne's home offices for details of the original design's R and D. But the fact that they refuse to give us that information strikes us as a pretty strong indicator that it didn't come out of their own shop...and that they think we'd be just a bit unhappy with them if we found out who handed it to them."

The assembled flag officers nodded in sober understanding. None of the data Honor had brought back from Ganymede indicated the original source of the Cataphract design, and the Technodyne headquarters on Mesa had suffered a mysterious fire before Michelle Henke could seize their records. There was a clear paper trail indicating how the Cataphract had morphed into the Hasta—all the work on that had been done at Ganymede—but no trace of where the initial Cataphract design had come from.

"I bring this up because it illustrates a point we need to keep very clearly in mind," she continued with a wintry smile. "Commodore Tremaine may have provided us with a lot of data on the positions and energy signatures of El Dorado's orbital platforms, and we may have what we believe are good counts on their mobile units, but all of you know we have no intelligence at all on these people's actual hardware. The Cataphract and the graserhead missiles we've already encountered are clear empirical proof that they have weapons none of us have ever faced in combat, however, and Commodore Tremaine's drones detected grav pulses indicating El Dorado has a substantially more sophisticated FTL com capability than the Solarian League had, so at the very least, their doctrine for their missile pods almost has to be more sophisticated than the League's was.

"We've spent the last month refining our plans for this operation, but we've known from the outset that our ability to project threats is suspect. I intend to do everything we can to expand and update our current data files after we make our alpha translation and begin openly deploying recon drones, but electronic intelligence and visual observation will be able to tell us only so much. We won't be able to peek inside their missiles or know how good their active defenses are until one side or the other opens fire.

"I wish we could expect the other side to be equally ignorant about *our* capabilities, but we know they had agents—highly placed, in some cases—inside our own militaries. We believe we've closed down those high-level conduits, but I don't believe anyone in this compartment is foolish enough to assume they don't continue to have penetration at lower levels. We're confident they haven't uncovered Bolthole's location, since there's been no attempt to duplicate the Yawata Strike on Refuge, but, unlike the Solarian League, there's no way in the galaxy that *these* people haven't moved heaven and earth to stay abreast of our doctrine and deployed weapons.

"That means they've had a huge advantage in terms of formulating tactics against the day they might have to defend *their* Bolthole, so expect me to approach this operation with caution. Understand me. If we can take these people down, we *will*." Her brown eyes were bleak and hard. "But if there's any dying to be done, I intend for the other side to do it. I will not give the people behind the millions of deaths we've already suffered—behind the Yawata Strike and the Beowulf Strike and behind all of the millions of spacers who died on both sides in the war they engineered—a single additional victim if I can avoid it. The 'Alignment' has visited more death and destruction on the human race than any other tyrant, any other dictatorship or totalitarian state, in the history of humankind.

"That *ends*." She tapped her right index finger on the tabletop. "It ends now. Maybe not instantly, if it turns out we've underestimated their defensive strength, but it *ends*." Her finger tapped again. "This isn't another star nation we're fighting. Not this time. This is a *cancer*, and we're going to cut it out and cauterize the wound. Whatever it takes, we will *do* it."

She let her final sentence settle into their bones, then folded her hands on the table and leaned forward.

"But we will not become them in the process," she said softly, quietly. "We'll remember who *we* are. We'll remember that *our* navies and *our* star nations fight with honor and a sense of decency. We will *destroy* the Mesan Alignment and consign it to the ash heap in the corner of Hell reserved for genocidal perversions. But when we do, we'll also remember that the initial labor force that built the Alignment's fortress consisted of slaves. Slaves who had no voice in what they did, or how they did it, or for whom.

Those slaves' descendants are undoubtedly still there, still with no voice, no choice, but to do the Alignment's bidding, and we will not massacre innocents just because the Alignment doesn't care who or how many of the people *we* loved it's killed. So, whatever else happens, there will be no Eridani Edict violations.

"Believe me when I say I understand the desire to turn their planets and their habitats into cinders. To pay them in their own coin. To stand back and watch as they burn to the ground. I've been there. I've wanted that so badly I could taste it, like poison. And I almost did it."

She tasted the surprise in more than one of those mind-glows as she admitted that, but she continued unflinchingly, meeting their eyes.

"In the end, I didn't, although I'm well aware there are people in Sol who fail to appreciate the restraint the Grand Alliance showed." Her smile was fleeting, and Sarnow snorted beside her. "But I didn't. Maybe I never would have. I don't know about that, but I do know I won't do it here. And I won't let any of you or any of our men and women carry the burden of having done it, either. We are who we are, and that's who I intend for us to be when the smoke clears."

She let that settle for a moment, then leaned back again.

"And now that that's out of the way," she smiled much more warmly, "Captain Jaruwalski has a few last-minute details for us to discuss."

GSNSS *Francis Crick*
Tschermak Orbit
Galton System

"TALK TO ME, DANIAR!" KONTREADMIRAL LEONARD SPADAFORA snapped as he stormed out of the lift shaft onto his command deck.

A mere OWP wasn't normally a rear admiral's command, but there was nothing "mere" about *Francis Crick*, and Korvetten-kapitän Quinzio, *Crick*'s tactical officer, looked up from his own displays at his CO's harsh-voiced command.

"All we have so far is the hyper footprint, Sir. It's sixteen light-minutes from Galton, just outside the hyper-limit. And it's big. *Very* big." Quinzio shook his head, his expression grim. "Whatever else it is, it's not a survey force."

"I see."

Spadafora crossed to the circular well, folded his hands behind him, and gazed down into the enormous holo display at the command deck's center. The massive hyper footprint's blood red icon pulsed at the display's perimeter, and his mouth tightened. It was, indeed, sixteen light-minutes from the system primary. But that was only *ten* light-minutes from Tschermak, perfectly positioned for a least-time course to Galton's only inhabited planet. Which meant Quinzio was right. This wasn't a survey force, not somebody *looking* for the Alignment.

This was somebody who knew where the Alignment was. Who knew the astrography of the system well enough to plot an approach that precise. He wondered how much *else* they knew about their enemy, because he was certain of at least one thing. That strobing icon never would have been there unless the ships it represented thought they had the firepower to kill that enemy now that they'd found it.

His face tightened. The Alignment's worst, darkest nightmare looked back at him from the plot, and despair flowed through him. *Crick* was the command center, the linchpin, of Galton's defenses. And because it was, Spadafora knew even better than most that the system was doomed. Concealment had been its one true defense, because there'd never been any point pretending it could hope to survive the massive power of the Grand Alliance's combined navies if they ever located the Alignment's heart.

Now, obviously, they had. And, equally obviously, the men and women prepared to die in the last, desperate defense of Leonard Detweiler's magnificent vision were about to do just that.

But then he inhaled deeply, squared his shoulders. Maybe they were. And maybe six hundred T-years of sweat, sacrifice, and devotion *were* about to die with them. But before they did, they would kill as many of the motherless bastards out there in that hyper footprint as they could.

"Tactical, spin up the wedge," he said.

"Yes, Sir!"

"And then, Com," he said coldly, "get me the Grossadmiral."

HMS *Imperator*
Grand Fleet
Galton System

"WELL, I IMAGINE THEY KNOW WE'RE HERE."

Honor Alexander-Harrington's tone was dry as she stood between Andrea Jaruwalski and Megan Petersen on *Imperator*'s flag deck, with Nimitz on her shoulder, and gazed at the master plot. It wasn't the first time she'd seen a display almost exactly like that one, but the others had been simulations in planning sessions and exercises, generated from recorded data. This one was live.

And this was no exercise.

"Oh, I think we can take that pretty much as a given, Your Grace." Jaruwalski's tone was even drier than Honor's. "What I'd like to know is how many of them feel a sudden urgent need to hit the head."

"I know *my* pucker factor would be just about off the scale," Peterson said. It had taken her a couple of weeks to settle in as Honor's ops officer, but she'd found her feet nicely in the end.

"I'm sure theirs is, too, Megan," Honor said, and turned from the plot to the master com display. It was divided into windows, one for each of her task force and task group commanders, and she smiled coldly at them.

"As Andrea and Megan have just observed, they know we're here and they're undoubtedly activating the defensive plans we all know they have. I suppose it's time we activated our *offensive* plans."

Heads nodded.

"All right, then, ladies and gentlemen. Let's be about it."

GSNSS *Irving Fischer*
Tschermak Orbit
Galton System

A MUSICAL TONE CHIMED, AND GROSSADMIRAL GUNTHER MON-talván turned from his com display, eyes seeking the plot as it updated.

The outermost sensor platforms light-speed data had come in seven minutes earlier. They could have had it even sooner, but Montalván wasn't prepared to give up the locations of any of his FTL relay platforms just yet. The nearest clusters of pre-spotted recon drones had been headed for the intruders for over eighteen minutes now, however, and he *had* authorized them to report through a single platform. He had enough of them to give up one without damaging his coverage.

"We have solid reads on them now, Sir," Kommodore Auberjonois, his operations officer said.

"How much coverage do we have?" Montalván asked.

"Virtually total." Auberjonois sounded more than a little bitter. "They're not even trying to knock back our drones. They *want* us to know what they have."

"Of course they do," Karoline Adebayo said from Montalván's com. He looked back at her, and she shrugged. "It's not like they ever thought they could sneak up on us. And when they're that far out-system, they must figure there's not much we can do with anything they show us. So they might as well make sure we know how big their hammer is. They may even hope we'll just throw in the towel if they do."

Montalván nodded, although he also wondered if the generalfeldmarshall was as calm as she sounded. The woman who was both Galton's governor and the commander-in-chief of its defenses couldn't allow herself to show anything but determination. She certainly couldn't show panic or despair, not if she expected her people to fight. On the other hand, Adebayo was as well aware as Montalván that the Alamo Contingency was upon them.

Of course, there was a certain liberating aspect to that, wasn't there? The two of them could make their plans, fight their battle, without any paralyzing uncertainty about their own fates.

"We can't confirm it, Generalfeldmarshall," Auberjonois said, "but we're certain they're flooding the system with recon platforms of their own. We've seen just a few weak impeller traces, but their drones are obviously just as hard to find as we thought they'd be."

"So they're not just letting us absorb their size and strength. They're getting a better read on ours, at the same time," Montalván said, acknowledging the ops officer's point. "I rather wish they'd gone ahead and tried to take out our drones, though."

Auberjonois nodded. They knew the Grand Alliance's reconnaissance drones were both highly stealthy and, courtesy of their onboard micro fusion plants, extraordinarily long-legged. The Alignment's stealth technology might actually be even better, however. It was certainly better than anything the Solarian League had ever had, and Galton's defenders had produced two different recon platforms. The Alpha Drones incorporated every upgrade the Alignment possessed, although their power budget remained badly limited compared to the Grand Alliance's Ghost Riders, while the Beta Drones were virtual clones of the SLN's current technology. At the moment, Auberjonois had deployed both Betas and Alphas to spy out the enemy's strength...and as a possible test of their own ability to penetrate the Grand Alliance's sensors. If the Grand Alliance had tried to knock out only the Betas, that might have been an indication it *couldn't* detect and target the Alphas. Not proof, of course, but at least an indication.

Which would have been good, since it might also give have given them some read on how readily their enemies might be able to detect the Alignment's equally upgraded Hasta.

"Where are we on Shuttlecock?" he asked.

"We should have the alpha launch in position in another fifty-two minutes, Sir."

"Well, in that case, the longer they're prepared to sit there, the happier I'll be."

"I'm a bit surprised we haven't already heard from them," Adebayo observed. "They've been here for almost twenty minutes now."

"Well, they know the system's not going anywhere," Montalván replied. "I can see where they might think hanging out there like some silent Sword of Damocles might have a . . . softening effect on our morale."

Their eyes met over the com, and Adebayo's smile was cold.

"Some things are more likely than others," she said.

HMS *Imperator*
Grand Fleet
and
GSNSS *Francis Crick*
Tschermak Orbit
Galton System

"—AND YOLANDA SAYS WE'RE GETTING GOOD DATA FROM THE Ghost Riders, Your Grace," Captain Rafael Cardones said from the com connecting Honor to *Imperator*'s command deck. "Not as much as we'd like, obviously. I've always been greedy." His flashing smile reminded Honor, for just a moment, of the young, inexperienced tactical officer who'd performed so well on Basilisk Station. And the far more experienced one who'd fought so brilliantly in Grayson. "But we're building a better profile on their mobile units at least."

"I agree, Your Grace." Megan Petersen stood beside Honor's command chair, looking into the com display with her. "One bit of good news—we've managed to confirm that most of their superdreadnoughts are pre-pod designs. Looks like they've got about three classes, so I'm guessing all of them were experimental. Or developmental, anyway. We've only IDed seventeen pod-layers, so far."

"I agree that's good news," Commander Yolanda Harriman, Cardones's tactical officer, said from off-screen over the same link. "It would be better news if we were looking at a *mobile* engagement, though."

"You've got that right, Yolanda." Andrea Jaruwalski had crossed the flag bridge to Honor just in time to hear Harriman's last comment. "And I'd feel a lot happier if we hadn't just confirmed Scotty's—I mean *Commodore Tremaine's*, of course—speculation about those damned forts. All of them are showing impeller wedges now."

"Unfortunate, but not unexpected," Honor replied.

Jaruwalski nodded, and no one would have guessed from her expression how hard she'd argued for an immediate missile strike on those OWPs, the moment Grand Fleet came out of hyper and had time to deploy pods. Unless the forts' impellers were continuously online, which was extraordinarily unlikely, given the power demand and relatively short operational life of impeller nodes *that* size, that strike would have gone home before they could bring up the protective bands of their wedges.

It was too late for that now, and Honor tasted Jaruwalski's regret for the lost opportunity. Well, Honor regretted it, too, and she'd completely understood Andrea's viewpoint. In fact, she'd shared it. The Alignment's own actions had put it beyond the pale, and the accepted rules of war recognized both the right of reprisal for violation of little things like the Eridani Edict. And they also recognized that, unlike orbital habitats, armed platforms of an enemy power were legitimate targets for immediate destruction. The Grand Alliance was under no obligation to allow the personnel aboard those forts to evacuate, or even surrender, in the wake of the Yawata and Beowulf strikes, and Honor was only too well aware of how much more difficult their destruction had become once those impeller wedges and sidewalls went up.

But she'd also meant what she'd said in that final pre-departure conference. The Grand Alliance wasn't the Alignment, and it wouldn't act like the Alignment. Not because of what it owed the Alignment, but because of what it owed to itself . . . and to history.

From a more pragmatic perspective, that quick a launch would have run far more risk of accidentally targeting the enormous constructs which were obviously habitats, some of them almost as big—and far more sprawling—than Beowulf Alpha had been before its destruction. Then there were the industrial platforms. Unless they were armed, they, too, were covered by the Eridani Edict's requirement that an attacking commander allow sufficient time for civilian personnel to be evacuated.

Honor glanced at Peterson as that thought ran through her mind. Megan was the one officer on her staff who'd argued strongly *against* the immediate missile strike. Which, given her experiences in Hypatia, hadn't surprised a single member of that staff.

"The inner system Ghost Rider platforms have deployed the Bloodhounds," Peterson said now, and Honor nodded.

The Bloodhound was one of the fruits of the Foraker/Hemphill Bolthole brain trust. Essentially, Bloodhounds were tiny parasite drones carried by modified Ghost Riders and deployed in constellations designed to penetrate hostile communications nets. Com lasers were impossible to detect without putting a platform directly into the path of the beam, and Bloodhound was designed to flood probable zones with enough platforms—moving very stealthily, in precisely calculated search patterns—to put one of their number exactly there. The interruption of signal, however brief, would tell an alert enemy the parasite had found one of her transmission paths, and its encrypted signals would still be impossible to read, but simply analyzing the density, complexity, and directions in which a command-and-control net extended could offer pattern analysis quite a lot of insight.

"We definitely don't have all their nets nailed down," Peterson continued. "Not even Bloodhound's going to let anyone do that! But Tristram—" Lieutenant Commander Tristram Jacoby was *Imperator*'s electronic warfare officer "—and I can confirm that Alpha, Beta, and Gamma are the command-and-control hubs for the entire system."

That was no surprise, Honor reflected, since the platforms they'd designated Alpha, Beta, and Gamma were the three largest fortresses in the entire system and just happened to be spaced equidistantly, a hundred and twenty degrees apart, around the inhabited planet. It was nice to have it confirmed, though.

"Do you and Tristram have any feel for which of them is the primary?"

"From what we've seen so far, we're inclined to think it's Beta, Your Grace. We can't guarantee that, but it appears to have more redundant links to the other two than either of them have to it or to each other. With the caveat, of course, that even Bloodhound's only giving us partial coverage."

"I'd tend to agree with their logic, Your Grace," Jaruwalski said, and Honor nodded.

"Anything else, Megan?" she asked.

"Not on what you might call the macro scale," Peterson replied. "One thing we've confirmed, though, is that their stealth is better than anything the Sollies had. Commodore Tremaine's recon had already suggested that, but I think it's even better than we'd assumed from his preliminary data. We *have* localized a few clusters of missile pods in what CIC is calling a Moriarty deployment, and I've got drones looking for the volumes where *we* would've put the missile stacks for something like that. But their pods are a lot harder sensor targets than anything we ever saw out of the League. In fact, I'd say they're at least as stealthy as our late-gen system-defense pods. Probably *more* stealthy, actually. And a star system's a big place. There's no way we're going to find all of them."

"All we can do is the best we can do," Honor said philosophically, "and I don't mind spending a little longer looking for them. I want to nail down every threat we can."

She glanced at the master plot. Grand Fleet's icons were an enormous globe at the center of that plot, rather than the conventional wall of battle which had been the norm for so many T-centuries. The capital ships at the heart of that globe had yet to deploy any missile pods of their own, but every starship's hyper generator was at instant readiness. From that start, an *Invictus*-class, like *Imperator*, could translate back into hyper in a bit less than four and a half minutes. A *Nike*-class battlecruiser could hyper out in just over a minute and a half, and a *Saganami-C* heavy cruiser could do it in just forty-three seconds. That should be plenty of cushion to evade anything the system's defenders could throw at them, but Honor was disinclined to rely on "should" where her people's lives were concerned. Her starships were surrounded by an intricate shield of LACs, configured and deployed in the missile defense role, and beyond the LACs, a shell of Ghost Rider platforms watched Argus-eyed for any threat.

"Your Grace, the communications buoy is coming up on the specified range in about two minutes," Lieutenant Commander Eriquez said, and Honor turned toward her com officer with a tight smile.

❖   ❖   ❖

"Generalfeldmarshall."

Karoline Adebayo turned from her conversation with Oberst Chuntao, her chief of staff.

"Yes, Zarmayr?"

"We have a communications request, Ma'am." Major Nerguizian's voice was taut. "It's addressed to the system commander."

"I see." Adebayo walked across to the com officer's station. "I suppose it's a case of better late than never."

Nerguizian smiled—briefly. But then he shook his head.

"I think I know what part of the delay was, Ma'am," he said. "The transmission's a standard com laser, but it's coming from a platform less than two hundred thousand kilometers from *Crick*. And sensors are picking up directional grav-pulses from the same platform."

"And we didn't know it was there until it started talking to us?"

"No, Ma'am."

"But they asked for the 'system commander,' not for any specific individual by name?"

"Yes, Ma'am. They did."

"I see," Adebayo repeated.

She stopped behind the com officer's chair and rested one hand on his shoulder.

"Get me Grossadmiral Montalván on a side link, Zarmayr."

"Yes, Ma'am!"

Gunther Montalván's face appeared on a secondary display, and he raised an eyebrow at Adebayo.

"They're finally talking to us," she told him. "I want you listening when I take the call."

"Of course, Ma'am."

"Two things before I do, though." She took her hand from Nerguizian's shoulder and folded her arms. "First, they got an FTL communications relay to within two hundred thousand kilometers of *Crick* without us ever seeing it coming. I'm inclined to think that's at least partly another deliberate statement of their capabilities. But they're also using a com laser, not an omnidirectional signal."

"So they know where you are?"

"Either that or they simply guessed correctly." She shrugged. "*Crick*, *Irving Fischer*, and *Zhou Jianren* are a third again the size of any of the other forts, so blind chance would give them a thirty percent chance of guessing right."

"Agreed." Montalván nodded.

"And the *second* thing," Adebayo said, "is that they're asking for the 'system commander.' They're not asking for me by name, or even for the 'system governor.' Which may or may not be significant."

"Given the way they seem to be deliberately emphasizing how hopeless they think our situation is," Montalván said thoughtfully, declining in front of other ears to mention that the Grand Alliance was entirely right about that, "it actually may be. It might not mean anything, of course, but it could suggest they stumbled across us more or less by accident, not through any systematic penetration."

"Exactly." Adebayo held his gaze for a moment, then looked back down at Nerguizian.

"All right, Zarmayr. Accept the request. And you might as well go ahead and tell them who we are."

"Yes, Ma'am."

The major tapped a touchpad and the image of a dark-haired, gray-eyed officer in a Royal Manticoran Navy uniform skinsuit with a lieutenant commander's insignia appeared on the main com display.

"This is Galton System Command," Nerguizian said.

Twenty-two seconds later—even with an FTL link, it took eleven seconds for a signal to travel ten light-minutes—those gray eyes narrowed as the Manty saw Nerguizian on her own display.

"I am Lieutenant Commander Eriquez, Royal Manticoran Navy, on behalf of the Grand Alliance," she said. "Is your commanding officer prepared to speak with my commanding officer?"

"Yes," Nerguizian said flatly.

"Stand by," Eriquez replied, twenty-two seconds later. And then her image disappeared, replaced by another officer. This one in the skinsuit of a fleet admiral but with a starship captain's white beret. An equally skinsuited treecat lay stretched across the back of her command chair, and Adebayo recognized those exotically angular dark eyes, those high cheekbones, and that strong chin instantly.

So the Grand Alliance had cared enough to send its very best, she thought wryly.

"Live mic, Generalfeldmarshall," Nerguizian said quietly, and Adebayo faced the pickup.

"Hello, Admiral Harrington," she said. "What can I do for you?"

"So you recognize me." Harrington smiled thinly after the inevitable delay. "That should make things simpler. May I ask who I'm speaking to?"

"I am Generalfeldmarshall Karoline Adebayo, the governor of this star system. In, as I assume your presence here indicates you already know, the name of the Mesan Alignment."

"No beating around the bush, I see. Good. In that case, I'll be brief. I represent the Star Empire of Manticore, the Republic of Haven, the Andermani Empire, and the Protectorate of Grayson, and the purpose of this conversation is to give you the opportunity to surrender to the forces of the Grand Alliance under my command. I would advise you to take it."

Harrington's soprano voice was colder than space, but her eyes were colder still.

"Why should I?" Adebayo asked calmly.

"Because if you don't, I will open fire and destroy every fortress and warship in this star system."

"Really. And what do you think the forces under *my* command will be doing while you do that, Admiral?"

"Dying," Harrington said flatly, twenty-two seconds later.

Adebayo's jaw tightened, and Harrington let the single, icy word linger, then shrugged.

"Understand me," she said then. "Nothing would give me greater personal satisfaction than to simply open fire and kill every man and woman under your command. My star nation and its allies—and I personally—hold you responsible for the millions of deaths your 'Alignment' has directly inflicted in the Manticore Binary System, Beowulf, *and* on Mesa, and for every Manticoran, Grayson, Havenite, and Solarian killed in the war you provoked between the Grand Alliance and the Solarian League. We intend to end that. We intend to end *you*...and we will."

Her chilled steel voice was calm, almost dispassionate, and that only made its sincerity even more terrible.

"Unlike the Alignment, however, we actually care about the blood on our hands. And because we do, I'm offering you this opportunity to surrender. Be advised, however, that if you do, every individual in a command position, at the very least, will face potential trial for crimes against humanity on a truly galactic scale. There are no promises of immunity, no guarantees. There's only the opportunity to at least spare your personnel. You have two hours to consider my offer. If you haven't accepted it at the end of that time, my forces will open fire.

"Harrington, clear."

The display blanked, and silence hovered on *Crick's* flag deck. Then Adebayo exhaled a long sigh and looked at Montalván.

"I think it's time for Shuttlecock," she said. "Execute as soon as you can."

HMS *Imperator*
Grand Fleet
Galton System

"CIC SAYS THE OUTER GHOST RIDERS ARE PICKING UP SOMETHING, Milady," Chief Petty Officer Ransom said. Megan Petersen looked at him, and he shook his head. "They're not sure what it is, but it's headed our way and it's moving faster than any of the other traces we've picked up."

Ransom's hands were busy at his command station as he spoke, and Petersen turned to her plot as he threw *Imperator*'s Combat Information Center's fresh datapoint onto it. The new icon blinked with the rapid strobe of an unidentified contact, and Ransom was right. It was headed towards Grand Fleet from the inner-system and moving a lot faster than the elusive recon drones they'd detected earlier. The Alignment had deployed two different types of recon platforms, one which was obviously virtually identical to the SLN's last-generation drones and one that was one hell of a lot stealthier. Petersen agreed with Duchess Harrington and Captain Jaruwalski that they wouldn't have mixed them that way if they hadn't hoped to learn how readily Grand Fleet could detect, lock up, and destroy their first-team platforms. Which was why Grand Fleet had declined to attempt anything of the sort.

Not that Peterson was at all confident that they could have taken the stealthy ones down if they had tried.

But this was coming in at a much higher velocity, sweeping toward the outermost drone shell at the next best thing to .42 cee, and the only reason the Ghost Riders had seen it was the bow wave of charged particles riding with it.

She frowned, and her frown tightened as the numerical

649

notation appended to the icon began to spin upward. Whatever it was, it wasn't alone.

The heel of her hand slammed down on a button and an alarm sounded raucously.

"All units, this is the Flag!" she snapped over the command net. "Bogies incoming, axis of threat-five-eight degrees, closing velocity one-two-three thousand KPS. Range two-two-point-eight million kilometers. Counter-missiles free. I repeat, counter-missiles free. Stand by to engage."

She sat back, the alarm still sounding, and only then looked over her shoulder.

Honor smiled briefly in approval as Petersen looked back at her. Megan had done exactly the right thing, and without waiting for anyone else's authorization, she thought, but her own attention was on the plot as the number beside that icon continued to climb.

She wished they'd detected whatever it was—and she had a bad feeling about that—earlier. At its current velocity, it would reach Grand Fleet in barely three minutes...which was ninety seconds longer than it would take *Imperator* to translate out. And it was her fault.

Whatever was coming at them was even stealthier than anything the Grand Alliance had. She'd allowed for that possibility in her planning, but it was obvious she hadn't made *sufficient* allowance for it. And, she realized now, that was because she'd never actually *believed* it would happen, whatever she'd told herself and her staff. She'd be a long time forgiving herself for that. It was too much like the SLN's hubris, its assumption that *no one* could have better tech than the invincible Solarian League.

You always knew that kind of thinking could carry its own penalty, a corner of her brain told her. *Did you* really *have to choose a moment like this to prove you were right?*

She didn't *know* what it was any more than Megan Petersen or CPO Ransom, but she was virtually certain those had to be missile pods. Probably an improved version of the SLN's Hasta. And that much she *should* have anticipated, given how hellishly difficult the Alignment's recon drones were to pin down. After all, the original Hasta had been little more than a recon drone converted into a missile carrier.

"Assume these things are armed with the same missile as the Sollies' Hasta," she said. "Display launch range."

The plot reconfigured almost instantly, and her jaw tightened. At their current velocity, the launch basket would be just under twenty million kilometers. And they'd reach it in another eleven seconds.

✦   ✦   ✦

As it happened, Honor Alexander-Harrington was exactly correct about what was coming at her command. The Hasta III was a distinct improvement upon the original Solarian version, with a far more robust main drive and stealth features that were better than anything the SLN had ever had. Not only that, each Hasta had been paired with a second, equally stealthy drone to serve as a "tug." The additional drone was reusable, and its function was purely to move Hastas undetectably about the system to concentrate them before launch, which was precisely what the Alignment's Plan Shuttlecock had done.

Now fourteen thousand of them came roaring into Grand Fleet's face on ballistic trajectories. The Hastas' main drives had burned out long since, but as they reached twenty million kilometers' range, their second stages separated and accelerated at over seven hundred KPS.

✦   ✦   ✦

"Vampire! Vampire!" Captain Lamar Ponferrada, HMS *Hylonome*'s COLAC, barked over the command net.

Hylonome was a unit of Carrier Squadron Seven, attached to Alice Truman's Task Group 1.1, and Ponferrada's command LAC, HMS *Despiadada*, was the senior LAC on the threat axis as the stealthy, nebulous targets Grand Fleet's missile defense officers had been tracking vanished into the blazing impeller signatures of missiles accelerating at the next best thing to seventy thousand gravities.

Few things in the galaxy could have been *less* stealthy than that, but even as he watched, decoys blossomed throughout the enormous salvo. The number of threats doubled, and then doubled again. The decoy platforms weren't as good as the Grand Alliance's Dragon's Teeth, but they were *damned* good, and other platforms hammered out massive spikes of jamming.

Grand Fleet's planners had assumed the Alignment's best would be better than anything the Solarian League had, and they weren't disappointed. On the other hand, the Grand Alliance's member navies were the most experienced, combat hardened fleets in existence. Quite possibly the most experienced and combat hardened in the entire history of interstellar warfare. The incoming missiles' capabilities had exceeded their base estimates for the Alignment's tech advantages, and they knew it. But there was no panic, and Grand Fleet's defenses swung into action with polished efficiency.

The counter-missile-armed LACs in the outer shell salvoed their fire-and-forget ordnance into the attack's teeth, then rolled ship sharply, interposing their wedges against any missiles which might have acquired them instead of one of their larger consorts. The starships behind them salvoed their own counter-missiles before *they* rolled ship against the threat axis. But unlike the LACs, the Keyhole-Two platforms deployed beyond their protective sidewalls were linked to their birds' telemetry. They took control of their defensive fire, coordinating it much more finely than the LACs could have, while Lorelei platforms sprang to life, decoying attack missiles away from their motherships, and Dazzlers sought to blind and baffle the attackers' sensors.

It was a defense in depth which had been developed and then honed over decades of the galaxy's bloodiest war, and for all their stealth, all their velocity and acceleration, the incoming missiles melted like snow in a blowtorch.

Thousands of them were blotted away by counter-missile impeller wedges, other thousands were diverted by the Loreleis, and still more were blinded by the Dazzlers, but the Alignment wasn't the Solarian League Navy. Eleven hundred of *its* missiles broke through everything Grand Fleet's outer defenses could throw at them. They streaked in on their targets, into the teeth of the fleet's massed point defense stations. Twelve thousand-plus laser clusters spat targeted lightning that shattered the survivors of the hurricane of counter-missiles, but four hundred and thirty of them broke through every active defense and reached attack range.

They weren't laserheads. They lacked the multiple lasing rods, the ability to fire clusters of X-ray lasers at their targets. But Galton's R&D had engineered the original graserhead down into something it could cram into an outsized conventional missile just small enough to fit into a Hasta III pod. It wasn't as powerful as the graser torpedoes which had savaged Manticore's industrial infrastructure in the Yawata Strike, but it was far more destructive than any X-ray laser, because its duration was measured in seconds, not milliseconds.

The capital ships' sidewalls blunted and attenuated the grasers' ferocity, and not even they could penetrate an impeller wedge. Armor shattered, atmosphere fumed from breached hulls, men and women died, and Honor Alexander-Harrington's face tightened as casualty and damage reports flooded her flag bridge.

GSNSS *Irving Fischer*
and
GSNSS *Francis Crick*
Tschermak Orbit
Galton System

"DAMAGE ESTIMATES ARE COMING IN, GROSSADMIRAL!" KOMMO-dore Auberjonois reported, and Gunther Montalván watched as the recon drones still spying on Grand Fleet updated *Irving Fischer*'s plot.

It was obvious the Grand Alliance hadn't seen the Hastas coming, at least not until the very last moment. He'd authorized Auberjonois to spin up two more of their precious FTL communications relays to feed *Irving Fischer*'s tactical officers data in near real-time, and he'd felt a fierce surge of anticipation as the stealthy platforms launched their attack birds and the torrent of fire had ripped straight into the Grand Alliance's teeth.

But now his jaw tightened as the huge fortress's CIC refined and updated its data.

Three ships. They'd destroyed *three* ships.

His hands closed into fists under cover of his console as that sank home. Only three.

"Grossadmiral, I—" Auberjonois's voice faltered, and Montalván nodded.

"I see it, Tomasz." He was astounded his own voice sounded so calm, and he tipped back in his command chair. "I'd hoped for more. Still, we just killed more Alliance superdreadnoughts in a single salvo than the Sollies managed in their entire war. And Shuttlecock was always at least partly a probe. A test of their defenses. And we got a lot of data on those. The next strike will use it."

"Yes, Sir!" Auberjonois sounded less than completely confident, Montalván noted. Not that he blamed the ops officer. Still, they truly had learned a great deal from the Allies' responses, and the next wave of Hastas would be much larger than the first one.

Of course, their enemies had learned a great deal, as well, and Harrington had always been a damnably fast learner.

✧   ✧   ✧

"We have a com request from the enemy, Generalfeldmarshall," Major Nerguizian announced.

"Really?" Karoline Adebayo smiled thinly. "Imagine that. Put it through."

Honor Alexander-Harrington appeared on Adebayo's display once again. Pity. The generalfeldmarshall had rather hoped Harrington's ship had been one of the ones which had just died.

"Admiral," she said.

"I see you've decided not to surrender," Harrington said. "Under the circumstances, I'm sure you'll forgive me if I don't wait the full two hours before I open fire on your defenses."

"It's not like you weren't going to all along," Adebayo replied.

"No," Harrington said. "No, it's not. But it does rather clarify the options for all concerned, doesn't it? And at least now—" her smile was a razor "—I won't have to second guess myself after I blow every single one of your forts to hell. Enjoy the ride, Generalfeldmarshall."

HMS *Imperator*
Grand Fleet
and
GSNSS *Irving Fischer*
Tschermak Orbit
Galton System

ꞌ "WE'LL GO WITH TSUSHIMA," HONOR TOLD THE ASSEMBLED, GRIM-faced flag officers on her master com display, and heads nodded.

She stood facing the display, holding Nimitz in her arms. She felt his fierce support, his own fury at the "evil-doers" of the Alignment, flowing into her, and just that moment, she needed the support of that loving rage.

The Alignment's massive attack hadn't quite constituted a violation of the laws of war. It had come close, but Adebayo hadn't promised not to open fire while she considered Honor's surrender demand. And it wasn't as if Honor hadn't anticipated the probability that she'd do exactly that.

But it had still hurt.

Grand Fleet had lost two superdreadnoughts—HMS *Brilliant* and IANS *Jingyi Nadelmann*—and the CLAC HMS *Damysus*, and over seven thousand men and women had died with their ships. That was bad enough, hurt fiercely enough, but the rest of the fleet hadn't gotten off unscathed, either. Thirty-six LACs—and three hundred and sixty more of her people—had fallen afoul of the missiles intended for the capital ships, and five more superdread-noughts and two of her carriers had taken enough damage that she'd sent them back into hyper. At least one of the SD(P)s was probably still combat capable, but she had more than sufficient strength without GNS *Protector Edward*...and no intention of exposing already damaged units to that sort of fire a second time.

Andrea Jaruwalski and Megan Petersen had reorganized around the missing ships, and despite her losses, Honor still commanded two hundred and ten superdreadnoughts and seventy-five carriers. That would be more than enough, she thought grimly.

She'd adjusted her defensive stance in the wake of the Hastas. Her LAC screen had been reinforced and pushed farther out. That put an additional strain on her carriers, working their LAC groups harder and reducing their reserve strength, but it also gave her outer defense zone thirty more light-seconds of depth. She'd deployed additional recon platforms, as well, thickening her close-in sensor shell and building a covered zone over four light-minutes deep beyond the LACs. And Grand Fleet's threat files had been updated with the data they'd acquired on the Hastas' stealth capabilities. The next wave would be detected much earlier. In fact, almost certainly early enough to buy Honor the four minutes she needed to whisk even her superdreadnoughts safely back into hyper, if she needed to.

Her new deployment was hideously expensive in terms of reconnaissance assets, but she was fine with that. The price tag in terms of money and industrial resources might be enormous, but the fleet train's freighters' holds were stuffed with missile pods, recon drones, even entire additional LACs. They'd been sent along to be used, to be expended instead of spending the blood of her people, and that was precisely what she intended to do.

"Should I designate Beta as the first target, Your Grace?" Megan Petersen asked, and Honor showed her teeth.

"I think that would be highly appropriate, Megan," she said.

"Pod deployment is almost complete," Petersen told her, and she nodded, watching the display as some of those freighters finished deploying five thousand Mk 17 missile pods. Honor had no intention of dipping into her mobile units' internal magazines as long as the fleet train was available, and she nodded again, in approval, as the freighters finished and translated back into hyper until she needed them to deploy the *next* attack wave.

"Very well," she said, turning back to her staff and her flag officers. "Whenever you're ready, Megan."

✧   ✧   ✧

"They've launched, Grossadmiral!" Auberjonois announced.

"I see it," Montalván replied, and looked down at the com display tied into *Francis Crick*'s flight deck.

"I suppose we'll find out shortly who they've picked as their first target," Karoline Adebayo said almost whimsically from the com, and he surprised himself with a snort of actual amusement.

✧   ✧   ✧

The range was ten light-minutes, but the Mark 23 multidrive missile didn't care.

Grand Fleet had deployed two thousand Mark 17 flatpack missile pods, and when Megan Petersen gave the command, they belched forth 18,000 Mark 23s. The big missiles accelerated for six minutes at an acceleration of 451 KPS² until their first two sets of impeller nodes burned out, 29,230,000 kilometers downrange, and they coasted onward at 162,387 KPS.

✧   ✧   ✧

"They've gone dark, Sir," Auberjonois reported. "Estimated ballistic time-of-flight seven hundred and three seconds, based on observed performance."

"Stand by Scutum," Montalván said, and Auberjonois nodded.

"Scutum is active, Sir."

✧   ✧   ✧

Honor stood gazing into the plot, still holding Nimitz, her expression almost serene, as eighteen thousand missiles streamed silently through space at fifty-four percent of the speed of light. She knew, better than almost anyone, what the Mark 23 could do. Ships under her command had almost certainly fired more of them than the ships of any other flag officer, and she was only too well aware of what those thousands upon thousands of laserheads would do to their target. How many human beings were about to be blotted out of existence, wiped away as if they'd never been.

And this time, she didn't care.

No, she admitted to herself from behind the serenity of her brown eyes, that wasn't true. This time she was looking forward to it, and she felt Nimitz sharing that merciless anticipation. But, to her own surprise, it wasn't with the icy hatred which had filled them both after the Beowulf Strike. She'd expected to feel that same bleakness. Not with the fury which had poured into her like poison when she'd thought Hamish and Samantha had died aboard Beowulf Alpha and Emily had died in her arms, perhaps, but the same icy, terrible hatred. After all, these were the people who'd engineered it all. The people whose sneak attack on Manticore had destroyed *Hephaestus* and virtually wiped out her family on Sphinx. If she'd ever doubted that, the graser-armed Hasta attack had proved they were. Just as it proved they were also the people who'd cleared the SLN's path for the Beowulf Strike... and planted the nuclear bombs which had actually destroyed the orbital habitats.

They were the ones responsible for *all* of it.

But what she and Nimitz felt in this moment was not fury. It wasn't even hatred.

It went beyond both of those emotions.

She'd told Hamish, more than once, that under the wrong circumstances she could have been a monster. Now she knew she'd been right. But there was a time and a place for monsters, for a woman who could stand on this command bridge, calmly, almost dispassionately, while she rained devastation upon her enemies. Could do it with a cold, calm, merciless eagerness born not of personal hatred but of an awareness that her enemies must be destroyed. Not defeated. Not conquered.

Destroyed.

"Third-stage activation in ten seconds," Megan Petersen announced.

✧   ✧   ✧

The tsunami roared down on *Francis Crick.*

The Mark 23-E Apollo platforms had been told exactly what to look for, and they'd been constantly updated by the Ghost Rider drones on their way in. They followed behind the phalanx of attack missiles and penetration platforms, their AIs woven together in a tightly coordinated but dispersed fire control network, murmuring back and forth as they refined the data...and their attack profiles.

Now eighteen thousand missiles streaked toward a single orbital fortress. Three thousand of them were EW platforms. Two thousand were Mark 23-Es. But the other thirteen thousand were laserhead-tipped destruction incarnate.

Yet the Galton Navy was not the SLN. It had known, from the beginning, what the Mark 23 could do, and it had devised its defenses accordingly.

Historically, counter-missiles had been designed to be cheap. Designed to operate under tight shipboard control and to be small enough that they could be carried in large numbers. Ship designers and tacticians always had to balance the larger size and expense of individually more capable weapons against the need to provide as many defensive missiles as a ship could carry.

But the Alignment had recognized that it must alter that traditional balance if it ever faced the sort of missile storms the Grand Alliance could generate. And so it had taken yet another page from its enemies and designed the Lorica, a counter-missile much too large to be carried in shipboard magazines. Its designers had stuffed it into missile pods, instead, then paired it with the system it called Scutum.

Scutum was, in many ways, derived from Shannon Foraker's original Moriarty concept. The Scutum platforms were far more capable than the original Moriarty had been, although they remained inferior to the Grand Alliance's current Mycroft system. On the other hand, Mycroft was designed to coordinate the fire of widely dispersed system-defense missile pods armed with shipkillers. Scutum was designed to coordinate the fire of tightly grouped pods armed with multidrive *counter*-missiles.

The first wave of Loricas launched at the preposterous range of 35,000,000 kilometers, barely a second after the Mark 23s' final stage lit off. That was ten times the Grand Alliance's best counter-missile range, and Honor's eyes narrowed as five thousand of them streaked to meet her own fire.

Even with Scutum, the Alignment's defensive fire control was unable to take full advantage of the Lorica's stupendous reach. Its tactical officers simply couldn't control and update their birds the way the Mark 23-E controlled and updated its attack missiles, because the Alignment remained unable to build an FTL link into something that size. But in recognition of that, they'd equipped the Lorica with a far more capable AI and sensor suite than any "traditional" counter-missile.

There was time for Grand Fleet to order the Mark 23-Es to spin up half of its Dragon's Teeth and light off a quarter of its Dazzlers before the Loricas reached them, and despite their improved AIs, the Loricas' accuracy plummeted in the face of that sort of countermeasures. But even hammered by the Allies' penetration aids, some of them got through, and they blotted almost a thousand Mark 23s from the face of the universe.

Worse, with Lorica's range and acceleration, Galton had time for two additional launches before the Mark 23s reached attack range, and each of them stripped away more of the penetration platforms, forced Grand Fleet's tactical officers and the Apollo birds to burn more Dragon's Teeth and Dazzlers just to stave off the Loricas.

Which meant those penaids weren't available when the attack birds hit the *standard* counter-missile defensive perimeter and plunged through it, into the waiting laser clusters.

And, there, too, the Alignment had learned from the Grand Alliance's example. The Royal Manticoran Navy's Keyhole had originated as a deployable point defense platform that could be extended beyond a ship's sidewalls and lay down the concentrated fire of multiple heavy laser clusters to intercept incoming missiles. During development, that original, purely defensive concept had evolved into the current Mark 20 Keyhole-Two, with its FTL fire control links.

Galton had taken the original concept and pushed it even farther and harder. They called it the Testudo, and each Testudo mounted more laser clusters than the entire broadside of an SLN *Scientist*-class superdreadnought. *Francis Crick* had deployed twelve of them beyond its sidewalls, supported by hundreds of internal and pod-launched conventional counter-missiles.

Eighty-seven of Grand Fleet's eighteen thousand missiles got through *Francis Crick*'s meticulously layered defenses.

Eighty-seven Mark 23s were nothing to take lightly, and even *Crick*'s mammoth bulk quivered and shook as X-ray lasers blasted through its sidewalls and deep into its hull. Men and women died, weapons and defensive systems were blasted into ruin, and leaking atmosphere haloed the fort, but it was still intact, and its emission signature still burned brightly in *Imperator*'s master plot.

✧   ✧   ✧

There was silence on the flag bridge as the damage estimates updated, and Honor tasted her staff's shock. It wasn't remotely close to panic, but it *was* its own form of dismay. A launch that size would have eviscerated any Solarian warship or fortress ever built, and no one had ever seen *that* kind of missile defense before.

"Well, that was certainly...enlightening," she said after a moment as the display finished updating and showed CIC's best estimate of their target's damage.

One or two of her officers blinked at her, and she chuckled dryly.

"We always knew the Sollies could have produced defenses

capable of standing up to—or at least blunting—our missile strikes, if they'd only realized in time that they needed to," she pointed out. "And that multidrive counter-missile of theirs looks like a more fully developed version of the one Admiral Foraker and Admiral Hemphill are working on at Bolthole. The counter-missile *pods* were an unexpected touch, though." She pursed her lips. "We probably should have been looking at something like that ourselves, but we've had such an advantage in offensive throw weight that we've been focused on killing platforms rather than missiles." She shrugged. "If you kill the pod-layer, you kill her pods—all her pods—right along with her. And, frankly, that's probably still the most effective way to deal with them. But these people can't match Apollo or the Mark 23's range, so they've had to focus on dealing with the missiles, instead."

"I suppose that's true, Your Grace," Jaruwalski said after a moment.

"Oh, believe me, it's something Bolthole's been looking at for a while," Honor replied. "Admiral Foraker and Admiral Hemphill are busy evolving an entirely new LAC doctrine using unmanned, expendable platforms, too, and I expect that will have a major impact, as well. I understand what they're looking at is basically a constellation of unmanned, stripped down Strikes and Ferrets, each controlled by a single command LAC through FTL links. Without crews, they could accelerate a *lot* faster, which ought to make them far better at penetrating someone's defenses, and the idea is to push them out closer to the enemy, use them to launch mass LAC strikes on enemy formations, without ever exposing our personnel to defensive fire. I'm sure the 'Demonic Duo' is also looking at ways to combine them with the multidrive counter-missile they have on the drawing board to push our missile defense zone even farther out, as well. But I have to admit that I hadn't anticipated the *Alignment* might have reacted quite this . . . comprehensively to its range disadvantage."

"I hadn't either," Michelle Henke said from her flag deck aboard *Vigilant*. "And, just between you and me, I find that I'm simply *delighted* the Sollies didn't do the same thing!"

"If their prewar planners had bothered to listen to operational analysis people like Captain al-Fanudahi, they *would* have, Mike," Honor said. "At which point, the people in this star system might have gotten what they wanted from the beginning. But they didn't, did they?" She showed her teeth. "And it doesn't really matter how good their defenses are. Not ultimately. We got almost ninety birds through Beta's defenses when we didn't know what they had waiting for us, and we did it with two thousand Mark Seventeen pods. We've got *five hundred thousand* of them aboard our missile colliers, and they've got fewer than forty forts, most of them a lot smaller than Beta."

Her eyes were bleak, hard, and Nimitz bared his fangs in her arms.

"We know about their improved Hasta now. They won't sneak another attack like that through our defenses. And now we've seen what their missile defense can do, too. So what we're going to do is take our time and analyze what they just showed us. We're going to factor that into our fire plans and into our penetration plans. Then we're going to give Beta another pasting and see how many of our birds they stop *this* time. And then we'll take the time to analyze *that* attack, carefully and fully, before we launch the *next* one."

She looked at her staff and the flag officers on her display, and her smile was liquid helium.

"I'm willing to bet we'll run out of targets before we run out of missiles," she told them.

GSNSS *Irving Fischer*
and
GSNSS *Francis Crick*
Tschermak Orbit
Galton System

GROSSADMIRAL GUNTHER MONTALVÁN CHECKED HIS SKINSUIT readouts. Another four hours of air, he saw. That was good.

He tightened the straps holding him into his command chair. The flag deck's gravity plates had gone out—what? Twelve hours ago? Longer than that? It was hard to remember. He knew when they'd lost pressure, though, and he looked at the ugly hole in the after bulkhead. It hadn't been a direct hit. If it had been, he'd be dead by now. But the internal secondary explosion that shredded the bulkhead had been bad enough. It had killed Tomasz Auberjonois, and wounded Marie-Françoise Monedero. The chief of staff had at least survived...so far. It seemed unlikely that anyone aboard *Irving Fischer* would survive a great deal longer.

Fregattenkapitän Kästner had taken over at tactical, and the com officer had done a damned good job. There wasn't much for him to do any longer, though, and Montalván looked at his remaining displays.

It hadn't been Honor Alexander-Harrington's sort of battle, he thought. He'd always considered her his most likely opponent if this day ever came, and he'd spent years analyzing her tactics and strategy. Especially after he'd discovered that the Harrington genome was one of the Alignment's "lost" Alpha lines. How bitterly ironic, he'd thought, and now he toyed with the notion of telling her where she'd truly come from, seeing how she reacted to *that*. But he couldn't, because that information was nowhere in any database in Galton.

Yet one thing he'd learned from studying her was her hatred for slogging matches. For battles of attrition. She believed in maneuver and mobility. Her tactics were always designed to minimize her own people's casualties, of course, but time after time, she'd demonstrated a matching determination to minimize even her adversaries' casualties, whenever she could, as well. There'd been times she couldn't, like her desperate defense of Grayson—both of her defenses of Grayson, really. Or like what had happened to Filareta's Second Fleet at Manticore...although it would appear the Alignment had forced her hand in that instance.

This time, she hadn't maneuvered at all.

She'd simply sat there, outside the hyper-limit, like some merciless, inviolable deity, pounding away with wave after wave of missile pods, hour after hour. Hell, day after *day!* She'd come to burn Galton to the ground, and that was precisely what she was going to do.

Montalván knew it. He'd known it before the first shot was fired, but he'd done his best. He'd expended every one of his Hastas in the process. He'd tried sneaking them into range again, but her sensor coverage was too good, her missile defense too deep. Her fleet had spotted each wave too early, too far out, and whittled it down into futility before its tattered survivors ever neared her starships. So then he'd piled every remaining Hasta into a single massive salvo and sent the next best thing to eighty thousand of them straight at her.

Only to have her sensor net warn her in time to take every single starship into hyper before they reached her. She'd been forced to leave her LACs behind, but LACs were fiendishly hard missile targets at the best of times, and the graserhead's lack of multiple lasing rods only made that worse. He'd killed another seventy or eighty of the agile little ships, and from Harrington's record, he suspected she'd find that painful to live with, but it was a piss poor result for the expenditure of that much firepower.

And once he'd used them up, she'd returned to n-space and resumed her methodical pounding.

She'd restricted her fire meticulously to the fortresses, at least. For that matter, she hadn't gone out of her way to simply obliterate her targets. Most of Montalván's forts *had* been destroyed over the past seventy-two hours, but once her recon platforms told her one of them had been silenced, she'd shifted her fire to other targets. He wondered if that was because even now, in some corner of her soul, she was still trying to reduce the death toll, the way she always had, or if it was simply a matter of economizing on ammunition. She'd used literally *millions* of multidrive missiles, after all. On the other hand, it was clear she'd brought even more of them with her than Montalván had believed she could.

Irving Fischer was one of the targets she was no longer shooting at, and little wonder. It was an incredible testimonial to her designers that *Fischer* hadn't simply broken up. The once proud fortress was a twisted mass of wreckage. She still had several dozen point defense clusters and a single Testudo, but aside from eight missile launchers and a grand total of two graser mounts, her offensive firepower was nonexistent, and at least sixty percent of her personnel had become casualties.

Zhou Jianren, unlike Montalván's flagship fortress, *had* broken up, but *Francis Crick* hadn't. Adebayo's command base was even more brutally damaged than *Fischer*, yet it was still there. And, incredibly, both he and Adebayo were still alive!

For now. Of course, that—

"Grossadmiral?"

Montalván shook himself, realized his mind had been wandering. Again.

"Yes, Abraham?"

"Grossadmiral, Harrington is asking for Generalfeldmarshall Adebayo on the com."

"Is she?" Montalván smiled through his visor. "Do you think she wants to surrender?"

Kästner gawked at him for a moment, and then—to his own obvious surprise—the fregattenkapitän actually chuckled.

"I fear not, Sir."

"Well, difficult to blame her, under the circumstances, I suppose." Montalván exhaled and shook himself. "Do we still have short range coms to *Crick*?"

"Yes, Sir. Only on the emergency channels, though."

Montalván grimaced. Harrington's merciless fire had stripped away all of *Crick*'s communications arrays along with every one of the fortress's weapons mounts.

"Very well," he said. "See if you can get me the Generalfeld-marshall."

"Yes, Sir."

It took the better part of five minutes, but then he heard Adebayo's voice over his skinsuit com.

"Yes, Gunther?"

"Harrington would like to speak to you," he said.

"Can you patch her through to me?"

"I think so. Give me a moment."

He looked at Kästner.

"Can you put Harrington through to my—" He paused, considering the crimson malfunction LEDs that decorated his command station. "To my Number Two display? I think that one's still up."

"A moment, Grossadmiral."

It was actually several minutes before the display he'd chosen blinked to life again. Which was a fairly emphatic indication of *Irving Fischer*'s damages, he supposed. Another several seconds passed, and then Honor Alexander-Harrington appeared on the display.

Obviously *she'd* taken the occasional nap, he thought through a dull burn of resentment. She looked fresh, well rested, and the spacious, orderly flag deck visible behind her was a far cry from the shattered, airless ruin of his own.

"Admiral Harrington," he said. "I am Grossadmiral Montalván."

"Grossadmiral." She nodded to him. "Are you now in command?"

"No," he replied. "Unfortunately, Generalfeldmarshall Adebayo's communications have been ... disrupted, however. I can patch you through to her, but I'm afraid the signal will be audio only."

"Then please do."

"It may take a moment," Montalván said, and nodded to Kästner.

A second or two passed, and then—

"This is Adebayo," the generalfeldmarshall's voice said.

"I gave you an opportunity, three days ago, to surrender your command intact," Harrington said coldly. "Your answer was to open fire. According to my recon platforms, you no longer have an intact command *to* surrender. I can complete the destruction of every one of your fortresses, but it's my opinion that enough people have already died. Which is why I am giving you one last opportunity to surrender. If you reject this offer, it will not be repeated, and I will destroy every military installation in the star system without permitting *any* of your personnel to surrender. The choice is yours, Generalfeldmarshall. I would suggest that you choose wisely."

Montalván gazed at the display, waiting as the seconds ticked past. And then, finally, Adebayo sighed.

"Very well, Admiral Harrington," she said heavily. "I'm prepared to surrender my surviving personnel."

"Understand that I intend to take no chances with the lives of my own people," Harrington said. "I will require that you evacuate the crews of your surviving secondary fortresses and any surviving starships and LACs and destroy them. I will further require that your two surviving command fortresses be surrendered intact, with their databases. And I formally inform you that my Marines will respond instantly with lethal force to any resistance when they board your fortresses. The same, I'm afraid, will apply to any resistance they encounter when we occupy your orbital habitats and industrial platforms. Do you understand what I've just said?"

"I assume you're speaking for the record," Adebayo replied. Her voice was bitter, which Montalván couldn't really fault her for. "And, also speaking for the record, yes. I understood what you said. Grossadmiral Montalván?"

"Yes, Generalfeldmarshall?"

"Be good enough to pass Admiral Harrington's conditions and...warning to all of our remaining personnel, and also to the habitats and industrial platforms."

"Yes, Generalfeldmarshall."

"In that case, my forces will proceed in-system once your secondary fortresses and remaining warships have been destroyed," Harrington said.

GSNSS *Francis Crick*
Tschermak Orbit
Galton System

KAROLINE ADEBAYO WATCHED THE DISPLAY, AND HER EYES WERE
bleak.

Damage Control had managed to restore a single connection to the sensor platforms. It had taken almost six hours, but there'd been ample time. It *took* time to evacuate so many personnel from the mangled wreckage of her handful of surviving secondary fortresses. From the superdreadnoughts and the LACs Harrington had simply ignored as she pounded remorselessly at the fixed defenses.

But it had been done eventually, and the forts and the starships and the LACs had been blown up, precisely as Harrington had demanded. And now her fleet was inbound in Adebayo's display, decelerating steadily as it prepared to take possession of its prize.

Even now, her professionalism showed, Adebayo thought. Every weapons platform, every deployed missile pod, had been destroyed before she ever crossed the hyper-limit, yet she was taking no chances. Her starships were covered by a swarm of more than a thousand LACs and surrounded by a dense shell of recon drones and an inner shell of defensive EW platforms. Adebayo never doubted that every counter-missile launcher and point defense cluster was manned and ready, as well.

It would have been nice if she were incompetent, the generalfeldmarshall reflected. *But if she were, she wouldn't be here at all, would she?*

And sometimes, it doesn't matter *how competent you are.*

She reached for the number pad on the arm of her command

chair, and a line from an ancient, Ante Diaspora novel ran through her mind as she entered the long, complex command code.

"'From hell's heart I stab at thee,'" she murmured. "'For hate's sake I spit my last breath at thee.'"

She pressed the enter key.

HMS *Imperator*
Grand Fleet
Galton System

HONOR ALEXANDER-HARRINGTON SAT IN HER COMMAND CHAIR
with Nimitz in her lap, watching the visual display as Grand Fleet
decelerated steadily towards rest relative to the system primary.
She had no intention of allowing her main body to come closer
than one light-minute to the habitable planet until her Marines
had secured all of the platforms in orbit around it, but the display's
magnification brought the planet and its infrastructure to arm's-
length. They gleamed before her in reflected sunlight, the gorgeous
emerald and sapphire jewel of the planet crowned with an orbital
diadem of diamonds, and she tried to parse her own feelings.

So many had paid so much to reach this moment, and those
habitats, that planet... they ought to look *different* somehow. There
should be some outward sign of the fanaticism and malevolence,
of the corruption which had brought her here, spattered the galaxy
with so much death, so much destruction and blood.

There wasn't, of course, and she knew it would have been
foolish to expect one. And yet, somehow, she did.

Triumph flowed through her, but there was no exultation. Not
after something like this. Completion, yes. And grim, unyielding satisfaction. But she'd seen so much blood—*shed* so much
blood. She remembered a conversation in King Michael's Tower.
Remembered telling Elizabeth Winton how tired she was. Well,
she was even tireder now, and what she felt—more than anything
else—was a desperate desire to go *home*. To feel Hamish's arms
around her and her own around Raoul, and Katherine, and
Andrew. To wrap herself in their love and her love for them.

To finally be *done* with the killing.

Her fingers moved slowly, rhythmically, caressing Nimitz's ears and tasting his love and matching heart-hunger. Yet there was more to his mind-glow than that. He understood what Honor felt with a clarity and precision only an empath could have imagined, but he wasn't her, and *his* satisfaction *was* fierce and exultant. The ones who had hurt and killed the people he loved, human and treecat alike, had finally paid, and that was enough for him.

Honor's lips twitched as she tasted that satisfaction. Treecats were such very *direct* souls, she thought, and Nimitz even more than most. She wondered sometimes if that was part of what had drawn them together. Or was it possible he'd become even more "direct" because of their bond? It had changed both of them in so many ways that—

The visual display flared suddenly as the two remaining command fortresses vanished in the eye-tearing brilliance of nuclear explosions.

Honor jerked upright in her chair, eyes widening.

"Missile launch!" Megan Petersen snapped.

✧   ✧   ✧

It was true that none of the Galton System's orbital habitats had mounted the weapons or the defenses its fortresses had. Aside from routine navigational systems, they mounted no sensor arrays, and only enough point defense to deal with orbital debris or the possibility of a rogue pilot in a cargo shuttle. Grand Fleet's recon drones had made that abundantly clear.

But what those drones had been unable to see were the completely inert pods disguised as standard cargo containers, scattered and hidden among the thousands of other cargo containers on those habitats' warehousing booms. Or the other pods floating equally inert in the component queues of the system's shipyards. Hidden among the holding tanks of the orbital gas farms.

The pods which spun up as *Francis Crick* and *Irving Fischer* vaporized and spat Karoline Adebayo's last eleven thousand missiles at Grand Fleet.

✧   ✧   ✧

There was no finesse to it.

There was no need for finesse. The range was down to barely twenty million kilometers, and the upgraded Cataphracts had a powered range of over *nineteen* million.

Even with a 1,630,000-kilometer ballistic phase, total flight time was only a hundred and fifty seconds. The attack missiles streaked towards their targets with no warning at all, and no one aboard any of those ships had guessed they might be coming.

But this was Grand Fleet.

Honor's command reacted almost instantly. Two and a half minutes was not much time by most humans' standards. By Grand Fleet's standards, it was far longer than that.

Indeed, it was almost long enough.

Almost.

Counter-missiles launched, LACs yawed around, volleying their own counter-missiles, bringing grasers and lasers to bear. Loreleis spun fully up, and point defense clusters tracked around onto the axes of threat. Space burned with dying missiles as the cloud of destruction streaked toward its target, and even taken totally by surprise, Grand Fleet destroyed ninety-one percent of the incoming fire short of its perimeter.

But nine percent of eleven thousand was still almost a thousand missiles.

They weren't armed with graserheads. Galton had exhausted its graserhead production arming the Hasta IIIs and the Cataphracts in the larger, more capable missile pods Adebayo had been forced to destroy before Honor crossed the hyper-limit. These were "only" laserheads, and they streaked in through the lattice of counter-missiles and point defense lasers at 173,000 KPS.

At that speed, with weapons of that power, it was all over in the blink of a thousand thermonuclear eyes, and eleven super-dreadnoughts, four LAC carriers, and seven battlecruisers of Grand Fleet were gone, destroyed outright or ripped into disintegrating wreckage, just as quickly.

HMS *Imperator* heaved as half a dozen X-ray lasers punched at her own sidewall. Massive armor shattered, and alarms shrilled as point defense clusters, counter-missile tubes, and grasers were torn apart. But she'd been designed and built to sustain damage exactly like that, and she was luckier than her sisters who died. She survived the holocaust, wounded but intact, and Honor Alexander-Harrington's eyes burned with a fire far colder than the one which had just savaged her command.

Back-plotted vectors in the master display showed exactly where those missiles had come from, and the sudden, brutal attack after the system had surrendered negated every restriction of the Eridani Edict and the laws of war. Those orbital habitats, those industrial platforms and shipyards, had just made themselves legitimate targets, and they lay helpless and exposed to the avenging sword of the Grand Alliance.

She tasted the vortex of her flag bridge personnel's fury. The blazing anger that demanded retribution upon the people who'd just murdered so many more thousands of their friends. That same vortex twisted in a spiral of killing rage in her own heart and soul, and all that justice required was a single command from her. Just two words. That was all her people needed, the words her dead deserved.

"Return fire." That was all she needed to say...

And she didn't.

She couldn't. She needed to say the words, just as terribly as the men and women around her needed to hear them. Needed to be released to avenge *all* of their dead, not just here, but in Manticore and Beowulf and every other star system where Manticoran and Havenite and Grayson and Andermani had died because of the Alignment's fanatic ambition.

But they were not the Alignment.

That was what stopped her. The promise she'd made her staff before they ever set out. Her adamantine refusal to *become* the Alignment, the very thing she hated with every fiber of her being.

And, even more, her refusal to let her people become that. To let them poison themselves with vengeance even if they could truthfully argue that it was also justice. Because there came a time when justice was too terrible a price for the people who inflicted it to endure.

When "justice" would turn them into the people they were never meant to be.

She stood on *Imperator*'s flight deck, hearing the background surf of damage control reports, of frantic search and rescue efforts, of fury controlled only by professionalism, and tasted those two words like unsaid splinters of bone in her throat.

"General broadcast, Ona," she said instead.

There was a heartbeat of silence. Then Lieutenant Commander Ona Eriquez cleared her own throat.

"General broadcast, yes, Your Grace." She tapped the command. "Live mic, Your Grace."

Honor faced the pickup and squared her shoulders, her face carved from stone and her eyes bleak.

"I am Admiral Honor Alexander-Harrington," she said flatly, "and I am speaking directly to every man and woman in this star system. You represent the Mesan Alignment, and your Alignment is responsible for millions upon millions of deaths. Despite that, the fleet under my command has taken every precaution to avoid the infliction of civilian deaths here in your star system. And our reward for that has been to have your system governor surrender, only to launch a final attack that has just killed thousands more of my personnel—*my* men and women. That attack was launched using missiles concealed in your orbital habitats, your shipyards. It was launched in violation of the laws of war and of the Eridani Edict. And that means that your system governor forfeited your protection under those laws and that edict. I have every legal right to destroy every platform from which a *single* missile was launched at my command, and that means that every person listening to my voice is legitimately sentenced to death the instant I choose to inflict it."

She paused to let that think in. For all of those ears hearing her voice to taste its iron sincerity. All of those eyes seeing her face to recognize the icy flint of her expression.

"Do *not* give me a reason—an excuse—to execute that sentence," she told them then, her voice very soft. "My Marines will board your platforms one at a time. While they do that, my light attack craft will move into position to fire upon you. And if a single shot is fired at one of my ships, if a single one of my Marines is killed or injured aboard one of your habitats or industrial platforms, I *will* order them to destroy the habitat from which that shot came. This is the only warning I will issue. For your own sake, and the sake of your children, I advise you to heed it."

She gazed into the pickup for two slow breaths. Then—

"Harrington, clear," she said.

June 1924 Post Diaspora

"Causes can be tricky masters. It's really
difficult to avoid checking your scruples at the
door when you buy into one of them."

—Honor Alexander-Harrington

HMS *Imperator*
Tschermak Planetary Orbit
Galton System

HONOR STOOD IN THE OBSERVATION DOME ON *IMPERATOR*'S SPINE. Her flagship was inverted, and her eyes were dark and thoughtful as she gazed up at the white-swirled sapphire of the planet called Tschermak.

It wasn't the first time she'd stood in this observation dome, looking up upon a surrendered planet in a star system ships under her command had conquered. But it wasn't the same, this time. Not the same at all.

That planet had been called Old Earth, the birthplace of humanity, capital of its oldest and largest star nation. It might have lost its way, its governance might have lapsed into corruption under the sway of entrenched bureaucrats who answered to no one. But it was the avatar of so much corruption—and so much greatness—that the infection which had brought the Grand Alliance to it had been only one more interlude, another small stain upon an escutcheon that showed so much more any human being could be proud to call her heritage.

And she'd killed so many fewer of its uniformed defenders.

She thought about Winston Kingsford, about the courage he'd shown—and the sanity—when she'd demanded his surrender. That surrender had been an act of mutiny, by some standards, but it had also been the act of a moral man who'd recognized when the slaughter had gone too far. When the cause for which his men and women bled had become too corrupt to be worthy of their sacrifice.

There'd been no Kingsford in Galton.

Perhaps there might have been someone of his stature, his

willingness to face reality, *somewhere* in the Galton chain of command, but if there had, no one would ever know it. What they knew was that the Galton Navy's officers had allowed their system governor to violate the surrender terms she'd been granted. To destroy herself and both of her surviving command forts in a nuclear furnace of Wagnerian megalomania. And to launch a final attack—one she must have known couldn't succeed, known could be only a final, posthumous gesture of vindictiveness—which would have justified Honor Alexander-Harrington in massacring every living person, almost three hundred million human beings, who made their homes aboard the habitats from which that attack had come.

Honor could almost—*almost*—understand Karoline Adebayo's suicide in the face of the destruction of all she'd believed in, lived for. But not the missile strike. That she could grasp as an intellectual fact, something Adebayo had done, but she would never truly *understand* it. How could someone sworn to protect, to defend, abandon every responsibility that was hers?

But perhaps it had been inevitable, because the planet Honor gazed up at now was nothing like Old Terra. It shared a similar atmosphere, a climate humanity found salubrious, and the presence on its surface of human cities and towns. But if Tschermak had an escutcheon, it was darkest black, unrelieved by the flashes of greatness which had illuminated humanity's history on its birth world.

And it didn't even realize that.

Her mouth tightened, and she felt Nimitz's disapproval of her mood from where he lay stretched along one of the dome's cushioned benches. He didn't disagree with her, he only disapproved of the bleakness of her emotions. The sense that there ought to have been a way to turn Tschermak into something else, something so much better. It wasn't guilt that she felt, because she'd had no hand in Tschermak's creation. No. What she felt was disappointment, regret... grief. And unlike her, Nimitz wasted no pity upon people who had embraced their own inner darkness.

The chime sounded, and she turned as Audrey O'Hanrahan walked into the observation dome. Simon Hawk and Clifford McGraw followed her, and so did Michael Anderle. He and Honor's armsmen had developed a comfortable working relationship over the last couple of T-months. She knew her Graysons liked

Anderle, and she and Nimitz approved of the protectiveness of his mind-glow where O'Hanrahan was concerned. There was a powerful strand of wariness where the Grand Alliance in general was concerned, and that extended to Honor, but she didn't begrudge him that. God knew there were enough Solarians who continued to hate and distrust the Grand Alliance, even though their own investigators were in the process of uncovering mountains of evidence which substantiated every charge the Allies had made against their own government. For that matter, there were still plenty of Manticorans and Havenites who remained a long way from forgiving one another, despite all the Grand Alliance had accomplished.

"Good morning, Audrey," she said, holding out her hand, and O'Hanrahan shook it.

"Good morning, Your Grace."

The reporter stood beside Honor and turned to look up at the planet with her, and the bitterness and anger—and horror—in O'Hanrahan's mind-glow surpassed anything Honor might feel.

"I'll be heading back to Manticore in a few days." Honor flashed a brief smile. "Elizabeth wants my firsthand report, and I'll be honest; I only went back on active duty for this." She waved a hand at the planet and the orbital habitats. "I've got three children and a husband waiting for me, and after this"—her lips tightened—"I really need them."

✧   ✧   ✧

Audrey O'Hanrahan nodded, still looking up at the planet her Alignment's evil twin had turned into a twisted lair of darkness. A darkness even worse because it had found its birth, at least, in the same bright cause to which O'Hanrahan had devoted her life. It was proof of what Leonard Detweiler's magnificent dream *could* have become—*had* become, at least here—and that filled her with a sense of crawling revulsion even someone as gifted with words as she would have found impossible to express.

She lowered her eyes from Tschermak and looked at the tall woman standing beside her, and a feeling of warmth flowed into her, pushing back some of that bleak anger and revulsion. She'd come to know Duchess Harrington well over the last couple of T-months, and Harrington had kept her word about access. O'Hanrahan had sat in on more than one of the duchess's staff meetings, listened to the frank discussions of honorable and forthright people trying to cope with something far beyond their own comprehension while retaining their own decency and sanity. And along the way, she'd discovered that every good thing she'd ever heard about Honor Alexander-Harrington was true.

She could think of only one or two other others, among the vast number of larger-than-life public figures she'd met, of whom she could have said that. In Harrington's case, she couldn't imagine *not* saying it. She knew—she'd viewed the recorded exchanges between Harrington and Adebayo, the message Harrington had broadcast after the final missile attack—that Grand Fleet would have been totally justified under the laws of war and the Eridani Edict if it had blown every orbital habitat in Galton into wreckage.

And Harrington hadn't.

There were undoubtedly billions of Solarians who would never forgive or forget the devastation of the Sol System's orbital infrastructure in Operation Nemesis. And the face they would always link with that devastation would be the one O'Hanrahan was looking at right now. But as more and more of the truth about the Alignment whose heart had been here in Galton came to light, the more O'Hanrahan came to appreciate the *restraint* Harrington and the Grand Alliance had shown in the Solarian League's case.

Yet that restraint was dwarfed by the restraint Harrington had shown here. Here where she'd known that, at last, the people responsible for all that death, all that destruction, were at her mercy. O'Hanrahan hadn't truly realized until she visited Manticore just how much of the enormous, extended Harrington family had died in the Yawata Strike, or that Honor Harrington's mother and infant son had very nearly died with them. Now she did, and the fact that a woman who'd lost that many people she'd loved so dearly hadn't ordered her fleet to fire on the habitats from which still more death had been spawned went far beyond the merely remarkable.

"I'll miss you, Your Grace," O'Hanrahan said now, and smiled. "I'll even miss Nimitz badgering me for celery!"

Nimitz bleeked a laugh from his cushioned perch, then leapt down and flowed over to rise high on his haunches and pat her thigh with a long-fingered true-hand. She looked down and stroked his ears, then looked back at Harrington, her expression serious.

"I want to thank you," she said. "You promised me access, and you gave me every single thing you said you would. But you didn't stop there." She shook her head. "I never expected to sit in on your staff meetings, or to join you and Countess Henke or your other flag officers for dinner. The opportunity to talk to *all* of you, under those circumstances—especially to Countess Henke, not just about Galton, but also about Mesa, and Baroness Arngrim about Hypatia—was...Well, it was *priceless*, Your Grace. It's the sort of access a journalist, especially a foreign journalist, could only dream of."

"Fair's fair, Audrey." Harrington smiled faintly. "I told you we wanted an honest Solarian perspective. But, obviously, we'll all be much happier if the honest Solarian perspective in question is...favorable, shall we say, to the Grand Alliance. Surely you've realized all of those dinners were just a way to lull any suspicions you might still have cherished and convince you we really were the good guys all along?"

"Oh, of course, Your Grace." O'Hanrahan rolled her eyes, then snorted. "I'll admit it did convince me of that, but I can't begin to tell you how many politicians and bureaucrats and admirals have *really* tried to play me. Trust me, I can tell the difference."

"Good." Harrington's smile broadened. "I see we succeeded even more completely than I'd hoped."

O'Hanrahan smiled back and returned her gaze to Tschermak.

"So Countess Henke will be remaining here?" she asked.

"For the immediate future." Harrington nodded, looking up at the planet with her. "It's probably cowardly of me to shuffle it off on her, but at least she had a month or two at home in Manticore before she got sent out to play conquistador again. And the truth is she's had more practice dealing with recalcitrant planets than just about anyone else in the Star Empire. She'll have Lester Tourville as her deputy, and Herzog von Rabenstrange's nominated Graf von Grauer Berg as the senior Andermani member of the Tschermak Occupation Command. Right now it's looking like Admiral Brigham will be less successful than I've been at wiggling out of the assignment. I think she's going to be Protector Benjamin's representative."

"So that's what it's going to be officially called? The 'Tschermak Occupation Command'?"

"For now, at least." Harrington shrugged. "It's not very sexy, but at least it's accurate. And it beats calling it the 'Cesspool Cleaning Committee.'"

O'Hanrahan grimaced in sour agreement.

"And what about you?" Harrington asked, turning back to face her. "Can I give you a lift back home—at least as far as Manticore—when I go?"

"I don't think so." O'Hanrahan shook her head.

"Really?" Harrington raised an eyebrow. "You're not eager to get home and get back on the boards?"

"Your Grace," O'Hanrahan chuckled, "you may know someone who *knows* newsies, but I can see you aren't one!"

"Oh?" Those dark eyes twinkled, and O'Hanrahan knew Harrington was "tasting" her own amusement.

"Your Grace, trust me—I'm already all *over* the boards back home. This is the biggest story in generations. The proof that there really was a vile, sinister conspiracy working to destroy the entire Solarian League? That your people were right the entire time about how the Mandarins were allowing themselves to be manipulated, getting so many millions of people killed? That's huge, and I'm the only Solarian reporter embedded in the fleet that conquered the star system that conspiracy called home. Who, just as an added flourish, has been granted personal access to the commander of that fleet and allowed to look at anything, anywhere, on the planet or on the orbital habitats, that I wanted to see. I have this *so* sewed up for the inside scoop that I'm pretty sure at least a dozen of my nearest peers dropped dead from sheer envy when my first recorded story broke. And I sent an entire month worth of additional reports to be dropped on a daily basis. *And* I'll be sending another month worth home with you, now that I know you're leaving."

She shook her head, her expression gleeful.

"You couldn't pull me out of Galton with a tractor beam, Your Grace."

"I hadn't really thought of it that way," Harrington said with a chuckle of her own. "Still, it's only fair, I guess. Especially since you were so good about not blowing the whistle on the entire operation early. It's good to have fresh evidence that there really are ethical reporters out there. I've had too much experience with the other sort, I'm afraid."

"So have I," O'Hanrahan acknowledged. "And I have to confess, I'm not always able to be as 'ethical' and aboveboard as I might wish. It comes with the territory."

Her regret was genuine, although she hoped Harrington would never realize just how much was subsumed in "the territory."

She looked back at Tschermak.

"So much *evil*," she said softly, with total sincerity. "I can understand people who're willing to commit their lives to a cause. *I'm* willing to do that. I have. And sometimes the causes we choose can require hard decisions, things we'd really rather not have to do. Like what you had to do here in Galton, I suppose. But to embrace the kinds of strategies and actions these people did—!"

"Causes can be tricky masters," Harrington sighed. "It's really difficult to avoid checking your scruples at the door when you buy into one of them. And what Mike Henke found on Mesa is proof of where these people started, at least. Obviously, they went to some very dark places along the way, but it's hard to fault the motives their founders probably had when they set out."

"You really mean that?" O'Hanrahan looked at her again, her expression surprised.

"Of course I do." Harrington sounded almost surprised herself at O'Hanrahan's reaction. "At the same time, though, good intentions are no excuse for horrible outcomes, and you're right about the evil down there—out there." She waved one arm to take in the orbital habitats. "The only people I've ever encountered who come close to the fanaticism of the Alignment, at least here in Galton, are the Masadans. And in a lot of ways, they're very much alike.

"For the Masadans, it's their own twisted interpretation of God that drives them to do terrible things. But because God decrees their intolerance and their determination to force everyone else to believe the way they do, *they're* not the ones committing acts of evil. They're only doing what God wants done, and that makes anyone who *opposes* them evil. And it also justifies anything they do to those opponents, because when *God* wants them to do something, any act, however vile, becomes automatically holy."

Her eyes were very dark now.

"And for the Alignment, it's their realization of how much more human potential could be realized, set free, if only narrow-minded, bigoted intolerance didn't stand in the way. The future they see is so bright, so glorious, that anything they have to do to achieve it partakes of that same brightness. And because they see it so clearly, because *they* understand it so completely, they can't really believe anyone else doesn't. I mean, the truth is the truth, isn't it, Audrey? So anyone who stands in the way of my truth must be inspired into doing what they *know* is morally wrong by selfishness, or bigotry, or greedy self-interest. And that justifies anything I have to do to them to achieve the glory they're dedicated to aborting."

"I can see that." O'Hanrahan nodded. "In fact, I might as well admit that from the first time I ever heard of Leonard Detweiler and what he wanted to accomplish, I thought it was probably the single greatest thing we might have aspired to. But from everything I've ever been able to find about his life, from his own writings and the testimony of the people who knew him, he would've been horrified by something like this."

"I'm sure he would have." Harrington nodded. "But that's another thing about causes. They have this nasty habit of getting away from their founders and morphing into things they'd never recognize."

They stood in silence for a minute or so, and then Harrington shook herself.

"Well! If you're going to be staying behind, you should probably join me, Mike, Alfred, Pascaline, and Chien-lu for dinner tonight. Anton Zilwicki will be there, too."

"He will?"

"And I think Damien Harahap and Indiana Graham will be, too," Harrington said with a nod. "Anton's crew will be hanging around, and the Ghost Hunters will be joining them. Captain al-Fanudahi and most of the others are still in transit from Sol, but they should be here in the next few days. Like Mike, they've had a lot of practice digging into conquered planets' secrets. And at least they've got a lot of data to mine."

O'Hanrahan nodded again. No doubt Adebayo had taken a great many of the Galton Alignment's military secrets to the grave with her, but the occupation force had sequestered literally T-centuries of detailed records from *Julian Huxley*, the oldest and largest of the Tschermak habitats. Digging through them would take even someone like Anton Zilwicki years.

"I'll ask Mike and Anton to keep you informed on what they dig up," Harrington continued. "I can't promise complete transparency, though." She shrugged. "Like I said before, there are undoubtedly some secondary nodes out there that we haven't found yet, and there's no telling what stray clue might warn one of them that we've found the breadcrumbs leading to them if it got out prematurely."

"I understand, and I realize you won't be calling the shots anymore, Your Grace," O'Hanrahan said, although she couldn't stifle a serious twinge of disappointment. And not just because she was a reporter. If what Phoebe had told her was accurate, no one in Galton should have had any suspicion her own Alignment even existed, but O'Hanrahan would have felt happier if she'd been able to confirm that for herself.

"Don't be so disappointed!" Harrington chided. "Mike's a reasonable woman. She's not going to shut you out just for the sake of shutting you out!"

"I know that," O'Hanrahan admitted. "And I promise to be reasonable. As long as she is."

"Well, that should keep her cooperative!" Harrington laughed. "Keep you in the pipeline or have the galaxy's nosiest muckraker digging up all the dirty laundry!"

"I never meant it *that* way, Your Grace," O'Hanrahan said innocently. "Mostly, anyway."

"I'm sure."

Harrington shook her head, then glanced at her chrono.

"I have a meeting with General Hibson in about fifteen minutes, so I need to head up to my briefing room. I'll expect you at eighteen hundred for dinner, if that's convenient?"

"Oh, I suppose I can make room in my crowded social calendar," O'Hanrahan replied.

"Good."

Harrington touched her lightly on the shoulder, bent to scoop up Nimitz, and then headed for the open hatch, her personal armsmen in tow.

O'Hanrahan watched her go, then glanced at Anderle before she looked back up at Tschermak.

She was rather bemused by how much she'd discovered that she *liked* Harrington, and she was glad the duchess could draw a clear distinction between the Alignment—the Engagement, now, she supposed—on Mesa and what she'd discovered here. And it would be O'Hanrahan's job to drive home that distinction for all the rest of the galaxy. It helped that what the Grand

Alliance had found in Galton was so twisted, so dark, that the distinction between the two iterations of the same dream would be easy to make.

All of that was true, but her personal motivation went even deeper than that. The reporter in her needed to rip off the scabs, open the wound and expose it to the healing light of public scrutiny. Not just because doing so would serve her own cause, but to punish anyone who could have turned her dream, *her* vision, into something so dark and twisted.

She'd have to head back to the League eventually, of course. But she already knew she'd be a frequent visitor here in Galton, continuing her own research, and despite the anger and disgust she knew would accompany her findings, she was eager to be about it.

July 1924 Post Diaspora

"I only met her once, many years ago. She was quite young. And already an asshole."

—Evelyn Adebayo

City of Leonard
Darius Gamma
Darius System

"HOW BAD WAS IT? DO WE KNOW YET?"

"In detail, no." Antwone Carpinteria shook his head. "And we won't know, until our own agents are able to provide us with firsthand data."

"And how soon will that be?"

"Hard to say, Evelyn. The security environment's gotten ferocious, and my understanding is that there are so many treecats helping out by now that any kind of penetration at the higher levels is virtually impossible. What we have so far is coming from Audrey O'Hanrahan's reportage. Apparently, she's the only Solarian newsy who got to go along for the ride." He shook his head. "I would judge, from the tone of her coverage, that she's not one of our greater admirers."

"Probably because she has a working brain," Evelyn Adebayo said sourly. "It's certainly looked that way to me from what I've seen of her stories, anyway."

"That's probably true," Mikolaj Ferran, one of the other men in the room, said. "And if she really wants to bury the Alignment, she's going about it the right way! Leading with documentation that we launched the Yawata Strike?"

"Actually, she's leading with documentation that *Galton* launched the Yawata Strike," Carpinteria pointed out, and grimaced. "Which they didn't, actually."

"Pointing the finger at Galton was probably the only semi-intelligent thing the Detweilers did about it," Ferran said in a tone of profound disgust. "What kind of idiot would think something like the Yawata Strike was a smart move?"

689

"The same kind of idiot who thinks a new speciation of the human race is a good idea," Adebayo said. "But to get back to my question, what's your best guess, Antwone?"

"Pretty damn bad, but not as bad as it could have been." Carpinteria shook his head. "Galton's just damned lucky somebody like Harrington was in command. O'Hanrahan's first story made that clear enough! She was pretty damn ruthless where the system defenses were concerned, but she was careful to kill as few civilians as possible. And speaking professionally, I have to admire her tactics. Assuming she didn't want to just kill everyone and let God sort them out, anyway." He shook his head again. "Personally, I probably would've done exactly that."

"Meaning what?" Ferran asked.

"Meaning that the really smart thing for her to have done would have been to translate out of hyper just long enough to deploy a shitpot of multidrive missile pods, send them off into the inner system in a fire-and-forget attack, and then vanish back *into* hyper while the attack went home. She'd have caught the fortresses with their wedges down, and she probably could have blown them all into dust bunnies without taking a single casualty of her own."

"Then why didn't she do that?" Adebayo asked. "I'm assuming from what you're saying that she did take casualties of her own?"

"Damn straight she did," Carpinteria said grimly. "O'Hanrahan didn't provide hard numbers, but reading between the lines, I'll be extremely surprised if it doesn't turn out that they took somewhere well north of ten thousand KIA. Admittedly, that's a pittance compared to what Galton took, but still..."

"And she could have avoided them?" Adebayo said. Carpinteria looked at her, and she shrugged. "Not every member of my family understands naval tactics, Antwone."

"Yes, she could have avoided them. But that sort of an attack would have run an excellent chance of taking out one or more of the orbital habitats, as well. And, like I said, she was obviously being very careful to avoid civilian casualties going in." He shook his head. "She had every legal justification to blow the hell out of the orbital habitats when the idiots ambushed her after they'd promised to surrender, and she didn't. I don't know for sure, but I wouldn't be too surprised if the brilliant masterminds who came up with this entire strategy hoped she *would*. Hoped she'd give them a fresh opportunity to blacken her and the Grand Alliance's reputation in the eyes of the galaxy. I don't know that for sure, but it's the kind of way they think.

"They still killed a hell of a lot of people, of course. But, like I said, it could have been a lot worse, at least from Galton's perspective. And that sort of brings me to the point I wanted to discuss."

"Which is?" Ferran asked in the tone of a man who already suspected the answer.

"Gail Weiss," Carpinteria said flatly. "The issue of what happens to her just got put on the front burner—and the heat's turned all the way up now. I'm in the same boat, in a lot of ways, of course, but I'm not blowing in the wind the way she is, and I'm already covered, at least as far as I can be. But after how well the Galton masquerade seems to have gone down, our lords and masters will be even more invested in propping it up. In 'proving' that Darius was always separate from Galton. That Darius was, in fact, created because of the way in which Galton had been 'corrupted.' Anybody or anything which might tend to undercut that narrative is far more at risk now that their precious 'Alamo Contingency' has actually come to pass. I'm too senior and too deep inside to be written off easily. Besides, I've done a damned good job of convincing The-Powers-That-Be of my total reliability. She hasn't. So at the very least, they're going to fully activate her suicide protocols. And it's possible—not likely, but possible—that they'll execute her outright."

One of the other women in the room who hadn't spoken yet sighed and gave the armrests of her chair the sort of stroke that was just a way to release tension.

"Antwone, I know this means a lot to you, and I know partly that's because she *is* 'in the same boat' as you, but I'm leery of taking any risks right now. The outcome at Galton may have been successful—" her fingers made air quotes around the word "successful" and then returned her hands to the armrests "—from the Detweilers' perspective, but as you just pointed out, they're still going to be edgy as hell and ready to jump at anything that seems like even a possible threat. Is this really a good time for us to be taking the risk of activating the Janus protocols—even for her, much less her partner? We can't do that without bringing them at least part of the way inside, you know."

Adebayo shook her head.

"Zuma, I understand why you want us to be cautious about bringing Weiss and McBryde into our confidence. And I'm not going to tell you there's no risk, because recruitment always poses a risk. But it's a risk we have to take, and from everything we've seen, I doubt you could find any two people—certainly not a couple—who'd be less of a risk than these two."

"Given McBryde's family's history on Mesa, I'm very strongly tempted to agree," Ferran said. "And I think you're the best candidate to approach them, Antwone."

"Funny you should say that." Carpinteria grinned. "Just this morning, Gail suggested that my wife and I should have dinner with her and Zach. At a restaurant they like called Xanadu."

✧   ✧   ✧

They didn't all leave at once.

They spaced their exits—and their order—at intervals of a few minutes, randomly selected by an app on Adebayo's uni-link.

She and Carpinteria ended up the last two in the room.

"I assume Generalfeldmarshall Adebayo was a relative of yours," he said. "God rest her soul."

"I wouldn't bet on it. I suppose I hope she got some satisfaction from her Gotterdammerung demise, but I'd like to think God has better taste than to associate with people like her." Adebayo grimaced. "Yes, we were related, although not closely. She was a third cousin. I only met her once, many years ago. She was quite young."

"And already an asshole."

Her uni-link buzzed, and she looked down at it.

"You're out of here, Antwone. Good luck. Keep us informed—safely, of course."

Xanadu Restaurant
City of Leonard
Darius Gamma
Darius System

"WELL, THAT WAS EXCELLENT," JANICE KARANJA SAID.

Her husband leaned back in his chair, pudgy hands clasped over his ample midriff, and nodded.

"Yes, it was," he said. "In retrospect, I wish I'd taken Zach's advice and ordered the *nakji bokkeum* the way you did. But my lamb was excellent."

"Face it, love," Janice said. "When it comes to food, you're a stick in the mud."

"I prefer the term 'conservative,'" he replied with a pained expression.

The two of them sat with Gail and Zach at their hosts' favorite table near the fountain, and now Janice smiled at the younger couple.

"Antwone can 'prefer' whatever he likes," she said. "He is so a stick in the mud where trying new dishes is concerned. But this really is a delightful place. Which one of you found it?"

"He did." Gail pointed to Zach with her thumb. "Zach's usually the one who turns up new restaurants for us. He's a foodie, which I'm really not." She gave Carpinteria a sympathetic glance. "I'm like Antwone when it comes to culinary radicalism—which is why I had a steak. We've come here more than half a dozen times, and I still haven't ordered the *nakji bokkeum*."

"No?" Janice said, and Gail grimaced.

"First, because I know it's *not* what they call '*nakji bokkeum*' back on Old Terra. It's made out of *moddoki*, instead, and I know what those look like in the wild. I'm not all that comfortable ordering

Old Terran octopus, much less something from the Savenko Sea that looks like a cross between a star fish with way too many arms and a massive version of a slug. Second, because I get nervous knowing that if the chef screws up and doesn't cook it right, I'm going to spend all night evacuating everything inside me."

"Oh, pfui." Zach shook his head. "A bit of indigestion is nothing compared to the risks the Japanese take eating *fugu*."

Carpinteria frowned.

"I'm almost afraid to ask, but...what is a '*fugu*'?"

"An old Earth delicacy, prized by all true gourmets," Zach told him with a gleaming smile. "It was—is, rather; they still cook it to this day, I'm told—a type of blowfish which is *extremely* poisonous. The critter's innards contain a poison which is more than a thousand times deadlier than cyanide. It's called terodotoxin, if I remember correctly, although I won't swear to it. One fish has enough of it to kill up to thirty people. It has to be prepared just right, by specially trained chefs."

"Foodieism is an especially pernicious type of mental illness," Gail said firmly. She extended her hand, as if holding up Zach as a piece of evidence, and Janice laughed.

"Oh, I think that's a little harsh!"

"I don't," Carpinteria said. "However, to change the subject, I have some good news, Gail."

"Yes?"

"The Powers-That-Be have okayed my request to have you permanently assigned to Tac Three. And while I can't discuss it here," he gave Zach an apologetic little nod "—top security, need-to-know, all that stuff—I think you'll find your new assignment a lot more congenial than the last one."

"Glad to hear it," she said. "On both counts."

"And to return, obliquely, to the previous subject," Carpinteria gave his wife a look of stern reproof, "the reason Janice downplayed your entirely rational characterization of foodie fanaticism is because she has a secret—well, sort of a secret—lunatic enthusiasm of her own."

"Oh?" Gail and Zach both looked at Janice, whose expression was that of a long-suffering spouse saddled with a stick-in-the-mud partner.

"Enthusiasm, yes," she said. "But I'd hardly call it '*lunatic*.' I like to glide, and I've become very good at it."

"Glide?" Zach seemed puzzled.

"What they call 'gliding' is when people turn up their noses at functional aircraft to fly in a gadget—I refuse to call it an 'aircraft' of any sort—that has no engine," Carpinteria told him. "No power source of any kind. And the most fragile construction you can imagine."

"That's twaddle," Janice said. "There's nothing 'fragile' about the wings and fuselage. It's just very light, that's all."

She looked back at Gail and Zach.

"It's true there's no engine. The way a glider works is that someone tows you aloft, releases you, and from then on you rely on wind currents—updrafts, especially—to keep you aloft. If you know what you're doing, which I do, it's perfectly safe. And if you're a wuss, like my beloved husband, you can always take along a counter-grav unit to lower yourself gently, daintily, and safely to the ground."

"Now I know what you're talking about," Gail said. "It was a sport back on Mesa, too, I believe. Although I never knew anyone who did it."

"'Gliding' is what threw me off," Zach said. "On Mesa, we called it 'soaring.' And I did know a couple of people who engaged in it. What they said they loved the most was the incredible silence of being suspended in midair by nothing but the movement of the wind—which didn't make any noise because you were moving with it."

"That's the one thing I treasure about my wife's mania," Carpinteria acknowledged. "And it's not just the silence, it's the privacy. You're up there all by yourself, and the one advantage to that cockleshell construction is that there's no place for anybody to smuggle in eavesdropping equipment that you won't spot easily."

Zach's eyes narrowed slightly.

"I don't know about that, Antwone. As it happens, electronic surveillance is one of my areas of professional expertise. I wouldn't be so confident about spotting the hardware."

"Yeah, I know." Carpinteria grinned. "But I have enough clout that I told the Powers-That-Be that if they tried to spy on me and Janice while she's engaged in her favorite sport, I'll see to it that any equipment on her craft is toast before we take off. Which—trust me—I know exactly how to do. Damn it, people need at least someplace they can be sure of not being snooped upon."

Zach's eyes got narrower, but Carpinteria only shrugged.

"They think I'm a little eccentric, of course. But they also know I'm not kidding."

"Why don't the two of you join us, the next time we go up?" Janice proposed. "My glider's big enough to seat four. It's not even cramped. And I'll pack us some lunch."

Zach's narrowed eyes widened, but Carpinteria wasn't looking his way. Instead, he was looking at his wife, with unabashed pride.

"She really is a good pilot," he said. "I've seen Janice keep that glider up for *hours*. Some of her fellow pilots—the hard-core competitors, I guess—have flown them for over a thousand kilometers. Your personal best is, what? Six hours?"

"Solo." Janice nodded. "I've never really gone for an endurance record, you know. But Otto and I combined for that fifteen-hour flight last year."

"See?" Carpinteria beamed at Gail and Zach, whose eyes had returned to normal. "Like I say, she really is a good pilot. I'll bet you wouldn't even break an arm, much less your necks! So, what do you say?"

"Sounds delightful!" Gail said.

"I look forward to it," Zach said.